Romance *of the* Three Kingdoms

VOLUME I

Romance *of the* Three Kingdoms

VOLUME I

Lo Kuan-chung

Translated by
C. H. BREWITT-TAYLOR

With an Introduction by
ROBERT E. HEGEL

TUTTLE PUBLISHING
Boston • Rutland, Vermont • Tokyo

Published by Tuttle Publishing, an imprint of Periplus Editions (HK) Ltd.

First published by Charles E. Tuttle Co. Inc., 1959
Completely reset and published with a new Introduction by Tuttle Publishing, 2002

ISBN: 0-8048-3467-9
Library of Congress Cataloging No. 2002102265

Printed in Singapore

10 09 08 07 06 05 04   8 7 6 5 4

Distributed by:

North America, Latin America & Europe
Tuttle Publishing
Airport Industrial Park
364 Innovation Drive
North Clarendon, VT 05759-9436
Tel: (802) 773-8930
Fax: (802) 773-6993
Email: info@tuttlepublishing.com

Japan
Tuttle Publishing
Yaekari Building, 3rd Floor
5-4-12 Osaki, Shinagawa-ku
Tokyo 141-0032
Tel: (03) 5437-0171
Fax: (03) 5437-0755
Email: tuttle-sales@gol.com

Asia Pacific
Berkeley Books Pte Ltd
130 Joo Seng Road
#06-01/03
Singapore 368357
Tel: (65) 6280-1330
Fax: (65) 6280-6290
Email: inquiries@periplus.com.sg

ROMANCE *of the Three Kingdoms* is China's oldest novel and still one of its most widely read works of literature. It is the first of a great tradition of historical fiction that remains undiminished in popularity today. The earliest printed edition of this novel appeared in 1522 CE, but it includes a Preface dated 1494, suggesting earlier composition. In fact, it shares subject matter with successive generations of plays popular among theater audiences since the middle of the thirteenth century. Likewise, the novel bears a close relation to an illustrated prose narrative that was printed in the 1320s entitled *San-kuo chih p'ing-hua* (Plain Tales from the *San-kuo chih*). It, and *Romance of the Three Kingdoms*, are clearly historical fiction; both are ostensibly indebted to the great *San-kuo chih* (Chronicles of the Three Kingdoms), completed by the historian Ch'en Shou (233–297 CE) during the last year of his life. All three of these texts focus on the individuals most centrally involved in those events, and each, in turn, places ever more responsibility on those individuals for the momentous events of their age. In this novel, especially, fiction takes clear precedence over historical fact.

History is always messy: there are so many individuals who play a role in major events, and each cries out to be examined. Historical novelists in China had no less difficulty than its historians in deciding whom to focus on. Unlike the historians, however, who could simply append biographical sketches to a chronology and let the reader somehow put the two together in some meaningful way, the novelist had to conceptualize the major movements in events and to demonstrate which figures deserve our attention. For the author of the "Plain Tales", the motivating element behind the rise of the Three Kingdoms was cosmic retribution: because of the sins of its founders, the Han dynasty deserved to fall into pieces. For the novelist behind *Romance of the Three Kingdoms*, however, the rationale was much more concrete. Here, events are shaped by human desires and aspirations, by laudatory hopes as well as by simple greed.

The players in this piece seem so numerous that initially it is difficult to understand the factions involved. The first chapter, however, introduces us to the novel's central figures: the noble Liu Pei (generally called Liu Yuan-te, who lived from 161 to 223 CE) and his sworn brothers Chang Fei (Chang I-te) and Kuan Yu (Kuan Yun-ch'ang, the "Beautiful Beard") who, in the year 184, swear brotherhood in a peach garden on the basis of their common sense of purpose. This group, along with Liu's primary advisor Chuko Liang (Chuko K'ung-ming, 181–234 CE, introduced in Chapter 38) and the mighty general Chao Yun (Chao Tzu-lung, especially Chapter 28), constitute the nucleus of the novel's anointed favorites, who ultimately form the state of Shu in western China. Because he shares the Han imperial surname and is, in fact, a distant descendant of the royal house, Liu Pei claims legitimacy for his state, and the novelist concurs. His special strength is his ability to inspire loyalty in others, despite his numerous failures in diplomacy and on the battlefield. Conversely, his curse is to use the loyalty of others without abusing them. This leads Liu Pei to the more compelling moral crises of the novel.

Chang Fei is the model warrior: tough, resourceful, fearless, and yet rash when it comes to issuing orders and dealing with underlings. Kuan Yu is the embodiment of courage and of faithful service to his lord; his individual exploits have enthralled readers (and theater audiences) for centuries. Always devoted, always diligent, the novelist allows him the strength of character to return in ghostly form after his death to take his revenge. This act reflects the awe he has always inspired: from early in China's medieval period, Lord Kuan has served as a powerful figure in the divine pantheon, becoming the paragon of fidelity. Statues of him appear in temples, shops and households throughout Chinese communities even today. For his part, Chuko Liang is often known as a wizard, but fans of this novel know him primarily as the crafty strategist who, through his keen insights into human nature, provides invaluable advice to his lord.

The second chapter introduces the figure who, to some readers, plays the dominant role in the novel. This is the upstart Ts'ao Ts'ao (Ts'ao Meng-te, sometimes called Ts'ao A-man, 155–220 CE), a man who, through cool calculations and pragmatic manipulations, takes control of the failing Han empire from the various other contenders at the capital and sets the stage for the creation of a new state. Ts'ao Ts'ao is a brilliant commander; his special strength is his unerring sense of the appropriate timing of action, and this brings him to the brink of success. However, his arrogance nearly spells his ruin. Yet, his strategy is simply to control the Han, not to destroy it. It remains to his elder son and successor, Ts'ao P'ei, to establish the state of Wei in north China.

The third of the three states evolves south of the Yangtze. This is Wu, governed by members of the Sun family, first Sun Chien (Chapter 5), then his son Sun Ts'e (introduced in Chapter 7 and again in Chapter 29), and then by his brother Sun Ch'uan (Chapter 38). Their ablest advisor, who figures prominently in the central battle of the novel fought during the year 208 (at Red Cliffs, Chapters 44 to 50), is Chou Yu, Sun Ch'uan's brother-in-law. Their advantage is provided by geography: protected by the Yangtze River, Wu remains unscathed despite various attacks from the other two states, from its formal establishment in 229 until all the rest of China is finally incorporated by the Ssuma family into the new Chin dynasty.

The History and How It Was Read

Ch'en Shou's "Chronicles of the Three Kingdoms" outlines the great and terrible events of the period from 168 to 280 CE, when China's first great dynasty, the Han (206 BCE–220 CE) was riven, through decades of bloody strife, into three separate states nearly constantly at war with each other. The period, and thus the novel, came to an end with the brief reunion of all China under the leadership of the Ssuma family and their dynasty, the Chin. As the "Plain Tales" reminds us, however, that dynasty, too, was divided after only a few decades. It was only in 589 with the final unification of the Sui (589–618) and its successor, the T'ang (618–906), that China again remained at least nominally united for an extended period.

Of grave concern to China's readers through time has been the succession: which of the three states was the legitimate dynasty? Which *should* have won this struggle? Historian Ch'en Shou, who lived through much of the period he wrote about, had no clear favorite, although word choice would suggest that he chose Wei, the northern state headed by the descendants of Ts'ao Ts'ao. Not all readers agreed with him. Especially during periods when China was threatened by invasion from the north—or was divided or occupied by northerners—sympathies tended to extend that favored position to Shu. Those who did not question the rectitude of the so-called "conquest dynasties" who took power by main force have generally remained pro-Wei in their reading of history; in times of national division, Liu Pei and his forces became emblematic of Han Chinese national sentiment. Thus, the novel has seldom been read for its historical fact; instead, it has often been read as a reflection on the readers' own times.

Authorship and the Formation of the Text

Ever since the 1522 edition, the name Lo Kuan-chung has been associated with the novel. Lo was apparently a playwright who lived from perhaps 1315 to nearly 1400; he is known to have compiled historical plays in the form popular during the period of Mongol rule in China (1279–1368 CE). There is no known author for the "Plain Tales" from which the novelist drew some of his material (the novel is ten times as long), nor is there any incontrovertible evidence for the existence of the novel before it was printed in 1522. Some interpret the novel as a product of the resurgence of Han (Chinese) nationalism as a response to Mongol domination that, as often has been the case, identified China's ethnic majority with the first great dynasty. Few would see the novel as any kind of allegory. The date of its first printing suggests that the novel circulated in manuscript form during the last decades of the fifteenth century at the latest, a hundred years after the shadowy Lo Kuan-chung was active. Scholarly opinion seems to favor composition during the late fifteenth century, given its uses of terms and its political concerns.

Could Lo Kuan-chung have written this first great Chinese novel? The answer can never be definitive, nor should we care, I believe. Authorship as we know it, is a relatively recent concept at both ends of the Eurasian landmass. Before then, "compiler" might be the best description for many authors in many cultures. As we have seen, the novelist adapted material from an earlier lengthy, but crude, narrative as well as formal historical accounts of the period. Undoubtedly, this shadowy figure, whoever he was, followed Confucius himself who claimed not "to create, but only to transmit" the wisdom of his predecessors. In the process, however, the Sage reshaped earlier ideas of Chinese tradition to make them his own philosophy. So, too, did our novelist reshape his raw materials into a tale quite unlike those source texts—if, in fact, we have only one author to thank for this work.

The original novel was named *San-kuo chih t'ung-su yen-i*, literally "Popular Elaborations on the Chronicles of the Three Kingdoms", presumably with the hope that readers would attribute to his version some of the respect generally accorded the official histories. It was divided into 240 unnamed sections, and, if we are to accept the word of the prefacers, it was meant to teach its readers about historical events and about such virtues as loyalty. By the middle of the sixteenth century, the novel passed into the realm of commerce and had spawned a rash of imitations, novels on other periods of Chinese history. By 1600, many editions of this work had appeared, some of them illustrated and some of them simplified and shortened, presumably to attract buyers less willing to tackle such a massive text. The version translated by Brewitt-Taylor, the one that drove all competitors from the market after its first appearance in the 1670s, is commonly titled *San-kuo chih yen-i* (Elaborations on Three Kingdoms), or as it has generally been known in the West, *Romance of the Three Kingdoms*. This edition was shortened somewhat from the 1522 version, and was slightly changed in content (the immortal words "Empires wax and wane..." cited below were their addition); it was divided into 120 chapters, each with its own summarizing title. More importantly, its editors, Mao Lun (b. c.1610, who lost his sight before the beginning of this project) and his son Mao Ts'ung-kang (c.1630–c.1705), included an extensive commentary, not reproduced in this reprint.

The Mao commentary, modeled on annotations to the classic texts of the Confucian tradition, emphasizes the question of legitimate succession. Moreover, it explains how the reader should appreciate the novel. It explores the novelist's craft, how events have been foreshadowed in earlier chapters, and how suggestions made in one place are realized later in the text. It discusses the morality of the characters' actions and draws attention to stylistic felicities throughout. Their commentary also emphasizes causality, the reasons why events work out as they did in fact. In the process, they clarify Liu Pei's great virtues, and their opposite in Ts'ao Ts'ao.

The Appeal of Chinese Historical Fiction

Like *Romance of the Three Kingdoms*, most traditional Chinese novels are set in periods of strife, and generally narrate the rise and fall of dynasties. This allows the novelist to build portraits of various contenders and explore the loyalty (or treachery) of their followers as the various groups jockey for position and power. This allows for the elaboration of complicated stratagems as alliances are made and broken. Many rebels begin as otherwise unknown local figures and rise to prominence through the relentless battles that dominate the narrative in these works. The popularity of these novels attests to the prevalence of a taste for action of a slightly subversive sort. Although the idea of loyalty to authority is intrinsic here, the glorification of members of the common mass to the detriment of inept civil officials regularly undercuts the official Confucian emphasis on order and tranquility—as well as the status of the educated. More importantly, by regular reference to the notion that periods of political disorder are inevitable, these works question the ability of rulers to maintain such order, even over short periods of time.

The great Confucian scholar Mencius (371–289? BCE) once commented, "Timing is less important than geographical advantage, and geographical advantage is less important than human unity." This is precisely how this great novel parcels out its favor: Ts'ao Ts'ao's timely action in Wei is allotted less favor than Wu in its security of location. Clearly, however, the novelist's sympathies lie with Liu Pei and his manifold humanity; his aspirations and his foibles ultimately shape this great work, and it is for his tragedy that the novel is primarily known.

Ultimately, the novel's appeal lies in its affirmation of the dynastic cycle. Even since the Han itself, historians and the general public have observed, as the novel says on its first page, "Empires wax and wane; states cleave asunder and coalesce," and on its last, "States fall asunder and re-unite; empires wax and wane." No matter how lengthy the division of China into separate political entities, a time for reunion will come. Thus, for modern readers, the novel seems to reflect the state of affairs that has existed since 1949 with China divided first into four (the mainland, Hong Kong, Macau and Taiwan) and, eventually, after 1999 only two parts, the mainland and its offshore competitor. This situation will come to an end, the concept affirms—but then that unity, too, will ultimately be replaced by another period of division.

Is this a reassuring scenario? Perhaps not, and yet it affirms the constant awareness of transience in Chinese culture, that nothing persists unchanged through time. Buddhist teachings only clarify a perception already age-old by the time of Confucius twenty-six centuries ago, that time flows like a river past our seeming position of stability on the bank. It has always been said that many tears were shed during the writing of this great tale. Surely many more have been shed during its reading, not only for its characters, but because we readers share their vain hopes, their grand aspirations, their terrible fears and their tragic weaknesses as well. As have they, so too must we disappear with the flow of time. Like all good fiction, *Romance of the Three Kingdoms* is not only about some characters long ago and far away; it is in large measure about us as well.

ROBERT E. HEGEL
Washington University
St. Louis, Missouri
December 2001

TRANSLATOR'S NOTE

The *San Kuo* is distinctly Eastern, a book adapted for the storyteller; one can almost hear him. It abounds in names and genealogies, which seem never to tire the Eastern reader or listener. Happily, English admits pronouns in place of so many strangely spelt names which ought to appear, and they have been used; and as most persons have at least a *tzu* in addition to the *hsing* and *ming* I have tried to lighten the burden on the foreign reader's memory by using only the *hsing* or the *hsing* and *ming* of a man, suppressing his *tzu* except in the case of very well-known characters.

Manchu, Japanese, Siamese, and possible other versions of the *San Kuo* have been made, and now to these I have attempted to add one in English, with what measure of success I leave to curious readers qualified to compare my rendering with the original.

The Wade system of romanisation, in which the vowels are pronounced as in Italian, has been used.

In conclusion, I wish to put on record my gratitude to Mr. Chen Ti Tsen, who typed the text, and Mr. E. Manico Gull, who has read the proofs, and to dedicate this translation to the memory of my son Raymond.

C. H. BREWITT-TAYLOR

Romance of the Three Kingdoms

VOLUME ONE

CHAPTER I

FEAST IN THE GARDEN OF PEACHES: BROTHERHOOD SWORN: SLAUGHTER OF REBELS: THE BROTHERS HEROES

Empires wax and wane; states cleave asunder and coalesce. When the rule of Chou weakened seven contending principalities sprang up, warring one with another till they settled down as Ts'in and when its destiny had been fulfilled arose Ch'u and Han to contend for the mastery. And Han was the victor.

The rise of the fortunes of Han began with the slaughter of the White Serpent. In a short time the whole Empire was theirs and their magnificent heritage was handed down in successive generations till the days of Kuang-Wu, whose name stands in the middle of the long line of Han. This was in the first century of the western era and the dynasty had then already passed its zenith. A century later came to the Throne the Emperor Hsien, doomed to see the beginning of the division into three parts, known to history as The Three Kingdoms.

The descent into misrule hastened in the reigns of the two Emperors Huan and Ling, who sat in the dragon seat about the middle of the second century. The former of these two paid no heed to the good men of his court, but gave his confidence to the palace eunuchs. He lived and died, leaving the sceptre to Ling, whose trusted advisers were the General Tou Wu and the Grand Tutor Ch'en Fan. These two, disgusted with the abuses resulting from the meddling of the eunuchs in affairs of State, plotted their destruction. But the chief eunuch Ts'ao Chieh was not to be disposed of easily. The plot leaked out and the two honest men fell, leaving the eunuchs stronger than before.

It fell upon the day of full moon of the fourth month, second year of the period Chien-Ning, that the Emperor went in state to the Wen-te Hall. As he drew near the Throne a rushing whirlwind arose in the corner of the hall and, lo! from the roof beams floated down a monstrous black serpent that coiled itself up on the very seat of majesty. The Emperor fell in a swoon. Those nearest him hastily raised and bore him to his palace while the courtiers scattered and fled. The serpent disappeared.

But there followed a terrific tempest, thunder, hail and torrents of rain, lasting till midnight and working havoc on all sides. Two years later the earth quaked in Loyang, while along the coast a huge tidal wave rushed in which, in its recoil, swept away all the dwellers by the sea. Another evil omen was recorded ten years later, when the reign-title was changed: certain hens suddenly developed male characteristics, a miracle which could only refer to the effeminate eunuchs meddling in affairs of State. At the new moon of the sixth month a long wreath of black vapour wound its way into the audience chamber, while in the following month a rainbow was seen in the Jade Chamber. Away from the capital a mountain fell in, leaving a mighty rift in its flank.

Such were some of various omens. The Emperor, greatly moved by these signs of the displeasure of Heaven, issued an edict asking his ministers for an explanation of the calamities and marvels. A certain Ts'ai Yung replied bluntly that showers of insects and changes of fowls' sexes were brought about by feminine interference in State affairs.

The Emperor read this memorial with deep sighs, and the chief eunuch Ts'ao Chieh, from his place behind the Throne, anxiously noted these signs of grief. An opportunity offering, he read the document and told his fellows its purport. Before long a charge was trumped up against the author, who was driven from court and forced to retire to his country house. With this victory the eunuchs grew bolder. Ten of them, rivals in wickedness and associates in evil deeds, formed a powerful party known as The Ten. One of them, Chang Jang, won such influence that he became the Emperor's most honoured and trusted adviser. The Emperor even called him Daddie. So the Government went quickly from bad to worse, till the country was ripe for rebellion and buzzed with brigandage.

At this time in Chulu was a certain Chang family, of whom three brothers bore the name of Chio, Pao and Liang respectively. The eldest was an unclassed graduate, who devoted himself to medicine. One day, while culling simples in the woods, he met a venerable old gentleman with very bright eyes and fresh complexion, who walked leaning on a staff. The old man beckoned Chio into a cave and there gave him three volumes of the "Book of Heaven." "This book" said he, "is the Way of Peace. With the aid of these volumes you can convert the world and rescue mankind. But you must be single-minded, or, rest assured, you will greatly suffer."

With a humble obeisance Chang took the book and asked the name of his benefactor.

"I am the Hsien of the Southern Land of Glory," was the reply, as the old gentleman disappeared in thin air.

The new possessor of the wonderful book studied it eagerly and strove day and night to reduce its precepts to practice. Before long he could summon the winds and command the rain, and became known as The Mystic of the Way of Peace. Soon he could test his other powers. With a change of reign-title appeared a terrible pestilence which ran throughout the land, whereupon Chang Chio distributed charmed remedies of which the success gained him the title of the Wise and Good Master. He began to have a following of disciples whom he initiated into the mysteries and sent abroad throughout all the land. They, like their master, could write charms and recite formulae and their fame increased his following. He began to organise his disciples. He established thirty six circuits, the larger with a myriad or more members, the smaller with about half that number. Each circuit had its chief who took the military title of General. They talked wildly of the death of the blue heavens and the setting up of the yellow; they said a new cycle was beginning and would bring universal good fortune, and they persuaded people to chalk the symbols for the first year of a cycle on the main door of their dwellings.

With the growth of the number of his supporters grew also the ambition of the "Wise and Good." He dreamed of empire. One of his partisans, Ma Yuan-i, was sent bearing gifts to gain the support of the eunuchs whereby to have allies within the palace. To his brothers Chang Chio said, "For schemes like ours always the most difficult part is to gain the popular favour. But that is already ours. Such an opportunity must not pass." And they began to prepare. Many yellow flags were made and a day was chosen to strike the first blow.

Then they wrote letters to the chief eunuch, Feng Hsu, and sent them by a follower, who alas! betrayed their trust and discovered the plot. The Emperor summoned his trusty General Ho Chin and bade him look to it. Ma Yuan-i was it once taken and put to death. Feng Hsu and many others were cast into prison.

The plot having thus become known the Changs were forced at once to take the field. They assumed grandiose titles, T'ien Kung, or Celestial Duke, Ti Kung, or Terrestrial Duke, Jen Kung, or Duke of Humanity, and in these names they put forth this manifesto:—

"The good fortune of the Hans is exhausted and the Wise Man has appeared. Discern the will of Heaven, O ye people, and walk in the way of righteousness, whereby alone ye may attain to peace."

Support was not lacking. On every side people bound their heads with a yellow turban and joined the army of the rebel Chang Chio, so that soon his strength was exceeding great and the official troops melted away at a whisper of his coming.

Ho Chin, Guardian of the Throne, memorialised for general preparations against the rebels and an edict called upon every one to fight against them. In the mean time Lu Chih, Huangfu Sung and Chu Chien marched against them in three directions with veteran soldiers.

It is now time to turn to Chang Chio. He led his army into Yuchow, the northern of the eight divisions of the country. The Prefect was one Liu Yen, a scion of the Imperial House through a certain Lu, Prince Kung of Chingling. Learning of the approach of the rebels, the Prefect called in the *Hsiao-yu* Tsou Ching to consult over the position. Said Tsou, "They are many and we few; you must enlist more men to oppose them."

The Prefect saw this was so and he put out notices calling for volunteers to serve against the rebels. One of these notices was posted up in the Cho district, where lived one of whom much will be heard later.

This man was no mere bookish scholar nor found he any pleasure in study. But he was liberal and amiable, albeit a man of few words, hiding all feeling under a calm exterior. He had always cherished a yearning for high emprise and had cultivated the friendship of men of mark. He was tall of stature. His ears were long, the lobes touching his shoulders, and his hands hung down below his knees. His eyes were very prominent, so that he could see backward past his ears. His complexion was clear as jade and he had rich red lips. He was a descendant of a Prince whose father was the grandson of the Emperor Ching, (the occupant of the dragon throne a century and a half B.C.) His name was Liu Pei, or more commonly Liu Yuan-te. Many years before one of his forbears had been Marquis of that very district, but had lost his rank for remissness in ceremonial offerings. However, that branch of the family had remained on in the place, gradually becoming poorer and poorer as the years rolled on. His father Liu Hung had been a scholar and an official but died young. The widow and orphan were left alone and Pei as a lad won a reputation for filial piety.

At this time the family had sunk deep in poverty and the son gained his living by the sale of straw sandals and weaving grass mats. The family home was in a village near the district city. Near the house stood a huge mulberry tree, and seen from afar its curved profile resembled the tilt of a waggon. Noting the luxuriance of its foliage a soothsayer had predicted that one day a man of distinction would come forth from the family. As a child Yuan-te, and the other village boys played beneath this tree and he would climb up into it, saying he was emperor and was mounting his chariot. The lad's uncle recognised that he was no ordinary boy and saw to it that the family did not come to actual want.

When Yuan-te was fifteen his mother sent him travelling for his education. For a time he served Cheng Yuan and Lu Chih as masters and he became great friends with Kungssun Tsan.

Yuan-te was twenty eight when the outbreak of the rebellion called for soldiers. The sight of the notice saddened him and he sighed as he read it. Suddenly a rasping voice behind him cried, "Noble Sir, why sigh if you do nothing to help your country?" Turning quickly he saw standing there a man about his own height, with a bullet head like a leopard's, large eyes, a pointed chin and a bristling moustache. He spoke in a loud bass voice and looked as irresistible as a runaway horse. At once Yuan-te saw he was no ordinary man and asked who he was.

"Chang Fei is my name; I am usually called I-te" replied the stranger. "I live near here where I have a farm; and I am a wine-seller and a butcher as well. And I like to become acquainted with worthy men. Your sighs as you read the notice drew me toward you."

Yuan-te replied, "I am of the Imperial Family, Liu by name, and my distinguishing name is Pei. An I could I would destroy these rebels and restore peace to the land, but alas! I am helpless."

"I am not without means," said Fei. Suppose you and I raised some men and tried what we could do."

This was happy news for Yuan-te and the two betook themselves to the village inn to talk over the project. As they were drinking, a huge, tall fellow appeared pushing a handcart along the road. At the threshold he halted and entered the inn to rest awhile and he called for wine. "And be quick," added he "for I am in haste to get into the town and offer for the army."

Yuan-te looked over the new-comer item by item and noted his huge frame, his long beard, his dark brown face and deep red lips. He had eyes like a phoenix and fine bushy eyebrows like silkworms. His whole appearance was dignified and awe-inspiring. Presently Yuan-te crossed over, sat down beside him and asked his name.

"I am Kuan Yu," said he; "I used to be known as Shou-ch'ang (Long as eternity), but now am usually called Yun-ch'ang (Long as a cloud). I am a native of the east side of the river, but I have been a fugitive on the waters for some five years, because I slew a ruffian who, since he was powerful, was a bully. I have come to join the army here."

Then Yuan-te told him his own intentions and all three went away to Chang Fei's farm where they could talk over the grand project.

Said Fei, "The peach trees in the orchard behind the house are just in full flower. Tomorrow we will institute a sacrifice there and solemnly declare our intention before Heaven and Earth. And we three will swear brotherhood and unity of aims and sentiments; thus will we enter upon our great task."

All three being of one mind, next day they prepared the sacrifices, a black ox, a white horse and wine for libation. Beneath the smoke of the incense burning on the altar they bowed their heads and recited this oath"—"We three Liu Pei, Kuan Yu and Chang Fei, though of different families, swear brotherhood, and promise mutual help to one end. We will rescue each other in difficulty, we will aid each other in danger. We swear to serve the state and save the people. We ask not the same day of birth but we seek to die together. May Heaven, the all-ruling, and Earth, the all-producing, read our hearts, and if we turn aside from righteousness or forget kindliness may Heaven and man smite us!"

They rose from their knees. The two others bowed before 'Yuan-te, as their elder brother and Chang Fei was to be the youngest of the trio. This solemn ceremony performed, they slew other oxen and made a feast to which they invited the villagers. Three hundred joined them and all feasted and drank deep in the Peach Garden.

The next day weapons were mustered. But there were no horses to ride. This was a real grief, but soon they were cheered by the arrival of two horse dealers with a drove of horses.

"Thus does Heaven help us," said Yuan-te and the three brothers went forth to welcome the merchants. They were from Changshan and went northwards every year to buy horses. They were now on their way home because of the rising. They also came to the farm, where wine was set before them, and presently Yuan-te told them of the plan to strive for tranquility. The two dealers were glad and at once gave them fifty good steeds, and beside, gold and silver and a thousand catties of steel fit for the forging of weapons.

After the merchants had taken their leave, armourers were summoned to forge weapons. For Yuan-te they made double sword.

Yun-ch'ang fashioned a long-handled, curved blade called "Black Dragon" or "Cold Beauty," which weighed a full hundredweight, and Chang Fei made himself an eighteen-foot spear. Each too had a helmet and full armour.

When these were ready the troop, now five hundred strong, marched to Tsou Ching, who presented them to Liu Yen. When the ceremony of introduction was over, Yuan-te declared his ancestry and Yen at once accorded him the favour due to a relation.

Before many days it was announced that the rebellion had actually broken out and the leader, Cheng Yuan-chih, had invaded the district with a huge army. Tsou Ching and the three heroes went out to oppose them with the five hundred men. Yuan-te joyfully undertook to lead the van and marched to the foot of the Tahsing Hills where they saw the rebels. The rebels wore their hair flying about their shoulders and their foreheads were bound with yellow turbans.

When the two armies had been drawn up opposite each other Yuan-te with his two brothers, one on each side, rode to the front and, flourishing his whip, began to hurl reproaches at the rebels and called upon them to surrender. Their leader, full of rage, sent out one Teng Mou to begin the battle. At once rode forward Chang Fei, his long spear poised to strike. One thrust and Teng rolled off his horse pierced through the heart. At this the leader himself whipped up his steed and rode forth with sword raised ready to slay Chang. But Kuan Yu swung up his ponderous weapon and rode at him. At the sight fear seized upon Cheng, and ere he could recover himself the great sword fell, cutting him in halves.

> Two heroes new to war's alarms,
> Ride boldly forth to try their arms.
> Their doughty deeds three kingdoms tell
> And poets sing how these befell.

Their leader fallen, the rebels threw away their weapons and fled. The official soldiers dashed in among them. Many thousands surrendered and the victory was complete. Thus this part of the rebellion was broken up.

On their return the Prefect met them and distributed rewards. But before long letters came from the prefecture of Chingchou saying that the rebels were laying siege to the chief city and it was near falling. Help was needed quickly.

"I will go," said Yuan-te as soon as he heard the news and he set out at once with his own men, reinforced by a large body under

Tsou Ching. The rebels seeing help coming at once attacked most fiercely. The relieving force being comparatively small could not prevail and retired some thirty *li*, where they made a camp.

"They are many and we but few," said Yuan-te to his brothers. "We can only beat them by superior strategy."

So they prepared an ambush. The two younger brothers, each with a goodly party, went behind the hills right and left and there hid. When the gongs beat they were to move out to support the main army.

These preparations made, the drums rolled for the advance. The rebels also came forward. Then Yuan-te suddenly retired. Thinking this was their chance the rebels pressed forward and were led over the hills. Then suddenly the gongs sounded for the ambush to discover itself and the rebels were attacked on three sides. They lost heavily and fled to the provincial city. But the Prefect led out the men he had to assist in the battle and the rebels were entirely defeated and many slain. Chingchou was no longer in danger.

> Tho' fierce as tigers soldiers be,
> Battles are won by strategy.
> A hero comes; he gains renown,
> Already destined for a crown.

After the celebrations in honour of victory were over Tsou Ching proposed to return home, but Yuan-te preferred to go to the aid of his old master Lu Chih, then struggling with a horde of rebels led by Chang Chio. So they separated and the three brothers with their troop made their way of Kuangtsung.

They found the Prefect in camp, were admitted to his presence and declared the reason of their coming. The Prefect received them with great joy and they remained with him while he made his plans.

At that time the rebels there were three to one and the two armies were facing each other. Neither had had any success. The Prefect said to Liu Pei, "I am surrounding these rebels here but the other two brothers Chang Liang and Chang Pao are strongly entrenched opposite Huangfu Sung and Chu Chien at Yingch'uan. I will give you a thousand more men and with these you can go to find out what is happening and we can then settle the moment to attack."

So Yuan-te set off and marched as quickly as possible. At that time the imperial troops were attacking with success and the rebels had retired upon Changshe. They had encamped among the thick grass, and, seeing this, Huangfu decided to attack them by fire. So he bade every man cut a bundle of dry grass and laid an ambush. That night the wind blew a gale and at the second watch they started a blaze. At the same time the rebels were attacked. Their camp was set on fire and the flames rose to the very heavens. The rebels were thrown into great confusion. There was no time to saddle horses or don armour; they fled in all directions.

The battle continued till dawn. Chang Liang and Chang Pao, with a few flying soldiers, found, as they thought, a way of escape. But suddenly a troop of soldiers with crimson banners appeared to oppose them. Their leader was a man of medium stature with small eyes and a long beard. He was one Ts'ao Ts'ao, also known as Ts'ao Meng-te, a P'eikuo man, holding the rank of Chi-tu-yu. His father was Ts'ao Sung, who had been born to the Hsiahou family, but he had been brought up by the eunuch Ts'ao T'eng and had taken his family name. This Ts'ao Ts'ao was Sung's son and, as a lad, bore the name of A-man.

As a young man Ts'ao Ts'ao had been fond of hunting and delighted in songs and dancing. He was resourceful and full of guile. An uncle, seeing the young fellow so unsteady, used to get angry with him and told his father Ts'ao Sung of his misdeeds. His father remonstrated with him.

But the youth was equal to the occasion. One day, seeing his uncle coming, he fell to the ground in a pretended fit. The uncle alarmed ran to tell his father, who came, and there was the youth in most perfect health.

"But your uncle said you were in a fit; are you better?"

"I have never suffered from fits or any such illness," said Ts'ao Ts'ao. "But I have lost my uncle's affection and he has deceived you."

Thereafter, whatever the uncle might say of his faults, his father paid no heed. So the young man grew up licentious and uncontrolled.

A certain man of the time said to Ts'ao Ts'ao, "Rebellion is at hand and only a man of the greatest ability can succeed in restoring tranquility. That man is yourself."

And Ho Yung of Nanyang said of him, "The dynasty of Han is about to fall. He who can restore peace is this man and only he."

Ts'ao Ts'ao went to enquire his future of a wise man of Junan.

"What manner of man am I?" asked Ts'ao.

The seer made no reply and again he put the question. Then he replied, "You are able enough to rule the world, but wicked enough to disturb it."

Ts'ao greatly rejoiced to hear this.

He graduated at twenty and began his career in a district near

Loyang. In the four gates of the city he ruled he hung up clubs of various sorts and any breach of the law met with its punishment whatever the rank of the offender.

Now an uncle of a eunuch was found one night in the streets with a sword and was arrested. In due course he was beaten. Thereafter no one dared to offend and Ts'ao's name became terrible. Soon he became a magistrate.

At the outbreak of rebellion he held the rank of Chi-tu-yu and was given command of five thousand horse and foot to help fight at Yingch'uan. He just happened to fall in with the newly, defeated rebels whom he cut to pieces. Thousands were slain and endless banners and drums and horses were captured and not a little money. However the two leaders got away and, after an interview with Huangfu Sung, Ts'ao went in pursuit of them.

We return now to Yuan-te. He and his brothers were hastening toward the point of danger when they heard the din of battle and saw flames rising high toward the sky. However they arrived too late for the fighting. They saw Huanfu and Chu to whom they told the intentions of Lu Chih.

"The rebel power is quite broken here," said the chiefs, "but they will surely make for Kuangtsung to join Chang Chio. You can do nothing better than hasten back."

The three brothers retraced their steps. Half way along the road they met a party of soldiers escorting a prisoner in a cage-cart. When they drew near the prisoner was no other than the man they were going to help. Hastily dismounting Liu Pei asked what had happened. Liu Chih explained, "I had surrounded the rebels and was on the point of smashing them, when Chang Chio employed some of his supernatural powers and prevented my victory. The Court sent down a eunuch to enquire into my failure and that official demanded a bribe. I told him how hard pressed we were and asked him where, in the circumstances, I could find a gift for him. He went away in wrath and reported that I was hiding behind my ramparts and would not give battle and I disheartened my men. So I was superseded by one Tung Cho and I have to go to the capital to answer the charge."

This story put Chang Fei into a rage. He was for slaying the escort and setting free the prisoner. But Yuan-te checked him.

"The Government will take the proper course," said he. "You must not act hastily." And they went their ways.

It was useless to continue on that road so Kuan Yu proposed to go back and they retook the road. Two days later they heard the thunder of battle behind some hills. Hastening to the top they beheld the government soldiers suffering great loss and they saw the countryside was full of Yellow Turbans. On their banners were the words, "Celestial Duke," writ large.

"We will attack this Chang Chio," said Yuan-te and they galloped out to join in the battle.

Chang Chio had worsted Tung Cho and was following up his advantage. He was in hot pursuit when the three brothers dashed into his army, threw his ranks into confusion and drove him back. Then they returned with the rescued general to his camp.

"What officers have you?" asked Tung Cho, when he had leisure to speak to the brothers.

"None," was the reply. And Tung treated them with disrespect. Yuan-te retired calmly, but Chang Fei was furious.

"We have just rescued this menial in a bloody fight," cried he, "and now he is rude to us! Nothing but his death can slake my anger."

He would have dashed into the tent and slain the insulter had not his elder brothers held him back.

> As it was in olden time so it is today,
> The simple wight may merit well,
>   officialdom holds sway;
> Chang Fei, the blunt and hasty,
>   where can you find his peer?
> But slaying the ungrateful would
>   mean many deaths a year.

Tung Cho's fate will be unrolled in later chapters.

CHAPTER II

AN OFFICIAL IS THRASHED:
UNCLE HO PLOTS TO KILL THE EUNUCHS

It must here be told who this Tung Cho was. Cho, or Chung-ying, was born in the west at Lint'ao in modern Shensi. His father was a prefect. He himself was arrogant and overbearing. But the day he had treated the three brothers with contumely had been his last had not the two elders restrained their wrathful brother.

"Remember he has the government commission;" said Yuan-te, "who are we to judge and slay?"

"It is bitter to take orders from such a wretch; I would rather slay him. You may stay here an you wish to, but I will seek some other place."

"We three are one in life and in death; there is no parting for us. We will all go hence."

So spake Yuan-te and his brother was satisfied. Wherefore all three set out and lost no time in travelling till they came to Chu Chien, who received them well and accepted their aid in attacking Chang Pao.

At this time Ts'ao Ts'ao had joined himself to Huangfu Sung and they were trying to destroy Chang Liang and there was a great battle at Chuyang. At the same time Chang Pao was attacked. The rebel had led his men to a strong position in the rear of the hills. An attack being decided upon Yuan-te was *hsien-feng*, or leader of the van. On the rebel side a subordinate leader, Kao Hsing, came out to offer battle. Chang Fei was sent to smite him. Out rode Fei at full speed, his spear ready set. After a few bouts he wounded Kao, who was unhorsed. At this the main army had the signal to advance. Then Chang Pao, while still mounted, loosened his hair, grasped his sword and uttered his incantations. Thereupon began the wind to howl and the thunder to roll, while a dense black cloud from the heavens settled upon the field. And therein seemed to be horse and footmen innumerable, who swept to attack the imperial troops. Fear came upon them and Yuan-te led off his men, but they were in disorder and returned defeated.

Chu Chien and Yuan-te considered the matter. "He uses magic," said Chien. "Tomorrow, then, will I prepare counter magic in the shape of the blood of slaughtered swine and goats and dogs. This blood shall be sprinkled upon their hosts from the precipices above by men whom they see not. Thus shall we be able to break the power of their black art."

So it was done. The two younger brothers took each a company of men and hid them on the high cliffs behind the hills, and they had a plentiful supply of the blood of swine and goats and dogs and all manner of filthy things. And so next day, when the rebels with fluttering banners and rolling drums came out to challenge, Yuan-te rode forth to meet them. At the same moment that the armies met, again Chang Pao began his magic and again the elements began to struggle together. Sand flew in clouds, pebbles were swept along the ground, black masses of vapour filled the sky and rolling masses of foot and horse descended from on high. Yuan-te turned, as before, to flee and the rebels rushed on. But as they pressed through the hills the trumpets blared and the hidden soldiers exploded bombs, threw down filth and spattered blood. The masses of men and horses in the air fluttered to the earth as fragments of torn paper, the wind ceased to blow, the thunder subsided, the sand sank and the pebbles lay still upon the ground.

Chang Pao quickly saw his magic had been countered and turned to retire. Then he was attacked on the flanks by the two younger brothers, and in rear by Yuan-te and Chu Chien. The rebels were routed. Yuan-te, seeing from afar the banner of the "Duke of Earth," galloped toward it but only succeeded in wounding the "Duke" with an arrow in the left arm. Wounded though he was, he got away into Yangch'eng, where he fortified himself and was besieged by Chu Chien.

Scouts, sent out to get news of Huangfu, reported that he had been very successful and Tung Cho had suffered many reverses. Therefore the Court had put Huangfu in the latter's place. Chang Chio had died before his arrival. Chang Liang had added his brother's army to his own but no headway could be made against Huangfu, whose army gained seven successive victories. And Chang Liang had been slain at Chuyang. Beside this Chang Chio's coffin had been exhumed, the corpse beheaded and the head, after exposure, had been sent to the capital. The common crowd had surrendered. For these services Huangfu had been promoted and now ruled in Ichou.

He had not forgotten his friends. His first act after he had attained to power was to memorialise concerning the case of Lu Chih, who was then restored to his former rank.

Ts'ao Ts'ao also had received advancement for his services and was preparing to go south to his new post.

Hearing these things Huangfu Sung pressed harder yet upon Yangch'eng and the approaching break-up of the rebellion became evident. Then one of Chang Pao's officers killed his leader and brought his head in token of submission. Thus rebellion in that part of the country was stamped out and Chu Chien made his report to the government.

However, the embers still smouldered. Three of the rebels Chao Hung, Han Chung and Sun Chung, began to murder and rob and burn, calling themselves the avengers of Chang Chio. The successful Chu Chien was commanded to lead his veteran and successful troops to destroy them. He at once marched toward Wanch'eng, which the rebels were attacking. When Chu arrived Han Chung was sent to oppose him. Chu Chien sent the three brothers, our heroes, to attack the south west angle of the city. Han Chung at once led the best of his men to beat them off. Meanwhile Chu Chien himself led two companies of armoured horsemen to attack the opposite corner. The rebels, thinking the city lost, abandoned the south west and turned back. The three brothers pressed hotly in their rear and they were utterly routed. They took refuge in the city which was then invested. When famine pressed upon the besieged they sent a messenger to offer to surrender but the offer was refused.

Said Yuan-te, "Seeing that the founder of the Han Dynasty could welcome the submissive and receive the favourable why reject these?"

"The conditions are different," replied Chu Chien. "In those days disorder was universal and the people had no fixed lord. Wherefore submission was welcomed and support rewarded to encourage people to come over. Now the Empire is united and the Yellow Turbans are the only malcontents. To receive their surrender is not to encourage the good. To allow brigands, when successful, to give way to every licence, and to let them surrender when they fail is to encourage brigandage. Your plan is not a good one."

Yuan-te replied, "Not to let brigands surrender is well. But the city is surrounded as by an iron barrel. If the rebels' request be refused they will be desperate and fight to the death and a myriad such men cannot be withstood. In the city there are many times that number, all doomed to death. Let us withdraw from one corner and only attack the opposite. They will all assuredly flee and have no desire to fight. We shall take them."

Chu Chien saw that the advice was good and followed it. As predicted the rebels ran out, led by Han Chung. The besiegers fell upon them as they fled and their leader was slain. They scattered in all directions. But the other two rebels came with large reinforcements, and as they appeared very strong, the government soldiers retired and the new body of rebels entered Wanch'eng.

Chu Chien encamped ten *li* from the city and prepared to attack. Just then there arrived a body of horse and foot from the east. They were led by one Sun Chien.

Sun Chien had a broad open face, was lithe and yet powerfully built. He was a native of Wu, a descendant of Sun Wu. His minor name was Wen-tai. When he was seventeen he was with his father on the Ch'ientang River and saw a party of pirates, who had been plundering a merchant, dividing their booty on the river bank.

"We can capture these," said he to his father.

So, gripping his sword, he ran boldly up the bank and cried out to this side and that as if he was calling his men to come on. This made the pirates believe the soldiers were on them and they fled, leaving their booty behind them. He actually killed one of the pirates.

In this way he became known and was recommended for official rank. Then, in collaboration with the local officials, he raised a band and helped to quell the rebellion of one Hsu Ch'ang, who called himself the Yangming Emperor. The rebel's son was also slain. For this he was commended in a memorial to the throne and received further promotion.

When the Yellow Turban rebellion began he gathered together the young men of his village, some of the merchant class, got a company and a half of veteran soldiers and took the field. Now he had reached the fighting area.

Chu Chien welcomed him gladly and ordered him to attack the south gate. Other gates were simultaneously attacked, but the east gate was left free to give the rebels a chance of exit. Sun Chien was the first to mount the wall and cut down a score of men with his own hand. The rebels ran, but Chao Hung their leader, rode directly at Sun Chien with his spear ready to thrust. Sun Chien leaped down from the wall, snatched away the spear and with it knocked the rebel from his horse. Then mounting the horse he rode hither and thither, slaying as he went.

The rebels fled north. Meeting Yuan-te they declined to fight and scattered. But Yuan-te drew his bow, fitted an arrow and wounded their leader Sun Chung, who fell to the ground. The main army came up, and after tremendous slaughter, the others surrendered. Thus was peace brought to the country about Nanyang.

Chu Chien led his army to the capital, was promoted to a General of Cavalry and received the governorship of Honan. He did not forget those who had helped him to win victory.

Sun Chien, having influential friends to support him, quickly got an appointment and went to it. But Yuan-te, in spite of Chu Chien's memorial, waited in vain for preferment and the three brothers became very sad.

Walking along one day Yuan-te met a Court official, Chang Chun by name, to whom he related his services and told his sorrows. Chang was much surprised at this neglect and one day at Court spoke to the Emperor about it.

Said he, "The Yellow Turbans rebelled because the eunuchs sold offices and bartered ranks. There was employment only for their friends, punishment only for their enemies. This led to rebellion. Wherefore it would be well to slay the eunuchs and expose their heads and proclaim what had been done throughout the whole empire. Then reward the worthy. Thereby the land would be wholly tranquil."

But the eunuchs fiercely opposed this and said the memorialist was insulting the Emperor and they bade the guard thrust him without.

However, the eunuchs took counsel together and one said, "Surely some one who rendered some service against rebels resents being passed over."

So they caused a list of unimportant people to be prepared for preferment by and by. Among them was Yuan-te, who received the post of magistrate of the Anhsi district, to which he proceeded without delay after disbanding his men and sending them home to their villages. He retained a score or so as escort.

The three brothers reached Anhsi, and soon the administration of the district was so reformed and the rule so wise that in a month there was no law-breaking. The three brothers lived in perfect harmony, eating at the same table and sleeping on the same couch. But when Yuan-te was in the company of others, the two younger brothers would stand in attendance, were it even a whole day.

Four months after their arrival there came out a general order for the reduction of the number of military officers holding civil posts, and Yuan-te began to fear that he would be among those thrown out. In due course the inspecting official arrived and was met at the boundary, but to the polite obeisance of Yuan-te he made no return, save a wave of his whip as he sat on his horse. This made the younger brothers furious; but worse was to follow.

When the inspector had arrived at his lodging, he took his seat on the dais leaving Yuan-te standing below. After a long time he addressed him.

"Magistrate Liu, what was your origin?"

Liu Pei replied, "I am descended from Prince Ching. Since my first fight with the Yellow Turban rebels at Chochun I have been in some score of battles, wherein I gained some trifling merit. My reward was this office."

"You lie about your descent and your statement of services is false," roared the inspector. "Now the Court has ordered the reduction of your sort of low class officials."

Yuan-te muttered to himself and withdrew. On his return to the magistracy he took council with his secretaries.

"This pompous attitude only means he wants a bribe," said they.

"I have never wronged the people to the value of a single stalk of stubble; then where is a bribe to come from?"

Next day the inspector had the minor officials before him and forced them to bear witness that their master had oppressed the people. Yuan-te time after time went to rebut this charge, but the doorkeepers drove him away and he could not enter.

Now Chang Fei had been all day drowning his sorrow in wine and had drunk far too much. Calling for his horse he rode out past the lodging of the inspector, and at the gate saw a small crowd of white-haired men weeping bitterly. He asked why. They said, "The inspector has compelled the underlings to bear false witness against our magistrate, with the desire to injure the noble Liu. We came to beg mercy for him, but are not permitted to enter. Moreover, we have been beaten by the doorkeepers."

This provoked the irascible and half intoxicated man to fury. His eyes opened till they became circles; he ground his teeth; in a moment he was off his steed, had forced his way past the scared doorkeepers into the building and was in the rear apartments. There he saw the inspector sitting on high with the official underlings in bonds at his feet.

"Oppressor of the people, robber!" cried Fei, "do you know me?"

But before he could reply Fei had him by the hair and had

dragged him down. Another moment he was outside and firmly lashed to the hitching post in front of the building. Then breaking off a switch from a willow tree Fei gave his victim a severe thrashing, only staying his hand when the switch was too short to strike with.

Yuan-te was sitting alone, communing with his sorrow, when he heard a shouting before his door. He asked what was the matter. They told him General Chang had bound somebody to a post and was thrashing him. Hastily going outside he saw who the unhappy victim was and asked the reason.

"If we do not beat this sort of wretch to death what may we expect?" said Fei.

"Noble Sir, save me," cried the victim.

Now Yuan-te had always been kindly and gracious, wherefore he bade his brother release the officer and go his way.

Then Kuan Yu came up saying, "Brother, after your magnificent services you only got this petty post and even here you have been insulted by this fellow. A thorn bush is no place for a phoenix. Let us slay this fellow, leave here and go home till we can evolve a bigger scheme."

Yuan-te contented himself with hanging the official seal about the inspector's neck saying, "If I hear that you injure the people I will assuredly kill you. I now spare your life and I return to you the seal. We are going."

The inspector went to the Prefect and complained, and orders were issued for the arrest of the brothers, but they got away to Taichou and sought refuge with Liu Hui, who sheltered them because of Liu Pei's noble birth.

But nothing will be here related of this. By this time the Ten Eunuchs had everything in their hands and they put to death all who did not stand in with them. From every officer who had helped to put down the rebels they demanded presents, and if these were not forthcoming he was removed from office. Huangfu and Chu both fell victims to these intrigues, while on the other hand the eunuchs received the highest honours. Thirteen of them were ennobled. The government grew worse and worse and every one was irritated.

Rebellion broke out in Changsha led by one Ou Hsing, and in other places. Memorials were sent up in number as snow flakes in winter, but the eunuchs suppressed them all. One day the Emperor was at a feast in one of the gardens with the eunuchs when a certain high minister Liu T'ao suddenly appeared showing very great distress. The Emperor asked what was the matter.

"Sire, how can you be feasting with these when the Empire is at the last gasp?" said Liu T'ao.

"All is well," said the Emperor, "Where is anything wrong?"

Said T'ao, "Robbers swarm on all sides and plunder the cities. And all is the fault of the Ten Eunuchs who sell offices and injure the people, oppress the prince and deceive their superiors. All virtuous men have left the services and misfortune is before our very eyes."

At this the eunuchs pulled off their hats and threw themselves at their master's feet.

"His Excellency disapproves of us," they said, "and we are in danger. We pray that our lives be spared and we may go to our homes. Lo! we yield our property to help defray military expenses."

And they wept bitterly. The Emperor turned angrily to the minister, saying, "You also have servants; why can you not bear with mine?"

And thereupon he called to the guards to eject T'ao and put him to death. Liu T'ao cried aloud, "My death matters nothing. The pity is that the Hans, after four centuries of reign, are falling fast."

The guards hustled him away and were just about to carry out their orders when another minister stopped them, saying, "Strike not! Wait till I have spoken with His Majesty."

It was the *Ssu-tu*, Cheng Tan. He went in to the Emperor, to whom he said, "For what fault is Liu the Censor to be put to death?" "He has vilified my servants; and has insulted me," said the Emperor.

"All the Empire would eat the flesh of the eunuchs if they could, and yet, Sire, you respect them as if they were your parents. They have no merit, but they are created nobles. Moreover, Feng Hsu was in league with the late rebels. Unless Your Majesty looks to it the State will fall.

"There was no proof against Feng," replied the Emperor. "Are there none faithful among the eunuchs?"

The minister beat his forehead on the steps of the throne and did not desist from remonstrance. Then the Emperor grew angry and commanded his removal and imprisonment with Liu T'ao. That night he was murdered.

Then a forged edict went forth making Sun Chien Prefect of Changsha, with orders to suppress the rebellion, and in less than two months he reported the district all tranquil. For this he was created Marquis of Wuch'eng. Further Liu Yu was made magistrate of Yuchow to move against Yuyang and suppress Chang Chu and Chang Shun. The Prefect of Taichow recommended Yuan-te to Liu

Yu, who welcomed him and gave him rank and sent him against the rebels. He fought with and worsted them, and entirely broke their spirit. Chang Shun was cruel and his men turned against him. One of his officers then slew him and brought in his head, after which the others submitted. The other leader Chang Chu saw that all was lost and committed suicide.

Yuyang being now tranquil Liu Pei's services were reported to the throne and he received full pardon for the insult to the inspector. He also became an official in Mich'eng. Then Sun Chien stated his previous good services and he was made *Pieh-pu Ssu-ma* and sent to Pingyuan.

This place was very prosperous and Yuan-te recovered something of his old manner before the days of adversity. Liu Yu also received preferment.

In the summer of the year A.D. 189 the Emperor became seriously ill and summoned Ho Chin into the palace to arrange for the future. This man Ho had sprung from a humble family of butchers, but a sister had become a concubine of rank and borne a son to the Emperor, named Pien. After this she became *Huang-hou* or Empress and Ho Chin became powerful. The Emperor had also greatly loved a beautiful girl named Wang who had borne him a son named Hsieh. The Empress Ho had poisoned the girl from jealousy, and the babe had been given into the care of the Empress Dowager Tung, who was the mother of the Emperor Ling. She was the wife of Liu Chang, the Marquis of Tu-ting. As time went on and the Emperor Huan had no son of his own he adopted the son of the marquis, who succeeded as the Emperor Ling. After his accession he had taken his own mother into the palace to live and had conferred upon her the title of *T'ai-hou*, or Empress Dowager.

The Dowager Empress had always tried to persuade her son to name Hsieh as the Heir Apparent, and in fact the Emperor greatly loved the boy and was disposed to do as his mother desired. When he fell ill one of the eunuchs said, "If Hsieh is to succeed, Ho Chin must be killed." The Emperor saw this too and commanded Ho Chin to come to him. But at the very gates of the palace Ho had been warned of his danger and had secreted himself. Ho had then called many of the ministers to his side and they met to consider how to put the eunuchs to death.

At this assembly Ts'ao Ts'ao had spoken saying, "The influence of the eunuchs dates back half a century and has spread like a noxious weed in all directions. How can we hope to destroy it? Above all keep this plot secret or you will be exterminated."

Ho Chin was very angry at this speech and cried, "What do inferiors like you, know of the ways of government?"

And in the midst of the confusion a messenger came to say the Emperor was no more. He also told them the eunuchs had decided to keep the death a secret and forge a command to Ho, the 'State Uncle,' to come into the palace to settle the succession. Meanwhile to prevent trouble they had inscribed the name of Hsieh on the roll. And as he finished speaking the edict arrived.

"The matter for the moment is to set up the rightful heir," said Ts'ao Ts'ao. "The other affair can wait."

"Who dares to join me?" asked Ho Chin.

At once one stood forward saying, "Give me five companies of veterans and we will break into the palace, set up the true heir, slay the eunuchs and sweep clean the government. Then will follow peace."

The energetic speaker was Yuan Shao, who then held the rank of *Hsiao-yu.*

Ho Chin mustered five companies of the guards. Shao put on complete armour and took command. Ho Chin, supported by a large number of ministers, went into the palace and in the hall where lay the coffin of the late Emperor they placed Pien on the throne. After the ceremony was over and all had bowed before the new Ruler. Yuan Shao went in to arrest the eunuch Chien Shih. Shih in terror fled into the palace garden and hid among the shrubs, where he was discovered and murdered by another eunuch. The guards under his command went over to the other side. Shao thought the moment most opportune to slay all the eunuchs and it had been well if his advice had been taken. But the eunuchs scented the danger and went to the Empress Dowager Ho.

They said, "The originator of the plan to injure your brother was Chien Shih; only he was concerned and no other. Now General Ho, on his lieutenant's advice, wishes to slay every one of us. We implore thy pity, O Grandmother."

"Fear not," said she, "I will protect you."

She sent for her brother, and said, "I and you are of lowly origin and we owe our good fortune to the eunuchs. The misguided Chien Shih is now dead and need you really put all the others to death as Yuan Shao advises?"

And Ho Chin obeyed her wish. He explained to his party that the real offender having met his fate they need not exterminate the whole party nor injure his colleagues.

"Slay them, root and branch," cried Shao, "or they will ruin you."

"I have decided," said Ho, coldly, "say no more."

Within a few days Ho became a President of a Board and his friends received offices.

Tung *T'ai-hou* summoned the eunuch Chang Jang and his party to a council. Said she, "It was I who first brought forward the sister of Ho Chin. Today her son is on the throne and all the officials are her friends/ and her influence is enormous. What can we do?"

Jang replied, "Madam should administer the state from 'behind the veil'; create the Emperor's son Hsieh a prince; give 'Uncle' Tung high rank and place him over the army and use us. That will do it."

Tung, *T'ai-hou* approved. Next day she held a court and issued an edict in the sense proposed. When Ho *T'ai-hou* saw this she prepared a banquet to which she invited her rival. In the middle of the feast, when all were well warmed with wine, she rose and offered a cup to her guest saying, "It is not fitting, that we two women should meddle in state affairs. Of old when Lu *T'ai-hou* laid hands upon the government all her clan were put to death. We ought to remain content, immured in our palaces, and leave state affairs to the statesmen. That would be well for the country and I trust you will act thus."

But the Empress Tung only got angry. "You poisoned the lady Wang out of jealousy. Now, relying upon the fact that your son sits on the throne and that your brother is powerful, you speak these wild words. I will command that your brother be beheaded and that can be done as easily as I turn my hand."

Then Empress Ho in her turn waxed wroth and said, "I tried to persuade you with fair words; why get so angry?"

"You low born daughter of a butcher, what do you know of offices?" cried her rival.

And the quarrel waxed hot.

The eunuchs persuaded the ladies to retire. But in the night Ho *T'ai-hou* summoned her brother into the palace and told him what had occurred. He went out and took counsel with the principal officers of state. Next morn a court was held and a memorial was presented saying that Tung *T'ai-hou*, being the consort of a "frontier" prince—only a collateral—could not properly occupy any part of the palace. She was to be removed into Hochien and was to depart immediately. And while they sent an escort to remove the lady a strong guard was placed about her brother's dwelling. They took away his seal of office and he, knowing this was the end, committed suicide in his private apartments. His dependents, who wailed his death, were driven off by the guards.

Two of the eunuchs having lost their patroness, sent large gifts to Ho Chin's younger brother Miao and his mother, and thus got them to put in a good word to the Empress Dowager Ho so as to gain her protection. And so they gained favour once more at court.

A few months later the secret emissaries of Ho Chin murdered Tung *T'ai-hou* in her residence in the country. Her remains were brought to the capital and buried. Ho Chin feigned illness and did not attend the funeral.

Yuan Shao went one day to see Ho Chin to tell him that two eunuchs, Chang Jang and Tuan Kuei, were spreading the report outside that Ho Chin had caused the death of the late empress dowager and was aiming at the throne. He urged Ho to make this an excuse to put them finally out of the way. Shao pointed out how Tou Wu had missed his chance because the secret had not been kept and urged upon him the ease with which they could be destroyed under the then favourable conditions. It was a heaven-sent opportunity.

But Ho Chin replied, "Let me think it over."

His servants secretly told the intended victims, who sent further gifts to the younger brother. Corrupted by these he went in to speak with his sister and said, "The General is the chief support of the new Emperor, yet he is not gracious and merciful but thinks wholly of slaughter. If he slay the eunuchs without cause, it may bring about revolution."

Soon after her brother entered and told her of his design to put the eunuchs to death. She argued with him. She said that they looked after palace affairs and were old servants. To kill the old servants just after the death of their master would appear disrespectful to the Dynasty. And as Ho was of a vacillating mind he murmured assent and left her.

"What about it?" said Shao on meeting him.

"She will not consent; what can be done?"

"Call up an army and slay them; it is imperative. Never mind her consent."

"That is an excellent plan," said Ho.

And he sent orders all round to march soldiers to the capital.

But the Recorder, Ch'en Lin, said, "Nay; do not act blindly. The proverb says 'To cover the eyes and snatch at swallows is to fool one's self.'" If in so small a matter you cannot attain your wish, what of great affairs? Now by virtue of the imperial prestige and with the army under your hand you may do as you please. To use such enormous powers against the eunuchs would resemble lighting up a furnace to burn a hair. But act promptly; use your powers and smite at once and all the Empire will be with you. But to summon forces to the capital, to gather many bold men into one spot, each with his own schemes, is to turn one's weapons against one's own person, to place one's self in the power of another. Nothing but failure can come of it, nothing but confusion."

"The view of a mere book-worm," said Ho with a smile.

Then one of those about him suddenly clapped his hands, crying

"It is as easy as turning over one's hand! why so much talk?"

The speaker was Ts'ao Ts'ao.

> Wouldst thou withdraw wicked men from thy prince's side
> Then seek counsel of the wise men of the State.

What Ts'ao Ts'ao said will be disclosed in later chapters.

CHAPTER III

TUNG CHO SILENCES TING YUAN:
LI SU BRIBES LU PU

What Ts'ao Ts'ao said was this: "The eunuch evil is of very old standing, but the real cause of the present trouble is in the improper influence allowed them by the ruler, and the misplaced favouritism they have enjoyed. But a gaoler would be ample force to employ against the evil. Why increase confusion by summoning troops from the provinces? Any desire to slay them will speedily become known and the plan will fail."

"Then Meng-te, you have some scheme of your own to further," said Ho with a sneer.

"Ho Chin is the man to throw the empire into confusion," retorted Ts'ao.

Then Ho Chin sent swift, secret letters far and wide.

It must be recalled here that the now powerful Tung Cho had failed in his attempt to destroy the Yellow Turban rebellion and would have been punished but for the protection of the Ten Eunuchs, whom he had bribed heavily. Later he obtained an important military command in the west. But he was treacherous and disloyal at heart. So when he received the summons to the capital he rejoiced greatly and lost no time in obeying it. He left a son-in-law Niu Fu to hold Shensi and set out for Loyang.

Li Ju, his adviser and son-in-law said, "Though a formal summons has come there are many obscurities in it. It would be well to send up a memorial stating plainly our aims and intentions. Then we can proceed." So he composed one something like this: "Thy servant knows that the continual rebellions owe their origin to the eunuchs who act counter to all recognised precept. Now to stop the ebullition of a pot the best way is to withdraw the fire; to cut out an abscess, though painful, is better than to nourish the evil.

I have dared to undertake a military advance on the capital, and now pray that Chang Jang and the other eunuchs be removed for the happiness of the Dynasty and of the whole land."

Ho Chin read this memorial and showed it to his partisans. Then said Cheng T'ai, "A fierce wild beast; if he come his prey will be men."

Ho Chin replied, "You are too timorous; you are unequal to great schemes."

But Lu Chih also said, "Long have I known this man; in appearance innocent, he is a very wolf at heart. Let him in and calamity enters with him. Stop him; do not let him come and thus will you avoid confusion."

Ho Chin was obstinate and both these men gave up their posts and retired, as did more than half the ministers of State, while Ho Chin sent a warm welcome to Tung Cho, who soon camped at Ying Pool.

The eunuchs knew this move was directed against them and recognised that their only chance for safety was to strike the first blow. So they first hid a band of armed ruffians in the palace at the Gate of Abundant Virtue and then went in to see the Empress.

They said, "The General, feigning to act under command, has called up armies to the capital to destroy us. We pray you, Grandmother, to pity and save us."

"Go to the General and confess your faults," said she.

"If we did then should we be cut to mincemeat. Rather summon the General into your presence and command him to cease. If he will not, then we pray but to die in your presence."

She issued the requisite command and Ho was just going to her when Ch'en Lin advised him not to enter, saying the eunuchs were certainly behind the order and meant him harm. But Ho could only see the command of the Empress and was blind to all else.

"The plot is no longer a secret"; and Yuan Shan, "still you may go if you are ready to fight your way in."

"Get the eunuchs out first," said Ts'ao Ts'ao.

"Silly children!" said Ho. "What can they do against the man who holds the forces of the Empire in the palm of his hand?"

Shao said, "If you will go, then we will come as a guard, just as a precaution."

Whereupon both he and Ts'ao chose a half company of the best men under their command, at whose head they placed a brother of Yuan Shao, named Shu.

Yuan Shu, clad in mail, drew up his men outside the Chingso Gate while the other two went as escort. When Ho Chin neared the palace the eunuchs said, "The orders are to admit the General and none other." So the escort was detained outside.

Ho Chin went in proudly. At the Gate of Abundant Virtue he was met by the two chief eunuchs and their followers quickly closed in around him. Ho began to feel alarmed. Then Chang Jang in a harsh voice began to revile him.

"What crime had Tung *T'ai-hou* committed that she should have been put to death? And when the Mother of the Country was buried, who feigned sickness and did not attend? We raised you and your paltry, huckstering family to all the dignity and wealth you have, and this is your gratitude! You would slay us. You call us sordid and dirty; who is the cleaner?"

Ho Chin was panic stricken and looked about for a way to escape, but the eunuchs closed him in and then the assassins appeared and did their bloody work.

> Closing the days of the Hans, and the years of their rule were near spent,
> Stupid and tactless was Ho Chin, yet stood he highest in office;
> Many were they who advised him, but he was deaf as he heard not:
> Wherefore fell he a victim under the swords of the eunuchs.

So Ho Chin died. Yuan Shao waited long. By and by, impatient at the delay, he called through the Gate, "Thy carriage waits, O General." For reply the head of the murdered officer was flung over the wall.

A decree was proclaimed that Ho Chin had contemplated treachery and therefore had been slain. It pardoned his adherents. Yuan Shao shouted, "The eunuchs have slain the minister. Let those who will slay this wicked party come and help me."

Then one of Ho Chin's officers set fire to the gate. Yuan Shu at the head of his men burst in and fell to slaying the eunuchs without regard to age or rank. Yuan Shao and Ts'ao Ts'ao broke into the inner part of the palace. Four of the eunuchs fled to the Blue Flower Lodge where they were hacked to pieces. Fire raged, destroying the buildings. Four of the eunuchs led by Chang Jang carried off the Empress, the heir apparent and the Prince of Ch'en-liu toward the north palace.

Lu Chih, since he had resigned office, was at home, but hearing of the revolution in the palace he donned his armour, took his spear and prepared to fight. He saw the eunuch Tuan Kuei hurrying the Empress along and called out "You rebels, how dare you abduct the Empress?" The eunuch fled. The Empress leaped out of a window and was taken to a place of safety.

Wu K'uang burst into one of the inner halls where he found Ho Miao, sword in hand.

"You also were in the plot to slay your brother," cried he. "You shall die with the others."

"Let us kill the plotter against his elder brother," cried many.

Miao looked around; his enemies hemmed him in on every side. He was hacked to pieces.

Shao bade his soldiers scatter and seek out all the families of the eunuchs, sparing none. In that slaughter many beardless men were killed in error.

Ts'ao Ts'ao set himself to extinguish the fires. He then begged Ho T'ai-hou to undertake the direction of affairs and soldiers were sent to pursue Chang Jang and rescue the young Emperor.

The two chief eunuchs, Chang Jang and Tuan Kuei, had hustled away the Emperor and the Prince of Ch'en-liu. They burst through the smoke and fire and travelled without stopping till they reached the Peimang Hills. It was then the third watch. They heard a great shouting behind them and saw soldiers in pursuit. Their leader was shouting "Stop, stop!" Chang Jang, seeing that he was lost, jumped into the river, where he was drowned.

The two boys ignorant of the meaning of all this confusion and terrified out of their senses, dared not utter a cry; they crept in among the rank grass on the river bank and hid. The soldiers scattered in all directions but failed to find them. So they remained till the fourth watch, shivering with cold from the drenching dew and very hungry. They lay down in the thick grass and wept in each other's arms, silently, lest any one should discover them.

"This is no a place to stay in," said the Prince, "we must find some way out."

So the two children knotted their clothes together and managed to crawl up the bank. They were in a thicket of thorn bushes and it was quite dark. They could not see any path. They were in despair when, all at once, millions of fireflies sprang up all about them and circled in the air in front of the Emperor.

"God is helping us," said the Prince.

They followed whither the fireflies led and gradually got into a road. They walked till their feet were too sore to go further, when, seeing a heap of straw near the road, they crept to it and lay down.

This heap of straw was close to a farm house. In the night, as the farmer was sleeping, he saw in a vision two bright red suns drop behind his dwelling. Alarmed by the portent he hastily dressed and went forth to look about him. Then he saw a bright light shooting up from a heap of straw. He hastened thither and then saw two youths lying behind it.

"To what household do you belong, young gentlemen?" asked he.

The Emperor was too frightened to reply, but his companion said, "He is the Emperor. There has been a revolution in the palace and we ran away. I am his brother Prince of Ch'en-liu."

The farmer bowed again and again and said, "I am the brother of a former official and my name is Ts'ui I. My brother was disgusted with the behaviour of the eunuchs and so resigned and hid away here."

The two lads were taken into the farm and their host on his knees served them with refreshment.

It has been said that Min Kung had gone in pursuit of the eunuch Tuan Kuei. By and by Kung overtook him and cried, "Where is the Emperor?"

"He disappeared. I do not know where he is."

Kung slew him and hung the bleeding head on his horse's neck. Then he sent his men searching in all directions and he rode off by himself on the same quest. Presently he came to the farm. Ts'ui I, seeing what hung on his horse's neck, questioned him and, satisfied with his story, led him to the Emperor. The meeting was affecting; all were moved to tears.

"The State cannot be without its ruler," said Min Kung. "I pray Your Majesty to return to the city."

At the farm they had but one sorry nag and this they saddled for the Emperor. The young prince was taken on Min Kung's charger. And thus they left the farm. Soon they fell in with other officials and the several guards and soldiers made up an imposing cavalcade. Tears were shed freely as the ministers met their Emperor.

A man was sent on in front to the capital there to expose the head of the eunuch Tuan Kuei.

As soon as they could they placed the Emperor on a better steed and the young prince had a horse to himself.

Thus the Emperor returned to Loyang and so it happened after all as the street boys' ditty ran:—

> Though the Emperor doesn't rule, though the prince no office fills,
> Yet a brilliant cavalcade comes along from Peimang Hills.

The cavalcade had not proceeded far when they saw coming towards them a large body of soldiers with fluttering banners hiding the sun and raising a huge cloud of dust. The officials turned pale and the Emperor was greatly alarmed. Yuan Shao rode out in advance and demanded who they were. From under the shade of an embroidered banner rode out an officer demanding if they had seen the Emperor. His Majesty was too panic-stricken to respond but the Prince of Ch'en-liu rode to the front and cried, "Who are you?"

Tung Cho replied giving his name and rank.

"Have you come to protect the chariot or to steal it?" said the prince.

"I have come to protect," said Tung Cho.

"If that is so the Emperor is here; why do you not dismount?"

Cho hastily dismounted and made obeisance on the left of the road. Then the prince spoke graciously to him.

From first to last the prince had carried himself most perfectly so that Cho in his heart admired his behaviour, and then arose the first desire to set aside the Emperor in favour of the prince.

They reached the palace the same day and there was an affecting interview with Ho T'ai-hou.

But when they had restored order in the palace the Hereditary Seal, the special seal of the Emperor, was missing.

Tung Cho camped without the walls but every day he was to be seen in the streets with an escort of mailed soldiers so that the common people were in a state of constant trepidation. He also went in and out of the palace careless of all the rules of propriety.

Pao Hsin spoke of his behaviour to Yuan Shao, saying, "This man harbours some evil design and should be removed."

"Nothing can be done till the government is more settled," said Shao."

Then he saw Wang Yun and asked what he thought.

"Let us talk it over," was the reply.

Pao Hsin said no more but he left the capital and retired to T'aishan. Tung Cho induced the soldiers of the two brothers Ho to join his command and privately spoke to his adviser about deposing the Emperor in favour of the Prince of Ch'en-liu.

"The government is really without a head; there can be no better time than this to carry out your plan. Delay will spoil all. Tomorrow assemble the officials in the Wenming Garden and address them on the subject. Put all opponents to death and your prestige is settled."

So spoke his adviser and the words pleased Tung Cho mightily.

So the next day he spread a feast and invited many guests. As all the officers went in terror of him no one dared be absent. He himself rode up to the garden last of all and took his place with his sword girded on. When the wine had gone round several times

Tung Cho stopped the service and the music and began to speak.

"I have something to say; listen quietly all of you."

All turned towards him.

"The Emperor is lord of all and if he lacks dignity and behaves in an unseemly manner he is no fitting inheritor of the ancestral prerogatives. He who is now on the throne is a weakling, inferior to the Prince of Ch'en-liu in intelligence and love of learning. The Prince is in every way fitted for the throne. I desire to depose the Emperor and set up the Prince in his place. What think you?"

The assembly listened in perfect silence, none daring at first to utter a word of dissent. But one dared; for suddenly a guest stood up in his place, smote the table and cried.

"No! No! who are you, that you dare utter such bold words? The Emperor is the son of the lawful consort and has done no wrong. Why then should he be deposed? Are you a rebel?"

The speaker was Ting Yuan, governor of Chinchow.

Cho glared at him. "There is life for those who are with me, death for those against," roared he.

He drew his sword and made for the objector. But the watchful Li Ju had noticed standing behind Ting Yuan a particularly dangerous looking henchman of his, who was now handling his spear threateningly, and whose eyes were blazing with anger. So he hastily interposed, saying, "But this is the banquet chamber and state affairs should be left outside. The matters can be fully discussed tomorrow."

His fellow guests persuaded Ting Yuan to leave, and after his departure Tung Cho said, "Is what I said just and reasonable?"

"You are mistaken, Illustrious Sir," said Lu Chih. "Of old* Tai Chia was unenlightened. Wherefore I Yin immured him in the T'ung Palace till he reformed. Later** Prince Ch'ang I ascended the throne, and in less than a month he committed more than three thousand categorical faults. Wherefore Ho Kuang, the regent, declared in the ancestral temple that he was deposed. Our present Emperor is young, but he is intelligent, benevolent and wise. He has not committed a single fault. You, Sir, are hot a metropolitan official and have had no experience in state administration. Neither have you the pure intentions of I Yin which qualified his actions. Without that justification such an act is presumption."

Tung Cho angrily drew his sword to slay the bold speaker, but another official remonstrated.

*1750 B.C. **80 B.C.

"President Lu is the cynosure of the whole country and his violent death would stir the hearts of all men," said P'eng Po.

Then Tung Cho stayed his hand.

Then said Wang Yun, "A great question like the deposition and substitution of Emperors is not one to be decided after a wine party. Let it be put off till another time."

So the guests dispersed. Cho stood at the gate with drawn sword watching them depart.

Standing thus he noticed a spearman galloping to and fro on a fiery steed and asked Li Ju if he knew him.

"That is Lu Pu, the adopted son of Ting Yuan. His ordinary name is Fenhsien. You must keep out of his way, my lord."

Tung Cho went inside the gate so that he could not be seen. But next day a man reported to him that Ting Yuan had come out of the city with a small army and was challenging to a battle. Tung Cho went forth to accept the challenge. And the armies were drawn up in proper array.

Lu Pu was a conspicuous figure in the forefront. His hair was arranged under a handsome headdress of gold and he had donned a beautiful embroidered fighting robe, a *t'ang-ni* helmet and breast plate, and round his waist was a *mang* belt with a lion's head clasp. With spear set he rode close behind his master.

Ting Yuan, pointing his finger at Tung Cho, began to revile him.

"Unhappy indeed was this State when the eunuchs became so powerful that the people were as if trodden into the mire under their feet. Now you, devoid of the least merit, dare to talk of deposing the rightful Emperor and setting up another. This is to desire rebellion and no less."

Tung Cho could not reply for Lu Pu, eager for the fight, rode straight at him. Tung Cho fled and Ting's army came on. The battle went in their favour and the beaten men retired and made another camp. Here Tung Cho called his officers to a council.

"This Lu Pu is a marvel," said Tung Cho. "If he was only on my side I would defy the whole world."

At this a man advanced saying, "Be content, O my lord! I am a fellow villager of his and know him well, his bravery, his stupidity, his cupidity and unscrupulousness. With this little, blarneying tongue of mine I can persuade him to put up his hands and come over to your side."

Tung Cho was delighted and gazed admiringly at the speaker, on Li Su a minor officer of his army.

"What arguments will you use with him?"

"You have a fine horse, the Hare, one of the best ever bred. I must have this steed, and gold and pearls to win his heart. Then will I go and persuade him. He will certainly abandon Ting Yuan's service for yours."

"What think you?" said Tung Cho to his adviser Li.

"One cannot grudge a horse to win an empire," was the reply.

So they gave the corrupter of morals what he demanded—a thousand taels of gold, ten strings of beautiful pearls and a jewelled belt, and these accompanied Li Su on his visit to his fellow villager. He reached the camp and said to the guard, "Please tell General Lu that a very old friend has come to visit him."

He was admitted forthwith.

"Worthy brother, have you been well since we last met?"

"How long it is since we last saw each other!" replied Pu, bowing in return. "And where are you now?"

"I am an officer in the Tiger Company. When I learned you were a strong supporter of the throne I could not say how I rejoiced. I have come now to present to you a really fine horse, a thousand *li* a day horse, one that crosses rivers and goes up mountains as if they were the level plain. He is called The Hare. He will be a fitting aid to your valour."

Lu Pu bade them lead out the horse. He was of a uniforrn colour like glowing charcoal; not a hair of another colour. He measured ten feet from head to tail and from hoof to neck eight feet. When he neighed the sound filled the empyrean and shook the ocean.

> Mark ye the steed swift and tireless, see the dust, spurned by his hoofs, rising in clouds;
> Now he swims the river, anon climbs the hill, rending the purple mist asunder;
> Scornful he breaks the rein, shakes from his head the jewelled bridle;
> He is as a fiery dragon descending from the highest heaven.

Pu was delighted with the horse and said, "What return can I hope to make for such a creature?"

"What return can I hope for? I came to you out of a sense of what is right."

Wine was brought in and they drank.

"We have seen very little of each other, but I am constantly meeting your honourable father," said Li Su.

"You are drunk," said Pu. "My father has been dead for years."

"Not so; I spoke of Ting Yuan, the man of the day."

Lu Pu started. "Yes, I am with him but only because I can do no better."

"Sir, your talent is higher than the heavens, deeper than the seas. Who in all the world does not bow before your name? Fame and riches and honours are yours for the taking. And you say you can do no better than remain a subordinate!"

"If I could only find a master to serve!" said Lu Pu.

"The clever bird chooses the branch whereon to perch; the wise servant selects the master to serve. Seize the chance when it comes, for repentance ever comes too late."

"Now you are in the government. Who think you is really the bravest of all?" asked Lu Pu.

"I despise the whole lot except Tung Cho. He is one who respects wisdom and reveres scholarship; he is discriminating in his rewards and punishments. Surely he is destined to be a really great man."

"I would that I could serve him, but there is no way, I fear." Then Su produced his pearls and gold and the jewelled belt and laid them out before his host.

"What is this? What does it mean?" said Lu Pu.

"Send away the attendants," said Li Su. And he went on, "Tung Cho has long respected your valour and sent these by my hand. The Hare was also from him."

"But, if he loves me like this, what can I do in return?"

"If a stupid fellow like me can be an officer in The Tigers, it is impossible to say what honours await you."

"I am sorry I can offer him no service worth mentioning."

"There is one service you can do, and an extremely easy one to perform; but you would not render that."

Lu Pu pondered long in silence. Then he said, "I might slay Ting Yuan and bring over his soldiers to Tung Cho's side; what think you of that?"

"If you would do that, there could be no greater service. But such a thing must be done quickly."

And Lu Pu promised his friend that he would do the deed and come over on the morrow.

So Li Su took his leave. That very night, at the second watch, Lu Pu entered, sword in hand, into his master's tent. He found Ting Yuan reading by the light of a solitary candle. Seeing who came in he said, "My son, what is afoot?"

"I am a bold hero," said Pu, "do you think I am willing to be a son of yours?"

"Why this change, Feng-hsien?"

As a reply Lu Pu made one cut at his protector and his head fell to the earth. Then he called the attendants and said, "He was an unjust man and I have slain him. Let those who back me stay; the others may depart."

Most ran away. Next day, with the head of the murdered man as his gift, Lu Pu betook himself to Li Su, who led him to Tung Cho. Cho received him with a warm welcome and had wine set before him.

"Your coming is welcome as the gentle dew to the parched grass," said Tung Cho.

Lu Pu made Cho seat himself and then made his obeisance, saying, "Pray let me bow to you as my adopted father."

Tung Cho gave his newly won ally gold and armour and silken robes and spread the feast of welcome. They then separated.

Thence Tung Cho's power and influence increased rapidly. He gave ranks of nobility to his brother and Lu Pu, who were leaders of the two wings, he himself being leader of the centre. The adviser Li Ju never ceased from urging him to carry out the design of deposing the young Emperor.

The now all-powerful general prepared a banquet in the capital at which all the officers of State were guests. He also bade Lu Pu post a company of armed men right and left ready for action. The feast began and several courses were served with nothing to distinguish that banquet from any other. Then suddenly the host arose and drew his sword, saying, "He who is above us being weak and irresolute is unfit for the duties of his high place. Wherefore I, as of old did I Yin and Ho Kuang, will set aside this Emperor giving him the title of Prince Hung-nung and I will place on the throne the present Prince of Ch'en-liu. And those who do not support me will suffer death."

Fear seized them in its grip and they were silent, all but Yuan Shao who said that the Emperor was innocent of any fault and to set him aside in favour of a commoner was rebellion and nothing else.

"The Empire is in my hands," cried Cho, "an I choose to do this thing who will dare say nay? Think you my sword lacks an edge?"

"If your sword is sharp, mine is never blunt," said Shao as his sword flashed out of the sheath.

The two men stood face to face amid the feasters:

> When Ting by treacherous murder died,
> The loss was great to Yuan's side.

The fate of Yuan Shao will be disclosed in later chapters.

CHAPTER IV

It is recorded that Tung Cho was on the point of slaying Yuan Shao, but his adviser checked him, saying, "You must not kill rashly while the business hangs in the balance."

Yuan Shao, his sword still unsheathed, left the assembly. He hung up the symbols of his office at the east gate and went to Ichow.

Tung Cho said to the *T'ai-fu* Yuan Wei, "Your nephew behaved improperly but I pardon him for your sake; what think you of my scheme."

"What you think is right," was the reply.

"If any one opposes the great scheme he will be dealt with by military law," said Tung Cho.

The ministers, thoroughly cowed, promised obedience and the feast came to an end. Tung asked Chou Pi and Wu Chiung what they thought of the flight of Yuan Shao.

"He left in a state of great anger. In such a state of excitement much harm may ensue to the present state of affairs, especially as the Yuan family have been noted for their kindness to the people for four generations, and their proteges and dependents are everywhere. If they assemble bold spirits and call up their clients, all the valiant warriors will be in arms and Shantung will be lost. You had better pardon him and give him a post. He will be glad at being forgiven and will do no harm."

Wu said, "Shao is fond of scheming, but he fails in decision and so is not to be feared. But it would be well to give him rank and thus win popular favour."

Tung Cho followed this advice and thereupon sent a messenger to offer Yuan Shao the command of Pohai.

In the ninth month the Emperor was invited to proceed to the Hall of Abounding Virtue where was a great assembly of officials. There Tung Cho, sword in hand faced the gathering and said, "The Emperor is a weakling unequal to the burden of ruling this land. Now listen ye to the document I have prepared."

And Li Ju read as follows:— "The dutiful Emperor Ling too soon left his people. The Emperor is the cynosure of all the people of this land. Upon the present Emperor Heaven has conferred but small gifts: in dignity and deportment he is deficient and in mourning he is remiss. Only the most complete virtue can grace the imperial dignity. The Empress Mother has trained him improperly and the whole State administration has fallen into confusion. The Empress Dowager, Jung-le, died suddenly and no one knew why. The doctrine of the three bonds and the continuity of celestial and terrestrial interdependence have both been injured. But Hsieh, Prince of Ch'en-liu, is sage and virtuous beside being of handsome exterior. He conforms to all the rules of propriety, his mourning is sincere; his speech is always correct. Eulogies of him fill the Empire. He is well fitted for the great duty of consolidating the rule of Han.

"Now therefore the Emperor is deposed and created Prince Hung-nung and the Empress Dowager retires from the administration.

"I pray the Prince to accept the throne in conformity with the decrees of Heaven, the desires of men and the fulfilment of the hopes of mankind."

This having been read Tung Cho bade the attendants lead the Emperor down from the throne, remove his seal and cause him to kneel facing the north, styling himself minister and requesting commands. Moreover he bade the Empress Dowager strip off her dress of ceremony and await the imperial command. Both victims of this oppression wept and every minister present was deeply affected. One put his discontent into words, crying, "The false Tung Cho is the author of this insult, which I will risk my life to wipe away." And with this he rushed at Tung Cho threatening him with his ivory bâton of office.

It was the President Ting Kuan and he was removed and summarily put to death. While he lived he ceased not to rail at the oppressor, nor was he frightened at death.

> The rebel Tung conceived the foul design
> To thrust the King aside and wrong his line.
> With folded arms the courtiers stood, save one
> Ting Kuan, who dared to cry that wrong was done.

Then the Emperor designate went to the upper part of the hall to receive congratulations. After this the late Emperor, his mother and the Lady in waiting T'ang were removed to the Palace of Perpetual Calm. The entrance gates were locked against all comers.

It was pitiful! There was the young Emperor, after reigning less than half a year, deposed and another put in his place. The new Emperor was Hsieh, the second son of the late Emperor and the name under which he reigned is Hsien. He was nine years of age and the reign-style was changed to Ch'u-P'ing or The Inauguration of Tranquillity.

As chief minister Tung Cho was arrogant beyond all reason. When he bowed before the throne he did not declare his name; in going to court he did not hasten. Booted and armed he entered the reception halls. Never had such a thing been seen before. Li Ju impressed upon him constantly to employ men of reputation so that he should gain public esteem. So when they told him Ch'ai Yung was a man of talent he was summoned. But he would not go. Cho sent a message to him that if he did not come he and his whole clan should be exterminated. Then Ch'ai gave in and appeared. Cho was very gracious to him and promoted him thrice in a month. He became a *Shih-chung* and seemed to be on most friendly terms with the tyrant.

Meanwhile the deposed ruler, his mother and the Lady T'ang were immured in the palace and found their daily supplies gradually diminishing. The deposed Emperor wept incessantly. One day a pair of swallows gliding to and fro moved him to verse.

> Spring! and the green of the tender grass,
> Flushes with joy as the swallows pass;
> The wayfarers pause by the rippling stream,
> And their eyes with new born gladness gleam;
> With lingering gaze the roofs I see
> Of the palace that one time sheltered me.

The messenger, sent by Tung Cho from time to time to the palace for news of the prisoners, got hold of this poem and showed it to his master.

"So he shows his resentment by writing poems, eh! A fair excuse to put them all out of the way," said Tung.

Li Ju was sent with ten men into the palace to consummate the foul deed. The three were in one of the upper rooms when he arrived. The Emperor shuddered when the maid announced the visitor's name.

Presently Li entered and offered a cup of poisoned wine to the Emperor. The Emperor asked what this meant.

"Spring is the season of blending and harmonious inter-change and the Minister sends a cup of the wine of longevity," said he.

"If it be the wine of longevity you may share it too; pledge me first," said the Empress.

Then Li became brutally frank.

"You will not drink!" cried he.

He called the men with daggers and cords and bade her look at them.

"The cup, or these?" said he.

Then said the Lady T'ang, "Let the handmaiden drink in place of her lord. Spare the mother and her son, I pray."

"And who may you be to die for a prince?" said Li.

Then he presented the cup to the Empress once more and bade her drink.

She railed against her brother, the feckless Ho Chin, the author of all this trouble. She would not drink.

Next Li approached the Emperor.

"Let me say farewell to my mother" begged he, and he did so in these lines:—

> The heaven and earth are changed alas! the sun and the moon leave
> their courses,
> I, once the centre of all eyes, am driven to the farthest confines.
> Oppressed by an arrogant minister my life nears its end,
> Everything fails me and vain are my falling tears.

The Lady T'ang sang:—

> Heaven is to be rent asunder, Mother Earth to fall away;
> I, handmaid of an Emperor, would grieve if I followed him not.
> We have come to the parting of ways, the quick and the dead walk
> not together;
> Alas! I am left alone with the grief in my heart.

When they had sung these lines they fell weeping into each others' arms.

"The minister is awaiting my report," said, Li, "and you delay too long. Think you that there is any hope of succour?"

The Empress broke into another fit of railing.

"The rebel forces us to death, mother and son, and Heaven has abandoned us. But you, the tool of his crime, will assuredly perish."

Thereupon Li grew more angry, laid hands on the Empress and

threw her out of the window. Then he bade the soldiers strangle Lady T'ang and forced the lad to swallow the wine of death.

He reported the achievement of the cruel deed to his master who bade them bury the victims without the city. After this Tung's behaviour was more atrocious than before. He spent his nights in the palace, defiled the virgins there and even slept on the imperial couch.

Once he led his soldiers out of the city to Yangch'eng when the villagers, men and women, were assembled from all sides for he annual festival. His men surrounded the place and plundered it. They took away booty by the cart load, and women prisoners and a large number of heads. The procession returned to the city and published a story that they had obtained a great victory over some rebels. They burned the heads beneath the walls and the women and jewellery were shared out among the soldiers.

An officer named Wu Fou was disgusted at this ferocity and sought a chance to slay the tyrant. He constantly wore a breastplate underneath his court dress and carried concealed a sharp dagger. One day when Tung came to court Fou met him on the steps and tried to stab him. But Cho was a very powerful man and held him off till Lu Pu came to his help. He struck down the assailant.

"Who told you to rebel?" said Tung.

Fou glared at him and cried, "You are hot my prince, I am not your minister: where is the rebellion? Your crimes fill the heavens and every man would slay you. I am sorry I cannot tear you asunder with chariots to appease the wrath of the world."

Tung Cho bade them take him out and hack him to pieces. He only ceased railing as he ceased to live.

> Men praise Wu Fou, that loyal servant of the latter days of Han.
> His valour was high as the Heavens, in all ages unequalled;
> In the court itself would he slay the rebel, great is his fame!
> Throughout all time will men call him a hero.

Thereafter Tung Cho always went well guarded.

At Pohai Yuan Shao heard of Tung Cho's misuse of power and sent a secret letter to Wang Yu.

"That rebel Cho outrages Heaven and has deposed his ruler. Men cannot bear to speak of him. Yet you suffer his aggressions as if you knew naught of them. How then are you a dutiful and loyal minister? I have assembled an army and desire to sweep clean the royal habitation, but I dare not lightly begin the task. If you are willing, then find an opportunity to plot against this man. If you would use force I am at your command."

The letter arrived but Wang Yun could see no chance. One day while among the throng in attendance, mostly men of long service, he said to his colleagues, "This is my birthday, I pray you come to a little party in my humble cot this evening."

"We certainly will," they cried, "and wish you long life."

That night the tables were spread in an inner room and his friends gathered there. When the wine had made a few rounds the host suddenly covered his face and began to weep.

The guests were aghast.

"Sir, on your birthday too, why do you weep?" said they.

"It is not my birthday," replied he. "But I wished to call you together and I feared lest Tung Cho should suspect, so I made that the excuse. This man insults the Emperor and does as he wishes so that the imperial prerogatives are in imminent peril. I think of the days when our illustrious founder destroyed Ts'in, annihilated Ch'u and obtained the Empire. Who could have foreseen this day when that Tung Cho has subjugated all to his will? That is why I weep."

Then they all wept with him.

Seated among the guests, however, was Ts'ao Ts'ao, who did not join in the weeping but clapped his hands and laughed aloud.

"If all the officers of the government weep till dawn, and from dawn weep till dark, will that slay Tung Cho?" said he.

His host turned on him angrily.

"Your forbears ate of the bounty of the Hans; do you feel no gratitude? You can laugh?"

"I laughed at the absurdity of an assembly like this being unable to compass the death of one man. Foolish and incapable as I am I will cut off his head and hang it at the gate as an offering to the people."

The host left his seat and went over to Ts'ao Ts'ao.

"These later days," Ts'ao continued, "I have bowed my head to Tung Cho with the sole desire of finding a chance to destroy him. Now he begins to trust me and so I can approach him sometimes. You have a 'seven precious' sword which I would borrow and I will go into his palace and kill him. I care not if I die for it."

"What good fortune for the world that this is so!" said the host.

With this he himself poured out a goblet for his guest who drained it and swore an oath. After this the sword was brought out and given to Ts'ao Ts'ao who hid it under his dress. He finished his wine, took leave of the guests and left the hall. Before long the others dispersed.

Soon after Ts'ao Ts'ao, with this short sword girded on, came to the palace of the minister.

"Where is the minister?" asked he.

"In the small guest room," replied the attendants.

So Ts'ao Ts'ao went in and found his host seated on a couch, Lu Pu was at his side.

"Why so late, Meng-te?" said Tung Cho.

"My horse is out of condition and slow," replied Ts'ao.

Cho turned to his henchman.

"Some good horses have come in from the west. You go and pick out a good one as a present for him." And Lu Pu left.

"He is doomed," thought Ts'ao Ts'ao. He ought to have struck then, but Ts'ao knew Cho was very powerful and he was afraid; he wanted to make sure of his blow.

Now Tung Cho's corpulence was such that he could not remain long sitting, so he rolled over and lay face inwards. "Now is the time," thought the assassin, and he gripped the good sword firmly. But just as he was going to strike, his victim happened to look up and in a mirror he saw the reflection of Ts'ao Ts'ao behind him with a sword in his hand.

"What are you doing, Meng-te?" said he turning suddenly. And at that moment Lu Pu came along leading a horse.

Ts'ao Ts'ao in a flurry dropped on his knees and said, "I have a choice sword here which I wish to present to Your Benevolence."

Tung Cho took it. It was a fine blade, over a foot in length, inlaid with the seven precious signs and very keen; a fine sword in very truth. He handed the weapon to Lu Pu while Ts'ao Ts'ao took off the sheath which he also gave to Lu Pu.

Then they went out to look at the horse. Ts'ao Ts'ao was profuse in his thanks and said he would like to try him. So Cho bade them bring saddle and bridle. Ts'ao led the creature outside, lept, into the saddle, laid oil his whip vigorously and galloped away eastward.

Lu Pu said, "Just as I was coming up it seemed to me as if that fellow was going to stab you, only a sudden panic seized him and he presented the weapon instead."

"I suspected him too," said Cho, Just then Li Ju came in and they told him.

"He has no family here but lodges quite alone and not far away," said he. "Send for him. If he comes forthwith the sword was meant as a gift, but if he makes any excuses he had bad intention. And you can arrest him."

They sent four prison warders to call Ts'ao Ts'ao. They were absent a long time and then came back saying Ts'ao Ts'ao had not returned to his lodging but had ridden in hot haste out of the eastern gate. To the gate-warden's questions he had replied that he was on a special message for the minister. He had gone off at full speed.

"His conscience pricked him and so he fled; there is no doubt that he meant assassination," said Li Ju.

"And I trusted him so well!" said Tung Cho in a rage.

"There must be a conspiracy afoot: when we catch him we shall know all about it," said Li Ju.

Letters and pictures of the fugitive were sent everywhere with orders to catch him. A large reward in money was offered and a patent of nobility, while those who sheltered him would be held to share his guilt.

Ts'ao Ts'ao travelled in hot haste toward Ch'iaochun. On the road at Chungmou he was recognised by the guards at the gate and made prisoner. They took him to the magistrate. Ts'ao declared he was a merchant, named Huangfu. The magistrate scanned his face most closely and remained in deep thought.

Presently he said, "When I was at the capital seeking a post I knew you as Ts'ao Ts'ao, why do you try to conceal your identity?"

He ordered him to the prison till the morrow when he could be sent to the capital and the reward claimed. He gave the soldiers wine and food as a reward.

About midnight he sent a trusty servant to bring the prisoner into his private rooms for interrogation.

"They say the Minister treated you well; why did you try to harm him?" said he.

"How can swallows and sparrows understand the flight of the crane and the wild goose? I am your prisoner and am to be sent to the capital for a reward. Why so many questions?"

The official sent away the attendants and turning to the prisoner said, "Do not despise me. I am no mere hireling, only I have not yet found the lord to serve."

Said Ts'ao Ts'ao, "My ancestors enjoyed the bounty of the Hans and should I differ from a bird or a beast if I did not desire to repay them with gratitude? I have bowed the knee to Tung Cho that thereby I might find an opportunity against him, and so remove this evil from the State. I have failed for this time. Such is the will of heaven."

"And where are you going?"

"Home to my village. Thence I shall issue a summons calling all the bold spirits to come with forces to kill the tyrant. This is my desire."

Thereupon the magistrate himself loosened the bonds of the prisoner, led him to the upper seat and bowed saying, "I am called

Ch'en Kung. My aged mother and family are in the east. I am deeply affected by your loyalty and uprightness and I will abandon my office and follow you."

Ts'ao Ts'ao was delighted with this turn of affairs. The magistrate at once collected some money for the expenses of their journey and gave his prisoner a different dress. Then each took a sword and rode away toward the home of Ts'ao. Three days later at eventide they reached Ch'engkao. Ts'ao Ts'ao pointed with his whip to a hamlet deep in the woods and said, "There lives my uncle, Lu Po-she, a sworn-brother of my father. Suppose we go and ask news of my family and seek shelter for the night?"

"Excellent!" said his companion and they rode over, dismounted at the farm gate and entered.

Their host said, "I hear the government has sent stringent orders on all sides to arrest you. Your father has gone into hiding to Ch'un Lu. How has this all come about?"

Ts'ao Ts'ao told him and said, "Had it not been for this man here with me I should have been already hacked to pieces."

Po-she bowed low to Ch'en Kung saying, "You are the salvation of the Ts'ao family. But be at ease and rest, I will find you a bed in my humble cottage."

He then rose and went into the inner chamber where he stayed a long time. When he came out, he said, "There is no good wine in the house, I am going over to the village to get some for you."

And he hastily mounted his donkey and rode away. The two travellers sat a long time. Suddenly they heard at the back of the house the sound of sharpening a knife.

Ts'ao Ts'ao said, "He is not my real uncle; I am beginning to doubt the meaning of his going off. Let us listen."

So they silently stepped out into a straw hut at the back. Presently some one said, "Bind before killing, eh?"

"As I thought," said Ts'ao Ts'ao, "now unless we strike first we shall be taken."

Suddenly they dashed in, sword in hand, and slew the whole household male and female; in all eight persons.

After this they searched the house. In the kitchen they found a pig bound ready to kill.

"You have made a huge mistake," said Ch'en Kung, "and we have slain honest folk."

They at once mounted and rode away. Soon they met their host coming home and over the saddle in front of him they saw two vessels of wine. In his hands he carried fruit and vegetables.

"Why are you going, Sirs?" he called to them.

"Accused people dare not linger," said Ts'ao.

"But I have bidden them kill a pig! Why do you refuse my poor hospitality? I pray you ride back with me."

Ts'ao Ts'ao paid no heed. Urging his horse forward he suddenly drew his sword and rode after Lu.

"Who is that coming along?"

Lu turned and looked back and Ts'ao at the same instant cut him down.

His companion was frightened.

"You were wrong enough before," cried he. "What now is this?"

"When he got home and saw his family killed, think you he would bear it patiently? If he had raised an alarm and followed us we should have been killed."

"To kill deliberately is very wrong," said Ch'en Kung.

"I would rather betray the world then let the world betray me," was the reply.

Ch'en Kung only thought. They rode on some distance by moonlight and presently knocked up an inn for shelter. Having first fed their horses, Ts'ao Ts'ao was soon asleep but his companion lay thinking.

"I took him for a true man and left all to follow him, but he is cruel as a wolf. If I spare him he will do more harm," thought Ch'en.

And he rose intending to kill his companion.

> In his heart lie cruelty and venom, he is no true man;
> In nought doth he differ from his enemy Tung Cho.

The further fortunes of Ts'ao Ts'ao will be told in later chapters.

CHAPTER V

At the close of the last chapter Ts'ao Ts'ao's companion was about to slay him. But the memory of why he had decided to join his fortunes with his companion's stayed his hand. Rising from his bed before dawn he mounted his horse and rode away toward his home in the east. Ts'ao Ts'io awoke with the day and missed his companion. Thought he, "He thinks me brutal because of a couple of egoistic phrases I used and so he has gone. I ought to push on too and not linger here."

So he travelled as quickly as possible toward home. When he saw his father he related what had happened and said he wanted to dispose of all the property and enlist soldiers with the money.

"Our possessions are but small"; said his father, and not enough to do anything with. However, there is a graduate here, one Wei Hung, careless of wealth but careful of virtue, whose family is very rich. With his help we might hope for success."

A feast was prepared and the rich man invited. Ts'ao made him a speech:— "The Hans have lost their lordship and Tung Cho is really a tyrant. He flouts his prince and is cruel to the people, who gnash their teeth with rage. I would restore the Hans but my means are insufficient. Sir, I appeal to your loyalty and public-spirit."

He replied, "I have long desired this but, so far, have not found a man fit to undertake the task. Since you, Meng-te, have so noble a desire I willingly devote all my property to the cause."

This was joyful news and the call to arms was forthwith prepared and sent far and near. So they established a corps of volunteers and set up a large white recruiting banner with the words "Loyalty and Right" inscribed thereon. The response was rapid and volunteers came in like rain drops in number.

One day came a certain Yo Chin whose minor name was Wen-ch'ien, and another Li Tien, also known as Man-ch'eng. These two were appointed to Ts'ao's personal staff. Another was one Hsiahou Tun. He was descended from Hsiahou Ying and had been trained from his early boyhood to use the spear and the club. When only fourteen he had been attached to a certain master-in-arms. One day some one spoke disrespectfully of his master and Tun killed him. For this deed, however, he had to flee and had been an exile for some time. Now he came to offer his services, accompanied by his brother. Each brought a company of trained men.

Really these two were brothers of Ts'ao Ts'ao by birth since his father was originally of the Hsiahou family, and had only been adopted into the Ts'ao family.

A few days later came two other brothers, Ts'ao Jen and Ts'ao Hung, each with a company. These two were accomplished horsemen and trained in the use of arms. Then drill began and Wei Hung spent his treasure freely in buying clothing, armour, flags and banners. From all sides poured in gifts of grain.

When Yuan Shao received Ts'ao Ts'ao's call to arms he collected all those under his command to the number of three legions. He came to take the oath to Ts'ao. Next a manifesto was issued:—

"Ts'ao and his associates, moved by a sense of duty, now make this proclamation. Tung Cho defies heaven and earth. He is destroying the State and injuring his prince. He pollutes the palace and oppresses the people. He is vicious and cruel. His crimes are heaped up. Now we have received a secret command to call up soldiers and we are pledged to cleanse the Empire and destroy the evil-doers. We will raise a volunteer army and exert all our efforts to maintain the dynasty and succour the people. Respond to this, O Nobles, by mustering your soldiers."

Many from every side answered the summons as the following list shows:—

The Prefect of Nanyang, Yuan Shu.
The Governor of Ichow, Han Fu.
The Governor of Yuchow, K'ung Yu.
The Governor of Yenchow, Liu Tai.
The Prefect of Honei, Wang K'uang.
The Prefect of Ch'en-liu, Chang Mo.
The Prefect of Tungchun, Chiao Mao.
The Prefect of Shanyang, Yuan I.
The *Hsiang* of Chipei, Pao Hsin.
The Prefect of Peihai, K'ung Yung.

The Prefect of Kuangling, Chang Ch'ao.

The Governor of Hsuchow, T'ao Ch'ien.

The Prefect of Hsiliang, Ma T'eng.

The Prefect of Peip'ing, Kungsun Tsan.

The Prefect of Shangtang, Chang Yang.

The Prefect of Ch'angsha, Sun Chien.

The Prefect of Pohai, Yuan Shao.

These contingents varied in size, but each was complete in itself with its officers, civil and military, and battle-leaders, and they assembled at Loyang.

The Prefect of Peip'ing, Kungsun Tsan, while on his way with his force of a legion and a half, passed through P'ingyuan. There he saw among the mulberry trees a yellow flag under which marched a small company. When they drew nearer he saw the leader was Liu Yuan-te.

"Good brother, what do you here?"

"You were kind to me once and on your recommendation I was made magistrate of this district. I heard you were passing through and came to salute you. May I pray my elder brother to enter into the city and rest his steed?"

"Who are these two?" said Tsan pointing to the other two brothers.

"These are Kuan Yu and Chang Fei, my sworn brothers."

"Were they fighting with you against the rebels?"

"All my success was due to their efforts," said Yuan-te.

"And what offices do they fill?"

"Kuan Yu is a mounted archer: Fei is a foot archer."

"Thus are able men buried!" said Tsan, sighing. Then he continued. "All the highest in the land are now going to destroy the rebellious Tung Cho. My brother would do better to abandon this petty place and join us in restoring the House of Han. Why not?"

"I should like to go," said Yuan-te.

"If you had let me kill him that other time you would not have this trouble today," said Chang Fei.

"Since things are so let us pack and go," said Kuan Yu.

So without more ado the three brothers, with a few horsemen, joined Kungsun Tsan and marched with him to join the great army.

One after another the feudal lords came up and encamped. Their camps extended over three hundred *li* and more. When all had arrived Ts'ao, as the head, prepared sacrificial bullocks and horses and called all the lords to a great assembly to decide upon their plan of attack.

Then spake the Prefect Wang saying "We have been moved by

a noble sense of right to assemble here. Now must we first choose a chief and bind ourselves to obedience."

Then said Ts'ao Ts'ao, "For four generations the highest offices of state have been filled by members of the Yuan family and his clients and supporters are everywhere. As a descendant of ancient ministers of Han, Yuan Shao is a suitable man to be our chief lord."

Yuan Shao again and again declined this honour. But they all said, "It must be he; there is no other." And then he agreed.

So a three-storeyed altar was built and they planted about it the five banners of the divisions of space. And they set up white yaks' tails and golden axes and emblems of military authority and the seals of leadership round about.

All being ready the chief lord was invited to ascend the altar. Clad in ceremonial robes and girt with a sword, Yuan Shao reverently ascended. There he burned incense, made obeisance and recited the oath:—

"The House of Han has fallen upon evil days, the bands of imperial authority are loosened. The rebel minister, Tung Cho, takes advantage of the discord to work evil, and calamity falls upon honourable families. Cruelty overwhelms simple folk. We, Shao and his confederates, fearing for the safety of the imperial prerogatives, have assembled military forces to rescue the State. We now pledge ourselves to exert our whole strength and act in concord to the utmost limit of our powers. There must be no disconcerted or selfish action. Should any depart from this pledge may he lose his life and leave no posterity. Almighty Heaven and Universal Mother Earth and the enlightened spirits of our forefathers, be ye our witnesses."

The reading finished, he smeared the blood of the sacrifice upon his lips and upon the lips of those who shared the pledge. All were deeply affected by the ceremony and many shed tears.

This done the oath-chief was supported down from the high place and led to his tent, where he took the highest place and the others arranged themselves according to rank and age. Here wine was served.

Presently Ts'ao Ts'ao said, "It behoves us all to obey the chief we have this day set up, and support the State. There must be no feeling of rivalry or superiority based upon numbers."

Shao replied, "Unworthy as I am, yet as elected chief I must impartially reward merit and punish offences. Let each see to it that he obeys the national laws and the army precepts. These must not be broken."

"Only thy commands are to be obeyed" cried all.

"My brother, Yuan Shu, is appointed Chief of the Commissariat. He must see to it that the whole camp is well supplied. But the need of the moment is a van-leader who shall go to Ssushui Pass and provoke a battle. The other forces must take up positions in support."

Then the Prefect of Ch'angsha offered himself for this service.

"You are valiant and fierce, and equal to this service," said Yuan Shao.

The force under Sun Chien set out and presently came to the Pass. The guard there sent a swift rider to the capital to announce to the tyrant the urgency of the situation.

Ever since Tung Cho had secured his position he had given himself up to luxury without stint. When the urgent news reached the adviser Li Ju, he at once went to his master, who much alarmed called a great council.

Lu Pu stood forth and said, "Do not fear, my father, I look upon all the lords without the Pass as so much stubble and with the men of our fierce army I will put every one of them to death and hang their heads at the gates of the capital."

"With your aid I can sleep secure," said Tung Cho.

But some one behind Lu Pu broke in upon his speech saying "A butcher's knife to kill a chicken! There is no need for the Marquis to go: I will cut off their heads every one as easily as I would take a thing out of my pocket."

Cho looked up and his eyes rested on a stalwart man of fierce mien, lithe and supple. He had a small round head like a leopard and shoulders like an ape's. His name was Hua Hsiung. Cho rejoiced at his bold words and at once gave him high rank and command over five legions of horse and foot. He, with Li Su, Hu Chen and Chao Ts'en hastily moved toward the Pass.

Among the feudal lords Pao Hsin was jealous lest the chosen van-leader should win too great honours. Wherefore he endeavoured to meet the foe first and so he secretly despatched his brother Chung with three companies by a bye road. As soon as this small force reached the Pass they offered battle. Hua Hsiung at the head of half a company of mail-clad horsemen swept down from the Pass crying "Flee not, rebel."

But Pao Chung was afraid and turned back. Hsiung came on, his arm rose, the sword fell, and Chung was cut down from his horse. Most of his company were captured. His head was sent to the minister's palace. Hua Hsiung was promoted to *Tu-tu*, or Commander in Chief.

Sun Chien presently approached the Pass. He had four captains: Ch'eng P'u, whose weapon was an iron-spined snaky lance; Huang

Kai, who wielded an iron whip; Han Tang, a swordsman, and Tsu Mou, who fought with a pair of swords.

The Commander Sun wore a helmet of fine silver wrapped round with a purple turban. He carried across his body his sword of ancient ingot iron and rode a dappled horse with flowing mane.

He advanced to the Pass and hailed the defenders, calling them helpers of a fool, and summoned them to surrender. A half legion under Hu Chen went out against him whom Ch'eng P'u with the snaky lance rode out and engaged. After a very few bouts Hu Chen was killed on the spot by a thrust through the throat. Then the signal was given for the main army to advance. But from the Pass they rained down showers of stones, which proved too much for the assailants and they retired into camp at Liangtung to await further help from Yuan Shao.

An urgent message for supplies was sent to the commissary. But one said to him, the Controller: "This Sun Chien is a very tiger. Should he take the capital and destroy Tung Cho we should have a tiger in place of a wolf. Do not send him grain. Starve his men and that will decide the fate of that army."

And Yuan Shu gave ear to the detractors and sent no grain or forage. Soon the hungry soldiers showed their disaffection by indiscipline and the spies bore the news to the defenders of the Pass, who decided upon a speedy attack in front and rear. They hoped to capture the Sun Chien.

So the soldiers of the attacking face were told off and given a full meal. At dark they left the Pass and crept by secret paths to the rear of Sun Chien's camp. The moon was bright and the wind cool. They arrived about midnight and the drums beat an immediate attack. Sun Chien hastily donned his fighting gear and rode out. He ran straight into Hua Hsiung and the two warriors engaged. But before they had exchanged many passes Li Su's men came up and set fire to whatever would burn.

Sun's army were thrown into confusion and fled like rats. A general melee ensued and soon only Tsu Mou was left at his chief's side. These two broke through the pass and fled. Hua Hsiung coming in hot pursuit, Sun Chien took his bow and let fly two arrows in quick succession, but both missed. He fitted a third arrow to the string, but drew the bow so fiercely that it snapped. He cast the magpie painted bow to the earth and set off at full gallop.

Then spake Tsu Mou saying, "My lord's purple turban is a mark that the rebels will too easily recognise. Give it to me and I will wear it."

So Sun Chien exchanged his silver helmet with the turban for his faithful friend's headpiece, and the two men parted, riding different ways. The pursuers looking only for the purple turban went after its wearer and Sun escaped along a bye-road.

Tsu Mou, hotly pursued, then tore off the headdress which he hung on the post of a half-burned house as he passed and dashed into the thick woods. Hua Hsiung's men seeing the purple turban standing motionless dared not approach, but they surrounded it on every side and shot at it with arrows. Presently they discovered the trick, went up and seized it.

This was the moment that the hidden man awaited. At once he rushed forth, his two swords whirling about, and dashed at the leader. But Hua Hsiung was too quick. With a loud yell he slashed at Tsu Mou and cut him down. Day had now broken and the victor led his men back to the Pass.

The three other leaders in time met their chief and the soldiers halted. Sun Chien was much grieved at the loss of his generous subordinate.

When news of the disaster reached Yuan Shao he was greatly chagrined and called all the lords to a council. They assembled and Kungsun Tsan was the last to arrive. When all were seated in the tent Yuan Shao said, "The brother of General Pao, disobeying the rules we made for our guidance, rashly went to attack the enemy; he was slain and with him many of our soldiers. Now Sun Wen-t'ai has been defeated. Thus our fighting spirit has suffered and what is to be done?"

Every one was silent. Lifting his eyes the chief looked round from one to another till he came to Kungsun Tsan and then he remarked three men who stood behind his seat. They were of striking appearance as they stood there, all three smiling cynically.

"Who are those men behind you?" said the chief.

Kungsun told Yuan-te to come forward, and said, "This is Liu Pei, magistrate of P'ingyuan and a brother of mine who shared my humble cottage."

"It must be the Liu Yuan-te who broke up the Yellow Turban rebellion," said Ts'ao.

"It is he," said his patron and he ordered Liu Pei to make his obeisance to the assembly, to whom he then related his services and his origin, all in full detail.

"Since he is of the Han line he should be seated," said the chief and he bade Liu Pei sit.

Liu Pei modestly thanked him.

Said Shao, "This consideration is not for your fame and office; I respect you as a scion of the imperial family."

So Liu Pei took his seat in the lowest place of the long line of lords. And his two brothers with folded arms took their stations behind him.

Even as they were at this meeting came in a scout to say that Hua Hsiung with a company of mail-clad horsemen was coming down from the Pass. They were flaunting Sun Chien's captured purple turban on the end of a bamboo pole. The enemy was soon hurling insults at those within the stockade and challenging them to fight.

"Who dares go out to give battle?" said the chief.

"I will go," said Yu She, a leader who belonged to the train of Yuan Shu.

So he went and almost immediately one came back to say that he had fallen in the third bout.

Fear began to lay its cold hand on the assembly. Then said another, "I have a brave warrior among my men. P'an Feng is his name and he could slay this Hua Hsiung."

So P'an was ordered out to meet the foe. With his great battle-axe in his hand he mounted and rode forth. But soon came the direful tidings that he too had fallen. The faces of the gathering paled at this.

"What a pity my two able leaders, Yen Liang and Wen Ch'ou, are not here! Then should we have some one who would not fear this man," said the chief.

He had not finished when from the lower end a voice cried, "I will go, take his head and lay it before you here."

All turned to look at the speaker. He was tall and had a long beard. His eyes were those of a phoenix and his eyebrows thick and bushy like caterpillars. His face was a swarthy red and his voice deep as the sound of a great bell.

"Who is he?" asked the chief.

Kungsun Tsan told them it was Kuan Yu, brother of Liu Yuan-te.

"And what is he?"

"He is in the train of Liu Yuan-te as a mounted archer."

"An insult to us all!" roared the chief's brother from his place. "Have we no leader? How dare an archer speak thus before us? Let us beat him forth!"

But Ts'ao Ts'ao intervened. "Peace, O Kung-lu! Since he, speaks great words, he is certainly, valiant. Let him try. If he fail, then you may reproach him."

"Hua Hsiung will laugh at us if we send a mere archer to fight him," said the chief.

"He looks no common person. And how can the enemy know he is but a bowman?" said Ts'ao Ts'ao.

"If I fail then can you take my head," cried Kuan.

Ts'ao Ts'ao bade them heat some wine and offered a stirrup cup to Kuan Yu as he went out.

"Pour it out," said Kuan. "I shall return in a little space."

He went with his sword in his hand and vaulted into the saddle. Those in the tent heard the fierce roll of the drums and then a mighty sound as if skies were falling and earth rising, hills trembling and mountains tearing asunder. And they were sore afraid. And while they were listening with ears intent, lo! the gentle tinkle of horse bells, and Kuan Yu threw at their feet the head of the slain leader, their enemy Hua Hsiung.

The wine was still warm!

This doughty deed has been celebrated in verse.

> The power of the man stands first in all the world;
> At the gate of the camp was heard the rolling of the battle drums:
> Then Yun-ch'ang set aside the wine cup till he should have displayed his valour,
> And the wine was still warm when the enemy had been slain.

Ts'ao Ts'ao was pleased at this success. But Chang Fei's voice was heard, shouting, "Brother, you slew the leader; why did you not break through the Pass and seize Tung Cho? Could there have been a better time?"

Again arose the voice of the peevish Yuan Shu, "We high officials are too meek and yielding. Here is the petty follower of a small magistrate daring to flaunt his prowess before us! Expel him from the tent, I say."

But again Ts'ao Ts'ao interposed, "Shall we consider the station of him who has done a great service?"

"If you hold a mere magistrate in such honour then I simply withdraw," said Yuan Shu.

"Is a word enough to defeat a grand enterprise?" said Ts'ao Ts'ao.

He told Kungsun Tsan to lead his three companions back to their own camp and the other chiefs then dispersed. That night he secretly sent presents of flesh and wine to soothe the three after this adventure.

When Hua Hsiung's men straggled back and told the story of defeat and death Li Su was greatly distressed. He wrote urgent letters to his master who called in his trusted advisers to a council. Li Ju summed up the situation. "We have lost our best leader and the rebel power has thereby become very great. Yuan Shao is at the head of this confederacy and Yuan Wei of the same family is holder of high office in the government. If those in the capital combine with those in the country we may suffer. Therefore we must remove them. So I request you, Sir Minister, to place yourself at the head of your army and break this confederation."

Tung Cho agreed and at once ordered Li Ts'ui and Kuo Ssu to take half a company and surround the residence of Yuan Wei, the *T'ai-fu*, slay every soul, and hang the head of the high officer outside the gate as a trophy. And Cho commanded twenty legions to advance in two armies. The first five legions were under Li Ts'ui and Kuo Ssu and they were to hold Ssushui Pass. They should not necessarily fight. The other fifteen legions under Tung Cho himself went to Tigertrap Pass.

This Pass is fifty *li* from Loyang and as soon as they arrived Tung Cho bade Lu Pu take three legions and make a strong stockade on the outside of the Pass. The main body with Cho would occupy the Pass.

News of this movement reaching the confederate lords the chief summoned a council. Said Ts'ao Ts'ao, "The occupation of the Pass would cut our armies in two, therefore must we oppose Tung Cho's army on the way."

So eight of the confederate lords went in the direction of the Pass to oppose their enemy. Ts'ao Ts'ao and his men were a reserve to render help where needed.

Of the eight, the Prefect of Honei was the first to arrive and Lu Pu went to give battle with three companies of mailed horsemen.

When Wang K'uang, Prefect of Honei, had ordered his army, horse and foot, in battle array he took his station under the great banner and looked over at his foe. There he saw Lu Pu, a conspicuous figure in front of the line. On his head was a triple curved headdress of ruddy gold. He wore a robe of Ssuch'uan silk embroidered with flowers and over that breast and back mail adorned with a gaping animal's head, joined by rings at the sides and girt to his waist with a belt fastened by a beautiful lion-head clasp. His bow and arrows were slung on his shoulders and he carried a trident-halberd (*hua-chi*). He was seated on his snorting steed "The Hare". Indeed he was the man among men, as his steed was the horse among horses.

"Who dares go out to fight him?" asked Wang K'uang turning to those behind him. In response a tried warrior named Fang spurred to the front, his spear set ready for battle. The two met: before the fifth bout Fang fell under a thrust of the halberd and Lu Pu dashed forward. Wang K'uang's men could not stand and scattered in all directions. Lu Pu went to and fro slaying all he met. He was quite irresistible.

Happily two other troops came up and rescued and wounded leader and his opponent retreated. The three having lost many men withdrew thirty *li* and made a stockade. And before long the remaining five lords came up and joined them. They held a council.

"This Lu Pu is irresistible," said they.

And while they sat there anxious and uncertain, it was announced that Lu Pu had returned to challenge them. Each mounted his horse and placed himself at the head of his force, each body in its station on lofty cliffs. Around them was the opposing army, innumerable horse and foot, their embroidered banners waving in the breeze.

They attacked. Mu Shun, a leader from Shangtang, rode out, but fell at the first encounter with Lu Pu. This frightened the others. Then galloped forth Wu An-kuo of the iron mace. Lu Pu whirling his halberd and urging on his steed came to meet him. The two fought, well matched for half a score bouts, when a blow from the halberd broke Wu An-Kuo's wrist. Letting his mace fall to the ground he fled. Then all eight of the lords led forth their men to his rescue and Lu Pu retired.

The fighting then ceased and after their return to camp another council met.

Ts'ao Ts'ao said, "No one can stand against the prowess of Lu Pu. Let us callup all the lords and evolve some good plan. If only Lu Pu were taken, his master could easily be killed."

While the council was in progress again came Lu Pu to challenge them and again they moved out against him. This time Kungsun Tsan, flourishing his spear, went to meet the enemy. After a very few bouts Tsan turned and fled, Lu Pu following at the topmost speed of "The Hare."

"The Hare" was a thousand-li-a-day horse, swift as the wind. As they watched "The Hare" gained rapidly upon the flying horseman and his rider's spear was poised ready to strike Tsan just behind the heart. Just then dashed in a third rider with round glaring eyes and a bristling moustache, and armed with a long snake-like spear.

"Stay, O thrice named slave!" roared he, "I, Chang Fei, await you."

Seeing this opponent Lu Pu left the pursuit of Tsan and engaged the new adversary. Fei fought with all his energies. They two were worthily matched and they exchanged half a hundred bouts with no advantage to either side. Then Kuan Yu rode out with his huge and weighty moon-curved sword and attacked Lu Pu on the other flank. The three steeds stood like the letter T and their riders battered away at each other for nearly two score bouts, yet still Lu Pu stood firm. Then Liu Yuan-te rode out to his brothers' aid, his double sword raised ready to strike. The steed with the flowing mane was urged in at an angle and now Lu Pu had to contend with three warriors at whom he struck one after another, and they at him, the flashing of the warriors' weapons looking like the revolving lamps suspended at the new year. And the spectators gazed rapt with amazement at such a battle.

But Lu Pu's guard began to weaken and fatigue seized him. Looking hard in the face of Yuan-te he feigned a fierce thrust thus making him suddenly draw back. Then, lowering his halberd, Lu dashed through the angle thus opened and got away.

But was it likely they would allow him to escape? They whipped their steeds and followed hard. The men of the eight armies cracked their throats with thunderous cheers and all dashed forward, pressing after Lu Pu as he made for the shelter of the Pass. And first among his pursuers were the three heroic brothers.

An ancient poet has told of this famous fight in these lines:

> The fateful day of Han came in the reigns of Huan and Ling,
> Their glory declined as the sun sinks at the close of day.
> Tung Cho, infamous minister of state, pulled down the youthful
>   sovereign from his throne.
> It is true Liu Hsieh was a weakling, too timid for his times.
> Then Ts'ao Ts'ao proclaimed abroad these wicked deeds,
> And the great lords, moved with anger, assembled their forces.
> In council met they and chose as their oath-chief Yuan Shao,
> Pledged themselves to maintain the ruling house and tranquillity.
> Of the warriors of that time peerless Lu Pu was the boldest.
> His valour and prowess are sung by all within the four seas.
> He clothed his body in silver armour like the scales of a dragon,
> On his head was a golden headdress, fastened with a massive pin,
> About his waist a shaggy belt, the clasp, two wild beasts' heads with
>   gripping jaws,
> His flowing, broidered robe fluttered about his form,
> His swift courser bounded over the plain, a mighty wind following,
> His terrible halberd flashed in the sunlight, bright as a placid lake.
> Who dared face him as he rode forth to challenge?
> The bowels of the confederate lords were torn with fear and their
>   hearts trembled within them.
> Then leaped forth Chang Fei, the valiant warrior of the north,
> Gripped in his mighty hand the long snakelike spear,

His moustache bristled with anger, standing stiff like wire.
His round eyes glared, lightning flashes darted from them.
Neither quailed in the fight, but the issue was undecided.
Kuan Yun-ch'ang stood out in front, his soul vexed within him,
Black Dragon his sword shone white as hoar frost in the sunlight,
His bright coloured fighting robe fluttered like butterfly wings,
Demons and angels shrieked at the thunder of his horse hoofs,
In his eyes was fierce anger, a fire to be quenched only in blood.
Next Yuan-te joined the battle, gripping his twin sword blades,
The heavens themselves trembled at the majesty of his wrath.
These three closely beset Lu Pu and long drawn out was the battle,
Always he warded their blows, never faltering a moment.
The noise of their shouting rose to the sky, and the earth
    re-echoed it,
The heat of battle ranged to the frozen pole star.
Worn out, feeling his strength fast ebbing, Lu Pu thought to flee,
He glanced at the hills around and thither would fly for shelter,
Then, reversing his halberd and lowering its lofty point,
Hastily he fled, loosing himself from the battle;
With head low bent, he gave the rein to his courser,
Turned his face away and fled to Hulaokuan.

The three brothers maintained the pursuit to the Pass. Looking up they saw an immense umbrella of black gauze fluttering in the west wind.

"Certainly there is Tung Cho," cried Chang Fei. "What is the use of pursuing Lu Pu? Better far seize the chief rebel and so pluck up the evil by the roots."

And he whipped up his steed toward the Pass.

To quell rebellion seize the leader if you can;
If you need a wondrous service then first find a wondrous man.

The following chapters will unfold the result of the battle.

CHAPTER VI

BURNING THE CAPITAL, TUNG CHO
COMMITS AN ATROCITY: HIDING THE SEAL,
SUN CHIEN BREAKS FAITH

Chang Fei rode hard up to the Pass but the defenders sent down stones and arrows like rain so that he could not enter and he returned. The eight lords all joined in felicitations to the three heroes for their services and the story of victory was sent to Yuan Shao, who ordered Sun Chien to advance.

Thereupon Sun with two trusty friends went over to the camp of Yuan Shu. Tracing figures on the ground with his staff Sun Chien said, "Tung Cho and I had no personal quarrel. Yet now I have thrown myself into the battle regardless of consequences, exposed my person to the risk of wounds and fought bloody battles to their bitter end. And why? That I might be the means of ridding my country of a rebel and—for the private advantage of your family. Yet you, heeding the slanderous tongues of certain enemies, formerly withheld the supplies absolutely necessary to me, and so I suffered defeat. How can you explain, General?"

Yuan Shu, confused and frightened, had no word to reply. He ordered the death of the slanderers to placate Sun.

Then suddenly they told Sun, "Some officer has come riding down from the Pass to see you, General; he is in the camp."

Sun Chien therefore took his leave and returned to his own camp where he found the visitor was an officer, much beloved of Tung Cho, named Li Ts'ui.

Wherefore come you?" said Chien.

He replied, "You are the one person for whom my master has respect and admiration, and he sends me to arrange a matrimonial alliance between the two families. He wishes that his daughter may become the wife of your son."

"What! Tung Cho, that rebel and renegade, that subverter of the throne! Would that I could destroy his nine generations as a thank-offering to the Empire! Think you I would be willing to have an alliance with such a family? I will not slay you as I ought, but go, and go quickly! Yield the Pass and I may spare your lives. If you delay I will grind your bones to powder and make mincemeat of your flesh."

Li Ts'ui threw his arms over his head and ran out. He returned to his master and told him what a rude reception he had met with. Cho asked his adviser Li Ju how to reply to this and he said that as Lu Pu's late defeat had somewhat blunted the edge of his desire for battle it would be well to return to the capital and remove the Emperor to Ch'angan, as the street boys had been lately singing:—

> "A Han on the west, a Han on the east.
> The deer will be safe in Ch'angan, poor beast."

Li continued "If you think out this couplet it applies to the present juncture. Half the first line refers to the founder of the dynasty, who became ruler in the western city, which was the capital during twelve reigns. The other half corresponds to Kuang-Wu who ruled from Loyang, the capital during twelve later reigns. The revolution of the heavens brings us to this moment and if the minister remove to Ch'angan there will be no need for anxiety."

Tung Cho was exceedingly pleased and said, "Had you not spoken thus I should not have understood."

Then taking Lu Pu with him he started at once for the capital. Here he called all the officials to a great council in the palace and addressed them thus:—

"After two centuries of rule here the royal fortune has been exhausted and I perceive that the aura of rule has migrated to Ch'angan, whither I now desire to move the court. All you had better pack up for the journey."

The minister Yang Piao said, "I pray you reflect. Within that city all is destruction. There is no reason to renounce the ancestral temples and abandon the imperial tombs here. I fear the people will be alarmed. It is easy to alarm them but difficult to pacify them."

"Do you oppose the State plans?" said Cho angrily.

Another official, Huang Yuan, supported his colleague, "In the rebellion of Wang Mang, in the days of Keng Shih and Fan Ch'ung of the Red Eyebrows, the city was burned and became a place of broken tiles. The inhabitants scattered all but a few. It is wrong to abandon these palaces for a desert."

Tung Cho replied, "East of the Pass is full of sedition and all the Empire is in rebellion. The city of Ch'angan is protected by Yaohan and very near Shensi, whence can be easily brought building material. In a month or so palaces can be erected. So an end to your wild words!"

Yet another raised a protest against disturbing the people but the tyrant overbore him also.

"How can I stop to consider a few common people when my scheme affects the Empire?"

That day the three objectors were degraded to the rank of ordinary people.

As Cho went out to get into his coach he met two other officers who made obeisance. They were the President, Chou Pi, and the Captain of the City Gate, Wu Ch'ing. Cho stopped and asked them what they wanted. Said the former, "We venture to try to dissuade you from moving the capital to Ch'angan."

Cho replied, "They used to say you two were supporters of Yuan Shao; now he has already turned traitor and you are of the same party."

And without more ado he bade his guards take both outside the city and put them to death.

The command to remove to the new capital immediately was issued. On the advice of Li Ju, who pointed out that money was short and the rich people of Loyang could be easily plundered and that it was a good occasion to remove the supporters of their opponents, Cho sent five companies out to plunder and slay. They captured very many wealthy folk and, having stuck flags on their heads saying they were traitors and rebels, drove them out of the city and put them to death. Their property was all seized.

The task of driving forth the inhabitants, some millions, was given to two of Tung Cho's creatures. They were sent off in bands of a hundred, each band between two parties of soldiers, who urged them forward. Enormous numbers fell by the road side and died in the ditches, and the escort plundered the fugitives and defiled the women. A wail of sorrow arose to the very sky. The tyrant's final orders as he left were to burn the whole city, houses, palaces and temples, and everything was devoured by the flames. The capital became but a patch of scorched earth.

Tung Cho sent Lu Pu to desecrate the tombs of the Emperors and their consorts for the jewels therein, and the common soldiers took the occasion to dig up the graves of officers and plunder the cemeteries of the wealth. The spoil of the city, gold and silver, pearls and silks, and beautiful ornaments, filled many carts and with these and the persons of the Emperor and his household Tung Cho moved off to the new capital.

The city being thus abandoned the commander at Ssushui Pass

evacuated that post of vantage, which Sun Chien at once occupied. The three brothers took Tigertrap Pass and the confederate lords advanced.

Sun Chien hastened to the late capital which was still in flames. When he arrived demise smoke hung all over it and spread for miles around. No living thing, not a fowl, or a dog, or a human being, remained. Sun told off his men to extinguish the fires and set out camping places for the confederate lords.

Ts'ao Ts'ao went to see the chief and said, "Tung has gone west; we ought to follow and attack without loss of time; why do you remain inactive?"

"All our colleagues are worn out and there is nothing to be gained by attack," said Yuan Shao.

Ts'ao Ts'ao urged him to strike a blow for the moment was most propitious in the utter confusion that reigned, palaces burned, the Emperor abducted, the whole world upset and no one knowing whither to turn. But all the confederate lords seemed of one mind and that mind was to postpone action. So they did nothing. However, Ts'ao Ts'ao and his subordinates, with a full legion of soldiers, started in pursuit.

The road to the new capital led through Jungyang, and when the cavalcade reached it the Prefect went to welcome Tung Cho. Li Ju said, "As there is some danger of pursuit it would be well to order the Prefect of this place to lay an ambush ready to cut off the retreat of our pursuers when our army beats them off. That will teach any others not to follow."

Then Lu Pu was ordered to command the rear guard. Very soon they saw Ts'ao Ts'ao coming up and Lu Pu laughed at his colleague's foresight. He set out his men in fighting order.

Ts'ao Ts'ao rode forward crying, "Rebels, abductors, drovers of the people, where are you going?"

Lu Pu replied, "Treacherous simpleton, what mad words are these?"

Then from Ts'ao Ts'ao's army rode against him Hsiahou Tun with his spear set and they two engaged. The combat had hardly begun when Li Ts'ui with a cohort came in from the left. Ts'ao Ts'ao bade Hsiahou Yuan meet this onslaught. However, on the other side appeared Kuo Ssu, against whom was sent Ts'ao Jen. The onrush on three sides was too much to withstand and Lu Pu showed no signs of being vanquished, so Hsiahou Tun had to retire to the main line. Thereupon Lu Pu's mail-clad men attacked and completed the defeat. The beaten men turned toward Jungyang.

They got as far as the foot of a bare hill in the second watch, about nine in the evening, and the moon made it as light as day. Here they halted to reform. Just as they were burying the boilers to prepare a meal there arose a great noise of shouting on all sides and out came the men from the ambush fresh to attack.

Ts'ao Ts'ao, thrown into a flurry, mounted and fled. He ran right in the way of the waiting Prefect. Then he dashed off in another direction, but the Prefect shot an arrow after him which struck him in the shoulder. The arrow still in the wound, he fled for his life. As he went over the hill two soldiers lying in wait among the grass suddenly dashed out and wounded his horse, which fell and rolled over, and as its rider slipped from the saddle he was seized and made prisoner.

Just then a horseman riding at full speed and whirling his sword came, up, cut down both the captors and rescued Ts'ao Ts'ao. It was his brother Ts'ao Hung.

Ts'ao Ts'ao said, "I am doomed, good brother, go and save yourself."

"My lord, mount my horse quickly; I will go afoot," said Hung.

"If those wretches come up, what then?"

The world can do without me, but not without you, my brother."

"If I live I shall owe you my life," said Ts'ao Ts'ao.

So he mounted. His brother tore off his own breastplate, gripped his sword and went on foot after the horse. Thus they proceeded till the fourth watch when they saw before them a broad stream, and behind they still heard the shouts of pursuers drawing nearer and nearer.

"This is my fate," said Ts'ao Ts'ao. "I am really doomed."

His brother helped him down from his horse. Then taking off his fighting robe he took the wounded man on his back and waded into the stream. When they reached the further side the pursuers had already gained the bank whence they shot arrows. Ts'ao Ts'ao all wet pushed on.

Dawn was near. They went on another thirty *li* and then sat down to rest under a precipice. Suddenly loud shouting was heard and a party of horse appeared. It was the Prefect of Jungpang who had forded the river higher up. Just at this moment Hsiahou Tun and his brother, with a half score men, came along.

"Hurt not my lord!" cried Hsiahou to the Prefect, who at once rushed at him. But the combat was short. The Prefect speedily fell under a spear thrust and his men were driven off. Before long Ts'ao

Ts'ao's other captains arrived. Sadness and joy mingled in the greetings. They gathered together the few hundreds of men left and then returned to Honei.

The story broke off leaving the confederate lords in their various camps at Loyang. Sun Chien, after extinguishing the fires, camped within the walls, his own tent being set up near the Chienchang Hall of the palace. His men cleared away the debris and closed the rifted tombs. The gates were barred. On the site of the Dynastic Temple he put up a mat shed containing three apartments, and here he begged the lords to meet and replace the sacred tablets, with solemn sacrifices and prayers.

This ceremony over, the others left and Sun Chien returned to his camp. That night the stars and moon vied with each other in brightness. As Sun sat in the open air looking up at the heavens he noticed a mist spreading over the stars of the Constellation Draco.

"The Emperor's stars are dulled," said he with a sigh, "No wonder a rebellious minister disturbs the State, the people sit in dust and ashes, and the capital is a waste."

And his tears began to fall. Then a soldier pointing to the south said, "There is a beam of coloured light rising from a well."

He bade his men light torches and descend into the well. Soon they brought up the corpse of a woman, not in the least decayed although it had been there many days. She was dressed in palace clothing and from her neck hung an embroidered bag. Opening this a red box was found, with a golden lock, and when the box was opened they saw a jade seal, square in shape, an inch each way. On it were delicately engraved five dragons intertwined. One corner had been broken off and repaired with gold. There were eight characters in the seal style of engraving which interpreted read, "I have received the command from Heaven: may my time be always prosperous."

Sun Chien showed this to Ch'eng P'u who at once recognised it as the hereditary seal of the Emperor.

He said, "This seal has a history. In olden days one P'ien Ho saw a phoenix sitting on a certain stone at the foot of Ching Hill. He offered the stone at court. King Wen of Ch'u split open the stone and found a piece of jade. Early in the Ts'in dynasty a jade cutter made a seal from it and Li Ssu engraved the characters. Two years later it was thrown overboard in a terrific storm on the Tungt'ing Lake as a propitiatory offering, and the storm immediately ceased. Ten years later again, when the Emperor was making a progress and had reached Huaying, an old man by the road side handed a seal to one of the attendants saying, "This is now restored to the ancestral dragon," and had then disappeared. Thus the jewel returned to Ts'in. The next year Emperor She died.

"Later Tzu-ying presented the seal to the founder of the Han dynasty. In Wang Mang's rebellion the Emperor struck two of the rebels with the seal and broke off a corner, which was repaired with gold. Kuang-Wu got possession of it at Iyang and it has been regularly bequeathed thereafter. I heard it had been lost during the trouble in the palace when 'The Ten' hurried off the Emperor. It was missed on His Majesty's return. Now my lord has it and certainly will come to the imperial dignity. But you must not remain here. Quickly go east where you can lay plans for the accomplishment of the great design."

"Your words exactly accord with my thoughts," said Sun Chien. "Tomorrow I will make an excuse that I am unwell and get away."

The soldiers were told to keep the discovery a secret. But who could guess that one among them was a compatriot of the elected chief of the confederacy? He thought this might be of great advantage to him so he stole away out of the camp and betrayed his master. He received a liberal reward and Yuan Shao kept him in his own camp. So when Sun Chien came to take leave saying "I am rather unwell and wish to return to Changsha." Shao laughed saying "I know what you are suffering from; it is called the Hereditary Seal!"

This was a shock to Sun Chien and he paled but he said, "Whence these words?"

Shao said, "The armies were raised for the good of the State and to relieve it from oppression. The seal is State property and since you have got hold of it you should publicly hand it over to me as chief. When Tung Cho has been slain it must go back to the government. What do you mean by concealing it and going away?"

"How could the seal get into my hands?"

"Where is the article out of the well?"

"I have it not: why harass me thus?"

"Quickly produce it, or it will be the worse for you."

Sun Chien pointing toward the heavens as an oath said, "If I have this jewel and am hiding it myself may my end be unhappy and my death violent!"

The lords all said, "After an oath like this we think he cannot have it."

Then Shao called out his informant. "When you pulled that thing out of the well, was this man there?" asked he of Sun.

Sun Chien's anger burst forth and he sprang forward to kill the man. The chief also drew his sword saying "You touch that soldier and it is an insult to me."

In a moment on all sides swords flew from their scabbards. But the confusion was stayed by the efforts of the others and Sun Chien left the assembly. Soon he broke up his camp and marched to his own place.

The chief was not satisfied. He wrote to Chingchou and sent the letter by a trusty hand to tell the governor to stop Sun Chien and take away the seal.

Just after this came the news of the defeat and misfortune of Ts'ao Ts'ao and when he was coming home Shao sent out to welcome him and conduct him into camp. They also prepared a feast to console him. During the feast Ts'ao Ts'ao said sadly, "My object was for the public good and all you gentlemen nobly supported me. My plan was to get Yuan Shu with his Honei men to approach Mengching and Suantsao while the others of you held Ch'eng-kao and took possession of the granaries and guarded Taku, and so controlled the points of vantage. Yuan Shao was to occupy Tanshi and go into Wukuan to help the three supports, all were to fortify their positions and not fight. Advantage lay in an uncertain military force showing the Empire's possibilities of dealing with the rebellion. Victory would have been ours at once. But then came delays and doubts and inaction and the confidence of the people was lost and I am ashamed."

No reply was possible and the guests dispersed. Ts'ao Ts'ao saw that the others mistrusted him and in his heart knew that nothing could be accomplished, so he led off his force to Yangchou.

Then Kungsun Tsan said to the three brothers, "This Yuan Shao is an incapable and things will go agley. We had better go too."

So he broke camp and went north. At P'ingyuan he left Liu Pei in command and went to strengthen his own position and refresh his men.

The Prefect of Yenchou wished to borrow grain of the Prefect of Tungchun. Being denied he attacked the camp, killed the leader and took over all his men. Yuan Shao seeing the confederacy breaking up also marched away and went east.

Now the Governor of Chingchou, Liu Piao, was a scion of the imperial house. As a young man he had made friends with many famous persons and he and his companions were called the Eight Dilettanti. The other seven were Ch'en Hsiang, Fan P'ang, K'ung Yu, Fan K'ang, T'an Fu, Chang Chien and Ts'en Ching. He was friends with all these. He had three famous men who helped him in the government of his district. They were K'uai Liang, K'uai Yueh and Ts'ai Mao.

When the letter detailing the fault of Sun Chien arrived the two K'uai and Ts'ai were sent with a legion of soldiers to bar the way. When Sun Chien drew near the force was arranged in fighting order and the leaders were in the front.

"Why are you thus barring the road with armed men?" asked Sun.

"Why do you, a minister of Han, secrete the Emperor's special seal? Leave it with me at once and you go free," said K'uai Yueh.

Sun Chien angrily ordered out a leader Huang Kai, who exchanged a few bouts with Ts'ao Mao and presently dealt him a blow with the iron whip just over the heart. Mao turned his steed and fled and Sun Chien got through with a sudden rush.

However, there arose the sound of gongs and drums on the hills behind and there was Prefect Liu in person with a large army. Sun Chien rode straight up to him and bowing low spoke thus. "Why did you, on the faith of a letter from Yuan Shao, try to coerce the chief of a neighbouring district?"

"You have concealed the State jewel and I want you to restore it," was Liu's reply.

"If I have this thing may I die a violent death!"

"If you want me to believe you let me search your baggage."

"What force have you that you dare come to flout me thus?"

And only the Prefect's prompt retirement prevented a battle.

Sun Chien proceeded on his way. But from the rear of the second hill an ambush suddenly discovered itself and K'uai and Ts'ai were still following. Sun Chien seemed entirely hemmed in.

> What doth it advantage a man to hold the imperial seal if its possession lead to strife?

How Sun Chien got clear of the difficulty will presently be told.

CHAPTER VII

YUAN SHAO FIGHTS WITH KUNGSUN
TSAN AT P'ANHO: SUN CHIEN ATTACKS
LIU PIAO

At the close of the last chapter Sun Chien was surrounded. However he eventually fought his way through, though with the loss of three of his best leaders and more than half his men and he returned to Chiangtung. Henceforward he and Liu Piao were open enemies.

Yuan Shao was in Honei. Being short of supplies he sent to borrow from Ichou, whence he obtained the wherewithal to support his army. Then his adviser, Feng Chi, said to him, "You are really the strongest power here about, why then depend upon another for food? Ichou is rich and wide; why not seize it?"

"I have no good plan," replied Yuan.

"You could secretly send a letter to Kungsun Tsan to attack, promising him your support. The Prefect Han Fu being incapable must ask you to take over his country and you will get it without lifting a finger."

So the letter was sent, and when Kungsun Tsan saw therein the proposal to make a joint attack and divide the territory, he agreed to give his help. In the meantime Yuan Shao had sent to warn Han Fu of his danger. Han sought advice from Hsun Shen and Hsin P'ing. The former said that if Kungsun came to attack them they could not stand against him, especially if he had the help of Liu and Chang. So he counselled getting aid from their powerful neighbour. "Yuan Pen-ch'u is bolder than most and he has many able and famous leaders under him. You cannot do better than ask him to assist in administering this district. He will certainly treat you with generosity and you need have no fear from Kungsun Tsan."

The Prefect agreed and sent a message to Yuan Shao. But the

commandant of the palace, Keng Wu, remonstrated with his master saying, "Yuan Shao is a needy man with a hungry army and as dependent on us for existence as an infant in arms on its mother. Stop the flow of milk and the infant dies. Why should you hand the district over to him? It is nothing less than letting a tiger into the sheepfold."

Han Fu replied, "I am one of the clients of the Yuan family and I know the abilities of Pen-ch'u. Why are you all so jealous? The ancients counselled yielding to the sage."

Keng Wu sighed, "Ichou is lost!" said he.

When the news got abroad two score of officers of Ichou left their employment and the city. However Keng and Kuan hid in the suburbs to await the arrival of Yuan Shao.

They had not long to wait. Soon Yuan Shao with his soldiers came and the two men tried to assassinate him. This attempt failed. Yen Liang killed one of them and Wen Ch'ou the other. Thus both died and the object of their hatred entered the prefecture.

His first act was to confer on Han Fu a high sounding title, but the administration was entrusted to four of his own confidants who speedily deprived the Prefect of all power. Full of chagrin Han soon abandoned all, even his family, and took refuge with the Prefect of Ch'enliu.

Hearing of Shao's invasion Kungsun Tsan sent his brother, Yueh, to see the usurper and demand his share of the district. The brother was sent back to request Kungsun himself to come, but on the homeward road he was killed by assassins who loudly proclaimed they belonged to the Minister, Tung Cho. Those of his followers who escaped carried the news to their late master's brother.

Kungsun Tsan was very angry and said, "He prevailed on me to attack and now he has taken possession. Also he pretends the murderers of my brother were not his men. Shall I not avenge my brother's injury?"

Then he brought up all his force to the attack. Yuan sent out his army and they met at P'anho. They halted on opposite sides of a stream, over which was a bridge. Kungsun Tsan took his station on the bridge and cried to his enemy, "Renegade, how dared you mislead me?"

Yuan rode to his end of the bridge and, pointing at Kungsun Tsan, replied, "Han Fu yielded place to me because he was unequal to the rule. What concern is it of yours?"

Kungsun replied, "Formerly you were regarded as loyal and

public spirited and we chose you chief of the confederacy. Now your deeds prove you cruel and base, wolf-hearted and currish in behaviour. How can you look the world in the face?"

"Who will capture him?" cried Yuan in a rage.

At once Wen Ch'ou rode out with his spear set. Kungsun Tsan rode down the bridge to the enemy's side, where the two engaged. Half a score bouts showed Tsan he had met his master so he drew off. The enemy came on. Tsan took refuge within his formation, but Wen Ch'ou cut his way in and rode this way and that, slaying right and left. The four best of Tsan's captains offered joint battle, but one fell under the first stroke of the doughty warrior and the other three fled, Wen Ch'ou following clear through to the rear of the army. Kungsun made for the mountains. Wen Ch'ou forced his horse to its utmost pace crying hoarsely, "Down! Dismount and surrender."

Kungsun fled for life. His bow and quiver dropped from his shoulders, his helmet fell off and his hair streamed straight behind him as he rode in and out between the sloping hills. Then his steed stumbled and he was thrown, rolling over and over to the foot of the slope.

Wen Ch'ou was now very near and poising his spear for the thrust. Then suddenly came out from the shelter of a grassy mound on the left a leader of youthful mien, but sitting his steed bravely and holding a sturdy spear. He rode directly at Wen Ch'ou and Kungsun crawled up the slope to look on.

The new warrior was of middle height with bushy eyebrows and large eyes, a broad face and a heavy jowl, a youth of commanding presence. The two exchanged some fifty bouts and yet neither had the advantage. Then Kungsun's rescue force came along and Wen Ch'ou turned and rode away. The youth did not pursue.

Kungsun Tsan hurried down the hill and asked the young fellow who he was.

He bowed low and replied that his name was Chao Yun, or Tzu-lung, and he was of Chengting.

"I first served Yuan Shao, but when I saw that he was disloyal to his prince and careless of the welfare of the people I left him and I was on my way to offer service to you. This meeting in this place is most unexpected."

Kungsun was very pleased and the two went together to the camp, where they at once busied themselves with preparations for a new battle.

Next day Kungsun prepared for fight by dividing his army into two portions, like the wings of a bird. He had five thousand cavalry, nearly all mounted on white horses and because he had formerly seen service against the frontier tribes, the *Ch'iang* (Ouigours) where he always placed his white horses in the van of his army, he had won the sobriquet of General of the White Horse. The tribes held him so much in fear that they always fled as soon as the white horses appeared.

On Yuan Shao's side Yen Liang and Wen Ch'ou were leaders of the van. Each had a company of archers and crossbowmen. They were set out half on either side, those on the left to shoot at Kungsun Tsan's right and those on the right to shoot at his left. In the centre was Ch'u I with a small company of bowmen and a legion and a half of foot. The chief took command of the reserve force in the rear.

In this fight Kungsun Tsan employed his new adherent Chao Yun for the first time and, as he did not feel assured of his good faith, put him in command of a company at the rear. The van-leader was Yen Kang and Kungsun himself commanded the centre. He took his place on horseback on the bridge beside an enormous red standard on which was displayed the word "General" in gold embroidery.

From *shen* (7 a.m.—9 a.m.) till *ssu* (9 a.m.—11 a.m.) the drums rolled for the attack, but Yuan's army made no move. Ch'u I made his bowmen hide under their shields. They heard the roar of explosions, the whistling of arrows and the rattle of the drums, as Yen Kang approached from the other side, but Ch'u I and his men lay closer than ever and never stirred. They waited till Yen Kang had got close on them and then, as the sound of a bomb rent the air, the whole company, eight hundred men, let fly their arrows in a cloud. Yen Kang was quite taken aback and would have retired, but Ch'u I rode furiously toward him, whirled up his sword and cut him down. So Kungsun's men lost that battle. The two wings that should have come to the rescue were kept back by the bowmen under Yen Liang and Wen Ch'ou and Yuan's men advanced right up to the bridge. Then Ch'u I rode forward, slew the standard bearer and hacked through the staff of the embroidered banner. Seeing this Kungsun Tsan turned his steed and galloped away.

Ch'u I followed. But just as he caught up the fugitive there came prancing forth Chao Yun, who rode directly at him with spear ready to strike. After a few passes the pursuer was laid in the dust. Then Chao Yun attacked the soldiers and turned the tide. Plunging forward on this side, dashing in on that, he went through as if there were no antagonists and, seeing this, Kungsun Tsan turned and came again into the fight. The final victory was on his side.

From the men sent to find out how the battle went Yuan Shao heard the good news of Ch'u I's success in slaying the standard bearer, capturing the flag and his pursuit. So he took no further care but rode out with his captains and a few guards to look on at the defeated enemy and enjoy his victory.

"Ha ha!" he laughed. "The poor fool! He is an incapable."

But even as he spoke he saw in front the redoubtable Chao Yun. His guards hastened to prepare their bows, but before they could shoot Chao with a few followers was in their midst and men were falling before him wherever he went. The others fled. Kungsun Tsan's army then gathered round and hemmed in Yuan Shao.

T'ien Feng then said to his master, "Sir, take refuge in this empty building here."

But Yuan dashed his helmet to the ground, crying "The brave man rather faces death in the battle than seeks safety behind a wall!"

This bold speech gave new courage to his men who now fought desperately and with such success that Chao Yun could nowhere force his way in. Shao was soon reinforced by the arrival of his main body and Yen Liang, so that Chao Yun could only just get his master safe out of the press. When clear they both returned to the bridge. But Yuan's men still came on and fought their way across the bridge, forcing multitudes of their adversaries into the water, where many were drowned.

Yuan was leading in person and his men still advanced. But not very far, for soon a great shouting was heard behind some hills, whence suddenly burst out a body of men led by the three brothers.

At P'ingyuan they had heard of the struggle between their protector and his enemy, Yuan Shao, and had at once set out to help. Now the three riders, each with his peculiar weapon, flew straight at Yuan, who was so frightened that his soul seemed to leave his body and fly beyond the confines of heaven. His sword fell from his hand and he fled for his life. He was chased across the bridge when Kungsun Tsan called in his men and they returned to camp.

After the usual greetings Kungsun said, "If you had not come to our help, we should have been in very bad case."

Yuan-te and Chao Yun were made acquainted with each other and a warm affection sprang up from the very first so that they were always together.

Yuan had lost that battle and Kungsun Tsan would hot risk

another. He strengthened his defences and the armies lay inactive for over a month. In the meantime news of the fighting had reached the capital and Tung Cho was told.

His adviser, Li Ju, went to see his master and said, "The two active warriors of today are Yuan Shao and Kungsun Tsan, who are at grips at P'anho. Pretend you have a command to make peace between them and both will support you out of gratitude for your intervention.

"Good!" said Tung Cho. So he sent a Grand Preceptor and a Court Chamberlain on the mission. When these men were arriving Yuan sent out to welcome them a hundred *li* from his headquarters and received the command with the greatest respect. Then the two officers went to Kungsun Tsan and made known their errand. Kungsun sent letters to his adversary proposing friendship. The two emissaries returned to report their task accomplished. Kungsun drew off his army. He also sent up a memorial eulogising Liu Yuan-te, who was raised in rank.

The farewell between Liu Pei and Chao Yun was affecting. They held each other's hands a long time, their eyes streaming with tears, and could not tear themselves apart.

Chao Yun said with a sob, "I used to think Kungsun noble, but I see now that he is no different from Yuan. They are both alike."

"But you are in his service, and we shall surely meet again." said Yuan-te.

Both men wept freely as they separated.

Now Yuan Shu, hearing that his brother had come into Ichou, sent to beg a thousand horses. The request was refused and enmity sprang up between the brothers. He also sent to Chingchow to borrow grain, which Liu Piao would not send. In his resentment he wrote to Sun Chien trying to get him to attack Liu Piao. The letter ran like this:—

"When Liu Piao stopped you on your way home it was at the instigation of my brother. Now the same two have planned to fall upon your district, wherefore you should at once strike at Liu Piao. I will capture my brother for you and both resentments will be appeased. You will get Chingchow and I shall have Ichou."

"I cannot bear Liu Piao," said Sun Chien as he finished reading this letter. "He certainly did bar my way home and I may wait many years for my revenge if I let slip this chance."

He called a council.

"You may not trust Yuan Shu; he is very deceitful," said Ch'eng P'u.

"I want revenge on my own part; what care I for his help?" said Chien.

He despatched Huang Kai to prepare a river fleet, arm and provision them. Some craft were to take horses on board. The force soon set out.

News of these preparations came to Liu Piao and he hastily summoned his advisers and warriors. K'uai Liang told him to be free from anxiety, and said, "Put Huang Tsu at the head of the Chianghsia army to make the first attack and you, Sir, support him. Let Sun Chien come 'riding the rivers and straddling the lakes;' what can he do?"

So Huang Tsu was bidden to prepare to march and a great army was assembled.

Here it may be said that Sun Chien had four sons, all the issue of his wife who was of the Wu family. Their names were Ts'e (Po-fu), Ch'uan (Chung-mou), I (Shu-pi) and K'uang (Chi-tso). His wife's sister was his second wife, and she bore him a son and daughter, the former called Lang (Tsao-an), the latter Jen. He had also adopted a son from the Yu family named Shao (Kung-li). And he had a younger brother named Ching (Yu-t'ai).

As Sun Chien was leaving on this expedition his brother with all his sons stood near his steed and dissuaded him, saying, "Tung Cho is the real ruler of the State for the Emperor is a weakling. The whole country is in rebellion, every one is scrambling for territory. Our district is comparatively peaceful and it is wrong to begin a war merely for the sake of a little resentment. I pray you, brother, to think before you start."

Chien replied, "Brother, say no more. I desire to make my strength felt everywhere and shall I not avenge my injuries?"

"Then father, if you must go, let me accompany you," said the eldest son.

His request was granted, and father and son embarked to go to ravage Fanch'eng.

Now Huang Tsu had placed archers and crossbowmen along the river bank. When the ships approached a flight of arrows met them. Sun ordered his men to remain under cover in the ships, which then sailed to and fro drawing the fire for three days. Several times a landing was tried, but showers of arrows repulsed each attempt. At last the arrows of the defenders were all shot away and Sun, who collected them, found he had many myriads. Then with a fair wind Sun's men shot them back at the enemy. Those on the bank were thrown into great disorder and retired. The army then landed and two divisions set out or Huang Tsu's camp along different roads. Between them marched Han Tang and under this triple attack Huang Tsu was worsted. He left Fanch'eng and hastened to Tengch'eng.

Leaving the ships under the command of Huang Kai, Sun led the pursuing force. Huang Tsu came out of his city and drew up for battle in the open country. When Sun had disposed his army he rode out to the standard. His son, clad in armour, placed himself beside his father.

Huang Tsu rode out with two captains Chang Hu and Ch'en Sheng. Flourishing his whip, the chief abused his enemy, "You swarm of rebels from Chiangtung, why do you invade the land of a scion of the ruling house?"

Chang Hu challenged to combat and Han Tang went out to accept. The two champions fought two score bouts and then Ch'en Sheng, seeing his fellow captain becoming exhausted, rode to his aid. Sun Chien saw him coming, laid aside his spear, reached for his bow and shot an arrow wounding Ch'en Sheng in the face. He fell from his horse. Panic seized upon Chang at the fall of his comrade and he could no longer defend himself. Then Han Tang with a slash of his sword clove his skull in twain.

Both having fallen, Ch'eng P'u galloped up to make prisoner of Huang Tsu, who threw off his helmet, slipped from his steed and mingled for safety among his men. Sun Chien led on the attack and drove the enemy to the Han water, where he ordered Huang Kai to make an immediate attack on Hanchiang.

Huang Tsu led his defeated men back and told Liu Piao they were no match for Sun Chien. K'uai Liang was called in to advise and he said, "Our newly defeated men have no heart for fighting now. Therefore we must fortify our position, while we seek help from Yuan Shao. Then we can extricate ourselves."

"A stupid move," said Ts'ai Mao. "The enemy is at the city gates; shall we fold our hands and wait to be slain? Give me men and I will go out and fight to the finish."

So he was placed in command of a legion and went out to the Hsien hills where he drew up his battle line. Sun Ts'e led the invaders, now flushed with success. When Ts'ai approached, Sun Chien looked at him and said, "He is brother-in-law to Liu Piao; who will capture him?"

Ch'eng P'u set his supple spear and rode out. After a few bouts Ts'ai Mao turned and fled. The Suns smote him till corpses filled the countryside and he took refuge in Hsiangyang.

K'uai Yen said, "Ts'ai ought to be put to death by military law. This defeat was due to his obstinacy." But Liu Piao was unwilling to punish the brother of his newly wedded wife.

Sun Chien surrounded Hsiangyang and assailed the walls daily. One day a fierce gale sprang up and the pole bearing his standard was broken.

"Very inauspicious!" said Han Tang. "We ought to go back."

His lord said, "I have won every battle and the city is on the point of falling. Shall I return because the wind breaks a flagstaff?"

He flouted the advice and attacked the walls still more vigorously.

Within the city they had seen an omen. It was told Liu Piao that a great star had fallen into the wild country without the city, and they had calculated that it inferred the fall of their enemy. Piao was advised to seek help from Yuan Shao.

So he wrote. But who would undertake to fight his way through with the letter? One Lu Kung, a warrior of great strength, offered himself for this service. K'uai Liang said, "If you undertake this service listen to my advice. You will have five hundred men; choose good bowmen. Dash through the enemy's formation and make for Hsien Hill. You will be pursued, but send a hundred men up the hill to prepare large stones and place a hundred archers in ambush in the woods. These are not to flee from the pursuers but to beguile them along devious ways round to the place where the boulders have along prepared. There stones will be rolled down and arrows shot. If you succeed, fire off a series of bombs as a signal and the men in the city will come out to help. If you are not pursued get away as fast as possible. Tonight will be suitable as there is very little moon. Start at dusk."

Lu Kung, having received these directions, prepared his force to carry them out. As soon as day began to close in he went quietly out at the east gate. Sun Chien was in his tent when he heard shouting and at once mounted and rode out with thirty men to discover the cause. Lu Kung's men had already hidden themselves in the thick woods. Chien rode ahead of his escort and soon he found himself alone and close to the enemy. He called out to them to halt. Lu at once turned back and came as if to fight. But they had only exchanged a single pass when he again fled, taking the road among the hills. Sun followed but soon lost sight of his foe.

Sun turned up the hill. Then the gongs clanged and down the hills fell showers of stones, while from among the trees the arrows flew in clouds. Sun was hit by several arrows and a huge stone crushed in his head. Both he and his steed were killed. And so his life ended at the age of thirty seven.

His escort was overpowered and every man of them slain. Then Lu let off a series of bombs, the sign of success, as agreed. At this signal three armies came out of the city and fell upon the Chiangtung men, throwing them into the utmost confusion.

When Huang Kai heard the sound of battle he led up the men from the ships. He met Huang Tsu and took him prisoner after a brief fight.

Ch'eng P'u set out to bear the sad news to Sun Ts'e. While he was seeking a way out he came across Lu Kung. He at once put his horse at full speed and engaged him. After a few bouts Lu went down under a spear thrust. The battle became general and continued till daylight broke, when each drew off his army. Liu Piao withdrew into the city and when Sun Ts'e returned to the river he heard that his father had perished in the fight, and his body had been carried within the enemy's, walls. He uttered a great cry and the army joined him with wailing and tears.

"How can I return home leaving my father's corpse with them?" cried Sun Ts'e.

Huang Kai said, "We have Huang Tsu as our prisoner. Let one enter the city and discuss peace, giving up our prisoner for our lord's body."

He had barely finished speaking when Huang K'ai offered himself as messenger saying he was an old friend of Liu Piao. So he went and peace was discussed. Liu Piao told him the body was already laid in a coffin and ready to be delivered as soon as Huang Tsu returned. "Let us both cease fighting and never again invade each other's district," said he.

Huan K'ai thanked him and took his leave. But as he went down the steps K'uai Liang suddenly broke in, saying, "No, No! Let me speak and I will see to it that not a single breastplate returns. I pray you first put this man to death and then employ my means."

> Pursuing his enemy, Sun Chien dies;
> Even on a peaceful mission Huang K'ai is threatened.

The fate of the ambassador will be disclosed in a later chapter.

CHAPTER VIII

GOVERNOR WANG PREPARES
THE "CHAIN" SCHEME: TUNG CHO'S RAGES
AT THE FENGI PAVILION

This is what K'uai Liang said, "Sun Chien is now gone and his sons are but youths. Seize this moment of weakness to break into Chiangtung and it is yours in one beat of the drum. If you return the corpse and make peace, you give them time to grow powerful and evil will ensue to this district."

"How can I leave Huang Tsu in their hands?" said the Prefect.

"Why not sacrifice this blundering warrior for a district?"

"But he is my dear friend and to abandon him is wrong."

So Huan K'ai was allowed to return to his own side with the understanding that Sun Chien's dead body should be given in exchange. Sun Ts'e freed his prisoner, brought away his father's coffin and the fighting ceased. Sun Chien was interred in the border of Chua and when the ceremonies were over Sun Ts'e led his army home again.

In his district Sun Ts'e set himself to the task of ruling well. He invited to his side men of wisdom and valour and so bore himself that all the best and bravest of the country gathered about him.

But this part of his story will not be told here. Tung Cho at the capital, when he heard of the death of the turbulent prefect, said, "An evil that pressed hard upon my heart has been removed." He asked what sons he had left and when they told him the eldest was but seventeen he dismissed all anxiety from his thoughts.

From this time forward his arrogance and domineering spirit waxed worse and worse. He styled himself Shang Fu or "Imperial Rector," a name full of honour, and in all his behaviour aped imperial state. He created his younger brother a marquis and made him Generalissimo of the Left. A nephew was placed in command of the Palace guards and everyone of his clan, young or old, was ennobled. At some distance from the capital he laid out a city, an exact replica of Ch'angan, with its palaces, granaries, treasuries and magazines, and employed a quarter of a million people to build it. Here he accumulated supplies sufficient for twenty years. He selected eight hundred of the most beautiful maidens and sent them to dwell in his new city. The stores of wealth in every form were incalculable. All his family and retainers found quarters in this new city named Meiwu.

Tung Cho visited his city at intervals of a month or so and every visit was like an imperial progress, with booths by the roadside to refresh the officials and courtiers who attended him to the Hengmen and saw him start.

On one occasion he spread a great feast for all those assembled to witness his departure and while it was in progress there arrived a large number of malcontents from the north who had voluntarily surrendered. The tyrant had them brought before him as he sat at table and meted out to them wanton cruelties. The hands of this one were lopped off, the feet of that; one had his eyes gouged out; another lost his tongue. Some were boiled to death. Shrieks of agony arose to the very heavens and the courtiers were faint with terror, but the author of the misery ate and drank, chatted and smiled as if nothing was going on.

Another day Tung Cho was presiding it a great gathering of officers who were seated in two long rows. After the wine had gone up and down several times Lu Pu entered and whispered a few words in his master's ear. Cho smiled and said, "He was always so. Take Chang Wen outside." The others all turned pale. In a little time a serving man brought the head of their fellow guest on a red dish and showed it to their host. They nearly died with fright.

"Do not fear," said Cho smiling. "He was in league with Yuan Shu to assassinate me. A letter he wrote fell by mistake into the hands of my son so I have had him put to death. You gentlemen, who have no reason, need have no fear."

The officials hastened to disperse. One of them, Governor Wang Yun, who had witnessed all this, returned to his palace very pensive and much distressed. The same evening, a bright moonlight night, he took his staff and went strolling in his private garden. Standing near one of the creeper trellises he gazed up at the sky and the tears rolled down his cheeks. Suddenly he heard a rustle in the peony pavilion and some one sighing deeply. Stealthily creeping near he saw there one of the household singing girls named Tiaoch'an or Sable Cicada.

This maiden had been brought up in his palace, where she had been taught to sing and dance. She was then just bursting into womanhood, a pretty and clever girl whom Wang Yun regarded more as a daughter than a dependent.

After listening for some time he suddenly called out, "What mischief are you up to there, you naughty girl?"

The maiden dropped on her knees in terror, "Would thy unworthy handmaid dare to do anything wrong?" said she. "Then what are you sighing about out here in the darkness?" "May thy handmaid speak from the bottom of her heart?"

"Tell me the whole truth; do not conceal anything."

And the girl said, "Thy handmaid has been the recipient of bountiful kindness. She has been taught to sing and dance and been treated so kindly that were she torn in pieces for her lord's sake it would not repay a thousandth part. She has noticed lately that her lord's brows have been knit in distress and knows it is on account of the State troubles. But she has not dared to ask. This evening he seemed more sad than ever and she was miserable on her lord's account. But she did not know she would be seen. Could she be of any use she would not shrink from a myriad deaths."

A sudden idea came to Wang and he stuck the ground with his staff. "Who would think that the fate of the Hans lay on your palm? Come with me!"

The girl followed him into the house. Then he summoned all the waiting women and girls, placed Sable Cicada on a chair and bowed before her. She was frightened and threw herself on the ground, asking in terror what it all meant.

Said he, "You can sympathise with the people of Han," and the fount of his tears opened afresh.

"As I said just now, use me in any way; I will never shrink.

Wang Yun knelt saying, "The people are on the brink of destruction, the prince and his officers are in jeopardy, and you, you are the only saviour. That wretch Tung Cho wants to depose the Emperor and not a man among us can find means to stop him. Now he has a son, a bold warrior it is true, but both father and son have a weakness for beauty and I am going to use what I may call the "chain" plan. I shall first propose you in marriage to Lu Pu and then, after you are betrothed, I shall present you to Tung Cho and you will take every opportunity to force them asunder and turn away their countenances from each other, cause the son to kill his adopted father and so put an end to the great evil. Thus you may restore the altars of the land that it may live again. All this lies within your power; will you do it?"

"Thy handmaid has promised not to recoil from death itself. You may use my poor self in any way and I must do my best."

"But if this gets abroad then we are all lost!"

"Fear not," said she, "if thy handmaid does not show gratitude, may she perish beneath a myriad swords!"

"Thank you; thank you!" said Wang Yun.

Then they took from the family treasury many pearls and bade a cunning jeweler make there with a fine golden headdress which was sent as a present to Lu Pu. He was delighted and came to thank the donor. When he arrived he was met at the gate by the host himself and within found a table full of dainties for his delectation. He was conducted into the private apartments and placed in the seat of honour.

He said, "I am but a simple officer in the palace of a minister; you are an exalted officer of State, why am I treated thus?"

"Because in the whole land there is no warrior your equal. Poor Yun bows not to an officer's rank; he bows to his ability."

This gratified Lu Pu mightily and his host continued to praise and flatter and ply him with wine and to talk of the virtues of the minister and his henchman.

Lu Pu laughed and drank huge goblets.

Presently most of the attendants were sent away, only a few kept to press the guest to drink. When the guest was very mellow Wang Yun suddenly said, "Let the child come in!"

Soon appeared two attendants, dressed in black, leading between them the exquisite and fascinating Sable Cicada.

"Who is this?" said Lu Pu startled into sobriety.

"This is my little girl, Cicada. You will not be annoyed at my familiarity, will you? But you have been so very friendly, I thought you would like to see her."

He bade the girl present a goblet of wine and her eyes met those of the warrior.

The host feigning intoxication said, "The little one begs you, Commandant, to take a cup or two. We all depend upon you, all our house."

Lu Pu begged the girl to sit down. She pretended to wish to retire. Her master pressed her to remain, saying that she might do so since the guest was a dear friend. So she took a seat modestly near her master.

Lu Pu kept his gaze fixed upon the maid while he swallowed cup after cup of wine.

"I should like to present her to you as a handmaid; would you accept?"

The guest started up. "If that is so you may rely upon my abject gratitude," said he.

"We will choose a propitious day ere long and send her to the palace."

Lu Pu was overjoyed. He could not keep his eyes off the girl and loving glances flashed from her liquid orbs.

However the time came for the guest to leave and Wang said, "I would ask you to remain the night but the Minister might suspect something."

The guest thanked him again and again and departed. Some few days later when Wang Yun was at court and Lu Pu was absent he bowed low before Tung Cho and said, "I would that you would deign to come to dine at my lowly cottage, could your noble thought bend that way!"

"Should you invite me I would certainly hasten," was the reply.

Wang Yun thanked him. He went home and prepared in the reception hall a feast in which figured every delicacy from land and sea. Beautiful embroideries surrounded the chief seat in the centre and elegant curtains were hung within and without. At noon next day, when the Minister arrived, his host met him at the gate in full court costume. He stood by while Tung Cho stepped out of his chariot and he and a host of armed guards crowded into the hall. Tung Cho took his seat at the top, his suite fell into two lines right and left, while the host stood humbly at the lower end. Tung Cho bade his people conduct Wang to a place beside himself.

Said Wang, "The great minister's abundant virtue is as the high mountains; neither I Yin nor Duke Chou could attain thereto."

Tung Cho smiled. They bore in the dishes and the wine and the music began. Wang Yun plied his guest with assiduous flattery and studied deference. When it grew late and the wine had done its work the guest was invited to the inner chamber. So he sent away his guards and went. Here the host raised a goblet and drank to his guest saying "From my youth up I have understood something of astrology and have been studying the aspect of the heavens. I read that the days of Han are numbered and that the great Minister's merits command the regard of all the world as when Shun succeeded Yao and Yu continued the work of Shun, conforming to the mind of heaven and the desire of man."

"How dare I expect this?" said Cho.

"From the days of old those who walk in the way have replaced those who deviate therefrom; those who lack virtue have fallen before those who possess it. Can one escape fate?"

"If indeed the decree of heaven devolve on me; you shall be held the first in merit," said Tung Cho.

Wang Yun bowed. Then lights were brought in and all the attendants were dismissed save the serving maids to hand the wine. So the evening went on.

Presently the host said, "The music of these everyday musicians is too commonplace for your ear, but there happens to be in the house a little maid that might please you."

"Excellent!" said the guest.

Then a curtain was lowered. The shrill tones of reed instruments rang through the room and presently some attendants led forward Cicada, who then danced on the outside of the curtain.

A poem says:—

> For a palace this maiden was born,
>> So timid, so graceful, so slender,
> Like a tiny bird flitting at morn
>> O'er the dew-laden lily-buds tender.
> Were this exquisite maid only mine,
> For never a mansion I'd pine.

Another poem runs thus:—

> The music calls; the dancer comes, a swallow gliding in,
>> A dainty little damsel, light as air;
> Her beauty captivates the guest yet saddens him within,
>> For he must soon depart and leave her there.
> She smiles; no gold could buy that smile, no other smileth so,
>> No need to deck her form with jewels rare,
> But when the dance is over and coy glances come and go,
>> Then who shall be the chosen of the fair?

The dance ended, Tung Cho bade them lead the maiden in, and she came, bowing low as she approached him. He was much taken with her beauty and modest grace.

"Who is she?" said he.

"A singing girl; we call her Sable Cicada."

"Then can she sing?"

The master bade her sing and she did so to the accompaniment of castanets. There is a measure describing her youthful beauty:—

> You stand, a dainty maiden,
>> Your cherry lips so bright,
>> Your teeth so pearly white,

Your fragrant breath love-laden;
Yet is your tongue a sword;
Cold death is the reward
Of loving thee, O maiden.

Tung Cho was delighted and praised her warmly. She was told to present a goblet of wine to the guest which he took from her hands and then asked her age.

She replied, "Thy unworthy handmaid is just sixteen."

"A perfect little fairy!" said Tung Cho.

Then Wang Yun rose and said, "If the Minister would not mind I should like to offer him this little maid."

"How could I be grateful enough for such a kindness?"

"She would be most fortunate if she could be your servant," said Wang.

Cho thanked his host warmly.

Then the orders were given to prepare a closed carriage and convey Sable Cicada to the palace.

Soon after Tung Cho took his leave and Wang Yun accompanied him the whole way.

After he had taken leave he mounted to ride homeward. Half way he met two lines of men with red lamps who were escorting Lu Pu on horseback and armed with his halberd. Seeing Wang Yun he at once reined in, stopped, seized him by the sleeve and said angrily, "You promised Cicada to me and now you have given her to the Minister: what foolery is this?"

Wang Yun checked him. "This is no place to talk; I pray you come to my house."

So they went together and he led Lu Pu into a private room. After the usual exchange of polite greetings Wang said, "Why do you find fault with me, Commander?"

"Somebody told me that you had sent Cicada to the Minister's palace in a covered carriage: what does it mean?"

"Of course you do not understand. Yesterday when I was at court the Minister told me he had something to talk to me about in my own house. So naturally I prepared for his coming and while we were at dinner he said, "I have heard something of a girl named Sable Cicada whom you have promised to my son Feng-hsien. I thought it was mere rumour so I wanted to ask if it was true. Beside I should like to see her." I could not say no, so she came in and made her bow to the lord of lords. Then he said that it was a lucky day and he would take her away with him and betroth her to you. Just think, Sir; when the Minister had come himself, could I stop him?"

"You were not so very wrong," said Pu, "but for a time I had misunderstood you. I owe you an apology."

"The girl has a small trousseau, which I will send as soon as she has gone over to your dwelling."

Pu thanked him and went away. Next day he went into the palace to find out the truth, but could hear nothing. Then he made his way into the private quarters and questioned the maids. Presently one told him that the Minister had brought home a new bedfellow the night before and was not up yet. Pu was very angry. Next he crept round behind his master's sleeping apartment.

By this time Cicada had risen and was dressing her hair at the window. Looking out she saw a long shadow fall across the little lake. She recognised the headdress and peeping around she saw it was indeed no other than Lu Pu. Thereupon she contracted her eyebrows, simulating the deepest grief, and with her dainty handkerchief she wiped her eyes again and again. Lu Pu stood watching her a long time.

Soon after he went in to give morning greeting. His master was sitting in the reception room. Seeing his henchman he asked if there was anything new.

"Nothing," was the reply and he waited while Tung Cho took his morning meal. As he stood beside his master he glanced over at the curtain and saw a woman there behind the screen showing a half face from time to time and throwing amorous glances at him. He felt it was his beloved and his thoughts flew to her. Presently Cho noticed his expression and began to feel suspicious.

"If there is nothing you may go," said he.

Lu Pu sulkily withdrew.

Tung Cho now thought of nothing but his new mistress and for more than a month neglected all affairs, devoting himself entirely to pleasure. He was a little indisposed and Cicada was constantly at his side, never even undressing to show her solicitude. She gratified his every whim. Cho grew more and more fond of her.

One day Lu Pu went to enquire after his father's health. Tung Cho was asleep and Cicada was sitting at the head of his couch. Leaning forward she gazed at the visitor, with one hand pointed to her heart, the other at Tung Cho asleep, and her tears fell. Lu Pu felt heartbroken. Cho drowsily opened his eyes, and seeing his son's gaze fixed on something behind him, turned over and saw who it was. He angrily rebuked Pu saying, "Dare you make love to my beauty?" He told the servants to turn him out and not allow him to come in again.

Lu Pu went off home very wrath. Meeting Li Ju he told him the cause of his anger. The adviser hastened to see his master and said, "Sir, you aspire to be ruler of the State, why then for a small fault do you blame the Marquis? If he turn against you, it is all over."

"Then what can I do?" said Cho.

"Recall him tomorrow; treat him well; overwhelm him with gifts and fair words and all will be well."

So Tung Cho did so. He sent for Lu Pu and was very gracious and said, "I was irritable and hasty yesterday owing to my illness and I wronged you, I know. Forget it."

He gave him ten catties of gold and twenty rolls of brocade. And so the quarrel was made up. But though Lu's body was with Tung his heart was with his promised bride.

Tung Cho having quite recovered went to court again and Lu Pu followed him as usual. Seeing Tung Cho deep in conversation with the Emperor, Lu Pu, armed as he was, went out of the palace and rode off to his chief's residence. He tied up his steed at the entrance and, halberd in hand, went to the private apartments to seek his love. He found her and she told him to go out into the garden where she would join him soon. He went, taking his halberd with him, and he leaned against the rail of the Phoenix Pavilion to wait for Cicada.

After a long time she appeared, swaying gracefully as she made her way under the drooping willows and parting the flowers as she passed. She was exquisite, a perfect little fairy from the Palace of the Moon. Tears were in her eyes as she came up and said, "Though I am not the Governor's real daughter yet he treated me as his own child. The desire of my life was fulfilled when he plighted me to you. But Oh! to think of the wickedness of the Minister, stealing my poor self as he did. I suffered so much. I longed to die, only that I had not told you the real truth. So I lived on, bearing my shame as best as I could but feeling it mean still to live. Now that I have seen you I can end it all. My poor sullied body is no longer fit to serve a hero. I can die before your eyes and so prove how true I am!"

Thus speaking she seized the curving rail as if to jump into the lily pond. Lu Pu caught her in his strong arms and wept as he held her close.

"I knew it; I always knew your heart," he sobbed. "Only we never had a chance to speak."

She threw her arms about Lu Pu. "If I cannot be your wife in this life I will in the ages to come," she whispered.

"If I do not marry you in this life, I am no hero," said he.

"Every day is a year long. O pity me! Rescue me!"

"I have only stolen away for a brief moment and I am afraid that old rebel will suspect something, so I must not stay too long," said Pu.

The girl clung to his robe.

"If you fear the old thief so much I shall never see another sunrise."

Lu Pu stopped. "Give me a little time to think," said he. And he picked up his halberd to go.

"In the deep seclusion of the harem, I heard the stories of your prowess; you were the one man who excelled all others. Little did I think that you of all men would rest content under the dominion of another."

And tears rained again!

A wave of shame flooded his face. Leaning his halberd against the railing he turned and clasped the girl to his breast, soothing her with fond words. The lovers held each other close swaying to and fro with emotion. How could they bring themselves to say farewell?

In the meantime Tung Cho missed his henchman and doubt filled his heart. Hastily taking leave of the Emperor, he mounted his chariot and returned to his palace. There at the gate stood Lu Pu's well known steed, riderless. He questioned the doorkeepers and they told him the Marquis was within. He sent away his attendants and went alone to the private apartments. Lu Pu was not there. He called Cicada, but she did not reply. He asked where she was and the waiting maids told him she was in the garden among the flowers.

So he went into the garden and there he saw the lovers in the pavilion in most tender talk. Lu Pu's halberd was leaning on the railing beside him.

A howl of rage escaped Tung Cho and startled the lovers. Lu Pu turned, saw who it was and ran away. Cho caught up the halberd and ran in pursuit. But Lu Pu was fleet of foot while his master was very stout. Seeing no hope of catching the runaway Cho hurled the halberd. Lu Pu fended it off and it fell to the ground. Cho picked it up and ran on. But by this time Lu Pu was far ahead. Just as Cho was running out at the garden gate he dashed full tilt against another man running in, and down he went.

> Surged up his wrath within him as the billows heavenward leap,
> Crashed his unwieldy body to earth in a shapeless heap.

We shall presently see who the other runner was.

CHAPTER IX

LU PU HELPS TO SUPPRESS DISORDER:
CHIA HSU COUNSELS AN ATTACK ON
THE CAPITAL

The person who collided with the irate Tung Cho was his most trusty adviser Li Ju. Li had not fallen in spite of the shock and at once helped his master to regain his feet and led him inside to the library, where they sat down.

"What were you coming about?"

"Happening to be passing your gates I heard that you had gone into your private garden to look for your adopted son. Then came Lu Pu running and crying out that you wanted to kill him, and I was coming in as fast as I could to intercede for him when I accidentally collided with you. I am very sorry. I deserve death."

"The wretch! How could I bear to see him toying with my fair one? I will be the death of him yet."

"Your Graciousness is making a mistake. It is the 'plucked tassel' story over again. But if you remember Prince Chuang of Ch'u made no fuss about the liberties taken with his lady love, although the hat-tassel in her hand betrayed the culprit. His restraint stood him in good stead, for the same man saved his life when he was hemmed in by the hosts of Ts'in. After all Cicada is only a woman, but Lu Pu is your trustiest friend and most dreaded commander. If you took this chance of making the girl over to him, your kindness would win his undying gratitude. I beg you, Sir, to think over it well."

Tung Cho hesitated a long time; he sat murmuring to himself. Presently he said, "What you say is right. I must think over it."

Li Ju felt satisfied. He took leave of his master and went away. Cho went to his private rooms and called Cicada.

"What were you doing there with Lu Pu?" said he.

She began to weep. "Thy handmaid was in the garden among the flowers, when he rushed in on me. I was frightened and ran away. He asked why I ran away from a son of the family and pursued me right to the pavilion, where you saw us. He had that halberd in his hand all the time. I felt he was a vicious man and would force me to his will so I tried to throw myself into the lily pond, but he caught me in his arms and held me so that I was helpless. Luckily just at that moment you came and saved my life."

"Suppose I send you to him."

She shrieked with terror.

"After having been yours to be given to a mere slave! Never! I would rather die."

And with this she snatched down a dagger hanging on the wall to kill herself. Tung Cho plucked it from her hand and, throwing his arms about her, cried, "I was only joking."

She lay back on his breast hiding her face and sobbing bitterly. "This is the doing of that Li Ju," said she. "He is much too thick with Lu Pu. He suggested that, I know. Little he cares for your reputation or my life. Oh! I would like to eat him alive."

"Do you think I could bear to lose you?"

"Though you love me yet I must not stay here. That Lu Pu will do me some harm if I do. I fear him."

"We will go to Meiwu tomorrow, you and J, and we will be happy together and have no cares."

She dried her tears and thanked him. Next day Li Ju came again to persuade Tung Cho to send the damsel to Lu Pu. "This is a propitious day," said he.

"He and I standing in the relation of father and son I cannot very well do that," said Tung Cho. "But I will say no more about his fault. You may tell him so and soothe him as well as you can."

"You are not being beguiled by the woman, are you?" said Li.

Tung Cho coloured. "Would you like to give your wife to some body else? Do not talk about this any further. It would be better not to."

Li left the chamber. When he got outside he cast his eyes up to heaven, saying, "We are dead men, slain by the hand of this girl."

When a certain student of history reached this episode he wrote a verse or two:—

> Just introduce a woman,
>   Conspiracies succeed;
> Of soldiers, or their weapons,
>   There really is no need.
> They fought their bloody battles,

And doughty deeds were done;
But in a garden summer house
The victory was won.

The order was given to journey to Meiwu and the whole body of officers assembled to add lustre to the start. Cicada, from her carriage, saw Lu Pu among the crowd. She at once dropped her eyes and assumed an appearance of deepest melancholy. After the cavalcade started and when her carriage had almost disappeared in the distance, the disappointed lover reined in his steed on a mount whence he could watch the dust that rose around it. Unutterable sadness filled his heart.

Suddenly a voice said, "Why do you not accompany the Minister, Marquis, instead of standing here and sighing?"

It was Wan Yun. "I have been confined to the house by illness these few days," continued he, "so I have not seen you. But I had to struggle out today to see the Minister set off. This meeting is most fortunate. But why were you sighing?"

"Just on account of that damsel of yours," said Lu Pu.

Feigning great astonishment he said, "So long a time and yet not given to you!"

"The old ruffian has fallen in love with her himself."

"Surely this cannot be true."

Lu Pu related the whole story while Wang Yun listened, silent, but stamping on the ground as with irritation and perplexity. After a long time he said, "I did not think he was such a beast."

Taking Lu Pu by the hand he said, "Come to my house and we will talk it over."

So they went away together to the house and retired to a secret room. After some refreshments, Lu Pu told the whole story of the episode in the garden just as it happened.

"He seems to have corrupted my little girl and has stolen your wife. He will be an object of shame and ridicule to the whole world. And those who do not laugh at him will laugh at you and me. Alas! I am old and powerless and can do nothing. More's the pity! But you, Commander, you are a warrior, the greatest hero in the world. Yet you have been put to this shame and exposed to this contempt."

A wave of fierce wrath rolled up in Lu Pu. Banging the table he shouted and roared. His host ostentatiously tried to calm him saying, "I forgot myself. I should not have spoken like that. Do not be so angry, I pray."

"I will kill the wretch, I swear it. In no other way can I wash away my shame."

"No, no! Do not say such a thing," said Wang, putting his hand over the other's mouth. "You will bring trouble on poor me."

"When a man is born great he cannot be patient for long under another man's domination," said Lu Pu.

"It needs some one greater than the Minister to limit the scope of such talents as voters."

Lu Pu said, "I would not mind killing the old wretch were it not for the relation in which we stand. I fear to provoke the hostile criticism of posterity."

His host smiled. "Your name is Lu; his is Tung. Where was the paternal feeling when he threw the halberd at you?"

"I had been misled if you had not said that," said Lu hotly.

Wang Yun saw the effect of his words and continued, "It would be a loyal deed to restore the House of Han, and history would hand down your name to posterity perpetually fragrant. If you lend your aid to Tung Cho you will be a traitor and your name will stink through all the ages."

Lu Pu rose from his place and bowed to Wang Yun. "I have decided," said he. "You need not fear, Sir."

"But yet you may fail and bring upon yourself misfortune," said Wang.

Lu Pu drew his dagger and pricking his arm swore by the blood that flowed.

Wang fell on his knees and thanked him. "Then the Han sacrifices will not be cut off and you will be their saviour. But this must remain a secret and I will tell you how the plot shall be worked out."

Lu Pu took leave with great emotion.

Wang Yun took into his confidence two colleagues, Sun Jui and Huang Yuan. The former said, "The moment is favourable. The Emperor has just recovered from his illness and we can despatch an able talker to Meiwu to persuade Tung Cho to come here to discuss affairs. Meanwhile we will obtain a secret decree as authority for Lu Pu. Lay an ambush just inside the palace gates to kill Cho as he enters. This is the best plan to adopt."

"But who would dare to go?"

"Li Su would go. He belongs to the same district as Lu Pu and is very angry with the Minister for not advancing him. His going would excite no suspicions."

"Good," said Wang Yun. "Let us see what Lu Pu thinks of it."

When Pu was consulted he told them that this man's persuasion had led him to kill Ting, his former benefactor. "If he refuse this mission I will kill him," said he.

So they sent for Li Su. When he arrived Lu Pu said, "Formerly you talked me into killing Ting and going over to Tung Cho. Now we find Tung Cho means evil for the Emperor and is an oppressor of the people. His iniquities are many and he is hated of gods and men. You go to Meiwu, say you have a command from the Emperor to summon Tung Cho to the palace. He will come and he will be put to death. You will have the credit of being loyal and restoring the Hans. Will you undertake this?"

"I also wish to slay him," was the reply. "But I could not find any to assist me. How can I hesitate? Your intervention is directly from heaven."

And he snapped an arrow in twain as register of his oath.

"If this succeed, what glorious rank will be yours!" said Wang Yun.

Next day Li Su, with a small escort, set out for Meiwu and announced himself as bearer of a decree. He was conducted into Tung Cho's presence. After he had made his obeisance Tung asked what the decree was.

"His Majesty has recovered and wishes his ministers to meet him in the palace to consider the question of his abdication in your favour. That is what this summons means."

"What does Wang Yun think of the scheme?"

"Wang Yun has already begun the construction of the Terrace of Abdication and only awaits my lord's arrival."

"Last night I dreamed a dragon coiled round my body," said Tung Cho greatly pleased, "and now I get this happy tidings! I must not neglect the opportunity."

So he gave instructions for the safekeeping of his city and announced his intention of starting on the morrow.

"When I am Emperor you shall be my Precursor," said he.

"Your minister thanks you," said Li.

Cho went to bid farewell to his aged mother. "Whither are you going, my son?"

"I go to receive the abdication of Han; and soon you will be Empress Dowager."

"I have been feeling nervous and creepy these few days. It is a bad sign."

"Any one about to become the mother of the State must have premonitions," said her son.

He left her with these words. Just before starting he said to Cicada, "When I am Emperor, you shall be *Kuei-fei*, the first of my ladies." She bowed low thanking him, but she knew and inwardly rejoiced.

He went out and mounted his carriage, and began his journey to the Capital with an imposing escort. Less than half way the wheel of his carriage broke. He left it and mounted a horse. Soon after the horse snorted and neighed, threw up his head and snapped the reins.

Tung Cho turned to Li Su and asked what these things portended.

"It means that you are going to receive the abdication of the Hans, which is to renew all things, to mount the jewelled chariot and sit in the golden saddle."

And Cho believed him. During the second day's journey a violent gale sprang up and the sky became covered with a thick mist. The wily Li Su had an interpretation for this also. "You are ascending to the place of the dragon; there must be bright light and lurid vapour to dignify your majestic approach."

Cho had no more doubts. He presently arrived and found many officials waiting without the city gate to receive him, all but Li Ju who was ill and unable to leave his chamber. He entered and proceeded to his own palace, where Lu Pu came to congratulate him.

"When I sit on the throne, you shall command the whole armies of the Empire, horse and foot," said he.

That night Cho slept in a tent in the midst of his escort. In the suburbs that evening some children at play were singing a little ditty and the words drifted in on the wind.

> "The grass in the meadow looks fresh now and green,
> Yet wait but ten days, not a blade will be seen."*

The song sounded ominous but Li Su was again prepared with a happy interpretation. "It only means that the Lius are about to disappear and the Tungs to be exalted."

Next morning at the first streak of dawn Tung Cho prepared for his appearance at court. On the way he saw a Taoist, dressed in a black robe and wearing a white turban, who carried in his hand a tall staff with a long strip of white cloth attached. At each end of the cloth was drawn a mouth.

"What is the meaning of this?" said Tung Cho.

"He is a madman," said Li Su, and he told the guards to drive the fellow away.

---

* The grass in the meadow is an ingenious quip on Tung Cho's surname; as is the "ten days" on his distinguishing name.

Tung Cho went in and found all the officials in court dress lining the road. Li Su walked beside his carriage, a sword in his hand. When he reached the side room on the north he found soldiers drawn up outside and only the pushers of the palace carriage, a score or so, were allowed to proceed further. When he arrived near the Reception Hall he saw that Wang Yun and all the other officials standing at the door were armed.

"Why are they all armed?" said he to Li Su. Li Su was silent. The pushers urged the carriage forward swiftly to the entrance.

Suddenly Wang Yun shouted, "The rebel is here! where are the executioners?"

At this call sprang from both sides men armed with halberds and spears who attacked Tung Cho. He had not put on the breastplate he usually wore and a spear pierced his breast. He sank down in the carriage calling loudly for his son, "Where is Feng-hsien?"

"Here, and with a decree to deal with a rebel," said Lu Pu savagely, as he appeared in front of his "father."

Thereupon he thrust his halberd through his victim's throat. Then Li Su hacked off the head and held it up. Lu Pu, his left hand holding his halberd, thrust his right hand into his bosom whence he drew the decree, crying, "The decree was to slay the rebel Tung Cho; no other."

The whole assembly shouted, "Live for ever! O Emperor."

A sympathetic poet has written a few lines in pity:—

> Await the time, O noble, and be king,
> Or failing, reap the solace riches bring;
> Heaven n'er is partial, but severely just,
> Meiwu stood strong yet now it lies in dust.

The lust of blood awakened, Lu Pu urged the slaughter of Li Ju, who had been the confidant of the murdered Minister and Li Su volunteered to go in search of him. But just then a shouting was heard at the gates and it was told them that a household slave had brought their intended victim in bonds. Wang Yun ordered his immediate execution in the market place.

Tung Cho's head was exposed in a crowded thoroughfare. He was very fat and the guards made torches by sticking splints into the body. The passers-by pelted the poor head and spurned the body with their feet.

A large force under Lu Pu was sent to destroy Meiwu. His first captive was Cicada. Then they slew every member of the Tung family, sparing none, not even his aged mother. Some of his particular adherents, with the "Flying Bear" force, fled to

Chingchou. In Meiwu were hidden many young ladies of good family. These were set free. The spoil was enormous; stores of wealth in all its forms had been collected there.

When they returned to report success Wang Yun rewarded and feasted the soldiers. Banquets were held in the halls to which all the officials were invited. They drank and congratulated each other. While the feasting was in progress it was announced that some one had come and was wailing over the corpse exposed in the market place.

"Tung Cho has been put to death," said Wang Yun, angrily. "Every body is glad to be rid of him and yet one is found to lament over him. Who is this?"

So he gave orders to arrest the mourner and bring him in. Soon be was brought in and when they saw him all were startled. For he was no other than Ts'ai Yung the *Shih-chung*.

Wang Yun spoke to him angrily, "Tung Cho has been put to death as a rebel and all the land rejoices. You, a Han Minister, instead of rejoicing, weep for him. Why?"

Yung confessed his fault. "I am without talent, yet know I what is right. Am I the man to turn my back on my country and toward Tung Cho? Yet once I experienced his kindness and I could not help mourning for him. I know my fault is grave but I pray you to regard the reasons. If you will leave my head and only cut off my feet, you may use me to continue the History of Han, whereby I may have the good fortune to be allowed to expiate my fault."

All were sorry for him, for he was a man of great talents and they begged that he might be spared. The Preceptor Ma secretly interceded for him, pointing out that he was famous as a scholar, that he could write glorious history, and that it was inadvisable to put to death a man renowned for rectitude. But in vain. The Great Councillor was now strong and obdurate.

"Ssu-ma Ch'ien was spared and employed on the annals, with the result that many slanderous stories have been handed down to us. This is a trying period of great perplexity and we dare not let a specious fellow like this wield his pencil in criticism of those about the court of a youthful prince and abuse us as he will."

Remonstrance and appeal being vain Ma retired. But he said to his colleagues, "Is Wang Yun then careless of the future? Worthy men are the mainstay of the State: laws are the canons of action. To destroy the mainstay and nullify the laws is to hasten destruction."

As was just said Wang Yun was obdurate. The man whose offence was an expression of gratitude was thrown into prison and there strangled. The people of that day wept for him, for they refused to see any offence in what he had done and death was a harsh punishment.

> Tung, the harsh dictator,
> Tyrannised the State,
> Fell and his sole mourner
> Shared his direful fate.
> Chuko in seclusion
> Was content to dream,
> Felt his worth and never
> Helped a traitor's scheme.

Those of his adherents whom Tung Cho had left to guard his city fled when their master was slain and went into Shensi. Thence they sent in a memorial entreating amnesty. But Wang Yun would not hear of it. Four of them were the chief instruments of Cho's aggressions. Now though a general amnesty were proclaimed these men should be excluded from its benefit.

The messenger returned and told the four there was no hope of pardon and they could only flee.

Adviser Chia Hsu said, "If we throw away our arms and flee singly then we shall fall easy victims to any village beadle who may seize us. Rather let us cajole the Shensi people to throw in their lot with us and make a sudden onslaught on the capital and so avenge our master. If we succeed, we control the court and the country. It will be time enough to run away if we fail."

The plan was adopted and they spread abroad the story that Wang Yun intended to harry the district. Having thus thrown the people into a state of terror they went a step farther and said, "There is no advantage in dying for nothing. Revolt and join us." So they cajoled the people into joining them and gathered a host equal to ten legions. This horde was divided into four parts and they all set out to raid the capital. On the way they fell in with a son-in-law of their late chief, with a number of soldiers. He had set out to avenge his father-in-law and he became the van-leader of the horde.

As they advanced the news came to Wang Yun and he consulted Lu Pu.

"They are a lot of rats," said he. "Never mind how many there are of them. Be not in the least anxious."

So Lu Pu and Li Su went to oppose them. The latter was in advance and met Niu Fu. They fought; Niu Fu was outmatched and retired. But unexpectedly Niu Fu returned in a night attack, found

Li Su quite unprepared and drove his force some thirty *li*, slaying many.

Li went to tell his chief who raged at him saying, "You have sullied my reputation as a warrior and destroyed my prestige."

And he put Li Su to death, exposing his head at the camp gate.

Next day Lu Pu advanced his own force and engaged Niu Fu. Could the result be the least dubious? Niu Fu was driven off. That night he called in his friend Hu Ch'ih-erh to advise him.

Lu Pu is too doughty a fighter for us to hope to overcome him. Our case is hopeless. Our best course is to desert these four men, secrete our valuables and leave the army with just a few of our followers."

The plan of Niu Fu was adopted and the two traitors that very night packed up and made their way out of camp. They were only half a dozen. They came to a river and, while crossing, Hu Ch'ih-erh, tempted by the lust of wealth, slew his companion. Then he went to offer the head to Lu Pu. Lu Pu enquired into the matter and when a follower told him the truth, he put the double traitor to death.

Then he advanced against the rebels and fell in with Li Ts'ui's force. Without giving them time to form in battle array, he attacked. Horses curvetting and spears set, the men dashed in irresistibly and Li Ts'ui, making no stand, fell back a long way. He took up a position under a hill and thence sent to call his fellows to council.

Li Ts'ui said, "Lu Pu though brave in battle is no strategist and so not really formidable. I will lead my men to hold the mouth of the gorge and every day I will incite him to attack and, when lie comes toward me, Commander Kuo can smite his rear, after the manner of P'eng Yueh when he fought against Ch'u. While thus I am alternating attack and retreat you other two will march off in different directions toward Ch'angan. Such an attack at two points must end in his defeat."

They set themselves to carry out this scheme. As soon as Lu Pu reached the hills a force came out to attack him. Pu made an angry dash toward the enemy, who retired up the hill, whence they shot arrows and hurled stones like rain. Lu Pu's men halted. At this moment the report came that the rear was being attacked and there appeared Kuo Ssu. At once Lu Pu wheeled toward the new enemy, but immediately the rolling drums gave the signal to retire and Lu Pu could not come to blows with them. As he called in his men the gongs clanged on the other side and his former opponent came as if to smite him. But before he could join battle his rear was again threatened by Kuo, who in his turn drew off without striking a blow.

Thus Lu Pu was baited till his bosom was near bursting with rage. The same tactics continued for several days. He could neither strike his enemies nor escape them; his men had no rest.

In the midst of these distracting manoeuvres a messenger rode up in hot haste to say that the capital was in imminent danger from a double attack. He at once ordered a march to save the capital, which became a rout when both his opponents came in pursuit. His loss was heavy.

He soon reached Ch'angan and found the rebels there in enormous numbers and the city quite surrounded. Lu Pu's attack had but little effect and as his temper became more savage under defeat many of his men went over to the rebels.

He fell into deep melancholy. Then a remnant of Tung Cho's adherents still in the city, led by Li Meng and Wang Fang, began to lend aid to the attackers and by and by they secretly opened the city gate and the beseigers poured in. Lu Pu exerted himself to the utmost but could not stem the tide. At the head of a few horse he dashed over to the Chingao Gate, or "Gate of the Black Lock," and called out to Wang Yun, who was on the other side, that the case was desperate and bade him mount and ride to a place of safety.

Wang Yun replied, "If I am gifted with the holy spirit of the State I shall succeed in restoring the tranquility which I desire, but if I have it not, then I offer my body a sacrifice. I will not quail before dangers. Thank the noble supporters east of the pass for their efforts and bid them remember their country."

Lu Pu urged him again and again, but he would not leave. Soon flames started up all over the city and Lu Pu had to leave, abandoning his family to their fate. He fled and joined Yuan Shu.

Li Ts'ui and his fellow leaders gave full licence to their ruffians, who robbed and murdered their fill. Many high officers perished. In time they penetrated to the inner palace and the eunuchs begged the Emperor to proceed to the Hsuanp'ing Men (the Gate of Pervading Peace) to try to quell the rioting. At sight of the yellow umbrella Li Ts'ui and Kuo Ssu checked their men and they all shouted "Long life O Emperor!" (*Wan-sui!*). The Emperor stood by the tower and addressed them, "Nobles, what means it that you enter the capital in this unruly manner and without my summons?"

The two leaders looked up and said, "Tung Cho, Your Majesty's Minister, has been slain by Wang Yun and we are here to avenge him. We are no rebels, Sire. Let us only have Wang Yun and we draw off our men."

Wang Yun was actually among the courtiers and at the Emperor's side. Hearing this demand he said, "The plan was made for the benefit of the Throne, but as this evil has grown therefrom Your Majesty will not grudge losing me. I have brought about evil and I will go down to these rebels."

The Emperor was torn with sorrow and wavered. But the faithful Minister leaped from the wall crying, "Wang Yun is here."

The two leaders drew their swords, crying, "For what crime was our master slain?"

"His crimes filled the heavens and covered the earth; no tongue can tell them. The day he died was a day of rejoicing in the whole city as you well know,' said Wang.

"And if he was guilty of some crime what had we done not to be forgiven?"

"Seditious rebels, why bandy words? I am ready to die."

And he was slain at the foot of the tower.

> Moved by the people's sufferings,
> Vexed at his prince's grief,
> Wang Yun compassed the traitor's death,
> That they might find relief.
> Every one knows him a hero,
> Leal to the State always:
> Living he guarded the princely towers,
> His soul keeps guard today.

Having done the loyal Minister to death at his master's feet they proceeded to exterminate also his whole family. Every one mourned.

Then said the ruffians to each other, "Having gone so far what could be better than to make away with the Emperor and complete our scheme?"

> The traitor condoned his crime,
> Rebellion ought to cease;
> But his licentious followers
> Disturb the Empire's peace.

The fate of the Emperor will be disclosed in the next chapter.

CHAPTER X

MA T'ENG SERVES HIS COUNTRY WELL: TS'AO TS'AO AVENGES HIS FATHER'S MURDER

In the last chapter the two arch rebels proposed to murder the Emperor Hsien, but their followers Chang and Fan opposed this. "No; the people will not approve of his death now. Restore him to power and get the leaguers inside the gates. Remove his supporters and then we can compass his death. And we shall be able to do what we wish."

So they ceased the attack. The Emperor again spoke from the tower, saying, "Why do you still remain? You have slain Wang Yun now withdraw these soldiers."

Then Li and Kuo replied, "Your servants desire rank us a reward for their good service to your dynasty."

"And what rank, Sirs?"

All four wrote their wishes and handed them up to the Emperor who had no choice but to accede to the request and they were created "Generals" (*Chiang-chun*) and received ranks of nobility and thereupon they went away and camped at Ssunung. The inferior leaders also were gratified with ranks. And once more the capital was free of troops.

Tung Cho's followers having so far succeeded did not forget their late leader. They sought his corpse for burial, but only a few fragments were discoverable. Then they graved an image of fragrant wood in his likeness, laid that out in proper form and instituted a noble's sacrifices and prayers. The remains were dressed in the robes of a prince laid in a princely coffin for burial. They selected Meiwu for his tomb and having found an auspicious day conveyed the coffin thither.

But a terrific thunder storm came on at the time of inhumation and the ground was flooded. The coffin was riven asunder and the poor remains thrown out. A second time they buried the coffin, but a similar thing happened in the night. And yet a third time in another place but the earth rejected the remains. Meanwhile the thunder-fire had entirely consumed them. So it may be said justly that Heaven was exceeding angry with Tung Cho.

So now Li Ts'ui and Kuo Ssu wielded the real power of the sceptre and they were hard upon the people. They also removed the attendants from the palace and replaced them by their own creatures, who maintained a most perfect watch over every movement of the Emperor so that he was greatly hampered and embarrassed. All appointments were made by the late rebels. For the sake of popularity they especially summoned Chu Chien to court, made him a High Chamberlain and associated him with the government.

One day came a report that Ma T'eng, the Prefect of Hsiliang, and Han Sui, with ten legions, were rapidly approaching the capital with the intention of attacking the rebels.

Now these men from the west had laid careful plans. They had sent trusty friends to the capital to find out who would support them. They had conspired with three officials to be their inside allies and plot against the rebels. These three obtained from the throne two secret edicts conferring the ranks of Commander, "Conqueror of the West," on Ma T'eng and Commander, "Warden of the West," on Han Sui. With these powers the two officials joined forces and began their march.

The four leaders of the party in power held a consultation as to how to meet the attack. The adviser, Chia Hsu, said, "Since the attackers are coming from a distance our plan is to fortify and wait till shortage of food shall work for us. In a hundred days their supplies will be consumed and they must retire. We can pursue and we shall capture them."

Li Meng and Wang Fang rose and said, "This plan is bad. Give us a legion and we will put an end to both of them and offer their heads before your ensign."

"To fight forthwith means defeat," said the adviser.

The other two cried with one voice, "If we fail we are willing to lose our heads, but if we win then your head is forfeit."

Chia Hsu then said, "Two hundred *li* west of the capital stand the Chouchih Hills. The passes are narrow and difficult. Send Generals Chang and Fan to occupy this point of vantage and fortify themselves so that they may support Li and Wang.

Li Ts'ui and Kuo Ssu accepted this advice. They told off a legion and a half of horse and foot and Li and Wang left. They made a camp two hundred and eighty *li* from Ch'angan.

The force from the west arrived and the two officers led out their men to the attack. They found their opponents in battle array. The two leaders, Ma T'eng and Han Sui, rode to the front side by side. Pointing to the rebel leaders they abused them, calling them traitors and asking who would capture them.

Hardly were the words spoken when there came out a youth with a clear, white complexion, eyes like shooting stars, lithe of body and strong of limb. He was armed with a long spear and bestrode an excellent steed. This young leader was Ma Ch'ao, son of Ma T'eng, then seventeen years of age.

Though young he was valiant and skilful. Wang Fang, despising him on account of his youth, galloped forth to fight him. Before they had exchanged many passes Wang Fang was disabled and fell to a thrust of the young man's spear. The victor turned to retire into the formation, but Li Meng rode after him to avenge his fallen colleague. Ma Ch'ao did not see him, but his father called out "You are followed!" Hardly had he spoken when he saw that the pursuer was a prisoner seated on his son's steed.

Now Ma Ch'ao had known he was followed, but pretended not to see, waiting till his enemy should have come close and lifted his spear to strike. Then he suddenly wheeled about. The spear thrust met only empty air, and as the horses passed Ma Ch'ao's powerful arm shot out and pulled Wang Fang from the saddle. Thus the soldiers were left leaderless and fled in all directions. The army dashed in pursuit and a complete victory was scored. They pressed into the pass and made a camp. They decapitated Li Meng and exposed his head.

When Li Ts'ui and Kuo Ssu heard that both the boastful captains had fallen under the hand of one young man they knew that Chia Hsu had given good advice and was gifted with clear prescience. So they valued his plans the more highly and decided to act on the defensive. They refused all challenges to combat.

Surely enough after a couple of months the supplies of the Hsiliang men were all exhausted and the leaders began to consider retreat.

Just at this juncture a household servant of Ma Yu's family betrayed his master and told of the conspiracy of the three men to assist the attackers. The two chief rebels in revenge seized the three conspirators, with every member of their households, and beheaded them in the market place. The heads of the three were exposed at the gate.

Being short of food and hearing of the destruction of their three adherents in the city, the only course for Ma and Han was to retreat. At once Chang Chi went in pursuit of Ma T'eng and Fan Ch'ou followed Han Sui. The retreating army under Ma was beaten and only by Ma Ch'ao's desperate efforts were the pursuers driven off.

Fan Ch'ou pursued the other army and when he had come close Han Sui rode boldly up and addressed him, saying "You and I, Sir, are fellow villagers. Why then behave so unfriendly?"

Ch'ou replied, "I must obey the commands of my chief."

"I am here for the service of the State; why do you press me so hard?" said Han.

At this Fan Ch'ou turned his horse, called in his men and left him in peace. Unwittingly a nephew of Li Ts'ui had been a witness of this scene and when he saw the enemy allowed to go free he returned and told his uncle. Angry that his enemy had escaped, Li would have wreaked vengeance on his lieutenant, but his adviser again came in saying it was dangerous to provoke another war. He proposed inviting the defaulting officer to a banquet and, while the feast was in progress, executing him for dereliction of duty. This seemed good to Li so the banquet was prepared. The two officers accepted their invitations and went cheerfully. Toward the latter part of the entertainment a sudden change came over their host and he suddenly asked Fan Ch'ou, "Why have you been intriguing with Han Sui? You are turning traitor, eh?"

The unhappy guest was taken aback and before he could frame his words to reply he saw the assassins rush out with swords and axes. In a moment all was over and his head lay beneath the table.

Scared beyond measure his fellow-guest grovelled on the floor. "He was a traitor," said the host, raising him by the arm, "and he has his deserts; you are my friend and need not fear."

He gave Chang Chi command of the murdered man's troop with which he returned to Hungnung. No one of the nobles among the leaguers dared attempt an attack on the party newly risen from Tung Cho's disaffection, while on the other hand Chia Hsu never ceased to urge his masters to exert themselves for the welfare of the people and thus to tempt wise men to join them. And by these means the government began to prosper.

However, a new trouble arose in the shape of a resurgence of Yellow Turbans. They came, without apparent head or leader, in large numbers and plundered any place they reached. Chu Chien said he knew of one who could destroy this sedition, and when asked who was the man he proposed he said, "You want to destroy this horde of rebels; you will fail unless you get the services of Ts'ao Meng-te."

"And where is he?" asked Li Ts'ui.

"He is Prefect of Tung Chun. He has a large army and you have only to order him to act; the rising will be broken."

A messenger went post haste with a command for Ts'ao Ts'ao and Pao Hsin to act together in quelling the rebellion. As soon as Ts'ao Ts'ao received the court command he arranged with his colleague first to attack the rebels at Shouyang. Pao Hsin made a dash right into their midst, inflicting damage wherever he could, and Ts'ao Ts'ao pursued them as they fled. So many surrendered. Then he put his quondam enemies in the van and when his army reached any place many more surrendered and joined him. After three months of these tactics they had won over many thousands, both of soldiers and ordinary folk.

Of these new adherents the strongest and boldest were made soldiers and the others were sent home to their fields. In consequence of these successes Ts'ao Ts'ao's prestige and fame became very great and increased daily. He reported his success to the capital and was rewarded with the title of Commander, "Warden of the East."

At his headquarters in Yenchow Ts'ao Ts'ao welcomed wise counsellors and bold warriors, and many gathered around him. Two clever men, uncle and nephew, came at the same time, both Yingchow men, named Hsun Yu and Hsun Yu. The uncle had once been in the service of Yuan Shao. Ts'ao Ts'ao rejoiced when he had won the elder Hsun to his side saying he was his teacher. The nephew was famed for his ability and had been in the court service but had abandoned that career and retired to his village.

The uncle said to Ts'ao Ts'ao, "There is a certain wise man of Yenchow somewhere, but I do not know in whose service he is."

"Who is he?"

"Ch'eng Yu; he belongs to the eastern district."

"Yes; I have heard of him," said Ts'ao. So a messenger was sent to his native place to enquire. He was away in the hills engaged in study, but he came at Ts'ao Ts'ao's invitation.

"I shall prove unworthy of your recommendation," said he to his friend Hsun, "for I am rough and ignorant. But have you forgotten a fellow villager of yours, Kuo Chia? He is really able. Why not spread the net to catch him?"

"I had nearly forgotten," said Hsun Yu suddenly. So he told his master of this man, who was at once invited. Kuo, discussing the world at large with his master, spoke in high terms of one Liu Yeh; and when he had arrived he was the means of inviting two more, Man Ch'ung and Lu Ch'ien, who were already known to Ts'ao Ts'ao by reputation. These two brought to their new master's notice the name of Mao Chieh, who also came and was given office. Then a famous leader, with his troop of some hundreds, arrived to offer service. This was Yu Chin of T'aishan, an expert horseman and archer, and skilled beyond his fellows in every form of military exercise. He was made an army inspector.

Then another day Hsiahou Tun brought a really fine, handsome fellow to present to Ts'ao Ts'ao.

"Who is he," asked Ts'ao.

"He is from Ch'en-liu and is named Tien Wei. He is the boldest of the bold, the strongest of the strong. He was one of Chang Mo's men, but quarrelled with his tent companions and killed a lot of them with his fists. Then he fled to the mountains where I found him. I was out shooting and saw him follow a tiger across a stream. I persuaded him to join my troop and I recommend him."

"I see he is no ordinary man," said Ts'ao. "He is handsome and straight and looks very powerful and bold."

"He is. He killed a man once to avenge a friend and carried his head through the whole market place. Hundreds saw him, but dared not come near. The weapon he uses now is a two branched spear over a hundred pounds in weight, and he vaults into the saddle with this under his arm."

Ts'ao Ts'ao bade the man give proof of his skill so he galloped to and fro carrying the spear. Then he saw away among the tents a huge banner swaying dangerously with the force of the wind and on the point of falling. A crowd of soldiers were vainly struggling to keep it steady. Down he leaped, shouted to the men to clear out and held the staff quite steady with one hand, keeping it perfectly upright in spite of the strong wind.

"This is old Wu Lai again," said Ts'ao Ts'ao. He gave the strong man a post in the army and besides made him presents of an embroidered robe and a swift steed with a handsome saddle.

Thus Ts'ao Ts'ao encouraged able men to assist him and he had advisers on the civil side and valiant captains in the army. He became famous through all Shantung.

Ts'ao's father, Sung, was living at Langya, whither he had gone as a place free from the turmoil of the partizan struggles and, as a dutiful son, Ts'ao sent the Prefect of T'aishan to escort his father to Yenchow. The old man read the letter with joy and the family prepared to move. They were some forty in all, with a train of a hundred servants and many carts.

Their road led through Hsuchou where the Prefect, T'ao Ch'ien, was a sincere and upright man who had long wished to get on good terms with Ts'ao Ts'ao but, hitherto, had found no means of effecting a bond of union. Hearing that the family of the great man was passing through his district he went to welcome them, treated them with great cordiality, feasting and entertaining them for two days, and when they left he escorted them to his boundary. Further he sent with them one Chang K'ai with a special escort.

The whole party reached Huafei. It was the end of summer, just turning into autumn, and at this place they were stopped by a tremendous storm of rain. The only shelter was an old temple and thither they went. The family occupied the main rooms and the escort the two side wings. The men of the escort were drenched, angry and discontented. The leader called some of his petty officers to a secret spot and said, "We are old Yellow Turbans and only submitted to T'ao because there was no help for it. We have never got much out of it. Now here is the Ts'ao family with no end of gear and we can be rich very easily. We will make a sudden onslaught tonight at the third watch and slay the whole lot. Then we shall have plenty of treasure and we will get away to the mountains."

They all agreed. The storm continued into the night and as Ts'ao Sung sat waiting anxiously for signs of clearing he suddenly heard a hubbub at the west end of the temple. His brother Ts'ao Te, drawing his sword, went out to see what it was about and was at once cut down. Ts'ao Sung seized one of the concubines by the hand, rushed with her through the passage toward the back of the temple so that they might escape. But the lady was stout and could not get through the narrow doors so the two hid in one of the small outhouses at the side. However, they were seen and slain.

The unhappy Prefect fled for his life to Yuan Shao. The murderers fled into Huainan with their plunder after having set fire to the old temple.

> Ts'ao Ts'ao, whom the ages praise,
> Slew the Lus in former days;
> Nemesis ne'er turns aside,
> Murdered too his family died.

Some of the escort escaped and took the evil tidings to Ts'ao Ts'ao. When he heard it he fell to the earth with a great cry. They raised him. With set teeth he muttered, "His men have slain my father: no longer can the same sky cover us. I will sweep Hsuchou off the face of the earth. Only thus can I satisfy my vengeance."

Leaving one small army to guard the east he set forth with all the remainder to destroy Hsuchou and avenge his father.

Now the Prefect of Kiukiang was a close friend of T'ao Ch'ien.

Hearing Hsuchou was threatened he set out with half a legion to his friend's aid. Ts'ao sent Hsiahou Tun to cut him off while still on the march. At this time Ch'en Kung was in office in the east and he was also on friendly terms with T'ao. Hearing of Ts'ao's design to destroy the whole population he came in haste to see his former companion. Ts'ao knowing his errand put him off at first and would not see him. But he could not forget the kindness he had formerly received and presently the visitor was called to his tent.

Ch'en Kung said, "They say you go to avenge your father's death on Hsuchou, to destroy its people. I have come to say a word. The Prefect is humane and a good man. He is not looking out for his own advantage, careless of the means and of others. Your worthy father met his unhappy death at the hands of Chang K'ai. T'ao Ch'ien is guiltless. Still more innocent are the people and to slay them would be an evil. I pray you to think over it."

Ts'ao retorted angrily, "You once abandoned me and now you have the impudence to come to see me! T'ao Chien slew my whole family and I will tear his heart out in revenge. I swear it. You may speak for your friend and say what you will. I shall be as if I heard not."

Intercession had failed. He sighed and took his leave. "Alas! I cannot go to T'ao and look upon his face." So he rode off to the Ch'en-liu district.

Ts'ao Ts'ao's army of revenge laid waste whatever place it passed through, slaying the people and desecrating their cemeteries.

When T'ao Ch'ien heard the terrible tidings he looked up to heaven saying, "I must be guilty of some fault before Heaven to have brought this evil upon my people." He called together his officials to consult. One of them, Ts'ao Pao, said, "Now the enemy is upon us, we cannot sit and await death with folded hands. I for one will help you to make a fight."

The army went out. From a distance the enemy spread abroad like hoar frost and rushed far and wide like snow. In their midst was a large white flag and on both sides was written "Vengeance."

When he had ranged his men Ts'ao Ts'ao rode out dressed in mourning white and abused T'ao Ch'ien. But T'ao advanced and from beneath his ensign bowed low and said, "I wished to make friends with you, Illustrious Sir, and so I sent Chang K'ai to escort your family. I knew not that his rebel heart was still unchanged. The fault does not lie at my door as you must see."

"You old fool, you killed my father and now you dare to mumble this nonsense," said Ts'ao Ts'ao. And he asked who would go out and seize him.

Hsiahou Tun undertook this service and rode out. The Prefect fled to the inner portion of his array and as Hsiahou Tun came on Ts'ao Pao went to meet him. But just as the two horses met a hurricane burst over the spot and the flying dust and pebbles threw both sides into the utmost confusion. Both drew off.

The Prefect retired into the city and called his officers to council. "The force against us is too strong," said he. "I will give myself up as a prisoner and let him wreak his vengeance on me. I may save the people."

But a voice was heard saying, "You have long ruled here and the people love you. Strong as the enemy are they are not necessarily able to break down our walls, especially when defended by you and your people. I have a scheme to suggest that I think will make Ts'ao Ts'ao die in a place where he will not find burial."

These bold words startled the assembly and they eagerly asked what the scheme was.

> Making overtures for friendship he encountered deadly hate,
> But, where danger seemed most threatening, he discovered safety's gate.

The next chapter will disclose who the speaker was.

CHAPTER XI

LIU, THE EMPEROR'S UNCLE,
RESCUES K'UNG JUNG: LU, MARQUIS
OF WEN, DEFEATS TS'AO TS'AO

It was one Mi Chu who said he knew how to defeat Ts'ao Ts'ao utterly. He came of a wealthy family of merchants trading in 'Loyang. One day travelling homeward from that city in a carriage he met an exquisitely beautiful lady trudging along the road, who asked him to let her ride. He stopped and yielded his place to her. She invited him to share the seat with her. He mounted, but sat rigidly upright never even glancing in her direction. They travelled thus for some miles when she thanked him and alighted. Just as she left she said, "I am the embodied spirit of the Southern Heat. I am on my way to execute a decree of the Supreme to burn your dwelling, but your extreme courtesy has so deeply touched me that I now warn you. Hasten homeward, remove your valuables for I must arrive tonight."

Thereupon she disappeared. Mi Chu hastily finished his journey and as soon as he arrived moved everything out of his house. Sure enough that night a fire started in the kitchen and involved the whole house. After this he devoted his wealth to relieving the poor and comforting the afflicted. T'ao Ch'ien gave him the office he then held.

The plan he proposed was this. "I will go to Pohai and beg K'ung Jung to help; another should go to Ch'ingchow on a similar mission, and if the armies of these two places march on our enemy he will certainly retire."

The Prefect accepted the plan and wrote letters. He asked for a volunteer to go to Ch'ingchow and a certain Ch'en Teng offered himself and, after he had left, Mi Chu was formally entrusted with the mission to the north. Meanwhile they would hold the city as they could.

This K'ung was a native of Ch'ufou in the old state of Lu, one of the twentieth generation in descent from the great Teacher Confucius. He had been noted as a very intelligent lad, somewhat precocious. When ten years old he had gone to see Li Ying, the Governor, but the doorkeeper demurred to letting him in. But when he said, "I am Minister Li's intimate friend," he was admitted. Li asked him what relations had existed between their families that might justify the term intimate. The boy replied, "Of old my ancestor (K'ung) questioned yours (Lao Tzu, whose name was Li Erh) concerning ceremonies. So our families have known each other for many generations." His host was astonished at the boy's ready wit.

Presently another visitor of high rank came in, to whom Li Ying told the story of his youthful guest. "He is a wonder, this boy," said Li.

The visitor replied, "It does not follow that a clever boy grows up into a clever man."

The lad took him up at once saying "By what you say, Sir, you were certainly one of the clever boys."

They all laughed. "The boy is going to be a noble vessel," said they.

Thus from boyhood he was famous. As a man he rose to be a Chung-lang Chiang, and was sent as Governor to Pohai, where he was renowned for hospitality. He used to quote the lines:—

> "Let the rooms be full of friends,
> And the cups be full of wine."

"That is what I like," said he.

After six years at Pohai the people were devoted to him. The day that Mi Chu arrived he was, as usual, seated among his guests and the messenger was ushered in without delay. In reply to a question about the reason of the visit he presented his letter which said that Ts'ao Ts'ao was pressing on the city and the Prefect prayed for help.

Then said K'ung Jung, "Your master and I are good friends and your presence here constrains me to go to his aid. However I have no quarrel with Ts'ao Meng-te either, so I will first write to him to try to make peace. If he refuses my offer, then I must set the army in motion."

"Ts'ao Ts'ao will not listen to proposals of peace; he is too certain of his strength," said the messenger.

K'ung Jung wrote his letter and also gave orders to muster his men. Just at this moment happened another rising of the Yellow

Turbans, and the ruffians began to rob and murder at Pohai. It was necessary to deal with them first and K'ung led his army outside the city.

The rebel leader rode out to the front saying, "I know this district is fruitful and can well spare ten thousand 'stone' of grain. Give me that and we retire: refuse, and we will batter down the city walls and destroy every soul."

The Prefect shouted back, "I am a servant of the great Hans, entrusted with the safety of their land. Think you I will feed rebels?"

The leader Kuan Hai whipped his steed, whirled his sword around his head and rode forward. Tsung Pao, one of K'ung's captains, set his spear and rode out to give him battle, but after a very few bouts was cut down. Soon the soldiers fell into confusion and rushed pell-mell into the city for protection. The rebels then laid seige to the city on all sides. K'ung Jung was very down-hearted and Mi Chu, who now saw no hope for the success of his mission, was grieved beyond words.

The sight from the city wall was exceeding sad, for the rebels were there in enormous numbers. One day as the Prefect stood on the wall, he saw a man armed with a spear riding hard in among his enemies and scattering them before him like chaff before the wind. Before long he had reached the foot of the wall and called out, "Open the gate!" But the defenders would not open to an unknown man and in the delay a crowd of rebels gathered round the rider along the edge of the moat. Suddenly wheeling about, the warrior dashed in among them and bowled over half a score at which the others fell back. At this the Prefect ordered the wardens to open the gates and let the stranger enter. As soon as he was inside he dismounted, laid aside his spear, ascended the wall and made humble obeisance to K'ung Jung.

He said his name was T'aishih Tz'u and he came from Laihuang. His aged mother had sent him out of gratitude for the kindness shown her by K'ung. "I only returned home yesterday from the north and then I heard that your city was in danger from a rebel attack. My mother said you had been very kind to her and told me I should try to help. So I set out all alone and here I am."

This was cheering. The Prefect already knew T'aishih by reputation as a valiant fighting man although they two had never met. The son being far away from his home the Prefect had taken his mother, who dwelt a few miles from the city, under his especial protection and saw that she did not suffer from want. This had won the old lady's heart and she had sent her son to show her gratitude.

K'ung showed his appreciation by treating his guest with the greatest respect, making him presents of clothing and armour, saddles and horses.

Presently said T'aishih, "Give me a company and I will go out and drive off these fellows."

"You are a bold warrior, but these are very numerous. It is a serious matter to go out among them," said K'ung.

"My mother sent me because of your goodness to her. How shall I be able to look her in the face if I do not raise the siege? I would prefer to conquer or perish."

"I have heard Liu Yuan-te is one of the finest warriors in the world and if we could get his help there would be no doubt of the result. But there is no one to send."

"I will go as soon as I have received your letter."

So K'ung wrote letters and gave them to his new helper. T'aishih put on his armour, mounted his steed, attached his bow and quiver to his girdle, took his spear in his hand, tied his packed haversack firmly to his saddle bow and rode out at the city gate. He went quite alone.

Along the moat a large party of the besiegers were gathered and they came to intercept the solitary rider. But he dashed in among them and cut down several and so finally fought his way through.

The rebel leader, hearing that a rider had left the city, guessed what his errand would be and followed T'aishih with a party of horsemen. He spread them out so that the messenger rider was entirely surrounded. Then T'aishih laid aside his spear, took his bow, adjusted his arrows one by one and shot all round him. And as a rider fell from his steed with every twang of his bowstring, the pursuers dared not close in.

Thus he got clear away and rode in hot haste to Liu Yuan-te. He reached P'ingyuan and after greeting his host in proper form he told how K'ung Pohai was surrounded and had sent him for help. Then he presented the letter which Liu Pei read.

"Who are you?" asked he.

"I am T'aishih Tz'u, a stupid fellow from Tunghai. I am not related by ties of kin to K'ung Jung, nor even by ties of neighbourhood, but I am by the bonds of sentiment and I share his sorrows and misfortunes. The rebel Kuan has invested his city and he is distressed with none to turn to and destruction is very near. You are known as humane and righteous and you are able to rescue him. Therefore at his command I have braved all dangers and fought my way through his enemies to pray you to save him."

Liu Yuan-te smiled, saying, "And does he know of my existence?"

So the three brothers told off three companies and set out to help raise the siege. When the rebel leader saw these new forces arriving he led out his army to fight them, thinking he could easily dispose of so small a force.

The brothers and T'aishih Tz'u with them sat on their horses in the forefront of their array. Kuan Hai, the rebel leader, hastened forward. T'aishih held back to allow Kuan Yu to open the combat. He rode forth and the two steeds met. The soldiers set up a great shout, for how could there be any doubt of the result? After a few bouts Black Dragon rose and fell, and with the stroke fell the rebel leader.

This was the signal for the two other warriors to take a share and they advanced side by side. With their spear ready they dashed in and Yuan-te urged forward his men. The besieged Prefect saw his doughty rescuers laying low the rebels as tigers among a flock of sheep. None could withstand them and he then sent out his own men to join in the battle so that the rebels were between two armies. The rebels' force was completely broken and many men surrendered, while the remainder scattered in all directions.

The victors were welcomed into the city and as soon as possible a banquet was prepared in their honour. Mi Chu was presented to Liu Yuan-te and he related the story of the murder of Ts'ao Sung by Chang K'ai and Ts'ao's vengeful attack on Hsuchou and his coming to beg for assistance.

Yuan-te, said, "T'ao Kung-tsu is a kindly man of high character, and it is a pity that he should suffer this wrong for no fault of his own."

"You are a scion of the imperial family," said the Prefect, "and this Ts'ao Ts'ao is injuring the people, a strong man abusing his strength. Why not go with me to rescue the sufferers?"

"I dare not refuse, but my force is weak and I must act cautiously," said Liu Pei.

"Though my desire to help arises from an old friendship, yet it is a righteous act as well. Is it that your heart is not inclined toward the right?" said K'ung.

Liu Pei said, "This being so, you go first and give me time to see Kungsun Tsan from whom I may borrow more men and horses. I will come anon."

"You surely will not break your promise?" said the Prefect.

"What manner of man think you that I am?" said Yuan-te. "The wise one said, 'Death is common to all: the man without truth cannot maintain himself.' Whether I get the men or not, certainly I shall myself come."

So the plan was agreed to. Mi Chu set out to return forthwith while K'ung Jung prepared for his expedition.

T'aishih Ts'u took his leave saying, "My mother bade me come to your aid and now happily you are safe. Letters have come from my fellow townsman, Liu Yu, Governor of Yang-chou, calling me thither and I must go. I will see you again."

K'ung pressed rewards upon him but he would accept nothing and went away. When his mother saw him she was pleased at his success saying she rejoiced that he had been to prove his gratitude, and after this he departed for Yangchou.

Here nothing will be said of the departure of the relieving force. But Yuan-te went away to his friend Kungsun Tsan and laid before him his design to help Hsuchou.

"Ts'ao Ts'ao and you are not enemies; why do you spend yourself for the sake of another?" said Tsan.

"I have promised," he replied, "and dare not break faith."

"I will lend you two companies, horse and foot," said Tsan.

"Also I wish to have the services of Chao Tzu-lung," said Yuan-te.

Tsan agreed to this also.

They marched away, their own men being in the front and Chao Tzu-lung, with the borrowed men, being in rear.

In due course Mi Chu returned saying that K'ung Jung had also obtained the services of the three warrior brothers. The other messenger, Ch'en Yuan-lung, came back and reported that T'ien K'ai would also bring help. Then was the Prefect's heart set at ease.

But both the leaders, though they had promised aid, greatly dreaded their antagonist and camped among the hills at a great distance, fearful of coming to close quarters. Ts'ao Ts'ao knew of their coming and divided his army into parts to meet them, so postponing the attack on the city itself. Presently Liu Pei came up and went to see K'ung Jung, who said, "The enemy is very powerful and Ts'ao Ts'ao handles his army skilfully. We must be cautious. Let us make most careful observations before we strike a blow."

"What I fear is famine in the city," said Liu Pei. "They cannot hold out very long. I will put my men with yours under your command while I with Chang Fei make a dash through to see T'ao Ch'ien and consult with him."

K'ung Jung approved of this, so he and T'ien K'ai took up positions on the "ox horn formation," with Kuan Yu and Chao Yun on either side to support them.

The day that Liu Pei and his company made their dash to get

through Ts'ao's army they got as far as the flank of his camp when there arose a great beating of drums, and horse and foot rolled out like billows on the ocean. The leader was Yu Chin. He checked his steed and called out, "You mad men from somewhere, where are you going?"

Chang Fei heard him but deigned no reply. He only rode straight to attack the speaker. After they had fought a few bouts Yuan-te waved his double sword as signal for his men to come on and they drove Yu Chin before them. Chang Fei led the pursuit and in this way they reached the city wall.

From the city wall the besieged saw a huge banner embroidered in white with the name of Liu Pei and the Prefect bade them open the gate for the rescuers to enter. The leader was made very welcome, conducted to the residency and a banquet prepared in his honour. The men also were feasted.

T'ao Ch'ien was delighted with Liu Pei, admiring his noble appearance and clear speech. He bade Mi Chu offer him the seal and insignia of office. But the visitor shrank back startled.

What does this mean?" said he.

T'ao said, "There is trouble on every side and the kingly rule is no longer maintained. You, Sir, are a member of the family and eminently fitted to support them and their prerogatives. I am verging on senility and I wish to retire in your favour. I pray you not to decline and I will report my action to the Court."

Liu Pei started up from his seat and bowed before his host saying, "Scion of the family I may be, but my merit is small and my virtue meagre. I doubt my fitness even for my present post and only a feeling of doing right sent me to your assistance. To hear such speech makes me doubt. Surely you think I came with greed in my heart. May God help me no more if I cherished such a thought."

"It is a poor old man's real sentiment," said T'ao Ch'ien.

Time after time T'ao Ch'ien renewed his offer to retire, but how could Liu Pei accept it?

In the midst of this came Mi Chu to say the enemies had reached the wall and something must be done to drive them off. The matter of one officer retiring in favour of the other could await a more tranquil time.

Said Liu Pei, "I ought to write to Ts'ao Ts'ao to press him to raise the siege. If he refuse, we will attack forthwith."

Orders were sent to the three camps to remain quiescent till the letters could reach Ts'ao Ts'ao.

It happened that Ts'ao Ts'ao was holding a council when a

messenger with a war letter was announced. The letter was brought in and handed to him and, when he had opened and looked at it, he found it was from Liu Pei.

This is the letter, very nearly:—"Since meeting you outside the pass, fate has assigned us to different quarters of the world and I have not been able to pay my respects to you. Touching the death of your noble father, the Marquis, it was owing to the vicious nature of Chang K'ai and due to no fault of T'ao Kung-tsu. Now while the remnant of the Yellow Turbans is disturbing the provinces and Tung Cho's partizans have the upper hand in the capital, I would that you, illustrious Sir, would regard the critical position of the Court rather than your personal grievances and so divert your forces from the attack on Hsuchou to the rescue of the State. Such would be for the happiness of that city and the whole world."

Ts'ao Ts'ao gave vent to a torrent of abuse. "Who is this Liu Pei that he dares write and exhort me? Beside, he means to be satirical."

He issued orders to put the bearer of the letter to death and to press on the siege. But Kuo Chia remonstrated, "Liu Pei has come from afar to help T'ao and he is trying the effect of politeness before resorting to arms. I pray you, my master, reply with fair words that his heart may be lulled with a feeling of safety. Then attack with vigour and the city will fall."

Ts'ao found this advice good, so he spared the messenger telling him to wait to carry back his reply. While this was going on a horseman came with news of misfortune. Lu Pu had made a raid on Yenchou.

When Li and Kuo, the two partizans of Tung Cho, succeeded in their attack on the capital Lu Pu had fled to Yuan Shu, who however looked askance at him for his instability, and refused to receive him. Then he had tried Yuan Shao, who had made use of him in an attack upon Chang Yen in Ch'angshan. But his success filled him with pride and his arrogant demeanour so annoyed the other commandants that Shao was on the point of putting him to death. To escape this he had gone away to Chang Yang, who accepted his services.

About this time P'ang Hsu, who had been protecting Lu's family since his disappearance, restored them to him, which deed angered Li and Kuo so that they put P'ang to death and wrote to Lu Pu's protector to serve him the same. To escape this Lu Pu once again had to flee and this time joined himself to Chang Mo.

He arrived just as Chang Mo's brother was introducing Ch'en Kung. Kung said to Mo, "The disrupture of the Empire has begun and warriors are seizing what they can. It is strange that you, with all the advantages you enjoy, do not strike for independence. Ts'ao Ts'ao has gone on an expedition against the east leaving his own district defenceless. Lu Pu is one of the fighting men of the day. If you and he together attacked and got Yenchow you could then proceed to the dominion."

Chang Mo was pleased and resolved to try. Soon Lu Pu was in possession of Yenchou and its neighbourhood, all but three small departments, which were desperately defended. Ts'ao Jen had fought many battles but was always defeated and the messenger with the evil tidings had come from him asking help.

Ts'ao Ts'ao was greatly disturbed by this and said, "If my own city be lost I have no home to return to. I must do something at once."

"The best thing would be to become friends with Liu Pei at any cost and return to Yenchou," said Kuo Chia.

Then he wrote to Liu Pei, gave the letter to the waiting messenger and broke camp. The news that the enemy had left was very gratifying to the Prefect, who then invited his various defenders into the city and prepared banquets and feasts in token of his gratitude.

At one of these, when the feasting was over, he proceeded with his scheme of retirement in favour of Liu Pei. Placing him in the seat of highest honour he bowed before him and then addressed the assembly.

"I am old and feeble and my two sons lack the ability to hold so important an office as this. The noble Liu is a descendant of the imperial house. He is of lofty virtue and great talent. Let him then take over the rule of this district and only too willingly I shall retire to have leisure to nurse my health."

Liu Pei replied, "I came at the request of K'ung Wen-chu because it was the right thing to do. Hsuchou is saved, but if I take it surely the world will say I am a wicked man."

Mi Chu said, "You may not refuse. The House of Han is failing, their realm is crumbling and now is the time for doughty deeds and signal services. This is a fertile district, well populated, and you are the man to rule over it."

"But I dare not accept."

"The Prefect is a great sufferer," said Ch'en Teng, "and cannot see to matters. You may not decline, Sir."

Said Yuan-te, "Yuan Shu belongs to a family of rulers and the highest offices of state were held four times in three generations. The whole empire respects him, why not invite him to this task?"

"Because he is a rotting bone in a dark tomb; not worth talking about. This opportunity is a gift from Heaven and you will never cease to regret its loss," said K'ung.

So spake K'ung Jung, but still Liu Pei obstinately refused. T'ao Ch'ien besought him with tears. "I shall die if you leave me and there will be none to close my eyes."

"Brother, you should accept the offer thus made," said Kuan Yu.

"Why so much fuss?" said Chang Fei. "We have not taken the place; it is he who wishes to give it you."

"You all persuade me to do what is wrong," said Liu Pei.

Thrice did T'ao entreat Liu Pei and thrice was he refused. Then he said, "As he is set in his determination perhaps he will consent to encamp at Hsiaop'ei. It is only a little town, but thence he can keep watch and ward over this city."

They all with one voice prayed Liu Pei to consent so he gave in. The feast of victory being now ended the time came to say farewell. When Chao Yun took his leave Liu Pei held his hands alternately while dashing away the falling tears. K'ung Jung and his leader went home to their own place.

When Liu Pei and his brothers took up their abode in Hsiaop'ei, they first repaired the defences and then they put out proclamations in order to calm the inhabitants.

In the meantime Ts'ao Ts'ao had marched toward his own district. His cousin, Ts'ao Jen, met him and told him Lu Pu was very strong and he had Ch'en Kung as adviser. Yenchou was as good as lost, with the exception of three small districts which had been desperately defended.

Ts'ao Ts'ao said, "I own that Lu Pu is a bold fighter but nothing more; he has no craft. So we need not fear him seriously."

Then he gave orders to make a strong camp till they could think out some victorious plan. Lu Pu, knowing of Ts'ao Ts'ao's return, called two of his subordinate captains, Hsueh Lan and Li Feng, to him and assigned to them the task of holding Yenchou, saying "I have long waited for opportunity to employ your skill: now I give you a legion and you are to hold the city while I go forth to attack Ts'ao Ts'ao."

They made no objection. But Ch'en Kung, the strategist, came in hastily saying, "You are going away; whither?"

"I am going to camp my men at Puyang, that vantage point."

"You are making a mistake," said Ch'en Kung. "The two you have chosen to defend this are unequal to the task. For this expedition remember that about one hundred and eighty *li* due south, on the road to T'aishan, is a very advantageous position where you should place your best men in ambush. Ts'ao Ts'ao will hasten homeward by double marches when he hears what has happened and if you strike when half his men have gone past this point you may seize him."

Said Lu Pu, "I am going to occupy Puyang and see what develops. How can you guess?"

So he left the two captains in command at Yenchou and went away.

Now when Ts'ao Ts'ao approached the dangerous part of the road near T'aishan, Kuo Chia warned him to take care as there was doubtless an ambush. But his master laughed, "We know all his dispositions. Do you think he has laid an ambush? I shall tell Ts'ao Jen to besiege Yenchou and I shall go to Puyang."

When Ch'en Kung heard of the enemy's approach he spoke, saying "The enemy will be fatigued with long marches so attack quickly before they have time to recover."

Lu Pu replied, "I, a single horseman, am afraid of none. I go and come as I will. Think you I fear this Ts'ao Ts'ao? Let him settle his camp; I will take him after that."

Now Ts'ao Ts'ao neared Puyang and he made a camp. And soon after he led out his commanders and they arrayed their men in open and desert country. Ts'ao Ts'ao took up his station on horseback between the two standards, watching while his opponents arrived and formed up in a circular area. Lu Pu was in front, followed by eight of his captains, all strong men. Two were called Chang Liao and Tsang Pa; and there were six others. They had five legions.

The drums began their thunderous roll and Ts'ao, pointing to his opponent, said, "You and I had no quarrel, why then did you invade my land?"

"The Empire of Han is the possession of all; what is your special claim?" said Lu.

So saying he ordered Tsang Pa to ride forth and challenge. From Ts'ao's side the challenge was accepted by Yo Chin. The two steeds approached each other, two spears were lifted both together and they exchanged near two score blows with no advantage to either. Then Hsiahou Tun rode out to help his colleague and, in reply, out went Chang Liao from Lu Pu's side. And they four fought.

Then fierce anger seized upon Lu Pu. Setting his spear he urged his steed forward to where the fight was waging. Seeing him approach Hsiahou and Yo both fled, but Lu Pu pressed on after them and Ts'ao Ts'ao's army lost the day. Retiring a long way they made a new camp. Lu Pu called in and mustered his men.

The day having gone against him Ts'ao Ts'ao called a council and Yu Chin said, "From the hill tops today I saw a camp of our enemies on the west of Puyang. They were but few men therein, and tonight after today's victory, it will not be defended. Let us attack and if we can take the camp we shall strike fear into the heart of Lu Pu. This is our best plan."

Ts'ao thought so too. He and six of his lieutenants and two legions left that night by a secret road for the camp.

In Lu Pu's camp was rejoicing for that day's victory when Ch'en Kung reminded him of the west camp and its importance, and said that it might be attacked, Lu Pu replied that the enemy would not dare approach after that day's defeat.

"Ts'ao Ts'ao is a very able commander," replied Kung. "You must keep a good lookout for him lest he attack our weak spot."

So arrangements were made for defence. At dusk Ts'ao Ts'ao reached the camp and began an immediate attack on all four sides. The defenders could not hold him off. They ran in all directions and the camp was captured. Near the fourth watch, when the party told off to help defend the camp reached it, Ts'ao Ts'ao sallied forth to meet them and met Kao Shun. Another battle then began and waged till dawn. About that time a rolling of drums was heard in the west and they told Ts'ao that Lu Pu himself was at hand. Thereupon Ts'ao Ts'ao abandoned the attack and fled.

They pursued him, Lu Pu taking the lead. Two of Ts'ao's lieutenants attacked the pursuers but could not check them. Ts'ao went away north. But from behind some hills came out more of Lu Pu's army and as they could not be beaten off Ts'ao sought safety in the west. Here again his retreat was barred.

The fight became desperate. Ts'ao Ts'ao dashed at the enemy's array. The din was terrible. Arrows fell like pelting rain upon them and they could make no headway. He was desperate and cried out in fear, "Who can save me?"

Then from the crush dashed out Tien Wei with his double lance, crying "Fear not, my master." He leapt from his steed, leaned his double lance against a wall and laid hold of a handful of darts. Turning to his followers he said, "When the ruffians are at ten paces, call out to me."

Then he set off with mighty strides, plunging forward careless of the flying arrows. Lu Pu's horsemen followed and when they got near the followers shouted, "Ten paces!"

"Five, then call!" shouted back Tien Wei, and went on.

Presently, "Five paces!"

Then Tien Wei spun round and flung the darts. With every fling a man fell from the saddle and never a dart missed.

Having thus slain half a score the remainder fled and Tien

quickly remounted his steed, set his twin lance and rushed again into the fight with a vigour that none could withstand. One by one his opponents yielded and he was able to lead Ts'ao Ts'ao safely out of the press of battle. Ts'ao and his captains went to their camp.

But as evening fell the noise of pursuit fell on their ears and soon appeared Lu Pu himself. "Ts'ao, you rebel, do not flee!" shouted he as he approached with his halberd ready for a thrust.

All stopped and looked in each others' faces: the men were weary, their steeds spent. Fear smote them and they looked around for some place of refuge.

> You may lead your lord safely out of the press,
> But what if the enemy follow?

We cannot say here what Ts'ao Ts'ao's fate was, but the next chapter will relate.

CHAPTER XII

THE PREFECT T'AO THRICE OFFERS
HIS CHARGE: TS'AO TS'AO FIGHTS
A GREAT BATTLE

The last chapter closed with Ts'ao Ts'ao in great danger. However, help came. Hsiahou Tun with a small body of soldiers found his chief, checked the pursuit, and fought with Lu Pu till dusk. Rain fell in torrents swamping everything and as the daylight waned they drew off and Ts'ao Ts'ao reached camp. He rewarded Tien Wei richly and advanced him in rank.

When Lu Pu reached his camp he called in his adviser Ch'en Kung. The latter proposed a new stratagem. He said, "In Puyang there is a rich family, T'ien by name, who number thousands, enough to populate a whole district in themselves. Make one of these people go to Ts'ao Ts'ao's camp with a pretended secret letter about Lu Pu's ferocity, and the hatred of the people, and their desire to be rid of him. End by saying that only Kao Shun is left to guard the city and they would help any one who would come to save them. Thus our enemy will be inveigled into the city and we will destroy him either by fire or ambush. His skill may be equal to encompassing the universe but he will not escape."

Lu Pu thought this trick might be tried and they arranged for the T'ien family letter to be sent. Coming soon after the defeat, when Ts'ao Ts'ao felt uncertain what step to take next, the secret letter was read with joy. It promised help and said the sign should be a white flag with the word "Rectitude" written thereon.

"Heaven is going to give me Puyang," said Ts'ao joyfully. So he rewarded the messenger very liberally and began to prepare for the expedition.

Then came Liu Hua saying, "Lu Pu is no strategist but Ch'en Kung is full of guile; I fear treachery in this letter and you must be careful. If you will go, then enter with only one third your army leaving the others outside the city as a reserve."

Ts'ao agreed to take this precaution. He went to Puyang, which he found gay with fluttering flags. Looking carefully he saw among them, at the west gate, the white flag with the looked-for inscription. His heart rejoiced.

That day, just about noon, the city gates opened and two bodies of soldiers appeared as if to fight. Ts'ao Ts'ao told off two of his captains to oppose them. Neither body, however, came on to engage but fell back into the city. By this move the assailants had been drawn close up to the drawbridge. From within the city several soldiers were seen taking any chance of confusion to escape and come outside. To Ts'ao Ts'ao they said they were clients of the T'ien family and they gave him secret letters stating the signal would be given about watch setting by beating a gong. That would be the time to attack. The gates would be opened.

So the rescuers were stationed and four trusty captains told off to accompany Ts'ao Ts'ao into the city. One of these Li Tien, pressed upon his master the precaution of letting him go first. But Ts'ao Ts'ao bade him be silent. "If I do not go, who will advance?" And so at the time appointed he led the way. The moon had not yet arisen.

As he drew near the west gate they heard a crackling sound, then a loud shouting, and then torches moved hither and thither. Next the gates were thrown wide open and Ts'ao Ts'ao, whipping up his steed, galloped in.

But when he reached the residence he noticed the streets were quite deserted and then he knew he had been tricked. Wheeling round his horse he shouted to his followers to retire. This was the signal for another move. An explosion of a signal-bomb was heard close at hand and it was echoed from every side in a deafening roar. Gongs and drums beat all around with a roar like rivers rushing backward to their source and the ocean boiling up from its depths. From two sides came bodies of soldiers eager to attack.

Ts'ao dashed off toward the north only to find his way barred; he tried for the south gate, but met enemies led by Kao Shun and Hou Ch'eng. His trusty henchman Tien Wei, with fierce eyes and gritting teeth, at last burst through and got out, with the enemy close after him.

But when he reached the drawbridge he glanced behind him and missed his master. Immediately he turned back and cut his way inside. Just within he met Li Tien.

"Where is our lord?" cried he.

"I am looking for him."

"Quick! get help from outside," shouted Tien Wei. "I will seek him."

So one hastened for aid and the other slashed his way in, looking on every side for Ts'ao Ts'ao. He was not to be found. Dashing out of the city Tien Wei ran up against Yo Chin, who asked where their lord was.

"I have entered the city twice in search of him, but cannot find him," said Tien.

"Let us go in together," said Yo Chin.

They rode up to the gate. But the noise of bombs from the gate tower frightened Yo Chin's horse, so that it refused to pass. Wherefore Tien Wei alone went in, butting through the smoke and dashing through the flames. But he got in and searched on every side.

When Ts'ao Ts'ao saw his sturdy protector cut his way out and disappear leaving him surrounded, he again made an attempt to reach the north gate. On the way, sharply outlined against the glow, he saw the figure of Lu Pu coming toward him with his halberd ready to kill. Ts'ao Ts'ao covered his face with his hand, whipped up his steed and galloped past. But Lu Pu came galloping up behind him and tapping him on the helmet with the halberd cried, "Where is Ts'ao Ts'ao?"

Ts'ao turned and, pointing to a dun horse well ahead, cried, "There; on that dun! that's he."

Hearing this Lu Pu left pursuing Ts'ao Ts'ao to gallop after the rider of the dun.

Thus relieved Ts'ao Ts'ao set off for the east gate. Then he fell in with Tien Wei, who took him under his protection and fought through the press leaving a trail of death behind till they reached the gate. Here the fire was raging fiercely and burning beams were falling on all sides. The earth element seemed to have interchanged with the fire element. Tien Wei warded off the burning pieces of wood with his lance and rode into the smoke making a way for his lord. Just as they were passing through the gate a flaming beam fell from the gate tower. Ts'ao just warded it off with his arm but it struck his steed on the quarters and knocked him down. Ts'ao's hand and arm were badly burned and his hair and beard singed.

Tien Wei turned back to his rescue. Luckily Hsiahou Yuan came along just then and the two raised Ts'ao and set him on Yuan's horse. And thus they got him out of the burning city. But the fighting went on till daybreak.

Ts'ao Ts'ao returned to his camp. His officers crowded about his tent, anxious for news of his health. He soon recovered and laughed when he thought of his escape.

"I blundered into that fool's trap, but I will have my revenge," said he.

"Let us have a new plan soon," said Kuo Chia.

"I will turn his trick to my own use. I will spread the false report that I was burned in the fire and that I died at the fifth watch. He will come to attack as soon as the news gets abroad and I will have an ambush ready for him in Maling Hills. I will get him this time."

"Really a fine stratagem!" said Kuo.

So the soldiers were put into mourning and the report went everywhere that Ts'ao Ts'ao was dead. And soon Lu Pu heard it and he assembled his men at once to make a surprise attack, taking the road by the Maling Hills to his enemy's camp.

As he was passing the hills he heard the drums beating for an advance and the ambushed soldiers leapt out all round him. Only by desperate fighting did he get out of the melee and with a sadly diminished force returned to his camp at Puyang. There he strengthened the fortifications and could not be tempted forth to battle.

This year locusts suddenly appeared and they consumed every green blade. There was a famine and in the east grain rose to fifty "strings" a *hu* (bushel). People even took to cannibalism. Ts'ao Ts'ao's army suffered from want and he marched them to Chuangch'eng. Lu Pu took his men to Shanyang. Perforce therefore the fighting ceased.

It is time to return to Hsuchou. T'ao Ch'ien, over sixty years of age, suddenly fell seriously ill and he summoned his confident, Mi Chu, to his chamber to make arrangements for the future. As to the situation the adviser said, "Ts'ao Ts'ao abandoned his attack on this place because of his enemy's seizure of Yenchou and now they are both keeping the peace solely because of the famine. But Ts'ao will surely renew the attack in the spring. When Liu Yuan-te refused to allow you to vacate office in his favour you were in full vigour. Now you are ill and weak and you can make this a reason for retirement. He will not refuse again."

So a message was sent to the little garrison town calling Liu Pei to a counsel on military affairs. This brought him with his brothers and a slender escort. He was at once called in to the sick man's chamber. Quickly disposing of the enquiries about his health T'ao soon came to the real object of his call for Liu Pei.

"Sir, I asked you to come for the sole reason that I am dangerously ill and like to die at any time. I look to you, illustrious Sir, to consider the Hans and their Empire as more important than anything else, and so to take over the symbols of office of this district, the commission and the seal, that I may close my eyes in peace."

"You have two sons, why not depute them to relieve you?" said Liu Pei.

"Both lack the requisite talents. I trust you will instruct them after I have gone, but do not let them have the guidance of affairs."

"But I am unequal to so great a charge."

"I will recommend to you one who could assist you. He is Sun Ch'ien who could be appointed to some post."

Turning to Mi Chu he said, "The noble Liu here is the most prominent man of the time and you should serve him well."

Still would Liu Pei have put from him such a post, but just then the Prefect, pointing to his heart to indicate his sincerity, passed away.

When the ceremonial wailings of the officials were over, the insignia of office were brought to Liu Pei. But he would have none of them. The following days the inhabitants of the town and country around crowded into the residence bowing and with tears calling upon Liu to receive the charge. "If you do not we cannot live in peace," said they. To these requests his brothers added their persuasion, till at length he consented to assume the administrative duties. He forthwith appointed Sun and Mi as his official advisers and Ch'en Teng his secretary. His guard came up from Hsiaop'ei and he put forth proclamations to reassure the people.

He also attended to the burial ceremonies, he and all his army dressing in mourning. After the fullest sacrifices and ceremonies a burial place for the late Prefect was found close to the source of the Yellow River. The dead man's testament was forwarded to Court.

The news of the events in Hsuchou duly reached the ears of Ts'ao Ts'ao, then in Chuanch'eng. Said he, angrily, "I have missed my revenge. This Liu has simply stepped into command of the district without expending half an arrow; he sat still and attained his desire. But I will put him to death and then dig up T'ao's corpse in revenge for the death of my noble father."

Orders were issued for the army to prepare for a new campaign against Hsuchou. But an adviser, Hsun Yu, remonstrated with Ts'ao saying, "When the founder of the Han dynasty secured Kuanchung and his illustrious successor on the throne, Kuang-wu, took Honei, they both first consolidated their position whereby they could command the whole Empire. Their whole progress was from success to success. Hence they accomplished their great designs in spite of difficulties. Illustrious Sir, your Kuanchung and your Honei are Yenchow, which you had first, and Hochi which is of the utmost strategic value. If you undertake this expedition against Hsuchou leaving many men here, you will not accomplish your design; if you leave too few, Lu Pu will fall upon us. And finally if you lose this and fail to gain Hsuchou whither will you retire? That prefecture is not vacant. Although T'ao has gone, Liu Pei holds it, and since the people support him they will fight to the death for him. To abandon this place for that is to exchange the great for the small, to barter the trunk for the branches, to leave safety and run into danger. I would implore you to reflect well."

Ts'ao Ts'ao replied, "It is not a good plan to keep soldiers idle here during such scarcity."

"If that is so it would be more advantageous to attack the east and feed your army on their supplies. Some remnant of the Yellow Turbans are there with stores and treasures of all kinds that they have amassed by plundering wherever they could. Rebels of their stamp are easily broken. Break them, and you can feed your army with their grain. Moreover, both the Court and the common people will join in blessing you."

This new design appealed strongly to Ts'ao Ts'ao and he quickly began his preparations to carry it out. He left Hsiahou Tun and Ts'ao Jen to guard Chuanch'eng while his main body, under his own command, marched to seize Ch'ench'eng. This done they went to Juying.

Now when the Yellow Turbans knew that Ts'ao Ts'ao was approaching they came out in a great body to oppose him. They met at Goat Hill. Though the rebels were numerous, they were a poor lot, a mere pack of foxes and dogs without organisation and lacking discipline. Ts'ao Ts'ao ordered his strong archers and vigorous crossbowmen to keep them in check.

Tien Wei was sent out to challenge. The rebel leader chose a second-rate champion for his side, who rode out and was vanquished in the third bout. Then Ts'ao Ts'ao's army pushed forward and they made a camp at Goat Hill.

The following day the rebel Huang Shao himself led forth his army and made his battle array along a circle. A leader advanced on foot to offer combat. He wore a yellow turban on his head and a green robe. His weapon was an iron mace. He shouted, "I am Ho Man the Yakcha who shoots across the sky; who dare fight with me?"

Ts'ao Hung uttered a great shout and jumped from the saddle to accept the challenge. Sword in hand he advanced on foot and the two engaged in fierce combat in the face of both armies. They exchanged some scores of blows, neither gaining the advantage. Then Ts'ao Hung feigned defeat and ran away. Ho Man went after him. Just as he closed Hung tried a feint and then suddenly wheeling about, wounded his adversary. Another slash, and Ho Man lay dead.

At once Li Tien dashed forward into the midst of the enemy and laid hands on the rebel chief whom he carried off captive. Ts'ao Ts'ao's men then set on and scattered the rebels. The spoil of treasure and food was immense.

The other leader, Ho I, fled with a few horsemen toward Kopei.

While on their road thither there suddenly appeared a force led by a certain swashbuckler, who shall be nameless for the moment. This bravo was a shortish man, thickset and stout, with a waist ten span in girth. He used a long sword.

He barred the way of retreat. The rebel leader set his spear and rode toward him. But at the first encounter the bravo caught him under his arm and bore him off a prisoner. All his men were terror-stricken, dropped from their horses and allowed themselves to be bound. Then the victor drove them like cattle into an enclosure with high banks.

Presently Tien Wei, still pursuing the rebels, reached Kopei. The swashbuckler went out to meet him.

"Are you also a Yellow Turban?" said Tien Wei.

"I have some hundreds of them prisoners in an enclosure here."

"Why not bring them out?" said Tien.

"I will if you win this sword from my hand."

This annoyed Tien Wei who attacked him. They engaged and the combat lasted for two long hours and then was still undecided. Both rested a while. The swashbuckler was the first to recover and renewed the challenge. They fought till dusk and then, as their horses were quite spent, the combat was once more suspended.

In the meantime some of Tien Wei's men had run off to tell the story of this wondrous fight to Ts'ao Ts'ao who hastened in amazement, followed by many officers to watch it and see the result.

Next day the unknown warrior rode out again and Ts'ao Ts'ao saw him. In his heart he rejoiced to see such a doughty hero and desired to gain his services for his own side. So he bade his champion feign defeat.

Tien Wei rode out in answer to the challenge and some score of bouts were fought. Then Tien Wei turned and fled toward his own side. The bravo followed and came quite close. But a flight of arrows drove him away.

Ts'ao Ts'ao hastily drew off his men for some distance and then secretly sent a certain number to dig a pitfall and sent hookmen to lie in ambush.

The following day Tien Wei was sent out with a small company of horse. His adversary nothing loth came to meet him.

"Why does the defeated leader venture forth again?" cried he laughing.

The swashbuckler spurred forward to join battle but Tien Wei, after a faint show of fighting, turned his horse and rode away. His adversary intent upon capture, took no care and he and his followers all blundered into the pitfall. The hook-men took them all captive, bound them and carried them before their chief.

As soon as he saw the prisoners, Ts'ao advanced from his tent, sent away the soldiers and with his own hands loosened the leader's bonds. Then he brought out clothing and dressed him, bade him be seated and asked who he was and whence he came.

"I am named Hsu Ch'u, and by my near friends called Chungk'ang. I am from Chao.* When the rebellion broke out I and my relations built a stronghold within a rampart for protection. One day the robbers came but I had stones ready for them. I told my relatives to keep on bringing them up to me and I threw them, hitting somebody every time I threw. This drove off the robbers."

"Another day they came and we were short of grain. So I agreed with them to an exchange of plough oxen against grain. They delivered the grain and were driving away the oxen when the beasts took fright and tore off to their pens. I seized two of them by the tail, one with each hand, and hauled them backwards a hundred or so paces. The robbers were so amazed that they thought no more about oxen but went their way. So they never troubled us again."

"I have heard of your mighty exploits," said Ts'ao Ts'ao. "Will you join my army?"

"That is my strongest desire," said Hsu.

So he called up his clan, some hundreds in all, and they formally submitted to Ts'ao Ts'ao. The strong man received the rank of *Tu-yu* and received ample rewards. The two rebel leaders were executed.

Juying being now perfectly quiet Ts'ao Ts'ao withdrew his army. His lieutenants came out to welcome him and they told him that spies had reported Yenchou to be left defenceless, all its garrison having given themselves up to plundering the surrounding country, and they wanted him to go against it without loss of time. "With

* Modern Anhui.

these soldiers fresh from victory the city will fall at a tap of the drum," said they.

So the army was marched to the city. An attack was quite unexpected but the two leaders, Hsueh and Li, hurried out their few soldiers to fight. Hsu Ch'u, the latest recruit, said he wished to capture these two and he would make of them an introductory gift.

The task was given him and he rode forth. Li Feng with his halberd advanced to meet Hsu Ch'u. The combat was brief as Li fell in the second bout. His colleague retired with his men. He found the drawbridge had been seized so that he could not get shelter within the city. He led his men toward Chuyeh. He was followed and slain. His soldiers scattered to the four winds. And thus Yenchou was recaptured.

Next an expedition was prepared to take Puyang. The army moved out in perfect order with van leaders, commanders of the flanks and rear guard. Ts'ao Ts'ao led the centre; Tien Wei and Hsu Ch'u were van leaders. When they approached Puyang, Lu Pu wished to go out in person and alone to attack but his adviser protested, begging him to await the arrival of his officers.

"Whom do I fear?" said Lu.

So he threw caution to the winds and went. He met his foes and he began to revile them. The redoubtable Hsu Ch'u went to fight with him, but after a score of bouts neither combatant was any the worse.

"He is not the sort that one man can overcome," said Ts'ao Ts'ao, and he sent Tien Wei to assist. Lu Pu stood the double onslaught. Soon after the flank commanders joined in and Lu Pu had six opponents. These proved really too many for him so he turned his horse and rode back to the city.

But when the members of the T'ien family saw him coming back beaten they raised the drawbridge. Pu shouted to open the gates, but the T'iens said, "We have gone over to Ts'ao Ts'ao." This was hard to hear and the beaten man abused them roundly before he left. The faithful Ch'en Kung got away through the east gate taking with him the general's family.

Thus Puyang came into Ts'ao Ts'ao's hands and for their present services the T'ien family were pardoned their previous fault. However, Liu Hua said that savage Lu Pu left alive was a great danger and he should be hunted down. Wherefore Ts'ao Ts'ao determined to follow Lu Pu to Tingt'ao whither he had gone for refuge.

Lu Pu and many of his captains were assembled in the city, but certain of them were out foraging. Ts'ao Ts'ao's army arrived but did not attack for many days and presently he withdrew a long way and made a stockade. It was the time of harvest and he set his men to cut the wheat for food. The spies having reported this to Lu Pu he came over to see, but when he saw that Ts'ao Ts'ao's stockade lay near a thick wood he feared an ambush and retired. Ts'ao Ts'ao heard that he had come and gone and guessed the reason.

"He fears an ambush in the wood," said he. "We will set up flags there and deceive him. There is a long embankment near the camp but behind it there is no water. There we will lay an ambush to fall upon Lu Pu when he comes to burn the wood."

So he hid all his soldiers behind the embankment except half a hundred drummers, and he got together many peasants to loiter within the stockade as though it was empty.

Lu Pu rode back and told his adviser what he had seen. "This Ts'ao Ts'ao is very crafty and full of wiles," said the adviser; "great care in necessary."

"I will use fire this time and burn out his ambush," said Lu Pu.

Next morning he rode out and there he saw flags flying everywhere in the wood. He ordered his men forward to set fire on all sides. But to his surprise no one rushed out to make for the stockade. Still he heard the beating of drums and doubt filled his mind. Suddenly he saw a party of soldiers move out from the shelter of the stockade. He galloped over to see what it meant.

Then the signal-bombs exploded; out rushed the men and all their leaders dashed forward. Lu Pu was at a loss and fled into the open country. One of his captains was killed by an arrow. Two thirds of his men were lost and the beaten remainder went to tell Ch'en Kung what had come to pass.

"We had better leave" said he. "An empty city cannot be held."

So he and Kao Shun, taking their chief's family with them, abandoned Tingt'ao. When Ts'ao Ts'ao's soldiers got into the city they met with no resistance, one leader burned himself to death, the other fled to Yuan Shu.

Thus the whole of Shantung fell under the power of Ts'ao Ts'ao.

How he tranquillised the people and rebuilt the cities will not be told here. But Lu Pu in his retreat fell in with his foragers and Ch'en Kung also rejoined him so that he was by no means broken.

"I have but few men," said he, "but still enough to break Ts'ao Ts'ao." And so he retook the backward road.

> Thus does fortune alternate, victory, defeat,
> The happy conqueror today, tomorrow, must retreat.

What was the fate of Lu Pu will appear later.

CHAPTER XIII

GREAT BATTLE BETWEEN LI TS'UI AND KUO SSU: THE EMPEROR RESCUED

The last chapter told of the defeat of Lu Pu, and his gathering the remnant of his army at Haipin. When all his lieutenants had joined him he began to feel strong enough to try conclusions with Ts'ao Ts'ao once again.

Said Ch'en Kung, who was opposed to this course, "He is too strong; seek some place where you can rest a time before trying."

"Suppose I went to Yuan Shao," said Lu Pu.

"Send first to make enquiries."

Lu Pu agreed. The news of the fighting between Ts'ao and Lu Pu had reached Ichou and one of Yuan's advisers, Shen P'ei, warned him saying, "If this savage Lu Pu gets possession of Yenchou he will certainly attempt to add this district to it. For your own safety you should help to crush him."

Wherefore Yen Liang, with five legions, was sent. The spies heard this and at once told Lu Pu, who was greatly disturbed and called in the faithful Ch'en Kung.

"Go over to Liu Pei, who has lately succeeded to Hsuchou."

Hence Lu Pu went thither. Some one urged Liu Pei to go out to meet such a warrior and receive him with honour. Mi Chu was strongly against receiving him at all saying he was a cruel, bloodthirsty beast.

But Pei replied, "How would misfortune have been averted from this place if he had not attacked Yenchou? He cannot be our enemy now that he comes seeking an asylum."

"Brother, your heart is really too good. Although it may be as you say yet it would be well to prepare," said Chang Fei.

The new Prefect with a great following met Lu a long way outside the city gates and the two chiefs rode in side by side. They proceeded to the residence and there, after the elaborate ceremonies of reception were over, they sat down to converse.

"After Wang Yun's plot to slay Tung Cho and my misfortune in the Li-Kuo sedition, I drifted about from one place to another and none of the nobles seemed willing to receive me. When Ts'ao Ts'ao wickedly invaded this district and you, Sir, came to its rescue, I aided you by attacking Yenchou and thus diverting a portion of his force. I did not think then that I should be the victim of a vile plot and lose my leaders and my soldiers. But now if you will I offer myself to you that we may together accomplish great designs."

Liu Pei replied, "When the late Prefect died there was no one to administer Hsuchou and so I assumed that task for a time. Now since you are here, General, it is most suitable that I retire in your favour."

Whereupon he handed the insignia and the seal to Lu Pu. Lu was on the point of accepting them when he saw Kuan and Chang, who stood behind the Prefect, glaring at him with angry eyes, so he put on a smile and said, "Lu may be something of a fighting man but he could not rule a place like this."

Yuan-te repeated his offer. Ch'en Kung said, "The strong guest does not oppress his host. You need not fear, O Prince Elect."

Then Yuan-te desisted. Banquets were held and dwelling places prepared for the guest and his retinue. As soon as convenient Lu Pu returned the feast. Liu Pei went with his two brothers. Half through the banquet Lu Pu requested his guest to retire to one of the inner private rooms, whither the brothers followed him. There Lu Pu bade his wife and daughters bow as to their benefactor. Here also Yuan-te showed excessive modesty and Pu said, "Good younger brother, you need not be so very modest."

Chang Fei heard what he said and his eyes glared. "What sort of a man are you that dares call our brother, 'younger brother'?" cried he. "He is one of the ruling family (a golden branch, a jade leaf). Come out; and I will fight you three hundred bouts for the insult."

Yuan-te hastily checked the impulsive one and Kuan Yu persuaded him to go away. Then the host apologised saying, "My poor brother talks wildly after he has been drinking. I hope you will not blame him."

Lu Pu nodded, but said nothing. Soon after the guests departed. But as the host escorted Liu Pei to his carriage he saw Chang Fei galloping up armed as for a fray.

"Lu Pu, you and I will fight that duel of three hundred!" shouted he.

Liu Pei bade Kuan Yu check him. Next day Lu Pu came to take leave of his host. "You, O Prince, kindly received me but I fear your brothers and I cannot agree. So I will seek some other asylum."

"General, if you go, my brother's fault becomes grave. My rude brother has offended and must eventually apologise. In the meantime what think you of a temporary sojourn at the town where I was encamped for some time, Hsiao-p'ei? The place is small and mean, but it is near and I will see to it that you are supplied with all you need."

Lu Pu thanked him and accepted this offer. He led his men there and took up residence. After he had gone Liu Pei buried his annoyance and Chang Fei did not again refer to the matter.

That Ts'ao Ts'ao had subdued Shantung has been stated before. He memorialised the throne and was rewarded with the title of General with the epithet "Firm Virtue" and a marquisate. At this time the rebellious Li Ts'ui had made himself *Ta-ssu-ma*, or Minister of War, and his colleague styled himself Grand Commander. Their conduct was abominable but no one dared to criticise them. The *Tai-yu* Yang Piao and the Minister of Agriculture, Chu Chien, privately talked with the Emperor Hsien and said, "Ts'ao Ts'ao has twenty legions of soldiers and many capable advisers and leaders; it would be well for the Empire if he would lend his support to the imperial family and help to rid the government of this evil party."

His Majesty wept, "I am weary of the insults and contempt of these wretches and should be very glad to have them removed," said he.

"I have thought of a plan to estrange Li and Kuo and so make them destroy each other. Then Ts'ao could come and cleanse the Court," said Piao.

"How will you manage it?" asked the Emperor.

"Kuo's wife is very jealous and we can take advantage of her weakness to bring about a quarrel."

So Yang Piao received instruction to act, with a secret edict to support him.

Piao's wife made an excuse to visit Madam Kuo at her palace and, in the course of conversation, said "There is talk of secret liaison between the General, your husband, and the wife of the Minister Li. It is a great secret, but if the Minister knew it he might try to harm your husband. I think you ought to have very little to do with that family."

Madam Kuo was surprised but said, "I have wondered why he has been sleeping away from home lately, but I did not think there was anything shameful connected with it. I should never have known if you had not spoken. I must put a stop to it."

By and by, when Madam Yang took her leave, her hostess thanked her warmly for the information she had given.

Some days passed and Kuo Ssu was going over to the dwelling of his colleague to a dinner. His wife did not wish him to go and she said, "This Ts'ui is very deep and one cannot fathom his designs. You two are not of equal rank and if he made away with you, what would become of your poor handmaid?"

Kuo Ssu paid no attention and his wife could not prevail on him to stay at home. Late in the afternoon some presents arrived from the Li palace and Kuo's wife secretly put poison into the delicacies before she set them before her lord. He was going to taste at once but she said, "It is unwise to consume things that come from outside. Let us try on a dog first."

They did and the dog died. This incident made Kuo doubt the kindly intentions of his colleague.

One day, at the close of business at Court, Li invited Kuo to his palace. After Kuo arrived home in the evening, rather the worse for too much wine, he was seized with a colic. His wife said she suspected poison and hastily administered an emetic, which relieved the pain. Kuo Ssu began to feel angry.

"We did everything together and helped each other always. Now he wants to injure me. If I do not get in the first blow, I shall suffer some injury."

So Kuo began to prepare his guard for any sudden emergency. This was told to Li and he in turn grew angry, saying, "So Kuo is doing so and so."

Then he got his guard under way and came to attack Kuo. Both houses had several legions and the quarrel became so serious that they fought a pitched battle under the city walls. When that was over both sides turned to plunder the people.

Then a nephew of Li's suddenly surrounded the palace, put the Emperor and Empress Dowager Fu in two carriages and carried them off. The palace attendants were made to follow on foot. As they went out of the rear gate they met Kuo's army who began to shoot at the cavalcade with arrows. They killed many attendants before Li's army came up and forced them to retire.

It is unnecessary to say how the carriages were got out of the palace but they eventually reached Li's camp, while Kuo's men plundered the palace and carried off all the women left there to their camp. Then the palace was set on fire.

As soon as Kuo Ssu heard of the whereabouts of the Emperor he came over to attack the camp. The Emperor between these two opposing factions was greatly alarmed.

Slowly the Hans had declined but renewed their vigour with
Kuang-Wu,
Twelve were the rulers before him, followed him also twelve others.
Foolish were two of the latest, dangers surrounded the altars,
These were degenerate days, with authority given to eunuchs.
Then did Ho Chin the simple, the inept, who commanded
the army,
Warriors call to the capital, wishing to drive out the vermin;
Though they drove out the leopard, tigers and wolves quickly
entered,
All kinds of evil were wrought by a low class creature from Hsichou.
Wang Yun, honest of heart, beguiled this wretch with a woman,
Much desired of his henchman, thus sowing seeds of dissension.
Strife resulted, and peace no longer dwelt in the Empire.
No one suspected that Li and Kuo would continue the evil,
Much to the sorrow of China; yet they strove for a trifle.
Famine stalked in the palace, grief for the clashing of weapons;
Why did the warriors strive? Why was the land thus partitioned?
We had turned aside from the way appointed of Heaven.
Kings must ponder these things; heavy the burden lies on them,
Chiefest in all the realm theirs is no common appointment,
Should the King falter or fail, calamities fall on the people,
The Empire is drenched with their blood, grisly ruin surrounds
them.
Steeped in sorrow and sad, read I the ancient records,
Long is the tale of years; the tale of sorrow is longer.
Wherefore he who would rule, chiefly must exercise forethought.
This and his keen-edged blade, these must suffice to maintain him.

Kuo Ssu's army arrived and Li Ts'ui went out to give battle. Kuo's men had no success and retired. Then Li Ts'ui removed the imperial captives to Meiwu with his nephew as gaoler. Supplies were reduced and famine showed itself on the faces of the eunuchs. The Emperor sent to Li to request five measures of rice and five sets of bullock bones for his attendants. Li angrily replied, "The Court gets food morning and evening; why do they ask for more?"

He sent putrid meat and rotten grain and the Emperor was very vexed at the new insult.

Yang Piao counselled patience. "He is a base creature but, under the present circumstances, Your Majesty must put up with it. You may not provoke him."

The Emperor bowed and was silent, but the tears fell on his garments. Suddenly some one came in with the tidings that a force of cavalry, their sabres glittering in the sun, was approaching to rescue them. Then they heard the gongs beat and the roll of the drums.

The Emperor sent to find out who it was. But it was Kuo Ssu, and the sadness fell again. Presently arose a great din. For Li had gone out to do battle with Kuo, whom he abused by name.

"I treated you well and why did you try to kill me?" said Li.

"You are a rebel, why should I not slay you?" cried Kuo.

"You call me rebel when I am guarding the Emperor?"

"You have abducted him; do you call that guarding?"

"Why so many words? Let us forgo a battle and settle the matter in single combat, the winner to take the Emperor and go."

They two fought in front of their armies but neither could prevail over the other. Then they saw Yang Piao come riding up to them, crying, "Rest a while, O Commanders! for I have invited a party of officers to arrange a peace."

Wherefore the two leaders retired to their camps. Soon Yang Piao, Sun Ch'ien and three score other officials came up and went to Kuo's camp. They were all thrown into confinement.

"We came with good intentions," they moaned, "and we are treated like this."

"Li Ts'ui has run off with the Emperor but I have got his officers," said Kuo.

"What does it mean? One has the Emperor, the other his officers. What do you want?" said the peace-maker, Yang Piao.

Kuo lost patience and drew his sword, but a certain Yang Mi persuaded him not to slay the speaker. Then he released Yang Piao and Sun Ch'ien; but kept the others in the camp. "Here are we two officers of the throne and we cannot help our lord. We have been born in vain," said Yang Piao.

Throwing their arms about each other they wept and fell swooning to the earth. Sun Ch'ien went home, fell seriously ill and died.

Thereafter the two adversaries fought every day for nearly three months each losing many men.

Now Li Ts'ui was irreligious and practised magic. He often called witches to beat drums and summon spirits, even when in camp. Chia Hsu used to remonstrate with him, but quite uselessly.

A certain Yang Chi said to the Emperor, "That Chia Hsu, although a friend of Li's, never seems to have lost the sense of loyalty to Your Majesty."

Soon after Chia Hsu himself arrived. The Emperor sent away his attendants and said to him weeping the while, "Can you not pity the Hans and help me?"

Chia prostrated himself, saying, "That is my dearest wish. But, Sire, say no more, let they servant work out a plan."

The Emperor dried his tears and soon Li Ts'ui came in. He wore a sword by his side and strode straight up to the Emperor, whose face became the colour of clay. Then he spoke.

"Kuo Ssu has failed in his duty and imprisoned the court officers. He wished to slay Your Majesty and you would have been captured but for me."

The Emperor joined his hands together in salute and thanked him. He went away. Before long Huangfu Li entered and the Emperor, knowing him as a man of persuasive tongue and that he came from the same district as Li, bade him go to both factions to try to arrange peace. He accepted the mission and first went to Kuo, who said he was willing to release the officers if Li Ts'ui would restore the Emperor to full liberty. He then went to the other side.

To Li he said, "Since I am a Hsiliang man the Emperor and the officers have selected me to make peace between you and your adversary. He has consented to cease the quarrel; will you agree to peace?"

"I overthrew Lu Pu; I have upheld the government for four years and have many great services to my credit as all the world knows. That other fellow, that horse-thief, has dared to seize the officers of state and to set himself up against me. I have sworn to slay him. Look around you. Do you not think my army large enough to break him?"

"It does not follow," said Huangfu Li. "In ancient days in Yuch'ing, Hou I, proud of and confident in his archer's skill, gave no thought to gathering difficulties and so perished. Lately you yourself have seen the powerful Tung Cho betrayed by Lu Pu, who had received many benefits at his hands. In no time his head was hanging over the gate. So you see mere force is not enough to ensure safety. Now you are a General, with the axes and whips and all the symbols of rank and high office, your descendants and all your clan occupy distinguished positions. You must confess that the State has rewarded you liberally. True, Kuo has seized the officers of State, but you have done the same to "The Most Revered." Who is worse than the other?"

Li angrily drew his sword and shouted, "Did the Son of Heaven send you to mock and shame me?"

But Yang Feng checked him. "Kuo Ssu is still alive," said he, "and to slay the imperial messenger would be giving him a popular excuse to raise an army against you. And all the nobles would join him."

Others also persuaded Li and gradually his wrath cooled down. The messenger of peace was urged to go away. But he would not be satisfied with failure. He remained there and cried loudly, "Li Ts'ui will not obey the Emperor's command. He will kill his Prince to set up himself."

Hu Miao tried to shut his mouth saying, "Do not utter such words. You will only bring hurt upon yourself."

But Huangfu Li shrieked at him also. "You also are an officer of state and yet you even back up the rebel. When the prince is put to shame the minister dies. If it be my lot to suffer death at the hands of Li Ts'ui, so be it!"

And he maintained a torrent of abuse. The Emperor heard of the incident, called in Huangfu Li and sent him away to his own country.

Now more than half Li Ts'ui's men were from Hsiliang and he had also the assistance of the *Ch'iang*, or tribes beyond the border. The stories spread by Huangfu Li, that Li Ts'ui was a rebel and so were those who helped him, and that there would be a day of heavy reckoning, were readily believed and the soldiers were much disturbed. Li Ts'ui sent one of his officers to arrest Huangfu Li, but the officer had a sense of right and instead of carrying out his orders returned to say he could not be found.

Chia Hsu tried to work on the feelings of the barbarian tribes. He said to them. "The Emperor knows you are loyal to him and have bravely fought and suffered. He has issued a secret command for you to go home and then he will reward you."

The tribesmen had a grievance against Li Ts'ui for not paying them, so they listened readily to the insidious persuasions of Chia Hsu and deserted. Then Chia represented to the Emperor the covetous nature of Li and asked that honours be heaped upon him now that he was deserted and enfeebled. So he was raised to the rank of President of a Board of State. This delighted him greatly and he ascribed his promotion to the potency of his wise women's prayers and incantations. He rewarded those people most liberally.

But his army was forgotten. Wherefore Yang Feng was angry and he said to one Sung Kuo, "We have taken all the risks and exposed ourselves to stones and arrows in his service, yet instead of giving us any reward he ascribes all the credit to those witches of his."

"Let us put him out of the way and rescue the Emperor," said Sung.

"You explode a bomb within as signal and I will attack from outside."

So the two agreed to act together that very night in the second watch. But they had been overheard and the eavesdropper told Li Ts'ui. The traitorous Sung was seized and put to death. That night Yang waited outside for the signal and while waiting, out came Li himself and found him. Then a fight began, which lasted till the fourth watch. But Yang Feng got away and fled to Hsian (Sian) in the west.

But from this time Li Ts'ui's army began to fall away and he felt more than ever the losses caused by Kuo's frequent attacks. Then came news that Chang Chi, at the head of a large army, was coming down from the west to make peace between the two factions. Chang said he would attack the one who was recalcitrant. Li Ts'ui tried to gain favour by hastening to send to tell Chang Chi he was ready to make peace. So did Kuo Ssu.

So the strife of the rival factions ended at last and Chang Chi memorialised asking the Emperor to go to Hungnung near Loyang. He was delighted saying he had longed to go back to the east. Chang Chi was rewarded with the title of General of Cavalry and was highly honoured. He saw to it that the Emperor and the Court had good supplies of necessaries. Kuo Ssu set free all his captive officers and Li Ts'ui prepared transport for the Court to move to the east. He told off companies of his veterans to escort the cavalcade.

The progress had been without incident as far as Hsinfung. Near Paling the west wind of autumn came on to blow with great violence, but soon above the howling of the gale was heard the trampling of a large body of horse. They stopped at a bridge and barred the way.

"Who comes?" cried a voice.

"The Imperial Chariot is passing and who dares stop it?" said Yang Chi, riding forward.

Two leaders advanced, "General Kuo has ordered us to guard the bridge and stop all spies. You say the Emperor is here; we must see him and then we will let you pass". So the beaded curtain was raised and the Emperor said, "I the Emperor am here. Why do you not retire to let me pass, Gentlemen?" They all shouted, "Long Life! Long Life!" and fell away to allow the cortege through.

But when they reported what they had done Kuo was very angry. "I meant to outwit Chang Chi, seize the Emperor and hold him in Meiwu. Why have you let him get away?"

He put the two officers to death and set out to pursue the cavalcade, and overtook it just at Huayin. The noise of a great shouting arose behind the travellers and a loud voice commanded the chariot to stop. The Emperor burst into tears.

"Out of the wolf's den into the tiger's mouth!" said he.

No one knew what to do, they were all too frightened. But when the rebel army was just upon them they heard the beating of drums and from behind some hills came into the open a cohort of soldiers preceded by a great flag bearing the well known name of that trusted leader, Yang Feng.

Now after Yang Feng's defeat he had camped under Chung nanshan and had come up to guard the Emperor as soon as he knew of his journey. Seeing it was necessary to fight now, he drew up his line of battle and Ts'ui Jung, one of Kuo's leaders, rode out and began a volley of abuse. Yang Feng turned and said, "Where is Kung-ming?"

In response out came a valiant warrior gripping a heavy battleaxe. He galloped up on his fleet bay, making directly for Ts'ui Jung, whom he felled at the first blow. At this the whole force dashed forward and routed Kuo. The defeated army went back some twenty *li*, while Yang Feng rode forward to see the Emperor who graciously said, "It is a great service you have rendered; you have saved my life."

Yang bowed and thanked him and the Emperor asked to see the actual slayer of the rebel leader. So he was led to the chariot where he bowed and was presented as "Hsu Huang, also known as Hsu Kung-ming, of Yangchun."

Then the cavalcade went forward, Yang Feng acting as escort as far as Huayin the halting place for the night. The General there supplied them with clothing and food and the Emperor passed the night in Yang Feng's camp.

Next day Kuo Ssu, having mustered his men, appeared in front of the camp and Hsu Huang rode out to engage. But Kuo threw his men out so that they entirely surrounded the camp and the Emperor was in the middle. The position was very critical, when help appeared in the person of a galloping horseman from the south-east and the rebels fell away. Then Hsu Huang smote them and so scored a victory.

When they had time to see their helper they found him to be

Tung Ch'eng, the "State Uncle." The Emperor wept as he related his sorrows and dangers.

Said Tung, "Be of good courage, Sire. We pledge ourselves to kill both the rebels and so purify the world."

The Emperor bade them travel east as soon as possible and so they went on night and day till they reached their destination.

Kuo led his defeated army back and meeting Li Ts'ui told him of the rescue of the Emperor and whither he was going. "If they reach Shantung and get settled there, they will send out proclamations to the whole country, calling up the nobles to attack us and we and our families will be in danger."

"Chang Chi holds Ch'angan and we must be careful. There is nothing to prevent a joint attack on Hungnung when we can kill the Emperor and divide the country between us," said Li.

Kuo found this a suitable scheme, so their armies came together in one place and united in plundering the countryside. Wherever they went they left destruction behind them. Yang and Tung heard of their approach when they were yet a long way off so they turned back to meet them and fought the rebels at Tungchien.

The two rebels had previously made their plan. Since the loyal troops were few as compared with their own horde they would overwhelm them like a flood. So when the day of battle came they poured out covering the hills and filling the plains. The two leaders devoted themselves solely to the protection of the Emperor and the Empress. The officials, the attendants, the archives and records and all the paraphernalia of the Court were left to care for themselves. The rebels ravaged Hungnung, but the two faithful soldiers got the Emperor safely away into the north of Shensi.

When the rebels showed signs of pursuit Yang and Tung sent to offer to discuss terms of peace, at the same time sending a secret edict to Hotung calling upon the old "White Wave General" Han and Li Yueh and Hu Ts'ai for help. Li Yueh was actually a brigand but the need for help was desperate.

These three being promised pardon for their faults and crimes and a grant of official rank, naturally responded to the call and thus the loyal side was strengthened so that Hungnung was recaptured. But meanwhile the rebels laid waste whatever place they reached, slaying the aged and weakly, forcing the strong to join their ranks. When going into a fight they forced these people-soldiers to the front and they called them the "Dare-to-die" soldiers.

The rebel force was very strong. When Li Yueh, the late brigand, approached, Kuo Ssu bade his men scatter clothing and valuables along the road. The late robbers could not resist the temptation so a scramble began. The rebels fell upon the disordered ranks and did much damage. Yang and Tung could not save them so they took the Emperor away to the north.

But the rebels pursued. Li Yueh said, "The danger is grave. I pray Your Majesty to mount a horse and go in advance."

The Emperor replied, "I cannot bear to abandon my officers."

They wept and struggled on as best they could. Hu Ts'ai was killed in one attack. The enemy came very near and the Emperor left his carriage and went on foot to the river where they sought a boat to ferry him to the other side. The weather was very cold and the Emperor and Empress cuddled up close to each other shivering. They reached the river but the banks were too high and they could not get down into the boat. So Yang Feng proposed to fasten together the horses' bridles and lower down the Emperor slung by the waist. However, some rolls of white silk were found and they rolled up the two imperial personages in the silk and thus they lowered them down near the boat. Then Li Yueh took up his position in the prow leaning on his sword. The brother of the Empress carried her on his back into the boat.

The boat was too small to carry everybody and those unable to get on board clung to the cable, but Li Yueh cut them down and they fell into the water. They ferried over the Emperor and then sent back the boat for the others. There was a great scramble to get on board and they had to chop off the fingers and hands of those who persisted in clinging to the boat.

The lamentation rose to the heavens. When they mustered on the farther bank many were missing, not a score of the Emperor's suite were left. A bullock cart was found in which the Emperor travelled to Tayang. They had no food and at night sought shelter in a poor, tile-roofed house. The cottagers gave them some boiled millet but it was too coarse to be swallowed.

Next day the Emperor conferred titles on those who had protected him so far and they pushed on. Soon two officers of rank came up with the cortege and they bowed before His Majesty with many tears. They were Yang Piao and Han Jung. The Emperor and Empress lifted up their voices and wept with them.

Said Han Jung to his colleague, "The rebels have confidence in my words. You stay as guard of the Emperor and I will take my life in my hands and try to bring about peace."

After he had gone the Emperor rested for a time in Yang's camp and then was requested to make Anihsien the capital. But the town contained not a single lofty building and the court lived in grass huts devoid even of doors. They surrounded these with a fence of thorns as a protection, and within this the Emperor held counsel with his ministers. The soldiers camped round the fence.

Li Yueh and his fellow ruffians showed their true colours. They wielded the powers of the Emperor as they wished and officials who offended them were beaten or abused even in the presence of the Emperor. They purposely provided thick wine and coarse food for the Emperor's consumption. He struggled to swallow what they sent. Li Yueh and Han Hsien joined in recommending to the throne the names of convicts, common soldiers, sorcerers, leeches and such people who thus obtained official ranks. There were more than two hundred of such people. As seals could not be engraved pieces of metal were hammered into some sort of a shape.

Now Han Jung went to see the two rebels who listened to him and set free the officials and palace people.

A famine occurred that same year and people were reduced to eating grass from the roadside. Starving they wandered hither and thither but food and clothing were sent to the Emperor from the surrounding districts and the Court began to enjoy a little repose.

Tung Ch'eng and Yang Feng sent workmen to restore the palaces in Loyang with the intention of moving the Court thither. Li Yueh was opposed to this and when argued with, that Loyang was really the capital as opposed to the paltry town of Ani, and removal would be but reasonable, he wound up by saying, "You may get the Court to remove but I shall remain here."

But when the consent of the Emperor had been given and a start made Li Yueh secretly sent to arrange with Li Ts'ui and Kuo Ssu to capture him. However, this plot leaked out and the escort so arranged as to prevent such a thing and they pressed on to Chikuan as rapidly as possible. Li heard this and without waiting for his colleagues to join him set out to act alone.

About the fourth watch, just as the cavalcade was passing Chikuan, a voice was heard shouting, "Stop those carriages! Li and Kuo are here."

This frightened the Emperor greatly and his terror increased when he saw the whole mountain side suddenly light up.

> The rebel party, erstwhile split in twain,
> To work their wicked will now join again.

How the Son of Heaven escaped this peril will be told in the next chapter.

CHAPTER XIV

TS'AO MENG-TE MOVES THE COURT:
LU FENG-HSIEN RAIDS HSUCHUN

The last chapter closed with the arrival of Li Yueh who shouted out falsely that the army was that of the two arch rebels Li and Kuo come to capture the imperial cavalcade. But Yang Feng recognised the voice of Li Yueh and bade Hsu Huang go out to fight him. He went and in the first bout the traitor fell. His men scattered and the travellers got safely through Chikuan. Here the Prefect, Chang Yang, supplied them plentifully with food and other necessaries and escorted the Emperor to Chihtao. For his timely help the Emperor conferred upon Chang Yang the rank of a *Ta-ssu-ma*, or President, and he went and camped at Yehwang.

Loyang was presently entered. Within the walls all was destruction. The palaces and halls had been burned, the streets were overgrown with grass and brambles and obstructed by heaps of ruins. The palaces and courts were represented by broken roofs and toppling walls. A small "palace" however was soon built and therein the officers of court presented their congratulations, standing in the open air among thorn bushes and brambles. The reign style was changed from Hsing-P'ing to Chien-An (firm tranquillity).

The year was a year of grievous famine. The Loyang people, even reduced in numbers as they were to a few hundreds, had not enough to eat and they prowled about stripping the bark off trees and grubbing up the roots of plants to satisfy their starving hunger. Officers of the Government of all but the highest ranks went out into the country to gather fuel. Many people lay down and died quietly behind the ruined walls of their houses. At no time during the decadence of Han did misery press harder than at this period.

A poem written in pity for the sufferings of that time says:—

Mortally wounded, the serpent poured forth his life blood at
    Mantang;
Blood-red pennons of war waved then in every quarter,
Chieftain with chieftain strove and raided each other's borders,
'Midst the turmoil and strife the Kingship even was threatened.
Wickedness stalks in a country when the King is a weakling,
Brigandage always is rife, when a dynasty's failing,
Had one a heart of iron, wholly devoid of feeling,
Yet would one surely grieve at the sight of such desolation.

The *Tai-yu* Yang Piao memorialised the Throne saying, "The decree issued to me some time ago has never been acted upon. Now Ts'ao Ts'ao is very strong in Shantung and it would be well to associate him in the government that he might support the ruling house."

The Emperor replied, "There was no need to refer to the matter again. Send a messenger when you will."

So the decree went forth and a messenger bore it into Shantung. Now when Ts'ao had heard that the Court had returned to Loyang he called together his advisers to consult. Hsun Yu laid the matter before him and the council thus:— "Of old Duke Wen supported Prince Hsiang of the Chou dynasty and all the feudal lords backed him. The founder of the Hans won the popular favour by wearing mourning for the Emperor I (who never really sat on the throne). Now the Emperor has been a fugitive on the dusty roads. To take the lead in offering an army to restore him to honour is to have an unrivalled opportunity to win universal regard. But you must act quickly or some one will get in before you."

Ts'ao Ts'ao understood and at once prepared his army to move. Just at this moment an imperial messenger was announced with the very command he wanted and he immediately set out.

At Loyang everything was desolate. The walls had fallen and there were no means of rebuilding them, while rumours and reports of the coming of Li and Kuo kept up a state of constant anxiety.

The frightened Emperor spoke with Yang Feng saying, "What can be done? There is no answer from Shantung and our enemies are near."

Then Yang Feng and Han Hsien said, "We, your ministers, will fight to the death for you."

Tung Ch'eng said, "The fortifications are weak and our military resources small, so that we cannot hope for victory and what does defeat mean? I see nothing better to propose than a move into Shantung."

The Emperor agreed to this and the journey began without further preparation. There being few horses, the officers of the Court had to march afoot. Hardly a bowshot outside the gate they saw a thick cloud of dust out of which came all the clash and clamour of an advancing army. The Emperor and his Consort were dumb with fear. Then appeared a horseman; he was the messenger returning from Shantung. He rode up to the chariot, made an obeisance and said, "General Ts'ao, as commanded, is coming with all the military force of Shantung, but hearing that Li and Kuo had again approached the capital he has sent Hsiahou Tun in advance. With him are many capable leaders and five legions of proved soldiers. They will guard Your Majesty."

All fear was swept away. Soon after Hsiahou Tun and his staff arrived and they were presented to the Emperor who graciously addressed them.

Then one came to say a large army was approaching from the east and at the Emperor's command Hsiahou Tun went to ascertain who these were. He soon returned saying they were Ts'ao Ts'ao's infantry.

In a short time Ts'ao Hung and his officers came to the chariot and their names having been duly communicated the chief said, "When my brother heard of the approach of the rebels he feared that the advance guard he had sent might be too weak so he sent me to march quickly and reinforce him."

"General Ts'ao is indeed a trusty servant," said the Emperor.

Orders were given to advance, the escort leading. By and by scouts came to say that the rebels were coming up very quickly. The Emperor bade Hsiahou Tun divide his force into two parts to oppose them, whereupon the armies threw out two wings with cavalry in front and foot behind. They attacked with vigour and beat off the rebels with great loss. Then they begged the Emperor to return to Loyang and Hsiahou Tun guarded the city.

Soon Ts'ao Ts'ao came with his great army and having got them duly camped he went into the city to audience. He knelt at the foot of the steps, but was called up hither to stand beside the Emperor and be thanked.

Ts'ao replied, "Having been the recipient of great bounty thy servant owes the State much gratitude. The measure of evil of the two rebels is full, I have a score of legions of good soldiers to oppose them and they are fully equal to securing the safety of Your Majesty and the Throne. The preservation of the state sacrifice is the matter of real moment."

High honours were conferred on Ts'ao Ts'ao.

The two rebels wished to attack Ts'ao Ts'ao's army while fatigued from its long march, but their adviser Chia Hsu opposed this, saying there was no hope of victory. In fact he advised submission. Li Ts'ui was angry at the suggestion, saying that the adviser wished to dishearten the army and drew his sword on Chia. But the other officers interceded and saved him. That same night Chia stole out of the camp and, quite alone, took his way home to his native village.

Soon the rebels decided to offer battle. Ts'ao sent out in reply a small company of horse with three warriors as leaders. These dashed into the rebels army but quickly retired. This manoeuvre was repeated, and again repeated before the real battle array was formed. Then Li Hsien and Li Pieh, nephews of Li Ts'ui, rode out. At once from Ts'ao's side dashed out Hsu Ch'u and cut down the former. Li Pieh was so startled that he fell out of the saddle. He too was slain. The victor rode back to his own side with the two heads. When he offered them to the chief, Ts'ao Ts'ao patted him on the back crying, "You are really my Fan K'uai! (Preserver)."

Next a general move forward was made, Hsiahou Tun and Ts'ao Jen leading the two wings and Ts'ao Ts'ao in the centre. They advanced to the roll of the drum. The rebels fell back before them and presently fled. They were pursued, Ts'ao himself leading, sword in hand. Many were killed and many more surrendered. The two leaders went west, flying in panic like dogs from a falling house. Having no place of refuge they took to the hills and hid among the brushwood.

The army returned and camped again near the city. Then Yang Feng and Han Hsien said one to another, "This Ts'ao has done a great service and he will be the man in power. There will be no place for us." So they represented to the Emperor that they wished to pursue the rebels and under this excuse withdrew and camped at Taliang.

One day the Emperor sent to summon Ts'ao Ts'ao to audience. The messenger was called in. Ts'ao noticed that he looked remarkably well and could not understand it seeing that everyone else looked hungry and famine stricken. So he said, "You look plump and well, Sir, how do you manage it?"

"Only this; I have lived *maigre* for thirty years."

Ts'ao nodded. "What office do you hold?"

"I am a graduate. I had an office under Yuan Shao, but came here when the Emperor returned. Now I am one of the secretaries. I am a native of Tingt'ao called Tung Chao."

Ts'ao got up from his place and crossed over saying, "I have heard of you. How happy I am to meet you!"

Then wine was brought into the tent and Hsun Yu was called in and introduced. While they were talking a man came in to report that a party was moving eastward. Orders were given to find out whose men these were but the visitor knew at once. "They are old leaders under the rebels, Yang Feng and the "White Wave General" Han. They are running off because you have come, Illustrious Sir!"

"Do they mistrust me?" said Ts'ao.

"They are not worthy of your attention. They are a poor lot."

"What of this departure of Li and Kuo?"

"Tigers without claws, birds without wings will not escape you very long. They are not worth thinking about."

Ts'ao Ts'ao saw that he and his guest had much in common so he began to talk of affairs of State.

Said Tung Chao, "You, Illustrious Sir, with your noble army have swept away rebellion and have become the mainstay of the throne, an achievement worthy of the five chieftains. But the officials will look at it in very different ways and not all favourably to you. I think you would not be wise to remain here and I advise a change of capital to Hsutu in Honan. However, it must be remembered that the restoration of the capital has been published far and wide and the attention of all the people is concentrated on Loyang, hoping for a period of rest and tranquillity. Another move will displease many. However, the performance of extraordinary service may mean the acquisition of extraordinary merit. It is for you to decide."

"Exactly my own inclination!" said Ts'ao Ts'ao, seizing his guest's hand. "But are there not dangers? Yang Feng at Taliang and the Court officials?"

"That is easily managed. Write to Yang and set his mind at rest. Say plainly that there is no food in the capital here and so you are going to another place where there is, and where there is no danger of scarcity. When the higher officials hear it they will approve."

Ts'ao Ts'ao had now decided and as his guest took leave he seized his hands once more saying, "All my success I shall only owe to you."

Tung Chao thanked and left. Thereafter Ts'ao and his advisers secretly discussed the change of capital.

Now as to that a certain official named Wang Li, who was a student of astrology, said to one Liu Ai, "I have been studying the stars. Since last spring Venus has been nearing the 'Guard' star in the neighbourhood of the 'Measure,' and the 'Cowherd'* crossing the River of Heaven.† Mars has been retrograding and came into conjunction with Venus in the Gate of Heaven,⁎ so that 'Metal' and 'Fire' are mingled. Thence must emerge a new ruler. The aura of the Hans is exhausted and Chin and Wei must increase."

A secret memorial was presented to the Emperor Hsien saying, "The Mandate of Heaven has its course and the five elements are out of proportion. 'Earth' is attacking 'Fire' and the successor to the Empire of Han is in Wei."

Ts'ao heard of these sayings and memorials and sent a man to the astrologer to say, "Your loyalty is well known, but the ways of Heaven are past finding out. The less said the better."

Hsun, the adviser, expounded the meaning thus: "The virtue of Han was fire; your element is earth. Hsutu is under the influence of earth and so your fortune depends on getting there. Fire can overcome earth, as earth can multiply wood. Tung Chao and the astrologer agree and you have only to bide your time."

So Ts'ao made up his mind. Next day at Court he said, "The capital is deserted and cannot be restored nor can it be supplied easily with food. Hsutu is a noble city, standing close to a fruitful district. It is everything that a capital should be. I venture to request that the Court move thither."

The Emperor dared not oppose and the officials were too overawed to have any independent opinion so they chose a day to set out. Ts'ao commanded the escort and the officials all followed. When they had travelled a few stages they saw before them a high mound and from behind this there arose the beating of drums. Then Yang and Han came out and barred the way. In front of all stood Hsu Huang, who shouted, "Ts'ao Ts'ao is stealing away the Emperor!"

Ts'ao rode out and took a good look at this man. He seemed a fine fellow and in his secret soul Ts'ao greatly admired him, although he was an enemy. Then he ordered Hsu Ch'u to go and fight him. The combat was axe against broadsword and the two men fought more than half a hundred bouts without advantage to either side. Ts'ao then beat the gongs and drew off his men.

---

* The Great Bear and Vega.
† The Milky Way.
⁎ A star in Taurus.

In the camp a council was called. Ts'ao said, "The two rebels themselves need not be discussed; but Hsu Huang is a fine captain and I was unwilling to use any great force against him. I want to win him over to our side."

An officer, Man Ch'ung, replied, "Do not let that trouble you; I will have a word with him. I shall disguise myself as a soldier this evening and steal over to the enemy's camp to talk to him. I shall incline his heart toward you."

That night Man Ch'ung, duly disguised, got over to the other side and made his way to the tent of Hsu Huang, who sat there by the light of a candle. He was still wearing his coat of mail. Suddenly Ch'ung ran out in front and saluted saying, "You have been well since we parted, old friend?"

Hsu jumped up in surprise, gazed into the face of the speaker a long time and presently said, "What! you are Man Po-ning of Shanyang? What are you doing here?"

"I am an officer in General Ts'ao's army. Seeing my old friend out in front of the army today I wanted to say a word to him. So I took the risk of stealing in this evening and here I am."

Hsu Huang invited him in and they sat down. Then said Man Ch'ung, "There are very few as bold as you on the earth; why then do you serve such as your present chiefs? My master is the most prominent man in the world, a man who delights in wise men and appreciates soldiers as every one knows. Your valour today won his entire admiration and so he took care that the attack was not vigorous enough to sacrifice you. Now he has sent me to invite you to join him. Will you not leave darkness for light and help him in his magnificent task?"

Hsu Huang sat a long time pondering over the offer. Then he said, with a sigh, "I know my masters are doomed to failure, but I have followed their fortunes a long time and do not like to leave them."

"But you know the prudent bird selects its tree and the wise servant chooses his master. When one meets a worthy master and lets him go one is a fool."

"I am willing to do what you say," said Hsu, rising.

"Why not put these two to death as an introductory gift?" said Man.

"It is very wrong for a servant to slay his master. I will not do that."

"True; you are really a good man."

Then Hsu, taking only a few horsemen of his own men with him, left that night and deserted to Ts'ao Ts'ao. Soon some one took the news to Yang Feng, who at the head of a strong company of horsemen, set out to capture the deserter. He called out to him to come back.

But when Yang was getting near he fell into an ambush. Suddenly the whole mountain side was lit up with torches and out sprang Ts'ao's men, he himself being in command. "I have been waiting here a long time; do not run away," cried he.

Yang Feng was completely surprised and tried to draw off, but was quickly surrounded. His colleague came to his rescue and a confused battle began. Yang Feng succeeded in escaping, while Ts'ao Ts'ao kept up the attack on the disordered army. A great number of the rebels gave in and the leaders found they had too few men left to maintain their independence so they betook themselves to Yuan Shu.

When Ts'ao Ts'ao returned to camp the newly surrendered man was presented and well received. Then again the cavalcade set out for the new capital. In due time they reached it and they built palaces and halls and an ancestral temple and an altar, terraces and public offices. The walls were repaired, storehouses built and all put in order.

Then came the rewards for Ts'ao Ts'ao's adherents. Thirteen were raised to rank of hou, or marquis. All good service was rewarded; certain others again, who deserved it, were punished, all according to Ts'ao Ts'ao's sole decision. He himself was made a Generalissimo and Marquis of Wup'ing. The advisers became Presidents of Boards and filled such offices. Mao Chieh and Jen Hsun were put over the military stores. Tung Chao was made magistrate of Loyang and Man Ch'ung of Hsutu. All good service received full recognition.

Ts'ao Ts'ao was then the one man of the Court. All memorials went first to him and were then submitted to the Throne.

When State matters were in order a great banquet was given in his private quarters to all Ts'ao's advisers, and affairs outside the capital were the subject of discussion. Then Ts'ao Ts'ao said, "Liu Pei has his army at Hsuchou and he carries on the administration of the prefecture. Lu Pu fled to him when defeated and Pei gave him Hsiaop'ei to live in. If these two agreed to join forces and attack, my position would be most serious. What precautions can be taken?"

Then rose Hsu Ch'u, saying, "Give me five legions and I will give the Minister both their heads."

Hsun Yu said, "O Leader, you are brave, but you are no strategist. You cannot start sudden war just as the capital has been

changed. However, there is a certain ruse known as The Rival
Tigers. Liu Pei has no decree authorising him to govern the district.
You, Illustrious Sir, can procure one for him, and when sending it,
and so conferring upon him right in addition to his might, you can
enclose a private note telling him to get rid of Lu Pu. If he does,
then he will have lost a vigorous warrior from his side and he could
be dealt with as occasions serve. Should he fail, then Lu Pu will slay
him. This is The Rival Tiger ruse; they wrangle and bite each other."

Ts'ao agreed that this was a good plan so he memorialised for
the formal appointment, which he sent to Liu Pei. Pei was created
General "Conqueror of the East" and a Marquis as well. At the same
time a private note was enclosed.

When Liu Pei heard of the change of capital he began to
prepare a congratulatory address. In the midst of this an imperial
messenger was announced and was met which all ceremony outside
the gate. When the epistle had been reverently received a banquet
was prepared for the messenger.

The messenger said, "This decree was obtained for you by the
Minister Ts'ao."

Yuan-te thanked him. Then the messenger drew forth his secret
letter. When he had read this Liu Pei said, "This matter can be
easily arranged."

The banquet over and the messenger conducted to his lodging
to seek repose, Yuan-te, before going to rest, called in his
councillors to consider the letter.

"There need be no compunction about putting him to death,"
said Chang Fei; "he is a bad man."

"But he came to me for protection in his weakness, how can I put
him to death? That would be immoral," said Liu Pei.

"If he was a good man; it would be difficult," replied Fei.

Liu Pei would not consent. Next day, when Lu Pu came to offer
congratulations, he was received as usual. He said, "I have come to
felicitate you on the receipt of the imperial bounty."

Liu Pei thanked him in due form. But then he saw Chang Fei
draw his sword and come up the hall as if to slay Lu Pu. He hastily
interfered and stopped him. Lu Pu was surprised and said, "Why do
you wish to slay me, I-te?"

"Ts'ao Ts'ao says you are immoral and tells my brother to kill
you," shouted Chang Fei.

Liu Pei shouted again and again to him to go away, and he led
Lu Pu into the private apartments out of the way.

Then he told him the whole story and showed him the secret
letter. He wept as he finished reading.

"This is that miscreant's scheme for sowing discord between us."

"Be not anxious, elder brother," said Liu Pei. "I pledge myself not to be guilty of such an infamous crime."

Lu Pu again and again expressed his gratitude and Liu Pei kept him for a time. They remained talking and drinking wine till late.

Said the other two brothers, "Why not kill him?"

Liu Pei said, "Because Ts'ao Meng-te fears that Lu and I may attack him, he is trying to separate us and get us to 'swallow' each other, while he steps in and takes the advantage. Is there any other reason?"

Kuan nodded assent, but Chang Fei said, "I want to get him out of the way lest he trouble us later."

"That is not what a noble man should do," said his elder brother.

Soon the messenger was dismissed and returned to the capital with the reply from Liu Pei. The letter only said the plan would be made later. But the messenger, when he saw Ts'ao Ts'ao, told him the story of Liu Pei's pledge to Lu Pu. Then said Ts'ao Ts'ao, "The plan has failed; what next?"

Hsun Yu replied, "I have another trick called 'The Tiger and the Wolf' in which the tiger is made to gobble up the Wolf."

"Let us hear it," said Ts'ao.

"Send to Yuan Shu to say that Liu Pei has sent up a secret memorial that he wishes to subdue the southern districts. Shu will be angry and attack him. Then you will order Pei to dispose of Shu and so set them destroying each other. Lu Pu will certainly think that is his chance and turn traitor. This is The Tiger-Wolf trick."

Ts'ao thought this good and sent the messenger and also sent a false edict to Liu Pei. When this came the messenger was received with all the ceremonies and the edict ordered the capture of Yuan Shu. After the departure of the bearer Liu called Mi Chu who pronounced it a ruse.

"It may be," said his master, "but the royal command is not to be disobeyed."

So the army was prepared and the day fixed. Sun Ch'ien said that a trusty man must be left on guard and Pei asked which of his brothers would undertake this task.

"I will guard the city," said Kuan Yu.

"I am constantly in need of your advice so how can we part?"

"I will guard the city," said Chang Fei.

"You will fail," said Pei. "After one of your drinking bouts you will get savage and flog the soldiers. Beside you are rash and will not listen to any one's advice. I shall be uneasy all the time."

"Henceforth I drink no more wine. I will not beat the soldiers and I will always listen to advice," said Fei.

"I fear the mouth does not correspond to the heart," said Mi Chu.

"I have followed my elder brother these many years and never broken faith; why should you be contemptuous!" said Fei.

Yuan-te said, "Though you say this I do not feel quite satisfied. I will order friend Yuan-lung to help you and keep you sober. Then you will not make any mistake."

Ch'en Teng was willing to undertake this duty and the final orders were given. The army of three legions, horse and foot, left Hsuchou and marched toward Nanyang.

When Yuan Shu heard that a memorial had been presented proposing to take possession of this district he broke out into abuse of Liu Pei. "You weaver of mats! You plaiter of straw shoes! You have been smart enough to get possession of a large district and elbow your way into the ranks of the nobles. I was just going to attack you and now you dare to scheme against me! How I detest you!"

So he at once gave orders to prepare an army of ten legions, under Chi Ling, to attack Hsuchou. The armies met at Hsui, where Liu Pei was encamped in a plain with hills behind and a stream on his flank, for his army was small.

Chi Ling, his opponent, was a native of Shantung. He used a very heavy three-edged sword. After he had made his camp he rode out and began abusing his opponents "Liu Pei, you rustic bumpkin, how dare you invade this land?"

"I have a decree ordering me to destroy the minister who behaves improperly. If you oppose you will be assuredly punished?" replied Pei.

Chi angrily rode out brandishing his weapon. But Kuan Yu cried, "Fool, do not attempt to fight!" and rode out to meet him. Then they two fought and after thirty bouts neither had an advantage. Then Chi cried out for a rest. So Kuan turned his horse away, rode back to his own array and waited for him.

When the moment came to renew the combat Chi sent out one of his officers to take his place. But Kuan said, "Tell Chi Ling to come: I must settle with him who shall be cock and who shall be hen."

"You a reputationless leader and unworthy to fight with our general," replied the officer, Hsun Cheng.

This reply angered Kuan, who made just one attack on Hsun and brought him to the ground. At this success Liu Pei urged on the army and Chi Ling's men were defeated. They retired to the mouth of the Huaiyin River and declined all challenges.

However, many of their men came privately into Liu Pei's camp to try to do what mischief they could and many, so found, were slain.

But the armies will be left facing each other while we relate what happened in Hsuchou.

After Liu Pei had started on his expedition Chang Fei placed his colleague and helper in charge of the administration of Hsuchou, keeping military affairs under his own supervision. After thinking over the matter for some time he gave a banquet to all the military officers and when they were all seated he made a speech. "Before my brother left he bade me keep clear of the wine cup for fear of accidents. Now, gentlemen, you may drink deep today but from tomorrow wine is forbidden for we must keep the city safe. So take your fill." And with this he and all his guests rose to drink together.

The wine bearer came to one Ts'ao Pao who declined it, saying he never drank as he was forbidden of heaven.

"What! a fighting man not drink wine!" said the host. "I want you to take just one cup."

Ts'ao Pao was afraid to offend so he drank.

Now the host drank huge goblets with all his guests on every hand and so swallowed a huge quantity of liquor. He became quite intoxicated. Yet he would drink more and insisted on a cup with every guest. It came to the turn of Ts'ao Pao who declined.

"Really, I cannot drink," said Pao.

"You drank just now: why refuse this time?"

Chang Fei pressed him, but still Ts'ao Pao resisted. Then Fei in his drunken madness lost control of his temper and said, "If you disobey the orders of your general you shall be beaten." And he called in his guards.

Here Ch'en Yuan-lung interfered reminding him of the strict injunctions of his brother.

"You civilians attend to your civil business and leave us alone," said Fei.

The only way of escape for the guest was to beg remission and he did so, but added, "Sir, if you saw my son-in-law's face you would pardon me."

"Who is your son-in-law?"

"Lu Pu."

"I did not mean to have you really beaten, but if you think to frighten me with Lu Pu I will. I will beat you as if I was beating him," said Fei.

The guests interposed to beg him off, but their drunken host was obdurate and the unhappy guest received fifty blows. Then at the earnest prayers of the others the remainder of the punishment was remitted.

The banquet came to an end and the beaten man went away burning with resentment. That night he sent a letter to Hsiaop'ei relating the insults he had received from Chang Fei. The letter told Lu Pu of the prefect's absence and proposed that a sudden raid should be made that very night before Chang Fei had recovered from his drunken fit. Lu Pu at once summoned Ch'en Kung and told him.

"This is only a place to occupy temporarily," said Kung. "If you can seize Hsuchou, do so. It is a good chance."

Lu Pu got ready at once and soon on the way with half a company, ordering Ch'en Kung to follow him with the main body. Kao Shun was to follow him.

Hsiaop'ei being only about forty *li* away, one gets there almost as soon as one is mounted and Lu Pu was under the walls at the fourth watch. It was clear moonlight. No one on the ramparts saw him. Pu came up close to the wall and called out, "Liu Pei's secret messenger has arrived."

The guards on the wall were Ts'ao Pao's men and they called him. He came and when he saw who was there he ordered the gates to be opened. Lu Pu gave the secret signal and the soldiers entered shouting.

Chang Fei was in his apartment sleeping off the fumes of wine. His servants hastened to arouse him and told him an enemy had got the gates open and was in the city. Chang savagely got into his armour and laid hold of his mighty spear, but as he was mounting his horse at the gate the soldiers came up. He rushed at them but being still half intoxicated made but a poor fight. Lu Pu knowing his prowess did not press him hard and Chang Fei made his way, with a small escort, to the east gate, and there went out, leaving his brother's family to their fate.

Ts'ao Pao, seeing Chang had but a very small force and was still half drunk as well, came in pursuit. Fei saw who it was and was mad with rage. He galloped toward him and drove him off after a few passes. He followed Pao to the moat and wounded him in the back. His frightened steed carried him into the moat and he was drowned.

Once well outside the city Chang Fei collected his men and they rode off toward the south.

Lu Pu having surprised the city set himself to restore order. He put a guard over the residence of Liu Pei so that no one should disturb the family.

Chang Fei with his few followers went to his brother's camp and told his story of treachery and surprise. All were greatly distressed.

"Success is not worth rejoicing over; failure is not worth grieving over," said Liu Pei with a sigh.

"Where are our sisters?" asked Kuan.

"They shared the fate of the city."

Liu Pei nodded his head and was silent.

Kuan Yu with an effort controlled his reproaches and said, "What did you say when you promised to guard the city and what orders did our brother give you? Now the city is lost and therewith our sisters-in-law. Have you done well?"

Chang Fei was overwhelmed by remorse. He drew his sword to kill himself.

> He raised the cup in pledge,
>   None might say nay;
> Remorseful, drew the sword,
>   Himself to slay.

Chang Fei's fate will be told in the next chapter.

In the last chapter it was recorded that Chang Fei was about to end his life with his own weapon. But his brother rushed forward and caught him in his arms, snatched away the sword and threw it on the earth saying, "Brothers are hands and feet; wives and children are as clothing. You may mend your torn dress, but who can re-attach a lost limb? We three, by the Oath of the Peach Garden, swore to seek the same deathday. The city is lost, it is true, and my wife and little ones, but I could not bear that we should die ere our course be run. Beside, the city was not really mine and Lu Pu will not harm my family but will rather seek to preserve them. You made a mistake, worthy brother, but is it one deserving of death?"

And he wept. His brothers were much affected and their tears fell in sympathy.

As soon as the news of Lu Pu's successful seizure of his protector's district reached Yuan Shu, he sent promises of valuable presents to Lu to induce him to join in a further attack on Liu Pei. The presents are said to have been fifty thousand measures of grain, five hundred horses, ten thousand taels of gold and silver and a thousand pieces of coloured silk. Lu Pu swallowed the bait and ordered Kao Shun to lead forth five legions. But Liu Pei heard of the threatened attack, so he made inclement weather an excuse to disband his few soldiers and left Hsui, before the attacking force came up.

However, Kao Shun demanded the promised reward through Chi Ling, who put him off saying, "My lord has gone away, I will settle this as soon as I can see him and get his decision."

With this answer Kao Shun returned to Lu Pu, who could not

decide what to do. Then came a letter from Yuan Shu saying that although Kao Shun had gone to attack Liu Pei, yet Pei had not been destroyed and no reward could be given till he was actually taken. Lu Pu railed at what he called the breach of faith and was inclined to attack Yuan Shu himself. However, his adviser opposed this course, saying, "You should not; he is in possession of Shouch'un and has a large army, well supplied. You are no match for him. Rather ask Liu Pei to take up his quarters at Hsiaop'ei as one of your wings and, when the time comes, let him lead the attack. Then both the Yuans will fall before you and you will be very powerful."

Finding this advice good he sent letters to Yuan-te asking him to return.

The story of Liu Pei's attack on Kuangling, the attack on his camp and his losses, has been told. On his way back he met the messenger from Lu Pu, who presented the letter. Yuan-te was quite content with the offer but his brothers were not inclined to trust Lu.

"Since he treats me kindly, I cannot but trust him," replied Yuan-te.

So he went back to Hsuchou. Lu Pu, fearing that Liu Pei might doubt his sincerity, restored his family and when the ladies, Kan and Mi, saw their lord they told him that they had been kindly treated and guarded by soldiers against any intrusion, and provisions had never been wanting.

"I knew he would not harm my family," said Yuan-te to Kuan and Chang.

However, they were not pleased and would not accompany their brother into the city when he went to express his thanks. They went to escort the two ladies to Hsiaop'ei.

At the interview Lu Pu said, "I did not wish to take the city, but your brother behaved very badly, drinking and flogging the soldiers, and I came to guard it lest some evil should befall."

"But I had long wished to yield it to you," said Yuan-te.

Thereupon Lu Pu pretended to wish to retire in favour of Yuan-te who, however, would not hear of it. He returned and took up his quarters in Hsiaop'ei, but his two brothers would not take the situation kindly and were very discontented.

Said Yuan-te, "One must bow to one's lot. It is the will of Heaven and one cannot struggle against fate."

Lu Pu sent presents of food and stuffs and peace reigned between the two houses.

But there is no need to write of this. As the story runs, Yuan Shu prepared a great banquet for his soldiers on the occasion of a victory gained by Sun Ts'e over Lu K'ang, the Prefect of Luchiang.

Yuan Shu summoned the victor, who made obeisance at the foot of the hall of audience. Shu, sitting in State, asked for details of the campaign and then invited Sun Ts'e to the banquet.

After the unhappy death of his father Sun Ts'e had returned to Chiangnan, where he had devoted himself to peaceful ends, inviting to his side good men and able scholars. Afterwards when a quarrel broke out between his mother's uncle, the Prefect of Tanyang, and T'ao Ch'ien, he removed his mother with all the family to Ch'ua, he himself taking service under Yuan Shu, who admired and loved him greatly.

"If I had a son like him," said Shu, "I should die without regret."

He employed Sun Ts'e as a soldier and sent him on various expeditions, all of which were successful. After this banquet to celebrate the victory over Lu K'ang, Sun Ts'e returned to his camp very bitter over the arrogant and patronising airs of his patron. Instead of retiring to his tent he walked up and down by the light of the moon.

"Here am I, a mere nobody and yet my father was such a hero!" And he cried out and wept in spite of himself.

Then suddenly appeared one who said, laughing loudly, "What is this, O Po-fu? While your noble father enjoyed the light of the sun he made free use of me and if his son has any difficulty to resolve why does he not refer it to me also instead of weeping here alone?"

Looking at the speaker Sun Ts'e saw it was one Chu Chih, whose less formal name was Chun-li, a native of that district, who had been in his father's service. Sun Ts'e then ceased weeping and they two sat down.

"I was weeping from regret at being unable to continue my father's work," said he.

"Why stay here bound to the service of a master? Why not get command of an army under the pretence of an expedition to relieve Chiangtung? Then you can accomplish great things."

While these two were talking another man suddenly entered saying, "I know what you two are planning, noble Sirs. Under my hand is a band of bold fellows ready to help Po-fu in whatever he wishes to do."

The speaker was one of Yuan Shu's advisers named Lu Fan. They three then sat and discussed schemes.

"The one fear is that the soldiers will be refused," said the newcomer.

"I still have the Imperial Seal that my father left me; that should be good security."

"Yuan Shu earnestly desires that jewel," said Chu Chih. "He will certainly lend you men on that pledge."

The three talked over their plans, gradually settling the details, and not many days after Sun Ts'e obtained an interview with his patron. Assuming the appearance of deep grief he said, "I have been unable to avenge my father. Now the Prefect of Yangchow is opposing my mother's brother and my mother and her family are in danger. Wherefore I would borrow a few companies of fighting men to rescue them. As perhaps, Illustrious Sir, you may lack confidence in me I am willing to deposit the Imperial Seal, left me by my late father, as a pledge."

"Let me see it, if you have it," said Shu. "I do not want the jewel really, but you may as well leave it with me. I will lend you three companies and five hundred horses. Return as soon as peace can be made. As your rank is hardly sufficient for such powers I will memorialise to obtain for you higher rank with the title of General, 'Exterminator of Brigands,' and you can soon start."

Ts'e thanked his patron most humbly and soon put the army in motion, taking with him his two new friends as well as his former captains. When he reached Liyang he saw a body of troops in front of him, at their head a dashing leader of handsome and refined mien. As soon as this man saw Sun Ts'e he dismounted and made obeisance. It was Chou Yu.

When Sun Chien was opposing the tyrant Minister Tung Cho, the Chou family had removed to Shu, in modern Anhui, and as Chou Yu and Sun Ts'e were of the same age all but two months, they became exceedingly good friends and sworn brothers, Ts'e being the "elder" in virtue of his two months' seniority. Chou Yu was on his way to visit Sun Ts'e's uncle, Prefect of Tanyang, when the happy meeting took place.

Naturally Sun Ts'e confided his projects and inmost ideas to his friend, who at once promised fidelity and service. They would work out the grand design together.

"Now that you have come the design is as good as accomplished," said Sun.

Chou Yu was introduced to Chu Chih and Lu Fan.

Chou Yu said, "Do you know of the two Changs of Chiangtung? They would be most useful men in working out your schemes."

"Who are they, the two Changs?" said Sun.

"They are men of transcendent genius who are living near here for the sake of tranquillity in these troublous times. Their names are Chang Chao and Chang Hung. Why not invite them to help you, brother?"

Sun Ts'e lost no time in sending letters and gifts, but they both declined. Then he visited them in person, was greatly pleased with their speech and by dint of large gifts and much persuasion, got them to promise to join him. They were given substantial offices.

The plan of the attack upon Yangchou was the next matter for discussion. The Prefect, Liu Yu, was of Tunglai, a scion of the Imperial family and brother of the governor of Yenchow. He had long ruled in Yangchou, but Yuan Shu had forced him to leave his usual abiding city and retire to Ch'ua.

Hearing of the meditated attack on him he summoned his captains to take counsel. Said Chang Ying, "I will take an army and entrench at Niuchu. No army can get past that, whatever its strength."

He was interrupted by another who shouted, "And let me lead the van!"

All eyes turned to this man; is was T'aishih Tzu who, after raising the siege of Pohai, had come on a visit to the Prefect and stayed on.

Hearing him offer to undertake the hazardous post of van-leader Liu Yu said, "But you are still young and not yet equal to such a charge. Rather stay by my side and obey my orders."

T'aishih Tzu withdrew in high dudgeon. Soon Chang Ying led his army to Niuchu, leaving his stores of grain at Tiko. When Sun Ts'e approached, Chang Ying went to meet him and the two armies faced each other above Niuchut'an, (Bullock Island Rapid). Chang Ying roundly abused his opponent and Huang Kai rode out to attack, but before the combat had proceeded far there arose an alarm of fire in Chang Ying's camp. Chang Ying turned back and then Sun Ts'e advanced in full force, compelling the enemy to abandon their possession. The defeated general fled to the hills.

Now the incendiaries who had brought about this result were two, named Chiang Ch'in and Chou T'ai, both from the Kiukiang district, who in these troublous times had got together a band of kindred spirits and lived by plundering the country along the Yangtse River. They knew Sun Ts'e by reputation as a man who treated able men very liberally and wished to join him. So they came with their band, three hundred strong, and helped him in this way as an introduction. Sun Ts'e welcomed them and gave the leaders rank. After taking possession of the stores of all kinds abandoned by the runaways, and enlisting a large number of those who surrendered into his own ranks, he moved forward to attack Shent'ing.

After his defeat Chang Ying returned to his master and told his misfortune. Liu Yu was going to punish his failure by death, but listened to his advisers, who asked for mercy for the unfortunate man, and sent him to command the garrison in Lingling. He himself set out to meet the invaders. He camped under the hills at Lingnan. Sun Ts'e camped on the opposite side of the hills.

Sun Ts'e enquired if there was a temple to Kuang-Wu, of the Hans, in the vicinity, and was told there was a temple on the summit of the hills.

"I dreamed last night that he called me so I will go and pray there," said Ts'e.

He was advised not to go as the enemy was on the other side and he might fall into an ambush.

"The spirit will help me; what need I fear?"

So he put on his armour, took his spear and mounted, taking with him twelve of his officers as an escort. They rode up the bills, dismounted, burned incense and they all bowed in the shrine. Then Ts'e knelt and made a vow saying, "If I, Sun Ts'e, succeed in my task and restore the authority of my late father then will I restore this temple and order sacrifices at the four seasons."

When they had remounted he said, I am going to ride along the ridge and reconnoitre the enemy's position."

His followers begged him to refrain but he was obstinate and they rode away together, noting the villages below. A soldier going along a bye road quickly reported the presence of horsemen on the ridge and Liu Yu said, "It is certainly Sun Ts'e trying to inveigle us to battle. But do not go out."

T'aishih Tzu, the bold, jumped up saying, "What better chance to capture him?"

So, without orders he armed himself and rode through the camp crying, "If there be any valiant men among you follow me!"

No one moved save a subaltern who said, "He is a valiant man and I will go with him." So he also went. The others only laughed at the pair.

Now having seen all he wished Sun Ts'e thought it time to return and wheeled round his horse. But when he was going over the summit some one shouted, "Stay, Sun Ts'e!"

He turned; two horsemen were coming at full speed down the next hill. He halted and drew up his little escort right and left, he himself with his spear ready.

"Which is Sun Ts'e?" shouted T'aishih.

"Who are you?" was the reply.

"I am T'aishih Tzu, of Tunglai, come to take him prisoner."

"Then I am he," said Sun Ts'e laughing. "Come both of you

together; I am not afraid of you. If I was, I should not be Po-fu."

"You and all your crowd come on and I will not blench," cried T'aishih putting his horse at a gallop and setting his spear.

Sun braced himself for the shock and the battle began. Fifty bouts were fought and still neither combatant had the advantage. Sun Ts'e's followers whispered to each other their admiration and amazement. T'aishih saw that the spearmanship of his opponent showed no weak point whereby he could gain the advantage so he decided to resort to guile. Feigning defeat he would lead Sun to pursue. T'aishih however did not retire along the road by which he had come, but took a path leading around the hill instead of over it. His antagonist followed, shouting, "He who retreats is no worthy son of Han!"

But T'aishih thought within himself, "He has twelve others at his back and I only one. If I capture him, the others will retake him. I will inveigle him into some secret spot and then try." So flying and fighting by turns he led Sun Ts'e, an eager pursuer, down to the plain.

Here T'aishih suddenly wheeled about and attacked. Again they exchanged half a hundred bouts, without result. Then Sun made a fierce thrust which his opponent evaded by gripping the spear under his oxter, while T'aishih did the same with his opponent's spear. Neither was wounded but each exerting his utmost strength to pull the other out of the saddle they both came to the ground.

Their steeds galloped off they knew not whither while the two men, each dropping his spear, began a hand to hand struggle. Soon their fighting robes were in tatters. Sun gripped the short lance that T'aishih carried at his back, while T'aishih tore off the other's helmet. Sun tried to stab with the short lance but T'aishih fended off the blow with the helmet as a shield.

Then arose a great shouting. Liu Yu had come up with a company of soldiers. Sun seemed now in sore straits. His twelve followers came up and each combatant let go his hold. T'aishih quickly found another steed, seized a spear and mounted. Sun Ts'e, whose charger had been caught by Ch'eng P'u, also mounted, and a confused battle began between the handful of men on one side and a whole company on the other. It swayed and drifted down the hill side. However, soon Chou Yu came to the rescue, and as evening drew on a tempest put an end to the fight. Both sides drew off and returned to camp.

Next day Sun Ts'e led his army to the front of Liu Yu's camp and the challenge was accepted. The armies were drawn up. Sun hung the short lance he had seized from T'aishih Tzu at the end of his spear and waved it in front of the line of battle and ordered his soldiers to shout, "If the owner of this had not fled he would have been stabbed to death."

On the other side they hung out Sun's helmet and the soldiers shouted back "Sun Ts'e's head is here already."

Both sides thus yelled defiance at each other, one side boasting, the other bragging. Then T'aishih rode out challenging Sun to a duel to the death and Sun would have accepted, but Ch'eng P'u said, "My lord should not trouble himself, I will take him," and he rode forth.

"You are no antagonist for me," said T'aishih. "Tell your master to come out."

This incensed Ch'eng, who rode at his opponent, and they two fought many bouts. The duel was stopped by the gongs of Liu Yu.

"Why did you sound the retreat?" said T'aishih. "I was just going to capture the wretch."

"Because I have just heard that Ch'ua is threatened. Chou Yu is leading a force thither and a certain Ch'en Wu is in league with him to betray the city. The loss would be irremediable. I will hasten to Moling to get the help of Hsueh Li and Chai Jung."

The army retired, T'aishih Tzu with it, without being pursued. On the other side Chang Chao said to Sun Ts'e, "Chou Yu's threatened attack is the cause of this move; they are in no mood to fight. A night raid on their camp would finish them."

The army was divided into five divisions for the night surprise and hastened toward the camp where they were victorious. Their opponents scattered in all directions. T'aishin alone made a determined stand and as he could not withstand a whole army he fled with a few followers to Chinghsien.

Now Sun Ts'e acquired a new adherent in the person of Ch'en Wu. He was a soldier of middle height, sallow of complexion and dark eye, an odd looking man. But Sun held him in high esteem, gave him rank and put him in the van for the attack on Hsueh Li. As van-leader he and half a score horsemen made a dash into the enemy's formation, where they slew half a hundred men. So Hsueh Li would not fight but remained within his defences. As Sun was attacking the city a spy came in with the news that Liu Yu and Chai Jung had gone to attack Niuchu, which made Sun move thither in haste. His two opponents were ready for battle.

"I am here," said Sun Ts'e, "you had better give in."

A horseman came out from behind the two leaders to accept the challenge. It was Yu Mi. But in the third bout Sun Ts'e made him prisoner and carried him off to the other side.

Seeing his colleague thus captured Fan Neng rode out to the rescue and got quite close. But just as he was going to thrust, all the soldiers shouted "There is a man behind you going to strike secretly!" At this Sun Ts'e turned and shouted so thunderously loud that Fan Neng fell out of his saddle from mere fright. He split his skull and died. When Sun Ts'e reached his standard he threw his prisoner to the ground. And he was also dead, crushed to death between the arm and the body of his captor. So in a few moments Sun Ts'e had disposed of two enemies, one crushed to death and one frightened to death. Thereafter Sun Ts'e was called the Little Prince.

After Liu Yu's defeat the greater portion of his force surrendered and the number of those put to death exceeded ten thousand. Liu Yu himself sought safety with Liu Piao.

An attack on Moling was the next move. As soon as Sun Ts'e arrived at the moat he summoned the commander, Hsueh Li, to surrender. Some one let fly a furtive arrow from the wall which wounded Sun in the left thigh so severely that he fell from his steed. Hastily his officers picked up their wounded chief and returned to the camp where the arrow was pulled out and the wound dressed with the medicines suitable for injuries by metals.

By Sun Ts'e's command the story was spread abroad that the hurt had been fatal and all the soldiers set up cries of lamentation. The camp was broken up. The defender of the city made a night sortie, but fell into a carefully prepared ambush and presently Sun himself appeared on horseback shouting "Sun Ts'e is here still."

His sudden appearance created such a panic that the soldiers dropped their weapons and fell on their faces. Sun gave orders not to kill them but their leaders fell, one from a spear thrust as he turned to run away, another wounded by an arrow, and the commander in chief was slain in the first rush. Thus Sun Ts'e got possession of Moling. Having calmed the people he sent his soldiers away to Chinghsien, where T'aishih Tzu was in command.

T'aishih Tzu had assembled two companies of veterans in addition to his own troop for the purpose of avenging his master. Sun Ts'e and Chou Yu on the other hand consulted how to capture him alive. The latter's plan was to attack the city on three sides, leaving the east gate free for flight. Some distance off an ambush would be prepared, when their victim, his men fatigued and horses spent, would fall an easy victim.

The latest recruits under T'aishih Tzu's banner were mostly hillmen and unaccustomed to discipline. Beside the walls of the city were pitiably low. One night Sun ordered one Ch'en Wu to strip off his long dress, leave his arms save a dagger, clamber up the ramparts and set fire to the city. Seeing the flames spreading the commander made for the east gate and, as soon as he got outside, Sun Ts'e followed in pursuit. The pursuit was maintained for some thirty *li* when the pursuers stopped. T'aishih Tzu went on as long as possible, finally halting to rest in a spot surrounded by reeds. Suddenly a tremendous shouting arose. T'aishih was just starting when tripping ropes arose all round, his horse was thrown and he found himself a prisoner.

He was taken to camp. As soon as Sun Ts'e heard the news he himself rode out to meet the successful man and ordered the guards to leave the prisoner, whose bonds he loosened with his own hands. Then he took off his own embroidered robe and put it on the captive. They entered the camp together.

"I knew you were a real hero," said Sun. "That worm of a Liu Yu had no use for such as you and so he got beaten."

The prisoner, overcome by this kindness and good treatment, then formally surrendered.

Sun Ts'e seized his hand and said, laughing, "If you had taken me at that fight we had near the shrine, would you have killed me?"

"Who can say?" said T'aishih smiling.

Sun Ts'e laughed also and they entered his tent, where the captive leader was placed in the seat of honour at a banquet.

T'aishih said, "Can you trust me so far as to let me go to muster as many as I can of the soldiers of my late master? Under the smart of this defeat they will turn against him and they would be a great help to you."

"Exactly what I most desire. I will make an agreement with you that at midday tomorrow you will return."

T'aishih agreed and went off. All the captains said he would never return.

"He is trustworthy and will not break his word," said the chief.

None of the officers believed he would come back. But the next day they set up a bamboo rod in the gate of the camp and just as the shadow marked noon T'aishih Tzu returned, bringing with him about a thousand men. Sun Ts'e was pleased and his officers had to confess that he had rightly judged his man.

Sun Ts'e had now several legions and Chiangtung was his. He improved the conditions of the people and maintained order so that his adherents and supporters daily increased. He was called Sun Lang (the Bright One). When his army approached the people used to flee in terror, but when it had arrived and they saw that no one was permitted to loot and not the least attempt was made on their houses, they rejoiced and presented the soldiers with oxen and wine, for which they were in turn duly rewarded. Gladness filled the country side. The soldiers who had followed Liu Yu were kindly treated. Those who wished to join Sun's army did so; those who preferred not to be soldiers were sent home with presents. And thus Sun Ts'e won the respect and praise of every one in Kiangnan and became very powerful.

Sun Ts'e then settled his mother and the remainder of the family in Ch'ua, setting his brother Ch'uan and Chou T'ai over the city.

Then he headed an expedition to the south to reduce the Wu districts. At that time there was a certain Yen Pai-hu, or the White Tiger, who styled himself Prince Te of Eastern Wu and ruled over the Wu districts. Hearing of Sun Ts'e's approach, the "Prince" sent his brother Yen Yu with an army against him and they met at Fengch'iao.

Yen Ye, sword in hand, took his stand on a bridge and this was reported to Sun Ts'e, who prepared to accept the challenge. Chang Hung tried to dissuade him saying, "Forasmuch as my lord's fate is bound up with that of the army, he should not risk a conflict with a mere robber. I would that you should remember your own value."

"Your words, O Elder One, are as gold and precious stones, but I fear that my soldiers will not carry out my commands unless I myself share their dangers."

Then he sent forth Han Tang to take up the challenge. Just as he reached the bridge, Chiang Ch'in and Ch'en Wu, who had dropped down the river in a small boat, passed under the bridge. Though the arrows fell in clouds on the bank, the two men rushed up and fiercely attacked Yen Yu as he stood on the bridge. He fled and Han Tang went in pursuit smiting up to the gate of the city into which he entered.

Sun Ts'e laid seige to Soochow both by land and water. For three days no one came out to offer battle. Then at the head of his army he came to the Ch'ang Gate and summoned the warden. An officer of inconsiderable rank came out and stood with one hand resting on a beam while with the other he gave point to his abuse of those below. Quickly T'aishih Tzu's hands sought his bow and an arrow was on the string.

"See me hit that fellow's hand," said he, turning to his companions.

Even as the sound of his voice died away, the bowstring twanged, the arrow sped and lodged in the beam, firmly pinning thereto the officer's hand. Both sides, those on the wall and those below it, marvelled at such marksmanship.

The wounded man was taken away and when the White Tiger heard of the exploit he said, "How can we hope to withstand an army with such men as this in it?"

And his thoughts turned toward a peace. He sent his brother Yu out to see Sun Ts'e, who received him civilly, invited him into the tent and set wine before him.

"And what does your brother propose?" said Sun.

"He is willing to share this district with you," was the reply.

"The rat! how dare he put himself on a level with me?" cried Sun.

He commanded to put the messenger to death. Yu started up and drew his sword, but out flew Sun Ts'e's blade and the unhappy messenger fell to the ground. His head was hacked off and sent into the city to his brother.

This had its effect. The White Tiger saw resistance was hopeless, so he abandoned the city and fled. Sun Ts'e pressed the attack. Huang Kai captured Chiahsing (Kashing) and T'aishih Tzu took Wuch'eng. The district was quickly subdued. The White Tiger rushed off toward Hangchow in the east, plundering on all sides, till a band of villagers under the leadership of one Ling Ts'ao checked his career of robbery there. He then went toward Kueichi.

The Lings, father and son, then went to meet Sun Ts'e, who took them into his service as a reward for their service and the joint forces crossed the river.

The White Tiger gathered his scattered forces and took up a position at the western ford, but Ch'eng P'u attacked him there and scattered the defenders, chasing them as far as Huichi. The Prefect of the place, Wang Lang, was on their side and inclined to support them actively. But, when he proposed this, one of his men stood forth saying, "No! No! Sun Ts'e as a leader is humane and upright, while the White Tiger is a savage ruffian. Rather capture him and offer his person as a peace offering to Sun Ts'e."

The Prefect turned angrily toward the speaker, who was an official named Yu Fan, and bade him be silent. He withdrew sighing deeply. And the Prefect went to the help of the White Tiger with whom he joined forces at Shanyin.

Sun Ts'e came up. When both sides were arrayed Sun Ts'e rode out and addressed Wang Lang, saying, "Mine is an army of good men and my aim is to restore peace to Chekiang, but you give your support to a rebel!"

Wang Lang replied, "Your greed is insatiable. Having got

possession of Wu you want also my district, and so as an excuse you have vengeance to wreak on the Yens."

This response greatly angered Sun Ts'e. Just as battle was to be joined T'aishih Tzu advanced and Wang Lang came toward him waving his sword. Before they had exchanged many passes Chou Hsin dashed out to help Wang. Thereupon Huang Kai rode out to make the sides more equal. These latter two were just engaging when the drums rolled on both sides and a general battle began.

Suddenly confusion was caused in the rear of Wang's army by the sudden onslaught of a small troop. Wang Lang galloped off to see to it. Then an attack was made on his flank, so that he was in a hopeless position, and he and the White Tiger, fighting desperately, only just managed to reach the shelter of the city. The drawbridges were raised, the gates closed and preparations made to sustain a siege.

Sun Ts'e followed right up to the walls and then divided his men so as to attack all four gates. Seeing that the city was being fiercely attacked Wang Lang was for making a sortie, but the White Tiger opposed this as hopeless against so strong a force outside. They could only strengthen their position and remain behind the shelter of the ramparts until hunger forced the besiegers to retire. Wang Lang agreed and the siege went on.

For several days a vigorous attack was maintained, but with little success. Taking counsel with his officers Sun Ching, who was the uncle of Sun Ts'e, said, "Since they are holding the city with such resolution it will be difficult to dislodge them. But the bulk of their supplies is stored at Ch'atu, distant only some score *li*. Our best plan is to seize this place, thus attacking where the enemy is unprepared, and doing what they do not expect."

Sun Ts'e approved saying, "My uncle's plan is admirable and will crush the rebels." So he issued orders to kindle watch fires at all the gates, and leave the flags standing to maintain the appearance of soldiers in position while the expedition went south.

Chou Yu came to utter a warning, "When you, my lord, go away the besieged will surely come out and follow you. We might prepare a surprise for them."

Sun Ts'e replied, "My preparations are complete and the city will be captured tonight."

So the army set out.

Wang Lang heard that the besiegers had gone and he went up to the tower to reconnoitre. He saw the fires blazing, the smoke rising, and the pennons fluttering in the breeze as usual and hesitated.

Chou Hsin said, "He has gone and this is only a stratagem. Let us go out and smite them."

The White Tiger said, "If he has gone, it is to attack Ch'atu. Let us pursue."

"The place is our base of supply," said Wang Lang, "and must be defended. You lead the way and I will follow with reserves."

So the White Tiger and Chou Hsin went forth with five companies and drew near their enemy about the first watch, at twenty *li* from the city. The road led through dense forest. Then suddenly the drums beat and lighted torches sprang up on all sides. The White Tiger was frightened, turned his horse and started to retreat. At once a leader appeared in front in whom, by the glare of the torches, he recognised Sun Ts'e. Chou Hsin made a rush at him but fell under Sun Ts'e's spear. The men surrendered. However, the White Tiger managed to cut his way out.

Wang Lang soon heard of the loss and not daring to return to the city retreated in all haste to Haiyu. And so Sun Ts'e got possession of the city.

Having restored order, a few days later a man came bringing the head of the White Tiger as an offering to Sun Ts'e. This man was a native of the district. He was of medium height, with a square face and wide mouth. He was named Tung Hsi, and was given an office. After this peace reigned in all the east and, having placed his uncle in command of the city and made Chu Chih Prefect, Sun Ts'e returned to his own place.

While Sun Ts'e was absent a band of brigands suddenly attacked Hsuanch'eng, left in the care of his brother Ch'uan and the leader Chou T'ai. As the onslaught was made on all sides at once, and in the night, the brigands got the upper hand. Chou T'ai took the youth in his arms and mounted a horse, but as the robbers came on with swords to attack him he dismounted, and though without mail, met the robbers on foot and slew them as they came up. Then came a horseman armed with a spear, but Chou T'ai laid hold of his spear and pulled him to the earth. Then he mounted the robber's horse and thrusting this way and that with the spear fought his way out. So Sun Ch'uan was preserved, but his saviour had received more than a dozen wounds.

These wounds being due to metal would not heal but swelled enormously, and the brave soldier's life hung in the balance. Sun Ts'e was deeply grieved. Then Tung Hsi said, "Once in an engagement with some pirates I received many spear wounds, but a certain wise man named Yu Fan recommended a surgeon who cured me in half a month."

"Surely this must be Yu Chung-hsiang," replied Sun Ts'e.

"That is he; he is so called."

"Yes, truly a wise man; I will employ him."

So Sun Ts'e sent two officers to invite him and he came at once. He was treated in most friendly fashion and appointed an official forthwith. Then the question of treating the wounded man was brought up.

"The surgeon is one Hua T'o, who has perfectly marvellous skill in the leech's art. I will get him to come," said Yu Fan.

Shortly the famous leech arrived, a man with the complexion of a youth and a snowy beard. He looked more like a saint who had passed the gates of this life. He was treated very handsomely and taken to see the sick soldier's wounds.

"The case is not difficult," said the surgeon and he prepared certain drugs that healed the wounds within a month. Sun Ts'e suitably acknowledged his care and skill and he was allowed to leave.

Next Sun Ts'e attacked the brigands and destroyed them, so restoring complete tranquillity to Chiangnan. After this he set garrisons at all the strategical points, and this done, memorialised what he had achieved. He came to an understanding with Ts'ao Ts'ao and sent letters to Yuan Shu demanding the return of the Seal he had left in pledge.

But Yuan Shu, secretly cherishing the most ambitious designs, wrote excuses and did not return the State jewel. In his own place he hastily summoned his officers to a council and said, "Sun Ts'e borrowed an army from me and set out on an expedition which has made him master of Chiangtung. Now he says nothing of repayment but demands the token of his pledge. Truly he is a boor and what steps can I take to destroy him?"

The Recorder, Yang Ta-chiang, replied, "You cannot do any thing against him for he is too strongly placed. You must first remove Liu Pei in revenge for having attacked you without cause, and then you may think about Sun Ts'e. I have a scheme to put the former into your hands in a very short time."

> He went not to destroy the tiger, but instead
> Against a dragon forth his army led.

The means he employed will be made plain in the next chapter.

"What is your plan of attack on Liu Pei?" said Shu. Yang Ta-chiang replied, "Though Liu Pei, now camped at Hsiaop'ei, could easily be taken, yet Lu Pu is strongly posted at the chief city near, and I think he would help Pei if it was only for the grudge he bears against you for not having given him the gold and stuffs, grain and horses you promised. First of all you should send Lu Pu a present whereby to engage his affections and keep him quiet while you deal with Liu Pei. You can see to Lu Pu after this is done."

Thereupon a large quantity of millet was sent, with letters, by the hand of Han Yin. The gift pleased Lu Pu greatly; and he treated the messenger with great cordiality. Feeling sure of no trouble from that quarter Yuan Shu told off the leaders of the expedition against Hsiaop'ei.

When Liu Pei heard these things he called his officers to take counsel. Chang Fei was for open war forthwith. Sun Ch'ien said their resources were too small: they must lay the position before Lu Pu and ask help.

"Do you think that fellow will do anything?" said Chang Fei cynically.

Liu Pei decided in favour of Sun's proposal and wrote as follows:—

"Humbly I venture to remind you that I am here by your orders and enjoy repose as the result of your kindness, extensive as the heavens. Now Yuan Shu, moved by a desire for revenge, is sending a force against this place and its destruction is imminent unless you intervene to save it. I trust you will send an army quickly to protect the town, and our happiness will be inexpressible."

Receiving this Lu Pu called in Ch'en Kung to whom he said, "I have just received gifts from Yuan Shu and a letter, with the intent of restraining me from helping Liu Pei. Now comes a letter from him asking help. It seems to me that Yuan-te where he is can do me no harm, but if Yuan Shu overcomes Liu Pei then the power of the north is so much nearer and I should be unable to resist the attacks of so many leaders and should never sleep secure. I will aid Liu Pei; that is the better course for me."

Now the force sent against Hsiaop'ei went thither as quickly as possible and soon the country to the southeast fluttered with pennons by day and blazed with watch fires by night, while the rolling of the drums reverberated from heaven to earth.

The few men at Liu Pei's disposal were led out of the city and arranged to make a brave show, but it was good news to him to hear that Lu Pu had arrived and was quite near. He camped only a *li* away to the south-west. When Yuan Shu's general, Chi Ling, heard of his arrival he wrote letters reproaching Lu Pu for his treachery. Lu Pu smiled as he read them.

"I know how to make both of them love me," said he. So he sent invitations to both leaders to come to a banquet. Liu Pei was for accepting the invitation and going, but his brothers dissuaded him saying, "There is some treachery in his heart."

"I have treated him too well for him to do me any harm," said Yuan-te.

So he mounted and rode away, the two brothers following. They came to the camp.

The host said, "Now by a special effort I have got you out of danger; I hope you will not forget that when you come into your own."

Yuan-te thanked him heartily and was invited to take a seat. The two brothers took up their usual place as guards.

But when Chi Ling was announced Yuan-te felt a spasm of fear and got up to go away.

"You two are invited for the particular purpose of a discussion," said the host. "Do not take it amiss."

Yuan-te, being quite ignorant of his intentions, was very uneasy. Presently his fellow guest entered. Seeing Yuan-te in the tent, and in the seat of honour, he was puzzled, hesitated and tried to withdraw. But the attendants prevented this and Lu Pu, advancing, laid hold of him and drew him into the tent as he had been a child.

"Do you wish to slay me?" asked he.

"Not at all," replied Lu Pu.

"Then you are going to slay Long-ears?"

"No; not that."

"Then what does it mean?"

"Yuan-te and I are brothers. Now, General, you are besieging him and so I have come to the rescue."

"Then slay me," said Chi Ling.

"There would be no sense in that. All my life I have disliked fighting and quarrels, but have loved making peace. And now I want to settle the quarrel between you two."

"May I ask how you think of doing so?"

"I have a means and one approved of heaven itself."

Then he drew Ling within the tent and led him up to Pei. The two men faced each other, full of mutual suspicion, but their host placed himself between them and they took their seats, Liu Pei on the right hand of the host.

The banquet began. After a number of courses almost in silence, Lu Pu spoke, saying, "I wish you two gentlemen to listen to me and put an end to your strife."

Liu Pei made no reply but Chi Ling said, "I have come with an army of ten legions at the express bidding of my master to take Liu Pei. How can I cease the strife? I must fight."

"What!" exclaimed Chang Fei drawing his sword. "Few as we are we regard you no more than a lot of children. What are you compared with a million Yellow Turbans? You dare to hurt our brother!"

Kuan Yu urged him to be silent. Let us see what General Lu has to say first; after that there will be time to go to our tents and fight."

"I beg you both to come to an understanding. I cannot let you fight," said Lu Pu.

Now on one side Chi Ling was discontented and angry; on the other Chang Fei was dying for a fight and neither of the two chiefly concerned would signify assent. Then suddenly the host turned to his attendants saying, "Bring my halberd!" They did so and he sat there gripping the graceful but effective weapon in his right hand. Both guests felt very ill at ease and turned pale. Lu Pu went on "I have tried to persuade you to make peace for that is the command of the Most High. It shall be put to the test."

He then bade his servants take the halberd outside beyond the gate and set it up. Then speaking to his two guests he said, "That gate is one hundred and fifty paces distant. If I can hit that centre branch of the halberd-head with an arrow, you will both withdraw your armies. If I miss, you can go away and prepare for immediate battle. I shall compel you to abide by what I say."

Chi Ling thought to himself, "That small mark at that distance! How could any one hit it?" So he assented, thinking he would have plenty of fighting after his host had missed the mark. Of course Liu Pei was willing.

They all sat down again and wine was served. When this had been drunk the host called for his bow and arrows. Yuan-te silently prayed that he would hit the mark.

Lu Pu turned back his sleeves, carefully fitted an arrow to the string and pulled the bow to its utmost stretch. A slight exclamation escaped him as the bow curved like the harvest moon sailing through the sky. "Twang!" went the bowstring and the arrow sped like a falling star. And it struck the slender tongue of the halberd head full and square. A roar of acclamation from all sides greeted the exploit.

> O Lu was a wonderful archer,
>   And the arrow he shot sped straight;
> By hitting the mark he saved his friend
>   That day at his yamen gate.
> Hou I, the archer of ancient days,
>   Brought down each mocking sun,
> And the apes that gibbered to fright Yuchi
>   Were slain by him, one by one.
> But we sing of Lu Pu that drew the bow,
>   And his feathered shaft that flew;
> For a myriad men could doff their mail
>   When he hit the mark so true.

Lu Pu laughed loud at the success of his shot. Dropping his bow he seized his guests by the hands saying, "The command of Heaven indeed! And now you cease from fighting!"

He ordered the soldier attendants to pour out great goblets of wine and each drank. Liu Pei in his inmost heart felt rather ashamed; his fellow guest sat silent, nodding his head. Presently he said, "I cannot disobey your command, General, but let me depart. What will my master say and will he believe me?"

"I will write a letter and confirm it," said Lu Pu.

After a few more rounds of the wine Chi Ling asked that he might have the letter and after that departed. When the brothers took their leave Lu Pu again reminded Liu Pei that he owed him his deliverance.

In a short time the soldiers had gone. Here nothing will be said of the entry of two of the actors in the drama into their own towns.

When Chi Ling had got back to Huainan and told the story of the feat of archery and the peace-making that followed, and had presented the letter, his lord was very wroth.

"He repays me for all my grain with this bit of play acting!" cried he. "He has saved Liu Pei, but I will lead a large army myself and settle him, and take Lu Pu too."

"Be careful, my lord," said Chi Ling. "He is braver and stronger than most men and has wide territory. He and Liu Pei together make a powerful combination, not easy to break. But there is another course. I have found out that his wife, the lady Yen, has a daughter just of marriageable age and as you have a son, you could arrange a marriage alliance with Lu Pu. If his daughter wedded your son he would certainly slay your enemy for you. This is the nothing-can-separate-relations plan."

This scheme appealed to Yuan Shu, who soon set about its accomplishment. He sent presents by the hand of Han Yin, who was to discuss the question. When Han saw Lu he spoke of the immense respect his master had for him and his desire to ensure perpetual alliance between the two families by a marriage, an alliance such as existed between the states Ts'in and Chin.

Lu Pu was well disposed toward the scheme, but went in to consult his wife. Now Lu Pu had two wives and one concubine. He first married a lady of the Yen family and she was the legal wife. Then he took Little Cicada as a concubine, and while he was living at Hsiaop'ei he had married a secondary wife, a daughter of Ts'ao Pao. She had died quite young leaving no issue. Neither had his concubine borne any children. So that he had but one child, this daughter, of whom he was dotingly fond.

When he broached the subject his wife said, "The Yuan's have dominated their part of the country these many years. They have a large army and are very prosperous. One day a Yuan will become Emperor and our daughter may hope to be an Empress. But how many sons has he?"

"Only this one."

"Then we should accept the offer. Even if our daughter does not become an Empress, Hsuchou is nothing to be sad about."

Lu Pu decided to accept and so treated the messenger with extreme generosity. Han Yin went back with a favourable answer. The wedding gifts were then prepared ready for Han Yin to take to the bride's family. They were received and banquets and merry-making filled all the time.

One day Ch'en Kung went to see the messenger in his lodging, and when the usual ceremonies and greetings had been exchanged, the two men sat down to talk. When the servants had been sent out of earshot Ch'en Kung said, "Who originated this scheme by which Yuan Shu and Lu Pu are to become connections by this marriage so that Liu Pei's head may fall?"

Han Yin was terrified. "I pray you not to let it get abroad," said he.

"I certainly shall keep it secret. But if there be any delay some other person will find it out and that spells failure."

"What had best be done?"

"I will see Lu Pu and get him to send the girl immediately so that the marriage may be concluded quickly."

"If it happened thus my master would indeed hold you in high respect."

With this Ch'en Kung took his leave and sought an interview with Lu Pu.

"I hear your daughter is to be married to Yuan Shu's son. That is capital, but no one knows when."

"That has yet to be considered."

"There were certain fixed rules as to the period between sending presents and consummation of the marriage; Emperors, a year; nobles, half a year; high officers, three months; and common people, one month."

Lu Pu replied, "As to Yuan Kung-lu, Heaven has already put into his hands one Imperial jewel and he will surely arrive at the dignity one day. So, I should think the Imperial rule would apply."

"No; it will not."

"The nobles' rule, then?"

"No; nor that."

"The high officers'?"

"Not even that."

Lu Pu laughed. Then you mean me to go by the rule for common people."

"Nor that either."

"Then what do you mean?"

"In the midst of the present troubles, when there is great rivalry between the nobles, do you not see that the others will be exceedingly jealous of your marriage alliance with such a family as the Yuans? Suppose you postpone the choice of the day, most likely when your fine morning arrives the wedding party will fall into an ambush on the road and the bride be carried off. Then what could be done? My opinion is that you would have done better to refuse. But since you have consented, then carry out the plan at once before the lords hear of it and so send the girl over without delay to Shouch'un. You can hire a lodging there till you have selected the wedding day and the odds are greatly against any failure."

"What you say is quite to the point," replied Lu.

He went into the private apartments to see his wife and told her the bride elect would set out immediately and the trousseau was to be prepared as far as it could be. On his side he chose some good horses and had a wedding carriage got ready. The escort consisted of Han Yin and two military officers. The procession went out of the city to the sound of music.

Now at this time Ch'en Kuei, father of Ch'en Teng (Yuanlung) was placidly waiting till the evening of his life passed into night. Hearing this burst of music he enquired the occasion and the servants told him.

"They are working on the 'Relatives-are-inseparable' device, then," said he. "Yuan-te is in danger."

Thereupon in spite of his many infirmities he went to see Lu Pu.

"Noble Sir, what brings you here?" asked Lu.

"I heard you were dead and I came to mourn," quavered the old man.

"Who said that?" exclaimed his host.

"Once upon a time you received grand presents from the Yuan's that you might slay Liu Pei, but you got out by that clever shot at your halberd. Now they suddenly seek a marriage alliance thinking to get hold of your daughter as a pledge. The next move will be an attack on Hsiaop'ei and, that gone, where are you? Whatever they ask in future, grain or men or anything else, and you yield, will bring your own end nearer, and make you hated all round. If you refuse, then you are false to the duties of a relative and that will be an excuse to attack you openly. Beside this Yuan Shu intends to call himself Emperor, which would be rebellion, and you would be of the rebel's family; something abominable, which the Empire would not suffer."

Lu Pu was much disturbed to hear this. "I have been misled!" cried he.

So he hurriedly sent Chang Liao to bring the wedding party back to the city. When they had come he threw Han Yin into prison and sent a reply to Yuan Shu saying curtly that the girl's trousseau was not ready and she could not be married till it was.

Han Yin was sent back to the capital. Lu Pu was hesitating what course to adopt, when he heard that Liu Pei was enlisting soldiers and buying horses for no apparent reason.

"He is simply doing his duty; there is nothing to be surprised at," said Lu Pu.

Then came two officers saying, "As you ordered us we went into Shantung to purchase horses. We had got three hundred when, on our way back, on the borders of Peihsien some robbers stole half of them. We hear that the real robbers were Chang Fei and his men, who took on the guise of brigands."

Lu Pu was very angry at this and began to prepare an expedition against Hsiaop'ei. When Liu Pei heard that an attack threatened he led out his army to oppose it and the two armies were arrayed. Liu Pei rode to the front and said, "Elder brother, why have you brought an army against me?"

Lu Pu began abusing him saying, "That shot of mine at the *yamen* gate saved you from grave danger; why then did you steal my horses?"

"I wanted horses and I sent out to buy them. Should I dare to take yours?" said Liu.

"You stole a hundred and fifty in the person of your brother Chang Fei. You only used another man's hand."

Thereupon Chang Fei, with his spear in rest, rode out saying, "Yes; I stole your good horses, and what more do you expect?"

Lu Pu replied, "You goggled-eyed thief! You are always treating me with contempt."

"Yes; I took your horses and you get angry. You did not say any thing when you stole my brother's city."

Lu Pu rode forward to give battle and Chang Fei advanced. A reckless fight began and the two warriors kept it up for a hundred bouts without a decisive stroke. Then Liu Pei, fearing some accident to his brother, hastily beat the gongs as a signal to retire and led his army into the city. Lu Pu then invested it.

Liu Pei called his brother and chid him as the cause of all this misfortune.

"Where are the horses?" said he.

"In some of the temples and courts," replied Fei.

A messenger was sent out to speak softly and offer to restore the stolen horses if hostilities were to cease. Lu Pu was disposed to agree but Ch'en Kung opposed. "You will suffer by and by if you do not remove this Liu Pei."

Under his influence the request for peace was rejected and the attack on the city pressed harder.

Liu Pei called Mi Chu and Sun Ch'ien to him to ask advice.

Said the latter, "The one person that Ts'ao Ts'ao detests is Lu Pu. Let us then abandon the city and take refuge with Ts'ao Ts'ao, from whom we may borrow men to destroy him."

"If we try to get away, who will lead the van?"

"I will do my best," said Chang Fei.

So he led the way. Kuan Yu was rearguard and in the centre was Liu Pei with the non-fighting portion. The cavalcade started and went out at the north gate. They met some opposition but the soldiers were driven off and the besieging force was passed without difficulty. Chang Liao pursued, but was held off by the rearguard. It seemed Lu Pu was not dissatisfied at the flight for he took no personal trouble to prevent it. He made formal entry into the city, settled local affairs and appointed a governor.

Liu Pei approached Hsutu and encamped outside the city, whence he sent Sun Ch'ien to see Ts'ao Ts'ao and relate the events that brought him there. Ts'ao was very friendly and said, "Liu Pei is as my brother." He invited him to enter the city.

Leaving his brothers at the camp Liu Pei, with Sun Ch'ien and Mi Chu, went to Ts'ao Ts'ao, who received him with the greatest respect. The story of Lu Pu's perfidy was again related.

"He has no sense of right," said Ts'ao Ts'ao. "You and I, my brother, will attack him together."

Yuan-te was very grateful. A banquet was then prepared and it was late evening before the visitor left for his own camp.

Hsun Yu then had an interview with his master and said, "If you are not on your guard Liu Pei will be your undoing. You ought to destroy him. He is too much of the hero."

Ts'ao made no reply and his adviser retired. Presently Kuo Chia came and Ts'ao Ts'ao said, "I have been advised to kill Liu Pei; what of such a scheme?"

"A bad scheme," said Kuo. "You are the popular champion, pledged to relieve the people from oppression and only by truth and rectitude can you secure the support of the nobleminded. Your only fear is lest they stay away. Now Liu Pei is famous. He has come to you for help and protection and to put him to death would be to alienate all good men and put fear into the hearts of all the able advisers. Hampered by these difficulties where will you find those whose help you need? To remove the dangers represented by one man and thereby injure yourself in the eyes of all mankind is a sure means of destruction. These conditions need careful consideration."

"What you say exactly fits in with what I think," said Ts'ao, greatly pleased with these remarks.

His next step was to memorialise the Emperor to give Liu Pei the governorship of Yuchou.

Again Ch'eng Yu said, "Liu Pei is certain to rise to the top; he will never remain in a subordinate position. You had better remove him."

"Now is just the time to make use of good men. I will not forfeit the regard of the world for the sake of removing one individual. Kuo Feng-hsiao and I both see this in the same light."

Wherefore he rejected all persuasion to work against Liu Pei but sent him soldiers and a large supply of grain, and set him on his way to Yu (Honan). He was to march to Hsiaop'ei, occupy it, call together his former soldiers and attack Lu Pu.

When Liu Pei reached Yuchou he sent to inform Ts'ao Ts'ao, who prepared to march an army to subjugate Lu Pu. But just then hasty news came that Chang Chi, who had gone to the attack of Nanyang, had been wounded by a stray arrow and had died. His nephew Hsiu had succeeded to the command of his army and with Chia Hsu as strategist, had joined Liu Piao and camped at Wanch'eng. They intended to attack the capital and get possession of the Emperor's person.

Ts'ao Ts'ao was placed in a quandary. He would go to attack this combination but he feared lest Lu Pu would attack the capital if he left it. So he sought the advice of Hsun Yu.

"Lu Pu has no notion of a policy. He is led astray by any little advantage that presents itself to his eyes. All you need do is to obtain promotion for him, giving him some additional title, and tell him to make peace with Yuan-te and he will do it."

"Good," said Ts'ao Ts'ao and he acted upon the hint and sent an officer with the official announcement and a letter urging peace, while he went on with preparations to meet the other danger. When ready he marched out in three divisions, Hsiahou Tun was the van-leader and they went to Yushui River and camped there.

Chia Hsu succeeded in persuading Chang Hsiu of the hopelessness of resistance.

"You would do well to surrender since his army is too large for you to oppose," said he.

Seeing the truth of this Hsiu sent his adviser to propose submission. Ts'ao Ts'ao was greatly pleased with the messenger, admiring his ready and fluent repartee, and tried to win him to his service.

"I was formerly with Li Ts'ui and was held guilty with him. Now I am with Chang who accepts my advice and I should not like to abandon him," said Chia Hsu.

He left and next day conducted his master into Ts'ao Ts'ao's presence. Ts'ao was generous. Then he entered Wanch'eng, the greater part of the army being put in camp outside where the lines extended some ten *li*. Great banquets were given every day and Ts'ao Ts'ao was always being entertained.

One day, when Ts'ao Ts'ao returned to his quarters in a more than usual merry mood, he asked the attendants if there were any singing girls in the city. The son of his elder brother heard the question and said, "Peeping through one of the partitions last evening I saw a perfectly beautiful woman in one of the courts. They told me she was the wife of Chang Hsiu's uncle. She is very lovely."

Ts'ao Ts'ao, inflamed by the description given him of the beauty, told his nephew to go and bring her to visit him. He did so supported by an armed escort and very soon the woman stood before him.

She was a beauty indeed and Ts'ao Ts'ao asked her name. She replied, "Thy handmaid was wife to Chang Chi; I was born of the Tsou family."

"Do you know who I am?"

"I have known the Minister by reputation a long time. I am happy to see him and be permitted to bow before him," said she.

"It was for your sake that I allowed Chang Hsiu to submit; otherwise I would have slain him and cut him off root and branch," said Ts'ao.

"Indeed, then, I owe my very life to you; I am very grateful," said she.

"To see you is a glimpse of paradise, but there is one thing I should like better. Stay here and go with me to the capital where I will see that you are properly cared for. What do you say to that?"

She could but thank him.

"But Chang Hsiu will greatly wonder at my prolonged absence and gossips will begin to talk," said she.

"If you like you can leave the city tomorrow."

She did so, but instead of going at once to the capital she stayed with him among the tents, where Tien Wei was appointed as a special guard over her apartments. Ts'ao was the only person whom she saw and he passed the days in idle dalliance with the lady, quite, content to let time flow by.

But Chang's people told him what had gone amiss and he was angry at the shame brought upon the family. He confided his trouble to Chia Hsu who said, "Keep this secret, wait till he appears again to carry on business and then. . . ."

A plan was arranged quite secretly.

Not long after this Chang Hsiu went into Ts'ao Ts'ao's tent to say that, as many of his men were deserting, it would be well to camp them in the centre and when permission was given the men of his old command were moved in and placed in four camps.

But Tien Wei, the especial guard of Ts'ao Ts'ao's tent, was a man to be feared, being both brave and powerful. It was hard to know how to attack him. So counsel was taken with an officer, Hu Ch'erh, a man of enormous strength and activity. He could carry a burden of six hundred pounds and travel seven hundred *li* in a day. He proposed a plan. He said, "The fearsome thing about Tien Wei is his double halberd. But get him to come to a party and make him quite drunk before you send him back. I will mingle among his escort and so get into his tent and steal away his weapon. One need not fear him then."

So the necessary arms were prepared and orders given in the various camps. This done the intended victim was invited and plied vigorously with wine so that he was quite intoxicated when he left. And, as arranged, the officer mingled with his escort and made away with his weapons.

That night, when Ts'ao Ts'ao was at supper with the lady, he heard the voices of men and neighing of horses and sent out to ask what it meant. They told him it was the night patrol going the rounds and he was satisfied.

Near the second watch of the night again was heard some noise in the rear of his tent and one of the fodder carts was reported to be burning.

"One of the men has dropped a spark; there is nothing to be alarmed at," said he.

But very soon the fire spread on all sides and became alarming. He called Tien Wei. But he, usually so alert, was lying down quite intoxicated.

However, the beating of gongs and rolling of drums mingling with his dreams awoke him and he jumped up. His trusty halberd had disappeared. The enemy was near. He hastily snatched up an infantryman's sword and rushed out. At the gate he saw a crowd of spearmen just bursting in. Tien Wei rushed at them slashing all around him and a score or more fell beneath his blows. The others drew back. But the spears stood around him like reeds on the river bank. Being totally without mail he was soon wounded in several places. He fought desperately till his sword snapped and was no longer of any use. Throwing it aside he seized a couple of soldiers and with their bodies as weapons felled half a score of his opponents. The others dared not approach, but they shot arrows at him. These fell thick as rain but he still maintained the gate against the assailants.

However, the mutineers got in by the rear of the camp and one of them wounded him in the back with a spear thrust. Uttering a loud cry he fell. The blood gushed from the wound in torrents and he died. Even after he was dead not a man, dared to come in by the main gate.

Ts'ao Ts'ao, relying on Tien Wei to hold the main gate, had fled in haste by the rear gate. His nephew accompanied him on foot. Then Ts'ao was wounded by an arrow in the arm and three arrows struck his horse. However, fortunately, the horse was a fine beast from Tawan full of spirit and, in spite of his wounds, he bore his master swiftly and well as far as the Yushui River.

Here some of the pursuers came up and his nephew was backed to pieces. Ts'ao Ts'ao dashed into the river and reached the further side, but there an arrow struck his steed in the eye and he fell. Ts'ao Ts'ao's eldest son dismounted and yielded his horse to his father, who galloped on. His son was killed but he himself got away. Soon after he met several of his officers who had rallied a few soldiers.

The soldiers under Hsiahou Tun seized the occasion to plunder the people. Yu Chin took his men fell upon them and slew many. Thus he protected and appeased the people. The plunderers, meeting Ts'ao Ts'ao on the road, knelt down howling and said Yu Chin had mutinied and attacked them. Ts'ao Ts'ao was surprised and when he met Hsiahou Tun, gave orders to attack Yu Chin.

Now when Yu Chin saw his master and a great company approaching he at once stopped the attack and set his men to make a camp. Hsun Yu asked him why.

"The Chingchou soldiers say you have turned traitor; why do you not explain now that the Minister has arrived? Why first make a camp?" said he.

He replied, "Our enemies are coming up in our rear and are very close. It is necessary to prepare for defence or we shall not withstand them. Explanation is a small matter, but defence is very important."

Soon after the camp was finished Chang Hsiu fell upon them in two divisions. Yu Chin himself rode out to face them. Chang drew back. The other leader, seeing Yu Chin advance thus boldly, also attacked and Chang Hsiu was overcome. They pursued him a great distance until his force was almost annihilated. With the miserable remnant he finally fled to Liu Piao.

Ts'ao Ts'ao's army reformed and the captains mustered. Then Yu Chin went to see his master and told him of the conduct of the Chingchou soldiers and their looting and why he had attacked them.

"Why did you not tell me before you made the camp?"

Yu Chin related what had occurred.

Said Ts'ao, "When the first thought of a leader in the time of greatest stress is to maintain order and strengthen his defences, giving no thought to slander but shouldering his burdens manfully, and when he thereby turns a defeat into a victory, who, even of the ancient leaders, can excel him?"

He rewarded Yu Chin with a service of plate and a marquisate. But he reprimanded Hsiahou Tun for his lack of discipline.

Sacrifices in honour of the dead warrior Tien Wei were instituted. Ts'ao himself led the wailing and paid due honours. Turning to his offices he said, "I have lost my first born son, but I grieve not so heavily for him as for Tien Wei. I weep for him."

All were sad at the loss of this captain. Then orders were issued to return but nothing will be said here of the march to the capital.

When Wang Tse, bearing the imperial decree, reached Hsuchou, he was met by Lu Pu, who conducted him into the residence where the decree was read. It conferred the title General, "Pacificator of the East," and a special seal accompanied the mandate. The private letter was also handed over and the messenger detailed the high appreciation in which Lu was held by the chief Minister of State.

Next came news that a messenger from Yuan Shu had arrived. When he had been introduced he said that Shu's project of declaring himself Emperor was advancing. He had already built a palace and would speedily choose an Empress and concubines and would come to Huainan.

"Has the rebel gone so far?" cried Lu Pu in a rage.

He put the messenger to death and Han Yin into the cangue. He drafted a memorial of thanks and sent it to the capital, at the same time sending, too, Han Yin, the unfortunate agent who had arranged the marriage alliance. He also replied to Ts'ao Ts'ao's private letter asking to be confirmed in his governorship.

Ts'ao was pleased to hear of the rupture of the marriage arrangement, and forthwith put Han Yin to death in the market place.

However, Ch'en Teng sent a secret remonstrance to Ts'ao Ts'ao, vilifying Lu Pu as cruel, stupid and facile and advising his destruction.

"I know Lu Pu quite well," said Ts'ao. "He is a wolf with a savage heart, and it will be hard to feed him for long. If it had not been for you and your father I should not have known all the circumstances and you must help me to get rid of him."

"Anything the Minister wishes to do shall have my assistance," was the reply.

As a reward Ts'ao Ts'ao obtained a grant of grain for the father and a prefecture for the son, who then took his leave. As he was saying farewell Ts'ao took him by the hand saying, "I shall depend upon you in the eastern affair."

Ch'en Teng nodded acquiescence. Then he returned to Lu Pu, who asked him how he had fared. Ch'en told him of the gifts to his father, which annoyed Pu.

"You did not ask Hsuchou for me, but you got something for yourself. Your father advised me to help Ts'ao Ts'ao by breaking off the marriage, and now I get nothing at all of what I asked while you and your father get everything. I have been victimised by your father."

He threatened Ch'en with his sword.

Ch'en Teng only laughed saying, "O how stupid you are, General!"

"I! How stupid?"

"When I saw Ts'ao, I said that to keep you going was like feeding a tiger. The tiger must be kept fully fed or he would eat men. But Ts'ao laughed and replied, 'No; not that. One must treat the marquis like a falcon. Not feed it till the foxes and hares are done. Hungry, the bird is of use; full fed it flies away.' I asked who were the quarry. He replied 'Yuan Shu, Sun Ts'e, Yuan Shao, Liu Piao, Liu Chang and Chang Lu; these are the foxes and hares.'"

Lu Pu threw aside his sword and laughed, saying, "Yes; he understands me."

But just about that time came news of the advance of Yuan Shu on Hsuchou and that frightened Lu Pu.

> When discord rose 'twixt Ts'in and Chin,
> They were attacked by Yueh and Wu,
> And when a promised bride ne'er came,
> An army marched to enforce the claim.

How all this fell out will be shown in the next chapter.

CHAPTER XVII

AN ARMY OF SEVEN DIVISIONS MARCHES OUT: THREE GENERALS ARE BROUGHT TOGETHER

Huainan was very fruitful, and Yuan Shu, as governor of such a large district, was very influential. He was not a little puffed up. The possession of the Imperial seal, pledged by Sun Ts'e, added to his pride. And he seriously thought of assuming the full style. As a preliminary he assembled all his officers and addressed them thus.—

"Of old Kao-Tsu, Founder of the Dynasty of Han, was only a very minor official and yet he became ruler of the Empire. The Dynasty has endured four centuries and its measure of fortune has run out. It no longer possesses authority; the cauldron is on the point of boiling over. My family has held the highest offices of State for four generations and is universally respected. Wherefore I wish, in response to the will of Heaven and the desire of the people, to assume the Imperial dignity. What think ye of the proposal, my officers?"

The Recorder, Yen Hsiang, rose in opposition at once. "You may not do this. Hou Chi, the Minister of the Chou Dynasty, was of distinguished virtue and held many offices, till in the time of Wen Wang he had two thirds of the Empire. Still he served and was loyal to the Yin Dynasty. Your house is honourable, but it is not so glorious as that of Chou. The Hans may be reduced, but they are not so abominably cruel as Tsou of the Yins. Indeed this should not be done."

Yuan Shu did not hear this with pleasure. "We Yuans came from Ch'en and he was a descendant of Shun (the Emperor). By the rule of interpreting the signs of fate the day has come when earth receives fire. Beside there is an oracle saying, 'He who replaces the Hans must wade through deep mire.' My name means 'the high road.' It fits exactly. Further than this, I possess the hereditary seal of State and must become lord of all or I turn from Heaven's own way. Finally I have made up my mind, so if any one says too much he will simply suffer death."

He arrogated himself the insignia of royalty. He set up officials with titles only given by an Emperor, and rode in a carriage decorated with the dragon and phoenix and offered sacrifices after the manner of an Emperor in the north and south suburbs. Also he appointed an "Empress" and an "Heir Apparent" (in the Eastern Palace) and pressed for the early wedding of Lu Pu's daughter with his son that the palace entourage might be complete.

But when he heard of the fate of his marriage ambassador he was very angry and began at once to plan for revenge. Chang Hsun was made Generalissimo having under his command more than twenty legions, in seven divisions under so many commanders, and each of these was instructed to make a certain town his objective. The Governor of Yenchou, Chin Shang, was ordered to superintend the commissariat, but he declined the office and so was put to death. Chi Ling was in command of the reserves to help wherever he was required. Yuan Shu led three legions and he appointed three tried officers to go up and down and see that the various armies did not lag behind.

Lu Pu found out from his scouts that his own city was Chang Hsun's objective; the other towns to be first attacked being Hsiaop'ei, Itu, Langya, Chiehshih, Hsiap'ei and Chunshan. The armies were marching fifty *li* a day, and plundering the countryside as they advanced.

He summoned his advisers to a council to which came Ch'en Kung, Ch'en Teng and his father. When all had assembled Ch'en Kung said, "This misfortune that has come to us is due to the two Ch'ens, who fawned upon the central government in order to obtain rank and appointments. Now remove the evil by putting these two to death and sending their heads to our enemy. Then he will retire and leave us in peace."

Lu Pu acquiesced and had the two arrested. But the son, Ch'en Teng, only laughed. "What is this anxiety about?" said he. "These seven armies are no more to me than so many heaps of rotting straw. They are not worth thinking about."

"If you can show us how to overcome them I will spare your life," said Lu.

"General, if you will listen to a poor stupid fool the city will be perfectly safe."

"Let us hear what you have to say."

"Yuan Shu's men are numerous but they are only a flock of crows; they are not an army under a leader. There is no mutual confidence. I can keep them at bay with the ordinary guards of the place and could overcome them by some unsuspected stratagem. If I should fail I have another plan by which I can not only protect the city but capture our enemy."

"Let us have it."

"Han Hsien and Yang Feng, two of the leaders of our enemies, are old servants of the Han dynasty who fled from fear of Ts'ao Ts'ao and, being homeless, sought refuge with Yuan Shu. He despises them and they are dissatisfied with his service. A little letter will secure their help as our allies, and with Liu Pei to help us on the outside we can certainly overcome Yuan."

"You shall take the letters yourself," said Lu.

He agreed and a memorial detailing his intentions was sent to the capital, letters to Yuchou to Liu Pei, and finally Ch'en Teng was sent, with a small escort, to wait for Han Hsien on the road to Hsiap'ei. When Han Hsien's army had halted and pitched camp Ch'en Teng went to see Han Hsien who said, "What are you here for? You belong to Lu Pu."

"I am a noble of the Court of the great Hans. Why do you call me a Lu Pu's man? If you, General, hitherto a Minister of State, now serve a traitor you nullify the grand services you rendered in protecting the Emperor and I despise you. Beside the suspicious Yuan Shu will assuredly do you some harm and you will regret not having taken this opportunity to work against him."

Han Hsien sighed. "I would return to my allegiance if there should be any opportunity."

Thereupon Ch'en Teng gave him the letter. Han read it and said, "Yes; I know. You may return to your master and say General Yang and I will turn our weapons and smite him. Look out for a signal-flare and let your master come to our aid."

As soon as Ch'en Teng had got back and reported his success, Lu Pu divided his men into five divisions and sent them to five points to meet his enemies. He himself led against the main body under Chang Hsun, leaving a guard in the city.

Lu Pu camped thirty *li* from the walls. When the enemy came up their leader thought Lu Pu too strong to attack with the force he had, so he retired twenty *li* to await reinforcements.

That night, in the second watch, Han Hsien and Yang Feng arrived and soon the flare was lighted as arranged. Lu Pu's men were admitted to the camp and caused great confusion. Then Lu Pu himself attacked and Chang Hsun was routed and fled. Lu Pu pursued till daylight when he fell in with one of the other bodies led by Chi Ling. Both sides faced each other, but at the very beginning of the engagement the two traitors also attacked and Chi Ling was forced to fly.

Lu Pu went in pursuit but soon another force came out from the rear of some hills. These looked very imposing. As the ranks opened he saw a leader's guard with flags bearing dragons and phoenixes and representations of the sun and moon, the four "measures,"* the five directions,† golden gourds, silver axes, yellow halberds, white yaks' tails, all Imperial emblems. And beneath a yellow silken parasol sat Yuan Shu on horseback, clad in silver mail with a sword handle showing at each wrist.

Standing out in front of the array he railed at his opponent calling him traitor and slave. Lu Pu said nothing but rode forward ready for battle and Li Feng, one of Yuan's leaders, advanced to take the challenge. They met, but at the third bout, Li was wounded in the hand, whereupon his spear fell to the ground and he fled. Lu Pu waved on the advance and his men prevailed. The other side fled, leaving much spoil, clothing, mail and horses.

Yuan Shu's defeated men had not gone far when a strong troop, led by Kuan Yu, appeared barring his way.

"Traitor! why have they not slain you?" cried Kuan Yu.

Whereat Yuan Shu fled in great trepidation and his army melted into fugitives in all directions. The new army fell upon them with great slaughter. Yuan Shu and the remnant of his army retreated into Huainan.

Victory being now secure, Lu Pu, in company with Kuan Yu, Yang Feng and Han Hsien returned to Hsuchou, where there were banquets and feastings and rewards for the soldiers. These over, Kuan took his leave and returned to his brother, while Han Hsien was appointed magistrate of Itu and his friend magistrate of Langya.

There had been a question of keeping these two in Hsuchou but Ch'en Kuei opposed it. "Let them hold those places in Shantung, which will be all yours within a year." So they were sent to these two cities in the meantime to await orders.

"Why not retain them here?" asked Ch'en Teng secretly of his father. "They would be a basis for our conspiracy against Lu Pu."

"But if they helped him, on the other hand, we should lengthen the tiger's claws and teeth," said his father.

So Teng could only approve of his father's precautions.

---

* Groups of stars similar to the Great Bear Constellation.
† Points of the compass, including the centre.

Yuan Shu returned home burning to avenge his defeat, so he sent to Chiangtung to ask a loan of men from Sun Ts'e. Ts'e said, "On the strength of holding the State Seal he secretly calls himself Emperor and rebels against the Hans. I would rather punish such a renegade than help him."

So he refused. The letter refusing help added to Yuan's anger. "What next from this callow youth?" cried he. "I will smite him before I deal with the other."

But Yang Ta-chiang dissuaded him from this course.

Having refused help to his powerful rival Sun Ts'e thought it wise to take measures for his own safety. So he stationed an army at Chiangk'ou. Soon after came a messenger from Ts'ao Ts'ao bearing his appointment as Prefect of Kueichi with orders to raise an army and reduce Yuan Shu.

Sun Ts'e was inclined to carry out these orders but he called a council at which Chang Chao opposed this course. Said he, "Although recently defeated Yuan Shu has many men and ample supplies. He is not to be attacked lightly. You had better write to Ts'ao Ts'ao persuading him to attack the south and we will be auxiliaries. Between the two armies Shu must certainly be defeated. If by the remotest chance we lose, we have Ts'ao Ts'ao to come to our rescue."

This plan was adopted and a messenger was sent to lay it before Ts'ao. In the meantime Ts'ao had reached Hsutu where his first thought was to institute sacrifices to his beloved lost leader Tien Wei. He conferred rank upon his son Tien Man and took him into his own palace to be cared for.

Presently arrived Sun Ts'e's messenger with letters and next came a report that Yuan Shu, being short of food, had made a raid on Ch'enliu. Ts'ao thought the moment opportune, so he issued orders for the expedition south, leaving Ts'ao Jen to hold the city. The army marched, horse and foot, seventeen legions, with commissariat waggons of food to the number of over a thousand. Messages were sent to summon Sun Ts'e, Liu Pei and Lu Pu to assemble on the Yuchang borders.

Liu Pei was the first to arrive and he was called in to the Minister's tent. After the usual salutations two human heads were produced.

"Whose are these?" asked Ts'ao in surprise.

"The heads of Han Hsien and Yang Feng."

"Why did this happen?"

"They were sent to control Itu and Langya and allowed their soldiers to plunder the people. Bitter complaints arose so I invited them to a banquet and my brothers despatched them when I gave the signal by dropping a cup. Their men gave in at once and now I have to apologise for my fault."

"You have removed an evil, which is a grand service: why talk of a fault?"

And he praised Yuan-te's action.

When the joint army reached Lu Pu's borders he came to meet it. Ts'ao Ts'ao spoke graciously to him and conferred upon him the title of Generalissimo of the Left, promising him a suitable seal as soon as he returned to the capital. Lu Pu was very pleased.

Then the three armies were made into one force, Ts'ao Ts'ao being in the centre and the other two on the wings. Hsiahou Tun and Yu Chin were leaders of the van.

On Yuan Shu's side Ch'iao Sui with five legions was appointed van leader. The armies met on the confines of Shouch'un. The two van leaders rode out and opened battle. Ch'iao Sui fell in the third bout and his men fled into the city.

Then came news that Sun Ts'e's fleet was near and would attack on the west. The other three land corps took each one face and the city was in a parlous state.

At this juncture Yuan Shu summoned his officers. Yang Ta-chiang explained the case. "Shouch'un has suffered from drought for several years and the people are on the verge of famine. Sending an army would add to the distress and anger the people, and victory would be uncertain. I advise not to send any more soldiers there, but to hold on till the besiegers are conquered by lack of supplies. Our noble chief, with his regiment of guards, will move over to the other side of the river, which is quite ready, and we shall also escape the enemy's ferocity."

So due arrangements being made to guard Shouch'un a general move was made to the other side of the Huai River. Not only the army went over but all the accumulated wealth of the Yuan family, gold and silver, jewels and precious stones, were moved.

Ts'ao Ts'ao's army of seventeen legions needed daily no inconsiderable quantity of food, and as the country around had been famine-stricken for several years nothing could be got there. So he tried to hasten the military operations and capture the city. On the other hand, the defenders knew the value of delay and simply held on. After a month's vigorous siege the fall of the city seemed as far off as it was at first and supplies were very short. Letters were sent to Sun Ts'e, who sent a hundred thousand measures of grain. When the usual distribution became impossible the Chief of the Commissariat, Jen Hsun, and the Controller of the

Granaries, Wang Hou, presented a statement asking what was to be done.

"Serve out with a smaller measure," said Ts'ao. "That will save us for a time."

"But if the soldiers murmur, what then?"

"I shall have another device."

As ordered the controllers issued grain in a short measure. Ts'ao sent secretly to find out how the men took this and when he found that complaints were general and they were saying that he was fooling them, he sent a secret summons to the controller. When he came Ts'ao said, "I want to ask you to lend me something to pacify the soldiers with. You must not refuse."

"What does the Minister wish?"

"I want the loan of your head to expose to the soldiery."

"But I have done nothing wrong!" exclaimed the unhappy man.

"I know that, but if I do not put you to death there will be a mutiny. After you are gone your wife and children shall be my care. So you need not grieve on their account."

Wang Hou was about to remonstrate further but Ts'ao Ts'ao gave a signal, the executioners hustled him out and he was beheaded. His head was exposed on a tall pole and a notice said that in accordance with military law Wang Hou had been put to death for peculation and the use of a short measure in issuing grain.

This appeased the discontent. Next followed a general order threatening death to the various commanders if the city was not taken within three days. Ts'ao Ts'ao in person went up to the very walls to superintend the work of filling up the moat. The defenders kept up constant showers of stones and arrows. Two inferior officers, who left their stations in fear, were slain by Ts'ao Ts'ao himself. Thereafter he went on foot to see that work went on continuously and no one dared be a laggard. Thus encouraged the army became invincible and no defence could withstand their onslaught. In a very short time the walls were scaled, the gates battered in and the besiegers were in possession. The officers of the garrison were captured alive and were executed in the market place. All the paraphernalia of imperial state were burned and the whole city wrecked.

When the question of crossing the river in pursuit of Yuan Shu came up Hsun Yu opposed it saying, "The country has suffered from short crops for years and we should be unable to get grain. An advance would weary the army, harm the people and possibly end in disaster. I advise a return to the capital to wait there till the spring wheat shall have been harvested and we have plenty of food."

Ts'ao Ts'ao hesitated and before he had made up his mind there came an urgent message saying Chang Hsiu, with the support of Liu Piao, was ravaging the country all round, that there was rebellion in Nanyang and Ts'ao Hung could not cope with it. He had been worsted already in several engagements and was in sore straits.

Ts'ao Ts'ao at once wrote to Sun Ts'e to command the river so as to prevent any move on the part of Liu Piao, while he prepared his army to go to deal with Chang Hsiu. Before marching he directed Liu Pei to camp at Hsiaop'ei, as he and Lu Pu, being as brothers, might help each other.

When Lu Pu had left for Hsuchou Ts'ao Ts'ao said secretly to Yuan-te, "I am leaving you at Hsiaop'ei as a pitfall for the tiger. You will only take advice from the two Ch'ens and there can be no mishap. You will find so-and-so your ally when needed."

So Ts'ao Ts'ao marched to Hsutu where he heard that Tuan Wei had slain Li Ts'ui and Wu Hsi had killed Kuo Ssu and they presented the heads of these two. Beside the whole clan of Li Ts'ui had been arrested and brought to the capital. They were all put to death at various gates and their heads exposed. People thought this very harsh dealing.

In the Emperor's palace a large number of officials were assembled at a peace banquet. The two successful leaders Tuan and Wu were rewarded with titles and sent to guard Ch'angan. They came to audience to express their gratitude and marched away.

Then Ts'ao Ts'ao sent in a memorial that Chang Hsiu was in rebellion and an army must be sent against him. The Emperor in person arranged the chariot and escorted his Minister out of the city when he went to take command of the expedition. It was the summer, the fourth month of the third year of the period Chien-An (199 A.D.). Hsun Yu was in chief military command in Hsutu.

The army marched away. In the course of the march they passed through a wheat district and the grain was ready for harvesting but the peasants had fled for fear and the corn was uncut. Ts'ao Ts'ao caused it to be made known all about that he was sent on the expedition by command of the Emperor to capture a rebel and save the people. He could not avoid moving in the harvest season but if any one trampled down the corn he should be put to death. Military law was so severe that the people need fear no damage. The people were very pleased and lined the road, wishing success to the expedition. When the soldiers passed wheat fields they dismounted and pushed aside the stalks so that none were trampled down.

One day, when Ts'ao Ts'ao was riding through the fields, a dove suddenly got up, startling the horse so that he swerved into the standing grain and a large patch was trampled down. Ts'ao at once called the Provost Marshal and bade him decree the sentence for the crime of trampling down corn.

"How can I deal with your crime?" asked the Provost Marshal.

"I made the rule and I have broken it. Can I otherwise satisfy public opinion?"

He laid hold of the sword by his side and made to take his own life. All hastened to prevent him and Kuo Chia said, "In ancient days, the days of the Spring and Autumn history, the laws were not applied to the persons of the most honourable. You are the supreme leader of a mighty army and must not wound yourself."

Ts'ao Ts'ao pondered for a long time. At last he said. "Since there exists the reason just quoted I may perhaps escape the death penalty."

Then with his sword he cut off his hair and threw it on the ground saying, "I cut off the hair as touching the head."

Then he sent a man to exhibit the hair throughout the whole army saying. "The Minister, having trodden down some corn, ought to have lost his head by the terms of the order; now here is his hair cut off as an attack on the head."

This deed was a stimulus to discipline all through the army so that not a man dared be disobedient. A poet wrote:—

> A myriad soldiers march along and all are brave and bold,
> And their myriad inclinations by one leader are controlled.
> That crafty leader shore his locks when forfeit was his head.
> O full of guile wert thou, Ts'ao Ts'ao, as every one has said.

One the first news of the approach of Ts'ao Ts'ao with an army Chang Hsiu wrote to Liu Piao for help. Then he sent out his men under command of Lei Hsu and Chang Hsien. When the array was complete Chang Hsiu took his station in front and pointing at Ts'ao Ts'ao railed at him saying, "O false and pretended supporter of benevolence and justice! O shameless one! You are just a beast of the forest, and absolutely devoid of humanity."

This annoyed Ts'ao Ts'ao who sent out Hsu Ch'u against the insulter. Chang Hsien came to meet him and fell in the third bout. Thence Chang Hsiu's men fled and were pursued to the very walls of Nanyang, only managing to get within just before the pursuit came up. The city was then closely besieged. Seeing the moat was so wide and deep that approach to the wall would be difficult they began to fill up the ditch with earth. Then with sand bags, brushwood and bundles of grass they built a great mound near the wall and on this erected steps so that they could look over into the city.

Ts'ao rode round the city closely inspecting the defences. Three days later he issued an order to make a mound of earth and brushwood at the north west angle, as he would mount the walls at that point. He was observed from within the city by Chia Hsu, who went to his chief and said, "I know what he intends and I can defeat him by a counter-move."

> E'en amongst the very foremost
> There is one who leads the way;
> Some one sees through your devices,
> Be as crafty as ye may.

What the counter-move was will be told in the next chapter.

CHAPTER XVIII

CHIA HSU ENGINEERS A GREAT VICTORY: HSIAHOU TUN LOSES AN EYE

Chia Hsu, as he had guessed the enemy's intention, had also devised a counter-move. So he went to his chief and said, "I saw Ts'ao Ts'ao very carefully reconnoitring round about the city and he certainly noticed that the south-east angle of the wall had been lately restored with mud bricks of a different kind and that the abatis is badly out of repair. He will try to effect an entrance there. Wherefore he is making a feint attack at the opposite point. He is piling up straw and making ostentatious preparations whereby to cajole us into withdrawing from the real point of attack to defend the north-west. His men will scale the walls in the darkness and try to enter at the south-east."

"Supposing your surmise is correct, what do you advise?" asked Chang Hsiu.

"The counter-move is plain. You issue an order for our best and bravest soldiers to fill their bellies, to take only the lightest outfit and conceal themselves in the houses near the south-east corner. Then disguise the towns people as soldiers and send them to pretend to defend the north-west. Tonight we will let the enemy climb up the walls and enter the city and, once they are fairly within, give the signal and the concealed soldiers will rush out upon them. We may even capture Ts'ao Ts'ao himself."

The stratagem was decided upon. Soon the scouts told Ts'ao that the defenders of the city had moved to the north-west where noisy preparations for defence were going on. The opposite corner was left undefended.

"They have fallen into my trap," said Ts'ao Ts'ao gleefully.

They prepared shovels and hooks and all the gear needed for scaling walls, and all day they kept up the attack on the north-west angle.

But at the second watch they despatched the veterans to the opposite corner, where they climbed the wall, broke up the abatis and got into the city apparently without disturbing any of the guards. There was no sign of life anywhere as they entered. But just as they were leaving the wall suddenly a bomb exploded and they found themselves in an ambush. They turned to retire, but Chang Hsiu immediately fell on the rear. Ts'ao's men were totally defeated and fled out of the gate into the country. Chang Hsiu kept up the pursuit till daybreak, when he retired into the city again.

Ts'ao Ts'ao then rallied his army and mustered his men. He had lost five legions and much baggage, while two of his captains, Lu Ch'ien and Yu Chin were wounded.

Ts'ao Ts'ao being thus worsted, Chang Hsiu wrote off to Liu Piao to cut off his retreat that he might be utterly destroyed.

An army was preparing for this purpose when a scout came to say that Sun Ts'e had encamped at Huk'ou. K'uai Liang urged the immediate departure of the expedition as he said this move of Sun Ts'e was part of Ts'ao Ts'ao's strategy and there would be never-ending regret if he were allowed to escape. Wherefore Liu Piao moved out with his army to Anchung, leaving Huang Tsu to hold the point of vantage. Chang Hsiu, having been informed of the movement to attack his enemy in the rear, went with Chia Hsu to smite him once more.

In the meantime Ts'ao Ts'ao's army, marching very leisurely, had arrived at Hsianch'eng. Walking one day beside the Yushui River he suddenly uttered a great cry, and when his officers asked the reason thereof he replied, "I remembered that here, only a year ago, I lost my great captain Tien Wei. Is that not a reason to grieve?"

Thereupon he gave orders to halt while he should make a great sacrifice and mourn for his lost leader. At the ceremony he himself burned incense and wailed and prostrated himself. The army was much affected by his devotion. After the sacrifices to the lost hero, he sacrificed to the names of his nephew Ts'ao An-ming and his eldest son Ts'ao An, both of whom had died at the same time. He also sacrificed to his lost soldiers and even to his steed which had been killed by an arrow.

Soon Hsun Yu wrote to tell him that Liu Piao had gone to help Chang Hsiu and was camped at Anchung, thereby cutting his road of retreat. Ts'ao replied to the letter saying, "I have been marching only a short distance each day and of course knew of the pursuit. But my plans are laid and, as I near Anchung, my enemy will be broken. You need not have any fears."

Then he hastened his march till he came near where Liu Piao had taken position. Chang Hsiu still followed. Ts'ao ordered his men during the night to open a secret way through a pass, where he laid an ambush.

With the first light of dawn Liu and Chang met. As Ts'ao Ts'ao's force looked small, they thought he had retired so they boldly advanced into the pass to smite him. Then the ambush was opened and both the attackers' forces were cut up. The fighting ended, Ts'ao's soldiers went outside the pass and encamped.

The two leaders on the other side restored order among their beaten men and then held a conference.

"How could we have foreseen such a wicked ruse?" said Liu Piao.

"Let us try again," said his colleague.

Wherefore they joined forces at Anchung.

But Hsun Yu discovered through his spies that Yuan Shao was preparing an attack on Hsutu, the then capital, so he at once wrote to Ts'ao Ts'ao who, much disturbed by this news, set out homeward at once. When Chang Hsiu heard this through his scouts he wished to follow the retreating army. Chia Hsu opposed it and said it would lead to a defeat. However Liu Piao was also of opinion that it was wrong to lose such a chance and so finally pursuit was decided upon.

They had not marched very far before they came upon Ts'ao's rear-guard, who fought with great vigour and bravery, so that the pursuers were beaten off and went home discomfited.

Chang Hsiu said to Chia, "This defeat comes from my not following your advice."

"Now set your army in order and pursue," said Chia.

"But we have just suffered defeat!" cried both leaders. "Do you now counsel pursuit?"

"Yes, and the result will be a great victory if you go now. I will venture my head on that," said Chia.

Chang Hsiu had confidence, but his colleague was afraid and would not accompany him. So one army only started in pursuit.

However, this was enough. Ts'ao Ts'ao's rear-guard was thoroughly routed and abandoned their waggons and their baggage in their hasty flight. Chang Hsiu pursued, but suddenly a troop came out from the shelter of some hills and checked him. Fearful to try further he hastened back to Anchung.

The other general, Liu Piao, asked the adviser to explain his apparent inconsistency. "When our veteran and brave soldiers were going to pursue those who retreated you said our men would lose the day; and when defeated men pursued the victors you foretold victory. You were right in both cases, but we wish you would enlighten us."

"It is easy to explain. You, Generals, although skilled leaders, are not a match for our enemy. Though the enemy had lost a battle he had able captains to keep the rear and guard against pursuit. Our men are good, but not a match for them. That is how I knew. Forasmuch as Ts'ao Ts'ao's hurried retreat was due to trouble in the capital and he had beaten off our men, I knew he would retire at his utmost speed and not take his usual precautions. I ventured to take advantage of his laxity."

Liu and Chang could not but affirm his complete understanding of the conditions.

On the advice of Chia Hsu then Liu Piao returned to Ching-chou, while Chang Hsiu took up his position at Hsiangch'eng so that each strengthened the other as the lips protect the teeth from cold.

When Ts'ao, during his retreat, heard that his army was being pursued he hastily turned back to support the rear-guard. Then he saw the pursuing army draw off. The soldiers of the beaten rear-guard said, "Had it not been for the troop that came out of the hills we should all have been lost."

"What troop?" asked Ts'ao Ts'ao in surprise.

The leader of the troop then advanced, slung his spear and, dismounting, made a low obeisance. He was Li T'ung, a captain of some rank and reputation from Chianghsia.

Ts'ao asked him why he had come.

Li T'ung replied, "I was in command at Junan when I heard of the struggle going on, so I came to lend you any help I could."

To show his gratitude Ts'ao conferred upon Li the title Marquis of Established Merit, and confirmed him in his command as a defence against Liu Piao. Then Li T'ung took his leave.

On his return to the capital Ts'ao Ts'ao presented a memorial on the good services rendered by Sun Ts'e and he was created Marquis of Wu with the title General "Captor of Rebels." The messenger bearing the decree bore also the order to repress Liu Piao.

Ts'ao Ts'ao went to his palace and there received the ceremonial calls of congratulation. These finished, Hsun Yu asked, saying, "You, Sir, marched very leisurely to Anchung; how came it that you felt certain of victory?"

Ts'ao replied, "He who retires and finds his retreat cut off fights desperately. I retired slowly to entice them into following whereby

I could do as I wished with them. Basing my movements on these considerations I felt secure."

Hsun bowed his head in admiration.

When Kuo Chia entered Ts'ao said, "Why so late, Sir?"

The visitor drew a letter from his sleeve saying to his master, "Yuan Shao sends this saying he desires to send an army to attack Kungsun Tsan and wishes you to lend provisions and men.

"I heard he was going to attack Hsutu; I suppose my return has made him change his intention," said Ts'ao.

Then he opened the letter and read it. It was couched in very arrogant terms.

"He is so exceedingly rude that I will attack him," said Ts'ao, "Only I think I am not quite strong enough. What should be done?"

"My lord, you know well who lost, and why, in the conflict between Liu Pang and Hsiang Yu; the former won only by superior wisdom. Hsiang Yu was the stronger, but in the end he was overcome. Your rival has ten weak points whereas you have ten strong ones, and, though his army is large, it is not terrible.

"Shao is over-much devoted to ceremony and deportment; while you are sympathetic and natural; this is an excellence in conduct. He is antagonistic and drives; you are conciliatory and lead; so you have the advantage of popular approval. For many years the government has been lax and he makes it more so: you strive vigorously after efficiency; this is the excellence of able administration. He is outwardly liberal but grudging at heart, and too given to nepotism: you appear exacting, but you understand and use men after their ability; this is the advantage of correct appreciation. He is a visionary and lacking in decision: you are a man of prompt decision and direct action; this is an advantage in policy. He loves to gather about him men of renown: you treat a man as you find him regardless of his reputation; this is where you excel in moral virtue. He is compassionate to those at hand, but careless about those out of sight: your care is all-embracing; this is where you excel in humanity. He lends a ready ear to calumny and is misled: you may be flooded with evil counsel, but you preserve independence; this is where you excel in perspicacity. His sense of right and wrong is confused: your appreciation is accurate and clear; this is where you excel in administrative capacity. He loves the make-believe force, but is ignorant of military essentials: you would overcome with far inferior numbers as you possess military genius; this is where you excel in war. With your ten superiorities you will have no difficulty in overcoming Shao."

"How can I be worth as much as you say?" said Ts'ao, smiling.

"What he has said about the ten points in your favour agrees exactly with what I think," said Hsun Yu. "Shao's army is not formidable in spite of its size."

"The real and dangerous enemy is Lu Pu," said Kuo Chia. "When Yuan Shao has gone north to destroy Kunsun Tsan, we ought to sweep away Lu Pu and so clear away our danger from that side, for if this is not done our attack on Shao will be the signal for an attempt on the capital. That would be most serious."

Ts'ao Ts'ao saw things in the same light as his advisers and began to discuss plans for an attack on Lu Pu. Sun Yu was of opinion that they should first secure the fidelity and aid of Liu Pei. So letters were written and they waited his assurance before moving a soldier. Then, in order to reassure Yuan Shao, his emissary was treated with great kindness and a memorial presented asking extra honours for him. With all this a private letter was written urging upon him to attack Kungsun and promising assistance. So Yuan Shao's army started.

In the meantime the two Ch'ens were playing their game. At every feast and gathering in Hsuchou they uttered the most fulsome praises of Lu Pu. Ch'en Kung was greatly displeased and took an opportunity to talk about them to his master. "They flatter you to your face, but what is in their hearts? You ought to be most carefully on your guard."

"Hold your tongue!" was the angry reply. "You are simply slandering them without the slightest excuse. You want to harm good men."

"No ears for loyal words"; said Ch'en Kung, as he went away sad at heart, "and we shall suffer."

He thought seriously of abandoning Lu Pu, but that would be too painful a wrench. Beside he feared people would laugh at him.

So the days passed sorrowfully for him. One day, with a few horsemen, he rode out to the country near Hsiaop'ei to hunt. On the high road he saw a messenger galloping along in hot haste and began to wonder what it might mean. He left the hunt, rode across country and intercepted the rider.

"Where are you from? Who sent you?" asked Ch'en Kung.

The messenger made no reply for he knew to what party his captors belonged. But they searched him and found a letter, the secret reply to Ts'ao Ts'ao's letter to Liu Pei. The messenger and the letter were both taken straight to Lu Pu. He questioned the man, who said he had been sent to Liu Pei with a letter and was now taking back the reply. He knew nothing more. He was ignorant of the contents of the letter. So Lu Pu tore it open and read:— "I have received your commands concerning the destruction of Lu Pu and dare I for a moment venture to disregard them? But my force is weak and I must act with extreme circumspection. If you move your main body, then I will hasten forward and in the meantime my men shall be got ready and weapons prepared. I await your command."

Lu Pu was really alarmed. "The wretch!" said he, "To dare to act thus!"

The unhappy messenger was put to death and counter-moves planned. Ch'en Kung and Tsang Pa went to enlist the help of the T'aishan bandits and take Yenchou in Shantung. Kao Shun and Chang Liao went to attack Liu Pei in P'eich'eng. Sung Hsieu and Wei Hsu went west to attack Juying and Lu Pu took command of a large body of men ready to afford help wherever needed.

The departure of the army under Kao Shun against Hsiaop'ei was told Liu Pei who assembled his officers at a council.

Sun Ch'ien advised sending a message to the capital to info Ts'ao Ts'ao of their danger and, in response to the chief's call. Chien Yung, a fellow-townsman of Liu Pei's, offered to take the message. Up to that moment he had served as a secretary. So a letter was written and the late secretary set out at once on his journey.

Then preparations were made for defence, Yuan-te commanding at the south gate and the two brothers and Sun Ch'ien taking each a gate. Mi Chu and his brother Fang commanded the family guard.

The two Mi's were put in command of the house guard because they were Liu Pei's brothers-in-law, he having taken a sister of Mi Chu as a second wife. Hence they were suitable men to guard the family.

In due course Kao Shun came to the south gate. Liu Pei ascended the tower and said, "I have no quarrel with your master, why do you come here with an army?"

"You have plotted with Ts'ao Ts'ao to injure my master as we know now; why should I not 'bind' you?"

So saying he gave the signal to attack. But Yuan-te did not go out to repulse him; he only kept the gate fast closed.

Soon after Chang Liao led an attack on the west gate, then kept by Yun-ch'ang, who addressed him from the wall.

"You are too good a man to waste yourself on rebels," said he.

Chang hung his head and made no reply.

Kuan Yu knew that he had a sound heart and high principles and said no more as he was unwilling to wound him. Nor did he go out to attack.

Chang Liao then drew off and proceeded to the east gate, and Chang Fei went out to give battle. Soon it was told Kuan Yu, who came over quickly. He saw Chang Fei going out, but Chang Liao was already withdrawing. Fei wished to pursue, but his brother held him back.

"He is afraid and so has gone away; it would be best to pursue," said Fei.

"No," said his brother. "As a warrior he is not inferior to either of us, but I have spoken a few straight words and they have sunk deep. He is repentant and that is why he will not meet us."

So Chang Fei understood and the gates were shut and orders given for careful defence.

When Liu Pei's messenger reached the capital he saw Ts'ao Ts'ao who told him what had happened. The advisers were called to discuss a plan. Ts'ao said, "I wish to attack Lu Pu. I fear not Yuan Shao, but Liu Piao and Chang Hsiu may attack me in the rear."

Hsun Yu replied. "Both these latter have been too recently defeated to do anything so rash. But Lu Pu is a bold fighting man, and if he joined forces with Yuan Shu and they set themselves to conquer Huai and Ssu* the problem would be difficult."

Then spoke Kuo Chia, "Let us take advantage of the moment before they have fully made up their mind. Smite before they are fully prepared." And Ts'ao Ts'ao did so. Five legions with four captains were sent in advance. Ts'ao commanded the rear army, which marched by divisions, and Chien Yung brought up the rear.

Soon the scouts informed Kao Shun. He sent flying messengers to Lu Pu, who detached two hundred horse to assist him. Kao Shun posted this reinforcement about thirty *li* from the city to meet Ts'ao's army. He followed close.

When Liu Pei saw the enemy retiring from the city he knew Ts'ao's army was close at hand. So, making arrangements for guarding the city within, he and his two brothers marched their men out of the city and made a camp, that they might be ready to assist.

Now the division of Ts'ao's army under Hsiahou Tun, having marched out in advance, first came into touch with Kao Shun. The former captain at once rode out with spear set and offered a challenge. It was accepted and the two leaders fought half a hundred bouts. Then Kao Shun began to weaken and had to own he had lost the day. His adversary pressed him hard and he rode

* The country about modern Kiangsu and south Shantung.

round to the rear of his array. Tun was not the man to quail so he followed right into the enemys country. Then Ts'ao Hsing, one of the captains, secretly strung his bow, fitted an arrow and, when Tun had come quite near, shot at him. The arrow hit Hsiahou Tun full in the left eye. He shrieked, and putting up his head, pulled out the arrow and with it the eye.

"Essence of my father, blood of my mother, I cannot throw this away," cried he, and he put the eye into the mouth and swallowed it.

Then resuming his firm grip of his spear he went after this new enemy.

There was no escape for Ts'ao Hsing. He was overtaken and fell with a spear wound full in the face. Both sides were stricken dumb with amazement.

Having thus slain the man who had wounded him Tun rode back toward his own side. Kao Shun went in pursuit and, waving on his men, attacked so vigorously that he won the day. Hsiahou Tun saved his elder brother, with whom he fled. The various divisions rallied at Chipei and made a camp there.

Kao Shun having scored this victory, returned to attack Liu Pei, and as Lu Pu opportunely arrived with Chang Liao, these three arranged their forces so that each attacked one of the brothers.

> Dauntless was Tun, that warrior hold,
> His courage had been proved of old;
> But smitten sore one hapless day,
> He might not in the battle stay.

The fate of Yuan-te will be told in the next chapter.

CHAPTER XIX

TS'AO TS'AO FIGHTS AT HSIAP'EI: LU PU PERISHES AT THE WHITE GATE TOWER

As was stated before, Kao Shun and Chang Liao together went to smite Kuan Yu, while Lu Pu attacked the younger brother's camp. Both brothers went out to give battle, while Liu Pei's force was held in reserve. Lu Pu attacked from the rear and the brothers were forced to flee. Liu Pei with a few score horsemen rushed back to P'eich'eng. As he approached the gate with Lu Pu pressing him close, he shouted to the soldiers on the wall to lower the drawbridge. Lu Pu was so close behind that the archers on the wall feared to shoot lest they should wound their lord and so Lu Pu got into the gate. The gate guards could not force him back so they scattered in all directions. Lu Pu led his force into the city.

Liu Yuan-te saw the position was too desperate for him to reach his residence and he must abandon all his family. So he hastened through the city and left by the west gate out at which he and his scanty following fled for very life.

When Lu Pu reached the residence he was met by Mi Chu who said, "The hero does not destroy a man's wife. Your rival for the Empire is Ts'ao Ts'ao, and my master, always mindful of the good turn you did him at your gate, would not be ungrateful. But he could not help going to Ts'ao Ts'ao and I think you will pity him."

Lu Pu replied, "We two are old friends; how could I bear to harm his wife and children?"

Whereupon he sent the family to Hsuchou with Mi Chu to take care of them. Next Lu led his army into Shantung to Yenchou, leaving Kao Shun and Chang Liao to guard Hsiao-p'ei.

During these troubles Sun Ch'ien had also fled out of the city and the two brothers, each with a handful of men, had got away to the hills. As Liu Pei with his few horsemen was making the best of their way from the scene of his defeat he heard some one coming up behind him. When he got closer the person proved to be Sun Ch'ien.

"Alas! I know not the fate of my brothers, whether they be alive or dead, and my wife and children are lost to me! What can I do?" said Liu Pei.

Sun replied, "I see nothing better than getting away to Ts'ao Ts'ao, whence we may be able to plan our future moves."

Liu Pei had no better plan to propose and the two men directed their way to Hsutu, choosing bye-roads rather than highways. When their small supplies ran out they entered a village to beg. But when the people of any place heard that Liu of Yuchou was the man who needed help they vied with each other in offering all that was required.

One day they sought shelter at a house whence a youth came out and made a low obeisance. They asked his name and he gave it as Liu An, of a well known family of hunters. Hearing who the visitor was the hunter wished to lay before him a dish of game, but though he sought for a long time nothing could be found for the table. So he came home, killed his wife and prepared a portion for his guest. While eating Liu Pei asked what flesh it was and the hunter told him "wolf." Yuan-te knew no better and ate his fill. Next day at daylight, just as he was leaving, he went to the stables in the rear to get his horse and passing through the kitchen he saw the dead body of a woman lying on the table. The flesh of one arm had been cut away. Quite startled he asked what this meant, and then he knew what he had eaten the night before. He was deeply affected at this proof of his host's regard and the tears rained down as he mounted his steed at the gate.

"I wish I could go with you," said Liu An, "but as my mother still lives I cannot go so far from home."

Liu Pei thanked him and went his way. The party took the road by Liangch'eng and as they were going out they saw not far off a thick cloud of dust. When the troop came nearer they found they were men of Ts'ao Ts'ao's army, and with them they travelled to the main camp where they found Ts'ao Ts'ao himself. He wept at the sad story of Liu's distress, the loss of the city, his brothers and wife and children. When he told him of the hunter who had sacrificed his wife to feed them Ts'ao sent the hunter a present of a hundred ounces of silver as a reward.*

* An editor here remarks in a note, "With a hundred ounces of silver Liu An could get himself another wife, but I am afraid no one would marry him. And what then? No woman could help reflecting that she might have to serve as the 'game' course in a chance visitor's dinner."

The march then was continued to Chipei, where Hsiahou Yuan welcomed them. They heard that his brother was still ill from the wound he had received in the eye. Ts'ao Ts'ao went to the sick man's bedside to see him and had him removed to Hsutu for skilled treatment.

Presently scouts, sent out particularly for tidings of Lu Pu, returned saying that he had allied himself with the bandits in the east and they were attacking Yenchou. At this Ts'ao Ts'ao despatched Ts'ao Jen with three companies to take P'eich'eng, while he, in conjunction with Liu Pei, moved against Lu Pu.

They went east. As they neared Artemisia Pass (Hsiao Kuan) they met the T'aishan brigands with three legions barring their road. However, they were easily beaten back and were chased right up to the pass.

The scouts told Lu Pu, who was then in Hsuchou, whither he had gone to start an expedition to save Hsiaop'ei. He left the protection of his city to Ch'en Kuei and set out with Ch'en Teng.

As this latter was starting Ch'en Kuei said to him, "Remember the words of Ts'ao Ts'ao, that the business of the east is in our hands. Now is our moment for Lu Pu is about to suffer defeat."

"Father, your son can look after the outside. But when he returns beaten you must arrange with Mi Chu to keep him out of the city. I shall find a means of escape," said Teng.

"His family is here and he has many friends. How about them?"

"I also have a scheme to settle them."

Then he went to see Lu Pu, to whom he said, "Hsuchou is surrounded and this city will be fiercely attacked. We ought to provide for possible retreat and I advise storing grain and money in Hsiaop'ei. We could retreat there if the day went adversely. Why not see about this in good time?"

"Your words are indeed wise. I will also send my wife and little ones thither," said Lu.

The family left under escort and with them was sent much grain and silver. And then the soldiers marched to the relief of the pass. About half way there Ch'en Teng said, "Let me go first to reconnoitre so that you, my lord, may advance with confidence."

Thus Ch'en Teng parted company with his chief and preceded him to the pass where he was received by Ch'en Kung. He said, "The Marquis greatly wonders why you do not advance. He is going to enquire into it."

"The enemy is in great force and we cannot be too careful," said Kung. "We are holding the pass and you should persuade our master to take steps to guard P'eich'eng."

Ch'en Teng muttered to himself and said no more. That evening he went up to the heights from which he could see Ts'ao's army, which was quite close to the pass. Then he wrote three notes, tied them to arrows and shot them into Ts'ao's camp.

Next day he left and hastened back to Lu Pu. "Those bandits are about to give up the pass to the enemy, but I have left Ch'en Kung to hold it. You had better make an attack tonight and hold him."

"Had it not been for you the pass would have been lost," said Lu.

Then he sent Ch'en Teng back to arrange a signal with Ch'en Kung for simultaneous action. So Teng returned to Kung to whom he said, "Ts'ao's men have found a secret way through the pass and I fear Hsuchou is already lost. You ought to go back at once."

At this the pass was abandoned and Kung began to retreat. Then the prearranged signal was given.

Lu Pu advanced in the darkness to the relief of the pass. Presently he met Ch'en Kun's men, and as neither recognised the other in the darkness a fierce battle ensued. Nor was the trick discovered till daylight came.

While these things were going on Ts'ao Ts'ao had noted the signal and advanced as fast as possible. The bandits, who alone remained to hold the pass, were easily driven out and scattered in all directions.

When daylight came and the trick was discovered Lu Pu and Ch'en Kung set off together for Hsuchou. But when they arrived and summoned the gate, instead of opening the doors the men on the wall saluted them with a thick flight of arrows. At the same time Mi Chu appeared on the defence tower and shouted, "You stole our master's city and now we are going to give it back to him. You will not enter here again."

"Where is Ch'en Kuei?" cried Lu Pu, angrily.

"We have slain him," was the reply.

"Where is that son of his?" said Pu turning to Ch'en Kung.

"Do you still hold to your delusion, General, that you ask where this specious rogue is?"

Lu Pu bade them search through all the ranks, but he was not to be found. Then they decided to go to Hsiaop'ei. But ere they had got half way there suddenly appeared the troops under the command of Kao Shun and Chang Liao. They said Ch'en Teng had come to them saying their lord was surrounded and wanted help so they had come at once.

"Another trick of that false rogue!" said Lu Pu. "Surely he shall die for this."

They went with all speed to the city, only to see as they drew near the ensigns of the enemy displayed all along the walls, for the city had been taken by Ts'ao Jen.

While Lu Pu stood at the foot of the rampart reviling the traitor Ch'en Teng, Teng himself appeared on the wall and pointing to Lu Pu cried, "Did you think that I, a Minister of the Dynasty, would serve a rebel like you?"

Lu Pu in his wrath was about to make a desperate attack but suddenly a great noise was heard and an army came up behind him. It was led by no other than Chang Fei.

Kao Shun went to engage him, but he had no chance of success. Lu Pu then joined in the fray. Then another army appeared, and the leader this time was Ts'ao Ts'ao himself, and his army rushed to the attack. Seeing that he had no hope of victory Lu Pu went away toward the east, with Ts'ao Ts'ao in pursuit. His army marched till they were worn out. Then appeared a new force under Kuan Yu. Holding his sword ready to strike he called out, "Do not flee, O Lu Pu, Kuan Yu is waiting for you."

Lu Pu joined battle; he was flurried and scarce knew what was happening. And soon Chang Fei came up once more. By desperate efforts Lu Pu and his men cut their way through the press and got free. After this they started for Hsiaop'ei as fast as they could travel and Hou Ch'eng helped to keep the pursuers at bay.

So the two brothers Kuan Yu and Chang Fei were together again after their separation. Both shed tears of joy as they told each other what they had seen and suffered.

"I was on the Haichow road when I heard of you," said Yun-ch'ang. "I lost no time in starting."

"And I had been camped in the Mangtang Hills for a long time. It is happiness to be together again."

So they talked. Then they marched off together to find their elder brother, and made their salutations with tears. In Yuan-te's heart sadness and joy intermingled. Next they were presented to Ts'ao Ts'ao and with him they went into the captured city.

Mi Chu soon came with the welcome news of the safety of the family. And the two Ch'en's, betrayers of Lu Pu, came to present their salutations. A grand banquet was prepared for the officers at which Ts'ao Ts'ao presided as host and Ch'en Kuei and Yuan-te occupied the seats of honour. At the close of the banquet Ts'ao Ts'ao paid the two Ch'ens the highest compliments on their success and rewarded them with the revenues of ten departments beside giving the son the title of *Fu-po Chang-chun* or General, "Queller of Waves."

Ts'ao Ts'ao was very pleased with his success and at once began to scheme for the taking of Hsiaop'ei, the sole place now left to Lu Pu, where he had taken refuge. Ch'eng Yu said the course was inadvisable.

"If Lu Pu be pressed too hard he may get clear by a desperate effort and throw himself into the arms of our especial enemy Yuan Shu. These two as allies would be difficult to overcome. Rather send a capable man to guard Huainan, one able to secure you against Lu Pu on one hand and to hold Yuan Shu on the other. Moreover the bandits are in Shantung and still our enemies. They must be watched."

Ts'ao replied, "I can keep the whole of Shantung and I will request Yuan-te to take the south."

"Could I dare withstand your command?" said Yuan-te.

So forthwith Liu Pei, leaving Mi Chu and Chien Yung at Hsuchou, went south, taking in his train his brothers and Sun Ch'ien. And Ts'ao led his army to Hsiaop'ei.

Lu Pu felt very secure in his refuge. He had good store of grain and he had the protection of the river, so he sat quiet, satisfied that he could maintain his defence. So he allowed Ts'ao's army to approach without molestation.

"You ought to attack Ts'ao's army as they come up before they have time to make camps and defences. They will only have fatigued men to oppose to your fresh troops and you will certainly defeat them."

So said Ch'en Kung but Lu Pu replied, "I have suffered too many defeats lately to take any risk. Wait till they actually attack and you will see them floating away on the waters."

So he neglected the confidant's advice and waited till the enemy had settled into their camp. This done, the attackers advanced against the city. From the foot of the wall Ts'ao Ts'ao called to Lu Pu to listen while he spoke. Lu Pu ascended to the wall where he stood.

Ts'ao addressed him, saying, "When I heard that your family and that of Yuan Shu were likely to be united by marriage I sent an army against you, for Yuan was guilty of treason while you had to your credit the destruction of Tung Cho. For what reason have you sacrificed all your merits to throw in your lot with a rebel? It will be over late to regret when this city shall have fallen. But if you surrender and help me to support the ruling house you shall not lose your rank of Marquis."

Lu Pu replied, "If the Minister will retire we may be able to discuss the matter."

But Ch'en Kung, standing near his master, began to rail at Ts'ao Ts'ao for a rebel and shot an arrow that struck his plumed helmet.

"My oath, but I will slay *you* at least!" cried Ts'ao, pointing his finger at Ch'en Kung.

Then the attack on the walls began.

"They have come from far and cannot maintain this for long," said Ch'en Kung. "General, go out with your horse and foot and take up a position outside, leaving me to maintain the defence with the remainder of our men. If he engages you, I will come out and strike at his rear ranks; if he attacks the city, you can come to our aid. In a few days their stores will fail and we can beat them off. This will place them between the horns."

"The advice seems good," said Lu Pu.

He went back to his palace and prepared his weapons. As it was the depth of winter he made his men take plenty of wadded clothing to keep them warm. His wife heard of it and came to ask whither he was going. He told her of Ch'en Kung's plan.

She said, "My lord, you are leaving an undamaged city, abandoning your wife and little ones and going with a paltry force. Should any untoward event happen will your handmaid and her lord ever meet again?"

Lu Pu hesitated, and for three days made no move. Then Ch'en Kung came to see him again and said, "The enemy are all round the city and unless you go out soon you will be quite hemmed in."

"I am thinking it would be better to maintain a stubborn defence," said Lu.

"Our enemies are short of food and have sent for supplies to Hsutu. These will soon arrive and you should go out with some veterans and intercept the convoy. That loss would be a heavy blow."

Lu Pu agreed and went in to tell his wife the new plan. She wept saying, "If you go do you think those others equal to the defence of the city? Should anything go wrong you would be very sorry. You abandoned me at Ch'angan and it was only through the fortunate kindness of P'ang Hsu that I was hidden from our enemies and rejoined you. Who would have thought you would leave me again? But go, go your way as far as you wish, and do not mind your wife?"

And she wept bitterly. Lu Pu very sadly went to take leave of Little Cicada who said, "You are my lord, you must not be careless and ride out alone."

"You need not fear; with my mighty halberd and the Hare, my swift steed, who dare come near me?"

He went out. He met Ch'en Kung and said, "That story about supplies for Ts'ao Ts'ao is all false, one of his many ruses I am not going to stir."

Ch'en Kung sighed; he felt all was lost.

"We shall die and no man shall know our burying place," said he.

Thereupon Lu Pu remained in his own quarters with his women folk, drinking freely to dissipate his sorrows. Two of his advisers went in and proposed that he should write to the powerful Yuan Shu for help. Yuan would hardly refuse to rescue the affianced bride of his son. So he wrote and bade these two take the letter.

Hsu Ssu said, "You ought to send a strong escort with us to force a way through."

So Lu told off a company and two captains to conduct his messenger beyond the pass. They started that same night at the second watch, Chang Liao leading and Ho Ming bringing up the rear. They got out of the city, crept past Yuan-te's camp and got beyond the danger zone. Then half the escort went on and Chang Liao led the remainder back toward the city. At the pass he found Yun-ch'ang waiting. However, at that moment Kao Shun came to his help and they all returned and re-entered the gates.

The two messengers presently reached Shouch'un, saw Yuan Shu and presented the letter.

"How is this?" said Shu. "Formerly he slew my messenger and repudiated the marriage; now he sends to ask for it.

"It is all due to the vile plans of that monster Ts'ao Ts'ao. I pray you, Illustrious Sir, to consider it carefully," replied Ssu.

"But if your master was not hemmed in by his enemy and in imminent danger he would never have thought of renewing this proposal of marriage."

The messengers said, "You may decide not to help him, but the teeth are cold when the lips are gone. It will not make for your happiness and comfort."

Said Shu, "Feng-hsien is unreliable; tell him that I will send soldiers after the girl has arrived here."

This was final and the two messengers took leave. When the party reached Yuan-te's camp they decided to try to get through in the darkness, the escort remaining behind to protect their rear. They tried that very night and the two messengers crept across without discovery. But the escort found themselves faced by Chang Fei. Ho Ming tried to fight but was captured in the very first bout and the men of his half company were either killed or they fled.

The prisoner was taken to Yuan-te, who forwarded him to the

main camp. There he told the story of the marriage and the scheme to save the city. Ts'ao Ts'ao was angry and ordered the execution of the prisoner at the main gate.

Then he sent orders to each camp to exercise the greatest diligence with threats of rigorous punishment of the officers of any corps that permitted any communication between the besieged and the outer world.

Every soldier felt mightily afraid. Yuan-te returned to camp and cautioned his brothers saying, "We are in the most important place with regard to Huainan and you must be very careful not to allow any breach of this command."

Chang Fei was inclined to grumble, "We have just captured one of the enemy's leaders," said he, "and there is no word of praise or reward for us; nothing but new orders and threats. What do you make of that?"

"You are wrong to complain," said Yuan-te. "These are orders of the Commander-in-Chief and what would happen were there no orders? Do not disobey them, brother."

They promised obedience and withdrew.

In the meantime the messengers had got back to Lu Pu and told him what Yuan Shu had said, that if the girl came the soldiers should go.

"But how can she be sent?" said Pu.

"That is the difficulty. Ho Ming's capture means that Ts'ao Ts'ao knows the whole plan of getting help from the south. I do not see how any one but you yourself could hope to get through the close siege."

"Suppose we tried, today?" said Lu Pu.

"This is an ill-omened day; you must not try today. Tomorrow is a very lucky day, especially in the evening, for any military action."

Then Lu Pu ordered Chang Liao and Kao Shun to get ready three companies for the venture and to prepare a light carriage. He would lead till they had got a couple of hundred *li* away. Thence they could escort the bride-elect the remainder of the way to her new home.

Next evening toward the second watch Lu Pu wrapped up his daughter in soft wadded garments, bound her about with a mailed coat and took her on his back. Then with his mighty halberd in hand, he mounted his steed and rode at the head of the cavalcade out of the city gate. The two captains followed.

In this order they approached Yuan-te's camp. The drums at

once beat the alarm and the two younger brothers barred the way.

"Stop!" they shouted.

Lu Pu had no desire to fight; all he wished was to get through so he made for a side road. Yuan-te came in pursuit and the two parties engaged. Brave as he might be, Lu Pu was almost helpless now that he was hampered by a girl on his shoulders, whom he was desperately anxious to preserve from hurt. Beside other parties came up all shouting and attacking and he had no alternative but to give up his project and return into the city. He reached his palace very sad at heart. The besiegers returned to camp well pleased that no one had got beyond their lines.

Lu Pu found consolation in the wine cup. The siege had gone on for two months and still the city stood, when they heard that Chang Yang, Prefect of Honei, had been inclined to come to the help of Lu Pu. But one of his subordinates had assassinated him and was bringing his head as an offering to Ts'ao Ts'ao, when he also had been slain by one of the Prefects friends. He had then gone to Tach'eng.

In the camp of the besiegers there now arose much murmuring. The officers grumbled saying, "Though Chang Yang, who meant to hurt us, is happily no more, yet we are threatened on the north by Yuan Shao and on the east Piao Hsiu is a menace. Here we meet with no success against the city. We are for leaving Lu Pu to his fate and returning home. We need a rest."

Among them Hsun Yu fought against this discontent. "You must not act like this," said he. "Lu Pu has lost much and his spirit is broken. The spirit of the leader expresses that of his men, and when the leader fails his men do not fight. Ch'en Kung is clever but nothing is done. Lu Pu broken, Ch'en Kung without decision, it only needs a sharp attack and we shall succeed."

"I have a plan to propose," said Kuo Chia, "a plan to overcome the city at once; it beats twenty legions."

"I suppose you mean drowning the city," said Hsun Yu.

"That is it," said the proposer, smiling.

Ts'ao Ts'ao accepted the suggestion with joy and set his men to cut the banks of the I and Ssu Rivers, and moved his men to the high ground whence they watched the drowning out of Hsiaop'ei. Only the east gate remained clear of water.

The besieged soldiers hastened to their leader. He said, "Why should I fear? My good horse can go as well through the water as over the land." And he again returned to the wine cup for consolation, drinking deeply with his wife and concubine.

The continual drinking bouts told at last and Lu Pu began to look dissipated. Seeing himself in a mirror one day he was startled at the change and said to himself, "I am injuring myself with wine; no more from this day forward."

He then issued an order that no one should drink wine under penalty of death.

Now one of his captains, Hou Ch'eng, lost fifteen horses, stolen by one Hou Ts'ao, who intended them for Yuan-te. The owner found out where they were, went out after them and recovered them. And his colleagues congratulated him on his success. To celebrate the occasion he brewed a few *catties* of wine to be drunk at the feast, but thinking his chief might find him in fault he sent the bottles of wine to his palace with a petition explaining that by virtue of his lord's warlike renown he had recovered his horses and asking that he and his comrades might be allowed a little wine at their feast.

Lu Pu took it very angrily saying, "When I have forbidden all wine you brew some and begin to give feasts; you are simply defying me." Whereupon he ordered the officer to instant execution. However, a number of his colleagues came in and interceded and after a time Lu Pu softened.

"You ought to lose your head for this disobedience, but for the sake of your colleagues the punishment shall be reduced to a hundred strokes."

They tried to beg him off this, but only succeeded in reducing the number of blows to one half.

When the sentence had been carried out and the offender was permitted to return home his colleagues came sadly to console him.

"Had it not been for you I should have been put to death," said Hou Ch'eng.

Sung Hsien replied, "All he cares for is his family, there is no pity for any one else. We are no more than the weeds by the roadside."

Wei Hsu said, "The city is besieged, the water is drowning us out. There will not be much more of this for we may die any day."

"He is a beast, with neither a sense of humanity nor of right. Let us leave him," said Hsien.

"He is not worth fighting for. The best we could do would be to seize him and hand him over to Ts'ao Ts'ao."

"I was punished because I got my horses back again, yet all he trusts in is his own steed. If you two will betray the gate and seize Lu Pu I will steal the horse and go out to Ts'ao's camp."

They settled how to carry out the plot and that very night Hou

Ch'eng sneaked into the stables and got the Hare away. He hastened to the east gate which was opened to let him through. The guard made a pretence of pursuing him but only a pretence.

Hou Ch'eng reached the besiegers' camp, presented the horse and told Ts'ao what had been arranged. They would show a white flag and open the gates to his army. Hearing this Ts'ao had a few notifications written out, which were attached to arrows and shot over the walls. This is one of them:— "The General Ts'ao Ts'ao has received a command to destroy Lu Pu. Those who interfere with the operations of his grand army, whatever their rank, shall be put to death in the gate on the day that the city shall be captured. Should any one capture Lu Pu or bring his head he shall be well rewarded. Let all take note of this."

Next day at daylight a tremendous hubbub was heard without the city and Lu Pu, halberd in hand, hasted to the wall to see what it meant. As he went from gate to gate inspecting the defences and guards he censured Wei Hsu for letting Hou Ch'eng escape and get away with his horse. He threatened to punish him. But just then the besiegers began a fierce attack as the white flag had just appeared and Lu Pu had to turn all his energies to defence. The assault lasted till noon, when the attacking force drew off for a time.

Lu Pu was taking a rest in the tower and fell asleep in his chair. Sun Hsien sent away his attendants, and when they had gone he stole his master's weapon, the halberd in which he trusted. Then he and Wei Hsu fell upon Lu together and before he was well awake had bound him with cords, trussing him 'so that he could not move. Lu Pu shouted for his men, but they were driven off by the two traitors and could not come near. Then a white flag was shown and the besiegers again approached the city. The traitors shouted out that Lu Pu was a prisoner. But Hsiahou Yuan could hardly believe it till they threw down the famous halberd.

The gates were flung open and the enemy entered the city. Kao Shun and Chang Liao, who were at the opposite gate, were surrounded and cut off by the water and helpless. They were captured. Ch'en Kung made a dash to the south gate but was also taken. Presently Ts'ao Ts'ao entered and at once gave orders to turn the streams back into their usual courses. He put out proclamations soothing the people.

He and Liu Pei seated themselves side by side in the White Gate Tower, with Kuan Yu and Chang Fei in attendance. The captives, to the number of a thousand, were brought before them. Lu Pu looked a pitiable object. Although a very tall man he was tied up in a veritable ball.

"The bonds are very tight," cried he, "I beseech you to loosen them."

"A bound tiger frets of course," replied Ts'ao.

Seeing the three traitors standing there looking pleased at their success Pu said, "I treated you all well enough; how could you turn against me?"

Said Sung Hsien, "You listened to the words of your women but rejected the advice of your captains. Was not that mean?"

Lu Pu was silent. Then Kao Shun was brought forward.

"What have you to say?" asked Ts'ao.

Shun sulkily held his tongue and was ordered out to execution.

Next Ch'en Kung was led in.

"I hope you have been well since we last saw each other, Kungt'ai?" said Ts'ao.

"Your ways were crooked and so I left you," said Ch'en.

"You say I was crooked; and what of your serving Lu Pu?"

"Though he was a fool, he did not resemble you in deceit and wickedness."

"You say you are able enough and clever, but what about your position today?"

Turning toward Lu Pu, Ch'en Kung said, "This man would not follow my advice. Had he done so he would not now be a captive."

"What think you ought to be done about this day's work?" said Ts'ao.

"There is death for me today and that is the end," shouted Ch'en Kung.

"Very well for you; but what of your mother and your wife?"

"It is said that he who rules with due regard to filial piety does not harm a man's family; he who would show benevolence does not cut off the sacrifices at a man's tomb. My mother and my wife are in your hands. But since I am your prisoner I pray you to slay me quickly and not to try to harrow my feelings."

Ts'ao's heart still leaned toward mercy, but Ch'en Kung turned and walked away, repulsing the attendants who would stop him. Ts'ao rose from his place and walked with him, the tears falling from his eyes. Ch'en Kung never looked at him. Turning to his men Ts'ao said, "Let his mother and family be taken to Hsutu and looked after. This insolent fellow must die."

The condemned man heard him but uttered no word. He stretched out his neck for the blow. Tears sprang to the eyes of all present. His remains were honourably coffined and buried in Hsutu.

A poem pitying his fate says:—

Neither hope of life nor fear of death moved him.
How brave was he, A hero indeed!
But his lord heeded not his words,
Wherefore in vain Possessed he great talents.
Nevertheless, in that he stood by his master,
To parting with wife and mother,
He merits our pity and profound respect.
Who would not resemble Kung-t'ai
That day he died at the White Gate?

While Ts'ao sadly escorted Ch'en Kung on the way to death, Lu Pu appealed to Yuan-te, "Noble Sir, you sit there an honoured guest while poor I lie bound at your feet. Will you not utter one word to alleviate my lot?"

Yuan-te nodded. As Ts'ao Ts'ao returned to his place his prisoner called out, "Your only trouble, Illustrious Sir, is myself and I am on your side now. You take the lead, I will help you and together the world is at our feet."

"What do you think?" said Ts'ao turning to Liu Pei.

"You are willing to forget the episodes of Ting Yuan and Tung Cho?"

"Truly the lout is not to be trusted," said Lu Pu, looking at Yuan-te.

"Strangle and expose," said Ts'ao.

As he was led away the prisoner turned once more to Yuan-te, "You long-eared lout, you forget now the service I rendered you that day at my *yamen* gate, when my arrow hit the mark."

Just then some one shouted, "Lu Pu, O fool! death is but death, and why are you scared at it?"

Every one turned to look; the lictors were hustling Chang Liao to the place of judgement.

A poet has written upon the death of Lu Pu:—

The flood spreads wide, the city drowns,
Its lord is captive. Nought avails
His courser's speed or halberd's thrust.
The tiger erstwhile fierce, now whines
For mercy. Ts'ao had meted him
Full well, a falcon flown at will
And hungry kept. Poor fool! He let
Ch'en Kung's advice be overborne
By harem tattle; vainly now
He rails against the Long-eared Childe.

And another poem says:—

> Bound is the hungry tiger, eater of men, for whom is no pity,
> Since the blood of his victims is fresh and not yet dry.
> Yuan-te spoke no word in favour of Lu Pu,
> To whom even a father's life was not sacred.
> How could he save him to be a menace to Ts'ao Man.

It was recorded earlier that the executioners were hustling Chang Liao forward. Pointing to him as he stood there Ts'ao said, "He has a fine face."

"You were not likely to forget me; you saw me before in P'uyang," said Liao.

"O, so you remember me, eh?"

"Yes; more's the pity."

"Pity for what?"

"That the fire that day was not fierce enough to burn you up, rebel that you are."

Ts'ao began to get angry. "How dare you insult me?" cried he and lifted his sword to kill the bold speaker.

The undaunted Chang Liao never changed colour, but stretched out his neck for the blow. Then a man behind Ts'ao Ts'ao caught his arm and in front of him another dropped on his knees, saying, "O Minister, I pray thee stay thy hand."

> Lu Pu whining was not spared,
> Railing Chang far better fared.

Who was it that saved Chang Liao? The next chapter will show.

CHAPTER XX

TS'AO A-MAN ORGANISES A HUNTING
EXPEDITION: TUNG, "STATE UNCLE,"
RECEIVES A COMMAND IN THE PALACE

The last chapter said that Ts'ao Ts'ao was checked in his angry attack upon Chang Liao. It was Liu Pei who held his arm and Kuan Yun-ch'ang who knelt before him.

"A man as generous-hearted as he is should be saved," said Liu.

Kuan said, "I know him well as loyal and righteous. I will vouch for him with my own life."

Ts'ao threw aside his sword. "I also know Wen-yuan to be loyal and good; I was just testing him," said he.

He loosed the prisoner's bonds with his own hands, had a change of dress brought in and clothed him therewith. Then he was led to a seat of honour. This kindly treatment sank deep into Chang's heart and he hastened to declare formally that he yielded. And then he was given a rank and the title of marquis. He was sent on a mission to win over Tsang Pa, who hearing what had happened, came forthwith and gave in his submission. He was graciously received and his former colleagues also yielded, with the exception of Chang Hsi, who remained obdurate. All these former enemies who came over were kindly treated and given posts of responsibility wherein they might prove the reality of their conversion. Lu Pu's family were sent to the capital.

After the soldiers had been rewarded with feastings the camp was broken up and the army moved away to Hsutu. Passing through Hsuchou the people lined the roads and burned incense in honour of the victors. They also petitioned that Liu Pei should be their governor.

Ts'ao Ts'ao replied, "Liu *Shih-chun* has rendered great services. You must wait till he has been received in audience and obtained his reward. After that he shall be sent here,"

Ch'e Chou, a General of Cavalry, was given command of

Hsuchou for the moment. After the army had arrived at the capital rewards were granted to all the officers who had been in the expedition. Liu Yuan-te was retained in the capital, lodging in an annexe to the Minister's palace. Soon after a Court was held and Ts'ao Ts'ao represented the services of Yuan-te who was presented to the Emperor Hsien. Dressed in Court robes he bowed at the lower end of the audience arena. The Emperor called him to the Hall and asked his ancestry.

Liu Pei replied, "Thy servant is the son of Liu Hung, grandson of Liu Hsiung, who was a direct descendant of Prince Ching of Chungshan, who was the great-great-grandson of His Majesty the Emperor Ching (about 150 B.C.)."

The Emperor bade them bring forth the Books of the Genealogies and therefrom a secretary read: "The filial Emperor Ching begat fourteen sons of whom the seventh was Liu Sheng, Prince Ching of Chungshan. Sheng begat Chen, Marquis (T'ing-hou) of Luch'eng; Chen begat Ang, Marquis P'ei; Ang begat Lu, Marquis Chang; Lu begat Lien, Marquis of Ishui; Lien begat Ying, Marquis of Ch'inyang; Ying begat Chien, Marquis Ankuo; Chien begat Ai, Marquis Kuanglu; Ai begat Hsien, Marquis of Chiaoshui; Hsien begat Hsu, Marquis of Tsuyi; Hsu begat I, Marquis of Ch'iyang; I begat Pi, Marquis of Yuantse; Pi begat Ta, Marquis of Yingch'uan; Ta begat Pu-i, Marquis of Fengling; Pu-i begat Hui, Marquis of Chich'uan; Hui begat Hsiung, Governor of the Eastern Districts; Hsiung begat Hung, who held no office or rank and Liu Pei is his son."

The Emperor compared this with the registers of the Imperial House and found by them that Liu Pei was his uncle by descent. He seemed greatly pleased and requested Liu Pei to go into one of the side chambers where he might perform the ceremonial obeisance prescribed for a nephew to his uncle. In his heart he rejoiced to have this heroic warrior-uncle as a powerful supporter against Ts'ao Ts'ao who really held all the power in his own hands. The Emperor knew himself to be a mere puppet. He conferred upon his uncle, the rank of General and the title of Marquis of Ich'eng.

When the banquet was concluded Yuan-te thanked the Emperor and went out of the palace. And from this time he was very generally styled Liu, "Uncle of the Emperor."

When Ts'ao Ts'ao returned to his palace Hsun Yu and his fellow advisers went in to see him. Hsun Yu said, "It is no advantage to you, Illustrious Sir, that the Emperor recognises Liu as an uncle."

"He may be recognised as uncle, but he is under my orders since I control the decrees of the throne. He will be all the more ready to obey. Beside I will keep him here under the pretence of having him near his sovereign and he will be entirely in my hands. I have nothing to fear. The man I fear is Yang Piao, who is a relative of the two Yuans. Should Yang conspire with them he is an enemy within and might do much harm. He will have to be removed."

Hence Ts'ao sent a secret emissary to say that Yang Piao was intriguing with Yuan Shu and on this charge Piao was arrested and imprisoned. And his death would have been compassed had his enemy dared.

But just then the Prefect of Pohai, K'ung Jung, was at the capital and he remonstrated with Ts'ao Ts'ao saying, "Yang comes from a family famed for virtue for at least four generations; you cannot trump up so foolish a charge as that against him."

"It is the Court," retorted Ts'ao.

"If Prince Ch'eng had put Duke Chao to death, could Duke Chou have pretended ignorance?"

So Ts'ao had to relinquish the attempt, but he took away Yang's offices and banished him to his family estate in the country.

A certain Chao Yen, a minor official but an opponent of the Minister, sent up a memorial impeaching Ts'ao for having removed a Minister of State from office without a decree. Ts'ao's reply to this was the arrest of Chao and his execution, a bold stroke which terrified the bulk of officers and reduced them to silence.

Ch'eng Yu advised Ts'ao to assume a more definite position. He said, "Illustrious Sir, your prestige grows daily; why not seize the opportunity to take the position of Chief of the Feudatory Princes?"

"There are still too many supporters of the Court," was the reply. "I must be careful. I am going to propose a royal hunt to try to find out the best line to follow."

This expedition being decided upon they got together fleet horses, famous falcons and pedigree hounds, and prepared bows and arrows in readiness. They mustered a strong force of guards outside the city.

When the Minister proposed the hunting expedition the Emperor said he feared it was an improper thing to do.

Ts'ao replied, "In ancient times rulers made four expeditions yearly at each of the four seasons in order to show their strength. They were called Sou, *Miao, Hsien* and *Shou,* in the order of the seasons. Now that the whole country is in confusion it would be wise to inaugurate a hunt in order to tram the army. I am sure Your Majesty will approve."

So the Emperor with the full paraphernalia for an Imperial hunt joined the expedition. He rode a saddle horse, carried an inlaid bow, and his quiver was filled with gold-tipped arrows. His chariot followed behind. The three brothers were in the Imperial train, each with his bow and quiver. Each wore a breastplate under the outer robe and held his especial weapon, while their escort followed them. Ts'ao Ts'ao rode a dun horse called "Flying Lightning" and the army was ten legions strong.

The hunt took place in Hsut'ien and the legions spread out as guards round the hunting arena which extended over some two hundred square *li*. Ts'ao Ts'ao rode even with the Emperor, the horses' heads alternating in the lead. The imperial suite immediately following were all in Ts'ao's confidence. The other officers, civil and military, lagged behind, for who dared press forward into the midst of Ts'ao's partizans?

One day the Emperor was riding near Hsut'ien and noticed his newly found uncle respectfully standing by the roadside.

"I should like to see my uncle display his hunting skill," said the Emperor.

Liu Pei mounted his steed at once. Just then a hare started from its form: Yuan-te shot and hit it with the first arrow.

The Emperor, much struck by this display, rode away over a slope. Suddenly a deer broke out of the thicket. He shot three arrows at it but all missed.

"You try," said the Emperor turning to Ts'ao.

"Lend me Your Majesty's bow," he replied, and taking the inlaid bow and the golden-barbed arrows he pulled the bow and hit the deer in the shoulder at the first shot. It fell in the grass and could not run.

Now the crowd of officers seeing the golden-barbed arrow sticking in the wound concluded at once that the shot was the Emperor's, so they rushed up and shouted "*Wansui!* O King, live for ever!" Ts'ao Ts'ao rode out pushing past the Emperor and acknowledged the congratulations.

They all turned pale. What did this mean? Liu Pei's brother Kuan who was behind him was especially angry. The sleeping caterpillar eyebrows stood up fiercely and the red phoenix eyes glared as, sword in hand, he rode hastily forth to cut down the audacious Minister for his impertinence. However, his elder brother hastily waved him back and shot at him a meaning glance so that he stopped and made no further move.

Yuan-te bowing toward Ts'ao said, "Most sincere felicitations! A truly supernatural shot, such as few have achieved !"

"It is only the enormous good fortune of the Son of Heaven!" said Ts'ao with a smile.

Then he turned his steed and felicitated the Emperor. But he did not return the bow; he hung it over his own shoulder instead.

The hunt finished with banqueting and when the entertainments were over they returned to the capital, all glad of some repose after the expedition. Kuan Yu was still full of the Minister's breach of decorum.

One day he said, "Brother, why did you prevent me from killing that rebel and so ridding the world of a scoundrel? He insults the Emperor and ignores everybody else."

"When you throw stones at a rat, beware of the vase," quoted Yuan-te. "Ts'ao Ts'ao was only a horse's head away from Our Lord and in the midst of a crowd of his partizans. In that momentary burst of anger, if you had struck and failed, and harm had come to the Emperor, what an awful crime would have been laid to us!"

"If we do not rid the world of him today, a worse evil will come of it," said Kuan.

"But be discreet, my brother. Such matters cannot be lightly discussed."

The Emperor sadly returned to his palace. With tears in his eyes he related what had occurred in the hunt to his consort the Empress Fu.

"Alas for me!" said he. From the first days of my access one vicious minister has succeeded another. I was the victim of Tung Cho's evil machinations; then followed the rebellion of Li Ts'ui and Kuo Ssu. You and I had to bear sorrows such as no others have borne. Then came this Ts'ao Ts'ao as one who would maintain the imperial dignity, but he has seized upon all real authority and does as he wishes. He works continually for his own glorification and I never see him but my back pricks. These last few days in the hunting field he went in front of me and acknowledged the cheers of the crowd. He is so extremely rude that I feel sure he has sinister designs against me. Alas, my wife, we know not when our end may come!"

"In a whole Court full of nobles who have eaten the bread of Han, is there not one who will save his country?" said she.

Thus spake the Empress, and at the same moment there stepped in a man who said, "Grieve not, O Imperial Pair! I can find a saviour for the country."

And who was this? It was none other than the father of the Empress, Fu Wan.

"Have you heard of Ts'ao Ts'ao's wanton and perverse behaviour?" said the Emperor, drying his eyes.

"You mean the deer shooting? Who did not see that indeed? But the whole Court is full of his clan or his creatures. With the exception of the relatives of your Consort there is not one loyal enough to deal with a rebel. I have no authority to do anything, but there is General Tung Ch'eng, the State Uncle, who could do it."

"Could Uncle Tung come in to consult about this? I know he has had much experience of State troubles."

Wan replied, "Every one of your attendants is a partizan of Ts'ao's and this sort of thing must be kept most profoundly secret or the consequence will be most serious."

"Then what can be done?" said the Emperor.

"The only plan I can think of is to send gifts of a robe and a jade girdle to Tung, and in the lining of the girdle hide a secret edict authorising him to take certain steps. When he gets home and has read the edict he can elaborate plans as quickly as possible and neither the spirits above nor the demons below will know anything about them."

The Emperor approved and Fu Wan went out. The emperor then with his own hand drew up a decree, writing it with blood drawn by biting his finger. He gave the document to his consort to sew into the purple lining of the girdle. When all was done he put on the robe and girded it with the girdle. Next he bade one of the attendants summon Uncle Tung to the palace.

Tung Ch'eng came and after the ceremonies were finished the Emperor said, "A few nights ago I was talking with the Empress of the terrible days of the rebellion and we thought of your good services then, therefore we have called you in to reward you."

The minister bowed his head in thanks. Then the Emperor led Tung out of the Reception Hall to the *T'ai Miao* or Temple of Ancestors, and they went to the gallery of Worthy Ministers, where the Emperor burned incense and performed the usual ceremonies. After this they went to see the portraits and among them was one of the Founder of the Dynasty, Han Kao-Tsu.

"Whence sprang our great ancestor and how did he begin his great achievement?" said the Emperor.

"Your Majesty is pleased to joke with thy servant," said Tung Ch'eng, rather startled at the question. "Who does not know the deeds of the Sacred Ancestor? He began life as a minor official in Ssushang. There gripping his sword he slew the White Serpent, the beginning of his struggle for the right. Speedily he mastered the Empire; in three years had destroyed Ts'in and, in five, also Ch'u. Thus he set up a Dynasty that shall endure for ever."

"Such heroic forefathers! such weakling descendants! How sad it is!" said the Emperor.

Pointing to the portraits right and left he continued, "Are not these two Chang Liang, Marquis Liu, and Hsiao Ho, Marquis Ts'uan?"

"Certainly. Your great ancestor was greatly assisted by these two."

The Emperor glanced right and left. His attendants were rather far away. Then he whispered to Tung Ch'eng, "You, like these two, must stand by me."

"My poor services are of no worth; I do not compare with those men," said the Uncle.

"I remember that you saved me at the western capital. I have never forgotten and I could never reward you." Then pointing to his own robe the Emperor continued, "You must wear this robe of mine, girded with my own girdle, and it will be as though you are always near your Emperor."

Tung Ch'eng bowed his gratitude while the Emperor, taking off the robe, presented it to his faithful Minister. At the same time he whispered, "Examine it closely when you get home, and help your Emperor carry out his intention."

Tung Ch'eng understood. He put on the robe and the girdle, took leave and left the chamber.

The news of the audience for Tung Ch'eng had been taken to the Minister, who at once went to the Palace and arrived as Tung Ch'eng was passing out at the gate. They met face to face and Tung Ch'eng could in nowise avoid him. He went to the side of the road and made his obeisance.

"Where are you from, State Uncle?" asked Ts'ao Ts'ao.

"His Majesty summoned me into the Palace and has given me this robe and beautiful girdle."

"Why did he give you these?"

"He had not forgotten that I saved his life in the old days."

"Take it off and let me see it."

Tung Ch'eng who knew that a secret decree was hidden away somewhere in the garments was afraid Ts'ao Ts'ao would notice a breach somewhere in the material, so he hesitated and did not obey. But the tyrant called his servants. So he took off the girdle. Then Ts'ao looked it over carefully. "It certainly is a very handsome girdle," said he. "Now take off the robe and let me look at that."

Tung Ch'eng's heart was melting with fear but he dared not disobey. So he handed over the robe. Ts'ao took it and held it up against the sun with his own hand and minutely examined every part of it. When he had done this he put it on, girded it with the girdle and turning to his suite said, "How is it for length?"

"Beautiful!" they chorussed.

Turning to Tung Ch'eng he said, "Will you give these to me?"

"My King's presents to me I dare not give to another. Let me give you another robe in its stead," said Tung.

"Is there not some intrigue connected with these presents? I am sure there is," said Ts'ao.

"How could I dare?" said Tung, trembling. "If you are so set upon it then I must give it up."

"How could I take away what your King has given you? It was all a joke," said the Minister.

He returned both robe and girdle and their owner made the best of his way home. When night came and he was alone in his library, he took out the robe and looked over every inch of it most carefully. He found nothing.

"He gave me a robe and a girdle and bade me look at them carefully. That means there is something to be looked for but I can find no trace of it. What does it mean?" he soliloquised.

Then he lifted the girdle and examined that. The jade plates were carved into the semblance of small dragons interlaced among flowers. The lining was of purple silk. All was sewn together most carefully and neatly and he could find nothing out of the common. He was puzzled. He laid the belt on the table. Presently he picked it up and looked at it again. He spent long hours over it but in vain. He leaned over on the small table, his head resting on his hands and was almost asleep, when a candle snuff fell down upon the girdle and burned a hole in the lining. He hastily shook it off, but the mischief was done: a small hole had been burned in the silken lining, and through this there appeared something white with blood red marks. He hastily ripped it open and drew out the decree written by the hand of the Emperor himself in characters of blood.

It read, "Of human relationships, that between father and son stands first; of the various social ties that between Prince and Minister stands highest. Today Ts'ao Ts'ao, the wicked is a real tyrant, treating even his Prince with indignity. With the support of his faction and his army he has destroyed the principles of government. By conferring rewards and inflicting punishments he has reduced the Emperor to a nonentity. I have grieved over this day and night. I have feared the Empire would be ruined.

"You are a high Minister of State and my own relative, You must recall the difficulties of the great Founder's early days and draw together the loyal and right-minded to destroy this evil faction and restore the prerogatives of the Throne. Such a deed would be indeed an extreme joy to the spirit; of my ancestors.

"This decree, written in blood drawn from my own veins, is

confided to a noble who is to be most careful not to fail in executing his Emperor's design.

" Given in the era Established Tranquillity, fourth year and the third month of Spring."

So ran the decree and Tung Ch'eng read it with streaming eyes. There was no sleep for him that night. Early in the morning he returned to his library and re-read it. No plan suggested itself. He laid the decree down on the table and sought in the depths of his mind for some scheme to destroy Ts'ao Ts'ao, but could not decide upon any. And he fell asleep leaning over his table.

It happened that a certain official, Wang Tzu-fu, with whom he was on terms of great intimacy, came to visit him and, as usual, walked into the house unannounced and went straight to the library. His host did not wake and Wang noticed, hardly hidden by his sleeve, the Emperor's writing. Wondering what this might be he drew it out, read it and put it in his own sleeve. Then he called out loud, "Uncle Cheng, are you not well? Why are you asleep at this time of day?"

Tung Ch'eng started up and at once missed the decree. He was aghast; he almost fell to the ground."

"So you want to make away with Ts'ao Ts'ao? I shall have to tell him,' said Wang.

"Then, brother, that is the end of the Hans," said his host,

"I was joking," said Wang. "My forefathers also served the Hans and ate of their bounty. Am I devoid of loyalty? I would help you, brother, as far as lies in my power."

"It is well for the country that you think like this," said Tung.

"But we ought to have a more private place than this to talk over such plans and pledge ourselves to sacrifice all in the cause of Han."

Tung Ch'eng began to feel very satisfied. He produced a roll of white silk and wrote his own name at the top and signed it, and Wang followed suit. Then the visitor said, "General Wu Tzu-lan is one of my best friends, he ought to be allowed to come in."

Ch'eng replied, "Of all the officials of the Court Ch'ung Chi and Wu Shih are my best friends. Certainly they would back me up."

So the discussion proceeded. Presently a servant announced no other than these very two men.

"This is providential," said Tung Ch'eng and he told his friend to hide behind a screen.

The two guests were led into the library and after the exchange of the ordinary civilities and a cup of tea, Ch'ung Chi referred to the incident at the hunt and the shooting of the stag. "Were you not angry at that?" said he.

Tung Ch'eng answered, "Though we be angry, what can we do?"

Wu Shih struck in, "I would slay this fellow, I swear, but I cannot get any one to back me up."

"Though one should perish for one's country one should not mind," said Ch'ung Chi.

At this moment Wang Tzu-fu appeared from behind the screen, saying, "You two want to kill Ts'ao! I shall have to let him know this. And Uncle Tung is my witness."

"A loyal Minister does not mind death. If we are killed we will be Han ghosts, which is better than being sycophants of a traitor."

Tung Ch'eng said, "We were just saying we wanted to see you two on this matter. Wang is only joking."

Then he drew forth the decree and showed it to the two new-comers, who also wept as they read it. They were asked to add their names.

Tzu-fu said, "Wait here a few moments till I get Wu Tzu-lan to come."

He left the room and very soon returned with his friend, who also wrote his name in the presence of all the others.

After this they went into one of the inner chambers to drink success to the new plot. While there a new visitor, Ma T'eng, Prefect of Hsiliang, was announced.

"Say I am indisposed," said the host, "and cannot receive visitors."

The doorkeeper took the message, whereat Ma angrily said, "Last night at the Tunghua Gate I saw him come out in robe and girdle. How can he pretend illness today? I am not come from mere idleness, why does he refuse to see me?"

The doorkeeper went in again and told his master what the visitor had said and that he was very angry. Then Ch'eng rose, excused himself saying he would soon return, and went to receive Ma T'eng. After the visitor had saluted and they were both seated, he said, "I have just come from a farewell audience and wished to bid you adieu. Why did you want to put me off?"

"My poor body was taken suddenly ill; that is why I was not waiting to welcome you," said Ch'eng.

"You do not look as if you were ill; your face wears the very bloom of health," said T'eng bluntly.

His host could say no more and was silent. The visitor shook out his sleeves and rose to depart. He sighed deeply as he walked down the steps, saying to himself, "Not one of them is any good: there is no one to save the country."

This speech sank deeply into Tung Ch'eng's heart. He stopped his guest, saying, "Who is no good to save the country? Whom do you mean?"

"That incident at the hunt the other day, the shooting of the stag, filled my breast with anger. But if you, a near relative of the Emperor, can pass your time in wine and idle dalliance without a thought of doing away with rebellion, where can any one be found who will save the dynasty?"

However, Tung Ch'eng's doubts were not set at rest. Pretending great surprise he replied, "The Minister is of high rank and has the confidence of the Court: why then does he utter such things?"

"So you find that wretch Ts'ao a good man, eh?"

"Pray speak lower: there are eyes and ears very near us."

"The sort of people who covet life and fear death are not those to discuss any great undertaking."

So saying he rose to go away. By this time his host's doubts were set at rest: he felt that Ma T'eng was loyal and patriotic. So he said, "Do not be angry any more. I will show you something."

Whereupon he invited Ma T'eng to go into the room where the others were seated and then showed him the decree. As Ma read it his hair stood on end, he ground his teeth and bit his lips till the blood came.

"When you move, remember the whole force of my army is ready to help," said he.

Tung Ch'eng introduced him to the other conspirators and then the pledge was produced and Ma T'eng was told to sign his name. He did so, at the same time smearing the blood as a sign of the oath and saying, "I swear to die rather than betray this pledge."

Pointing to the five he said, "We require ten for this business and we can accomplish our design."

"We cannot get many true and loyal men. One of the wrong sort will spoil all," said Tung Ch'eng.

Ma T'eng told them to bring in the list of officials. He read on till he came to the name Liu, of the Imperial clan, when clapping his hands he cried, "Why not consult him?"

"Whom?" cried they altogether.

Ma T'eng very slowly and deliberately spoke his name.

> To a very trusty servant comes an Emperor's decree,
> And a scion of the ruling house can prove his loyalty.

If the reader turns to the next chapter he will see who was Ma T'eng's hero.

CHAPTER XXI

TS'AO TS'AO DISCUSSES HEROES:
KUAN YU SLAYS CH'E CHOU

"Who is it?" was the question on the lips of the conspirators. Ma T'eng's reply was, "The Governor of Yuchow, Liu Pei. He is here and we will ask him to help."

"Though he is an uncle of the Empreor, he is at present a partizan of our enemy, and he will not join."

"But I saw something at the hunt," said Ma T'eng. "When Ts'ao Ts'ao advanced to acknowledge the congratulations due to the Emperor, Yuan-te's sworn brother Kuan Yu was behind him, and grasped his sword as if to cut down Ts'ao Ts'ao. However, Yuan-te signed to him to hold his hand and he did. He would willingly destroy Ts'ao, only he thinks his teeth and claws are too many. You must ask him and he will surely consent."

Here Wu Shih urged caution. "Do not go too fast," said he. "Let us consider the thing most carefully."

They dispersed. Next day after dark Tung Ch'eng went to Liu Pei's lodging taking with him the decree. As soon as he was announced Yuan-te came to greet him and led him into a private room where they could talk freely. The two younger brothers were there as well.

"It must be something unusually important that has brought you here tonight," said Pei.

"If I had ridden forth by daylight, Ts'ao might have suspected something so I came by night."

Wine was brought in and while they were drinking Tung Ch'eng said, "Why did you check your brother the other day at the hunt when he was going to attack Ts'ao Ts'ao?"

Yuan-te was startled and said, "How did you know?"

"Nobody noticed but I saw."

Yuan-te could not prevaricate and said, "It was the presumption of the man that made my brother so angry; he could not help it."

The visitor covered his face and wept. "Ah," said he, "if all the Court Ministers were like him, there would be no sighs for lack of tranquillity."

Now Yuan-te felt that possibly Ts'ao Ts'ao had sent his visitor to try him, so he cautiously replied, "Where are the sighs for lack of tranquillity while Ts'ao Ts'ao is at the head of affairs?"

Tung Ch'eng changed colour and rose from his seat. "You, Sir, are a relative of His Majesty and so I showed you my inmost feelings. Why did you mislead me?"

"Because I feared you might be misleading me, and I wanted to find out."

At this Tung Ch'eng drew out the decree he had received and showed it. His host was deeply moved. Then he produced the pledge. There were only six names to it and these were Tung Ch'eng, Wang Tzu-fu, Ch'ung Chi, Wu Shih, Wu Tzu-lan and Ma T'eng.

"Since you have a decree like this, I cannot but do my share," said Liu Pei and at Tung Ch'eng's request he added his name and signature to the others and handed it back.

"Now let us but get three more, which will make ten, and we shall be ready to act."

"But you must move with great caution and not let this get abroad," said Yuan-te.

The two remained talking till an early hour in the morning when the visitor left.

Now in order to put Ts'ao Ts'ao quite off the scent that any plot against him was in progress, Liu Pei began to devote himself to gardening, planting vegetables and watering them with his own hands. His brothers ventured to remonstrate with him for taking to such an occupation when great matters needed attention.

"The reason for this you may not know," replied he. And they said no more.

One day when the two brothers were absent and Yuan-te was busy in his garden, two messengers with an escort came from Ts'ao Ts'ao, saying, "The command of the Minister is that you come at once."

"What important affair is afoot?" asked he nervously.

"We know nothing: we were ordered to come and request your presence."

All he could do was to follow. When he arrived Ts'ao met him and laughingly said, "That is a big business you have in hand at home."

This remark made Liu Pei turn the colour of clay. But Ts'ao took him by the hand and led him straight to the private garden, saying, "The growth of vegetables that you are trying to learn is very difficult."

Yuan-te breathed again. He said, "That is hardly a business it is only a solace."

Tstao said, "I happened to notice the green plums on the trees today and suddenly my thoughts went back to a year ago when we were thrashing Chang Hsiu. We were marching through a parched district and every one was suffering from thirst. Suddenly I lifted my whip and pointing at something in the distance I said, "Look at those plum trees." The soldiers heard it and it made their mouths water. Now I owe something to the plums and we will pay it today. I ordered the servants to heat some wine very hot and sent to invite you to share it."

Yuan-te was quite composed by this time and no longer suspected any sinister design. He went with his host to a small summer house, where the wine cups were already laid out and green plums filled the dishes. After a goblet of wine had been swallowed they sat down to a confidential talk and enjoyment of their wine.

As they drank the weather gradually changed, clouds gathering and threatening rain. The servants pointed out a mass of cloud that looked like a dragon hung in the sky. Both host and guest went to the window and leaned over the rail looking at it.

"Do you understand the evolutions of dragons?" asked Ts'ao of the guest.

"Not in detail."

"A dragon can assume any size, can rise in glory or hide from sight. Bulky, it generates clouds and evolves mist; attenuated, it can scarcely hide a mustard stalk or conceal a shadow. Mounting, it can soar to the empyrean; subsiding, it lurks in the uttermost depths of the ocean. This is the mid-spring season and the dragon chooses this moment for his transformations, like a man realising his desires and overrunning the world. The dragon among animals compares with the hero among men. You, O Yuan-te, with your experience must know who are the heroes of the present day and I wish you would say who they are."

"How can a dullard like me know such things?"

"Do not be so modest."

"Thanks to your kindly protection I have a post at Court. But as to heroes I really do not know who they are."

"You may not have looked upon their faces, but you have heard their names."

"Yuan Shu, with his resources, is he one?"

His host laughed, "A rotting bone in a graveyard. I shall put him out of the way shortly."

"Well, Yuan Shao then. The highest offices of State have been held in his family for four generations and his clients are many. He is firmly posted in Ichou and he commands the services of many able men. Surely he is one."

"A bully, but a coward, he is fond of grandiose schemes, but is devoid of decision, he makes for great things but grudges the necessary toil. He loses sight of everything else in view of a little present advantage. He is not one."

"There is Liu Ching-sheng. He is renowned as a man of perfection, whose fame has spread on all sides. Surely he is a hero."

"He is a mere semblance, a man of vain reputation. No, not he."

"Sun Ts'e is a sturdy sort, the chief of all in the east. Is he a hero?"

"He has profited by his father's reputation, he is no hero."

"What of Liu Chang?"

"Though he is of the reigning family, he is nothing more than a watch dog. How could you make a hero of him?"

"What about Chang Hsiu, Chang Lu, Han Sui and all those?"

Tsiao clapped his hands and laughed very loudly. "Paltry people like them are not worth mentioning."

"With these exceptions I really know none."

"Now heroes are men who cherish lofty designs in their bosoms and have plans to achieve them, they have all-embracing schemes and the whole world is at their mercy."

"Who is such a man?" said Yuan-te.

Ts'ao pointed his finger first at his guest and then at himself, saying, "The only heroes in the world are you and I."

Yuan-te gasped and the spoon and chopsticks rattled to the floor. Now just at that moment the storm burst with a tremendous peal of thunder and rush of rain. Yuan-te stooped down to recover the fallen articles, saying, "What a shock! and it was quite close."

"What! are you afraid of thunder?" said Ts'ao.

Yuan-te replied, "The wise man paled at a sudden peal of thunder or fierce gust of wind. Why should one not fear?"

Thus he glossed over the real fact, that it was the words he had heard that had so startled him.

Constrained to lodge in a tiger's lair,
　　He played a waiting part,
But when Ts'ao talked of breaking men,
　　Then terror gripped his heart.
But he cleverly used the thunder peal
　　As excuse for turning pale;
O quick to seize occasions thus!
　　He surely must prevail.

The shower had passed and there appeared two men rushing through the garden, both armed. In spite of the attendants they forced their way to the pavilion where sat the two friends. They were Kuan Yu and Chang Fei.

The two brothers had been outside the city at archery practice when Ts'ao Ts'ao's invitation had come so peremptorily. On their return they heard that two officers had arrived and led away Yuan-te to the Minister. They hastened to his palace and were told their brother was with his host in the grounds and they feared something had happened. So they rushed in. Now when they saw their brother quietly talking with Ts'ao and enjoying a cup of wine, they took up their usual places and meekly stood waiting.

"Why did you come?" said Ts'ao Ts'ao.

"We heard that you, Sir, had invited our brother to a wine party and we came to amuse you with a little sword play," said they.

"This is not a Hungmen banquet," replied Ts'ao. "What use have we for two Hsiangs?"

Yuan-te smiled. The host ordered wine to be served to the two "Fan K'uai" to allay their excitement and, soon after, the three took their leave and returned homeward.

"We were nearly frightened to death," said Kuan Yu.

The story of the dropped chopsticks was told. The two asked what their brother intended by his actions and he told them that his learning gardening was to convince Ts'ao Ts'ao of his perfect simplicity and the absence of any ambition. "But," said he, "when he suddenly pointed to me as one of the heroes I was startled, for I thought he had some suspicions. Happily the thunder at that moment supplied the excuse I wanted."

"Really you are very clever," said they.

Next day Ts'ao again invited Yuan-te and while the two were drinking, Man Ch'ung, who had been despatched to find out what Yuan Shao was doing, came to present his report.

He said, "Kungsun Tsan has been completely defeated by Yuan."

"Do you know the details? I should like to know how," interrupted Liu Pei.

"They were at war and Tsan got the worst of it, so he acted on the defensive, building a high wall about his army and on that erecting a high tower, which he called the I-ching Tower. Therein he placed all his grain and took up his own quarters. His fighting men passed in and out without ceasing, some going out to give battle, others returning to rest. One of them was surrounded and sent to ask Kungsun to rescue him. Kungsun said, "If I rescue him, hereafter every one will want to be helped and will not exert himself." So he did not go. This disgusted his men and many deserted to the enemy so that his army diminished. He sent letters to the capital to crave help, but the messenger was captured. He sent to Chang Yen to arrange with him for a joint attack and those letters with the plans also fell into Shao's hands and the plans were adopted by his enemy, who gave the signals agreed upon. Thus Tsan fell into an ambush, lost heavily and retreated into the city. There he was besieged and a subterranean passage was pierced into the tower where he lodged. The tower was set on fire and Kungsun could not escape. So he slew his wife and little ones and committed suicide. The flames destroyed the bodies of the whole family.

"Yuan Shao has added the remnants of the vanquished army to his own and so become yet stronger. His brother Yuan Shu in Honan, however, has become so arrogant and cruel that the people have turned against him. Then he had sent to say he would yield the title of Emperor, which he had assumed, in favour of his brother. His brother Shao demanded the seal also and Yuan Shu promised to bring it in person. Now he has abandoned Huainan and is about to occupy Hopei. If he succeeded, the two brothers will control adjoining districts and be dangerous."

It was a sad story and Yuan-te remembered with sorrow that, in the days of success and prosperity, the dead chieftain had pushed his interest and shown him much kindness. Moreover he was anxious to know the fate of Chao Tzu-lung.

In his heart he thought, "What better chance am I likely to get of setting myself free?"

So he rose and said to Ts'ao Ts'ao, "If Yuan Shu goes over to join his brother he will surely pass through Hsuchou. I beg you to give me an army with which to smite him on the way. That will finish Yuan Shu."

"Memorialise the Emperor tomorrow and I will give you an army," said Ts'ao.

So next day Yuan-te went to an audience and Ts'ao gave him command of five legions, horse and foot, and sent Chu Ling and Lu Chao with him.

At parting with Liu Pei the Emperor shed tears. As soon as he reached his lodging he set about preparations for immediate departure, returning his seal as General and preparing his weapons. Tung Ch'eng went out some distance on the road to bid him farewell.

"You must not mind my going; this journey will assuredly help on the scheme," said Liu Pei.

"Keep your mind fixed on that," said Tung, "and never forget what His Majesty requires of us."

They parted. Presently his brothers asked him why he was in such a hurry to get away.

He replied, "I have been a bird in a cage, a fish in a net. This is like the fish regaining the open sea and the bird soaring into the blue sky. I suffered much from the confinement."

Now Kuo Chia and Ch'eng Yu had been absent inspecting stores and supplies when Liu Pei left. As soon as they heard of his expedition they went in to see their master, asking him why he had let Liu Pei go in command of an army.

"He is going to cut off Yuan Shu."

"Formerly, when he was governor of Yuchou, we recommended that he should be put to death but you would not hear of it. Now you have given him an army. You have allowed the dragon to reach the sea, the tiger to return to the mountains. What control will you have in future?"

So spoke Ch'eng Yu and Kuo Chia followed in the same strain.

"Even if you would not put him to death you need not have let him go. As the proverb says, 'Relax opposition for one day and age-long harm ensues.' You must admit the truth of this."

Ts'ao recognised that these were prudent counsels so he sent Hsu Ch'u with a half company and imperative orders to bring Yuan-te back again.

Liu Pei was marching as rapidly as possible when he noticed a cloud of dust in the rear and remarked to his brothers, "Surely they are pursuing us."

He halted and made a stockade and ordered his brothers to be in readiness, one on each flank. Presently the messenger arrived and found himself in the midst of an army ready for battle. He dismounted and entered the camp to speak with Yuan-te.

"Sir, on what business have you come?" asked Pei.

"The Minister has sent me to request you to return as he has further matters to discuss with you."

"When a general has once taken the field even the royal command is of no effect. I bade farewell to the Emperor, I received the Minister's commands and there can be nothing further to talk about. You may return forthwith and take that as my reply."

The messenger was undecided what action to take. He knew of the friendship that existed between the Minister and his late guest and he had no orders to kill. He could only return with this reply and ask further instructions. So he left. When he related what had occurred Ts'ao still hesitated to take any action. His advisers urged upon him that this refusal to return meant enmity.

"Still, two of my men are with him," said Ts'ao. "He will not dare do anything unfriendly, I think. Beside, I sent him and I cannot go back on my own orders."

So Yuan-te was not pursued.

> He took his arms, he fed his steed,
> And fared forth willingly,
> Intent to accomplish his King's behest
> Deep grayed on his memory.
> At least he had broken out of his cage,
> He heard not the tiger's roar,
> He had shaken the shackles from his feet,
> As a dragon on high could soar.

As soon as Ma T'eng heard that Liu Pei had set forth he reported that pressing business called him and marched back to his own district.

When Yuan-te reached Hsuchou the governor, Ch'e Chou, came to meet him, and when the official banquet was over, Sun Ch'ien and Mi Chu came to visit him. Then he proceeded to his residence to greet his family.

Scouts were sent out to see what Yuan Shu was doing. They came back with the intelligence that his arrogance had driven away his banditti allies, who had returned to their mountain fastnesses. His forces thus reduced he had written resigning the Imperial style he had assumed in favour of his brother Shao, who had at once commanded his presence. Thereupon he packed up the palace fittings he had had made, got the remnants of his army in order and marched west.

When he neared Hsuchou, Yuan-te led out his captains with the five legions to meet him. Yuan sent out Chi Ling to force a way through, But Chang Fei opposed him and attacked without a parley. In the tenth bout he cut down Chi Ling. The defeated soldiers fled in all directions.

Then Yuan Shu came up with his own army. Yuan-te placed his captains right and left, he himself being in the centre, and so met Yuan Shu. As soon as the enemy came near Yuan-te began to abuse him. "O rebellious one, and wicked, I have a command to destroy you. Yield, then, with good grace and so escape your punishment."

"Base weaver of mats and mean maker of straw sandals, how dare you make light of me?" replied Shu and he gave the signal for an attack.

Yuan-te retired and his captains from the flanks closed in. They smote the army of Shu till corpses littered the plain and blood flowed in streams. At the same time the bandits attacked the baggage train and completed the destruction. Shu tried to retreat to Shouch'un but the bandits barred the road.

He sought refuge in Chiangt'ing, with the small company left of all his army. And these were the weakly ones able neither to fight nor flee. It was then the height of summer and their food was nearly exhausted. The whole provision consisted of thirty measures of wheat. This was made over to the soldiers and the members of his household went hungry. Many died of actual starvation. Yuan Shu could not swallow the coarse food that the soldiers lived on. One day he bade his cook bring him some honey-water to quench his thirst.

"There is no water, save that tainted with blood," replied the cook. "Where can I get honey-water?"

This was the last straw. Shu sat up on his couch and rolled out on the floor with a loud cry. Blood gushed from his mouth and thus he died. It was the sixth month of the fourth year of "Established Tranquillity."

> The last days of Han approached and weapons clashed in every
> quarter,
> The misguided Yuan Shu, lost to all sense of honour,
> Forgetful of his forefathers, who had filled the State's highest
> Offices,
> Madly aspired to become himself Emperor,
> Resting his outrageous claim on the possession of The Seal,
> And arrogantly boasting that thus he fulfilled the design of Heaven.
> Alas! Sick unto death he vainly begged for a little honey-water;
> He died, alone.

Yuan Shu being dead, his nephew taking his coffin and his wife and children, sought shelter in Luchiang. There the magistrate, Hsu Ch'iu, slew all the survivors. Among the possessions he found the Imperial Seal, which he at once took to the capital and presented to Ts'ao Ts'ao, for which service he was made Prefect of Kaoling.

When Yuan-te heard that Yuan Shu was dead he prepared a report to the throne, and sent it to Ts'ao Ts'ao. He sent the two officers deputed by Ts'ao Ts'ao back to the capital, keeping the army to defend Hsuchou. He also personally went through the countryside commanding the people to resume their ordinary avocations.

Ts'ao Ts'ao was angry when his two officers returned without their man and was going to put them to death. Hsun Yu reasoned with him.

"The power was in Liu Pei's hands and so these two had no alternative," said he.

So they were pardoned.

"You should instruct Ch'e Chou to try to destroy him," said Yu.

Accordingly he sent secret orders to Ch'e Chou, who took Ch'en Teng into his confidence and asked his advice. Teng advised an ambush in the city gate to attack Liu Pei on his return from the country; he himself would attack the escort with arrows from the city walls. Ch'e agreed to try this.

Then Teng went to his father to tell him. His father Ch'en Kuei bade him go and warn the intended victim. He at once rode away to do so. Before long he met the two younger brothers, to whom he told his story.

Now Yuan-te was following some distance behind. As soon as Chang Fei heard of the plot he wanted to attack the ambush, but Yun-ch'ang said he had a better plan.

Said he, "The ambush will be a failure. And I think we can compass the death of Ch'e Chou. In the night we will pretend to be some of Ts'ao's men and entice him out to meet us. We will slay him."

Chang Fei approved of the plan. Now the soldiers still had some of Ts'ao Ts'ao's army banners and wore similar armour. About the third watch they came to the city wall and hailed the gate. Those on guard asked who they were. The men replied that they were Chang Wen-yuan's troop sent from the capital. This was told Ch'e Chou who sent hastily for Ch'en Teng to ask his advice.

"If I do not receive them they will suspect my loyalty," said he. "Yet if I go out I may be victim of a ruse."

So he went up on the wall and said it was too dark to distinguish friends from foes and they must wait till daylight. The men shouted back that Liu Pei must be kept in ignorance and they begged him to let them in. Still Ch'e Chou hesitated. They shouted louder than ever to open the gate.

Presently Ch'e girded on his armour, placed himself at the head of a company and went out. He galloped over the bridge, shouting, "Where is Wenyuan?"

Then lights blazed around and he recognised Kuan Yu with his sword drawn.

"Wretch!" cried Kuan Yu. "You would plot to slay my brother, would you?"

Ch'e Chou was too frightened to make good defence and he turned to re-enter the gate. But as he reached the drawbridge flights of arrows met him, wherefore he turned aside and galloped along under the wall. But Kuan Yu came quickly in pursuit. His sword was raised aloft and as it came down the fugitive fell to the earth. Kuan Yu cut off his head and returned, shouting, "I have slain the traitor. You others need not fear if you only surrender."

They threw aside their spears and gave in. As soon as the excitement had calmed Kuan Yu took the head to show Yuan-te and told him the story of the plot.

"But what will Ts'ao Ts'ao think of this?" said Yuan-te. "And he may come."

"If he does we can meet him," said Kuan Yu.

But Yuan-te was grieved beyond measure. When he entered the city the elders of the people knelt in the road to welcome him. When he reached his residence he found that Chang Fei had already exterminated the family of Ch'e Chou.

Yuan-te said, "We have slain one of his best friends and how will he stand that?"

"Never mind!" cried Ch'en Teng. "I have a plan."

> Just from grave danger extricated,
> An injured friend must be placated.

The plan proposed by Ch'en Teng will be disclosed next.

CHAPTER XXII

YUAN AND TS'AO BOTH TAKE THE FIELD:
THE TWO BROTHERS CAPTURE TWO CAPTAINS

This was the plan proposed to Yuan-te: "Yuan Shao is Ts'ao Ts'ao's terror. He is strongly posted in an extensive district with a hundred legions of fighting men and many able officers. Write letters and pray him to rescue you."

Liu Pei replied, "But we have never had any dealings with each other and he is unlikely to do such a thing for one who has just destroyed his brother."

"There is some one here whose family have been on intimate terms with the Yuans for a hundred years. Shao would surely come if he wrote."

"And who is this?"

"A man you know well and respect greatly; can you not guess?"

"You surely mean Cheng K'ang-ch'eng," said Liu Pei suddenly.

"That is he," said Ch'en Teng smiling.

Now Cheng K'ang-ch'eng's *ming* was Yuan. He was a student and a man of great talent, who had long studied under Ma Jung. Ma Jung was peculiar as a teacher. Whenever he lectured he let fall a curtain behind which were a circle of singing girls. The students were assembled in front of this curtain. Cheng Yuan attended these lectures for three years and never once let his eyes wander to the curtain.

Naturally the master admired his pupil. After Cheng Yuan had finished his studies and gone home Ma Jung praised him to the others, saying, "Only one man has penetrated the inner meaning of my instructions and that one is Cheng Yuan."

In the Cheng household the waiting maids were familiar with Mao's edition of the Odes. Once one of the maids opposed Yuan's wishes, so as punishment she was made to kneel in front of the steps. Another girl made fun of her, quoting from an ode;—

"What are you doing there in the mire?"

The kneeling girl capped the verse from another ode; quoth she:—

"Twas but a simple word I said,
Yet brought it wrath upon my head."

Such was the family in which he had been born. In the reign of the Emperor Huan he rose to the rank of President of a Board, but when the Ten Eunuchs began to control the government he gave up office and retired into the country to Hsuchou. Liu Pei had known him before, had consulted him on many occasions and greatly respected him.

Liu Pei was glad that he had remembered this man and without loss of time, in company with Ch'en Teng, he went to his house to ask him to draft this letter, which he generously consented to do.

Sun Ch'ien was entrusted with the task of delivery and set out at once. Shao read it and considered the matter long before speaking. "Liu Pei destroyed my brother and I ought not to help him, but out of consideration for the writer of this letter I must."

Whereupon he assembled his officers to consider an attack upon Ts'ao Ts'ao.

T'ien Feng said, "Do not raise an army. The people are worn out and the granaries are empty with these constant wars. Let us rather report the recent victory of Kungsun Tsan to the Throne. If that does not reach the Emperor, then memorialise that Ts'ao Ts'ao is hindering the government. Then raise an army: occupy Liyang, assemble a fleet in Honan, prepare weapons, send out your various divisions and within three years you will win all round."

The adviser Shen P'ei replied, "I do not agree. The military genius of our illustrious lord having overcome the hordes of the north, to dispose of Ts'ao is as simple as turning one's hand; it is not a matter of months."

Chu Shou said, "Victory is not always to the many. Ts'ao Ts'ao's discipline is excellent; his soldiers are brave and well drilled. He will not sit down quietly waiting to be surrounded as Kungsun Tsan did. Now you abandon the intention to inform the Throne of our success, which I find a good plan, but you intend to send out an army without any valid excuse. Our lord should not do that."

Then followed adviser Kuo T'u, "You are wrong. No expedition against Ts'ao Ts'ao can lack excuse. But if our master would take the chance now offering itself of coming into his own, he will accede to the request in the letter and ally himself with Liu Pei for the destruction of Ts'ao. This would win the approval of heaven and the affections of the people, a double blessing."

Thus the four advisers differed and wrangled and Yuan Shao could not decide which to follow. Then there came two others, Hsu Yu and Hsun Shen, and, seeing them, Shao said, "You two have wide experience, how would you decide?"

The two made their obeisance and Yuan Shao said, "A letter from Cheng the President has arrived, counselling me to support Liu Pei in an attack on Ts'ao Ts'ao. Now am I to send an army or not send an army?"

They both cried with one voice, "Send! Your armies are numerous enough and strong enough; you will destroy a traitor and help the dynasty."

"Your words just express my desire," said Shao and thenceforward the discussion turned on the expedition.

First Sun Ch'ien was sent back with Yuan Shao's consent and instructions for Liu Pei to make ready to co-operate. Officers were assigned divisions and advisers were told off. The army was to be composed of thirty legions, horse and foot in equal numbers. They were to march on Liyang.

When the arrangements were complete Kuo T'u went to his chief saying, "In order to manifest the righteousness of your attack on Ts,ao it would be well to issue a manifesto with a summary of his various crimes."

Yuan Shao approved of this and a certain Ch'en Lin, well known as a scholar, who had been a Recorder in the late Emperor's reign, was entrusted to compose such a document. This is the manifesto:—

"A perspicacious ruler wisely provides against political vicissitudes; a loyal minister carefully foresees the difficulties in the assertion of authority. Wherefore a man of unusual parts precedes an extraordinary situation, and of such a man the achievements will be extraordinary. For indeed the ordinary man is quite unequal to an extraordinary situation.

"In former days, after having gained ascendancy over a weakling King of the powerful Ts'in Dynasty, Chao Kao wielded the whole authority of the Throne, overruling the government. All dignity and fortune came through him and his contemporaries were restrained so that none dared to speak openly. Slowly but surely evolved the tragedy of the Wangi Temple, when the Emperor was slain and the Imperial tablets perished in the flames. He, the author of these crimes, has ever since been held up to obloquy as the arch example of an evil doer.

"In the later days of the Empress Lu of the Hans the world saw Lu Chan and Lu Lu, brothers of the Empress and fellows in wickedness, monopolising the powers of government. Within the capital they commanded two armies and without they ruled the feudal states of Liang and Chao. They arbitrarily controlled all State affairs and decided all questions in the council chamber and the Court. This dominance of the base and declension of the noble continued till the hearts of the people grew cold within them.

"Thereupon Chou P'o, Marquis of Chiang, and Liu Chang Marquis of Chuhsu, asserted their dignity and let loose their wrath. They destroyed the contumacious ministers and restored their Ruler to his royal state. Thus they enabled the kingly way to be re-established and the glory to be manifested. Here are two instances where ministers asserted their authority.

"This Ts'ao, now a minister, forsooth, had for ancestor a certain eunuch named T'eng, fitting companion of Tso Kuan and Hsu Huang. All three were prodigies of wickedness and insatiably avaricious and, let loose on the world, they hindered ethical progress and preyed upon the populace. This T'eng begged for and adopted Ts'ao's father who, by wholesale bribery, wagons of gold and cartloads of jewels presented at the gates of the influential, contrived to sneak his way into considerable office where he could subvert authority. Thus Ts'ao is the depraved bantling of a monstrous excrescence, devoid of all virtue in himself, ferocious and cunning, delighting in disorder and revelling in public calamity.

"Now I, Mu-fu, a man of war, have mustered my armies and displayed my might that I may sweep away and destroy the evil opponents of government. I have already had to deal with Tung Cho, the ruffian who invaded the official circle and wrested the government. At that time I grasped my sword and beat the drums to restore order in the east. I assembled warriors, selected the best and took them into my service. In this matter I came into relations with this Ts'ao and conferred with him to further my scheme. I gave him command of a subordinate force and looked to him to render such petty service as he was equal to. I suffered his stupidities and condoned his shortcomings, his rash attacks and facile retreats, his losses and shameful defeats, his repeated destruction of whole armies. Again and again I sent him more troops and filled the gaps in his depleted ranks. I even addressed a memorial to the Throne for him to be appointed Governor of Yenchou. I made him feared as he were a tiger. I added to his honours and increased his authority, hoping that eventually he would justify himself by a victory such as fell to Meng Ming of Ts'in.

"But Ts'ao availed himself of the opportunity to overstep all bounds, to give free rein to violence and evil. He stripped the common people, outraged the good and injured the virtuous. Pien Jang, Prefect of Kiukiang, was a man of conspicuous talent and of world-wide reputation. He was honest in speech and correct in demeanour. He spoke without flattery. He was put to death and his head exposed, and his family utterly destroyed. From that day to this scholars have deeply mourned and popular resentment has steadily grown. One man raised his arm in anger and the whole countryside followed him Whereupon Ts'ao was smitten at Hsuchou and his district was snatched by Lu Pu. He fled eastward without shelter or refuge.

"My policy is a strong trunk and weak branches, a commanding central government and obedient feudal lords. Also I am no partizan. Therefore I again raised my banners, donned my armour and moved forward to attack. My drums rolled for an assault on Lu Pu and his multitudes incontinently fled. I saved Ts'ao from destruction and restored him to a position of authority. Wherein I must confess to showing no kindness to the people of Yenchou although it was a great matter for Ts'ao.

"Later it happened that the imperial cortege moved west and a horde of rebels rose and attacked. The course of government was hindered. At that moment my territory was threatened from the north and I could not leave it. Wherefore I sent one of my officers to Ts'ao to see to the repair of the temples and the protection of the youthful sovereign. Thereupon Ts'ao gave the rein to his inclinations. He arbitrarily ordered the removal of the Court. He brought shame upon the ruling House and subverted the laws. He engrossed the presidency of the three highest offices and monopolised the control of the administration. Offices and rewards were conferred according to his will; punishment was at his word. He glorified whole families of those he loved; he exterminated whole clans of those he hated. Open critics were executed; secret opponents were assassinated. Officials locked their lips; wayfarers only exchanged glances. Presidents of Boards recorded levies and every government official held a sinecure.

"The late Yang Piao, a man who had filled two of the highest offices of State as President of two Boards, because of some petty grudge was, though guiltless, charged with a crime. He was beaten and suffered every form of cruelty. This arbitrary and impulsive act was a flagrant disregard of constitutional rules.

"Another victim was the Councillor Chao Yan. He was faithful in remonstrance, honest in speech, endowed with the highest principles of rectitude. He was listened to at Court. His words carried enough weight with the Emperor to cause him to modify his intention and confer reward for outspokenness. Desirous of diverting all power into his own hands and stifle all criticism, Ts'ao presumed to arrest and put to death this censor, in defiance of all legal procedure.

"Another evil deed was the destruction of the tomb of Prince Liang Hsiao, the brother of the late Emperor. His tomb should certainly have been respected, even its mulberries and *lindera* trees, its cypresses and its pines. Ts'ao led soldiers to the cemetery and stood by while it was desecrated, the coffin destroyed and the poor corpse exposed. They stole the gold and jewels of the dead. This deed brought tears to the eyes of the Emperor and rent the hearts of all men. Ts'ao also appointed 'Openers-of-Grave-Mounds' and 'Seekers-for-Gold,' whose tracks were marked by desecrated graves and exhumed bodies. Indeed, while assuming the position of the highest officer of State, he indulged the inclination of a bandit, polluting the State, oppressing the people, a bane to gods and men.

"He added to this by setting up minute and vexatious prohibitions so that there were nets and snares spread in every pathway, traps and pitfalls laid in every road. A hand raised was caught in a net, a foot advanced was taken in an entanglement. Wherefore the men of Yen and Yu waxed desperate and the inhabitants of the metropolis groaned and murmured in anger.

> Read down the names through all the years
> Of ministers that all men curse
> For greed and cruelty and lust;
> Than Ts'ao you will not find a worse.

"I have investigated the cases of evil deeds in the provinces, but I have been unable to reform him. I have given him repeated opportunities hoping that he would repent. But he has the heart of a wolf, the nature of a wild beast. He nourishes evil in his bosom and desires to pull down the pillars of the State, to weaken the House of Han, to destroy the loyal and true and to stand himself conspicuous as the chiefest of criminals.

"Formerly, when I attacked the north, Kungsun Tsan, that obstinate bandit and perverse bravo, resisted my might for a year. Before he could be destroyed this Ts'ao wrote to him that, under the pretence of assisting the Imperial armies, he would covertly lead them to destruction. The plot was discovered through his messengers and Tsan also perished. This blunted Ts'ao's ardour and his plans failed.

"Now he is camped at the Ao Granaries with the river to strengthen his position. Like the mantis in the story, who threatened the chariot with its forelegs, he thinks himself terrible. But with the dignity and prestige of Han to support me I confront the whole world. I have spearmen by millions, horsemen by thousands of squadrons, fierce and vigorous warriors strong as Chung Huang, Hsia Yu and Wu Huo, those heroes of antiquity. I have enlisted expert archers and strong bowmen. In Pingchou my armies have crossed the T'aihang Range and in Chingchou they have forded the Chi and T'a Rivers. They have coasted down the Yellow River to attack his van, and from Chingchou they have descended to Wanyeh to smite his rearguard. Thunder-like in the weight of their march, tiger-like in the alertness of their advance, they converge on Lot'ing. They are as flames let loose among light grass, as the blue ocean poured on glowing embers. Is there any hope that he escape destruction?

"Of the hordes of Ts'ao, those who can fight are from the north or from other camps and they all desire to return home. They weep whenever they look to the north. The others belong to Yen or Yu, being remnants of the armies of Lu Pu and Chang Yang. Beaten, stern necessity forced them to accept service, but they take it only as a temporary expedient. Every man who has been wounded is an enemy. If I give the signal to return and send my drums and shawms to the mountain tops, and wave the white flag to show them they may surrender, they will melt away like dew before the sun and no blood will be shed. The victory will be mine.

"Now the Hans are failing and the bonds of Empire are relaxed, The sacred Dynasty has no supporter, the Ministers are not strong enough to cope with the difficulties. Within the capital the responsible Ministers are crestfallen and helpless. There is no one to rely upon. Such loyal and high principled men as are left are browbeaten by a tyrannical Minister. How can they manifest their virtue?

"Ts'ao has surrounded the Palace with seven hundred veterans, the ostensible object being to guard the Emperor, but the covert design being to hold him prisoner. I fear this is but the first step in usurpation and so I take my part. Now is the time for loyal Ministers to sacrifice their lives, the opportunity for officers to perform meritorious deeds. Can I fail to urge you?

"Ts'ao has forged commands to himself to undertake the control of government affairs and, in the name of the State, sends out calls for military assistance. I fear lest distant districts may obey his behest and send troops to help him, to the detriment of the multitude and their everlasting shame. No wise man will do so.

"The forces of four prefectures are moving out simultaneously. When this call reaches Chingchou you will see their forces co-operate with those of Chang Hsiu. All districts and departments ought to organise volunteers and set them along their borders to demonstrate their force an prove their loyal support of the Dynasty. Will not this be rendering extraordinary service?

"The rank of Marquis, with feudal rights over five thousand households and a money reward of fifty millions, will be the reward of him who brings the head of Ts'ao. No questions will be asked of those who surrender. I publish abroad this notice of my bounty and the rewards offered that you may realise that the Dynasty is in real danger."

Shao read this effusion with great joy. He at once ordered copies to be posted everywhere, in towns and cities, at gates (tax stations) and ferries and passes. Copies found their way to the capital and one got into Ts'ao Ts'ao's palace. That day he happened to be in bed with a bad headache. The servants took the paper to the sick man's room. He read it and was frightened from the tips of his hair to the marrow of his very bones. He broke out into a cold perspiration and his headache vanished. He bounded out of bed and said to Ts'ao Hung, "Who wrote this?"

"They say it is Ch'en Lin's pencil," replied he.

Ts'ao laughed "They have the literary gift; they had better have the military too to back it up. This fellow may be a very elegant writer, but what if Yuan Shao's fighting capacity falls short?"

He called his advisers together to consider the next move. K'ung Jung heard of the summons and went to his master saying, "You should not fight with Yuan Shao; he is too strong. Make peace."

Hsun Yu said, "He is despicable: do not make peace."

Jung replied, "His land is wide and his people strong. He has many skilful strategists and he has loyal and able captains. You cannot say he is despicable."

Yu laughed saying, "His army is a rabble. One captain, T'ien Feng, is bold but treacherous; another, Hsu Yu, is greedy and ignorant; Shen P'ei is devoted but stupid; Feng Chi is steady but useless. And these four of such different temperaments, mutually incompatible, will make for confusion rather than efficiency. Yen Liang and Wen Ch'ou are worthless and can be disposed of in the first battle and the others are poor, rough stuff. What is the use even of their legions?"

K'ung Jung was silent and Ts'ao smiled. "They are even as Hsun Wen-jo describes," said he.

Then Ts'ao issued orders. Generals Liu Tai and Wang Chung were to lead an army of five legions, displaying the minister's banners, and march against Hsuchou to attack Liu Pei.

This Liu Tai had been governor of Yenchou but had surrendered and entered Ts'ao Ts'ao's service after the fall of the city. Ts'ao had given him a rank as supernumerary leader and now was disposed to make use of him.

Ts'ao Ts'ao himself took command of a large army of twenty legions for a simultaneous attack on Yuan Shao at Liyang.

A certain adviser said he thought the two captains sent against Liu Pei were unequal to their task.

"I know," said Ts'ao. "They are not meant to fight Liu Pei; it is merely a feint. They have orders not to make any real attack till I have overcome Yuan, Shao. Then Liu Pei will be next."

Liu Tai and Wang Chung went their way and Ts'ao Ts'ao marched out his grand army, which came into touch with the enemy, then eighty *li* distant, at Liyang. Both sides made fortified camps and waited watching each other. This went on for two months.

There was dissension in Yuan Shao's camp. Hsu Yu was at enmity with his colleague, Shen P'ei, and the strategist Chu Shou resented the rejection of his plan. So they would not attack. Yuan Shao also could not make up his mind. Tired of this state of inaction Ts'ao Ts'ao then gave certain commanders definite points to hold and marched back to Hsutu.

The five legions sent against Liu Pei went into camp a hundred *li* from Hsuchou. The camp made an imposing display of the banners of the Prime Minister but no attacks followed. Their spies were very busy north of the river. On the defensive side, Liu Pei, as he was uncertain of the strength of the force against him, dared not move.

Suddenly orders came for the Ts'ao army to attack and then discord showed itself.

Liu Tai said, "The Minister orders an attack; you advance."

Wang Chung replied, "You were named first."

"I am the Commander in Chief; it is not my place to go first."

"I will go with you in joint command," said Chung.

"Let us cast lots and he upon whom the lot falls must go," said Tai.

They drew lots and it fell to Wang Chung, who advanced toward Hsuchou with half the force.

When Yuan-te heard of the threatened attack he called Ch'en Teng to consult.

Yuan-te said, "There is dissension in Yuan Shao's camp at Liyang so they do not advance. We do not know where Ts'ao Ts'ao is but his own banner is not displayed in his Liyang camp. Why then is it shown here?"

Ch'en Teng replied, "His tricks take a hundred forms. It must be that he regards the north as most important and has gone there to look after its defence. He dares not show his flag there and I feel sure it is only meant to mislead us. He is not here.

Yuan-te then asked whether one of his brothers would find out the truth and Chang Fei volunteered to go.

"I fear you are unsuited for this," said Yuan-te. "You are too impetuous."

"If Ts'ao is there I will haul him over here," said Fei.

"Let me go first and find out," said Kuan Yu. .

"If you go I shall feel more at ease," said Yuan-te.

So Kuan Yu set out with three companies to reconnoitre. It was then early winter and snow was falling from a gloomy sky. They marched regardless of the snow and came near Wang Chung's camp with arms all ready to attack. Kuan Yu summoned Wang Chung to a parley.

"The Minister is here: why do you not surrender?" said Wang Chung.

"Beg him to come to the front for I would speak with him," replied Kuan Yu.

"Is he likely to come out to see such as you?"

Kuan Yu angrily dashed forward and Wang Chung set his spear to meet him. Yu rode till he came close to his antagonist, then suddenly wheeled away. Wang Chung went after him and followed up a slope. Just as they passed the crest, Yu suddenly wheeled again, shouted and came on flourishing the mighty sword. Wang Chung could not withstand that and fled. But Kuan Yu, changing the huge sword to his left hand, with his right laid hold of his victim by the straps of his breastplate, lifted him out of the saddle and rode away to his own lines with the captive laid across the pommel of his saddle. Wang Chung's men scattered.

The captive was sent to Hsuchou, where he was summoned into the presence of Liu Pei.

"Who are you? What office do you hold? How dare you falsely display the ensigns of the Minister Ts'ao Ts'ao?" said Liu Pei.

"What do you mean by falsely when I simply obeyed my orders?" said Wang. "My master wanted to produce the impression that he was present. Really he was not there."

Liu Pei treated him kindly, giving him food and clothing; but put him in prison till his colleague could be captured. Kuan Yu said that, knowing his brother had peaceful intentions in his mind, he captured the man instead of slaying him.

"I was afraid of Chang Fei's hasty and impulsive temper," said Liu Pei. "He would have slain this man. So I could not send him. There is no advantage in killing persons of this sort and while alive they are often useful in amicable settlements."

Here Chang Fei said, "You have got this Wang; now I will go and get the other man."

"Be careful," said his brother. "Liu Tai was once governor of Yenchou and he was one of the nobles who met at Tigertrap Pass to destroy Tung Cho. He is not to be despised."

"I do not think him worth talking about so much. I will bring him in alive just as my brother did this other."

"I fear that if his life be lost it may upset our designs," said Liu Pei.

"If I kill him I will forfeit my own life," said Fei.

So he was given three companies and went off quickly.

The capture of his colleague made Liu Tai careful. He strengthened his defences and kept behind them. He took no notice of the daily challenges and continual insults which began with Chang Fei's arrival.

After some days Fei evolved a ruse. He issued orders to prepare to rush the enemy's camp at night, but he himself spent the day drinking. Pretending to be very intoxicated he held a court martial and one soldier was severely flogged for a breach of discipline. The man was left bound in the midst of the camp, Fei saying, "Wait till I am ready to start tonight; you shall be sacrificed to the flag." At the same time he gave secret orders to the custodians to let the man escape.

The man found his opportunity, crept out of camp and went over to the enemy, to whom he betrayed the plan of a night attack. As the man bore signs of savage punishment Liu Tai was the more disposed to credit his desertion and tale and made his arrangements, putting the greater part of his men in ambush outside his camp so that it was empty.

That night, having divided his men into three parties, Chang Fei went to attack the camp. A few men were ordered to advance directly, dash in and set fire going. Two larger bodies of men were to go round to the rear of the camp and attack when they saw the fire well started. At the third watch (midnight) Chang Fei, with his veterans, went to cut off Liu Tai's road to the rear.

The thirty men told off to start a conflagration made their way into the camp and were successful. When the flames arose the ambushed men rushed out but only to find themselves attacked on both sides. This confused them and as they knew nothing of the number of their assailants they were panicstricken and scattered.

Liu Tai, with a company of footmen got clear of the fight and fled, but he went straight toward Chang Fei. Escape was impossible and the two men rode up each to attack the other. Chang Fei captured his opponent and the men surrendered.

Chang Fei sent news of this success to his brothers.

Yuan-te said, "Hitherto I-te has been rather violent, but this time he has acted wisely and I am very pleased."

They rode out to welcome their brother.

"You said I was too rough; how now?" said Fei to his brothers.

"If I had not put you on your mettle you would not have evolved this stratagem," said Liu Pei.

Fei laughed. Then appeared the captive Liu Tai, in bonds. Yuan-te at once dismounted and loosed the cords, saying, "My young brother was rather hasty, but you must pardon him."

So he was freed. He was taken into the city, his colleague was released and both were cared for.

Yuan-te said to them, "I could not help putting Ch'e Chou to death when he tried to kill me, but Ts'ao Ts'ao took it as disaffection and sent you two generals to punish me. I have received much kindness from him and certainly would not show ingratitude by killing you. I wish you to speak for me and explain when you get back."

"We are deeply grateful that you spare our lives and we will certainly do so in gratitude for what our wives and children owe you."

Next day the two leaders and their army were allowed to depart unscathed. But before they had got ten *li* from the boundary they heard a mighty shouting and there appeared Chang Fei barring the road.

"My brother made a mistake in letting you go: he did not understand. How could he give freedom to two rebels?"

This made the two men quake with fear, but as the fierce-eyed warrior with uplifted sword was bearing down upon them they heard another man galloping up and shouting, "Do not behave so disgracefully!"

The newcomer was Kuan Yu and his appearance relieved the unhappy men of all fear.

"Why do you stop them since our brother set them free?" cried he.

"If they are let go today they will surely come back," cried Fei.

"Wait till they do, then you may kill them," replied Kuan Yu.

The two leaders with one voice cried, "Even if the Minister slay our whole clan we will never come again. We pray you pardon us."

Said Fei, "If Ts'ao Ts'ao himself had come I would have slain him. Not a breastplate should have gone back. But for this time I leave you your heads."

Clapping their hands to their heads the two men scuttled off while the two brothers returned to the city.

"Ts'ao Ts'ao will certainly come," they said.

Sun Ch'ien said, "This is not a city that can hold out for long. We should send part of our forces to Hsiaop'ei and guard P'eich'eng as a corner stone of our position."

Yuan-te agreed and told off his brothers to guard P'eich'eng whither he also sent his two wives, the Ladies Kan and Mi. The former was a native of the place; the latter was Mi Chu's sister.

Four captains were left to defend Hsuchou and Yuan-te with Chang Fei went to Hsiaop'ei.

The two released leaders hastened home to Ts'ao Ts'ao and explained to him that Liu Pei was not disaffected. But their master was exceeding angry with them, crying "You shameful traitors, what use are you?"

He roared to the lictors to take them away to instant execution.

How can a dog or a pig expect
   To conquer in tiger strife?
Minnows and shrimps that with dragons contend
   Already have done with life.

The fate of the two leaders will be told in the next chapter.

CHAPTER XXIII

MI HENG SLIPS HIS GARMENT AND RAILS AT
TRAITORS: CRUEL PUNISHMENT OF THE
PHYSICIAN CHI

At the close of the last chapter the two unsuccessful leaders Liu and Wang were in danger of death. However, one of the advisers, K'ung Jung, remonstrated with Ts'ao saying, "You knew these two were no match for Liu Pei and if you put them to death because they failed you will lose the hearts of your men."

Wherefore the death sentence was not executed but they were deprived of rank and status. Ts'ao next proposed to lead an army himself to attack Liu Pei, but the weather was too inclement. So it was settled to await the return of spring. In the interval there would be time to arrange peace with Chang Hsiu and Liu Piao.

Wherefore Liu Yeh was sent to the former of these and in due time reached Hsiangch'eng. He first had an interview with Chia Hsu, whereat he dwelt upon Ts'ao's virtues so that Hsu was impressed, kept him as a guest and undertook to smooth his way.

Soon after he saw Chang Hsiu and spoke of the advantages of coming to terms with Ts'ao Ts'ao. While the discussion was in progress a messenger from Yuan Shao was announced and he was called in. He presented letters and, when they also proposed terms of peace, Chia Hsu asked what their success had been lately against Ts'ao.

"The war had ceased for the moment on account of the winter," replied the messenger. "As you, General, and Liu Piao are both well reputed officers of the State, I have been sent to request your help."

Chia Hsu laughed, "You can return to your master and say that as he could not brook rivalry of his brother he certainly would be sorely put to it with that of all the officers of the State."

The letter was torn into fragments before the messenger's face and he was angrily bidden begone.

"But his master, Yuan Shao, is stronger than Ts'ao Ts'ao,"

protested Chang Hsiu. "You have torn up his letter and are dismissing his man. What shall we say about such an insult should Yuan Shao come?"

"Better join hands with Ts'ao Ts'ao," said Chia Hsu.

"But there is still between us an unavenged enmity, we could not suffer each other."

Chia Hsu said, "There are three advantages in joining hands with Ts'ao. First, he has a command from the Emperor to restore peace. Secondly, as Yuan Shao is so strong our little help to him will be despised, while we shall loom large and be well treated by Ts'ao Ts'ao. Thirdly, Ts'ao is going to be Chief of the Feudal Lords and he will ignore all private feuds in order to show his magnanimity to all the world. I hope, General, you will see these things clearly and hesitate no longer."

Chang Hsiu, now convinced, became more reasonable and recalled the messenger, who, at the interview, extolled the many virtues of his master. "If the Minister had any thought of the old quarrel he would hardly have sent me to make friendly engagements: would he?" said he at the last.

So Chang and his adviser proceeded to the capital where formal submission was made. At the interview the visitor bowed low at the steps, but Ts'ao Ts'ao, hastening forward, took him by the hand and raised him saying "Forget that little fault of mine, I pray you."

Chang Hsiu received the title of *Yang-wu* General ("Prowess-in-War" General) and Chia Hsu that of *Chih Chin-wu* (Controller of the Ways).

Ts'ao then directed his secretaries to draft letters inviting the support of Liu Piao.

Chia Hsu said, "Liu Ching-sheng loves to have to do with famous people. If some famous scholar should be sent to him he would submit forthwith."

So Ts'ao enquired of Hsun Yu who was the best man to go as a messenger and he recommended K'ung Jung. Ts'ao agreed and sent him to speak with this officer. So he went to K'ung, saying, "A scholar of reputation is required to act as a messenger of State; can you undertake this task?"

K'ung Jung replied, "I have a certain friend, Mi Heng, whose talents are ten times mine. He ought to be constantly at the Court of the Emperor and not merely be sent as a State messenger. I will recommend him to the Emperor."

So he wrote the following memorial:—

"In ancient days, when the great waters were abroad, the Emperor pondered over their regulation and he sought out men of talent from all directions. In old time, when the Emperor Wu of the Hans desired to enlarge his borders, crowds of scholars responded to his call.

"Intelligent and holy, Your Majesty ascended the throne. You have fallen upon evil days, but have been diligent, modest and untiring in your efforts. Now the great mountains have sent forth spirits and men of genius appear.

"I, your humble servant, know of a certain simple scholar, Mi Heng by name, of P'ingyuan, a young man of twentyfour. His moral character is excellent, his talents eminent. As a youth he took a high place in study and penetrated the most secret arcana of learning. What he glanced at he could repeat, what he heard once he never forgot. He is naturally high principled and his thoughts are divine. Hung-yang's mental calculations and An-shih's mnemonical feats compared with Mi Heng's powers are no longer wonderful. Loyal, sincere, correct and straight-forward, his ambition is unsullied. He regards the good with trembling respect, he detests the evil with uncompromising hatred. Jen Tso in unflinching candour, Shih Yu in severe rectitude, never surpassed him.

"Hundreds of hawks are not worth one osprey. If Mi Heng be given a Court appointment notable results must follow. Ready in debate, rapid in utterance, his overwhelming intelligence wells up in profusion; in the solution of doubts and the unravelling of difficulties he has no peer.

"In former days Chia I begged to be sent on trial to a vassal State to be responsible for the arrest of Shan Yu; Chung Chun offered to bring the Prince of Nanyueh as with a pair of long reins. The generous conduct of these youths has been much admired. In our day Lu Tsui and Yen Hsiang, remarkable for their talents, have been appointed among the secretaries. And Mi Heng is no less capable. Should he be got, then all possibilities may be realised; the dragon may curvet through the celestial streets and soar along the Milky Way; fame will extend to the poles of the universe and hang in the firmament with rainbow glory. He would be the glory of all the present Ministers and enhance the majesty of the Palace itself. The air *Chun-t'ien* will acquire new beauties and the Palace will contain an excellent treasure. Men like Mi Heng are but few. As in the recitation of *Chi-ch'u* and the singing of *Yang-o* the most skilful performers are sought, and such fleet horses as *Fei-t'u* and *Yao-miao* were looked for by the famous judges of horses, Wang Liang and Pai Lo, so I, the humble one, dare not conceal this man. Your Majesty is careful in the selection of servants and should try him.

Let him be summoned as he is, simply clad in his serge dress, and should he not appear worthy then may I be punished for the fault of deception."

The Emperor read the memorial and passed it to his Minister, who duly summoned Mi Heng. He came, but after his formal salutations were over he was left standing and not invited to sit down. Looking up to heaven he sighed deeply, saying, "Wide as is the universe it cannot produce the man."

"Under my orders are scores of men whom the world call heroes. What do you mean by saying there is not the man?" said Ts'ao.

"I should be glad to hear who they are," said Mi.

"Hsun Yu and Hsun Yu, Kuo Chia and Ch'eng Yu are all men of profound skill and long views, superior to Hsiao Ho and Ch'en P'ing; Chang Liao and Hsu Chu, Li Tien and Yo Chin are bravest of the brave, better than Tsen P'eng and Ma Wu. Lu Ch'ien and Man Ch'ung are my secretaries, Yu Chin and Hsu Huang are my van-leaders; Hsiahou Tun is one of the world's marvels and Ts'ao Tzu-hsiao is the most successful leader of the age. Now say you there are not the men?"

"Sir, you are quite mistaken," said Mi Heng with a smile. "I know all these things you call men. Hsun Yu is qualified to pose at a funeral or ask after a sick man. Hsun Yu is fit to be a tomb guardian. Ch'eng Yu might be sent to shut doors and bolt windows, and Kuo Chia is a reciter of poems; Chang Liao might beat drums and clang gongs; Hsu Chu might lead cattle to pasture; Yo Chin would make a fair confidential clerk of the Court Li Tien could carry despatches and notices; Lu Ch'ien would be a fair armourer; Man Ch'ung could be sent to drink wine and eat brewers' grains; Yu Chin might be of use to carry planks and build walls; Hsu Huang might be employed to kill pigs and slay dogs; Hsiahou Tun should be styled 'Whole Body' General and Ts'ao Tzu-hsiao should be called 'Money-grubbing Prefect.' As for the remainder, they are mere clothes-horses, rice-sacks wine butts, flesh bags."

"And what special gifts have you?" said Ts'ao Ts'ao angrily.

"I know everything in heaven above and the earth beneath. I am conversant with the Three Religions and the Nine Systems of Philosophy. I could make my prince the rival of Yao and Shun and I myself could compare in virtue with K'ung and Yen. Can I discuss on even terms with common people?"

Now Chang Liao was present and he raised his sword to strike down the impudent visitor who spoke thus to his master, but Ts'ao Ts'ao said, "I want another drummer boy to play on occasions of congratulation in the Court. I will confer this office upon him."

Instead of indignantly declining this Mi Heng accepted the position and went out.

"He spoke very impertinently," said Liao; "Why did you not put him to death?"

"He has something of a reputation; empty, but people have heard of him and so, if I put him to death, they would say I was intolerant. As he thinks he has ability I have made him a drummer to mortify him."

Soon after Ts'ao instituted a banquet in the capital at which the guests were many. The drums were to be played and the old drummer were ordered to wear new clothes. But the new took his place with the other musicians clad in old and worn garments. The piece chosen was *Yu-yang* (or "Fishing") and from the earliest taps on the drum the effect was exquisite, profound as the notes from metal and stone. The performance stirred deeply the emotions of every guest, some even shed tears. Seeing all eyes turned on the shabby performer the attendants said, "Why did you not put on your new uniform?"

Mi Heng turned to them, slipped off his frayed and torn robe and stood there in full view, naked as he was born. The assembled guests covered their faces. Then the drummer composedly drew on his nether garments.

"Why do you behave so rudely at Court?" said Ts'ao Ts'ao.

"To flout one's prince and insult one's superiors is the real rudeness," cried Mi Heng. "I bare my natural body as an emblem of my purity."

"So you are pure! And who is foul?"

"You do not distinguish between the wise and the foolish; which is to have foul vision; you have never read the Odes or the Histories, which is to have foul speech; you are deaf to honest words, which is to have foul ears; you are unable to reconcile antiquity with today, which is to be foul without; you cannot tolerate the nobles, which is to be foul within; you harbour thoughts of rebellion, which is to have a foul heart. I am the most famous scholar in the world and you make me a drummer boy, that is as Yang Huo belittling *Chung-ni* (Confucius) or Tsang Ts'ang vilifying Meng, the Philosopher (Mencius). You desire to be chief and arbitrator of the great nobles, yet you treat me thus!"

Now K'ung Jung who had recommended Mi Heng for employment was among the guests and he feared for the life of his friend. Wherefore he tried to calm the storm.

"Mi Heng is only guilty of a misdemeanour like Hsu Mi's,"

cried he. He is not a man likely to disturb your dreams, illustrious Prince."

Pointing to Mi Heng the Minister said, "I will send you to Chingchou as my messenger and if Liu Piao surrender to me I will give you a post at Court."

But Heng was unwilling to go. So Ts'ao Ts'ao bade two of his men prepare three horses and they set Heng on the middle one and dragged him along the road between them.

It is also related that a great number of officers of all ranks assembled at the east gate to see the messenger start. Hsun Yu said, "When Mi Heng comes we will not rise to salute him."

So when Heng came, dismounted and entered the waiting room, they all sat stiff and silent. Mi Heng uttered a loud cry.

"What is that for?" said Hsun Yu.

"Should not one cry out when one enters a coffin?" said Mi Heng.

"We may be corpses," cried they altogether, "but you are a wandering ghost."

"I am a Minister of Han and not a partizan of Ts'ao's," cried he. "You cannot say I have no head."

They were angry enough to kill him, but Hsun Yu checked them. "He is a paltry fellow, it is not worth soiling your blades with his blood."

"I am paltry, am I? Yet I have the soul of a man and you are mere worms," said Mi Heng.

They went their ways all very angry. Mi Heng went on his journey and presently reached Chingchou, where he saw Liu Piao. After that, under pretence of extolling his virtue, he lampooned Piao, who was annoyed and sent him to Chianghsia to see Huang Tsu.

"Why did you not put the fellow to death for lampooning you?" said one to Liu Piao.

"You see he shamed Ts'ao Ts'ao, but Ts'ao did not kill him as he feared to lose popular favour. So he sent him to me, thinking to borrow my hand to slay him and so suffer the loss of my good name. I have sent him on to Huang Tsu to let Ts'ao see that I understood."

His clever caution met with general praise. At that time a messenger from Yuan Shao was also there with certain proposals for an alliance and it was necessary to decide which side to espouse All the advisers came together to consider the question. Then the secretary, Han Sung, said, "As you have now two offers you can please yourself and choose your own way to destroy your enemies, for if one refuse you can follow the other. Now Ts'ao Ts'ao is an able general and has many capable men in his train. It looks as though he may destroy Yuan Shao and then move his armies across the river. I fear, General, you would be unable then to withstand him. That being so it would be wise to support Ts'ao Ts'ao, who will treat you with respect."

Liu Piao replied, "You go to the capital and see how things tend. That will help me to decide."

Han Sung said, "The positions of master and servant are clearly defined. Now I am your man prepared to go all lengths for you and obey you to the last, whether in serving the Emperor or in following Ts'ao Ts'ao. But lest there should be any doubt you must remember that if the Emperor gives me any office then I shall become his servant and shall not be ready to face death for you."

"You go and find out what you can. I have ideas in my mind."

So Han Sung took his leave and went to the capital, where he saw Ts'ao. Ts'ao gave him rank and made him Prefect of Lingling. The adviser Hsun Yu remonstrated, saying, "This man came to spy out how things were moving. He has done nothing to deserve reward and yet you give him an office like this. There were no such suspicious rumours connected with poor Mi Heng and yet you sent him off and would never test his powers."

"Mi Heng shamed me too deeply before all the world. I am going to borrow Liu Piao's hand to remove him. And you need say no more," said Ts'ao.

Then Ts'ao sent Han Sung back to his former master to tell him what had happened. He came and was full of praise for the virtues of the Court and was keen on persuading Piao to espouse that side. Then Liu Piao suddenly turned angry, charged him with treachery and threatened him with death.

"You turn your back on me," cried Han Sung. "I did not betray you."

K'uai Liang remarked that Han Sung had foretold this possibility before he left, it was only what he expected. Liu Piao, who was just and reasonable, went no further.

Presently came the news that Mi Heng had been put to death by Huang Tsu on account of a quarrel begun over the wine cups. Both being worse for liquor they had begun to discuss the worth of people.

"You were in Hsutu," said Huang. "Who was there of worth?"

"The big boy was K'ung Jung and the little one Yang Te-tsu. There was no one else to count."

"What am I like?" said Huang.

"You are like a god in a temple; you sit still and receive sacrifice, but the lack of intelligence is pitiful."

"Do you regard me as a mere image?" cried Huang Tsu, angry.

So he put the impudent speaker to death. Even at the very point of death Mi never ceased his railing and abuse.

"Alas!" sighed Liu Piao, when he heard of his fate. He had the victim honourably interred near Yingwuchou. And a later poet wrote of him:—

> Huang Tsu could brook no rival; at his word
> Mi Heng met death beneath the cruel sword.
> His grave on Parrot Isle may yet be seen,
> The river flowing past it, coldly green.

Ts'ao Ts'ao heard of the young man's death with pleasure. "The putrid bookworm has just cut himself up with his own sharp tongue," said he.

As there was no sign of Liu Piao coming to join him, Ts'ao Ts'ao began to think of coercion. The adviser, Hsun Yu, dissuaded him from this course.

Said he, "Yuan Shao is not subjugated, Liu Pei is not destroyed. To attack Liu Piao would be to neglect the vital to care for the immaterial. Destroy the two chief enemies first and Chiang-han is yours at one blow."

And Ts'ao Ts'ao took the advice.

After the departure of Yuan-te, Tung Ch'eng and his fellow conspirators did nothing else day or night but try to evolve plans for the destruction of their enemy. But they could see no chance to attack. At the new year audience Ts'ao Ts'ao was odiously arrogant and overweening and the chief conspirator's disgust was so intense that he fell ill. Hearing of his indisposition the Emperor sent the Court physician to see his "State Uncle."

The Court physician at this time was a native of Loyang, named Chi T'ai, more commonly known as Chi P'ing. He was very famous. He devoted himself wholly to the treatment of his Court patient. Living in his Palace and seeing him at all times he soon found that some secret grief was sorely troubling Tung Ch'eng. But he dared not ask questions.

One evening, when the physician was just taking his leave, Tung Ch'eng kept him and the two men had supper together. They sat talking for some time and Tung by and by dropped off to sleep dressed as he was.

Presently Wang Tzu-fu and the others were announced. As they were coming in Wang cried, "Our business is settle!"

"I should be glad to hear how," said Tung.

"Liu Piao has joined Yuan Shao and fifty legions are on their way here by different routes. More than this, Ma T'eng and Han Sui are coming from the north with seventytwo legions, Ts'ao Ts'ao has moved every soldier outside Hsutu to meet the combined armies. There is a great banquet in the Palace to night and if we get together our young men and slaves, we can muster more than a thousand, and we can surround the palace, while Ts'ao Ts'ao is at the banquet, and finish him off. We must not miss this."

Tung Ch'eng was more than delighted. He called his slaves and armed them, put on his own armour and mounted his horse. The conspirators met, as they had arranged, just at the inner gate. It was the first watch. The small army marched straight in, Tung Ch'eng leading with his sword drawn. His intended victim was at table in one of the private rooms. Tung rushed in crying, "Ts'ao you rebel, stay!" and dashed at Ts'ao Ts'ao who fell at the first blow.

And just then he woke up and found it was all a dream, a dream as unreal as that of life in the kingdom of the ants. But his mouth was still full of curses.

"Do you really wish to destroy Ts'ao Ts'ao?" said Chi P'ing, going forward to his half awakened patient.

This brought him to his senses. Tung stopped, terror stricken, and made no reply.

"Do not be frightened, O Uncle," said the doctor, "Although I am a physician I am also a man, and I never forget my Emperor. You have seemed sad for many days but I have never ventured to ask the reason. Now you have shown it in your dream and I know your real feelings. If I can be of any use I will help. Nothing can daunt me."

Tung Ch'eng covered his face and wept. "I fear you may not be true to me," cried he.

Chi P'ing at once bit off a finger as a pledge of his faith. And then his host and patient brought forth the decree he had received in the girdle. "I am afraid our schemes will come to nought," said he. "Liu Yuan-te and Ma T'eng are gone and there is nothing we can do. That was the real reason I fell ill."

"It is not worth troubling you gentlemen with, for Ts'ao's life lies in these hands of mine," said Chi P'ing.

"How can that be?"

"Because he is often ill with deep seated pain in his head. When this comes on he sends for me. When next he calls me I only have to give him one dose and he will certainly die. We do not want any weapons."

"If only you could do it! You would be the saviour of the Dynasty; it depends upon you."

Then Chi P'ing went away leaving his late patient a happy man. Tung strolled into the garden and there he saw one of his slaves, Ts'in Ch'ing-t'ung, whispering with one of the waiting maids in a dark corner. This annoyed him and he called his attendants to seize them. He would have put them to death but for the intervention of his wife. At her request he spared their lives but both were beaten, and the lad was thrown into a dungeon. Sulky at his treatment the slave broke out of the cell in the night, climbed over the wall and went straight to Ts'ao Ts'ao's palace, where he betrayed the conspiracy.

Ts'ao Ts'ao at once had him taken into a secret chamber and questioned him. He gave the names of the conspirators and told as much as he knew of their doings. He said his master had a piece of white silk, with writing on it, but he did not know what it meant. Lately Chi P'ing had bitten off one of his fingers as a pledge of fidelity. He had seen that.

The runaway slave was kept in a secret part of the Palace while his late master, only knowing that he had run away, took no special means to find him.

Soon after this Ts'ao feigned a headache and sent for Chi P'ing as usual.

"The rebel is done for," thought Chi P'ing, and he mad a secret package of poison which he took with him to the palace of the Minister. He found Ts'ao in bed. The patient bade the doctor prepare a potion for him.

"One draught will cure this disease," said P'ing. He bade them bring him a pipkin and he prepared the potion in the room. When it had simmered for some time and was half finished the poison was added, and soon after the physician presented the draught. Ts'ao Ts'ao, knowing it was poisoned, made excuses and would not swallow it.

"You should take it hot," said the doctor. "Then there will be a gentle perspiration and you will be better."

"You are a scholar," said Ts'ao, sitting up, "and know what is the correct thing to do. When the master is ill and takes drugs, the attendant first tastes them; when a man is ill, his son first tastes the medicine. You are my confidant and should drink first. Then I will swallow the remainder."

"Medicine is to treat disease; what is the use of any one's tasting it?" said P'ing. But he guessed now the conspiracy had been discovered so he dashed forward, seized Ts'ao Ts'ao by the ear and tried to pour the potion down his throat. Ts'ao pushed it away and it spilt. The bricks upon which it fell were split asunder. Before Ts'ao Ts'ao could speak his servants had already seized his assailant.

Said Ts'ao, "I am not ill: I only wanted to test you. So you really thought to poison me."

He sent for a score of sturdy gaolers who carried off the prisoner to the inner apartments to be interrogated. Ts'ao took his seat in a pavilion and the hapless physician, tightly bound, was thrown to the ground before him. The prisoner maintained a bold front.

Ts'ao said "I thought you were a physician; how dared you try to poison me? Some one incited you to this crime and if you tell me I will pardon you."

"You are a rebel; you flout your Prince and injure your betters. The whole world wishes to kill you. Do you think I am the only one?"

Ts'ao again and again pressed the prisoner to tell what he knew, but he only replied that no one had sent him; it was his own desire.

"And I have failed and I can but die," added he.

Ts'ao angrily bade the gaolers give him a severe beating and they flogged him for two watches. His skin hung in tatters, the flesh was battered and the blood from his wounds ran down the steps. Then fearing he might die and his evidence be lost, Ts'ao Ts'ao bade them cease and remove him. They took him off to a quiet place where he might recover somewhat.

Having issued orders to prepare a banquet for next day Ts'ao invited all the conspirators thereto. Tung Ch'eng was the only one who excused himself, saying he was unwell. The others dared not stay away as they felt they would be suspected.

Tables were laid in the private apartments and after several courses the host said, "There is not much to amuse us today but I have a man to show you that will sober you."

"Bring him in," he said, turning to the gaolers, and the hapless Chi P'ing appeared, securely fastened in a wooden collar. He was placed where all could see him.

"You officials do not know that this man is connected with a gang of evil doers who desire to overturn the government and even injure me. However Heaven has defeated their plans, but I desire that you should hear his evidence."

Then Ts'ao ordered the lictors to beat their prisoner. They did so till he lay unconscious, when they revived him by spraying water over his face. As soon as he came to he glared at his oppressor and ground his teeth.

" Ts'ao Ts'ao you rebel! what are you waiting for? Why not kill me?" cried Chi.

Ts'ao Ts'ao replied, "The conspirators were only six at first; you made the seventh."

Here the prisoner broke in with more abuse, while Wang Tzu-fu and the others exchanged glances looking as though they were sitting on a rug full of needles. Ts'ao continued his torture of the prisoner, beating him into unconsciousness and reviving him with cold water, the victim disdaining to ask mercy. Finally Ts'ao realised he would incriminate none of his accomplices and so he told the gaolers to remove him.

At the close of the banquet, when the guests were dispersing, four of them, the four conspirators, were invited to remain behind to supper. They were terrified so that their souls seemed no longer to inhabit their bodies, but there was no saying nay to the invitation. Presently Ts'ao Ts'ao said, "Still there is something I want to speak about so I have asked you to stay for a time longer. I do not know what you four have been arranging with Tung Ch'eng."

"Nothing at all," said Wang.

"And what is written on the white silk?" asked Ts'ao.

They all said they knew nothing about it.

Then Ts'ao ordered the runaway slave to be brought in. As soon as he came Wang said, "Well, what have you seen and where?"

The slave Ch'ing-t'ung replied, "You six very carefully chose retired places to talk in and you secretly signed a white roll. You cannot deny that."

Wang replied, "This miserable creature was punished for misbehaviour with one of Uncle Tung's maids and now because of that he slanders his master. You must not listen to him."

"Chi P'ing tried to pour poison down my throat. Who told him to do that if it was not Tung?"

They all said they knew nothing about who it was.

"So far," said Ts'ao, "matters are only beginning and there is a chance of forgiveness. But if the thing grows, it will be difficult not to take notice of it."

The whole four vigorously denied that any plot existed. However Ts'ao called up his henchmen and the four men were put into confinement.

Next day Ts'ao Ts'ao with a large following went to the State

Uncle's Palace to ask after his health. Ch'eng came out to receive his visitor, who at once said, "Why did you not come last night?"

"I am not quite well yet and have to be very careful about going out," replied Ch'eng.

"One might say you were suffering from national sorrow, eh?" said Ts'ao.

Ch'eng started. Ts'ao continued, "Have you heard of the Chi P'ing affair?"

"No; what is it?"

Ts'ao smiled coldly. "How can it be you do not know?"

Ts'ao turned to his attendants and told them to bring in the prisoner while he went on talking to his host about his illness.

Tung Ch'eng was much put about and knew not what to do. Soon the gaolers led in the physician to the steps of the hall. At once the bound man began to rail at Ts'ao as rebel and traitor.

"This man," said Ts'ao, pointing to Chi P'ing, "has implicated Wang Tzu-fu and three others, all of whom are now under arrest. There is one more whom I have not caught yet."

"Who sent you to poison me?" continued he, turning toward the physician. "Quick, tell me."

"Heaven sent me to slay a traitor."

Ts'ao angrily ordered them to beat him again, but there was no part of his body that could be beaten. Tung Ch'eng sat looking at him, his heart feeling as if transfixed with a dagger.

"You were born with ten fingers; how is it you have now only nine?"

Chi P'ing replied, "I bit off one as a pledge when I swore to slay a traitor."

Ts'ao told them to bring a knife and they lopped off his other nine fingers.

"Now they are all off; that will teach you to make pledges."

"Still I have a mouth that can swallow a traitor and a tongue that can curse him," said Chi P'ing.

Ts'ao told them to cut out his tongue.

Chi P'ing said, "Do not. I cannot endure any more punishment I shall have to speak out. Loosen my bonds."

"Loose them. There is no reason why not," said Ts'ao.

They loosed him. As soon as he was free Chi P'ing stood up, turned his face toward the Emperor's Palace and bowed, saying, "It is Heaven's will that thy servant has been unable to remove the evil," then he turned and fell dead on the steps.

His body was quartered and exposed.

This happened in the first month of the fifth year of "Established Tranquillity" and a certain historian wrote a poem:—

> There lived in Han a simple leech.
> No warrior, yet brave
> Enough to risk his very life
> His Emperor to save.
> Alas! he failed; but lasting fame
> Is his; he feared not death;
> He cursed the traitorous Minister
> Unto his latest breath.

Seeing his victim had passed beyond the realm of punishment Ts'ao had the slave led in.

"Do you know this man, Uncle?"

"Yes," cried Tung Ch'eng. "So the runaway slave is here; he ought to be put to death."

"He just told me of your treachery; he is my witness," said Ts'ao. "Who would dare kill him?"

"How can you, the first Minister of State, heed the unsupported tale of an absconding slave?"

"But I have Wang and the others in prison," said Ts'ao Ts'ao. "And how can you rebut their evidence?"

He then called in the remainder of his followers and ordered them to search Tung Ch'eng's bedroom. They did so and found the decree that had been given him in the girdle and the pledge signed by the conspirators.

"You mean rat!" cried Ts'ao, "you dared do this?"

He gave orders to arrest the whole household without exception. Then he returned to his Palace with the incriminating documents and called all his advisers together to discuss the dethronement of the Emperor and the setting up of a successor.

> Many decrees, blood written, have issued, accomplishing nothing
> One inscribed pledge was fraught with mountains of sorrow.

The reader who wishes to know the fate of the Emperor must read the next chapter.

CHAPTER XXIV

MURDER OF A KUEI-FEI: LIU PEI DEFEATED: FLIGHT TO YUAN SHAO

The last chapter closed with the discovery of the "girdle" decree and the assembly of Ts'ao Ts'ao's advisers to consider the deposition of the Emperor Hsien. Ch'eng Yu spoke strongly against this saying, "Illustrious Sir, the means by which you impress the world and direct the government is the command of the House of Han. In these times of turmoil and rivalry among the nobles such a step as the deposition of the ruler will certainly bring about civil war and is much to be deprecated."

After reflection Ts'ao Ts'ao abandoned the project. But Tung Ch'eng's plot was not to go unpunished. All five of the conspirators with every member of their households, seven hundred at least, were taken and put to death at one or another of the gates of the city. The people wept at such merciless and wholesale slaughter.

> A secret decree in a girdle sewn,
> In red blood written, the Emperor's own,
> To the staunch and faithful Tung addressed,
> Who had saved him once when enemies pressed,
> And who, sore grieved at his Sovereign's fate,
> Expressed in dreams his ceaseless hate,
> Carried misfortune and death in its train
> But glory to him who died in vain.

Another poet wrote of the sad fate of Wang Tzu-fu and his friends:—

> Greatheartedly these signed the silken roll,
> And pledged themselves to save their King from shame.
> Alas! black death of them took heavy toll,
> To write their names upon the roll of fame.

But the slaughter of the conspirators and their whole households did not appease the wrath of the cruel Minister. The Emperor's *Kuei-fei* was a sister of Tung Ch'eng and, sword in hand, Ts'ao Ts'ao went into the palace determined to slay her also. The Emperor cherished her tenderly, the more so as she was then in the fifth month of pregnancy. That day, as they often did, the Emperor, his Consort and the *Kuei-fei* were sitting in their private apartments secretly talking of the decree entrusted to Tung Ch'eng and asking each other why nothing seemed to have been done. The sudden appearance of the angry Minister, armed as he was, frightened them greatly.

"Does Your Majesty know that Tung Ch'eng conspired against me?" said he.

"Tung Cho died long ago," replied the Emperor.

"Not Tung Cho; Tung Ch'eng," roared Ts'ao.

The Emperor's heart trembled but he gasped out, "Really I did not know."

"So the cut finger and the blood written decree are all forgotten, eh?"

The Emperor was silent. Ts'ao bade his lictors seize the *Kuei-fei.* The Emperor interposed asking pity for her condition.

"If Heaven had not interposed and defeated the plot I should be a dead man. How could I leave this woman to work evil to me by and by?"

Said the Emperor, "Immure her in one of the palaces till her confinement. Do not harm her now."

"Do you wish me to spare her offspring to avenge the mother?" said Ts'ao.

"I pray that my body may be spared mutilation and not put to shame," said Tung *Kuei-fei.*

Ts'ao bade his men show her the white silk cord. The Emperor wept bitterly.

"Do not hate me in the realms below the Nine Springs," said the Emperor to her.

His tears fell like rain. The Empress Fu also joined in the lament, but Ts'ao said, "You are behaving like a lot of children," and told the lictors to take her away and strangle her in the courtyard.

> In vain had the fair girl found favour in the sight of her lord,
> She died, and the fruit of her womb perished.
> Stern and calm her lord sat, powerless to save,
> Hiding his face while tears gushed forth.

When leaving the palace Ts'ao gave strict orders to the keepers saying "Any one of the Imperial relatives by marriage who enter the Palace will be put to death, and the guards will share the same punishment for lack of zeal."

To make more sure he appointed three companies of Imperial Guards from his own men and appointed Ts'ao Hung to the command.

Then said Ts'ao to his counsellor, Ch'eng Yu, "The conspirators in the capital have been removed, it is true, but there are yet two others, Ma T'eng and Liu Pei. These must not be left."

Ch'eng Yu replied, "Ma T'eng is strong in the west and would not be easily captured. He might be enticed to the capital by suave words and kindly praises, when he would be at your mercy. The other is at Hsuchou, strongly posted, and not to be lightly attacked. More than this, Yuan Shao is at Kuantu and his one desire is to attack you. Any attempt on the east will send Liu Pei to him for help and he will come here at once. Then what will you do?"

"You are at fault," replied Ts'ao Ts'ao. "Lu Pei is a bold warrior and if we wait till he is fully fledged and winged, he will be more difficult to deal with. Shao may be strong but he is not to be feared. He is too undecided to act."

As they were discussing these things Kuo Chia came in and Ts'ao Ts'ao suddenly referred the matter to him.

"If I attack Liu Pei, then Yuan Shao is to be feared: what do you think of it?"

"Shao by nature is dilatory and hesitating and his various advisers are jealous of each other. He is not to be feared. Liu Pei is getting together a new army and has not yet won their hearts. You could settle the east in one battle."

This advice being in harmony with Ts'ao Ts'ao's own opinion was pleasing to him and he prepared an army of twenty legions, to move in five divisions against Hsuchou.

Scouts took the news of these preparations to Hsuchou. Sun Ch'ien first went to Hsiap'i to tell Kuan Yu and then went to Hsiaop'ei to tell Yuan-te. The two discussed the position and decided that help must be sought. So letters were written to Yuan Shao and given to Sun Ch'ien, who went north, sought T'ien Feng and asked him to take him into the presence of Yuan Shao. He was introduced and presented his letters.

But Yuan Shao was of melancholy countenance and his dress was all awry. T'ien Feng said, "Why this disarray, my lord?"

"I am about to die," replied Shao.

"But why do you utter such words?"

"I have five sons, but only the youngest is clever enough to understand my ideas. Now he is suffering from a disease which places his life in jeopardy. Think you that I have any heart to talk over any other affairs?"

"But," said T'ien Feng, "the present combination of circumstances is unparalleled. Ts'ao Ts'ao is going to attack the east and Hsuch'ang will be empty. You can enter it with a few volunteers and so perform good service to the Emperor and save the people from sorrow. You have only to make up your mind to act."

"I know the chance is excellent but I am worried and distressed and fear failure."

"What are you distressed about?" said Feng.

"Among my sons only this special one is remarkable and if anything happens I am done."

Thus it became evident that no army would be despatched. In confirmation of this Yuan said to Sun Ch'ien, "Go home and tell Yuan-te the real reason and say that if anything untoward happen he can come over to me and I will find some means of helping him."

T'ien Feng struck the ground with his staff. "It is such a pity!" cried he. "Just as an unique opportunity presents itself everything is spoiled by the illness of a child."

He went out. Sun Ch'ien saw that no help could be hoped for and set out to return. When he had arrived and related what he had seen Yuan-te was quite alarmed and asked what could be done.

"Do not be troubled, brother," said Chang Fei. "We can destroy Ts'ao Ts'ao merely by a sudden attack before his army shall have time to camp."

"That would be according to the rules of war," said Yuan-te. "You have always been a bold warrior and that move against Liu Tai shows that you are becoming a strategist too."

So he gave his younger brother command of enough men to carry out his plan.

Now while Ts'ao Ts'ao was in the midst of his march toward Hsiaop'ei a tornado sprang up and the howling gale tore down one of the banners and broke the staff. Ts'ao Ts'ao called together his advisers and leaders to ask them what this portended. Hsun Yu said, "From what direction was the wind at the time and what was the colour of the flag?"

"The wind was from the south-east and the flag was blue and red."

"There is only one interpretation; there will be a raid on the camp tonight."

Ts'ao nodded. At that moment Mao Chih entered and reported a similar incident. Ts'ao asked him the portent.

"My foolishness tells me that it means a night raid," replied he.

> Alas for the weakness of this descendant of kings!
> He placed his faith on a night raid,
> But the broken staff of a banner warned his enemy.
> Why should the ancient of days favour the wicked?

"This is evidently providence," said Ts'ao Ts'ao and he began to make preparations. He told off nine bodies of men to take stations, leaving only one of them as if camped while he placed the others in ambush at eight points.

There was but little moonlight as Yuan-te and Chang Fei marched their respective armies toward Ts'ao Ts'ao's camp. They had left Sun Ch'ien to guard Hsiaop'ei. Chang Fei, since he was the originator of the stratagem, led the way with some light horse. As they drew near everything seemed very quiet and no one seemed moving. Then suddenly lights flashed out all about them and Chang Fei saw he had fallen into a trap. At once from all the eight directions came out the ambushed troops.

Chang Fei, dashing this way and rushing that, guarding his van and protecting his rear, vainly tried to clear himself. The soldiers he had, being originally Ts'ao Ts'ao's men, soon gave in and returned to their old leader. The position became very desperate.

Chang Fei met Hsu Huang and engaged him but his rear was also attacked by Yo Chin. At length he cut his own way out and with a half score of his men started to return to Hsiaop'ei. The retreat was cut off. He thought to make for Hsuchou but felt certain that way was also barred. No other way seemed open and so he made for the Mangyang Hills.

As Yuan-te drew near the camp he intended to attack he heard the din of battle. Then he was attacked in the rear and very soon had lost half his force. Next Hsiahou Tun came to attack. Thereupon Yuan-te bolted. He was pursued by Hsiahou Yuan. Presently he looked about him and found he had less than half a hundred men following him. He set his face in the direction of Hsiaop'ei.

But before long he saw that place was in flames. So he changed his plan and went toward Hsiap'i. However he found the whole countryside full of the enemy and he could not get through. So he bethought himself of the promise of Yuan Shao, that he would find refuge if things went agley, and determined to go to him till he could form some other plan. Wherefore he took the Ch'ingchou road. But it also was blocked and he went into the open country and made his way north, not without being pursued and losing the remainder of his few followers.

He hastened toward Ch'ingchou, travelling three hundred *li* a day. When he reached the city and summoned the gate the guards asked who he was and they told the governor, who was Yuan Shao's eldest son, T'an. Yuan T'an was greatly surprised, but he opened the gates and went to meet Yuan-te, whom he treated with due consideration.

Liu Pei told the story of his defeat and said he wished for harbour. He was given suitable quarters and hospitably entertained, while the young man wrote to inform his father. Then he provided an escort and sent Yuan-te on his journey as far as the boundary of P'ingyuan.

At Yehchun he was met by Yuan Shao in person, with a great escort. Yuan-te made a humble obeisance which Yuan Shao hastened to return and said, "I have been very distressed that, on account of my son's illness, I did not come to your aid. It is great joy to see you; the one desire of my life is satisfied."

Yuan-te replied, "The poor Liu Pei you see here has long desired to take refuge with you, but fate has hitherto denied him that privilege. Now, attacked by Ts'ao Ts'ao, my family lost, I remembered that you, General, would receive gentlemen from all sides. Wherefore I put my pride in my pocket. I trust that I may be found worthy and one day I will prove my gratitude."

Yuan Shao received him with much pleasure and treated him exceedingly well. And they both lived in Ch'ichou.

After the capture of Hsiaop'ei, Ts'ao Ts'ao pressed on toward Hsuchou, which, after a short defence and the flight of the defenders, was surrendered by Ch'en Teng. Ts'ao Ts'ao led his army into the city, restored order and pacified the people. Next he wanted to press on to Hsiap'i, where Kuan Yu was holding out and keeping guard of Liu Pei's family.

Hsun Yu said, "Kuan Yu is there, in charge of his brother's family, and he will defend the city to the last. If you do not take it quickly Yuan Shao will get it."

"I have always loved Kuan Yu, both for his warlike abilities and his intelligence. I would engage him to enter my service. I would rather send some one to talk him into surrender."

"He will not do that," said Kuo Chia; "his sense of right is too solid. I fear any one who went to speak with him would suffer."

Then suddenly a man stepped out, saying, "I know him slightly and I will go."

The speaker was Chang Liao. Hsun Yu looked at him and said, "Though you are an old acquaintance I do not think you are equal to talking over Kuan Yu. But I have a scheme that will so entangle him that he will have no alternative; he will have to enter the service of the Minister."

> They set the fatal spring beside the lordly tiger's trail,
> They hide the hook with fragrant bait to catch the mighty whale.

How Kuan Yu was to be entrapped will be told in the next chapter.

CHAPTER XXV

FROM T'USHAN CAMP KUAN YU MAKES
THREE CONDITIONS: THE RESCUE AT PAIMA
RELEASES TS'AO TS'AO

The plan to seduce Kuan Yu from allegiance to his brothers was now announced by its proposer. Since Kuan was far braver than ordinary men he could only be overreached by superior cunning. So it was proposed to send some of his soldiers who had lately been of Liu Pei's army into Hsiap'i, where they would say they had come back. They would thus be allies on the inside. Then an attack and a feigned defeat would entice Kuan to a distance from the city. And his return road would be cut.

Ts'ao Ts'ao accepted the scheme and a few score of the men who had lately been in Hsuchou were sent to the city. The commander believed the story they told and trusted them. So they were suffered to remain.

After this part of the game had been played, Hsiahou Tun led forward five companies against the city. At first Kuan Yu would not accept the challenge, but provoked by men sent to hurl insults at him from the foot of the wall, his wrath got the better of him and he moved out with three companies. After the leaders had exchanged a half score bouts Tun made to run away. Kuan Yu pursued. Tun stopped and made a stand; then he fled again. Thus alternately fighting and retiring, he enticed Kuan Yu twenty *li* from the city. Then Kuan suddenly remembering the risk to the city drew off his men to return homeward.

Soon, at the sound of a signal bomb, out moved two bodies of men who barred his way. Kuan Yu hastened along a road that seemed to offer retreat, but from both sides his ambushed enemies shot their crossbows and the arrows flew like locusts on the wing. No way past was found and he turned back. Then both bodies joined in attacking him. He drove them off and got into the road to his own city, but soon Hsiahou Tun came up again and attacked fiercely as before. Evening came and still Kuan was hemmed in, so he went up on a low hill upon which he encamped for a rest.

He was surrounded on all sides by enemies. By and by, looking toward his city, he saw the glow of fire. It meant that the traitors, who had come in to surrender, had opened the gate and the enemy had gone in force. They had made the fires in order to perplex and distress Kuan Yu and indeed the sight saddened him.

In the night he made efforts to escape from the hill, but every attempt was cheeked by flights of arrows. At daybreak he prepared for one more effort, but before moving he saw a horseman riding up at full speed and presently discerned Chang Liao. When within speaking distance, Kuan Yu said, "Are you come to fight me, Wen-yuan?"

"No," replied Chang Liao. "I am come to see you because of our old friendship."

Wherefore he threw aside his sword, dismounted and came forward saluting. And the two sat down.

"Then naturally you have come to talk me over," said Kuan Yu.

"Not so," said Chang Liao. "Sometime ago you saved me; can I help saving you?"

"Then you desire to help me."

"Not exactly that," replied Chang.

"Then what are you doing here if you have not come to help me."

"Nothing is known of the fate of your elder brother, nor whether your younger brother is alive or dead. Last night your city fell into the hands of Ts'ao Ts'ao, but neither soldiers nor people were harmed and a special guard was set over the family of Yuan-te lest they should be alarmed. I came to tell you how well they had been treated."

"This is certainly talking me over," said Kuan testily. "Though escape is impossible yet I am not perturbed. I look upon death as going home. You had better depart quickly and let me go down and begin the struggle again."

"Surely you must know everybody will ridicule you when they hear of this," said Chang, laughing loud.

"I shall die for loyalty and righteousness. Who will laugh?" said Kuan.

"You would be guilty of three faults if you died."

"Tell me them," said Kuan.

"First of all you and your elder brother pledged yourselves in the Peach Garden to die or to live together. Now your brother has been defeated and you want to fight to the death. Therefore, if your brother appear again by and by and wants your help, he will seek it in vain. Is this anything else than betraying the Peach Garden oath? Secondly you are in charge of your brother's family and, if you fought and died, the two women would be left forlorn and without a protector. That would be a betrayal of trust. Thirdly your military skill stands out conspicuous and will go down in history. If you do not aid your brother in his noble attempt to maintain the Dynasty then all your labours and sufferings will have been spent to win a worthless reputation as a valiant fool. Where is the sense in that? I feel it my duty to point out these three faults to you."

Kuan Yu remained silent and thought for some time. Then he said, "You have spoken of my three faults, What do you desire?"

"You are surrounded with the certainty of death if you do not yield. There is no advantage in a useless death. Wherefore your best course is to yield to Ts'ao Ts'ao till you hear news of Liu Pei and can rejoin him. Thus you will ensure the safety of the two ladies and also keep inviolate the Peach Garden compact. You will preserve a useful life. Brother, you must reflect on these things."

"Brother, you have spoken of three advantages; now I have three conditions. If the Minister concede these then will I doff my armour. If he refuse, then I prefer to be guilty of the three faults and die."

"Why should the Minister not concede them? He is most liberal and large minded. I pray you to let me hear your conditions."

"The first is that as I and the Imperial Uncle have sworn to support the Hans I now submit to the Emperor and not to his minister Ts'ao. The second condition is that suitable provision be made for the two ladies under my care and that no one shall be allowed to approach them. The third is that I shall be allowed to set off to rejoin Uncle Liu so soon as I shall hear where he is, whether it be far or near. I require all these to be satisfied; failing a single one, I will not submit. Wherefore, Wen-yuan, I pray you hasten back and announce them."

Chang Liao lost no time but rode back to Ts'ao Ts'ao. When he spoke of Kuan Yu's intention to submit to the Hans but not to Ts'ao Ts'ao, the latter smiled, saying, "As I am the Minister of Han, so am I Han. I grant that."

Chang then spoke of provision due to their rank and security from molestation for the ladies, to which Ts'ao replied, "I will give them twice the regular amount for an Uncle of the Emperor; as for securing them from molestation, that is simple. The ordinary domestic law is enough. Why should there be any doubt?"

Then said Chang, "Whenever he shall get news of the whereabouts of Yuan-te, he must go to him."

At this Ts'ao shook his head, saying, "Then I am merely to feed Yun-ch'ang. What is the use of this? I cannot consent."

Chang replied, "You must know of the difference in Yu Jang's behaviour brought about by difference of treatment? Yuan-te treats Yun-ch'ang just kindly and liberally; you can surely engage his heart and support by being kinder and more liberal."

"What you say is much to the point. I will grant the three conditions," said Ts'ao.

Whereupon Chang Liao left to carry the news to Kuan Yu, still on the summit of the hill.

"Now I expect the army to withdraw so that I may enter the city to tell the two ladies what has been arranged. After that I submit at once."

Chang Liao rode back once more with this request and the order was given for the army to retire ten *li*.

"Do not do this," said Hsun Yu. "I fear treachery."

"He will certainly not break faith," said Ts'ao Ts'ao. He is too high principled."

The army retired and Kuan Yu with his force reentered the city, where he saw that the people were following their ordinary avocations in tranquillity. He came to the palace and went in to see the two ladies, who hastened to meet him. He bowed to them below the steps and said, "I apologise for having caused you to feel alarmed."

"Where is the Uncle?" asked they.

"I know not whither he has gone."

"What do you intend to do, brother-in-law?"

"I went out of the city to try a last battle. I was surrounded on a hill top and Chang Liao has urged me to yield. I proposed three conditions, all of which were conceded, and the enemy drew off to allow me to return to the city. Unless I have your decision, sisters-in-law, I scarcely dare to take any final step."

They asked what were the conditions and were told. Then Kan *Fu-jen* said, "When Ts'ao's army came in we took it to mean certain death. But it is scarcely credible that not a hair of our heads has been disturbed, not a soldier has dared enter our doors. You have accepted the conditions, brother-in-law, and there is no need to ask our consent. Our only fear is that he will not let you go by and by to search for the Uncle."

"Sisters-in-law, you need not be anxious. I will see to that."

"You must decide everything and need not ask us women-kind."

Kuan Yu withdrew and then, with a small escort, went to his interview with Ts'ao Ts'ao. Ts'ao came to the outermost gate to welcome him and Kuan Yu dismounted and made obeisance. Ts'ao returned his salute with the greatest cordiality.

"The leader of a defeated army is grateful for the graciousness that has preserved his life," said Kuan Yu.

"I have so long admired your loyalty and high principles that this happy meeting gratifies the desire of my whole life," replied Ts'ao.

"As the Minister has granted the three requests which my friend petitioned for on my behalf there is now but little to discuss," said Kuan.

"As I have spoken, so be it; I could not break faith," replied Ts'ao.

"Whenever I hear where Uncle Liu is I must certainly go to him, even if through fire and water. It may be that there will be no opportunity of taking leave. I trust you will understand the reason."

"If Liu Pei should prove to be alive you must certainly be allowed to go to him. But I fear that in the confusion he may have lost his life. You may set your mind at rest and let me make enquiries."

Kuan Yu thanked him. Then a banquet was prepared in his honour. Next day the army started on its homeward march.

For the journey to the capital a carriage was prepared for the two ladies and Kuan Yu was its guard. On the road they rested at a certain post station and Ts'ao Ts'ao, anxious to compromise Kuan by beguiling him into forgetfulness of his duty, assigned him to the same apartment as his sisters-in-law. Kuan stood the whole night before the door with a lighted candle in his hand. Not once did he yield to fatigue. Ts'ao Ts'ao's respect for him could not but increase.

At the capital the Minister assigned a dignified residence to Kuan Yu, which he immediately divided into two enclosures, the inner one for the two ladies and the other for himself. He placed a guard of eighteen of his veterans over the women's quarters.

Kuan Yu was presented to the Emperor Hsien who conferred upon him the rank of General. Soon after Ts'ao made a great banquet, inviting all his advisers and fighting men, solely in honour of Kuan Yu, who sat in the seat of honour. Beside this he received presents of silks and gold and silver vessels, all of which were sent into the ladies' quarters for their use and keeping. In fact from the day of arrival in the capital Kuan Yu was treated with marked respect and distinction, banquets and feasts following each other in quick succession.

Ts'ao Ts'ao also presented him with ten most lovely serving girls; these also were sent within to wait upon his two sisters-in-law.

Every third day Kuan Yu went to the door of the women's quarters to enquire after their welfare, and then they asked if any news of the wanderer had come. This ceremony closed with the words "Brother-in-law, you may retire when you wish."

Ts'ao heard of this extremely correct behaviour and thought all the more of the man for it.

One day Ts'ao noticed that the robe Kuan Yu was wearing was old and frayed. Taking his measurements Ts'ao had a new one made of fine brocade and presented it to him. He took it and put it on under the old robe, so that the latter covered it.

"Why so very thrifty?" laughed Ts'ao.

"It is not thrift," was his reply. "The old robe was a gift from my brother and I wear it because it reminds me of him. I could not allow the new gift to eclipse his old one."

"How very high principled!" said Ts'ao Ts'ao sighing.

But he was not pleased with the man or a his conduct. One day when Kuan Yu was at home there came a messenger to say that the two women had thrown themselves on the ground and were weeping. They would not say why. Kuan Yu set his dress in order, went over and knelt by the door saying, "Why this grief, sisters-in-law?"

Kan *Fu-jen* replied, "In the night I dreamed that the Uncle had fallen into a pit. I woke up and told Mi *Fu-jen* and we think he must be dead. So we weep."

"Dreams are not to be credited," he replied. "You dreamed of him because you were thinking of him. Pray do not grieve."

Just then Kuan Yu was invited to another banquet so he took leave of the ladies and went. Seeing Kuan look sad and tearful his host asked the reason.

"My sisters-in-law have been weeping for my brother and I cannot help being sad in sympathy."

Ts'ao smiled and tried to cheer up his guest. He plied him with wine so that he became quite intoxicated and sat stroking his beard and saying, "What a useless thing am I! I could do no service for my country and I have parted from my elder brother."

"How many hairs in your beard?" suddenly asked his host.

"Some hundreds, perhaps. In the autumn a few fall out, but in the winter it is fullest. Then I use a black silk bag to keep the hairs from being broken," replied Kuan.

Ts'ao had a bag made for him to protect his beard. Soon after when they were at Court the Emperor asked what was the bag he saw on Kuan Yu's breast.

"My beard is rather long. Your Majesty," said Kuan. "So the Minister gave me a bag to protect it."

The Emperor bade him take off the bag and show his beard in all its fullness and it fell in rippling waves below his breast.

"Really a most beautiful beard!" said the Emperor.

This is why people call him "The Duke with the Beautiful Beard."

Another time, after a banquet, Ts'ao was seeing his guest start from the gate of his palace when he noticed that his charger was very thin.

"Why is he so thin?" said Ts'ao.

"My worthless body is rather heavy and really too much for him. He is always out of condition."

Ts'ao at once told his men to bring out a certain steed and before long he appeared. He was red, like glowing charcoal, and a handsome creature in every way.

"Do you recognise him?" asked Ts'ao.

"Why, it is no other than 'Red Hare!'" cried Kuan Yu.

"Yes; it is he," said Ts'ao, and he presented the horse, all fully caparisoned, to his guest. Kuan Yu bowed many times and thanked him again and again, till Ts'ao began to feel displeased and said, "I have given you many things, lovely handmaids and gold and silks and never won a bow of gratitude from you before. This horse seems to please you better than all the rest. Why do you think so poorly of the damsels and so much of the steed?"

"I know the horse, and his speed, and I am very lucky to get him. Now as soon as I find out where my brother is I can get to him in a single day," said Kuan.

Ts'ao grumbled to himself and began to repent of his gift, but Kuan Yu took his leave and went away.

> Fortune dealt a stunning blow, still he played his part;
> Partitioning his dwelling proved his purity of heart.
> The crafty Minister desired to win him to his side,
> But felt that failure was foredoomed however much he tried.

Said Ts'ao Ts'ao to Chang Liao, "I have treated him pretty liberally, but he still cherishes the desire to leave me. Do you know if it is really so?"

"I will try to find out," was the reply.

So he took an early opportunity of seeing Kuan Yu and when

the politenesses of the visit were over, Liao said, "I recommended you to the Minister and you have not lost much by that."

"I am deeply affected by his kindness and bounty," said Kuan Yu, "but, though my body is here, yet I am always thinking of my brother."

"Your words do not express present conditions quite correctly. One who lives in the world without discrimination and consideration of his relations with others is not the most admirable type of man. Even Yuan-te never treated you better than does the Minister. Why then do you maintain this desire to get away?"

"I know only too well that he has been most kind, but I have also received great kindness from Uncle Liu. Beside we have sworn to die together and I cannot remain here, but before I go I must try to render him some signal service to prove my gratitude."

"Supposing Yuan-te should have left the world, whither will you go?" said Chang.

"I will follow him to the realms below."

There could no longer be the least doubt as to Kuan Yu's intentions and Chang Liao told Ts'ao Ts'ao just how matters stood. Ts'ao sighed. "To serve one's chief with unswerving fidelity is a proof of the highest principle of all," said he.

Said Hsun Yu, "He spoke of performing some act of service before leaving. If he gets no chance of such a thing, he will not be able to go."

Ts'ao Ts'ao agreed that this was so.

The story of Yuan-te broke off at the point when he went to Yuan Shao for refuge. Here he was always sorrowful and, when asked the reason, said he did not know where his brothers were nor what had happened to his family since they fell into the hands of Ts'ao Ts'ao.

"Why should I not be sad when I have failed towards my country and my family?" said he.

"I have long wished to attack Hsutu," said Yuan Shao. "Now it is autumn and just the time for an expedition, so let us discuss plans for the destruction of Ts'ao Ts'ao."

T'ien Feng at once opposed this. "When Ts'ao Ts'ao attacked Hsuchou and Hsutu was undefended you let the chance slip by. Now that Hsuchou has been captured and the soldiers are flushed with victory it would be madness to attempt it. It is necessary to await another chance."

"Let me think about it," said Yuan Shao.

He asked advice from Yuan-te, whether to attack or to hold on.

Yuan-te replied, "Ts'ao is a rebel. I think you are failing in your duty if you do not attack him."

"Your words are good," said Shao.

He made up his mind to move. But again the adviser T'ien intervened. Then Shao grew angry, saying, "You fellows who cultivate literature and despise war have made me miss a lot."

T'ien Feng bowed his head and said, "Neglect your servant's wise words and you will fail in the field."

Yuan Shao was so angry that he wanted to put him to death. However Yuan-te begged him off and he was only imprisoned.

Seeing the fate of his colleague another adviser, Chu Shou by name, assembled his clan and distributed among them all his possessions, saying, "I go with the army. If we succeed, then nothing can exceed our glory, but if we are defeated, the risk I run is great."

His friends wept as they said farewell.

Yen Liang was appointed to the command of the advance guard, to go to attack Paima. Then Chu Shou first protested, "His mind is too narrow for such a post. He is brave but unequal to such a trust."

"You are not the sort of man to measure my best generals," replied Shao.

The army marched to Liyang and the Prefect sent an urgent call to Hsuch'ang for aid. Ts'ao moved his armies hastily. As soon as the news of battle got about Kuan Yu went to see the Minister and asked that he might go with the first body.

"I scarcely dare put you to such inconvenience, but presently, if need arises, I will call upon you."

So Kuan Yu retired and fifteen legions marched out in three directions. On the road the letters from Liu Yen arrived praying for help and the first five legions went to Paima and took up a position supported by the hills. In the wide plains in front of them Yen Liang was encamped with ten legions of veterans.

Ts'ao Ts'ao was frightened at the force opposed to him and, returning to camp, spoke to Sung Hsien, who had once served under Lu Pu, saying, "You are one of Lu Pu's famous veteran generals; can you give battle to this Yen?"

Sung Hsien agreed to try. He armed himself, mounted and rode to the front. Yen Liang was there on horseback his sword lying crossways. Seeing an opponent approaching he uttered a loud shout and galloped toward him. The two met, but after only three bouts, Sung Hsien fell under a mighty slash from the other's sword.

"What a terrible leader!" said Ts'ao.

"He has slain my comrade, I want to go and avenge him," then cried Wei Hsu.

Ts'ao bade him go and he rode out, spear in rest, and in front of the army railed at Yen Liang.

Yen Liang replied not a word, but their two steeds came together and at the first blow from Yen's sword this second champion fell.

"Now, who again dares face him?" cried Ts'ao.

Hsu Huang took up the challenge and he went out. The combat endured a score of bouts and then Hsu fled back to his own side. The other captains were now greatly depressed at their failure. Yen Liang however had marched off his men leaving Ts'ao very sad at the loss of two captains in quick succession.

Then Ch'eng Yu went to see him saying, "I can produce a man the equal of Yen Liang."

"Who?" cried Ts'ao.

"No other than Kuan Yu."

"I am afraid that if he is given an opportunity to perform that return service he spoke of he will leave me."

"If Liu Pei is still alive he is with Yuan Shao. If you get Kuan Yu to defeat Yuan Shao's army Shao will look askance at Liu Pei and put him to death. Liu Pei gone, where can Kuan Yu go?"

This argument appealed to Ts'ao Ts'ao at once and he sent to request Kuan Yu to come.

Previous to obeying the call Kuan went to say farewell to his sisters-in-law.

"You may get news of the Uncle on the journey," said they.

"Yes," said Kuan and left them.

Armed with his famous Black Dragon, riding on the swift steed "Red Hare," and having but a slender following, Kuan Yu was not long in arriving at Paima. He saw Ts'ao Ts'ao, who told him what had happened. Yen Liang was too valiant for any to face.

"Let me look at him," said Kuan.

Then wine was served for his refreshment and while they were drinking, it was reported that Yen Liang once again offered a challenge. So Ts'ao and his guest and staff went to the summit of a hill whence the enemy could be seen. These two sat on the hill top and the captains stood about them. Ts'ao pointed out Yen Liang's men arrayed on the plains below. The ensigns and banners waving fresh and bright amid the forest of spears and swords made a grand and imposing spectacle.

"See what fine fellows these northmen are," said Ts'ao.

"I regard them as so many clay fowls and mud dogs," said Kuan.

Ts'ao Ts'ao pointed out Yen Liang, saying, "There he is under that umbrella."

He was wearing an embroidered robe and a silver breastplate and rode on horseback. His hand gripped his sword.

"His head looks as though it was stuck on a pole for sale," said Kuan, just glancing over the army at his feet.

"You must not despise him," said Ts'ao.

Kuan rose, saying, "I am a poor thing but I will go over and bring you his head if you like."

"Joking is not allowed in this army," interposed Chang Liao. "Be careful what you say."

Kuan Yu quickly mounted, turned down his mighty weapon and galloped down the hill, his phoenix eyes rounded and his heavy eyebrows fiercely bristling. He dashed straight into the enemy's array and the northmen opened like water before him, a wave spreading right and left. He made directly for the general.

Now Yen Liang sitting there in state saw a horseman rushing toward him and just as he began to ask who the rider of the red horse was, lo! the horseman was there. Taken utterly by surprise the leader could make no defence. Kuan's arm rose and the mighty weapon fell. And with it fell Yen Liang.

Leaping from the saddle Kuan Yu cut off his victim's head and hung it to his horse's neck. Then he mounted and rode out, just as if there was no army there.

The northern men, panic stricken, made no fight. Ts'ao's army attacked with vigour and slew great numbers of them. They captured many horses and weapons and much military gear. Kuan Yu rode quickly back up the hill and laid the proof of his prowess at the feet of the Minister.

"You are more than human, General!" cried Ts'ao.

"What have I done to talk about?" said Kuan. "My brother, Chang I-te, did the same thing in an army of a hundred legions, and did it easily."

Ts'ao Ts'ao marvelled at the statement and turning to those about him said, "If you meet this brother be careful." And he bade them make a note on the overlap of their robes so that they should remember.

The beaten army returning northward met Yuan Shao on the road and told their story. "A red-faced warrior with a long beard, wielding a huge sword, broke into the army, cut off the general's head and bore it off," said they.

"Who was this?" asked Shao

Chu Shou said, "It must have been Liu Yuan-te's brother; it could be nobody else."

Yuan Shao was very angry and, pointing to Liu Pei, he said, "Your brother has slain my beloved leader. You are in the plot too. Why should I save you alive?"

He bade the lictors take him away and behead him.

> Morning saw him guest on high,
> Evening, prisoner, doomed to die.

His actual fate will be told in the next chapter.

CHAPTER XXVI

YUAN SHAO IS DEFEATED AND LOSES A LEADER: KUAN YU ABANDONS RANK AND WEALTH

As the last chapter closed Yuan-te had been condemned to die. He spoke up, however, and said, "Pray hear one word, Illustrious Sir, before you decide. I have lost sight of my brother since my misfortune at Hsuchou and know not whether Yun-ch'ang be dead or alive. There are many men in the world who resemble him. Is every red-faced man with a beard named Kuan? Should you not rather seek some evidence?"

Now Yuan Shao was impulsive and facile by nature and when Yuan-te spoke thus, he suddenly turned upon Chu Shou, saying, "By wrongly regarding what you said I nearly killed an innocent man."

Then he requested Yuan-te once more to resume his seat in the tent and advise him how to avenge Yen Liang.

Soon from the lower end a voice was heard, saying, "Yen Liang and I were as brothers and can I allow any other to avenge his death?"

The speaker was a man of middle height with a face like a unicorn, a famous leader from Hopei, named Wen Ch'ou.

Yuan Shao was pleased and said, "You are the only man who can do it. I will give you ten legions and you can cross the Yellow River, and quickly smite that rebel Ts'ao.

"You cannot do it; he will fail," said Chu Shou. "The proper course is to hold Yenching and detach a force to Kuantu. If you rashly cross the river and anything goes wrong not a soul will return."

Yuan Shao said, "That is always the way with you fellows, always delaying and taking the dash out of the soldiers. You put off today and postpone tomorrow till success has become impossible. Do you forget that promptitude is what the soldier honours?"

The adviser withdrew sadly, saying. "Superiors do not curb their ambitions: inferiors must strive to render service. Eternal is the Yellow River, shall I cross it?"

Thereafter he feigned illness and went no more to the Council.

Yuan-te said, "I have received much kindness at your hands and have been unable to show my gratitude. I would accompany General Wen that I may repay your bounty and also that I may hear news of my brother."

Yuan Shao gladly consented and ordered Wen Ch'ou to share his command with Yuan-te. But the former objected saying that Yuan-te had been so often defeated that it would augur ill for success this time. He proposed to give Yuan-te command of the rear guard, and this being approved, three legions were told off under Liu Pei's special command to follow the main body.

The prowess displayed by Kuan Yu in the bold attack on Yen Liang redoubled Ts'ao Ts'ao's respeet for him and he memorialised the throne that Kuan Yu receive the title of Marquis of Hanshout'ing and a seal was cast for him.

Just then came the unexpected news that Yuan Shao's army had moved toward the Yellow River and was in position above Yenching. Ts'ao first sent to transfer the inhabitants to Hsiho and then led out an army to oppose Yuan Shao. He issued an order to face about, thus placing the rear companies in front. The commissariat wagons were also placed in the van.

"What is this reversal for?" asked Lu Ch'ien.

Ts'ao replied, "When the supplies are in rear they are liable to be plundered. So I have put them first."

"But if you meet the enemy and they steal them?"

"Wait till the enemy appears; I shall know what to do."

Lu Ch'ien was much exercised at this new move of the Minister's. In the meantime the supply train moved along the river toward Yenching. Presently the foremost troops raised a great shout and Ts'ao sent to see what it meant. The messenger came back to say Wen Ch'ou's army was approaching, and the supply train had been abandoned and was at the mercy of the enemy. Thereupon Ts'ao pointed to two mounds saying, "We will take refuge here for the present."

All those near him hastened to the mounds. There Ts'ao ordered them all to loosen their dress, lay aside their breastplates and rest a time. The horsemen turned their steeds loose.

Wen Ch'ou's men approached under cover. As they drew near one after another the officers told Ts'ao saying, "The rebels are near: we ought to catch the horses and go back to Paima."

But the adviser, Hsun Yu, checked them saying, "These are a bait for the enemy: why retire?"

Ts'ao glanced across at him and said, "He understands; do not say anything."

Now having got possession of the supply carts the enemy next came to seize the horses. By this time they had all broken ranks and were scattered, each man going his own way. Then suddenly Ts'ao gave the order to go down from the mounds and smite them.

The surprise was complete. Wen Ch'ou's army was in confusion and Ts'ao's men surrounded them. Wen Ch'ou made a stand, but those about him trampled each other down and he could do nothing but flee. And he fled.

Then standing on the top of a mound Ts'ao pointed to the flying leader calling out, "There is one of the most famous captains of the north; who can capture him?"

Chang Liao and Hsu Huang both mounted and dashed after him, crying, "Wen Ch'ou, do not run away!"

Looking round, the fugitive saw two pursuers and then he set aside his spear, took his bow and adjusted an arrow, which he shot at Chang Liao.

"Cease shooting, you rebel!" shouted Hsu Huang. Chang Liao ducked his head and the shaft went harmlessly by, save that it carried away the tassel of his cap. He only pressed harder in pursuit. The next arrow however struck his horse in the head and the animal stumbled and fell, throwing his rider to the earth.

Then Wen Ch'ou turned to come back. Hsu Huang, whirling his battle axe, stood in his way to stop him. But he saw behind Wen several more horsemen coming to help him and as they would have been too many for him he fled. Wen pursued along the river bank. Suddenly he saw coming toward him with banners fluttering in the breeze, a small party of horse, and the leader carried a great sword.

"Stop!" cried Yun-ch'ang, for it was he, and he attacked at once. At the third bout Wen Ch'ou's heart failed him and he wheeled and fled, following the windings of the river. But Kuan Yu's steed was fast and soon caught up. One blow, and the hapless Wen Ch'ou fell.

When Ts'ao Ts'ao saw from the mound that the leader of the enemy had fallen, he gave the signal for a general onset and many of the northmen were driven into the river. And the carts with supplies and all the horses were quickly recovered.

Now Kuan Yu, at the head of a few horsemen, was thrusting here and striking there at the moment when Yuan-te, with the three reserve legions, appeared on the battle field. At once they told him that the red-faced, long-bearded warrior was there and had slain

Wen Ch'ou. He hastily pressed forward to try to get a look at the warrior. He saw across the river a large body of horse and the banners bore the words "Kuan Yun-ch'ang, Marquis of Hanshout'ing."

"Then it is my brother and he is really with Ts'ao Ts'ao," said Yuan-te, secretly thanking God that he was safe.

He made an attempt to wait about till he could call to Kuan Yu, but a great mass of Ts'ao Ts'ao's soldiers came rushing down and he was forced to retire.

Yuan Shao, bringing reinforcements, reached Kuantu and built a stockade. Two advisers went in to see him and said, "Again that fellow Kuan has been in the battle; he killed Wen Ch'ou. Liu Pei pretends ignorance of him."

Their master was angry and railed at Pei. "The long-eared rebel! How dare he do such a thing?"

Soon Yuan-te appeared; again Shao ordered him out to instant execution.

"What crime have I committed?" asked Yuan-te.

"You sent your brother to slay one of my generals. Is that no crime?"

"Pray let me explain before I die. Ts'ao hated me and has always done so. Now he has found out where I am and, fearing that I may help you, has got my brother to destroy your two generals, feeling sure that when you heard of it you would be angry and put me to death. You cannot fail to see this."

"What he says is sense," said Shao, "and you two nearly brought on me the reproach of injuring the good."

He ordered his attendants to retire and asked Yuan-te to come and sit by him. Yuan-te came saying, "I am deeply thankful, Illustrious Sir, for your great kindness, for which I can never be sufficiently grateful. Now I desire to send some confidential messenger with a secret letter to my brother to tell him where I am, and I am sure he will come without a moment's delay. He will help you to destroy Ts'ao Ts'ao to make up for having destroyed your two officers. Do you approve of this?"

"If I got Yun-ch'ang he would be ten times better than the two men I have lost," replied Shao.

So Yuan-te prepared a letter. But there was no one to take it. Yuan Shao ordered the army to withdraw to Wu-yang, where they made a large camp. For some time nothing was done.

Then Ts'ao Ts'ao sent Hsiahou Tun to defend the strategical point at Kuantu while he led the bulk of the army back to the capital. There he gave many banquets in honour of the services of

Kuan Yu and then he told Lu Ch'ien that putting the supplies in the front of the army had been meant as a bait to draw the enemy to destruction. "Only Hsun Yu understood that," said he in conclusion.

Every one present praised his ingenuity. Even while the banquet was proceeding there arrived news of a rising of Yellow Turban rebels at Junan. They were very strong and Ts'ao Hung had been defeated in several engagements. Now he begged for help.

Kuan Yu, hearing this said, "I should like to have the opportunity of performing some service by destroying these rebels."

"You have already rendered noble services for which you have not been properly requited. I could hardly trouble you again," said Ts'ao.

"I have been idle too long; I shall get ill," said Kuan Yu.

Ts'ao encouraged him to go and gave him five legions with Yu Chin and Yo Chin as captains under him. They were to leave soon.

Then Hsun Yu said privily to his master, "He always cherishes the idea of returning to Liu Pei. He will leave you if he hears any news. Do not let him go on this expedition."

"If he does well this time I will not let him go into battle again," said Ts'ao.

In due time the force led by Kuan Yu drew near the rebels and made their camp. One night, just outside his camp, two spies were caught and taken in to Kuan who in one of them recognised Sun Ch'ien. The attendants being dismissed Kuan Yu questioned him.

"After we lost sight of each other I have heard not a word of you, what are you doing here?"

"After I escaped I drifted hither and thither till I had the good fortune to reach Junan and Liu P'i took me in. But why are you with Ts'ao Ts'ao, General? And where are your sisters-in-law? Are they well?"

Kuan Yu told him all that had happened.

"I have heard lately that Liu Pei is with Yuan Shao. I would have liked to go and join him, but I have not found a convenient opportunity. Now the two men I am with have taken the side of Yuan Shao against Ts'ao. By good luck you were coming here so I got command of a small party of scouts to be able to see you and tell you. Presently our two leaders will pretend to be defeated and you, and the two ladies, can go over to Yuan Shao. And you will see your brother."

"Since he is there I certainly must go at once to see him. But it is a misfortune that I have slain two of Yuan Shao's generals. I fear things are not in my favour," said Kuan.

"Let me go first and see how the land lies; I will come back and tell you."

"I would risk a myriad deaths to see my brother," said Kuan Yu. "But I must go to say farewell to Ts'ao Ts'ao."

Sun Ch'ien was sent away that night and next day Kuan Yu led out his men to offer battle. Kung Tu, in armour, went out to the front of the line of battle and Kuan Yu said, "You people, why have you risen against the government?"

"Why do you blame us when you have turned your back on your own lord?" replied Kung Tu.

"How have I turned my back on my lord?"

"Liu Yuan-te is with Yuan Pen-ch'u and you are with Ts'ao Ts'ao; what is that?"

Kuan Yu could not reply, but he whirled round his sword and rode forward. Tu fled and Kuan Yu followed. Tu turned and said to Kuan Yu, "I cannot forget my old chief's kindness. Now attack as soon as you can and I will give up the defences."

Kuan Yu understood and urged on his men. The leaders of the rebels pretended they were worsted and they all scattered. So the city was taken. Having pacified the people Kuan Yu quickly led his army back to the capital, where he was met by Ts'ao, congratulated on his success and feasted.

When this was all over Kuan Yu went to the dwelling of his sisters-in-law to pay his respects at their gate.

"Have you been able to get any news of Uncle Liu in your two expeditions?" asked the Lady Kan.

"None," replied Kuan Yu.

As he retired from the door he heard sounds of bitter weeping within.

"Alas he is dead," said they. "Our brother-in-law thinks we shall be greatly distressed and hides the truth from us."

One of the old soldiers, who acted as guard, hearing the sounds of perpetual grief, took pity on them and said, "Do not weep, ladies; your lord is with Yuan Shao in Hopei."

"How do you know that?" said they.

"I went out with General Kuan and one of the soldiers told me."

The two ladies summoned Kuan Yu and reproached him saying, "Uncle Liu never betrayed you and yet you remain here enjoying the bounty of Ts'ao Ts'ao and forgetting the old times. And you tell us falsehoods."

Kuan Yu bowed his head. "My brother really is in Hopei, but I dared not tell you, lest it should become known. Something must be done but done carefully and it needs time."

"Brother-in-law, you should hasten," said the Lady Kan.

Kuan Yu withdrew feeling that he must evolve some scheme of departure without further loss of time. It caused him much uneasiness.

Yu Chin, having found out that Liu Pei was in the north, told Ts'ao Ts'ao, who at once sent Chang Liao to find out Kuan Yu's intentions. Chang Liao entered jauntily and congratulated Kuan, saying, "They tell me you obtained news of your brother in the battlefield; I felicitate you."

"My lord was there indeed but I met him not. I see nothing to be glad about."

"Is there any difference between the relationship of you two and that of any other two brothers?"

Kuan replied, "You and I stand in the relationship of friends: Yuan-te and I are friends and brothers beside, and prince and minister in addition to both. Our relationship cannot be discussed in usual terms."

"Well, now that you know where your brother is, are you going to him?"

"How can I go back on what I said before? I am sure you will explain fully to the Minister."

Chang Liao went back and told his master who said, "I must find a way to keep him here."

While Kuan Yu was pondering over his difficulties they told him that a friend had come to enquire for him. The visitor was introduced but Kuan did not recognise him.

"Who are you?" asked Kuan.

"I am Ch'en Chen of Nanyang, in the service of Yuan Shao."

In great perturbation Kuan Yu sent away the attendants and, they being gone, said, "There is some special reason for your visit."

For reply the newcomer drew out a letter and handed it to his host, who recognised that it was from his brother Yuan-te.

"I, the writer, and you, Sir, pledged ourselves in the Peach Garden to die together. Why then are we apart and yet alive, our kindly feelings destroyed, our sense of right outraged? Surely you desire to obtain fame and acquire riches and honour by offering my head as a crowning act of merit. More might be said but I await your commands with great anxiety."

Kuan Yu finished the letter with a bitter cry. "I always wanted to find my brother, but I did not know where he was. How can he think such evil of me?" said he.

"Yuan-te looks for you very eagerly, and if you are still bound by the old pledge you should go quickly," said the messenger.

"Anyone born into the world without the one essential virtue of sincerity is no true man. I came here openly and can go in no other way. Now will I write a letter which I will ask you to bear to my brother, that as soon as I can take leave of Ts'ao Ts'ao I will bring the ladies and come to him."

"But what if Ts'ao Ts'ao refuses to let you go?" said Ch'en.

"Then would I rather die; I will not remain here."

"Then, Sir, quickly write your letter and relieve your brother from his anxiety."

So Kuan Yu wrote like this: "I, the humble one, know full well that a man of principle does not betray and a man of loyalty despises death. I have been a student in my youth and know somewhat of the proprieties. I sigh and weep at the memory of the fraternal affection that made Yang Chio-ai and Tso Po-t'ao die rather than separate. I was in charge of Hsiap'i but the place lacked provision and there was no help. I would have fought to the death but there was on my shoulders the responsibility for my sisters-in-law. Wherefore I had to take care of my body lest I betrayed my trust. And so I made a prisoner of myself, hoping to find a way of release. I heard of you lately in Junan. I must, however, bid farewell to Ts'ao Ts'ao and bring the ladies with me when I come. May I perish, victim to the superhuman powers, if I have harboured any traitorous thought. Pencil and paper are poor substitutes for what I would say, but I look to see you soon."

The visitor left with this missive and Kuan Yu went to tell the women. Then he proceeded to the Minister's palace to say farewell. But Ts'ao knew what he was coming for and he found at the gate the board intimating that no one could be received. So he had to return. However, he bade his own few soldiers prepare to start at any moment. He also gave orders that everything received from Ts'ao was to be left in the quarters; nothing was to be taken.

Next day he again proceeded to the palace to say farewell to his patron, but again found the board hanging there to show there was no admission. So it was several times; he could never enter. Then he went to see Chang Liao, but he was indisposed.

"This means he will not let me go," thought Kuan Yu. "But I am going and I shall hesitate no longer."

So he wrote this letter:—"As a young man I entered the service of the Imperial Uncle, and pledged myself to share his fortunes. Heaven and Earth witnessed this oath. When I lost the city I made three requests which you granted. Now I hear my brother is with Yuan Shao and I, remembering our pledge, cannot but go to him.

Though your bounty is great I forget not the bond of the past, wherefore I write this letter of farewell trusting that when you have read it you will be content for me to postpone to another season the proof of my gratitude."

He sealed and sent it to the Palace. Then he deposited in the treasury of his dwelling all the gold and silver he had received, suspended his seal of marquis in the reception hall and left, taking his sisters-in-law with him in a carriage. He rode "Red Hare" and carried Black Dragon in his hand. With a small escort of men, those formerly under his command, he left the city by the north gate.

The wardens would have stopped him but he frightened them with a fierce shout. Having got out he told the escort to go in front with the carriage while he would remain behind to guard against pursuit. So they pushed the carriage toward the high road.

In the city Kuan Yu's letter reached the Minister while he was consulting about what to do. He read it and exclaimed, "So he has left!"

Then the warden of the gate came to report that Kuan Yu had forced his way out, and was gone with a carriage, a horse and a score of guards. Next came the servants from his house to report that he had left, taking nothing of the treasure, nor any one of the waiting maids. Everything was left in the house. Even his seal was there. His only escort were the few men of his original force.

Suddenly from the assembly of men rose a voice saying, "With three companies of mailed horse I will bring him back alive."

Their eyes turned to the speaker, who was General Ts'ai Yang

> On the dragon's cave he turns his back,
> But numberless wolves infest his track.

What came of this offer to pursue will be seen in the next chapter.

CHAPTER XXVII

"BEAUTIFUL BEARD" RIDES ON A SOLITARY JOURNEY: AND SLAYS SIX MEN AT FIVE PASSES

Now of all the captains in Ts'ao Ts'ao's army, the only one friendly toward Kuan Yu, with the exception of Chang Liao, was Hsu Huang. The others treated him with respect, except Ts'ai Yang who was decidedly inimical. So this Ts'ai was ready to pursue and capture him as soon as he heard of his departure. But Ts'ao accepted his going as natural. "He does not forget his old leader and he was perfectly open in all his actions. He is a gentleman and you would do well to follow his example."

So he bade the would-be pursuer begone and say no more about pursuit.

"You were exceedingly good to Kuan Yu," said Ch'eng Yu, "but he went off very rudely. He certainly left a screed behind with his reasons, but he affronted you and that is no light matter. Now to let him join Yuan Shao is to add wings to a tiger. You had better catch him and put him to death so as to guard against future evil."

Ts'ao replied, "But he had my promise and can I break my word? Each has his master. Do not pursue." But he said to Chang Liao, "He has rejected all I gave him, so bribes were powerless with him in whatever shape. I have the greatest respect for such as he. He has not yet gone far and I will try to strengthen his attachment to me and make one appeal to sentiment. Ride after him and beg him to stop till I can come up and bid farewell and offer him a sum of money for his expenses and a fighting robe, that he may remember me kindly in after days."

So Chang rode out quite alone; Ts'ao followed him leisurely with an escort of a score or so.

Now the steed that Kuan Yu rode was "Red Hare" and he was very fast. No one could have come up with him but that there was the ladies' carriage to escort and so "Red Hare" had to be held in and go slow. Suddenly Kuan Yu heard a shout behind him, a voice crying, "Go slowly, Yun-ch'ang."

He turned and made out the person to be Chang Liao. Ordering the pushers of the carriage to press on along the high road, he reined in his steed, held Black Dragon ready for a stroke and waited for Chang Liao to come up.

"Of course you have come to take me back, Wen-yuan?" said he.

"No; the Minister, seeing that you are going a long journey, wishes to see you on your way and told me to hasten forward and beg you to wait till he can come up. That is the only thing."

"Seeing that he is coming along with mailed men I shall fight to the very last," said Kuan Yu and he took up his position on a bridge where he waited the approach of the party, who advanced quickly. Four of Ts'ao Ts'ao's captains followed close. Seeing Kuan Yu was ready to fight, Ts'ao ordered his escort to open out in two lines and then it was seen they carried no arms. This relieved his mind; for it proved to Kuan Yu they meant no attack.

"Why do you go in such haste, Yun-ch'ang?" asked Ts'ao.

Kuan Yu inclined his head but did not dismount.

"I informed you in writing that since my lord was in Hopei I had to leave at once. I went to your palace again and again but was refused admittance. So I wrote a letter of farewell, sealed up the treasure, resigned my marquis seal and left everything for you. I hope you recall the promise you once made me."

Ts'ao replied, "My desire is to keep my troth with all men; I cannot go back on my word. However, you may find the journey expensive and therefore I have here prepared a sum of money to help you."

Then from horseback he held out a packet of gold.

"I have sufficient left from your former bounty; keep that for presents to your soldiers."

"Why should you refuse this? It is but an insignificant return for great services."

"My services have been all trifling, not worth mentioning."

"Really, Yun-ch'ang, you are the most highprincipled of men. I am very sorry my luck is too poor to retain you at my side. Pray accept just this robe to show you I am not quite ungrateful," said Ts'ao, and one of his captains, dismounting, held up a silken coat in both hands. Kuan Yu even still fearful of what might happen, would not dismount, but he reached down his sword and took the robe on its point. Then he threw it over his shoulders and turned to thank the giver saying, "I thank you, Sir Minister, for the robe and trust we shall meet again."

So saying he went down from the bridge and bore away to the north.

"He is a very rude man," said Hsu Ch'u, who was of the escort. "Why do you not take him prisoner?"

Ts'ao replied, "He was absolutely alone facing scores of us; he was justified in being suspicious. But my word has gone forth and he is not to be pursued."

Ts'ao and his escort returned, the Minister very sad when he thought of the man who had gone.

But here we need say nothing more of Ts'ao's return. Kuan Yu went down from the bridge and started in the wake of the carriage carrying the two ladies, which should have gone about thirty *li* while this interview had been going on. He could see no signs of it and rode hither and thither looking on all sides.

Presently he heard some one shouting from a hill, calling him by name to halt. He saw a youth wearing a yellow turban and dressed in a silk robe. He held a spear in his hand and was mounted on a horse from the neck of which dangled a bloody head. Behind him were a hundred or so men on foot and they advanced quickly.

"Who are you?" asked Kuan Yu.

The young man dropped his spear, dismounted and made a low bow. Kuan feared this was some ruse so he only checked his horse and gripped his sword the more firmly, saying, "Sir Swashbuckler, I desire you to tell me your name."

"My family name is Liao and I am known as Liao Hua or Liao Yuan-chien. I belong to a Hsiangyang family. Since these troubled times began I have been an outlaw among the rivers and lakes and I and my comrades have lived by plunder. We are about five hundred in all. By chance my friend Tu Yuan came across two ladies in a carriage just now and, quite wrongly, he took them prisoners and brought them to the hold in the hills. I questioned the servants and so found out who they were and who was escorting them. So I wished them to be set free to pursue their journey. My friend opposed this and spoke so ill-mannerly that I killed him. And here is his head. I pray you to pardon me."

"Where are the two ladies?"

"They are among the hills," replied Liao.

"Bring them down here, at once," said Kuan.

In a short time a party of the brigands pushed the carriage down the hill and the ladies sat there before him.

Then Kuan Yu dismounted, laid aside his sword and stood respectfully before them with his arms crossed.

"Sisters, have you been alarmed?" asked he.

They replied, "We should have suffered at the hands of Tu Yuan had it not been for Liao Hua."

"How did Liao Hua come to save the ladies?" asked Kuan of those who stood by.

They said, "Tu carried off the ladies and proposed that he and Liao Hua should have one each as wife. But Liao Hua had found out they were of gentle birth and worthy, and was for treating them with respect. When Tu disagreed Liao slew him."

Hearing this Kuan Yu bowed to Liao Hua and thanked him. Liao then wanted to join himself and his troop to Kuan Yu, but the latter, seeing he was a Yellow Turban, would have nothing to do with him. So he simply thanked him for his kindness to the ladies. Liao offered some presents but these were also declined.

So Liao Hua took his leave and presently disappeared in a valley among the hills. Kuan Yu told his sisters the story of his interview with Ts'ao and the gift of a robe and then he urged the carriage on its way. Towards dark they came to a farm where they would rest. The farmer, an old greybeard, came out to welcome the party and asked who they were. Kuan Yu described himself as the brother of Liu Pei, and said his name was Kuan.

"Surely you are no other than the slayer of Yen Liang and Wen Ch'ou," said the venerable host.

"That is so," replied Kuan Yu.

"Come in," said the old man, joyfully.

"My two sisters-in-law are in the carriage" said Kuan Yu, "will you let your women-folk go out to receive them?"

As Kuan Yu remained standing there the host asked him to be seated, but he would not sit while the women were present and remained standing in a respectful attitude till the old man's wife had returned and ushered the ladies into the inner apartments. Then the old man set to the entertainment of his guest in the guest hall. Kuan Yu asked his name.

He replied, "I am called Hu Hua. In the days of the Emperor Huan I was an officer of the Court but I resigned and retired into private life. I have a son with the Prefect of Yungyang (in Szechuan) and if you should be going that way, General, I should like to send him a letter by you."

Kuan Yu said he would take the letter. Next day, after an early meal, the ladies got into their carriage, the host handed his letter to Kuan Yu, and the little party once more took the road. They went toward Loyang.

Presently they approached a pass known as the Tungling Pass, guarded by one K'ung Hsiu and half a company. When the soldiers saw a carriage being pushed toward the pass they ran to tell their commander, who came out to accost the travellers. Kuan Yu dismounted and returned the officer's salute and the latter said, "Whither are you going?"

"I have left the Minister to go into Hopei to find my brother."

"But Yuan Shao is my master's rival. You have authority from him to go thither?"

"I left hurriedly and could not get it."

"If you have no authority you must wait while I send to request orders."

"To remain while you send and receive an answer will delay me greatly," said Kuan.

"I must stand by my instructions; that is the only thing to do," said K'ung.

"Then you refuse to let me pass?"

"If you want to go through leave the family as a gage."

At this Kuan Yu got very angry and made to cut at the officer on the spot, but he withdrew into the gate and beat the drums for an attack. Thereupon the soldiers armed themselves, mounted and came down to oppose the passage, crying, "Dare you go through, eh?"

The carriage was sent off to a safe distance and then Kuan Yu rode at full speed directly at the commander of the guard, who set his spear and came to meet him. The two steeds met and the men engaged, but at the first stroke of Black Dragon the commander of the gate fell to the earth dead. His men fled.

"Soldiers, do not flee!" cried Kuan Yu. "I killed him because I could do no otherwise. I have nothing against you, but I would ask you to tell the Minister how this thing came to pass, that he wished to kill me and so I slew him in self-defence."

The men bowed before him and Kuan Yu, with the carriage, passed through the gates and they continued their way to Loyang. But one of the guards of the pass went quickly in advance and informed the Prefect of Loyang Han Fu, of the slaughter of K'ung Hsiu. Wherefore Han Fu assembled his officers to take counsel. Meng T'an, one of his captains, said, "This Kuan Yu must be a fugitive or he would have a safe conduct. Our only course is to stop him or we shall incur blame."

"The man is fierce and brave. Remember the fate of Yen and Wen. It seems vain to oppose him by force and so we must think out some trap for him," said Han Fu.

"I have a ruse ready," said Meng T'an. "I will close the gate with "deerhorns" (chevaux de frise) and I will go to fight with him. I will engage and then flee, and you can shoot him from an ambush along the road. If we can get him and his party and send them prisoners to the capital we ought to be well rewarded."

This course was determined upon and soon they heard that Kuan Yu was approaching. Han Fu strung his bow and filled his quiver with arrows and with one company took up position along the pass. Then as the party approached Han Fu said, "Who is the traveller who comes?"

Kuan Yu bowed low and said, "He is a certain Kuan, Marquis of Hanshout'ing, and he wishes to go through the pass."

"Have you a letter from the Minister?"

"In the hurry of departure I did not get any."

"My special orders from him are to hold this pass and make examination of all spies that may go to and fro. Any person without an authority must be a fugitive."

Then Kuan Yu began to be angry, and he told them what had happened to K'ung Hsiu. "Do you also seek death?" asked Kuan.

"Who will capture him for me?" cried Han Fu, and Meng T'an offered himself. He rode out, whirling his double swords and made straight for Kuan Yu.

Kuan Yu sent back the carriage out of danger and then rode toward Meng. They engaged, but very soon Meng turned his steed and fled. Kuan Yu pursued. Meng, intent only on leading his enemy toward the ambush, took no account of the speed of "Red Hare." Very soon he was caught up and a stroke of the mighty sword cut him in two pieces. Then Kuan Yu stopped and turned back. The archers in the gate shot their hardest and though it was a long way off one of them lodged an arrow in his left arm. He pulled it out with his teeth but the blood streamed down as he rode toward the Prefect, Han Fu. The men scattered. Kuan Yu rode straight at his next victim. He raised his sword and made an oblique cut which sliced off the head and shoulder of his opponent.

Then he drove off the soldiers and returned to escort the carriage. He bound up his wound, and, fearing lest any one might take advantage of his weakness, he made no long halts on the road but hurried toward Ishui Pass.

The warden of this pass was Pien Hsi of Pingchou, a warrior whose weapon was a comethammer. He had been a Yellow Turban and had gone over to Ts'ao, who had given him this post. As soon as he heard of the coming of the redoubtable warrior he cudgelled his brains for a ruse to use against him. He decided upon an ambush. In a temple at the pass he placed two hundred "axe and sword" men. He reckoned on enticing Kuan to the temple for refreshment and when he let fall a cup as signal the hidden men would rush out.

All being thus arranged and ready, he went out to welcome Kuan Yu in friendly guise and he dismounted at his coming. Pien Hsi began very amiably.

"Your name, General, makes the very earth tremble and every one looks up to you. This return to the Imperial Uncle proves you to be noble and true."

Kuan Yu in reply told him the story of the men he had slain. Hsi replied, "You slew them; that is well. When I see the Minister I will explain to him the inner reasons for these acts."

Kuan Yu thought he had found a friend and so mounted and rode through the pass. When he came to the temple a number of priests came out to meet him with clanging bells.

This temple, that of a Guardian of the State, had a courtyard in which the Emperor Ming had burned incense. In the temple were thirty priests and among these there happened to be one who came from the same village as Kuan Yu. His religious name was P'u-ching. Hearing who the visitor was, he came forward to speak with him.

"General," said he, "it is many a long year since you left Putung."

"Yes," said Kuan Yu, "nearly twenty years."

"Do you recognise this poor priest?"

"I left the village many years ago; I do not recognise you."

"My house and yours were only separated by a rivulet," said the priest.

Now Pien Hsi, seeing the priest holding forth about village matters, thought he would blab about the ambush, so he bade him be silent.

"I want to invite the General to a feast. You priest fellows seem to have a lot to say," said Pien.

"Not too much," said Kuan Yu. "Naturally when fellow villagers meet they talk of old times."

P'u-ching invited the visitor into the guest room to take tea, but Kuan Yu said, "The two ladies are out there in the carriage; they ought to have some first."

So the priest bade them take some tea to the ladies and then he led Kuan Yu within, at the same time lifting the priest knife which he wore at his side and looking meaningly at Kuan Yu. The latter understood and told his people to bring along his weapon and keep close at his side.

When Pien Hsi invited Kuan Yu to go into the Hall of the Law for some refreshment, Kuan Yu turned to him, saying, "Is this invitation with good intention or evil?"

His host was so taken aback that he could make no reply, and then Kuan Yu saw that many armed men were concealed behind the arras. Then he shouted loudly at Pien Hsi, saying, "What means this? I thought you an honourable man. How dare you?"

The traitor saw that his plot had failed and called to the assassins to come out and fall to, but Kuan Yu had a short sword in his hand and slashed at any one who came near. So they scattered. Their commander ran down the hall and tried to escape among the side buildings, but Kuan Yu threw aside the short sword, took up Black Dragon and went after Pien Hsi. The latter was trying to get into position to throw his comethammer, but Kuan Yu cut the cord and the weapon was useless. He followed Pien in and out and soon caught up with him. Then with one blow he cut him in halves.

The fight over he sought the two ladies, who were surrounded by soldiers. These fled at sight of the terrible warrior. Seeking out the priest, his fellow countryman, he thanked him for the timely warning which had saved him from death.

"I cannot remain here after this," said P'u-ching. "I shall pack up my few garments and my alms bowl and take to the road vague in my wanderings as the clouds in the sky. But we shall meet again and till then take care of yourself."

Then Kuan Yu took leave and retook the road to Yungyang. The Prefect of this city was named Wang Chih, and he was related to Han Fu by marriage. Hearing of the death of his relative he set about a scheme to kill Kuan Yu secretly. He sent men to guard the city gates and, when he heard that Kuan Yu approached, he went himself and received him with a smiling countenance and bade him welcome. Kuan Yu told him the object of his journey.

"You, General, have been able to get some exercise on the road, but the ladies in their carriage must be cramped and fatigued. I pray you to come into the city and all of you remain the night in the official travellers' quarters. Tomorrow you can set forth again."

The offer was tempting and his host seemed in earnest so the two ladies went into the city, where they found everything very comfortably prepared for them. And, though Kuan Yu declined the Prefect's invitations to a banquet, refreshments for the travellers were sent to their lodgings. Kuan Yu was fatigued from the trials of the journey and as soon as the evening meal was over he bade the ladies retire to rest while he sat down in the main room, quite alone, for he bade all to get repose while they could. His horse was given a good feed for once. He sat with his armour loosened in order to be more at ease.

Now the Prefect had a secretary named Hu Pan to whom he had entrusted the arrangements for the destruction of his guest. Said he, "This Kuan is a traitor to the Minister and a fugitive. On the road he has murdered several Commanders of Passes and is guilty of serious crimes. But he is too strong and valiant for any ordinary soldier to overcome. So this evening a whole company of men will surround his lodging, each one armed with a torch, and we will burn him. They will start the fire about midnight. Every one of the party will perish. I will come with a force to stand by and assist if necessary."

These orders received, Hu Pan passed them on to the men, who began secretly to prepare dry wood and other combustibles which they piled up at the gate of the rest-house. Hu Pan thought within him that he would like to know what manner of man was this Kuan Yu, whose fame had spread so far, so he determined to get a peep at him. He went to the rest-house and enquired where Kuan Yu was.

"The General is the man in the main hall reading," was the reply.

Hu Pan noiselessly made his way to the outside of the room and peeped in. He saw the famous warrior stroking his beard with his left hand while he read by the light of a lamp placed on a low table. An involuntary exclamation of wonder escaped at the majesty of the figure.

"Really a god!" he sighed.

"Who is there?" suddenly asked the reader at the sound.

Hu Pan entered and said he was the Prefect's secretary.

"Surely you are the son of Hu Hua, who lives outside Hsu-tu," said Kuan.

"I am he," replied Hu Pan.

Then Kuan Yu called up his followers and bade them look among the baggage for the letter, which they brought. Kuan Yu handed it to the secretary, who read it and then breathed long, saying, "I very nearly caused the death of a good man."

Then he betrayed the whole plot. "This Wang is a wicked man, who wanted to kill you. At this moment you are surrounded and at the third watch they will set fire to this place. Now I will go and open the city gates while you hastily prepare for flight."

Kuan Yu was greatly surprised, but he quickly buckled up his armour, got his steed ready, roused the two ladies and put them into their carriage. Then they left the rest-house and as they passed out they saw the soldiers all about them, each with a torch. The party hastened to the outskirts of the city and found the gate already open and they lost no time in getting clear of the city. Hu Pan returned to give orders to fire the rest house.

The fugitives pressed on but before long they saw lights coming up behind them and Wang Chih called out to them to stop. Kuan Yu reined in his horse and began to abuse him.

"Worthless fellow! What had you against me that you wished to burn me to death?"

Wang Chih whipped up his steed and set his spear, but Kuan Yu cut him through with the short sword he wore at his side and scattered his followers.

Then the carriage pushed on. Kuan Yu's heart was filled with gratitude to Hu Pan. When they drew near Huachou some one told Liu Yen, who rode out to welcome him. Kuan Yu did not dismount but bowed from horseback, saying, "Have you been quite well since we parted?"

"Whither are you going, Sir?" replied Liu Yen.

"I have left the Minister and am on my way to find my brother."

"Yuan-te is with Yuan Shao, who is at enmity with the Minister. How can you be allowed to go to him?" asked Liu Yen.

"That matter was settled long ago."

"The Yellow River ferry is an important point and is guarded by a lieutenant of Hsiahou Tun; he will not let you cross."

"But suppose then you provide boats for me?"

"Though there are boats I dare not give them to you."

"Well, formerly I slew Yen Liang and Wen Ch'ou and saved you from a grave danger. Now you refuse me a ferry boat!"

"I am afraid Hsiahou will know of it and make it a fault against me."

Kuan Yu perceived that no help was to be expected from this man so he pushed on and presently reached the ferry. There the commander of the guard, Ch'in Ch'i, came out to question him.

"I am one Kuan, Marquis of Hanshout'ing."

"Whither are you bound?"

"I go to Hopei to seek my brother, Liu Yuan-te, and I respectfully ask you to grant me a passage over the river."

"Where is the authority of the Minister?"

"I am not on a mission from the Minister so why should I have such an authority?"

"I have orders from my chief to guard the ferry and you will not cross; even if you grew wings you should not fly over."

Kuan Yu's choler arose. "Do you know that I have been the death of all those who have hitherto tried to stop me?" said he.

"You have only slain a few officers of no rank or reputation; but you dare not kill me."

"Where would you stand beside Yen Liang and Wen Ch'ou?"

The Ch'in Ch'i grew angry and he loosed his rein. Sword in hand he came at a gallop. The two met, but in the first encounter Ch'in Ch'i's head was swept off by the terrible Black Dragon.

"He who opposed me is dead; you others need not be afraid," cried Kuan Yu, "Be quick and prepare me a boat."

The boat was soon at the landing and the two women stepped on board, followed by Kuan Yu. They crossed, and were then in the country of Yuan Shao. In the course of his journey to this point Kuan Yu had forced five passes and slam six captains.

> His seal hung up, the treasury locked, his
> courtly mansion left,
> He journeyed toward his brother dear, too long
> from his side reft.
> The horse he rode was famed for speed as for
> endurance great,
> His good sword made a way for him and
> opened every gate.
> His loyalty and truth forth stand, a pattern
> unto all,
> His valour would frighten rushing streams and
> make high mountains fall.
> Alone he travelled lustily, 'twas death to meet
> his blade,
> He has been themed by myriads, his glory ne'er
> will fade.

"I did not willingly slay a single one of them," mused Kuan Yu as he rode along. "There was no help for it. Nevertheless when Ts'ao hears of it he will regard me as ungrateful for his bounty."

Before long he saw a rider on the road who soon hailed him and proved to be Sun Ch'ien.

"I have never heard a word from you since we lost sight of each other at Junan; how have you fared?" said Kuan Yu.

"After your departure the city fell. I was sent to Yuan Shao to try to make peace with him and succeeded, so that he invited your brother to go to him and share in the deliberations for an attack on Ts'ao Ts'ao. But to my disgust the leaders of Yuan Shao's army showed great jealousy of each other so that one got into gaol, another was degraded and others quarrelled. Then Yuan Shao vacillated and hesitated, so that your brother and I consulted how we might get away from them all. Now the Uncle is at Junan with Liu P'i and, thinking you could not know that and might suffer some harm if you unwillingly went to Yuan Shao, I have come to warn you. It is good fortune to find you like this. Now we can hasten to Junan and you will meet your brother."

Kuan Yu took Sun Ch'ien to make his bow to the ladies, who asked after his adventures and he told them of the risks Liu Pei had run from Yuan Shao's sudden bursts of anger. Now, however, he was out of his way and safe at Junan where they would meet him.

They covered their faces and wept at the recital of his dangers. Then the party no longer travelled north but took the road toward Junan. Not long after a great cloud of dust was noticed behind them and they presently made out a squadron of horsemen. These were led by Hsiahou Tun, who shouted out to Kuan Yu to stop.

> One by one the pass commanders stopped
>   his progress and were slain,
> The river crossed, another army comes and he
>   must fight again.

How finally Kuan Yu escaped death will appear in the succeeding chapter.

CHAPTER XXVIII

TS'AI YANG PUT TO DEATH, THE BROTHERS'
DOUBTS DISAPPEAR: MEETING AT KUCH'ENG,
LORD AND LIEGE FORTIFY EACH OTHER

Sun Ch'ien had joined Kuan Yu in escorting the two ladies and they were on the road to Junan when Hsiahou Tun suddenly determined to pursue. So with a couple of hundred horse he set out. When he was seen approaching, Kuan Yu bade Sun Ch'ien go ahead with the carriage while he remained to deal with the pursuers. When they were near enough Kuan Yu said, "In coming after me thus you do not reinforce the magnanimity of your master."

Replied Hsiahou Tun, "The Minister has sent no definite instructions. You have caused the death of several people, among them one of my lieutenants, and so I have come to capture you. You have behaved most grossly. He will decide."

Thereupon he dashed forward with his spear ready to thrust. But at that moment a rider came up behind him at full gallop crying, "You must not fight with Yun-ch'ang."

Kuan Yu stayed his steed at once and waited. The messenger came up, drew from his bosom an official letter and said to Hsiahou Tun, "The Minister loves General Kuan for his loyalty and honour, and fearing lest he might be stopped at the various passes, he sent me with this letter to show when necessary at any point on the road."

"But this Kuan has slain several commanders of the passes, does the Minister know that?" said Tun.

The messenger said these things were unknown.

"Then," said Tun, "I will arrest him and take him to the Minister, who may set him free or not as he wills."

"Do you think I fear anything you can do?" said Kuan Yu getting wrathful.

And he rode forward. Tun, nothing loth, set his spear and

prepared for battle. They met and had reached the tenth encounter when a second horseman came up at full speed, crying, "Generals, wait a little!"

Hsiahou Tun stayed his hand and asked the messenger, saying, "Am I to arrest him?"

"No" replied the messenger. "Fearing lest he should have difficulties at the passes the Minister has sent me with a despatch to say he is to be released."

"Did the Minister know that he had slam several men on the way?"

"He did not know."

"Since he was ignorant of that I may not let him go," and he gave the sjgnal to his men to close in round Kuan Yu.

But Kuan Yu flourished his sword and made to attack them and a fight was again imminent, when a third rider appeared who cried, "Yun-ch'ang, give way and do not fight!"

The speaker was Chang Liao. Both combatants made no further move but awaited his arrival.

He said, "I bring the Minister's order that since he has heard that Yun-ch'ang has slain certain men on the way he fears that some will hinder his passage. Wherefore he has sent me to deliver his command at each gate that Kuan Yu is to be suffered to pass freely."

Hsiahou Tun said, "Ch'in Ch'i was the son of Ts'ai Yang's sister, and he was confided to my especial care. Now this Kuan has killed him and how can I refrain?"

"When I see his uncle I will explain. But now the main point is that you have the Minister's orders to let Kuan Yu pass and you may not despise his wish."

So the only thing for Hsiahou Tun to do was to retire; and he did.

"Whither are you going?" then said Chang Liao to Kuan Yu.

"I fear my brother is no longer with Yuan Shao and now I am going to find him wherever he is."

"As you do not know where to go, why not return to the Minister?"

"Where is the sense of that?" said Kuan Yu with a smile. "But, Wen-yuan, you return, and try to arrange pardon for my faults."

With this he saluted Chang Liso and took his leave. Chang Liao retired and joined Hsiahou Tun.

Kuan Yu quickly regained the carriage, and as they went along side by side he told Sun Ch'ien what had happened. Several days later a heavy rain storm came on which soaked everything. Looking about for protection they noticed a farm under the shelter of a precipice and took their way thither. An old man came out to them, to whom they told their story. When they had finished, the old fellow said, "My name is Kuo Ch'ang and I have lived here many years. I am very pleased to greet the man whom I have known so long by reputation."

He quickly killed a sheep for their refreshment and brought out wine for the two men. The two ladies were entertained in the inner apartments. And while they refreshed themselves their baggage was put out to dry and their steeds were fed.

As the day closed in they saw several youths come along and their host said, "My son is come to pay his respects."

"This is my stupid son," said he, presenting a lad to Kuan Yu.

"What has he been doing?" asked Kuan.

"He has just come in from hunting."

The young fellow went out. The old man continued, "All my family have been farmers or scholars. He is my only son and instead of following in the footsteps of his ancestors he cares for nothing but gadding about and hunting, unhappily."

"Why unhappily?" said Kuan Yu. "In these days of disorder a good soldier can make a name for himself."

"If he would only learn the military arts that would be something of a career, but he is nothing but a vagabond and does everything he should not. He is a grief to me."

Kuan Yu sighed in sympathy. The old gentleman stayed till a late hour and when he took his leave his two guests began to prepare for rest.

Suddenly outside there arose a great hubbub, men shouting and horses neighing Kuan Yu called to his people, but as no one answered he and his companion drew their swords and went into the stable yard. There they found their host's son on the ground shouting to his followers to fight. Kuan Yu asked what it was all about and his men told him that the young fellow had tried to steal Red Hare, but had been badly kicked. They had heard shouting and had gone to see what it meant when the farm people, had set on them.

Kuan Yu was very wrathful "You mean thieves! Would you steal my horse?" cried he.

But before he could do anything his host came running out saying, "It was not with my consent that my son did this evil thing. I know he is very guilty and deserves death. But his mother loves him tenderly and I pray you to be generous and pardon him."

"Really he is unworthy of his father," said Kuan Yu. "What you told me shows he is a degenerate. For your sake I pardon him."

Then he told his own people to keep a better lookout, sent the farm people about their business and, in company with Sun Ch'ien, went away to rest.

Next morning both host and hostess were up betimes waiting to thank him for forgiving their son's mad freak. "My currish son has insulted your tiger dignity, I know, and I am deeply affected by your kindness in not punishing him," said the old man.

"Bring him here and I will talk to him," said Kuan Yu.

"He went out before daylight with a lot of his fellow-rogues and I know not where he is."

So Kuan Yu bade them farewell, got the ladies into their carriage and they moved out of the farmyard, the two warriors riding abreast as escort. They took the road toward the hills.

Before they had gone far they saw a large party of men, led by a couple of riders, pouring down one of the gullies. One of the riders wore a yellow turban and a battle robe. The other was Kuo Ch'ang's son. The wearer of the turban called out saying, "I am one of the captains of the Celestial Duke, Chang Chio. Whoever you may be, leave that horse you are riding for me. You may then go free."

Kuan Yu greeted the speech with a hearty laugh.

"O you mad ignoramus! If you had ever been with Chang Chio as a bandit you would have learned to know Liu, Kuan and Chang, the three brothers."

"I have heard of the ruddy long beard called Kuan but I have never seen him. Who may you be?"

Kuan Yu then laid aside his sword, stopped his horse and drew off the bag that covered his beard thus showing its magnificence.

The turban wearer immediately slipped out of the saddle, laid an angry hand on his companion and they both bowed low in front of Kuan Yu's steed.

"Who are you?" asked Kuan Yu.

"I am P'ei Yuan-shao. After the death of Chang Chio I was left forlorn and I got together a few others like myself and we took refuge in the forests. This morning early this fellow came to tell us that a guest at his father's farm had a valuable horse and proposed to me to steal it. I did not think I should meet you, General."

The wretched youth Kuo implored that his life might be spared and Kuan Yu pardoned him for his father's sake. He covered his face and crept away.

"You did not recognise me; how then did you know my name?" asked Kuan Yu.

P'ei replied, "Not far from here is a mountain called the Sleeping

Bull, where lives a certain Chou Ts'ang, a very powerful man who came from the west. He has a stiff curly beard and looks very handsome. He also was a captain in the rebel army, who took to the forest when his leader perished. He has told me a lot about you but I have never had the happiness of seeing you."

Said Kuan Yu, "Under the greenwood tree is no place for a hero's foot. You had better abandon this depraved life and return to the path of virtue. Do not work out your own destruction."

As they were talking a troop of horsemen appeared in the distance. They were the men of Chou Ts'ang, as P'ei said, and Kuan Yu waited for them to approach. The leader was very dark complexioned, tall and armed with a spear. As soon as he drew near enough to see he exclaimed joyfully, "This is General Kuan."

In a moment he had slipped out of the saddle and was on his knees by the roadside.

"Chou Ts'ang renders obeisance," said he.

Said Kuan Yu, "O warrior, where have you known me?"

"I was one of the Yellow Turbans and I saw you then. My one regret was that I could not join you. Now that my good fortune has brought me here I hope you will not reject me. Let me be one of your foot soldiers to be always near you to carry your whip and run by your stirrup. I will cheerfully die for you.

As he seemed thoroughly in earnest Kuan Yu said, "But if you follow me, what of your companions?"

"They may do as they please; follow me or go their ways."

Thereupon they all shouted, "We will follow."

Kuan Yu dismounted and went to ask the ladies what they thought of this. The Lady Kan replied, "Brother-in-law, you have travelled thus far alone and without fighting men; you have safely passed many dangers and never wanted their assistance. You refused the service of Liao Hua, why then suffer this crowd? But this is only a woman's view and you must decide."

"What you say, sister-in-law, is to the point."

Therefore returning to Chou Ts'ang he said, "It is not that I am lacking in gratitude but my sisters-in-law do not care for a large following. Wherefore return to the mountains till I shall have found my brother when I will surely call you."

Chou Ts'ang replied, "I am only a rough uncouth fellow, wasting his life as a brigand. Meeting you, General, is like seeing the full sun in the skies and I feel that I can never bear to miss you again. As it might be inconvenient for all my men to follow you I will bid my companion lead them away, but I will come and follow you on foot wherever you go."

Kuan Yu again asked his sisters-in-law what they thought of this. Lady Kan said one or two made no difference and so Kuan Yu consented. But P'ei Yuan-shao was not satisfied with this arrangement and said he wished also to follow.

Chou said, "If you do not stay with the band they will disperse and be lost. You must take command for the moment and let me accompany General Kuan. As soon as he has a fixed abode I will come to fetch you."

Somewhat discontentedly P'ei Yuan-shao accepted the situation and marched off, while his one-time colleague joined the train of Kuan Yu and they went toward Junan. They travelled quickly for some days and then they saw a city on a hill. From the natives they heard that the city was called Kuch'eng and that a few months before a warrior had suddenly appeared, driven out the magistrates and taken possession. Then he had begun to recruit men, buy up horses and lay in stores. The warrior's name was Chang Fei. Now he had a large force and no one in the neighbourhood dared face him.

"To think that I should find my brother like this!" said Kuan Yu, delighted. "I have had never a word of him, nor knew I where he was since Hsu-chou fell."

So he despatched Sun Ch'ien into the city to tell its new commander to come out to meet him and provide for their sisters-in-law.

Now, after being separated from his brothers, Chang Fei had gone to the Mangyang Hills, where he had remained a month or so while he sent far and near for tidings of Yuan-te. Then as he happened to pass Kuch'eng he had sent in to borrow some grain, but had been refused. In revenge, he had driven away the magistrate and taken possession of the city. He found the place well suited to his needs at the moment.

As directed by Kuan Yu, Sun Ch'ien entered the city and, after the usual ceremonies, told Chang Fei the news of both his brothers; that Yuan-te had left Yuan Shao and gone to Junan and that Kuan Yu, with their sisters-in-law, was at his gates. Chang Fei listened without a word till he came to the request to go out to meet him. At that point he called for his armour and, when he had put it on, laid hold of his long spear, mounted and rode out with a large company at his back. Sun Ch'ien was too astonished to ask what this meant and simply followed.

Kuan Yu was very glad when he saw his brother coming, put up his weapons and, with Chou Ts'ang at his back, rode toward him at full speed. But as he approached he saw all the signs of fierce anger on his brother's face and he roared as he shook his spear, threatening his brother.

Kuan Yu was entirely taken aback and called out anxiously, "Brother, what does this mean? Is the Peach Garden Pledge quite forgotton?"

"What impudence is this that you come to see me since your disgraceful behaviour?" shouted Chang.

"What disgraceful behaviour has been mine?" said Kuan Yu.

"You have betrayed your brother, you have surrendered to Ts'ao Ts'ao and you have received title and office at his hands. And now you are come to exploit me. One of us shall die."

Kuan said, "Really you do not understand and it is hard for me to explain. But ask the two ladies here, worthy brother, and they will tell you."

At this the ladies lifted the curtain of the carriage and called out, "Brother, why is this?"

Fei said, "Wait a while, sisters, and see me slay this traitor. After that I will conduct you into the city."

Said the Lady Kan, "Since he knew not where you were our brother took shelter with Ts'ao Ts'ao. And since he knew that his elder brother was at Junan he has braved every danger to escort us thus far on the road. Pray take a correct view of his conduct."

The Lady Mi also chimed in, "When your brother went to Hsutu no other course was open to him."

"Sisters, do not let him blind you to the truth. Real loyalty prefers death to dishonour. No good man can serve two masters."

Kuan Yu said, "Brother, cease to wrong me I pray you."

Sun Ch'ien said, "Yun-ch'ang came expressly to seek you."

"How much more nonsense will you talk?" roared Chang Fei. "How can he be true-hearted? He came to capture me, I say."

"Had I come to capture you, I should have come with men and horses," said Kuan Yu.

"And are there not men and horses?" said Chang Fei pointing to a point behind Kuan Yu.

Kuan Yu turned and there he saw a cloud of dust rising as though a squadron of horse was coming. And soon they were near enough and from their trumpets and banners they showed themselves to be of Ts'ao Ts'ao's army.

"Now will you try to cajole me further?" cried Chang Fei in a rage.

He set his long spear and was just coming on when Kuan Yu said, "Brother, wait a while; see me slay the leader of these that I may prove myself no traitor."

"Well, if you are really true, prove it by slaying that leader, whoever he may be, before I have finished three rolls of the drum."

Chang Fei's condition was accepted. Soon the attacking force was near enough to make out the leader to be Ts'ai Yang. Sword in hand he rode at full speed, crying, "So I have found you, slayer of my nephew! I have a command to capture you and will execute it."

Kuan Yu made no reply. Raising his sword ready to strike he moved out and the drums began to beat. Before a roll could be completed the fight was over and Ts'ai Yang's head had rolled on the ground. His men scattered and fled. Kuan Yu, however, captured the young ensign-bearer and questioned him. The youth said that in very truth the Minister had not given an order. Incensed at the loss of his nephew, Ts'ai wished to pursue and attack Kuan Yu although the Minister refused permission. To satisfy him he had sent Ts'ai to attack Junan and the meeting at this place was entirely an accident.

Kuan Yu bade him repeat this story to his brother. Chang Fei also questioned him concerning all that had happened in the capital and the recital of the whole story satisfied him of the fidelity of Kuan Yu.

Just then messengers came from the city to Chang Fei to say that some scores of horsemen had arrived at the south gate. They seemed in a great hurry but no one knew them. Chang Fei, with still a lingering doubt in his mind, went to look at the newcomers and there saw a score or two of mounted archers with light bows and short arrows. Hastily dismounting to see them better he found they were Mi Chu and Mi Fang. Quickly slipping out of the saddle they came up and Mi Chu said, "After the dispersal at Hsu-chou when we lost sight of you we returned to our village whence we sent all around for news of you. We heard that Kuan Yu had surrendered to Ts'ao Ts'ao and our lord was in Hopei. The one of whom we could hear nothing was yourself. But yesterday, while on our way, we fell in with some travellers who told us a certain General Chang, of such and such an appearance, had suddenly occupied Kuch'eng and we felt it must be you. So we came to enquire and we happily fell in with you here."

Fei replied, "Kuan Yu and Sun Ch'ien are here and my two sisters are with them. They had heard where my elder brother was."

This news added to the joy of the two newcomers who went to see Kuan Yu and the women and then they all entered the city. When the ladies had settled down a little they related the whole story of the adventures on the road at which Chang Fei was overcome with remorse and bowed before his brother bitterly weeping. The brothers Mi were greatly affected. Then Chang Fei related what had happened to him.

A day was spent in banquets and next day Chang Fei wished his newly found brother to go with him to Junan to see their elder brother Yuan-te. But Kuan Yu said, "No; you take care of the ladies here while Sun Ch'ien and I go to get news."

So Kuan Yu and Sun Ch'ien with a small escort set out. When they reached Junan they were received by Liu P'i who told them their brother was no longer in the city. After waiting some days he had come to the conclusion that the soldiers were too few and had gone back to Yuan Shao to consult with him.

Kuan Yu was greatly disappointed and his companion did his best to console him. "Do not be sorrowful; it only means the trouble of another journey into Hopei to tell Uncle Liu and then we can all meet at Kuch'eng."

So spoke Sun Ch'ien and Kuan Yu accepted it. They took leave of Liu P'i and returned to Kuch'eng where they related what had happened. Chang Fei wanted to go with them into Hopei, but Kuan Yu opposed this, saying, "Seeing you have this city it makes a rallying point for us and a resting place. We must not abandon it lightly. We two will go and while away we look to you to keep the city safe."

"How can you go after killing the two generals, Yen Liang and Wen Ch'ou?"

"That will not stop me. And after I am there I can act according to circumstances."

Then he summoned Chou Ts'ang and asked him, saying, "How many men are there with P'ei at Sleeping Bull Mountain?"

"I should think four or five hundred."

"Now," said Kuan Yu, "I am going to take the shortest road to find my brother. Can you go to summon your men and lead them along the high road to assist me?"

With instructions to bring up these men Chou Ts'ang left, while Kuan Yu and Sun Ch'ien and their small escort went off to the north. When they drew near the boundary Sun Ch'ien said, "You must be careful how you go over; you ought to stop here while I go in, see Uncle Liu and take the necessary steps."

Seeing the wisdom of this Kuan Yu stopped there and sent his companion in advance, he and his followers going up to a nearby farm as an abiding place.

When they got to the farm out came a venerable man leaning

on a staff. After exchanging salutes Kuan Yu told the old man all about himself.

"My name is also Kuan; my personal name being Ting," said the old man. "I know your reputation and I am very happy to meet you."

He sent for his two sons to come and make their bow. He put up Kuan in his house and provided for his escort in the farm buildings.

In the meantime Sun Ch'ien had made his way to Ch'ichow and seen Yuan-te, who said, "Chien Yung also is here. We will send for him secretly to talk over this matter."

They did so, and when the usual salutes had been exchanged, they three began to consider the means of getting away.

"You see Yuan Shao personally," said Yung, "and say you wish to go to Chingchou to see Liu Piao about a scheme for the destruction of our enemy. That will give an excuse."

"That seems best," said Liu Pei, "but will you go with me?"

"I have another plan to extricate myself," said Yung.

Having settled their plans, Yuan-te soon went in to see his protector and suggested that, as Liu Piao was strong and well posted, his help should be sought against their enemy.

"I have sent messengers repeatedly to ask his help, said Shao, "but he is unwilling."

"As he and I are of the same family he will not refuse me if I go and ask him," said Liu Pei.

"Certainly he is worth much more than Liu P'i; you shall go."

"I have just heard," Shao continued, "that Kuan Yun-ch'ang has left Ts'ao Ts'ao and wants to come here. If he does I will put him to death out of revenge for my two officers."

"Illustrious Sir, you wished to employ him and so I sent for him. Now you threaten to put him to death. The two men he slew were but deer compared with such a tiger as he is. When you exchange a couple of deer for a tiger you need not complain of the bargain."

"Really I like him," said Shao. "I was only joking. You can send another messenger for him and tell him to come soon."

"May I send Sun Ch'ien for him?"

"Certainly."

After Yuan-te had gone Chien Yung came in and said to Shao, "If Yuan-te goes he will not come back. I had better go to speak to Liu Piao. And I can keep a watch on Liu Pei."

Yuan Shao agreed and issued orders for both to go.

On the subject of the mission Kuo T'u came in to his chief to dissuade him. Said he, "He went to speak to Liu P'i, but he accomplished nothing. Now you are sending Chien Yung with him and I am sure neither will ever return."

"Do not be too suspicious," said Shao. "Chien Yung is clever enough."

That was the end of the interview. Forthwith Yuan-te sent Sun Ch'ien back to Kuan Yu and then, with Chien Yung, took leave of Yuan Shao and rode out of the city. As soon as they reached the border line they met Sun Ch'ien and all three rode off to Kuan Ting's farm to meet Kuan Yu. He came out to welcome them, bowed and then seized his brother's hands while tears streamed down his face.

Presently the two sons of their host came to bow to the visitors. Liu Pei asked their names.

"These are of the same name as myself," said Kuan Yu. "The sons are Kuan Ning, who is a student, and Kuan P'ing, who is to be a soldier."

"I have been thinking of sending the younger in your train, General," said old Kuan, "would you take him?"

"What is his age?" said Liu Pei.

"He is eighteen "

Liu Pei said, "Since, O Senior, you are so kind I venture to suggest that your son should be adopted by my brother, who has no son of his own. What think you of that?"

Kuan Ting was perfectly willing, so he called his younger son and bade him make a son's obeisance to Kuan Yu and to style Yuan-te, "Uncle."

Then it was time to get on their way lest they should be pursued and with them went Kuan P'ing in the train of his "father." The lad's real father escorted them a short distance and then left. They took the road to Sleeping Bull Hill. Before they had gone very far they met Chou Ts'ang with a small party. He was wounded. He was introduced to Yuan-te who asked him how it was. He replied, "Before I reached the Hill a certain warrior, all alone, had fought with my friend P'ei and killed him. Then many of our men surrendered to him and he occupied our old camp. When I reached it I tried to allure the soldiers back to my side but only succeeded with a few. The others were too afraid. I got angry and engaged the interloper, who however worsted me time after time and wounded me thrice."

"Who is the warrior? what does he look like?" asked Yuan-te.

"All I know he is a doughty fighter, I do not know his name."

Thereafter they advanced toward the hill with Kuan Yu in front and Yuan-te in rear. When they drew near Chou Ts'ang began to abuse his enemy, who soon appeared, mailed and armed, coming down the hills.

Suddenly Yuan-te rode out waving his whip and shouting, "You, O Comer, are surely Tzu-lung?"

The rider, for it was Chao Tzu-lung, (Chao Yun), instantly slipped out of the saddle and bowed by the roadside.

The brothers dismounted to talk with him and ask how he came to be there.

"When I left you I had no idea that Kungsun Tsan was a man who would listen to no reason. The result was disaster and he perished in the flames. Yuan Shao invited me to him several times, but I thought too little of him to go. Then I wanted to go to Hsuchou to you, but you had lost that place and Yun-ch'ang had gone over to Ts'ao Ts'ao and you had joined Yuan Shao. Several times I thought of coming to you but I feared Yuan Shao. So I drifted from one place to another with nowhere to rest till I happened to come this way and P'ei Yuan-shao tried to steal my horse. So I slew him and took possession of his camp. I heard I-te was in Kuch'eng but thought it might be only a rumour. And so the days have passed till this happy meeting."

Yuan-te told him all that had happened to him since they parted and so did Kuan Yu.

Said Liu P'ei, "The first time I saw you I felt drawn to you and did not want to part from you. I am very happy to meet you again."

"In all my wanderings, trying to find a lord worth serving, I have seen no one like you. Now I have reached your side that is enough for all my life. I care not what may happen to me."

Next they burned the camp, after which they all took the road back to Kuch'eng where they were welcomed They exchanged the stories of their several adventures and the two ladies related the valiant deeds of Kuan Yu whereat Yuan-te was too affected to speak.

Then they performed a great sacrifice to Heaven and Earth with the slaughter of a bull and a horse.

The soldiers also were recompensed for their toils. Yuan-te surveyed the conditions around him and found therein much to rejoice at. His two brothers were restored to his side and none of his helpers were missing. Moreover he had gained Chao Yun, and his brother Kuan Yu had acquired an adopted son P'ing. Another captain had joined his ranks in the person of Chou Ts'ang. There was every occasion for feasting and gratification.

Scattered wide were the brothers, none knew another's retreat,
Joyfully now they foregather, dragon and tiger meet.

At this time the forces under the command of the three brothers
and their adherents numbered four or five thousand men. Yuan-te
was in favour of leaving Kuch'eng and occupying Junan and just
then Liu P'ei and Kung Tu, commanders of that city, sent to invite
him to go there. So they went. There they devoted all their efforts
to strengthen their army both horse and foot, but nothing will be
said of the recruiting purchase of horses and such matters.

However it must be noted that Yuan Shao was much annoyed
when Yuan-te did not return and at first was for sending a force
after him. However Kuo T'u dissuaded him.

"Liu P'ei need cause you no anxiety; Ts'ao Ts'ao is your one
enemy and must be destroyed. Even Liu Piao, though strongly
posted on the river, is none too terrible. There is Sun Po-fu on the
east of the river, strong, feared, with wide territory, a large army
and able counsellors and leaders; you should make an alliance there
against Ts'ao Ts'ao."

He won his chief to his view and wrote to Sun; sending the
letter by Ch'en Chen.

Just as one warrior leaves the north,
Another from the east comes forth.

Future chapters will reveal the outcome of these dispositions.

CHAPTER XXIX

We may tell here how Sun Ts'e gradually became supreme on the east of the river. In the fourth year of the period "Established Peace,"* he took Luchiang by the defeat of the Prefect Liu Hsun. He despatched Yu Fan with a despatch to the Prefect of Yuchang,† Hua Hsin, and he surrendered. Thence his renown increased and he boldly sent a memorial on his military successes to the Emperor by the hand of Chang Hung.

Ts'ao Ts'ao saw in him a powerful rival and said he was a lion difficult to contend with. So he betrothed his niece, daughter of Ts'ao Jen, to Sun K'uang, the youngest brother of Sun Ts'e, thus connecting the two families by marriage. He also retained Chang Hung near him in the capital.

Then Sun Ts'e sought the title of *Ta Ssu-ma*, or Minister of War, one of the highest offices of State, but Ts'ao Ts'ao prevented the attainment of this ambition, and Sun Ts'e keenly resented it. Henceforward his thoughts turned toward an attack on Ts'ao Ts'ao.

About this time the Prefect of Wuchun sent a secret letter to the capital to Ts'ao Ts'ao, saying that Sun Ts'e was a turbulent fellow of the Hsiang Chi type and the government ought, under the appearance of showing favour to him, to recall him to the capital for he was a danger in the provinces. But the bearer of this letter was captured on the Yangtse River and sent to Sun Ts'e, who immediately put him to death. Then he treacherously sent to ask the author of the letter, Hsu Kung by name, to come and consult over some affair. The unsuspecting man came. Sun Ts'e produced the letter, saying. "So you wish to send me to the land of the dead, eh?" and thereupon the executioners came in and strangled him. The family of the victim scattered, but three of his clients determined to avenge him if only they could find some means of attacking Sun.

Their chance came in the hunting field. One day Sun went hunting in the hills to the west of Tant'u. A stag was started and Sun pressed after it at topmost speed and followed it deep into the forest. Presently he came upon three armed men standing among the trees. Rather surprised to see them there he reined in and asked who they were.

"We belong to Han Tang's army and are shooting deer," was the reply.

So Sun Ts'e shook his bridle to proceed. But just as he did so one of the men thrust at him with a spear and wounded his thigh. Sun drew the sword at his side, dashed forward and cut down the aggressor. The blade of his sword suddenly fell to the ground, only the hilt remaining in his hand. Then one of the assassins drew his bow and an arrow wounded Sun in the cheek. He plucked out the arrow and shot at the offender, who fell, but the other two attacked him furiously with their spears, shouting, "We are Hsu Kung's men and his avengers!"

Sun Ts'e then understood. But he had no weapons save his bow against them. He tried to draw off, keeping them at bay by striking with his bow, but the fight was getting too much for him and both he and his steed were wounded in several places. However, just at the critical moment, some of his own men came up and they made short work of the remaining two avengers.

But their lord was in a sorry plight. His face was streaming with blood and some of the wounds were very severe. They tore up his robe and therewith bound up his wounds and they carried him home.

A poem in praise of the three avengers says:—

> O Sun Ts'e was a warrior and a stranger he to fear,
> But he was basely murdered while hunting of the deer.
> Yet were they leal who slew him, to avenge a murdered lord,
> Self immolated like Yu-jang, they dreaded not the sword.

Badly wounded, Sun Ts'e was borne to his home. They sent to call the famous physician, Hua T'o, but he was far away and could not be found. However, a disciple of his came and the wounded man was committed to his care.

"The arrowheads were poisoned," said the physician, "and the poison has penetrated deep. It will take a hundred days of perfect repose before danger will be past. But if you give way to passion or anger the wounds will not heal."

Sun's temperament was hasty and impatient and the prospect of such a slow recovery was very distasteful. However, he remained quiet for some twenty of the hundred days. Then came a messenger from the capital and he insisted on seeing and questioning him.

"Ts'ao Ts'ao fears you, my lord, very greatly," said the messenger, "and his advisers have exceeding respect for you; all except Kuo Chia."

"What did he say?" asked the sick chieftain.

The messenger remained silent, which only irritated his master and caused him to demand to be told. So the messenger had to speak the truth. He said, "The fact is Kuo Chia told Ts'ao Ts'ao that he need not fear you, that you were frivolous and unready, impulsive and shallow, just a stupid swaggerer who would one day come to his death at the hands of some mean person."

This provoked the sick man beyond endurance.

"How dare he say this of me, the fool!" cried Sun Ts'e. "I will take the capital from Ts'ao, I swear."

It was no more a question of repose. Ill as he was he wanted to begin preparations for an expedition at once. They remonstrated with him, reminded him of the physician's orders and urged him to rest.

"You are risking your priceless self in a moment's anger," said Chang Chao.

Then arrived Ch'en Chen, the messenger from Yuan Shao, and Sun would have him brought in. He said, "My master wishes to ally himself with Wu in an attack on Ts'ao Ts'ao."

Such a proposal was just after Sun's heart. At once he called a great meeting of his officers in the wall tower and prepared a banquet in honour of the messenger. While this was in progress he noticed many of his captains whispering to each other and they all began to go down from the banquet chamber. He could not understand this and enquired of the attendants near him what it meant. They told him that Saint Yu had just gone by and the officers had gone down to pay their respects to him. Sun Ts'e rose from his place and went and leaned over the railing to look at the man. He saw a Taoist priest in snowy garb leaning on his staff in the middle of the road, while the crowd about him burnt incense and made obeisance.

"What wizard fellow is this? Bring him here!" said Sun.

"This is Yu Chi," said the attendants. "He lives in the east and goes to and fro distributing charms and draughts. He has cured many people as everybody will tell you, and they say he is a saint. He must not be profaned."

This only angered Sun the more and he told them to arrest the man at once or disobey at their peril. So there being no help for it they went down into the road and hustled the saint up the steps.

"You madman! How dare you incite men to evil?" said Sun Ts'e.

"I am but a poor priest of the Lanyeh Palace. More than half a century ago, when gathering simples in the woods, I found near the Chuyang Spring a book called "The Way of Peace." It contains a hundred and more chapters and taught me how to cure the diseases of men. With this in my possession I had only one thing to do, to devote myself to spreading its teachings and saving mankind. I have never taken any thing from the people. Can you say I incite men to evil deeds?"

"You say you take nothing; whence came your clothes and your food? The fact is you are one of the Yellow Turban kidney and you will work mischief if you are left alive." "Take him away and put him to death," continued he to his attendants.

Chang Chao interceded, "The Taoist has been here in the east these many years. He has never done any harm and does not deserve death or punishment."

"I tell you I will kill these wizard fellows just as I would cattle."

The officials in a body interceded, even the guest of honour Ch'en Chen, but in vain; Sun Ts'e refused to be placated. He ordered the Taoist to be imprisoned.

The banquet came to an end and the messenger retired to his lodging. Sun Ts'e also returned to his palace.

His treatment of the Taoist Holy Man was the theme of general conversation and soon reached the ears of his mother. She sent for her son to the ladies' apartments and said to him, "They tell me you have put the Taoist in bonds. He has cured many sick people and the common folk hold him in great reverence. Do not harm him."

"He is simply a wizard who upsets the multitude with his spells and craft. He must be put to death," replied Ts'e.

She entreated him to stay his hand, but he was obstinate. "Do not heed the gossip of the street, mother," said he. "I must be judge of these matters."

However, he sent to the prison for the Taoist in order to interrogate him. Now the gaolers having a great respect for Yu Chi and faith in his powers were very indulgent to him and did not keep him in the collar. However when Ts'e sent for him he went with collar and fetters all complete.

Ts'e had heard of their indulgence and punished the gaolers so that the prisoner thereafter lay in constant torture. Chang Chao and some others, moved by pity, made a petition which they humbly presented and they offered to become surety for him.

Sun Ts'e said to them, "Gentlemen, you are all great scholars, but why do you not understand reason? Formerly in Chiao chou was a certain Governor Chang Ching, who was deluded by these vicious doctrines into beating drums, twanging lyres, burning incense and such things. He wore a red turban and represented himself as able to ensure victory to an army. But he was slain by the enemy. There is nothing in all this, only none of you will see it. I am going to put this fellow to death in order to stop the spread of this pernicious doctrine.

Lu Fan interposed, "I know very well this Yu Chi can control the weather. It is very dry just now, why not make him pray for rain as an amercement?"

"We will see what sort of witchcraft he is equal to," said Sun Ts'e.

Whereupon he had the prisoner brought in, loosed his fetters and sent him up to an altar to intercede for rain.

The docile Taoist prepared to do as he was bidden. He first bathed himself, then dressed himself in clean garments. After that he bound his limbs with cord and lay down in the fierce heat of the sun. The people came in crowds to look on.

Said he, "I will pray for three feet of refreshing rain for the benefit of the people, nevertheless I shall not escape death thereby."

The people said, "But if your prayer be efficacious our lord must believe in your powers."

"The day of fate has come for me and there is no escape."

Presently Sun Ts'e came near the altar and announced that if rain had not fallen by noon he would burn the priest. And to confirm this he bade them prepare the pyre.

As it neared noon a strong wind sprang up and the clouds gathered from all quarters. But there was no rain.

"It is near noon," said Sun Ts'e. "Clouds are of no account without rain. He is only an impostor."

He bade his attendants lay the priest on the pyre and pile wood around him and apply the torch. Fanned by the gale the flames rose rapidly. Then appeared in the sky above a wreath of black vapour followed by roaring thunder and vivid lightning, peal on peal and flash on flash. And the rain fell in a perfect deluge. In a short time the streets became rivers and torrents. It was indeed a three feet fall.

Yu Chi, who was still lying upon the pile of firewood, cried in a loud voice, "O clouds, cease thy rain, and let the glorious sun appear!"

Thereupon officials and people helped the priest down, loosened the cord that bound him and bowed before him in gratitude for the rain.

But Sun Ts'e boiled with rage at seeing his officers and the people gathered in groups and kneeling in the water regardless of the damage to their clothing.

"Rain or shine are as nature appoints them and the wizard has happened to hit upon a moment of change; what are you making all this fuss about?" cried he.

Then he drew his sword and told the attendants to smite the Taoist therewith. They all besought him to hold his hand.

"You want to follow Yu Chi in rebellion, I suppose," cried Sun Ts'e.

The officers, now thoroughly cowed by the rage of their lord, were silent and showed no opposition when the executioners seized the unhappy Taoist and beheaded him.

They saw just a wreath of black smoke drift away to the northeast where lay the Langyeh Mountains.

The corpse was exposed in the market place as a warning to enchanters and wizards and such people. That night there came a very violent storm and when it calmed down at daylight there was no trace of the body. The guards reported this and Sun Ts'e in his wrath sentenced them to death. But as he did so he saw Yu Chi calmly walking toward him as if he were still alive. He drew his sword and darted forward to strike at the wraith, but he fainted and fell to the ground.

They carried him to his chamber and in a short time he recovered consciousness. His mother, the Lady Wu, came to visit him and said, "My son, you have done wrong to slay the holy one and this is your retribution."

"Mother, when I was a boy I went with my father to the wars, where men are cut down as one cuts hempen stalks. There is not much retribution about such doings. I have put fellow to death and so checked a great evil. Where does retribution come in?"

"This comes of want of faith," she replied. "Now you must avert the evil by meritorious deeds."

"My fate depends on Heaven: wizards can do me no harm, so why avert anything?"

His mother saw that it was useless to try persuasion, but she told his attendants to do some good deeds secretly whereby the evil should be turned aside.

That night about the third watch, as Sun Ts'e lay in his chamber, he suddenly felt a chill breeze, which seemed to extinguish the lamps for a moment, although they soon brightened again, an he saw in the lamp light the form of Yu Chi standing near his bed.

Sun said, "I am the sworn foe of witchcraft and I will purge the world of all such as deal in magic. You are a spirit and how dare you approach me?"

Reaching down a sword that hung at the head of his bed he hurled it at the phantom, which then disappeared. When his mother heard this story her grief redoubled. Sun Ts'e, ill as he was, did his utmost to reassure his mother.

She said, "The Holy One says, 'How abundantly do spiritual beings display the powers that belong to them!' and 'Prayer has been made to the spirits of the upper and lower worlds.' You must have faith. You sinned in putting Master Yu to death and retribution is sure. I have already sent to have sacrifices performed at the Jadepure Monastery and you should go in person to pray. May all come right!"

Sun Ts'e could not withstand such mandate from his mother so, mustering all his strength, he managed to get into a sedan chair and went to the monastery, where the Taoists received him respectfully and begged him to light the incense. He did so, but he returned no thanks. To the surprise of all the smoke from the brazier, instead of floating upwards and dissipating, collected in a mass that gradually shaped itself into an umbrella and there on the top sat Yu Chi.

Sun Ts'e simply spat abuse and went out of the temple. As he passed the gates, lo! Yu Chi stood there gazing at him with angry eyes.

"Do you see that wizard fellow?" said he to those about him.

They said they saw nothing. More angry than ever he flung his sword at the figure by the gate. The sword struck one of his escort who fell. When they turned him over they saw it was the executioner who had actually slain the Taoist. The sword had penetrated his brain and his life drained out through the seven channels of perception. Sun Ts'e told them to bury the man. But as he went out of the courtyard he saw Yu Chi walking in.

"This temple is nothing more than a lurking place for sorcerers and wizards and such people," said he.

Whereupon he took a seat in front of the building and sent for half a company of soldiers to pull the place down. When they went up on the roof to strip off the tiles he saw Yu Chi standing on the main beam flicking tiles to the ground. More angry than ever he told them to drive out the priests belonging to the place and burn it. They did so and when the flames rose their highest he saw the dead Taoist Yu Chi standing in the midst of the fire.

Sun Ts'e returned home still in a bad humour, which increased when he saw the form of Yu Chi standing at his gate. He would not enter but mustered his army and went into camp outside the city walls. And there he summoned his officers to meet him and talk over joining Yuan in an attack on Ts'ao.

They assembled, but they remonstrated with him and begged him to consider his precious health. That night he slept in the camp and again saw Yu Chi, this time with his hair hanging loose. He raged at the vision without cessation.

Next day his mother called him into the city and he went. She was shocked at the change in his appearance; he looked so utterly miserable. Her tears fell.

"My son," said she, "how wasted you are!"

He had a mirror brought and looked at himself; he was indeed so gaunt and thin that he was almost frightened and exclaimed, "How do I come to look so haggard?"

While he spoke, Yu Chi appeared in the mirror. He struck it and shrieked. Then the half healed wounds reopened and he fainted.

He was raised and borne within. When he recovered consciousness he said, "This is the end; I shall die."

He sent for Chang Chao and his other chief officers and his brother, Sun Ch'uan, and they gathered in his chamber. He gave them his dying charge, saying, "In the disordered state of the Empire Wu and Yueh, with their strong defence of the Three Chiang, have a brilliant future. You, Chang Chao, must assist my brother."

So saying he handed his seal to Sun Ch'uan saying, "For manipulating the might of Chiangtung so as to make it the deciding force between two factions and then obtaining the whole Empire you are not so suited as I; but in encouraging the wise and confiding in the able and getting the best out of every one for the preservation of this district, I should not succeed as you will. Remember with what toil and labour your father and I have won what we possess and take good care thereof."

Sun Ch'uan wept as he knelt to receive the seal and the dying chief turned to his mother, "Mother, the days allotted of Heaven have run out and I can no longer serve my tender mother. I have given over the seal to my brother and trust that you will advise him early and late, and see that he lives worthy of his predecessors."

"Alas! your brother is full young for such a task," said his mother weeping. "I know not what may happen."

"He is far abler than I and fully equal to the task of ruling.

Should he have doubts upon internal affairs, he must turn to Chang Chao; for outer matters he must consult Chou Yu. It is a pity Chou Yu is absent so that I cannot give him my charge face to face."

To his brothers he said, "When I am gone you must help your brother. Should any discord arise in the family let the others punish the wrong-doer and let not his ashes mingle with those of his ancestors in the family vaults."

The young men wept at these words. Then he called for his wife, the famous beauty of the Ch'iao family, and said, "Unhappily we have to part while still in the full vigour of life. You must care for my mother. Your sister will come to see you presently and you can ask her to tell Chou Yu to help my brother in all things and make him keep to the way I have taught him to walk in."

Then he closed his eyes and soon after passed away. He was only twenty-six.

> Men called him first of the chieftains,
>> The east had felt his might,
> He watched like a tiger crouching,
>> Struck as a hawk in flight.
> There was peace in the lands he ruled,
>> His fame ran with the wind,
> But he died and left to another,
>> The great scheme in his mind.

As his brother breathed his last Sun Ch'uan sank by his bed and wept.

"This is not the time to mourn," said Chang Chao. "First see to the funeral ceremonies and that the government is safe."

So the new ruler dried his tears. The superintendence of the funeral was confided to Sun Ching and then Chang Chao led his young master to the hall to receive the felicitations of his officers.

Sun Ch'uan was endowed with a square jaw and a large mouth; he had blue eyes and a dark brown beard. Formerly, when Liu Yuan had gone to Wu to visit the Sun family, he said of the family of brothers, "I have looked well at them all and they are all clever and perspicacious, but none of them have the very ultimate degree of good fortune. Only the second has the look of a deep thinker. His face is remarkable, and his build unusual, and he has the look of one who will come to great honour. But none of them will attain to the blessing of a great age."

History says that when Sun Ch'uan succeeded to his brother and his brother's might, there was still some reorganization to be done. Soon Chou Yu had arrived. The young ruler received him very graciously and said, "I need have no anxiety now that you have come."

It will be remembered that Chou Yu had been sent to hold Pachiu. When he heard that his chief had been wounded by an arrow he thought it well to return to see how he was. But Sun Ts'e had died before Chou Yu could arrive. He hurried to be present at the funeral.

When he went to wail at the coffin of his late chief, Wu *Fu-jen*, the dead man's mother, came out to deliver her son's last injunctions. When she had told him the last charge he bowed to the earth, saying, "I shall exert the puny powers I have in your service as long as I live."

Shortly after Sun Ch'uan came in, and, after receiving Chou Yu's obeisance, said, "I trust you will not forget my brother's charge to you."

Chou bowed saying, "I would willingly suffer any form of death for you."

"How best can I maintain this grave charge which I have inherited from my father and brother?"

"He who wins men, prospers; he who loses them, fails. Your present plan should be to seek men of high aims and farseeing views and you can establish yourself firmly."

"My brother bade me consult Chang Chao for internal administration, and yourself on external matters," said Ch'uan.

"Chang Chao is wise and understanding and equal to such a task. I am devoid of talent and fear to take such responsibility, but I venture to recommend to you as a helper one Lu Su, named Tzu-ching, a man of Tungch'uan. This man's bosom hides strategy and his breast conceals tactics. He lost his father in early life and has been a perfectly filial son to his mother. His family is rich and renowned for charity to the needy. When I was stationed at Ch'ao-ch'ang I led some hundreds of men across the Linhuai. We were short of grain. Hearing that the Lu family had two granaries there, each holding three thousand measures, I went to ask for help. Lu Su pointed to one granary and said, 'Take that as a gift.' Such was his generosity!"

"He has always been fond of fencing and horse archery. He was living in Chuo. His grandmother died while he was there and he went to bury her in Tungch'eng and then his friend, Liu Tzu-yang, wished to engage him to go to Ch'aohu and join Cheng Pao. However, he hesitated about that and has not gone yet. You should invite him without loss of time."

Sun Ch'uan at once sent Chou Yu to engage the services of this man and he set out. When the obeisances were over he laid before his friend the inducements that his own master held out. He replied that as he had been engaged by Liu Tzu-yang to go to Ch'aohu he was just starting thither.

Said Chou Yu, "Of old Ma Yuan said to Kuang-Wu, 'This is an age when not only do princes select their ministers, but ministers choose their princes.' Now our General Sun calls to him the wise and treats his officers well. Thus he engages the help of the wonderful and gets the services of the extraordinary in a way that few others do. But if you are not engaged elsewhere come with me to Wu as the best thing to do."

Lu Su returned with him and saw Sun Ch'uan, who treated him with the greatest deference and with him discussed affairs very fully. The conference proved so interesting that it went on all day and neither felt fatigue.

One day at the close of the usual reception, the chief kept Lu Su to dine with him. They sat up late and by and by slept on the same couch as would the closest of friends. In the dead of night Sun Ch'uan said to his bedfellow, "The Dynasty is failing and everything is at sixes and sevens. I have received a great charge from my father and brother and I am thinking of imitating the actions of Huan and Wen and becoming the leader of the feudal lords and I pray you instruct me."

Lu Su replied, "Of old Han Kao-Tsu wished to honour and serve the Emperor I, but could not on account of Hsiang Yu's evil doings. Now Ts'ao Ts'ao can be compared with Hsiang Yu; how can you be Huan and Wen? My humble opinion is that the Hans have fallen beyond hope of recovery and Ts'ao Ts'ao cannot be destroyed and that the only key to your schemes is to secure your present position in order to keep the master hand and control the combinations among the others. Now take advantage of the turmoil in the north to smite Huang Tsu and attack Liu Piao. Thereby you will command the whole length of the Great River (Yangtse). Then you may style yourself Emperor or King and thereafter as may be. This was how Kao-Tsu acted."

Hearing this Sun Ch'uan was very greatly pleased. He threw on some clothing, got up and thanked his new-found adviser. Next day Sun Ch'uan gave him costly gifts and sent robe and hangings to his mother.

Lu Su then recommended a friend of his to the young man's notice, a man of wide reading and great ability. He was also a filial son. His double name was Chuko Chin and he came from

Nanyang. Sun Ch'uan treated him as a superior guest. This man dissuaded Sun Ch'uan from making common cause with Yuan Shao, but advised him rather to favour Ts'ao Ts'ao, against whom he could plan when occasion served. Sun Ch'uan therefore sent back the messenger Ch'en Chen with despatches that broke off all negotiations.

Hearing of Sun Ts'e's death, Ts'ao Ts'ao was for sending an expedition against Chiangnan. But a certain historian, Chang Hung, dissuaded him, saying that it would be mean to take advantage of the period of mourning.

"And if you should not overcome him you will make him an enemy instead of being a friend. It would be preferable to treat him generously "

So Ts'ao memorialised the throne and obtained for Sun Ch'uan the title of Generalissimo and Prefect of Kueichi, while Chang Hung was appointed under him as *Tu-yu*.

And a seal of office was sent him. The new appointment pleased Sun Ch'uan and he was also glad to get Chang Hung back again. He was sent to act jointly with Chang Chao.

Chang Hung was the means of getting another into Sun Ch'uan's service. His friend was Ku Yung, known also as Yuan-t'an, a disciple of the historian Ts'ai Yung. He was a man of few words and an abstainer from wine. He was very correct in all things. Sun Ch'uan employed him in the administration.

Henceforward Sun Ch'uan's rule was very prosperous and he waxed mightily in influence and won the love of all the people.

When Ch'en Chen had returned and related the events in Wu, and told of the honours that Ts'ao Ts'ao had obtained for the young man in return for his support, Yuan Shao was very wroth and he set about preparing for an attack on the capital with a force of seventy legions of northern men.

> Although in the south they rest from war,
> They rattle the spears 'neath the northern star.

Later it will be seen which side conquered.

CHAPTER XXX

YUAN SHAO DEFEATED AT THE FERRY: TS'AO TS'AO BURNS THE WUCH'AO GRANARIES

Hearing that Yuan Shao was hastening to attack at Kuantu, Hsiahou Tun wrote to the capital urgently asking for reinforcements, and Ts'ao Ts'ao told off seventy legions with which he marched. Hsun Yu was left to guard the capital.

Just as Yuan's army was starting T'ien Feng sent out a remonstrance from his prison cell denouncing the policy of attack and counselling Shao to wait upon such times as Heaven should appoint.

An enemy said to Yuan, "Why does this T'ien Feng utter ill-omened words? My lord is sending forth an army in the cause of humanity and justice."

Easily moved to anger Yuan Shao was going to execute T'ien, but this time he forebore at the entreaties of many of his officers. However, he was not appeased, for he said, "I will punish him when I return from conquering Ts'ao Ts'ao."

Meanwhile he hastened to start. The banners of his host filled the horizon, their swords were as trees in the forest. They marched to Yangwu and there made a strong camp.

Then Chu Shou once more opposed any hasty movement, saying, "Though our soldiers are many they are not so bold as the enemy; however, veterans as are the enemy they have not ample supplies. Therefore they will wish to force on a speedy battle, while our policy is to hold them off and delay. If we can keep from a decisive battle long enough the victory will be ours without fighting."

This advice did not appeal to the General. Said he, threateningly, "T'ien Feng spake discouraging words to my armies and I will assuredly put him to death on my return. How dare you follow in the same way?"

He summoned the lictors and sent away the adviser in chains, saying, "When I have overcome Ts'ao then will I deal with you and T'ien Feng together."

The huge army was camped in four divisions, one toward each point of the compass. The camps were ninety *li* in circuit. Scouts and spies were sent out to discover the strong and the weak points of the enemy.

Ts'ao's army arrived and were smitten with fear when they heard of the strength of their enemy. The leader called together his council. Then said the adviser Hsun Yu, "The enemy are many but not terrible. Ours is an army of veterans, every man worth ten, but our advantage lies in a speedy battle for unhappily our stores are insufficient for a long campaign."

"You speak to the point," said Ts'ao. "I think the same."

Therefore he issued orders to press forward and force on a battle. Yuan Shao's men took up the challenge and the two sides were arrayed. On Yuan's side a legion of crossbow men were placed in ambush on the two wings, while half a legion of archers held the centre. The signal for general attack was a bomb and the onset was to continue through three rolls of the drum.

Yuan Shao wore a silver helmet and breastplate and an embroidered robe held in by a jewelled belt. He took up his post in the centre with his numerous captains ranged right and left. His banners and ensigns made a brave show.

When the Ts'ao army centre opened and the banners moved aside the great captain appeared on horseback with his staff of doughty leaders all fully armed. Pointing with his whip at Yuan Shao he cried, "In the presence of the Emperor I pressed your claims to consideration and obtained for you the title of Generalissimo; why do you now plan rebellion?"

Yuan replied, "You take the title of a minister of Han, but you are really a rebel against the House. Your crimes and evil deeds reach to the heavens, and you are worse than the usurper Mang and the rebel Cho. What are these slanderous words about rebellion that dare you address to me?"

"I have a command to make you prisoner."

"I have the Girdle Decree to arrest rebels," replied Yuan.

Then Ts'ao became wrathful and bade Chang Liao ride forth as his champion. From the other side rode Chang Ho on a curvetting steed. The two champions fought four or five bouts with no advantage to either. In his heart Ts'ao thought the contest amazing. Then Hsu Ch'u whirled up his sword and went to help. To match him rode out Kao Lan with his spear in rest, and the contestants were now four, battling two and two. Then Ts'ao ordered three companies under Hsiahou Tun and Ts'ao Hung to attack the opponents' array. Thereupon on Yuan's side the signal for attack was also given and the legion of crossbow men on the wings shot and the centre archers let fly all together. The arrows flew all over the field in front and Ts'ao's men could not advance. They hastened away toward the south. Yuan threw his soldiers on their rear and they were broken. They went away toward Kuantu and Yuan advanced another stage. He camped near them.

Then Shen P'ei said, "Now send ten legions to guard Kuantu and get near Ts'ao's camp, then throw up observation mounds to get a clear view of the enemy and choose vantage points whence to shoot arrows into the midst of their host. If we can force him to evacuate this place we shall have gained a strategical point whence Hsuch'ang can be attacked."

Yuan adopted this suggestion. From each of the camps they sought out the strongest veterans who dug with iron spades and carried earth to raise mounds near Ts'ao's camp.

Ts'ao's men saw what their enemies were doing and were anxious to make a sortie and drive them off. But the archers and crossbow men came out commanding the narrow throat through which it was necessary to attack and stayed them. At the end of ten days they had thrown up more than half a hundred mounds and on the summit of each was a lofty tower, whence the archers could command their opponents' camp. Ts'ao's men were greatly frightened and held up their bucklers to keep off the various missiles. From the mounds the arrows flew down, pang! pang! like a fierce rain. The men of the Yuan army laughed and jeered when they saw their enemies crouching under their shields and crawling on the ground to avoid their missiles.

Ts'ao saw that his soldiers were getting out of hand under this attack so he called a council. Liu Yeh spoke up saying, "Let us make ballistae and so destroy them."

Ts'ao at once had models brought and set cunning workmen to make these machines. They soon constructed some hundreds and placed them along the walls of the camp inside, just opposite the high ladders on the enemy's mounds.

Then they watched for the archers to ascend the towers. As soon as they began to shoot all the ballistae began to heave their stone balls into the skies and they wrought great havoc. There was no shelter from them and enormous numbers of the archers were killed. Yuan's men called these machines "Rumblers" and after their appearance the archers dared not ascend the mounds to shoot.

Then Shen P'ei, the strategist, thought out another plan. He set men to tunnel under the walls into the midst of Ts'ao's camp and called this corps "The Sappers." Ts'ao's men saw the enemy digging out pits behind the mounds and told the chief, who at once sought a counter plan from Liu Yeh.

"As Yuan Shao can no longer attack openly he is attacking secretly and is tunnelling a road under ground into the midst of our camp," said he.

"But how to meet it?"

"We can surround the camp with a deep moat which renders their tunnel useless."

So a deep moat was dug as quickly as possible and when the enemy sappers arrived thereat, lo! their labour had been in vain and the sap was useless.

It is recorded that Ts'ao held Kuantu throughout the eighth and ninth months when, the men being worn out and provisions failing, he began to think of giving up and returning to the capital. As he could not make up his mind he referred his difficulties by letter to Hsun Yu, whom he had left to guard Hsuch'ang. The reply he got was to this effect:— "I have received your command to decide whether to continue the campaign or retire. It appears to me that Yuan Shao assembled such large forces at Kuantu with the expectation of winning a decision. You, Sir, are very weak while he is very strong and if you cannot get the better of him he will be able to work his will on you for this is a crisis of empire. Your opponents are indeed numerous, but their leader knows not how to use them. With your military genius and discernment where are you not sure to succeed? Now though your numbers are small it is not as when Ch'u and Han were between Jungyang and Ch'engkao. You are securely intrenched with your hands on his throat, and even if you cannot advance, that state of things cannot endure for ever but must change. This is the time to play some unexpected move and you must not miss it. The device I leave to your illustrious ingenuity."

This letter greatly pleased Ts'ao and he urged upon his men to use every effort to maintain the position.

Yuan having retired some thirty *li*, Ts'ao sent out scouts to ascertain his new dispositions. One of Hsu Huang's officers captured an enemy spy and sent him to his chief, who interrogated him and found out that a convoy of supplies was expected and that this spy and others had been sent to find out what were the risks of the route. Hsu Huang went at once to tell Ts'ao. When the adviser Hsun Yu heard that the commander of the convoy was Han Meng he said, "That fellow is a valiant fool. A few companies of light horse sent to intercept him can capture the whole train and cause much trouble in the enemy's camp."

"Whom should I send ?" asked Ts'ao.

"You might send Hsu Huang; he is capable of such a task."

So Hsu was deputed and he took with him Shih Huan, who had captured the spy, and his company. And this party was supported by Chang Liao and Hsu Ch'u.

It was night when the commissariat train of many thousands of carts drew near Yuan Shao's camp. As they passed through a defile Ts'ao's men came out and stopped the train. Han Meng galloped up to give battle but was soon overcome. The guard was scattered and soon the whole train was in flames. The escort and their leader got away.

The glow of the flames seen from Shao's camp caused great consternation, which became fear when the escaped soldiers rode in and told their tale.

Yuan sent out Chang Ho and Kao Lan to try to intercept the raiders and they came upon Hsu Huang and his company. Just as they were attacking reinforcements came up and the Yuan men were between two fires. They were cut to pieces and the successful captains rode back to Kuantu, where they were richly rewarded.

As an additional safeguard Ts'ao made a supporting outpost in front of the main camp to be the apex of a triangle of defence.

When Han Meng returned with his woeful tidings Yuan Shao was angry and threatened to put him to death. His colleagues begged him off.

Then said Shen P'ei, "Food is very important for an army in the field and must be defended with the greatest diligence. Wuch'ao is our main depot and must be carefully guarded."

"My plans being complete," said Shao, "you may as well return to Yehtu and undertake the control of the supplies. Let there be no shortage." So Shen P'ei left the army.

Then a force of two legions under six captains was told off to defend the depot. One of these captains, Shunyu Ch'iung, was a hard man and a heavy drinker, who in his cups was a terror to the men. Under the idle life of guarding the supply depot the leaders gave themselves up to indulgence and drank heavily.

In Ts'ao's army also food was getting scarce and a message was sent to the capital to send grain quickly. The messenger with the letter, however, had not gone far when he fell into the hands of Shao's men, who took him to the adviser Hsu Yu. Seeing from the letter that Ts'ao was short of supplies the adviser went to his master and told him saying, "Ts'ao Ts'ao and we have been at grips here for a long time and the capital must be undefended. A small army sent quickly could take it and at the same moment an attack here would deliver Ts'ao into our hands. Now is the moment to strike, for his supplies are short."

Shao replied, "Ts'ao is full of ruses and this letter is artfully designed to bring about a battle to suit himself."

"If you do not take this chance he will do you some injury by and by."

Just at this juncture in came a despatch from Yehchun in which, after some details regarding the forwarding of grain, Shen P'ei said he had discovered that Hsu Yu had been in the habit of receiving bribes while in Ch'ichou and had winked at his relatives collecting excess taxes. One son and nephew were then in prison.

At this Yuan Shao turned on Hsu Yu angrily and said, "How can you have the face to stand before me and propose plans, you extortionate fellow? You and Ts'ao Ts'ao have old likings for each other and he has bribed you to do his dirty work for him and help his base schemes. Now you want to betray my army. I ought to take off your head, but temporarily I will let your neck carry it away. Get out and never let me see you again."

The discredited adviser sighed and went out, saying, "Faithful words offend his ear. He is a pest and unworthy of advice from me. And now that Shen P'ei has injured my son and nephew how can I look my fellow men in the face again?"

And he drew his sword to end his life. But his people prevented that. They said, "If Yuan Shao rejects your honest words then assuredly he will be taken by Ts'ao Ts'ao. You are an old friend of Ts'ao's; why not abandon the shade for the sunlight?"

Just these few words awakened him to consciousness of his position and he decided to leave Yuan Shao and go over to Ts'ao Ts'ao for he was an old friend.

> Vainly now for chances lost
> Yuan sighs; once he was great.
> Had he taken Hsu's advice,
> Ts'ao had not set up a State.

Hsu Yu stealthily left the camp and set out for Ts'ao's lines. He was captured on the way. He told his captors he was an old friend of the Minister's and asked them to tell him that Hsu Yu of Nanyang wished to see him.

They did so. Ts'ao was resting in his tent, his clothing loose and comfortable after the toils of the day. When he heard who wished to see him he arose quite joyfully and dressed himself hastily to receive Hsu. He went forth to greet him. They saw each other in the distance and Ts'ao Ts'ao clapped his hands with gladness bowing to the ground when near enough to his visitor, Hsu Yu hastened to help him rise, saying, "Sir, you, a great Minister, should not thus salute a simple civilian like me."

"But you are my old friend and no name or office makes any difference to us," replied Ts'ao.

"Having been unable to choose the lord I would serve I had to bow my head before Yuan Shao. But he was deaf to my words and disregarded my plans. Wherefore I have left him and come now to see my old friend from whom I hope employment."

"If Tzu-yuan is willing to come then have I indeed a helper," said Ts'ao. "I desire you to give me a scheme for the destruction of Yuan Shao."

"I counselled him to send a light force to take the capital so that head and tail be both attacked."

Ts'ao was alarmed. "If he does so, I am lost."

"How much grain have you in store?" said the new adviser.

"Enough for a year."

"I think not quite," said Yu smiling.

"Well, half a year."

The visitor shook out his sleeves, rose and hurried toward the door of the tent, saying, "I offer him good counsel and he repays me with deceit. Could I have expected it?"

Ts'ao held him back. "Do not be angry," said he. "I will tell you the truth. Really I have here only enough for three months."

"Everybody says you are a marvel of wickedness and indeed it is true," said Yu.

"But who does not know that in war there is no objection to deceit?" replied Ts'ao. Then whispering in the other's ear he said, "Actually here I have only supplies for this month's use."

"O do not throw dust in my eyes any more. Your grain is exhausted and I know it."

Ts'ao was startled, for he thought no one knew of the straits he was in.

"How did you find that out?" said he.

Hsu Yu produced the letter, saying, "Who wrote that?"

"Where did you get it?"

Whereupon he told Ts'ao the story of the captured messenger. Ts'ao seized him by the hand saying, "Since our old friendship has brought you to me I hope you have some plan to suggest to me."

Hsu Yu said, "To oppose a great army with a small one is to walk in the way of destruction unless you inflict quick defeat. I can propose a plan which will defeat the innumerable hordes of Yuan Shao without fighting a battle. But will you follow my advice?"

"I desire to know your plan," said Ts'ao.

"Your enemy's stores of all kinds are at Wuch'ao, where the commander of the guard is that drunkard Shunyu Ch'iung. You can send some of your trusty veterans to pretend they belong to Chiang Chi, one of Yuan's generals, sent to help guard the depot. These men can find an opportunity to fire the grain and stores of all kinds, which will upset all Yuan Shao's calculations."

Ts'ao approved. He treated Hsu Yu very liberally and kept him in his camp. Forthwith he chose five companies of horse and foot ready for the expedition. Chang Liao protested the enterprise would be futile as the grain depot would certainly be well guarded and he suggested treachery on the part of the newly arrived strategist."

"Hsu Yu is no traitor," said Ts'ao. "He has come sent by Heaven to defeat Yuan Shao. If we do not get grain it will be hard to hold out and I have either to follow his advice or sit still and be hemmed in. If he was a traitor he would hardly remain in my camp. Moreover this raid has been my desire for a long time. Have no doubts; the raid will certainly succeed."

"Well, then, you must look out for an attack here while the camp is undefended."

"That is already well provided for," said Ts'ao gleefully.

The defenders of the camp were then told off. Among them was Hsu Yu.

The arrangements for the raid on the grain depot were made with extreme care to ensure success. When all was ready they set out, Ts'ao himself in the centre. The army showed the ensigns of their opponents. The men carried bundles of grass and faggots to make a blaze. The men were gagged and the horses tied round the muzzles so as to prevent any noise.

They set out at dusk. The night was fine and the stars shone brightly Chu Shou, still a prisoner in Yuan Shao's camp, saw the stars were very brilliant and told his gaolers to conduct him out to the central pavilion whence he could study them. While watching he saw the planet Venus invade the quarter of the Bear and Lyra, which startled him very greatly.

"Some misfortune is near," said he.

So although it was still night he went to see his master. But Yuan Shao was sleeping after indulgence in too much wine and was in bad humour. However, when they had roused him saying that the prisoner had a secret message to deliver, he got up.

"While I happened to be studying the aspect of the heavens," said the night visitor, "I saw Venus, then between Hydra and Cancer, suddenly shoot into the neighbourhood of the Bear and Lyra. There is danger of a robber raid and special precautions must be taken at the grain depot. Lose no time in sending good soldiers and vigorous leaders thither and keep a lookout on the byeways among the hills that you may escape the wiles of Ts'ao Ts'ao."

"You are a criminal," said Shao. "How dare you come with such wild nonsense to upset my armies."

And turning to the gaolers he continued, "I bade you confine him; why did you let him come?"

Then he issued orders to put the gaolers to death and appointed others to keep the prisoner in close custody.

Chu Shou went away, wiping his falling tears and sighing deeply. "Our soldiers' destruction is at hand and I know not where my poor corpse may find a resting place."

> Blunt truth offended Yuan Shao,
> Too stupid any plan to make,
> His stores destroyed 'tis evident
> That Ch'ichou also is at stake.

Ts'ao Ts'ao's raiding party went along through the night. Passing one of Yuan Shao's outpost camps they were challenged Ts'ao sent forward a man to say, "Chiang Chi has orders to go to Wuch'ao to guard the grain stores."

Seeing that the raiders marched under the ensigns of Yuan Shao the guard had no suspicions and let them pass. At every post this ruse was effective and they got safely through.

They reached their objective at the end of the fourth watch, the straw and wood were placed in position without loss of time and the blaze started. Then the captains beat to attack.

At the time of the attack Shunyu Ch'iung and his companions were all asleep after a heavy drinking bout. However, when the alarm was given, they sprang up and asked what was the matter. The hubbub was indescribable. Very soon the fuddled officers were caught with hooks and hauled out of their camp.

Mu Yuan-chin and Chao Jui were just returning from taking grain to the camp and seeing the flames arise, they hastened to assist. Some of Ts'ao's soldiers ran to tell him that some of the enemy were coming up in the rear and ask him to send reinforcements, but he only replied by ordering the generals to press on to the front till the enemy was actually close at hand and then face about. So the attack was pressed and they all hastened forward.

Very soon the fire gained strength and thick smoke hung all around filling the sky. When Mu and Chao drew near, Ts'ao turned about and attacked them. They could not stand this for a moment and both captains were killed. Finally the stores of grain and forage were utterly destroyed.

The commander, Shunyu Ch'iung, was made prisoner and taken to Ts'ao who ordered him to be deprived of ears, nose and hands. He was bound on a horse and sent, thus horribly mutilated, to his master.

From Yuan's camp the flames of the burning depot were seen away in the north and they knew what they meant. Yuan hastily summoned his officers to a council to send a rescue party. Chang Ho offered to go with Kao Lan but Kuo T'u said, "You may not go; it is certain that Ts'ao Ts'ao is there in person, wherefore his camp is undefended. Let loose our soldiers on the camp and that will speedily bring Ts'ao back again. This is how Sun Pin besieged Wei and thereby rescued Han."

But Chang Ho said, "Not so; Ts'ao is too wily not to have fully prepared against a chance attack. If we attack his camp and fail and Shunyu Ch'iung should be caught we shall all be captured too."

Kuo T'u said, "Ts'ao will be too intent on the destruction of the grain to think of leaving a guard. I entreat you to attack his camp."

So five companies under Chang Ho and Kao Lan were sent to attack Ts'ao's camp and Chiang Chi was sent to try to recover the grain store.

Now after overcoming Shunyu, Ts'ao's men dressed themselves in the armour and clothing of the defeated soldiers and put out their emblems, thus posing as defeated men running back to their own headquarters. And when they happened upon Chiang Chi's rescue legion they said they had been beaten at Wuch'ao and were retreating. So they were suffered to pass without molestation while Chiang Chi hastened on. But soon he came to Chang Liao and Hsu Chu who cried out to him to stop. And before he could make any opposition Chang Liao had cut him down. Soon his men were killed or dispersed and the victors sent false messengers to Shao's camp to say that Chiang Chi had attacked and driven away the defenders of the granaries. So no more reliefs were sent that way. However, reinforcements were sent to Kuantu,

In due course the Yuan men came down upon Ts'ao's camp at

Kuantu and the defenders at once came out and fought them on three sides so that they were worsted. By the time reinforcements arrived Ts'ao's army, returning from the raid, had also come and Yuan's men were attacked in the rear. So they were quite surrounded. However, Chang Ho and Kao Lan managed to force their way out and got away.

When the remains of the defenders of the gram stores reached their master's camp they were mustered. Seeing the mutilated state of their one time leader, Shao asked how he had come to betray his trust and to suffer thus and the soldiers told their lord that their commander had been intoxicated at the time of the attack. So Shun-yu was forthwith executed.

Kuo T'u, fearing lest Chang Ho and Kao Lan would return and testify the whole truth, began to intrigue against them. First he went to his lord saying, "Those two, Chang and Kao, were certainly very glad when your armies were defeated."

"Why do you say this?" asked Yuan.

"O they have long cherished a desire to go over to Ts'ao Ts'ao, so when you sent them on the duty of destroying his camp they did not do their best and so brought about this disaster."

Shao accordingly sent to recall these two to be interrogated as to their faults. But Kuo T'u, their enemy, sent a messenger in advance to warn them, as though in friendly guise, of the adverse fate that awaited them. So when the orders reached them to return to answer for their faults they asked why they were recalled. When the messenger disclaimed all knowledge of the reasons, Kao Lan drew his sword and killed him. Chang Ho was stupefied at this demonstration but Lan said, "Our lord has allowed some one to malign us and say we have been bought by Ts'ao Ts'ao. What is the sense in our sitting still and awaiting destruction? Rather let us surrender to Ts'ao Ts'ao in reality and save our lives."

"I have been wanting to do this for some time," replied Chang Ho.

Wherefore both, with their companies, made their way to Ts'ao Ts'ao's camp to surrender.

When they arrived, Hsiahou Tun said to his master, "These two have come to surrender but I have doubts about them."

Ts'ao replied, "I will meet them generously and win them over even if they have treachery in their hearts."

The camp gates were opened to the two officers and they were invited to enter. They laid down their weapons, removed their armour and bowed to the ground before Ts'ao who said, "If Yuan Shao had listened to you he would not have suffered defeat. Now you two coming to surrender are like Wei Tzu going to Yin and Han Hsin going over to Han."

He gave both men the rank of general and the title of marquis, which pleased them much.

And so as Yuan Shao had formerly driven away his adviser, Hsu Yu, so now he had alienated two captains and had lost his stores at Wuch'ao and the army was depressed and downhearted.

When Hsu Yu advised Ts'ao to attack as promptly as he could the two newly surrendered men volunteered to lead the way. So these two were sent to make a first attack on the camp, and left in the night with three divisions. The fighting went on confusedly all night but stayed at dawn. Shao had lost heavily.

Then Hsun Yu suggested a plan saying, "Now is the moment to spread a report that a party of men will go to take Suantsao and attack Yehchun, and another to take Liyang and intercept the enemy's retreat. Yuan Shao, when he hears of this, will be alarmed and tell off his men to meet this new turn of affairs, and while he is making these new dispositions we can have him at great disadvantage."

The suggestion was adopted and care was taken that the report spread far around. It came to the ears of Yuan's soldiers and they repeated it in camp. Yuan Shao believed it and ordered Yuan Shang with five legions to rescue Yehchun, and Hsin Ming with another five to go to Liyang and they marched away at once. Ts'ao heard that these armies had started and at once despatched eight divisions to make a simultaneous attack on the nearly empty camp. Yuan Shao's men were too dispirited to fight and gave way on all sides.

Yuan Shao without waiting to don his armour went forth in simple dress with an ordinary cap upon his head and mounted his steed. His son Shang followed him. Four of the enemy captains with their men pressed in his rear and Shao hastened across the river, abandoning all his documents and papers, baggage, treasure and stores. Only eight hundred men followed him over the stream. Ts'ao Ts'ao's men followed hard but could not come up with him; however, they captured all his impedimenta and they slew many thousands of his men so that the watercourses ran blood and the drowned corpses could not be counted. It was a most complete victory for Ts'ao and he made over all the spoil to the army.

Among the papers of Yuan Shao was found a bundle of letters showing secret correspondence between him and many persons in the capital and army. Ts'ao's personal staff suggested that the names of those concerned should be abstracted and the persons arrested, but their lord said, "Shao was so strong that even I could not be sure of safety; how much less other men?"

So he ordered the papers to be burned and nothing more was said.

Now when Yuan Shao's men ran away Chu Shou, being a prisoner, could not get away and was captured. Taken before Ts'ao, who knew him, he cried aloud, "I will not surrender."

Said Ts'ao, "Yuan Shao was foolish and neglected your advice; why still cling to the path of delusion? Had I had you to help me I should have been sure of the Empire."

The prisoner was well treated in the camp but he stole a horse and tried to get away to Yuan Shao. This angered Ts'ao who put him to death, which he met with brave composure.

"I have slain a faithful and righteous man, then said Ts'ao sadly. And the victim was honourably buried at Kuantu. His tomb bore the inscription "This is the tomb of Chu the loyal and virtuous."

> Chu honest was and virtuous,
> The best in Yuan's train,
> From him the stars no secrets held,
> In tactics all was plain.
> For him no terrors had grim death,
> Too lofty was his spirit,
> His captor slew him, but his tomb
> Bears witness to his merit.

Ts'ao Ts'ao now gave orders to attack Ch'ichou.

> In feeling over confident, that's where one's weakness lay;
> The other bettered him by plans which never went agley.

The following chapter will tell who won the next campaign.

CHAPTER XXXI

TS'AO TS'AO OVERCOMES YUAN SHAO: LIU PEI SEEKS SHELTER WITH LIU PIAO

Ts'ao lost no time in taking advantage of Yuan Shao's flight, but smote hard at the retreating men. Yuan Shao without helmet or proper dress, and with few followers, crossed hastily to the north bank at Liyang. He was met by his General, Chiang I-chu, who took him in and comforted him and listened to the tale of misfortunes. Next Chiang called in the scattered remnants of the army, and when the soldiers heard that their old lord was alive they swarmed to him like ants so that he quickly became strong enough to attempt the march to Ch'ichou. Soon the army set out and at night halted at Huang Hills.

That evening, sitting in his tent, Shao seemed to hear a far off sound of lamentation. He crept out quietly to listen and found it was his own soldiers telling each other tales of woe. This one lamented an elder brother lost, that one grieved for his younger brother abandoned a third mourned a companion missing, a fourth, a relative cut off. And each beat his breast and wept. And all said, "Had he but listened to T'ien Feng we had not met this disaster."

And Yuan Shao, very remorseful, said, "I did not hearken unto T'ien Feng and now my men have been beaten and I was nearly lost. How can I return and look him in the face?"

Next day the march was resumed and he met Feng Chi with reinforcements, to whom he said, "I disregarded T'ien Feng's advice and have brought myself to defeat. Now shall I be greatly ashamed to look him in the face."

This tribute to T'ien Feng's prescience roused the jealousy of Feng Chi, who replied, "Yes; when he heard the news of your defeat, though he was a prisoner, he clapped his hands for joy and said, 'Indeed, just as I foretold!'"

"How dare he laugh at me, the blockhead? Assuredly he shall die," said Yuan.

Whereupon he wrote a letter and sent therewith a sword to slay the prisoner.

Meanwhile T'ien's gaoler came to him one day saying, "Above all men I felicitate you."

"What is the joyful occasion and why felicitate?" said T'ien Feng.

The gaoler replied, "General Yuan has been defeated and is on his way back; he will treat you with redoubled respect."

"Now am I a dead man," said T'ien.

"Why say you that, Sir, when all men give you Joy?"

"The General appears liberal but he is jealous and forgetful of honest advice. Had he been victorious he might have pardoned me; now that he has been defeated and put to shame I may not hope to live."

But the gaoler did not believe him. Before long came the letter and the sword with the fatal order. The gaoler was dismayed, but the victim said, "I knew all too well that I should have to die."

The gaoler wept. T'ien Feng said, "An able man born into this world who does not recognise and serve his true lord is ignorant. Today I die, but I am not deserving of pity."

Whereupon he committed suicide in the prison.

> Chu Shou but yesterday was killed,
> T'ien ends his life his fate fulfilled;
> Hopei's main beams break one by one,
> Mourn ye that House! its day is done.

Thus died T'ien Feng, pitied of all who heard of his fate. When Yuan Shao came home it was with troubled mind and distorted thoughts. He could not attend to the business of government and became so ill that his wife, who came of the Liu family, besought him to make his last dispositions.

Now three sons had been born to him, T'an the eldest, who was commander at Ch'ingchou; Hsi, who ruled over Yuchou; and Shang, borne to him by his second wife, who still lived. This youngest son was very handsome and noble looking, and his father's favourite. So he was kept at home. After the defeat at Kuantu the lad's mother was constantly urging that her son should be named as successor and Shao called together four of his counsellors to consider this matter. These four happened to be divided in their sympathies, Shen P'ei and Feng Chi being in favour of the youngest son, and Hsin P'ing and Kuo T'u supporters of the eldest.

When they met to consult, Yuan Shao said, "As there is nought but war and trouble outside our borders it is necessary that tranquillity within be early provided for and I wish to appoint my successor. My eldest son is hard and cruel, my second is mild and unfit. The third has the outward form of a hero, appreciates the wise and is courteous to his subordinates. I wish him to succeed, but I would that you tell me your opinions."

Kuo T'u said, "T'an is your first born and he is in a position of authority beyond your control. If you pass over the eldest in favour of the youngest you sow the seeds of turbulence. The prestige of the army has been somewhat lowered and enemies are on our border. Should you add to our weakness by making strife between father and son, elder and younger brothers? Rather consider how the enemy may be repulsed and turn to the question of the heirship later."

Then the natural hesitation of Yuan Shao asserted itself and he could not make up his mind. Soon came news that his sons, T'an and Hsi, and his nephew, Kao Kan, were coming with large armies to help him and he turned his attention to preparations for fighting Ts'ao Ts'ao.

When Ts'ao Ts'ao drew up his victorious army on the banks of the Yellow River a certain aged native brought an offering of food and sauce to bid him welcome. His venerable and hoary appearance led Ts'ao to treat him with the highest respect and he invited him to be seated and said to him, "Venerable Sir, what may be your age?"

"I am nearly a hundred," replied the ancient.

"I should be very sorry if my men had disturbed your village," said Ts'ao.

"In the days of the Emperor Huan a yellow star was seen over by way of Ch'u and Sung in the southwest. A certain man of Liaotung, Yin K'uei, who was learned in astrology, happened to be passing the night here and he told us that the star foretold the arrival in these parts, fifty years hence, of a true and honest man from Lian and P'ei. Lo! that is exactly fifty years ago. Now Yuan Pen-ch'u is very hard on the people and they hate him. You, Sir, having raised this army in the cause of humanity and righteousness, out of pity for the people and to punish crimes, and having destroyed the hordes of Yuan Shao at Kuantu, just fulfil the prophecy of Yin K'uei and the millions of the land may look now for tranquillity."

"How dare I presume that I am he?" said Ts'ao with a smile.

Wine was served and refreshments brought in and the old gentleman was sent away with presents of silk stuffs. And an order was issued to the army that if any one killed so much as a fowl or a dog belonging to the villagers he should be punished as for murder.

And the soldiers obeyed with fear and trembling while Ts'ao rejoiced in his heart.

It was told Ts'ao that the total army from the four prefectures under the Yuan family amounted to twenty-three legions and they were camped at Ts'ang-t'ing. Ts'ao then advanced nearer them and made a strong camp.

Soon after the two armies were arrayed over against each other. On one side Ts'ao rode to the front surrounded by his captains, and on the other appeared Yuan Shao supported by his three sons, his nephew and his officers.

Ts'ao spoke first, "Pen-ch'u, your schemes are poor, your strength is exhausted, why still refuse to think of surrender? Are you waiting till the sword shall be upon your neck? Then it will be too late."

Yuan Shao turned to those about him saying, "Who dares go out?"

His son Shang was anxious to exhibit his prowess in the presence of his father so he flourished his pair of swords and rode forth. Ts'ao pointed him out to his officers and asked if any one knew him and they replied that he was the youngest son. Before they had finished speaking from their own side rode out one Shih Huan, armed with a spear. The two champions fought a little while and suddenly Shang whipped up his horse, made a feint and fled. His opponent followed. Yuan Shang took his bow, fitted an arrow, turned in his saddle and shot at Shih Huan, wounding him in the left eye. He fell from the saddle and died on the spot.

Yuan Shao seeing his son thus get the better of his opponent, gave the signal for attack and the whole army thundered forward. The onslaught was heavy, but presently the gongs on both sides sounded the retire and the battle ceased.

When he had returned to camp Ts'ao took counsel to find a plan to overcome Yuan Shao. Then Ch'eng Yu proposed the plan of the Ten Ambushes and persuaded Ts'ao to retire upon the river, placing men in ambush as he went. Thus would Shao be inveigled into pursuit as far as the river, when Ts'ao's men would be forced to make a desperate stand or be driven into the water.

Ts'ao accepted this suggestion and told off five companies to lie in ambush on one side of the road of retreat and five on the other, while Hsu Chu commanded the advanced front.

Next day the ten companies started first and placed themselves right and left as ordered. In the night Ts'ao ordered the advanced front to feign an attack on the camp, which roused all the enemy in all their camps. This done Hsu Chu retreated and the Shao army came in pursuit. The roar of battle went on without cessation and at dawn Ts'ao's army rested on the river and could retreat no farther. Then Ts'ao shouted, "There is no road in front, so all must fight to the death."

The retreating army turned about and advanced vigorously. Hsu Chu simply flew to the front, smote and killed a half score captains and threw Yuan Shao's army into confusion. They tried to turn and march back, but Ts'ao Ts'ao was close behind. Then the drums of the enemy were heard and right and left there appeared a company, one pair of the ambushed parties. Yuan Shao collected about him his three sons and his nephew and they were enabled to cut their way out and flee. Ten *li* further on they fell into another ambush and here many men were lost so that their corpses lay over the country-side and the blood filled the water courses. Another ten *li* and they met the third pair of companies barring their road.

Here they lost heart and bolted for an old camp of their own that was near, and bade their men prepare a meal. But just as the food was ready to eat down came Chang Liao and Chang Ho and burst into the camp.

Yuan Shao mounted and fled as far as Ts'angt'ing, when he was tired and his steed spent. But there was no rest, for Ts'ao came in close pursuit. It seemed now a race for life. But presently Shao found his onward course again blocked and he groaned aloud.

"If we do not make most desperate efforts we are all captives," said he, and they plunged forward. His second son and his nephew were wounded by arrows and most of his men were dead or had disappeared. He gathered his sons into his arms and wept bitterly. Then he fell into a swoon. He was picked up, but his mouth was full of blood which ran forth in a bright scarlet stream. He sighed saying, "Many battles have I fought and little did I think to be driven to this. Heaven is afflicting me. You had better return each to his own and swear to fight this Ts'ao to the end."

Then he bade Hsin P'ing and Kuo T'u as quickly as possible follow Yuan T'an to his district and prepare to give battle to the enemy lest he should invade, Yuan Hsi was told to go to Yuchou and Kao Kan to Pingchou.

So each started to prepare men and horses for repulsing Ts'ao Ts'ao. Yuan Shao with his youngest son and the remnant of his officers went away to Ch'ichou and military operations were suspended for a time.

Meanwhile Ts'ao Ts'ao was distributing rewards to his army for the late victory and his men were scouting all about Ch'ichou. He soon learned that Yuan Shao was ill and that his youngest son and

Shen P'ei were in command of the city, while his brothers and cousin had returned each to his own. Ts'ao's advisers were in favour of a speedy attack. But he objected, saying "Ch'ichou is large and well supplied; Shen P'ei is an able strategist and it behoves me to be careful. I would rather wait till the autumn when the crops have been gathered in so that the people will not suffer."

While the attack was being talked over there came letters from Hsun Yu saying that Liu Pei was strengthening himself at Junan and, when he had heard that Ts'ao was going to attack Ch'ichou, he had said he would take the opportunity to march on the capital. Wherefore the Minister would do well to hasten homeward to defend it. This news disconcerted Ts'ao Ts'ao. He left Ts'ao Hung in command on the river bank, with orders to maintain the appearance of strength there, while he led the main part of his army to meet the threatened attack from Junan.

It has to be said now that Liu Pei, his brothers and supporters, having gone forth with the intention of attacking the capital, had reached a point near Jang Hills when Ts'ao came upon them. So Liu Pei camped by the hills and divided his army into three, sending his brothers with one division each to entrench themselves south-east and south-west respectively of the main body which he and Chao Yun commanded.

When Ts'ao came near, Yuan-te beat his drums and went out to where Ts'ao had already arrayed his men. Ts'ao called Liu Pei to a parley, and when the latter appeared under his great standard, Ts'ao pointed his whip at him and railed saying, "I treated you as a guest of the highest consideration; why then do you turn your back on righteousness and forget kindness?"

Yuan-te replied, "Under the name of Minister you are really a rebel. I am a direct descendant of the family and I have a secret decree from the throne to take such offenders as you."

As he said these words he produced and recited the decree which is known as the "Girdle Mandate."

Ts'ao grew very angry and ordered Hsu Ch'u to go out to battle, and, as Liu Pei's champion, out rode Chao Yun with spear ready to thrust. The two warriors exchanged thirty bouts without advantage to either. Then there arose an earth-rending shout and up came the two brothers, Yun-ch'ang from the south-east and Fei from the south-west. The three armies then began a great attack, which proved too much for Ts'ao's men, fatigued by a long march, and they were worsted and fled. Yuan-te having scored this victory returned to camp.

Next day he sent out Chao Yun again to challenge the enemy,

but it was not accepted and Ts'ao's army remained ten days without movement. Then Chang Fei offered a challenge which also was not accepted. And Yuan-te began to feel anxious.

Then unexpectedly came news that the enemy had stopped a train of supplies and at once Chang Fei went to the rescue. Worse still was the news that followed, that an army had got in behind to attack Junan.

Quite dismayed, Yuan-te said, "If this be true I have enemies in front and rear and have no place to go."

He then sent Yun-ch'ang to try to recover the city and thus both his brothers were absent from his side. One day later a horseman rode up to say Junan had fallen, its defender Liu P'i was a fugitive and Yun-ch'ang surrounded. To make matters worse the news came that Chang Fei, who had gone to rescue Kung Tu, was in like case.

Yuan-te tried to withdraw his men, fearing all the time an attack from Ts'ao Ts'ao. Suddenly the sentinels came in saying Hsu Ch'u was at the camp gate offering a challenge, but no one dared accept it or go out. They waited till dawn, and then Yuan-te bade the soldiers get a good meal and be ready to start. When ready the foot went out first, the horsemen next, leaving a few men in the camp to beat the watches and maintain an appearance of occupation.

After travelling a short distance they passed some mounds. Suddenly torches blazed out and on the summit stood one who shouted, "Do not let Liu Pei run away; I, the Minister, am here awaiting him."

Liu Pei dashed along the first clear road he saw.

Chao Yun said, "Fear not, my lord, only follow me," and setting his spear he galloped in front opening a lane as he went. Yuan-te gripped his double sword and followed close. As they were winning through, Hsu Ch'u came in pursuit and engaged Chao Yun, and two other companies bore down as well. Seeing the situation so desperate Yuan-te plunged into the wilds and fled. Gradually the sounds of battle became fainter and died away while he went deeper and deeper into the hills, a single horseman fleeing for his life. He kept on his way till daybreak, when a company suddenly appeared beside the road. Yuan-te saw these men with terror at first, but was presently relieved to find they were led by the friendly Liu P'i. They were a company of his defeated men escorting the family of their chief. With them also were Sun Ch'ien, Chien Yung and Mi Fang.

They told him that the attack on their city had been too strong to be resisted and so they had been compelled to abandon the defence, that the enemy had followed them and only Kuan's timely arrival had saved them.

"I do not know where my brother is," said Liu Pei.

"All will come right if you will push on," said Liu P'ei.

They pushed on, Before they had gone far the heating of drums was heard and suddenly appeared Chang Ho with a company of soldiers. He cried, "Liu Pei, quickly dismount and surrender."

Yuan-te was about to retire when he saw a red flag waving from a rampart on the hills and down came rushing another body of men under Kao Lan. Thus checked in front and his retreat cut off, Yuan-te looked up to Heaven and cried, "O Heaven, why am I brought to this state of misery? Nothing is left me now but death." And he drew his sword to slay himself.

But Liu P'i stayed his hand saying, "Let me try to fight a way out and save you."

As he spoke Kao Lan's force was on the point of engaging his. The two leaders met and in the third bout Liu P'i was cut down. Liu Pei at once rushed up to fight, but just then there was sudden confusion in the rear ranks of the opponents and a warrior dashed up and thrust at Kao Lan with his spear. Kao Lan fell from his steed. The newcomer was Chao Yun.

His arrival was most opportune. He urged forward his steed thrusting right and left, and the enemy's ranks broke and scattered. Then the first force under Chang Ho came into the fight and the leader and Chao Yun fought thirty or more bouts. However, this proved enough, for Ho turned his horse away recognising that he was worsted. Yun vigorously attacked, but was forced into a narrow space in the hills where he was hemmed in. While seeking for some outlet they saw Yun-ch'ang, Kuan P'ing and Chou Ts'ang, with three hundred men, coming along. Soon Chang Ho was driven off and then they came out of the narrow defile and occupied a strong position among the hills where they made a camp.

Yuan-te sent Yun-ch'ang for news of the missing brother. Chang Fei. He had been attacked by Hsiahou Yuan, but had vigorously resisted, beaten him off and followed him up. Then Yo Chin had come along and surrounded Chang Fei. In this pass he was found by Yun-ch'ang, who had heard of his plight from some of his scattered men met on the way. Now they drove off the enemy. The two brothers returned. Soon they heard of the approach of a large body of Ts'ao Ts'ao's army. Yuan-te then bade Sun Ch'ien guard his family and sent him on ahead, while he and the others kept off the enemy, sometimes giving battle and anon marching. Seeing that Yuan-te was retiring, Ts'ao Ts'ao let him go and left the pursuit.

When Yuan-te collected his men he found they numbered only a thousand, and this halting and broken force marched as fast as possible to the west. Coming to a river they asked the natives its name and were told it was the Han, and near it Yuan-te made a temporary camp. When the local people found out who was in the camp they presented flesh and wine.

A feast was given upon a sandy bank of the Han. After they had drunk awhile, Yuan-te addressed his faithful followers, saying, "All you, fair Sirs, have talents fitting you to be advisers to a monarch, but your destiny has led you to follow poor me. My fate is distressful and full of misery. Today I have not a spot to call my own and I am indeed leading you astray. Therefore I say you should abandon me and go to some illustrious lord where you may be able to become famous."

At these words they all covered their faces and wept. Yun-ch'ang said, "Brother, you are wrong to speak thus. When the great Founder of Han contended with Hs'ang Yu he was defeated many times, but he won at Chiuli Hill and that achievement was the foundation of a Dynasty that endured for four centuries. Victory and defeat are but ordinary events in a soldier's career and why should you give up?"

"Success and failure both have their seasons, said Sun Ch'ien, "and we are not to grieve Chingchou, which your illustrious relative, Liu Piao, commands, is a rich and prosperous country. Liu Piao is of your house, why not go to him?"

"Only that I fear he may not receive me," said Liu Pei.

"Then let me go and prepare the way. I will make Liu Ching-hsing come out to his borders to welcome you."

So with his lord's approval Sun Ch'ien set off immediately and hastened to Chingchou. When the genuflexions and ceremonies of greeting were over Liu Piao asked the reason of the visit.

Said Sun, "The Princely Liu is one of the heroes of the day although just at the moment he may lack soldiers and leaders. His mind is set upon restoring the Dynasty to its pristine glory, and at Junan the two commanders, Liu and Kung, though bound to him by no ties, were content to die for the sake of his ideals. You, illustrious Sir, like Liu Pei, are a scion of the Imperial stock. Now the Princely One has recently suffered defeat and thinks of seeking a home in the east with Sun Chung-mou (Sun Ch'uan). I have ventured to dissuade him, saying that he should not turn from a relative and go to a mere acquaintance; telling him that you, Sir, are well known as courteous to the wise and condescending to scholars, so that they flock to you as the waters flow to the east, and that certainly you would show kindness to one of the same ancestry. Wherefore he has sent me to explain matters and request your commands."

"He is my brother," said Piao, "and I have long desired to see him, but no opportunity has occurred. I should be very happy if he would come."

Ts'ai Mao, who was sitting by, here broke in with "No, no! Liu Pei first followed Lu Pu, then he served Ts'ao Ts'ao, and next he joined himself to Yuan Shao. And he stayed with none of these, so that you can see what manner of man he is. If he come here Ts'ao Ts'ao will assuredly come against us and fight. Better cut off this messenger's head and send it as an offering to Ts'ao Ts'ao, who would reward you well for the service."

Sun Ch'ien sat unmoved while this harangue was pronounced, saying at the end, "I am not afraid of death. Liu, the Princely One, is true and loyal to the State and so out of sympathy with Lu Pu, or Ts'ao Ts'ao, or Yuan Shao. It is true he followed these three, but there was no help for it. Now he knows your chief is a member of the family, so that both are of the same ancestry, and that is why he has come far to join him. How can you slander a good man like that?"

Liu Piao bade Ts'ao Mao be silent and said, "I have decided and you need say no more."

Whereat Ts'ai Mao sulkily left the audience chamber.

Then Sun Ch'ien was told to return with the news that Yuan-te would be welcome and Prefect Liu Piao went thirty *li* beyond his boundaries to meet his guest. When Yuan-te arrived he behaved to his host with the utmost politeness and was warmly welcomed in return. Then Liu Pei introduced his two sworn brothers and friends and they entered Chingchou, where Liu Pei finally was lodged in the Prefect's own residence.

As soon as Ts'ao Ts'ao knew whither his enemy had gone he wished to attack Liu Piao, but Ch'eng Yu advised against any attempt so long as Yuan Shao, the dangerous enemy, was left with power to inflict damage. He advised return to the capital to refresh the men so that they might be ready for a campaign in the mild spring weather.

Ts'ao accepted his advice and set out for the capital. In the first month of the eighth year of the period "Established Tranquillity," Ts'ao Ts'ao once again began to think of war, and sent to garrison Junan as a precaution against Liu Piao. Then, after arranging for the safety of the capital, he marched a large army to Kuantu, the camp of the year before.

As to Yuan Shao, who·had been suffering from blood-spitting

but was now in better health, he began to think of measures against Hsutu, but Shen P'ei dissuaded him saying, "You are not yet recovered from the fatigues of last year. It would be better to make your position impregnable and set to improving the army."

When the news of Ts'ao's approach arrived, Yuan said, "If we allow the foe to get close to the city before we march to the river we shall have missed our opportunity. I must go out to repel this army."

Here his son interposed, "Father, you are not sufficiently recovered for a campaign and should not go so far. Let me lead the army against this enemy."

Yuan consented, and he sent to Ch'ingchou and Yuchou and Pingchou to call upon his other two sons and his nephew to attack Ts'ao Ts'ao at the same time as his own army.

> Against Junan they beat the drum,
> And from Ch'ichou the armies come.

To whom the victory will be seen in the next chapter.

CHAPTER XXXII

CH'ICHOU TAKEN: YUAN SHANG STRIVES:
THE CHANG RIVER CUT:
HSU YU'S SCHEME

Yuan Shang was puffed up with pride after his victory over Shih Huan and, without deigning to wait the arrival of his brothers, he marched out to Liyang to meet the army of Ts'ao Ts'ao. Chang Liao came out to challenge him, and Yuan Shang, accepting the challenge rode out with spear set. But he only lasted to the third bout when he had to give way. Chang Liao smote with full force and Shang, quite broken, fled pell mell to Ch'ichou. His defeat was a heavy shock to his father, who had a severe fit of hemorrhage at the news and swooned.

The Lady Liu, his wife, got him to bed as quickly as possible, but he did not rally and she soon saw it was necessary to prepare for the end. So she sent for Shen P'ei and Feng Chi that the succession might be settled. They came and stood by the sick man's bed, but by this time he could no longer speak; he only made motions with his hands. When his wife put the formal question, whether Shang was to succeed, he nodded his head. Shen P'ei at the bedside wrote out the dying man's testament. Presently he uttered a loud moan, a fresh fit of bleeding followed and he passed away.

> Born of a line of nobles famous for generations,
> He himself in his youth was wayward always and headstrong,
> Vainly he called to his side captains skilled and courageous,
> Gathered beneath his banner countless legions of soldiers,
> For he was timid at heart, a lambkin dressed as a tiger,
> Merely a cowardly chicken, phoenix-feathered but spurless.
> Pitiful was the fate of his house; for when he departed
> Brother with brother strove and quarrels arose in the household.

Shen P'ei and some others set about the mourning ceremonies

for the dead man. His wife, the Lady Liu, put to death five of his favourite concubines, and such was the bitterness of her jealousy that, not content with this, she shaved off the hair and slashed the faces of their poor corpses lest their spirits should meet and rejoin her late husband in the land of shades beneath the Nine Springs. Her son followed up this piece of cruelty by slaying all the relatives of the unhappy concubines lest they should avenge their death.

Shen P'ei and Feng Chi declared Yuan Shang successor with the titles of Minister of War and General Governor of the four prefectures of Ch'i, Ch'ing, Yu and Ping and sent in a report of the death of the late governor.

At this time Yuan T'an, the eldest son, had already marched out his army to oppose Ts'ao Ts'ao, but hearing of his father's death he called in Kuo T'u and Hsin P'ing to consult as to his course of action.

"In your absence, my lord," said Kuo T'u, the two advisers of your younger brother will certainly set him up as lord, wherefore you must act quickly."

"Those two Shen and Feng, have already laid their plans," said Hsin P'ing. "If you go you will meet with some misfortune."

"Then what should I do?" asked T'an.

Kuo T'u replied, "Go and camp near the city and watch what is taking place while I enter and enquire."

Accordingly Kuo T'u entered the city and sought an interview with the young governor.

"Why did not my brother come?" asked Shang after the usual salutes.

Kuo T'u said, "He cannot come as he is in the camp unwell."

"By the command of my late father I take the lordship. Now I confer upon my brother the rank of General of Cavalry and I wish him to go at once to attack Ts'ao Ts'ao, who is pressing on the borders. I will follow as soon as my army is pressing on the borders. I will follow as soon as my army is in order."

"There is no one in our camp to give advice," said Kuo T'u. "I wish to have the services of Shen P'ei and Feng Chi."

"I also need the help of these two," said Shang, "And as I am always working at schemes I do not see how I can do without them."

"Then let one of these two go," replied T'u.

Shang could do no other than accede to this request so he bade the two men cast lots who should go. Feng Chi drew the lot and was appointed, receiving a seal of office. Then he accompanied

Kuo T'u to the camp. But when he arrived and found T'an in perfect health he grew suspicious and resigned. T'an angrily refused to accept his resignation and was disposed to put him to death, but Kuo T'u privately dissuaded him saying, "Ts'ao Ts'ao is on the borders and he must be kept here to allay your brother's suspicions. After we have beaten Ts'ao we can at once make an attempt on Ch'ichou."

Yuan T'an agreed and forthwith broke up his camp to march against the enemy. He reached Liyang and lost no time in offering battle. He chose for his champion Wang Chao and, when he rode out, Ts'ao Ts'ao sent Hsu Huang to meet him. These two had fought but a few bouts when Wang Chao was slain. At once Ts'ao's army pressed forward and T'an suffered a severe defeat. He drew off his army and retired into Liyang, whence he sent to his brother for reinforcements.

Shang and his adviser Shen P'ei discussed the matter and half a legion only was sent. Ts'ao hearing of the despatch of this meagre force sent two generals to waylay them and the half legion was destroyed. When T'an heard of the inadequate force sent and their destruction he was very wrath and roundly abused Feng Chi. Feng replied, "Let me write to my lord and pray him to come himself."

So Feng Chi wrote and the letter was sent. When it arrived Shang again consulted Shen P'ei who said, "Kuo T'u, your elder brother's adviser, is very guileful. Formerly he left without discussion because Ts'ao was on the border. If Ts'ao be defeated there will certainly be an attempt on you. The better plan is to withhold assistance and use Ts'ao's hand to destroy your rival."

Shang took his advice and no help was sent. When the messenger returned without success T'an was very angry and showed it by putting Feng Chi to death. He also began to talk of surrendering to Ts'ao. Soon spies brought news of this to Shang and again Shen P'ei was called in. Said he, "If he goes over to Ts'ao they will both attack Ch'ichou and we shall be in great danger." Finally Shen P'ei and Su Yu were left to take care of the defence of the city and Yuan Shang marched his army to the rescue of his brother.

"Who dares lead the van?" said Yuan Shang.

Two bothers named Lu volunteered and three legions were given them. They were the first to reach Liyang.

T'an was pleased that his brother had made up his mind to play a brotherly part and come to his aid, so he at once abandoned all thought of going over to the enemy. He being in the city, Yuan Shang camped outside, making that an angle of their strategic position. Before long Yuan Hsi, the second brother, and their cousin, Kao Kan, arrived with their legions and also camped outside the city.

Engagements took place daily and Shang suffered many defeats. On the other hand Ts'ao was victorious and elated. In the second month of the eighth year, Ts'ao made separate attacks on all four armies and won the day against each. Then they abandoned Liyang and Ts'ao pursued them to Ch'ichou, where T'an and Shang went into the city to defend it, while their brother and cousin camped about thirty *li* away making a show of great force. When Ts'ao had made many attacks without success Kuo Chia proffered the following plan.

He said, "There is dissension among the Yuans because the elder has been superseded in the succession. The brothers are about equally strong and each has his party. If we oppose them they unite to assist each other, but if we have patience they will be weakened by family strife. Wherefore send first a force to reduce Liu Piao in Chingchou and let the fraternal quarrels develop. When they have fully developed we can smite them and settle the matter."

Ts'ao approved of the plan. So leaving Chia Hsu as Prefect of Liyang and Ts'ao Hung as guard at Kuantu the army went way toward Chingchou.

The two brothers T'an and Shang congratulated each other on the withdrawal of their enemy, and their brother Hsi and cousin marched their armies back to their own districts.

Then the quarrels began. T'an said to his confidants, "I, the eldest, have been prevented from succeeding my father, while the youngest son, born of a second wife, received the main heritage. My heart is bitter."

Said Kuo T'u, "Camp your men outside, invite your brother and Shen P'ei to a banquet and assassinate them. The whole matter is easily settled."

And T'an agreed. It happened that a certain Wang Hsiu came just then from Ch'ingchou whom T'an took into his confidence. Wang opposed the murder plan saying, "Brothers are as one's limbs. How can you possibly succeed if at a moment of conflict with an enemy you cut off one of your hands? If you abandon your brother and sever relationship, whom will you take in all the world as a relation? That fellow Kuo is a dangerous mischief maker, who would sow dissension between brothers for a momentary advantage, and I beg you to shut your ears and not listen to his persuasions."

This was displeasing to T'an and he angrily dismissed Wang,

while he sent the treacherous invitation to his brother.

His brother and Shen P'ei talked over the matter. Shen P'ei said, "I recognise one of Kuo T'u's stratagems and if you go, my lord, you will be the victim of their plot. Rather strike at them at once."

Whereupon Shang rode out to battle. His brother T'an seeing him come with five legions, knew that his treachery had been discovered, so he also took the field, and when the forces were near enough T'an opened on Shang with a volley of abuse.

"You poisoned my father and usurped the succession; now you come out to slay your elder brother?"

The battle went against T'an. Shang himself took part in the fight, risking the arrows and the stones. He urged on his men and drove his brother off the field. He took refuge in P'ingyuan. Yuan Shang drew off his men to his own city.

Yuan T'an and Kuo T'u decided upon a new attack and this time they chose Ts'en Pi as leader. Yuan Shang went to meet him. When both sides had been arrayed and the banners were flying and the drums beating, Ts'en Pi rode out to challenge and railed at his opponent. At first Shang was going to answer the challenge himself but Lu K'uang actually went out. Lu and Ts'en met but had fought only a few bouts when the latter fell. T'an's men were once more defeated and ran away to P'ingyuan. Shen P'ei urged his master to press home the advantage and T'an was driven into the city, where he fortified himself and would not go out. So the city was besieged on three sides.

T'an asked his strategist what should be done next and he said, "The city is short of food, the enemy is flushed with victory and we cannot stand against them. My idea is to send some one to offer surrender to Ts'ao Ts'ao and thus get him to attack Ch'ichou. Your brother will be forced to return thither, which will leave you free to join in the attack. We may capture Shang. Should Ts'ao begin to get the better of your brother's army we will lend our force to help him against Ts'ao Ts'ao, and as Ts'ao's base of supply is distant we shall drive him off. And we can seize on Ch'ichou and begin our real career."

"Supposing this scheme be attempted, who is the man for a messenger?"

"I have one, Hsin P'i, Hsin P'ing's younger brother; he is magistrate here in this very place. He is a fluent speaker and good scholar and suited to your purpose."

So Hsin P'i was summoned and came readily enough. Letters were given him and an escort of three companies took him beyond the border. He travelled as quickly as possible.

At that time Ts'ao's camp was at Hsip'ing and he was attacking Liu Piao, who had sent Yuan-te out to offer the first resistance. No battle had yet taken place.

Soon after his arrival Hsin P'i was admitted to the Minister's presence, and after the ceremonies of greeting Ts'ao asked the object of the visit. Hsin P'i explained that Yuan T'an wanted assistance and presented his despatches. Ts'ao read them and told the messenger to wait in his camp while he called his officers to a council.

The council met. Ch'eng Yu said, "Yuan T'an has been forced into making this offer because of the pressure of his brothers attack. Put no trust in him."

Lu Ch'ien and Man Ch'ung said, "You have led your armies here for a special purpose; how can you abandon that and go to assist Yuan T'an?"

"Gentlemen, not one of you is giving good advice," interposed Hsun Yu. "This is how I regard it. Since there is universal trouble, in the midst of which Liu Piao remains quietly content with his position between Chiang and Han, it is evident that he has no ambition to enlarge his borders. The Yuans hold four *Chou* and have many legions of soldiers. Harmony between the two brothers means success for the family and none can foresee what will happen in the Empire. Now take advantage of this fraternal conflict and let them fight till they are weakened and have to yield to our Minister. Then Yuan Shang can be removed, and when the times are suitable, Yuan T'an can be destroyed in his turn. Thus peace will ensue. This present combination of circumstances is to be taken advantage of to full measure."

Ts'ao realised the truth of this and treated the messenger well. At a banquet he said, "But is this surrender of Yuan T'an real or false? Do you really think that Shang's army is sure to overcome him?"

Hsin P'i replied, "Illustrious one, do not enquire into the degree of sincerity; rather regard the situation. The Yuans have been suffering military losses for years and are powerless without, while their strategists are put to death within. The brothers seize every chance to speak evil of each other and their country is divided. Add to this famine, supplemented by calamities and general exhaustion, and everybody, wise as well as simple, can see that the catastrophe is near, the time ordained of Heaven for the destruction of the Yuans is at hand. Now you have a force attacking Yeh, and if Yuan Shang will not return to give aid the place of refuge is lost. If he help, then T'an will follow up and smite him, making use of your power to destroy the remnant of his brother's army, just as the autumn gale sweeps away the fallen leaves. If he do not, then he will attack Chingchou. Now Chingchou is rich, the government peaceful, the people submissive and it cannot be shaken. Moreover, there is no greater threat to it than Hopei. If that be reduced then the task is complete. I pray you, Sir, think of it."

"I am sorry that I did not meet you earlier," said Ts'ao, much gratified with this speech.

Forthwith orders were given to return and attack Ch'ichou. Yuan-te, fearing this retirement was only a ruse, allowed it to proceed without interference and himself returned to Chingchou.

When Yuan Shang heard that Ts'ao had crossed the river he hastily led his army back to Yeh, ordering the two Lus to guard the rear. His brother T'an started from P'ingyuan with a force in pursuit. He had not proceeded far when he heard a bomb and two bodies of men came out in front of him and checked his progress. Their leaders were Lu K'uang and Lu Hsiang. T'an reined in and addressed them, saying, "While my father lived I never treated you badly; why do you support my brother and try to injure me?"

The two men had no reply to make, but they dismounted and bowed before him yielding submission.

T'an said, "Do not surrender to me but to the Minister," and he led them back to camp, where he waited the arrival of Ts'ao and then presented the pair. Ts'ao received them well. He promised his daughter to T'an to wife and he appointed the two brothers as advisers.

When T'an asked Ts'ao to attack Ch'ichou the reply was "Supplies are short and difficult to transport. I must turn the waters of the Chishui into the Paiho from Chiho whereby to convey my grain and afterwards I can advance."

Ordering T'an to remain in P'ingyuan, Ts'ao retired into camp at Liyang. The two brothers Lu, who were renegades from Yuan Shang, were now raised to noble rank and followed the army as supernumeraries.

Kuo T'u noted this advancement and said to T'an, "He has promised you a daughter to wife. I fear that bodes no good. Now he has given titles of nobility to the two Lus and taken them with him. This is a trap for the northern people but he intends evil toward us. You, my lord, should have two generals' seals engraved and send them secretly to the brothers so that you may have friends at court ready for the day when Ts'ao shall have broken your brother's power and we can begin to work against him."

The seals were engraved and sent. As soon as the brothers

received them they informed Ts'ao Ts'ao, who smiled saying, "He wants your support so he sends you seals as officers. I will consider it as soon as Yuan Shang has been dealt with. In the meantime you may accept the seals till I shall decide what to do."

Thenceforward T'an was doomed. Shen P'ei and his master also discussed the situation.

"Ts'ao is getting grain into Paikou, which means an attack on Ch'ichou; what is to be done?" asked Shang.

Shen P'ei replied, "Send letters to Yin Kai, Chief of Wuan, bidding him camp at Maoch'eng to secure the road to Shangtang and direct Chu Ku to maintain Hantan as a distant auxiliary. Then you may advance on P'ingyuan and attack Ts'ao Ts'ao."

The plan seemed good. Yuan Shang left Shen P'ei and Ch'en Lin in charge of Ch'ichou, appointed two captains Ma Yen and Chang K'ai as van leaders, and set out hastily for P'ingyuan.

When T'an heard of the approach of his brother's army he sent urgent messages to Ts'ao, who said to himself, "I am going to get Ch'ichou this time."

Just at this time it happened that Hsu Yu came down from the capital. When he heard that Yuan Shang was attacking his brother T'an he sought Ts'ao and said, "You, Sir Minister, sit here on guard; are you waiting till Heaven's thunder shall strike the two Yuans?"

"I have thought it all out," said Ts'ao.

Then he ordered Ts'ao Hung to go and fight against Yeh, while he led another army against Yin Kai. Kai could make no adequate defence and was killed by Hsu Ch'u. His men ran away and presently joined Ts'ao's army. Next he led the army to Hantan and Chu Ku came out to fight him. Chang Liao advanced to fight with Chu and after the third encounter the latter was defeated and fled. Liao went after him and when their two horses were not far apart, Liao took his bow and shot. The fleeing soldier fell as the bowstring twanged. Ts'ao sent Ma Yen to complete the rout and Chu Ku's force was broken up.

Now Ts'ao led his armies to an attack on Ch'ichou. Ts'ao Hung went close to the city and a regular siege began. The army encompassed the city and began by throwing up great mounds. They also tunnelled subterranean ways.

Within the city Shen P'ei turned his whole care to the defence and issued the severest commands. The captain of the east gate, one Feng Li, got intoxicated and failed to keep his watch for which he was severely punished. He resented this, sneaked out of the city, went over to the besiegers and told them how the place could be attacked.

"The earth within the T'umen is solid enough to be tunnelled and entrance can be effected there," said the traitor.

So Feng Li was sent with three hundred men to carry out his plan under cover of darkness.

After Feng Li had deserted to the enemy Shen P'ei went every night to the wall to inspect the men on duty. The night of the sapping he went there as usual and saw that there were no lights outside the city and all was perfectly quiet. So he said to himself, "Feng is certain to try to come into the city by an underground road." Whereupon he ordered his men to bring up stones and pile them on the cover of the tunnel opening. The opening was stopped up and the attacking party perished in the tunnel they had excavated. Ts'ao having failed in this attempt abandoned the scheme of underground attack. He drew off the army to a place above the Hengshui to await till Yuan Shang should return to relieve the city.

Yuan Shang heard of the defeat of Yin Kai and Chu Ku, and the siege of his own city, and bethought himself of relieving it. One of his captains, Ma Yen, said, "The high road will surely be ambushed; we must find some other way. We can take a bye-road from the Western Hills and get through at Fushuik'ou, whence we can fall upon Ts'ao's camp."

The plan was acceptable and Shang started off with the main body, Ma Yen and Chang K'ai being rear guard.

Ts'ao's spies soon found out this move and when they reported it he said, "If he comes by the high road I shall have to keep out of the way; if by the Western Hills bye-road I can settle him in one battle. And I think he will show a blaze as a signal to the besieged that they may make a sortie. I shall prepare to attack both." So he made his preparations.

Now Yuan Shang went out by the Fushui Pass east toward Yangp'ing and near this he camped. Thence to his own city was seventeen *li*. The Fushui stream ran beside the camp. He ordered his men to collect firewood and grass ready for the blaze he intended to make at night as his signal. He also sent Li Fu, a civil officer, disguised as an officer of Ts'ao Ts'ao's army, to inform Shen P'ei of his intentions.

Fu reached the city wall safely and called out to the guards to open. Shen P'ei recognised his voice and let him in. Thus Shen P'ei knew of the arrangements for his relief and it was agreed that a blaze should be raised within the city so that the sortie could be simultaneous with Shang's attack. Orders were given to collect inflammables.

Then said Fu, "As your food supply is short it would be well for the old men, the feeble soldiers and the women to surrender. This will come upon them as a surprise and we will send the soldiers out behind them."

Shen P'ei promised to do all this and next day they hoisted on the wall a white flag with the words "The populace of Ch'ichou surrender" on it.

"Ho ho! This means no food," said Ts'ao. "They are sending away the non-combatants to escape feeding them. And the soldiers will follow behind them."

So on two sides he laid an ambush of three companies while he went near the wall in full state. Presently the gates were opened and out came the people supporting their aged folk and leading their little ones by the hand. Each carried a white flag. As soon as the people had passed the gate the soldiers followed with a rush.

Then Ts'ao Ts'ao showed a red flag and the ambushed soldiers fell upon the sortie. The men tried to return and Ts'ao's men made a direct attack. The chase continued to the drawbridge, but there they met with a tremendous shower of arrows and crossbow bolts which checked the advance. Ts'ao's helmet was struck and the crest carried away.

So the men retired. As soon as Ts'ao had changed his dress and mounted a fresh horse he set out at the head of the army to attack Yuan Shang's camp.

Yuan Shang led the defence. The attack came simultaneously from many directions, the defenders were quite disorganised and presently defeated. Shang led his men back by the hills and made a camp under their shelter. Thence he sent messengers to urge Ma Yen and Chang K'ai to bring up the supports. He did not know that Ts'ao had sent the two Lus to persuade these two into surrender and that they had already passed under Ts'ao's banner, and he had made them marquises.

Just before going to attack the Western Hills he sent the two Lus with Ma Yen and Chang K'ai to seize the source of Yuan Shang's supplies. Shang had realised he could not hold the hills so he went by night to Ik'ou. Before he could get camped he saw flaring lights springing up all around him and soon an attack began. He was taken aback and had to oppose the enemy with his men half armed, his steeds unsaddled. His army suffered and he had to retreat another fifty *li*. By that time his force was too enfeebled to show any resistance and as no other course was possible he sent to ask that he might surrender. Ts'ao feigned to consent, but that night he sent a force to raid Shang's camp. Then it became flight, abandoning everything, seals, emblems of office and even personal clothing. He made for the hills.

Then came an attack on Ch'ichou and to help out this Hsu Yu suggested drowning the city by turning the course of the River Chang. Ts'ao adopted the suggestion and at once sent a small number of men to dig a channel to lead the water to the city. All told, it was forty *li*.

Shen P'ei saw the diggers from the city wall and noticed that they made only a shallow channel. He chuckled, saying to himself, "What is the use of such a channel to drown out the city from a deep river?"

So he made no preparations to keep out the water.

But as soon as night came on Ts'ao increased his army of diggers tenfold and by daylight the channel was deepened to twenty feet and the water was flowing in a great stream into the city where it already stood some feet deep. So this misfortune was added to the lack of food.

Hsin P'i now displayed the captured seal and garments of Yuan Shang hung out on spears, to the great shame of their late owner, and called upon the people of the city to surrender. This angered Shen P'ei, who avenged the insult by putting to death on the city wall the whole of the Hsin family who were within the city. There were nearly a hundred of them and their severed heads were cast down from the walls. Hsin P'i wept exceedingly.

Shen P'ei's nephew Shen Yung, one of the gate wardens, was a dear friend of Hsin P'i and the murder of P'i's family greatly distressed him. He wrote a secret letter offering to betray the city and tied it to an arrow, which he shot out among the besiegers. The soldiers found it, gave it to Hsin P'i and he took it to his chief.

Ts'ao issued an order that the family of the Yuans should be spared when the city should be taken and that no one who surrendered should be put to death. The next day the soldiers entered by the west gate, opened for them by Shen's nephew. Hsin P'i was the first to prance in on horseback and the men followed.

When Shen, who was on the southeast of the city, saw the enemy within the gates he placed himself at the head of some horsemen and dashed toward them. He was met and captured by Hsu Huang who bound him and led him outside the city. On the road they met Hsin P'i, who ground his teeth with rage at the murderer of his relatives and then struck the prisoner over the head with his whip and abused him as a murderer. Shen retorted by calling him traitor and saying how sorry he was not to have slain him before.

When the captive was taken into Ts'ao's presence Ts'ao said, "Do you know who opened the gate to let me in?"

"No; I know not."

"It was your nephew Shen Yung who gave up the gate," said Ts'ao.

"He was always unprincipled; and it has come to this!" said Shen.

"The other day when I approached the city why did you shoot so hard at me?"

"I am sorry we shot too little."

"As a faithful adherent of the Yuans you could do no otherwise. Now will you come over to me?"

"Never; I will never surrender."

Hsin P'i threw himself on the ground with lamentations, saying, "Eighty of my people murdered by this ruffian; I pray you slay him, O Minister!"

"Alive, I have served the Yuans," said Shen, "dead, I will be their ghost. I am no flattering time-server as you are. Kill me!"

Ts'ao gave the order; they led him away to put him to death. On the execution ground he said to the executioners, "My lord is in the north, I pray you not to make me face the south." So he knelt facing the north and extended his neck for the fatal stroke.

> Who of all the official throng
> In Hopei was true like Shen?
> Sad his fate! he served a fool,
> But faithful, as the ancient men.
> Straight and true was every word,
> Never from the road he swerved.
> Faithful unto death, he died
> Gazing toward the lord he'd served.

Thus died Shen P'ei and from respect for his character Ts'ao ordered that he be buried honourably on the north of the city.

Ts'ao Ts'ao then entered the city. As he was starting he saw the executioners hurrying forward a prisoner who proved to be Ch'en Lin.

"You wrote that manifesto for Yuan Shao. If you had only directed your diatribe against me, it would not have mattered. But why did you shame my forefathers?" said Ts'ao.

"When the arrow is on the string, it must fly," replied Lin.

Those about Ts'ao urged him to put Ch'en Lin to death, but he was spared on account of his genius and given a small civil post.

Now Ts'ao's eldest son was named P'ei, otherwise Tzu-heng. At the taking of the city he was eighteen years of age. When he was born a dark purplish halo hung over the house for a whole day. One who understood the meaning of such manifestations had secretly told Ts'ao that the halo belonged to the Imperial class and portended honours which could not be put into words.

At eight the lad could compose very skilfully and he was well read in ancient history. Now he was an adept at all military arts and very fond of fencing. He had gone with his father on the expedition to Ch'ichou. He led his escort in the direction of the Yuan family dwelling, and when he reached it he strode in sword in hand. When some one would have stayed him, saying that by order of the Minister no one was to enter the house, he bade them begone. The guards fell back and he made his way into the private rooms, where he saw two women weeping in each other's arms. He went forward to slay them.

> Four generations of honours, gone like a dream,
> Fate follows on ever surely, though slow she seem.

The fate of the two women will be told in the next chapter.

CHAPTER XXXIII.

TS'AO P'EI FINDS A WIFE:
A PLAN FOR SETTLING LIAOTUNG

As was said, Ts'ao P'ei, having made his way into the Yuan Palace, saw two women there whom he was about to kill. Suddenly a red light shone in his eyes, and he paused. Lowering his sword he said, "Who are you?"

"Thy handmaid is the widow of the late Yuan Shao, *nee* Liu," said the elder of the two, "and this is the wife of Hsi, his second son. She was of the Chen family. When Hsi was sent to command in Yu her family objected to her going so far from home and she stayed behind."

Ts'ao P'ei drew her toward him and looked at her closely. Her hair hung disordered, her face was dusty and tear-stained, but when, with the sleeve of his inner garment, he had wiped away these disfigurements he saw a woman of exquisite loveliness, with a complexion clear as jade touched with the tender bloom of a flower petal, a woman indeed beautiful enough to ruin a kingdom.

"I am the son of the Minister Ts'ao," said he turning to the elder woman. "I will guarantee your safety so you need fear nothing."

He then put by his sword and sat down at the upper end of the room.

As the great Minister Ts'ao was entering the gate of the conquered city Hsu Yu rode up very quickly, passed him and pointed with his whip at the gate saying, "A-man, you would not have been here but for my plans."

Ts'ao laughed, but his captains were very annoyed. When he reached the Yuan residence he stopped at the gate, and asked if any one had gone in. The guard at the gate said, "Your son is within." Ts'ao called him out and chid him, but the wife of the late Prefect interposed, saying, "But for your son we had not been saved. I desire to present to you a lady, of the Chen family, as a handmaid to your son."

Ts'ao bade them bring out the girl and she bowed before him. After looking at her intently he said, "Just the wife for him!" and he told Ts'ao P'ei to take her to wife.

After the conquest of Ch'ichou had been made quite sure, Ts'ao made a ceremonial visit to the Yuan family cemetery, where he sacrificed at the tomb of his late rival, bowed his head and lamented bitterly.

Turning to his captains he said, "Not long ago when Pen ch'u and I worked together in military matters he asked me, saying, 'If this disturbance continue what districts should be held?' and I replied asking him what he thought. He said, 'To the south I would hold the river, on the north, guard against Yen and Tai and the hordes from the Shamo. Thence south-ward I would try for the Empire and do you not think I might succeed?' I replied saying, I depended upon the wisdom and force of the world directed by *Tao*; then every thing would be possible. These words seem as if spoken only yesterday, and now he is gone. Thinking over it I cannot refrain from tears."

His officers were deeply affected. Ts'ao treated the widow generously, giving her gold and silks and food to her content.

He also issued a further order that the taxes in Hopei would be remitted in consideration of the sufferings of the people during the warlike operations. He sent up a memorial and formally became Governor of Ch'ichou.

One day Hsu Ch'u, riding in at the east gate, met Hsu Yu, who called out to him "Would you fellows be riding through here if it had not been for me?"

Hsu Ch'u replied, "We fellows, those who survive and those who perished, risked our lives in bloody battle to get this city, so do not brag of your deeds."

"You are a lot of blockheads, not worth talking about," said Yu.

Ch'u in his anger drew his sword and ran him through. Then he took his head and went to tell Ts'ao the reason.

Said Ts'ao, "He and I were old friends and we could joke together. Why did you kill him?"

He blamed Hsu Ch'u very severely and gave orders that the corpse should be buried honourably.

He enquired for any wise and reputable men who were known to be living in the district and was told of a certain cavalry officer named Ts'ui Yen, of Tungwu City, who had on many occasions given valuable advice to Yuan Shao. As the advice was not followed Yen had pleaded indisposition and remained at home.

Ts'ao sent for this man, gave him an office and said to him, "According to the former registers there are three hundred thousand households in the district so that one may well call it a major district."

Yen replied, "The Empire is rent and the country is torn; the brothers Yuan are at war and the people have been stripped naked. Yet, Sir, you do not hasten to enquire after local conditions and how to rescue the people from misery, but first compute the possibilities of taxation. Can you expect to gain the support of our people by such means?"

Ts'ao accepted the rebuke, changed his policy, thanked him and treated him all the better for it.

As soon as Ch'ichou was settled, Ts'ao sent to find out the movements of Yuan T'an. He heard he was ravaging Kanling and the places near it in the south and west. Moreover, the scouts brought the news that Yuan Shang had fled to the hills. An expedition had been sent against him but Shang would not face a battle. He had gone away to Yuchou to his brother Hsi.

T'an, having surrendered with all his army, yet prepared for another attempt on Ch'ichou. Whereupon Ts'ao summoned him. T'an refused to come and Ts'ao sent letters breaking off the marriage with his daughter. Soon after Ts'ao led an expedition against T'an and marched to P'ingyuan, whereupon T'an sent to Liu Piao to beg assistance. Piao sent for Liu Pei to consult about this and he said, "Ts'ao is very strong now that he has overcome Ch'ichou and the Yuans will be unable to hold out for long. Nothing is to be gained by helping this man and it may give Ts'ao the loophole he is always looking for to attack this place. My advice is to keep the army in condition and devote all our energies to defence."

"Agreed; but what shall we say?" said Piao.

"Write to both the brothers as peacemaker in gracious terms."

Accordingly Liu Piao wrote thus to Yuan T'an:—"When the superior man would escape danger he does not go to an enemy State. I heard recently that you had crooked the knee to Ts'ao, which was ignoring the enmity between him and your father, rejecting the duties of brotherhood and leaving behind you the shame of an alliance with the enemy. If your brother, the successor to Ch'ichou, has acted unfraternally, your duty was to bend your inclination to follow him and wait till the state of affairs had settled. Would it not have been very noble to bring about the redress of wrongs?"

And to Yuan Shang he wrote:— "Your brother, the ruler of Ch'ingchou, is of an impulsive temperament and confuses right with wrong. You ought first to have destroyed Ts'ao in order to put an end to the hatred which your father bore him and, when the situation had become settled, to have endeavoured to redress the wrongs. Would not that have been well? If you persist in following this mistaken course, remember the hound and the hare, both so wearied that the peasant got the hare."

From this letter Yuan T'an saw that Liu Piao had no intention of helping him, and feeling he alone could not withstand Ts'ao, he abandoned P'ingyuan and fled to Nanp'i, whither Ts'ao pursued him. The weather was very cold and the river was frozen, so that his grain boats could not move. Wherefore Ts'ao ordered the inhabitants to break the ice and tow the boats. When the peasants heard the order they ran away. Ts'ao angrily wished to arrest and behead them. When they heard this they went to his camp in a body and offered their heads to the sword.

"If I do not kill you, my order will not be obeyed," said Ts'ao, "Yet supposing I cut off your heads—but I cannot bear to do that. Quickly flee to the hills and hide so that my soldiers do not capture you."

The peasants left weeping.

Then Yuan T'an led out his army against Ts'ao. When both sides were arrayed Ts'ao rode to the front, pointed with his whip at his opponent and railed at him saying, "I treated you well; why then have you turned against me?"

T'an replied, "You have invaded my land, captured my cities and broken off my marriage; yet you accuse me of turning against you."

Ts'ao ordered Hsu Huang to go out and give battle. T'an bade P'eng An accept the challenge. After a few bouts P'eng An was slain and T'an, having lost, fled and went into Nanp'i, where he was besieged. T'an, panic stricken, sent Hsin P'ing to see Ts'ao and arrange surrender.

"He is nothing but a fickle minded child," said Ts'ao. "He is never of the same mind two days running and I cannot depend upon what he says. Now your brother is in my employ and has a post of importance, you had better remain here also."

"Sir Minister, you are in error," said Hsin P'ing. "It is said that the lord's honour is the servant's glory, the lord's sadness is the servant's shame. How can I turn my back on the family I have so long served?"

Ts'ao felt he could not be persuaded and sent him back. P'ing returned and told T'an the surrender could not be arranged and T'an turned on him angrily calling him a traitor. At this unmerited reproach such a huge wave of anger welled up in the man's breast that he was overcome and fell in a swoon. They carried him out, but the shock had been too severe and soon after he died. T'an regretted his conduct when it was too late.

Then Kuo T'u said, "Tomorrow when we go out to battle we will drive the people out in front as a screen for the soldiers and we must fight a winning battle."

That night they assembled all the common people of the place and forced into their hands swords and spears. At daylight they opened the four gates and a huge party with much shouting came out at each, peasantry carrying arms in front, and soldiers behind them. They pushed on toward Ts'ao's camps and a melee began which lasted till near midday. But this was quite indecisive, although heaps of dead lay everywhere.

Seeing that success was at best only partial Ts'ao rode out to the hills near and thence had the drums beaten for a new attack under his own eye. Officers and men, seeing that he could observe them in person, exerted themselves to the utmost and T'an's army was severely defeated. Of the peasantry driven into the battle field multitudes were slain.

Ts'ao Hung, who displayed very great valour, burst into the press of battle and met Yuan T'an face to face. The two slashed and hammered at each other and T'an was killed.

Kuo T'u saw that his side was wholly disorganised and tried to withdraw into the shelter of the city. Yo Chin saw this and opened a tremendous discharge of arrows so that the moat was soon filled with dead.

The city fell to Ts'ao; he entered and set about restoring peace and order. Then suddenly appeared a new army under one of Yuan Hsi's captains. Ts'ao led out his men to meet them, but the two commanders laid down their arms and yielded. They were rewarded with the rank of marquis.

Then Chang Yen, the leader of the Black Hills Brigands, came with ten legions and gave in his submission. He was made a General, *Chiang-chun*.

By an order of Ts'ao Ts'ao's the head of Yuan T'an was exposed and death was threatened to any one who should lament for him.

Nevertheless a man dressed in mourning attire was arrested for weeping below the exposed head at the north gate. Taken into Ts'ao's presence he said he was Wang Hsiu and had been an officer in Ch'ingchou. He had been expelled because he had remonstrated with T'an, but when the news of T'an's death came he had come to weep for him.

"Did you know of my command?"

"I knew it."

"Yet you were not afraid?"

"When one has received favours from a man in life it would be wrong not to mourn at his death. How can one stand in the world if one forgets duty through fear? If I could bury his body I would not mind death."

Ts'ao said, "And there were many such as this in this district. What a pity that the Yuan family could not make the best of them! But if they had done so I should never have dared to turn my eyes toward this place."

The intrepid mourner was not put to death. The remains of Yuan T'an were properly interred and Wang Hsiu was well treated and even given an appointment.

In his new position he was asked for advice about the best way to proceed against Yuan Shang, who had fled to his brother, but he held his peace, thereby winning from Ts'ao renewed admiration for his constancy. "He is indeed loyal!" said Ts'ao.

Then he questioned Kuo Chia, who named certain officers who should be sent to bring about the surrender of the Yuans. Then five captains, to attack Yuchou along three routes, and other armies, were sent against Pingchou.

The two brothers Shang and Hsi heard of Ts'ao's advance with dismay for they had no hope of successful resistance. Therefore they abandoned the city and hastily marched into Liaohsi to the Governor Wuhuan Ch'u. But the governor was not disposed to incur the enmity of the powerful Ts'ao Ts'ao so he called his subordinates together to swear them to support him and said, "I understand that Ts'ao Ts'ao is the most powerful man of the day and I am going to support him and those who do not go with me I shall put to death."

Each in turn smeared his lips with the blood of sacrifice and took the oath till it came to the turn of Han Heng. Instead he dashed his sword to the ground crying, "I have received great benefits from the Yuans. Now my lord has been vanquished; my knowledge was powerless to save him, my bravery insufficient to cause me to die for him; I have failed in my duty. But I refuse to commit the crowning act of treachery and ally myself with Ts'ao."

This speech made the others turn pale. The chief said "For a great undertaking there must be lofty principles. However, success does not necessarily depend upon universal support and since Han Heng is actuated by such sentiments then let him follow his conscience." So he turned Han Heng out of the assembly.

Wuhuan Ch'u then went out of the city to meet and welcome Ts'ao Ts'ao's army and rendered his submission. He was well received and the title given him of Guardian of the North.

Then the scouts came to say that the three captains had marched to Pingchou but that Kao Kan had occupied Hukuan Pass and could not be dislodged. So Ts'ao marched thither himself. The defender still maintaining his position Ts'ao asked for plans. Hsun Yu proposed that a band should go over pretending to be deserters. Ts'ao assented and then called the two brothers Lu, to whom he gave whispered orders. They left with their companies.

Soon they came near the pass and called out, saying, "We are old officers in Yuan's armies forced into surrender to Ts'ao. We find him so false and he treats us so meanly that we want to return to help our old master. Wherefore quickly open your gates to us."

Kao Kan was suspicious, but he let the two officers come up to the pass, and when they had stripped off their armour and left their horses they were permitted to enter. And they said to Kao Kan, "Ts'ao's men are new to the country and not settled; you ought to fall upon their camp this very evening. If you approve we will lead the attack."

Kao Kan decided to trust them and prepared to attack, giving the two brothers the leadership. But as they drew near Ts'ao's camp a great noise arose behind them and they found themselves in an ambush attacked on all sides. Realising too late that he had been the victim of a ruse, Kao retreated to the pass, but found it occupied by the enemy. Kao Kan then made the best of his way to the barbarian chieftain Shanyu. Ts'ao gave orders to hold the passes and sent companies in pursuit.

When Kao Kan reached the boundary of Shanyu's territory he met *Tso-hsien*, Prince of the northern tribesmen. Kao Kan dismounted and made a low obeisance saying, "Ts'ao is conquering and absorbing all the borders and your turn, O Prince, will come quickly. I pray you help me and let us smite together for the safety of the northern regions."

The Prince replied, "I have no quarrel with Ts'ao, why then should he invade my land? Do you desire to embroil me with him?"

He would have nothing to do with Kao Kan and sent him away.

At his wits' end Kan decided to try to join Liu Piao and got so far on his journey as Shanglu when he was taken prisoner and put to death by Wang Yen. His head was sent to Ts'ao Ts'ao and Wang was created a marquis for this service.

Thus Pingchou was conquered. Then Ts'ao Ts'ao began to discuss the overthrow of Wuhuan on the west. Ts'ao Hung, speaking in the name of his brother officials, said, "The two brothers Yuan are nearly done for and too weak to be feared. They have fled far into the Sea of Sand and if we pursue them thither it may bring down Liu Piao and Liu Pei upon the capital. Should we be unable to rescue it the misfortune would be immense. Wherefore we beg you to return to Hsutu."

But Kuo Chia was of different advice. "You are wrong," said he. "Though the prestige of our lord fills the Empire, yet the men of the desert, relying upon their inaccessibility, will not be prepared against us. Wherefore I say attack, and we shall conquer them. Beside Yuan Shao was kind to the nomads and the two brothers have been more so. They must be destroyed. As for Liu Piao he is a mere gossip, who need not cause the least anxiety. And Liu Pei is unfit for any heavy responsibility and will take no trouble over a light one. You may leave the State with perfect safety and make as long an expedition as you choose. Nothing will happen."

"You speak well, O Feng-hsiao," said Ts'ao. He led his legions, heavy and light, to the edge of the desert, with many waggons.

The expedition marched into the desert. The rolling ocean of yellow sand spread its waves before them and they saw far and near the eddying sand pillars, and felt the fierce winds that drove them forward. The road became precipitous and progress difficult. Ts'ao began to think of returning and spoke thereof to Kuo Chia, who had advised the journey. Kuo had speedily fallen victim to the effects of the climate, and at this time he lay in his cart very ill.

Ts'ao's tears fell as he said; "My friend, you are suffering for my ambition to subdue the Shamo. I cannot bear to think you should be ill."

"You have always been very good to me, said the sick man, "and I can never repay what I owe you."

"The country is exceedingly precipitous and I am thinking of going back; what think you?"

Chia replied, "The success of an expedition of this kind depends upon celerity. To strike a sudden blow on a distant spot with a heavy baggage train is difficult. To ensure success the need is light troops and a good road to strike quickly before an enemy has time to prepare. Now you must find guides who know the road well."

Then the sick adviser was left at Ichou for treatment and they sought among the natives for some persons to serve as guides. One of Yuan Shao's old captains knew those parts well and Ts'ao called him and questioned him. He said, "Between autumn and summer this route is under water, the shallow places too heavy for wheeled traffic, the deep parts insufficient for boats. It is always difficult. Therefore you would do better to return and at Lulungk'ou cross the Pait'an Pass into the desert. Then advance to Liuch'eng (Willow City) and smite before there is time to prepare. One sudden rush will settle Mao Tun."

For this valuable information and plan T'ien Ch'ou was made a "Pacificator of the North" General, and went in advance as leader and guide. Next after him came Chang Liao and Ts'ao brought up the rear. They advanced by double marches.

T'ien Ch'ou led Chang Liao to White Wolf Hill, where they came upon the two Yuans with Mao Tun and a large force of cavalry. Chang Liao galloped to inform his chief and Ts'ao rode up to the top of an eminence to survey the foe. He saw a large mass of cavalry without any military formation advancing in a disorderly crowd.

Said he, "They have no formation, we can easily rout them."

Then he handed over his ensign of command to Chang Liao who, with Hsu Ch'u, Yu Chin and Hsu Huang, made a vigorous attack from four different points, with the result that the enemy was thrown into confusion. Chang Liao rode forward and slew Mao Tun and the other captains gave in. The brothers Yuan with a few companies of horse got away into Liaotung.

Ts'ao Ts'ao then led his army into Liuch'eng. For his services he conferred upon T'ien Ch'ou the rank of marquis of Liut'ing and put him over the city. But T'ien Ch'ou declined the rank, saying with tears, "I am a renegade and a fugitive. It is my good fortune that you spared my life and how can I accept a price for Lulung camp? I would rather die than accept the marquisate."

Ts'ao recognised that reason was on his side and conferred upon him another office. Ts'ao then pacified the Shanyu chieftains; collected a large number of horses and at once set out on the homeward march.

The season was winter, cold and dry. For two hundred *li* there was no water, and grain also was scanty. The troops fed on horse flesh. They had to dig very deep, thirty to forty *chang*,* to find water.

---

* A *chang* is ten feet.

When Ts'ao reached Ichou he rewarded those who had remonstrated with him against the expedition.

He said, "I took some risk in going so far but by good fortune I have succeeded; with the aid of Heaven I have secured victory. I could not be guided by your advice but still they were counsels of safety and therefore I reward you to prove my appreciation of advice and that hereafter you may not fear to speak your minds."

The adviser, Kuo Chia, did not live to see the return of his lord. His coffin was placed on the bier in a hall of the government offices and Ts'ao went thither to sacrifice to his manes. Ts'ao mourned for him, saying, "Alas! Heaven has smitten me; Feng-hsiao is dead."

Then turning to his officers he said, "You, gentlemen, are of the same age as myself, but he was very young to die. I needed him for the future and unhappily he has been torn from me in the flower of his age. My heart and my bowels are torn with grief."

The servants of the late adviser presented his last testament, which they said his dying hand had written, and he had told them to say, "If the Minister shall follow the advice given herein then Liaotung will be secure."

Ts'ao opened the cover and read, nodding his head in agreement and uttering deep sighs. But no other man knew what was written therein.

Shortly after, Hsiahou Tun at the head of a delegation presented a petition saying, "For a long time Kungsun K'ang, the Prefect of Liaotung, has been contumacious and it bodes ill for peace that the brothers Yuan have fled to him. Would it not be well to attack before they move against you?"

"I need not trouble your tiger courage, gentlemen," said Ts'ao smiling. "Wait a few days and you will see the heads of our two enemies sent to me."

They could not believe it.

As has been related the two brothers Yuan escaped to the east with a few squadrons of horse. The Prefect of Liaotung was a son of General Kungsun Tu, "the Warlike," as his title ran, He was a native of Hsiangp'ing. When he heard that the Yuans were on their way to his territory he called a council to decide upon his plan. At the council Kungsun Kung rose saying "When Yuan Shao was alive he nourished the plan of adding this district to his own. Now his sons, homeless, with a broken army and no officers, are coming here; it seems to me like the dove stealing the magpie's nest. If we offer them shelter they will assuredly intrigue against us. I advise that they be inveigled into the city, put to death and their heads sent to Ts'ao, who will be most grateful to us."

Said the Prefect, "I have one fear; Ts'ao will come against us. If so, it would be better to have the help of the Yuans against him."

"Then you can send spies to ascertain whether the army is preparing to attack us. If it is then save them alive; if not, then follow my advice."

It was decided to wait till the spies came back. In the meantime the two Yuans had taken counsel together as they approached Liaotung, saying, "Liaotung has a large army strong enough to oppose Ts'ao Ts'ao. We will go thither and submit till we can slay the Prefect and take possession. Then when we are strong enough we will attack and recover our own land."

With these intentions they went into the city. They were received and lodged in the guests' quarters, but when they wished to see Kungsun K'ang he put them off with the excuse of indisposition. However, before many days the spies returned with the news that Ts'ao Ts'ao's army was quiescent and there was no hint of any attack.

Then Kungsun K'ang called the Yuans into his presence. But before they came he hid swordmen and axemen behind the arras in the hall. When the visitors came and had made their salutations, K'ang bade them be seated.

Now it was bitterly cold and on the couch where Shang was sitting were no coverings. So he asked for a cushion. The host surlily said, "When your heads take that long, long journey, will there be any cushions?"

Before Shang could recover from his fright K'ang shouted, "Why do you not begin?"

At this out rushed the assassins and the heads of the two brothers were cut off as they sat. Packed in a small wooden box they were sent to Ts'ao Ts'ao at Ichou.

All this time Ts'ao had been calmly waiting, and when his impatient officers had petitioned in a body that he would march to the capital if he intended no attack on the east, he told them what he was waiting for. He would go as soon as the heads arrived.

In their secret hearts they laughed. But then, surely enough, a messenger soon came from Liaotung bringing the heads. Then they were greatly surprised and when the messenger presented his letters Ts'ao cried, "Just as Feng-hsiao said!"

He amply rewarded the messenger and the Governor of Liaotung was made a marquis and General of the Left Wing; and when the officers asked what had happened, Ts'ao told them what the late adviser had predicted. He read to them the dead officer's testament, which ran something like this:—"Yuan Shang and his brother are going to Liaotung. Illustrious Sir, you are on no account to attack for Kungsun K'ang has long lived in fear lest the Yuans should absorb his country. When they arrive K'ang will hesitate. If you attack, he will save the Yuans to help him; if you wait, they will work against each other. This is evident."

The officers simply jumped with surprise to see how perfectly events had been foreseen.

Then Ts'ao at the head of all his officers performed a grand sacrifice before the coffin of the wise Kuo Chia. He had died at the age of thirty-eight, after eleven years of meritorious and wonderful service in the wars.

> When Heaven permitted Kuo Chia's birth,
> It made him ablest man on earth.
> He knew by rote all histories,
> From him war kept no mysteries.
> Like Fan's, his plans were quite decisive,
> As Ch'en's, his strokes were most incisive.
> Too soon he ran his earthly race,
> Too soon the great beam fell from place.

When Ts'ao returned to Ch'ichou he sent off the coffin of his late adviser to the capital where it was interred.

Then certain of his officers said that as the north had been overcome it was time to settle Chiangnan. Ts'ao was pleased and said that had long occupied his thoughts.

The last night he spent in Ch'ichou he went to one of the corner towers and stood there regarding the sky. His only companion was Hsun Yu. Presently Ts'ao said, "That is a very brilliant glow there in the south. It seems too strong for me to do anything there."

"What is there that can oppose your heaven high prestige?" said Yu.

Suddenly a beam of golden light shot up out of the earth. "Surely a treasure is buried there," remarked Yu.

They went down from the city wall, called some men and led them to the point whence the light proceeded. There the men were ordered to dig.

> The southern skies with portents glow,
> The northern lands their treasures show.

What the diggers found will appear in the next chapter.

CHAPTER XXXIV

A WOMAN OVERHEARS A SECRET:
A WARRIOR LEAPS A STREAM

The story says that the diggers at the spot whence the golden light proceeded presently unearthed a bronze bird. Looking at it, Ts'ao turned to his companion, saying, "What is the portent?"

"You will remember that Shun's mother dreamed of a jade bird before his birth, so certainly it is a felicitous omen," said Hsun Yu.

Ts'ao was very pleased and he ordered forthwith the building of a lofty tower to celebrate the find, and they began to dig foundations and cut timber, to burn tiles and to smooth bricks for the Bronze Bird Tower on the banks of the Chang River. Ts'ao set a year for the building.

His younger son, Chih, said, "If you build a terraced tower you should add two others, one on each side. The centre tower and the tallest should be called The Bronze Bird Tower; the side towers named Jade Dragon Tower and Golden Phoenix Tower. Then connect these by flying bridges and the effect will be noble."

"My son, your words are very good and by and bye when the building is complete I can solace my old age therein."

Ts'ao Ts'ao had five sons, but this one Chih was the most clever and his essays were particularly elegant. His father was very fond of him and, seeing that the young man took an interest in the building, Ts'ao left him with his brother P'ei at Yehchun to superintend the work, while he led the army that had recently conquered the Yuans back to the capital. When he arrived he distributed rewards liberally and memorialised the throne obtaining the title of "The Pure Marquis" for the late Kuo Chia. And he took Kuo's son to be brought up in his own family.

Next he began to consider the reduction of Liu Piao's power. Hsun Yu said, "The Grand Army has only just returned from the north and needs rest. Wait half a year that the men may recover from the fatigue of the campaign and both Liu Piao and Sun Ch'uan will fall at the first roll of the drums."

Presently Ts'ao approved of this plan and to rest his men he assigned certain lands to them to till while they rested.

Liu Piao had been very generous to Liu Pei ever since he had come, a fugitive seeking shelter. One day at a banquet there came news that two captains, who had tendered their submission, had suddenly begun plundering the people in Chianghsia. They evidently meant rebellion. "If they really rebel it will cause a lot of trouble," said Piao, rather dismayed.

"Do not let that trouble you, I will go and settle it," said P'ei.

Pleased with this proposal, Piao told off three legions and placed them under his friend, and the army marched as soon as the orders were issued. In a short time it reached the scene and the two malcontents came out to fight, Yuan-te and his two brothers took their stand beneath the great banner and looked over at the enemy. The two leaders were riding handsome prancing horses and Yuan-te said, "They certainly have fine steeds."

As he spoke Chao Yun galloped out with his spear set and dashed toward the enemy. Chang Wu, one of the leaders, came out to meet him, but the combat was very brief for Chang was soon killed. Thereupon Chao Yun laid a hand upon the bridle of the fallen man's horse to lead him back to his own side. The slain rebel's companion Ch'en Sun at once rode after him, whereupon Chang Fei uttered a loud shout and rode out to meet him. With one thrust he slew the rebel. Their followers now scattered and Yuan-te speedily restored order and returned.

Liu Piao, grateful for this service, rode out to the boundary to welcome the victors. They reentered the city and grand banquets were instituted, at which they emptied great goblets in congratulations over the victory. At one of these banquets the Prefect said, "With such heroism as my brother has shown Chingchou has one upon whom to rely. But a source of sorrow is the south country Yueh, from which a raid may come at any time. Chang Lu and Sun Ch'uan are to be feared."

"But I have three bold captains," said Yuan-te, "quite equal to any task you can set them. Send Chang Fei to keep ward on the southern marches, Kuan Yu to guard the city against Chang Lu and Chao Yun will protect you from Sun Ch'uan. Why need you grieve?"

The scheme appealed strongly to the Prefect, but Ts'ai Mao did not approve. So he spoke to his sister, Liu Piao's wife, and insisted on the danger of putting these men in such commanding positions all round the prefecture. The lady Ts'ai, thus influenced by her brother, undertook to remonstrate and that night began by saying, "The Chingchou men seem to have a great liking for Liu Pei; they are always coming and going. You ought to take precautions. I do not think you should let them stay in the city. Why not send them on some mission?"

"Yuan-te is a good man," replied the Prefect.

"I think others differ from you" said the lady.

The Prefect said nothing but muttered to himself. Soon after he went out of the city to see Yuan-te and noticed he was riding a very handsome horse. They told him it was a prize taken from the recently conquered rebels, and as he praised it very warmly, the horse was presented to him. Liu Piao was delighted and rode it back to the city. K'uai Yueh saw it and asked where it had come from. The Prefect told him it was a gift from Liu P'ei and Yueh said, "My brother knew horses very well and I am not a bad judge. This horse has tear-tracks running down from his eyes and a white blaze on his forehead. He is called a *tilu* and he is a danger to his master. That is why Chang Wu was killed. I advise you not to ride him.

The Prefect began to think. Soon after he asked Yuan-te to a banquet and in the course of it said, "You kindly presented me with a horse lately and I am most grateful, but you may need him on some of your expeditions and, if you do not mind, I would like to return him."

Yuan-te rose and thanked him. The Prefect continued, "You have been here a long time and I fear I am spoiling your career as a warrior. Now Hsinyeh in Hsiangjang is no poverty-stricken town; how would you like to garrison it with your own men?"

Yuan-te naturally took the offer as a command and set out as soon as he could, taking leave of the Prefect the next day. And so he took up his quarters in Hsinyeh. When he left the city he noticed in the gate a person making him emphatic salutations and the man presently said, You should not ride that horse."

Yuan-te looked at the man and recognised in the speaker one of the secretaries named I Chi, a native of Shanyang. So he hastily dismounted and asked why. I Chi replied, "Yesterday I heard that K'uai Yueh told the Prefect that that horse was a *tilu* and brought disaster to its owner. That is why it was returned to you. How can you mount it again?"

"I am deeply touched by your affection," replied Yuan-te, "but a man's life is governed by fate and what horse can interfere with that?"

I Chi admitted his superior view, but thereafter he followed Yuan-te wherever he went.

The arrival of Liu P'ei in Hsinyeh was a matter of rejoicing to all the inhabitants and the whole administration was reformed.

In the spring of the twelfth year the Lady Kan gave birth to a son who was named Ch'an. The night of his birth a crane settled on the roof of the house, screeched some forty times and then flew away westward.

Just at the time of birth a miraculous incense filled the chamber. Lady Kan one night had dreamed that she was looking up at the sky and the constellation of the Great Bear, Peitou, had fallen down her throat. As she conceived soon after she gave her son the milk-name of O-tou.

While Ts'ao Ts'ao was absent from the capital on his northern expedition, Liu P'ei went to Liu Piao and said to him, "Why do you not take this opportunity to march against the capital? An empire might follow from that."

"I am well placed here," was the reply, "Why should I attempt other things?"

Yuan-te said no more. Then the Prefect invited him into the private apartments to drink and while they were so engaged he suddenly began to sigh despondently.

"O brother, why do you sigh thus?" asked Yuan-te.

"I have a secret sorrow that is difficult to speak about," said Piao.

Yuan-te was on the point of asking what it was when the Lady Ts'ai came and stood behind the screen, whereat Piao hung his head and became silent. Before long host and guest bade each other farewell and Liu P'ei went back to his own place.

That winter they heard that Ts'ao Ts'ao had returned from Liuch'eng and Liu P'ei sighed when he reflected that his friend had paid no heed to his advice.

Unexpectedly a messenger came from the principal city with a request that Liu P'ei would go thither to consult with the Prefect. So he started at once with the messenger. He was received very kindly, and when the salutations were over, the two men went into the private quarters at the rear to dine. Presently the host said, "Ts'ao has returned and he is stronger than ever. I am afraid he means to absorb this district. I am sorry I did not follow your advice for I have missed an opportunity."

"In this period of disruption, with strife on every side, one cannot pretend that there will be no more opportunities. If you only take that what offers there will be nothing to regret."

"What you say, brother, is quite to the point," replied Liu Piao.

They drank on for a time till presently Liu P'ei noticed that his host was weeping, and when he asked the cause of these tears, Piao replied, "It is that secret sorrow I spoke of to you before; I wished to tell you, but there was no opportunity that day."

"O brother, what difficulty have you, and can I assist you? I am entirely at your service."

"My wife, of the Ch'en family, bore me a son Ch'i, my eldest. He grew up virtuous but weakly and unfitted to succeed me in my office. Later I took a wife of the Ts'ai family, who bore me a son named Ts'ung, fairly intelligent. If I pass over the elder in favour of the younger there is the breach of the rule of primogeniture, and if I follow law and custom there are the intrigues of the mother's family and clan to be reckoned with. Further, the army is in the hollow of their hands. There will be trouble and I cannot decide what to do."

Liu P'ei said, "All experience proves that to set aside the elder for the younger is to take the way of confusion. If you fear the power of the Ts'ai faction, then gradually reduce its power and influence, but do not let doting affection lead you into making the younger your heir."

Piao agreed. But the Lady Ts'ai had had a suspicion why her lord had summoned Liu P'ei and what was the subject of discussion, so she had determined to listen secretly. She was behind the screen when the matter was talked over and she conceived deep resentment against Liu P'ei for what he had said. On his side he felt that his advice had fallen upon deaf ears and he arose and walked across the room. As he did so he noticed that he was getting heavy and stiff and a furtive tear stole down his cheek as he thought of the past. When he returned and sat down his host noticed the traces of weeping and asked the cause of his sorrow.

"In the past I was always in the saddle and I was slender and lithe. Now it is so long since I rode that I am getting stout and the days and months are slipping by, wasted; I shall have old age on me in no time and I have accomplished nothing. So I am sad."

"I have heard a story that when you were at Hsucheng at the season of green plums you and Ts'ao Ts'ao were discussing heroes. You mentioned this name and that to him as men of parts and he rejected every one of them. Finally he said that you and he were the only two men of real worth in the whole country. If he with all his power and authority did not dare to place himself in front of you, I do not think you need grieve about having accomplished nothing."

At this flattering speech Liu P'ei pretended that the wine was getting the better of him and in a half maudlin manner he replied, "If I only had a starting point then I would not trouble about any one in a worldful of fools."

His host said no more and the guest, feeling that he had slipped up in speech, rose as if drunk, took leave and staggered out saying he must return to his lodging to recover.

The episode has been celebrated in a poem:—

> When with crooking fingers counting,
> Ts'ao Ts'ao reckoned up the forceful
> Men of real determination,
> Only two he found; and one was
> Yuan-te. But by inaction
> He had grown both fat and slothful;
> Yet the months and years in passing
> Fretted him with nought accomplished.

Though Liu Piao kept silence when he heard the words of Yuan-te, yet he felt the more uneasy. After the departure of his guest he retired into the inner quarters where he met his wife. The Lady Ts'ai said, "I happened to be behind the screen just now and so heard the words of Liu P'ei. They betray scant regard for other people and mean that he would take your country if he could. If you do not remove him it will go ill with you."

Her husband made no reply, but only shook his head. Then the Lady Ts'ai took counsel with her kinsman Ts'ai Mao, who said, "Let me go to the guest-house and slay him forthwith, and we can report what we have done."

His sister consented and he went out, and that night told off a party of soldiers to do the foul deed.

Now Yuan-te sat in his lodging by the light of a single candle till about the third watch, when he prepared to retire to bed. He was startled by a knock at his door and in came I Chi, who had heard of the plot against his new master and had come in the darkness to warn him. He related the details of the plot and urged speedy departure.

"I have not said farewell to my host; how can I go away?" said Liu P'ei.

"If you go to bid him farewell you will fall a victim to the Ts'ai faction," said I Chi.

So Yuan-te said a hasty good-bye to his friend, called up his escort and they all mounted and rode away by the light of the stars toward Hsinyeh. Soon after they had left the soldiers arrived at the guest-house, but their intended victim was already well on his way.

Naturally the failure of the plot chagrined the treacherous Ts'ai Mao, but he took the occasion to scribble some calumnious verses on one of the partitions. Then he went to see Liu Piao to whom he said, "Liu P'ei has treacherous intentions, as can be seen from some lines written on the wall. And his hurried departure is suspicious."

Liu Piao felt doubtful, but he went to the guest-house and there on the wall he read this poem:

> Too long, far too long I have dreamed life away,
> Gazing at scenery day after day.
> A dragon can never be kept in a pond,
> He should ride on the thunder to heaven and beyond.

Greatly angered by what he read, Liu Piao drew his sword and swore to slay the writer. But before he had gone many paces his anger hard already died down and he said to himself, "I have seen much of the man, but have never known him write verses. This is the handiwork of some one who wishes to sow discord between us."

So saying he turned back and with the point of his sword scraped away the poem. Then, putting up his sword, he mounted and rode home. By and bye Ts'ai Mao reminded him that the soldiers were awaiting orders and asked whether they could go to Hsinyeh and arrest Liu P'ei.

"There is no hurry," he replied.

Ts'ai Mao saw his brother-in-law's hesitation and again sought his sister. She said, "Soon there is to be the great gathering at Hsiangyang and we can arrange something for that day."

Next day Ts'ai Mao petitioned the Prefect, saying, "I pray you, Sir, to attend the Full Harvest Festival at Hsiangyang; it would be an encouragement to the people."

"I have been feeling my old trouble lately; I certainly cannot go," replied he, "but my two sons can go to represent me and receive the guests."

"They are full young," replied Mao, "They may make some mistakes."

"Then go to Hsinyeh and request Liu P'ei to receive the guests," said Piao.

Nothing could have pleased Ts'ai Mao more, for this would bring Liu P'ei within reach of his plot. Without loss of time he sent to Yuan-te requesting him to go to preside at the Festival.

It has been said that Yuan-te made the best of his way home to

Hsinyeh. He felt that he had offended by that slip in speech, but determined to keep silence about it and attempt no explanation. So he discussed it with nobody. Then came the message asking him to preside at the Festival, and he needed counsel.

Sun Ch'ien said, "You have seemed worried and preoccupied lately and I think something untoward happened at Chingchou. You should consider well before you accept this invitation."

Thereupon Yuan-te told his confidants the whole story.

Kuan Yu said, "You yourself think your speech offended the Prefect, but he said nothing to show displeasure. You need pay no attention to the babble of outsiders. Hsiangyang is quite near and, if you do not go, Liu Chinchou will begin to suspect something really is wrong."

"You speak well," said Yuan-te.

Said Chang Fei, "Banquets are no good; gatherings are no better; it is best not to go."

"Let me take three hundred horse and foot as escort; there will be no trouble then," said Chao Yun.

"That is the best course," said Yuan-te.

They soon set out for the gathering place and Ts'ai Mao met them at the boundary and was most affable and courteous. Soon arrived the Prefect's sons at the head of a great company of officers, civil and military. Their appearance put Yuan-te more at ease. He was conducted to the guest-house and Chao Yun posted his men so as to guard it completely, while he himself, armed, remained close to his chief.

Liu Ch'i said to Yuan-te, "My father is feeling unwell and could not come, wherefore he begs you, Uncle Liu, to preside at the various ceremonies and conduct the inspections."

"Really I am unfit for such responsibilities," said Yuan-te, "But my brother's command must be obeyed."

Next day it was reported that the officials from the forty-one departments of the nine districts had all arrived.

Then Ts'ai Mao said to K'uai Yueh, "This Liu P'ei is the villain of the age and if left alive will certainly work harm to us. He must be got rid of now."

"I fear you would forfeit everybody's favour if you harmed him," replied K'uai.

"I have already secretly spoken in these terms to Prefect Liu," said Ts'ai, "and I have his word here."

"So it may be regarded as settled; then we can prepare."

Ts'ai Mao said, "One of my brothers is posted on the road to the Hsien Hills from the east gate and the others are on the north and south roads. No guard is needed on the west as the T'an Torrent is quite safeguard enough. Even with legions he could not get over that."

K'uai replied, "I notice that Chao Yun never leaves him. I feel sure he expects some attack."

"I have placed five hundred men in ambush in the city."

"We will tell Wen P'ing and Wang Wei to invite all the military officers to a banquet at one of the pavilions outside the city, and Chao Yun will be among them. Then will be our opportunity."

Ts'ai Mao thought this a good device for getting Chao Yun out of the way.

Now oxen and horses had been slaughtered and a grand banquet prepared. Yuan-te rode to the residence on the horse of ill omen and when he arrived the steed was led into the back part of the enclosure and tethered there. Soon the guests arrived and Yuan-te took his place as master of the feast, with the two sons of the Prefect, one on each side. The guests were all arranged in order of rank. Chao Yun stood near his lord sword in hand as a faithful henchman should do.

Then Wen and Wang came to invite Chao Yun to the banquet they had prepared for the military officers. But he declined. However, Yuan-te told him to go, and, after some demur, he went. Then Ts'ai Mao perfected his final arrangements, placing his men surrounding the place like a ring of iron. The three hundred guards that formed the escort of Yuan-te were sent away to the guest-house.

All were ready and awaiting the signal. At the third course, I Chi took a goblet of wine in his hands and approached Yuan-te, at the same time giving him a meaning look. Then in a low voice he said, "Make an excuse to get away."

Yuan-te understood and presently rose as if stiff with long sitting and went outside. There he found I Chi, who had gone thither after presenting the cup of wine. I Chi then told him more of the plot and that all the roads were guarded except that to the west. And he advised him to lose no time.

Yuan-te was quite taken aback. However, he got hold of the horse of ill omen, opened the door of the garden and led him out. Then he took a flying leap into the saddle and galloped off without waiting for the escort. He made for the west gate. At the gate the wardens wanted to question him, but he only whipped up his steed and rode through. The guards at the gate ran off to report to Ts'ai Mao, who quickly went in pursuit with a half company of soldiers.

As has been said Yuan-te burst out at the west gate. Before he had gone far there rolled before him a great river barring the way. It was the T'an, many score feet in width, which pours its waters into the Hsiang. Its current was very swift.

Yuan-te reached the bank and saw the river was unfordable. So he turned his horse and rode back. Then, not far off, he saw a cloud of dust and knew that his pursuers were therein. He thought that it was all over. However, he turned again toward the swift river, and seeing the soldiers now quite near, plunged into the stream. A few paces, and he felt the horse's fore legs floundering in front while the water rose over the skirt of his robe. Then he plied the whip furiously, crying, "Tilu, Tilu, I trust to you."

Whereupon the good steed suddenly reared up out of the water and, with one tremendous leap, was on the western bank. Yuan-te felt as if he had come out of the clouds.

In after years the famous court official, Su T'ung-p'o, wrote a poem on this leap over the T'an Torrent:—

> I'm growing old, the leaves are sere,
> My sun slopes westward, soon will sink,
> And I recall that yester year
> I wandered by T'an River brink.
>
> Irresolute, anon I paused,
> Anon advanced, and gazed around,
> I marked the autumn's reddened leaves,
> And watched them eddying to the ground.
>
> I thought of all the mighty deeds
> Of him who set the House of Han
> On high, and all the struggles since,
> The battlefields, the blood that ran.
>
> I saw the nobles gathered round
> The board, set in the Banquet Hall;
> Amid them, one, above whose head
> There hung a sword about to fall.
>
> I saw him quit that festive throng
> And westward ride, a lonely way;
> I saw a squadron follow swift,
> Intent the fugitive to slay.
>
> I saw him reach the River T'an,
> Whose swirling current rushes by;
> Adown the bank he galloped fast,
> "Now leap, my steed!" I heard him cry.

His steed's hoofs churn the swollen stream;
What recks he that the waves run high?
He hears the sound of clashing steel,
Of thundering squadrons coming nigh.

And upward from the foaming waves
I saw two peerless beings soar;
One was a destined western king,
And him another dragon bore.

The T'an still rolls from east to west,
Its roaring torrent ne'er dry.
Those dragons twain, Ah! where are they?
Yes, where? But there is no reply.

The setting sun, in dark relief
Against the glowing western sky,
Throws out the everlasting hills
While, saddened, here I stand and sigh.

Men died to found the kingdoms three,
Which now as misty dreams remain.
Of greatest deeds the traces oft
Are faint that fleeting years retain.

Thus Liu P'ei crossed the rolling river. Then he turned and looked back at the other bank which his pursuers had just gained.

"Why did you run away from the feast?" called out Ts'ai Mao.

"Why did you wish to harm one who has done you no injury?" replied Yuan-te.

"I have never thought of such a thing; do not listen to what people say to you."

But Yuan-te saw that his enemy was fitting an arrow to his bowstring, so he whipped up his steed and rode away south-west.

"What spirits aided him?" said Ts'ai Mao to his followers.

Then he turned to go back to the city, but in the gate he saw Chao Yun coming out at the head of his company of guards.

By wondrous leap the dragon steed his rider's life could save,
Now follows him, on vengeance bent, his master's henchman brave.

The next chapters will tell what fate befell the traitor.

Just as Ts'ai Mao was going into the city he met Chao Yun and his three hundred coming out. It had happened that, while at the banquet, Chao Yun had noticed some movement of men and horses and had at once gone to the banquet-hall to see if all was well with his lord. Missing him from his place he had become anxious and gone to the guest-house. There he heard that Ts'ai Mao had gone off to the west gate with troops. So he quickly took his spear, mounted and went, he and the escort, in hot haste along the same road. Meeting Ts'ai Mao near the gate he said, "Where is my lord?"

"He left the banquet-hall quite suddenly and I know not whither he has gone," was the reply.

Now Chao Yun was cautious and careful and had no desire to act hastily, so he urged his horse forward till he came to the river. There he was checked by a torrent without ford or bridge. At once he turned back and shouted after Ts'ai Mao, "You invited my lord to a feast; what means this going after him with a squadron of horse?"

Mao replied, "It is my duty to guard the officials who have assembled here as I am the chief captain."

"Whither have you driven my lord?" asked Chao.

"They tell me he rode quite alone out through the west gate, but I have not seen him."

Chao Yun was anxious and doubtful. Again he rode to the river and looked around. This time he noticed a wet track on the farther side. He thought to himself that it was almost an impossible crossing for a man and a horse, so he ordered his men to scatter and search. But they also could find no trace of Liu Pei.

Chao Yun turned again to the city. By the time he had reached the wall Ts'ai Mao had gone within. He then questioned the gate wardens, and they all agreed in saying that Liu Pei had ridden out at full gallop. That was all they knew. Fearing to re-enter the city lest he should fall into an ambush, Chao started for Hsienyeh.

After that marvellous life-saving leap over the torrent, Yuan-te felt elated but rather dazed. He could not help feeling that his safety was due to an especial interposition of Providence. Following a tortuous path, he urged his steed toward Nanchang. But the sun sank to the west and his destination seemed yet a long way off. Then he saw a young cowherd seated on the back of a buffalo and playing on a short pipe.

"If I were only as happy!" sighed Yuan-te.

He checked his horse and looked at the lad, who stopped his beast, ceased playing on the pipe and stared fixedly at the stranger.

"You must be Yuan-te, the General who fought the Yellow Turbans," said the boy presently.

Yuan-te was taken aback.

"How can you know my name, a young rustic like you living in such a secluded place?" said he.

"Of course I do not know you, but my master often has visitors and they all talk about Yuan-te, the tall man whose hands hang down below his knees and whose eyes are very prominent. They say he is the most famous man of the day. Now you, General, are just such a man as they talk about, and surely you are he."

"Well, who is your master?"

"My master's name is Ssuma, a compound surname, and his *ming* is Hui; his other name is Te-ts'ao. He belongs to Ying-chou and his Taoist appellation is Shui-ching, 'The Water-mirror.'"

"Who are your master's friends that you mentioned?"

They are P'ang Te-kung and P'ang T'ung of Hsiangyang."

"And who are they?"

"Relatives. P'ang Te-kung is ten years older than my master; the other is five years younger. One day my master was up in a tree picking mulberries when P'ang T'ung arrived. They began to talk and kept it up all day, my master did not come down till the evening. My master is very fond of P'ang T'ung and calls him brother."

"And where does your master live?"

"In that wood there, in front," said the cowherd pointing to it. There he has a farmstead."

"I really am Liu Yuan-te and you might lead me to your master that I may salute him."

The cowherd led the way for about two *li*, when Liu Pei found himself in front of a farm house. He dismounted and went to the centre door. Suddenly came to his ear the sound of a lute most skilfully played and the air was extremely beautiful. He stopped his guide and would not allow him to announce a visitor, but stood there rapt by the melody.

Suddenly the music ceased. He heard a deep laugh and a man appeared, saying, "Amidst the clear and subtle sounds of the lute there suddenly rang out a high note as though some noble man was near."

"That is my master," said the lad pointing.

Liu Pei saw before him a tall figure, slender and straight as a pine tree, a very "chosen vessel." Hastening forward he saluted. The skirt of his robe was still wet from the river.

"You have escaped from a grave danger today, Sir," said "Water-mirror."

Yuan-te was startled into silence, and the cowherd said to his master, "This is Liu Yuan-te."

"Water-mirror" asked him to enter and when they were seated in their relative positions as host and guest, Yuan-te glanced round the room. Upon the bookshelves were piled books and manuscripts. The window opened upon an exquisite picture of pines and bamboos and a lute lay upon a stone couch. The room showed refinement in its last degree.

"Whence come you, illustrious Sir?" asked the host.

"By chance I was passing this way and the lad pointed you out to me. So I came to bow in your honoured presence. I cannot tell what pleasure it gives me."

"Water-mirror" laughed. "Why this mystery? Why must you conceal the truth? You have certainly just escaped from a grave danger."

Then the story of the banquet and the flight was told.

"I knew it all from your appearance," said his host. "Your name has long been familiar," continued he, but whence comes it that, up to the present, you are only a homeless devil?"

"I have suffered many a check during my life," said Liu Pei, "and through one of them am I here now."

"It should not be so; but the reason is that you still lack the one man to aid you."

'I am simple enough in myself, I know; but I have Sun Ch'ien, Mi Chu and Chien Yung on the civil side, and for warriors I have Kuan Yu, Chang Fei and Chao Yun. These are all most loyal helpers and I depend upon them not a little."

"Your fighting men are good: fit to oppose a legion. The pity is you have no really able adviser. Your civilians are but pallid students of books, not men fitted to weave and control destiny."

"I have always yearned to find one of those marvellous recluses who live among the hills till their day arrive. So far I have sought in vain."

"You know what the Master said, 'In a hamlet of ten households there must be one true man.' Can you say there is no man?"

"I am simple and uninstructed; I pray you enlighten me."

"You have heard what the street boys sing:—

> In eight and nine begins decay,
>   Four years, then comes the fateful day,
> When destiny will show the way,
>   And the dragon files out of the mire O!

This song was first heard when the new reign-style was adopted. The first line was fulfilled when Liu Piao lost his first wife, and when his family troubles began. The next line relates to the approaching death of Liu Piao and there is not a single man among all his crowd of officers who has the least ability. The last two lines will be fulfilled in you, General."

Yuan-te started up in surprise, crying, "How could such a thing be?"

"Water-mirror" continued, "At this moment the marvellously clever ones of all the earth are all here and you, Sir, ought to seek them."

"Where are they? Who are they?" said Yuan-te quickly.

If you could find either Fu-lung (Hidden Dragon) or Feng-ch'u (Phoenix Fledgeling), you could restore order in the Empire."

"But who are these men?"

His host clapped his hands, smiled and said, "Good; very good."

When Yuan-te persisted and pressed home his questions "Water-mirror" said, "It is getting late. You might stay the night here, General, and we will talk over these things tomorrow."

He called to a lad to bring wine and food for his guest and his horse was taken to the stable and fed. After Yuan-te had eaten he was shown to a chamber opening off the main room and went to bed. But the words of his host would not be banished and he lay there only dozing till far into the night.

Suddenly he became fully awake at the sound of a knock at the door and a person entering. And he heard his host say "Where are you from, Yuan-chih?"

Liu Pei rose from his couch and listened secretly. He heard the man reply, "It has long been said that Liu Piao treated good men as good men should be treated and bad men as they should be treated.

So I went to see for myself. But that reputation is undeserved. He does treat good men correctly but he cannot use them, and he treats wicked men in the right way, all but dismissing them. So I left a letter for him and came away; and here I am."

"Water-mirror" replied, "You, capable enough to be the adviser of a king, ought to be able to find some one fit to serve. Why did you cheapen yourself so far as to go to Liu Piao? Beside there is a real hero right under your eyes and you do not know him."

"It is just as you say," replied the stranger.

Liu Pei listened with great joy for he thought this visitor was certainly one of the two he was advised to look for. He would have shown himself then and there, but he thought that would look strange. So he waited till daylight, when he sought out his host and said, "Who was it came last night?"

"A friend of mine," was the reply.

Yuan-te begged for an introduction. "Water-mirror" said, "He wants to find an enlightened master and so he has gone elsewhere."

When the guest asked his name his host only replied, "Good, good." And when he asked who they were who went by the names of Fu-lung and Feng-ch'u he only elicited the same reply.

Yuan-te then, bowing low before his host, begged him to leave the hills and help him to bring about the restoration of the ruling house to its prerogatives. But he replied, "Men of the hills and deserts are unequal to such a task. However, there must be many far abler than I who will help you if you seek them."

While they were talking they heard outside the farm the shouts of men and neighing of horses, and a servant came in to say that a captain with a large company of men had arrived. Yuan-te went out hastily to see who these were and found Chao Yun. He was much relieved and Chao dismounted and entered the house.

"Last night, on my return to our city," said Chao, "I could not find my lord, so I followed at once and traced you here. I pray you return quickly as I fear an attack on the city."

So Yuan-te took leave of his host and the whole company returned to Hsinyeh. Before they had gone far another troop appeared, and, when they had come nearer, they saw the two brothers. They met with great joy and Yuan-te told them of the wonderful leap his horse had made over the torrent. All expressed surprise and pleasure.

As soon as they reached the city a council was called and Chao Yun said, "You ought first of all to indite a letter to Liu Piao telling him all these things."

The letter was prepared and Sun Ch'ien bore it to the seat of government. He was received, and Liu Piao at once asked the reason of Yuan-te's hasty flight from the festival. Whereupon the letter was presented and the bearer related the machinations of Ts'ai Mao and told of the escape and the amazing leap over the torrent. Liu Piao was very angry, sent for Ts'ai Mao and berated him soundly, saying, "How dare you try to hurt my brother?" and he ordered him out to execution.

Liu Piao's wife, Ts'ao Mao's sister, prayed for a remission of the death penalty, but Liu Piao refused to be appeased. Then spoke Sun Ch'ien, saying, "If you put Ts'ai to death, I fear Uncle Liu will be unable to remain here."

Then he was reprieved, but dismissed with a severe reprimand.

Liu Piao sent his elder son back with Sun Ch'ien to apologise. When Ch'i reached Hsinyeh, Yuan-te welcomed him and gave a banquet in his honour. After some little drinking, the chief guest suddenly began to weep and presently said, "My stepmother always cherishes a wish to put me out of the way, and I do not know how to avoid her anger. Could you advise me, Uncle?"

Yuan-te exhorted him to be careful and perfectly filial and nothing could happen. Soon after the young man took his leave, and wept at parting. Yuan-te escorted him well on his way and, pointing to his steed, said, "I owe my life to this horse: had it not been for him I had been already below the Springs."

"It was not the strength of the horse, but your noble fortune, Uncle."

They parted, the young man weeping bitterly. On re-entering the city Yuan-te met a person in the street wearing a hempen turban, a cotton robe confined by a black girdle, and black shoes. He came along singing a song.

> The universe is riven, alack! now nears the end of all,
> The noble mansion quakes, alack! what beam can stay the fall?
> A wise one waits his lord, alack! but hidden in the glen,
> The seeker knows not him, alack! nor me, of common men.

Yuan-te listened. "Surely this is one of the men 'Water-mirror' spoke of," thought he.

He dismounted, spoke to the singer and invited him into his residence. Then when they were seated he asked the stranger's name.

"I am from Yingshang and my name is Tan Fu. I have known you by repute for a long time and they said you appreciated men of ability. I wanted to come to you but every way of getting an introduction seemed closed. So I bethought me of attracting your notice by singing that song in the market place."

Yuan-te thought he had found a treasure and treated the newcomer with the greatest kindness. Then Tan Fu spoke of the horse that he had seen Yuan-te riding and asked to look at him. So the animal was brought round.

"Is not this a *tilu?*" said Tan Fu. "But though he is a good steed he risks his master. You must not ride him."

"He has already fulfilled the omens," said Yuan-te, and he related the story of the leap over the torrent.

"But this was saving his master, not risking him; he will surely harm some one in the end. But I can tell you how to avert the omen."

"I should be glad to hear it," said Yuan-te.

"If you have an enemy against whom you bear a grudge, give him this horse and wait till he has fulfilled the evil omens on this man: then you can ride him in safety."

Yuan-te changed colour. "What, Sir! You are but a new acquaintance and you would advise me to take an evil course and to harm another for my own advantage? No, Sir! I cannot listen."

His guest smiled. "People said you were virtuous. I could not ask you directly, so I put it that way to test you."

Yuan-te's expression changed. He rose and returned the compliment, saying, "But how can I be virtuous while I lack your teaching?"

"When I came here, I heard the people saying:

> Since Liu came here, O blessed day!
> We've had good luck: long may he stay!

So you see the effects of your virtue extend to the ordinary people."

Thereupon Tan Fu was made Organiser in Chief of the army.

The one idea that held Ts'ao Ts'ao after his return from Ch'ichou was the capture of Chingchou. He sent Ts'ao Jen and Li Tien, with the two brothers Lu who had surrendered, to camp at Fanch'eng with three legions and so threaten Chingchou and Hsiangyang. Thence he sent spies to find out the weak points.

Then the two Lus petitioned Ts'ao Jen saying, "Liu Pei is strengthening his position at Hsinyeh and laying in large supplies. Some great scheme is afoot and he should be checked. Since our surrender we have performed no noteworthy service and, if you will give us half a legion, we promise to bring you the head of Liu Pei."

Ts'ao Jen was only too glad, and the expedition set out. The scouts reported this to Yuan-te who turned to Tan Fu for advice.

Tan Fu said, "They must not be permitted to cross the boundary. Send your two brothers right and left, one to attack the enemy on the march, the other to cut off the retreat. You and Chao Yun will make a front attack."

The two brothers started and then Yuan-te went out at the gate with three companies to oppose the enemy. Before they had gone far they saw a great cloud of dust behind the hills. This marked the approach of the brothers Lu. Presently, both sides being arrayed, Yuan-te rode out and stood by his standard. He called out, "Who are you who thus would encroach on my territory?"

"I am the great general Lu K'uang, and I have the orders of the minister to make you prisoner," said the leader.

Yuan-te ordered Chao Yun to go out, and the two captains engaged. Very soon Chao had disposed of his opponent and Yuan-te gave the signal to attack. Lu Hsiang could not maintain his position and led his men off. Soon his men found themselves attacked by an army rushing in from the side led by Kuan Yu. The loss was more than a half and the remainder fled for safety.

About ten *li* farther on they found their retreat barred by an army under Chang Fei, who stood in the way with a long spear ready to thrust. Crying out who he was, he bore down upon Lu Hsiang, who was slain without a chance of striking a blow. The men again fled in disorder. They were pursued by Yuan-te and the greater part killed or captured.

Then Yuan-te returned into his own city where he rewarded Tan Fu and feasted his victorious soldiers. Some of the defeated men took the news of the deaths of the leaders and the capture of their comrades to Ts'ao Jen.

Ts'ao Jen, much distressed, consulted his colleague who advised staying where they were and holding on till reinforcements could arrive.

"Not so," said Ts'ao Jen. "We cannot support calmly the death of two leaders and the loss of so many men. We must avenge them quickly. Hsinyeh is but a crossbow-slug of a place and not worth disturbing the Minister for."

"Liu Pei is a man of metal," said Li Tien. "Do not esteem him lightly."

"What are you afraid of?" said Jen.

"The Rule of War says 'To know your enemy and yourself is the secret of victory,'" replied Tien. "I am not afraid of the battle, but I do not think we can conquer."

"You are a traitor!" cried Jen angrily. "Then I will capture Liu Pei myself."

"Do so; and I will guard this city," said Tien.

"If you do not go with me, it is a proof that you are a traitor," retorted Ts'ao Jen.

At this reproach, Li Tien felt constrained to join the expedition. So they told off two and a half legions with which they crossed the river for Hsinyeh.

> The officers all keenly felt the shame of many slain,
> The Chief determines on revenge and marches out again.

What measure of success the expedition met with will be related in the next chapter.

CHAPTER XXXVI

CAPTURE OF FANCH'ENG:
CHUKO LIANG RECOMMENDED

In hot anger, Ts'ao Jen lost no time in marching out to avenge the loss of so many of his army. He hastily crossed the river to attack Hsingyeh and trample it in the dust.

When Tan Fu got back into the city he said to his master, "When Ts'ao Jen, now at Fanch'eng, hears of his losses, he will try to retrieve them and will come to attack us."

"What is the counter move?" asked Yuan-te.

"As he will come with all his force his own city will be left undefended; we will surprise it."

"By what ruse?"

The adviser leaned over and whispered to his chief. Whatever the plan was it pleased Yuan-te, who made arrangements. Soon the scouts reported Ts'ao Jen crossing the river with a mighty host.

"Just as I guessed," said Tan Fu, hearing of it.

Then he suggested that Yuan-te should lead out one army against the invaders. He did so, and, when the formation was complete, Chao Yun rode to the front as champion and challenged the other side.

Li Tien rode out and engaged. At about the tenth bout Li Tien found he was losing and retired toward his own side. Chao Yun pressed after him, but was checked by a heavy discharge of arrows from the wings. Then both sides stopped the battle and retired to their camps.

Li Tien reported to his chief that their opponents were brave, very full of spirit, and that they would be hard to overcome and advised a retreat on Fancheng.

Ts'ao Jen angrily replied, "You damped the men's spirits before we started, and now you betray us. You have been bought and you deserve death."

He called in the executioners and they led away their victim. But the other officers came to intercede and Tien was spared. However, he was transferred to the command of the rear, while Ts'ao Jen himself led the attack.

Next day the drums beat an advance and Ts'ao Jen, having drawn up his men, sent a messenger over to ask if his opponent recognised his plan of array. So Tan Fu went on a hill and looked over it. Then he said to Liu Pei "The arrangement is called 'The Eight Docked Gates,' and each 'gate' has a name. If you enter by one of the three named 'Birth,' 'Bellevue' and 'Expanse' you succeed; if by one of the 'gates' 'Wounds,' 'Fear,' or 'Annihilation,' you sustain injuries. The other two 'gates' are named 'Obstacles' and 'Death,' and to enter them means the end. Now, though the eight 'gates' are all there quite correct, the central 'key-post' is lacking and the formation can be thrown into confusion by entry from the south-east and exit due west."

Wherefore certain orders were issued and Chao Yun, leading half a company, rode out on his prancing steed to break the array. He burst in, as directed, at the south-east and, with great clamour and fighting, reached the centre. Ts'ao Jen made for the north, but Chao Yun, instead of following him, made a dash westward and got through. Thence he turned round to the south-east again and smote till Ts'ao Jen's army was in disarray. A general advance was signalled and the defeat was severe. The beaten enemy retired.

Tan Fu forbade pursuit and they returned.

The loss of the battle convinced Ts'ao Jen of the wisdom of his colleague and he sent for him to consult.

"They certainly have some very able person in Liu Pei's army since my formation was so quickly broken," said Ts'ao Jen.

"My chief anxiety is about Fanch'eng," said Li Tien.

"I will raid their camp this night," said Jen. "If I succeed we will decide upon what should be done next. If I fail, we will return to Fanch'eng."

"The camp will be well prepared against such a thing and you will fail," said Li.

"How can you expect to fight successfully when you are so full of doubts?" said Jen, angrily.

He held no more converse with his cautious colleague, but himself took command of the van and set out. Tien was relegated to the rear. The attack on the enemy's camp was fixed for the second watch.

Now as Tan Fu was discussing plans with his chief a whirlwind went by, which Fu said foretold a raid on the camp.

"How shall we meet it?" said Yuan-te.

"The plans are quite ready," was the reply.

He whispered them to the chief. So at the second watch, when the enemy arrived, they saw fires on all sides; the stockades and huts burning. Ts'ao Jen understood at once that all hope of a surprise was vain and he turned to get away as quickly as possible. This was the signal for Chao Yun to fall on and that cut his return road. He hastened north toward the river, and reached the bank, but, while waiting for boats to cross the stream, up came Chang Fei and attacked.

By dint of great efforts and with the support of his colleague he got into a boat, but most of the men were drowned in the stream. As soon as he got to the farther shore he bolted for Fanch'eng. He reached the wall and hailed the gate, but, instead of a friendly welcome, he heard the rolling of drums, which was soon followed by the appearance of a body of men. Kuan Yu led them.

"I took the city a long time ago," shouted Kuan Yu.

This was a severe shock to Jen, who turned to flee. As soon as he faced about Kuan Yu attacked and killed many of his men. The remnant hastened to Hsuch'ang. On the road the beaten general wondered who had advised his opponents with such success.

While the defeated general had to find his way back to the capital, Yuan-te had scored a great success. Afterwards he marched to Fanch'eng, where he was welcomed by the magistrate Liu Pi, himself a scion of the ruling family, who had been born in Changsha. He received Yuan-te as a guest in his own house and gave banquets and treated him exceedingly well.

In the train of the magistrate, Yuan-te saw a very handsome and distinguished-looking young man, and asked who he was.

Liu Pi replied, "He is my nephew, K'ou Feng, an orphan, whom I am taking care of."

Yuan-te had taken a great liking for the lad and proposed to adopt him, His guardian was willing, and so the adoption was arranged. The young man's name was changed to Liu Feng. When Yuan-te left, he took his adopted son with him. He was then made to bow before Kuan Yu and Chang Fei as uncles.

Kuan Yu was doubtful of the wisdom of adopting another son, saying, "You have a son; why do you think it neccessary to adopt another? It may cause confusion."

"How? I shall treat him as a father should and he will serve me as befits a son."

Kuan Yu was displeased. Then Yuan-te and Tan Fu began further discussions of strategy and they decided to leave a guard in Fanch'eng and to return to Hsinyeh.

In the meantime Ts'ao Ts'ao's defeated generals had gone back. When they saw the Minister, Ts'ao Jen threw himself on the ground weeping and acknowledging his faults. He told the tale of his losses.

"The fortune of war," said Ts'ao Ts'ao. "But I should like to know who laid Liu Pei's plans."

"That was Tan Fu," said Jen.

Ch'eng Yu said, "The man is not Tan Fu. When young this man was fond of fencing and used to take up the quarrels of other men and avenge their wrongs. Once, after killing his man, he let down his hair, muddied his face and was trying to escape when a lictor caught him and questioned him. He would not reply. So they carted him through the streets beating a drum and asking if any one recognised him. Nobody dared own to knowing him, if they did so. However, his companions managed to release him secretly and he ran away under some other name. Then he turned to study and wandered hither and thither wherever scholars were to be found. He was a regular disputant with Ssuma Hui. His real name is Hsu Shu (Yuan-chih) and he comes from Yingchou. Tan Fu is merely an assumed name."

"How does he compare with yourself?" asked Ts'ao.

"Ten times cleverer."

"It is a pity. If able men gather to Liu Pei his wings will soon grow. What is to be done?"

"Hsu Shu is there now; but if you wanted him it would not be difficult to call him," replied Hsun Yu.

"How could I make him come?" said Ts'ao.

"He is noted for his affection for his mother. His father died young, leaving his mother a widow with one other son. Now that son is dead and his mother has no one to care for her. If you sent and got his mother here and told her to write and summon her son he would surely come."

Ts'ao sent without loss of time and had the old lady brought to the capital, where he treated her exceedingly well. Presently he said, "I hear you have a very talented son, who is now at Hsinyeh helping on that rebel Liu Pei against the government. There he is like a jewel in a muck-heap; it is a pity. Supposing you were to call him, I could speak of him before the Emperor and he might get an important office."

Ts'ao bade his secretaries bring along the "four precious things of the study," with which the dame could write to her son.

"What sort of a man is Liu Pei?" asked she.

Ts'ao replied, "A common sort of person from P'eichun, irresponsible enough to style himself Imperial Uncle, and so claiming some sort of connection with the Hans. He is neither trustworthy nor virtuous. People say he is a superior man as far as externals go, but a mean man by nature."

The dame answered in a hard voice, "Why do you malign him so bitterly? Every one knows he is a descendant of one of the Han Princes and so related to the House. He has condescended to take a lowly office and is respectful to all men. He has a reputation for benevolence. Every one, young and old, cowherds and firewood cutters, all know him by name and know that he is the finest and noblest man in the world. If my son is in his service, then has he found a fitting master. You, under the name of a Han minister, are really nothing but a Han rebel. Contrary to all truth you tell me Yuan-te is a rebel, whereby you try to induce me to make my son leave the light for darkness. Are you devoid of all sense of shame?"

As she finished speaking she picked up the inkstone to strike Ts'ao Ts'ao. This so enraged him that he forgot himself and the need for caution and bade the executioners lead off the old woman and put her to death. The adviser Ch'eng Yu, however, stopped this act of folly by pointing out the effect it would have on his reputation and how it would enhance hers, beside adding a keen desire for revenge to the motives which led Hsu Shu to labour in the interest of Liu Pei. He closed his remarks saying, "You had better keep her here so that Hsu Shu's body and his thoughts may be in different places. He can not devote all his energies to helping our enemy while his mother is here. If you keep her I think I can persuade the son to come and help you."

So the outspoken old lady was saved. She was given quarters and cared for. Daily Ch'eng Yu went to ask after her health, falsely claiming to being a sworn brother of her son's, and so entitled to serve her and treat her as a filial son would have done. He often sent her gifts and wrote letters to her so that she had to write in reply. And thereby he learned her handwriting so that he could forge a "home" letter. When he could do this without fear of detection he wrote one and sent it by the hand of a trusty person to Hsinyeh.

One day a man arrived enquiring for one Tan Fu, a secretary; he had a letter from home for him. The soldiers led him to Tan Fu. The man said he was an official carrier of letters and had been told to bring this one. Tan Fu quickly tore it open and read:—

"On your brother's death recently I was left alone; no relative was near and I was lonely and sad. To my regret, the Minister Ts'ao Ts'ao inveigled me into coming to the capital, and now he says you are a rebel and he has thrown me into bonds. However, thanks to Ch'eng Yu, my life has been spared so far, and, if you would only come and submit too, I should be quite safe. When this reaches you, remember how I have toiled for you and come at once, that you may prove yourself a filial son. We may together find some way of escape to our own place and avoid the dangers that threaten me. My life hangs by a thread and I look to you to save me. You will not require a second summons."

Tears gushed from Hsu Shu's eyes as he read, and with the letter in his hand he went to seek his chief, to whom he told the true story of his life and how he had joined Yuan-te. "I heard that Liu Piao treated men well and went to him. I happened to arrive at a time of confusion. I saw he was of no use, so I left him very soon. I arrived at the retreat of Ssuma Shui-ching ('Water-mirror') late one night and told him, and he blamed me for not knowing a master when I saw one. Then he told me of you and I sang that wild song in the streets to attract your attention. You took me; you used me. But now my aged mother is the victim of Ts'ao Ts'ao's wiles. She is in prison and he threatens to do worse. She has written to call me and I must go. I hoped to be able to render you faithful service, but, with my dear mother a captive, I should be useless. Therefore I must leave you and hope in the future to meet you again."

Yuan-te broke into loud moans when he heard that his adviser was to leave.

"The bond between mother and son is divine," said he, "and I do not need to be reminded where your duty lies. When you have seen your venerable mother perhaps I may have again the happiness of receiving y our instruction."

Having said farewell, Hsu Shu prepared to leave at once. However, at Yuan-te's wish he consented to stay over the night.

Then Sun Ch'ien said privately to his master, "Hsu Shu is indeed a genius, but he has been here long enough to know all our secrets. If you let him go over to Ts'ao, he will be in his confidence and that will be to our detriment. You ought to keep him at all costs and not let him go. When Ts'ao sees he does not come he will put the mother to death, and that will make Hsu Shu the more zealous in your service, for he will burn to avenge his mother's death."

"I cannot do that. It would be very cruel and vile to procure the death of his mother that I might retain the son's services. If I kept him it would lead to a rupture of the parental lien, and that would be a sin I would rather die than commit."

Both were grieved and sighed. Yuan-te asked the parting guest to a banquet, but he declined saying, "With my mother a prisoner I can swallow nothing, nay, though it were brewed from gold or distilled from jewels."

"Alas! your departure is as if I lost both my hands," said Yuan-te. "Even the liver of a dragon or the marrow of a phoenix would be bitter in my mouth."

They looked into each other's eyes and wept. They sat silent till dawn. When all was ready for the journey the two rode out of the city side by side. At Long Pavilion they dismounted to drink the stirrup cup. Yuan-te lifted the goblet and said, "It is my mean fortune that separates me from you, but I hope that you may serve well your new lord and become famous."

Hsu Shu wept as he replied, "I am but a poor ignorant person whom you have kindly employed. Unhappily I have to break our intercourse in the middle, but my venerable mother is the real cause. Though Ts'ao Ts'ao use all manner of means to coerce me, yet will I never plan for him."

"After you are gone I shall only bury myself in the hills and hide in the forests," said Yuan-te.

Tan Fu said, "I had in my heart for you the position of leader of the chieftains, but my plans have been altogether upset by my mother. I have been of no advantage to you nor should I do any good by remaining. But you ought to seek some man of lofty wisdom to help you in your great emprise. It is unseemly to be downcast."

"I shall find none to help better than you, my master."

"How can I permit such extravagant praise?" said Tan Fu. "I am only a useless blockhead."

As he moved off he said to the followers, "Officers, I hope you will render the Princely One good service, whereby to write his name large in the country's annals and cause his fame to glow in the pages of history. Do not be like me, a man who has left his work half done."

They were all deeply affected. Yuan-te could not bring himself to part from his friend. He escorted him a little further, and yet a little further, till Shu said, "I will not trouble you, O Princely One, to come further. Let us say our farewell here."

Yuan-te dismounted, took Hsu Shu by the hands and said, "Alas! we part. Each goes his way and who knows if we shall meet again?"

His tears fell like rain and Shu wept also. But the last goodbyes were said and when the traveller had gone Yuan-te stood gazing after the little party and watched it slowly disappear. At the last glimpse he broke into lamentation.

"He is gone! What shall I do?"

One of the trees shut out the travellers from his sight and he testily pointed at it, saying, "Would that I could cut down every tree in the countryside!"

"Why?" said his men.

"Because they hinder my sight of Hsu Yuan-chih."

Suddenly they saw Hsu Shu galloping back.

Said Yuan-te, "He is returning; can it be that he is going to stay?"

So he hastened forward to meet him and when they got near enough he cried, "This return is surely for no slight reason."

Checking his horse, Hsu Shu said, "In the turmoil of my feelings I forgot to say one word. There is a man of wonderful skill living about twenty *li* from the city of Hsiangyang, why not seek him?"

"Can I trouble you to ask him to visit me?"

"He will not condescend to visit you; you must go to him. But if he consent you will be as fortunate as the Chous when they got the aid of Lu Wang, or Han when Chang Liang came to help."

"How does the unknown compare with yourself?"

"With me? Compared with him I am as a worn-out cart-horse to a *kilin*, an old crow to a phoenix. This man is of the same kidney as Kuan Chung and Yo I but, in my opinion, he is far their superior. He has the talent to measure the heavens and mete the earth; he is a man who overshadows every other in the world."

"I would know his name."

"He belongs to Yangtu of Langya; and his name, a double name, is Chuko Liang. His minor name is K'ung-ming. He is of good family. His father was an official but died young and the young fellow went with his uncle to Chingchou, the Prefect of which was an old friend of his uncle's, and he became settled there. Then his uncle died and he, with a younger brother, Chun, were farmers. They used to amuse themselves with the composition of songs in the 'Old Father Liang' style.

"On their land was a ridge of hills called the Sleeping Dragon and the elder of the two took it as a name and called himself 'Master Sleeping Dragon.' This is your man; he is a veritable genius. You ought really to visit him and if he will help you, you need feel no more anxiety about peace in the Empire."

"'Water-mirror' spoke that time of two men, Fu-lung and Feng-ch'u, and said if only one of them could be got to help me all would be well. Surely he, whom you speak of, is one of them."

"Feng-ch'u, or 'Phoenix Fledging,' is 'P'ang T'ung': and Fu-lung, or 'Hidden Dragon,' is 'Chako K'ung-ming.'"

Yuan-te jumped with delight, "Now at last I know who the mysterious ones are. How I wish they were here! But for you I should have still been like a blind man," said he.

Some one has celebrated in verse this interview where Hsu Shu from horseback recommended K'ung-ming:—

> Yuan-te heard that his able friend
> Must leave him, with saddened heart,
> For each to the other had grown very dear,
> Both wept when it came to part.
> But the parting guest then mentioned a name
> That echoed both loud and deep,
> Like a thunder clap in a spring-time sky,
> And there wakened a dragon from sleep.

Thus was the famous K'ung-ming recommended to the lord he was to serve, and Hsu Shu rode away.

Now Yuan-te understood the speech of the hermit Ssuma Hui, and he woke as one from a drunken sleep. At the head of his officers, he retook the road to the city and having prepared rich gifts set out, with his brothers, for Nanyang.

Under the influence of his emotions at parting Hsu Shu had mentioned the name and betrayed the retreat of his friend Now he thought of the possibility that K'ung-ming would be unwilling to play the part of helper in Yuan-te's scheme, so he determined to go to visit him. He therefore took his way to Reposing Dragon Ridge and dismounted at the cottage. Asked why he had come, he replied, "I wished to serve Liu Pei of Hsiangchou but my mother has been imprisoned by Ts'ao Ts'ao, and has sent to call me. Therefore I have had to leave him. At the moment of parting I commended you to him. You may expect him speedily and I hope, Sir, you will not refuse your aid but will consent to use your great talents to help him."

K'ung-ming showed annoyance and said, "And so you have made me the victim of your sacrifice."

So saying he shook out his sleeves and left the room. The guest shamefacedly retired, mounted his horse and hastened on his way to the capital to see his mother.

To help the lord he loved right well,
  He summoned the aid of another,
When he took the distant homeward way,
  At the call of a loving mother.

What was the sequel will appear in the following chapters.

CHAPTER XXXVII

ANOTHER SCHOLAR INTRODUCED:
THE THREE VISITS TO THE RECLUSE

As has been said Hsu Shu hastened to the capital. When Ts'ao
Ts'ao knew he had arrived he sent two of his confidants to
receive him and so he was led first to the minister's palace.

"Why did such an illustrious scholar as you bow the knee to Liu
Pei?" said Ts'ao.

"I am young and I fled to avoid the results of certain escapades.
I spent some time as a wanderer and so came to Hsinyeh where I
became good friends with him. But my mother is here and when I
thought of all her affection I could no longer remain absent."

"Now you will be able to take care of your mother at all times.
And I may have the privilege of receiving your instruction."

"Hsu Shu then took his leave and hastened to his mother's
dwelling. Weeping with emotion he made his obeisance to her at
the door of her room.

But she was greatly surprised to see him and said, "What have
you come here for?"

"I was at Hsinyeh, in the service of Liu of Yuchou when I
received your letter. I came immediately."

His mother suddenly grew very angry. Striking the table she
cried, "You shameful and degenerate son! For years you have been a
vagabond in spite of all my teaching. You are a student and know
the books. You must then know that loyalty and filial piety are
often opposed. Did you not recognise in Ts'ao a traitor, a man who
flouts his king and insults the mighty ones? Did you not see that Liu
Pei was virtuous and upright as all the world knows? Moreover, he
is of the House of Han and when you were with him you were
serving a fitting master. Now on the strength of a scrap of forged
writing, with no attempt at any enquiry, you have left the light and
plunged into darkness and earned a disgraceful reputation. Truly

you are stupid! How can I bear to look upon you? You have besmirched the fair fame of your forefathers and are of no use in the world."

The son remained bowed to the earth, not daring to lift his eyes while his mother delivered thing vilifying tirade. As she said the last word she rose suddenly and left the room. Soon after one of the servants came out to say she had hanged herself Her son rushed in to try to save her, but was too late.

A eulogy of her conduct has been written thus:—

> Wise Mother Hsu, fair is your fame,
> The storied page glows with your name,
> From duty's path You never strayed,
> The family's renown you made.
> To train your son no pains you spared,
> For your own body nothing cared.
> You stand sublime, from us apart,
> Through simple purity of heart.
> Brave Liu Pei's virtues you extolled,
> You blamed Ts'ao Ts'ao, the basely bold.
> Of blazing fire you felt no fear,
> You blenched not when the sword came near,
> But dreaded lest a wilful son
> Should dim the fame his fathers won.
> Yes, Mother Hsu was of one mould
> With famous heroines of old,
> Who never shrank from injury,
> And even were content to die.
> Fair meed of praise, while still alive,
> Was yours, and ever will survive.
> Hail! Mother Hsu, your memory,
> While time rolls on, shall never die.

At sight of his mother dead Hsu Shu fell in a swoon and only recovered consciousness after a long time. By and bye Ts'ao heard of it and sent mourning gifts, and in due course went in person to condole and sacrifice. The body was interred on the south of the capital and the dead woman's unhappy son kept vigil at her tomb. He steadily rejected all gifts from Ts'ao Ts'ao.

At that time Ts'ao was contemplating an attack on the south. His advisers dissuaded him, saying he should await milder weather; and he yielded. But he began to prepare, and led the river waters aside to form a lake, which he called the Training Lake, where he could accustom his men to fight on the water.

As has been said Yuan-te prepared gifts to offer to Chuko Liang on his visit. One day his servants announced a stranger of extraordinary appearance, wearing a lofty head-dress and a wide belt.

"Surely this is he" said Yuan-te, and, hastily arranging his dress, he went to welcome the visitor. But the first glance showed him that it was the recluse of the mountains, Ssuma Hui. However, Yuan-te was glad to see him and led him into the inner apartment as he would an old friend. There Pei conducted him to the seat of honour and made his obeisance, saying, "Since leaving you that day in the mountains I have been overwhelmed with military preparations and so have failed to visit you as courtesy demanded. Now that the brightness has descended upon me I hope this dereliction of duty may be pardoned."

"I hear Hsu Yuan-chih is here. I have come expressly to see him," replied the visitor bluntly.

"He has lately left for Hsuch'ang. A messenger came with a letter telling of the imprisonment of his mother."

"Then he has just fallen into Ts'ao Ts'ao's trap, for that letter was a forgery. I have always known his mother to be a very noble woman, and even if she were imprisoned by Ts'ao she would not summon her son like that. Certainly the letter was a forgery. If the son did not go, the mother would be safe; if he went, she would be a dead woman."

"But how?" asked Yuan-te, dismayed.

"She is a woman of the highest principles, who would be greatly mortified at the sight of her son under such conditions."

Liu Pei said, "Just as your friend was leaving he mentioned the name of a certain Chuko Liang. What think you of him?"

Hui laughed, saying, "If Yuan-chih wanted to go, he was free to go. But why did he want to provoke *him* into coming out and showing compassion for some one else?"

"Why do you speak like that?" asked Yuan-te.

He replied, "Five men, K'ung-ming, Ts'ui Chou-p'ing, Shih Kuang-yuan, Meng Kung-wei and Hsu Yuan-chih were the closest of friends. They formed a little coterie devoted to meditation on essential refinement. Only K'ung-ming arrived at a perception of its meaning. He used to sit among them with his arms about his knees muttering and then, pointing to his companions, he would say, 'You, gentlemen, would become governors and prefects if you were in official life.'

"When they asked him what was his ambition he would only smile and always compared himself with the great scholars Kuan Chung and Yo I. No one could gauge his talents."

"How comes it that Yingchou produces so many able men?" said Yuan-te.

"That old astrologer, Yin K'uei, used to say that the stars clustered thick over the district and so there were many wise men."

Now Kuan Yu was there and when he heard K'ung-ming so highly praised he said, "Kuan Chung and Yo I are the two most famous men mentioned in the 'Spring and Autumn.' They well overtopped the rest of mankind. Is it not a little too much to say that K'ung-ming compares with these two?"

"In my opinion he should not be compared with these two, but rather with two others," said Hui.

"Who are these two?" asked Kuan Yu.

"One of them is Chiang Tzu-ya, who laid the foundations of the Chou dynasty so firmly that it lasted eight hundred years, and the other Chang Tzu-fang, who made Han glorious for four centuries."

Before the surprise called forth by this startling statement had subsided, the visitor walked down the steps and took his leave. Liu Pei would have kept him if he could, but he was obdurate. As he stalked proudly away he threw up his head and said, "Though the 'Sleeping Dragon' has found his lord, he has not been born at the right time. It is a pity."

"What a wise hermit!" was Liu Pei's comment.

Soon after the three brothers set out to find the abode of the wise man. When they drew near the spot they saw a number of peasants in a field hoeing up the weeds, and as they worked they sang:—

> "The earth is a chequered board,
> And the sky hangs over all,
> Under it men are contending,
> Some rise, but a many fall.
> For those who succeed 'tis well,
> But for those who go under rough.
> There's a dozing dragon hard by,
> But his sleep is n't deep enough."

They stopped to listen to the song and, calling up one of the peasants, asked who made it.

"It was made by Master 'Sleeping Dragon,'" said the labourer.

"Then he lives hereabout. Where?"

"South of this hill there is a ridge called The Sleeping Dragon and close by is a sparse wood. In it stands a modest cottage. That is where Master Chuko takes his repose."

Yuan-te thanked him and the party rode on. Soon they came to the ridge, most aptly named, for indeed it lay wrapped in an atmosphere of calm beauty.

A poet wrote of it thus:—

> Not far from Hsiangyang's massive walls
> There stands, clear cut against the sky,
> A lofty ridge, and at its foot
> A gentle stream goes gliding by.
>
> The contour, curving up and down,
> Although by resting cloud it's marred,
> Arrests the eye; and here and there
> The flank by waterfalls is scarred.
>
> There, like a sleeping dragon coiled,
> Or phoenix hid among thick pines,
> You see, secure from prying eyes,
> A cot, reed-built on rustic lines.
>
> The rough-joined doors, unshed by the wind,
> Swing idly open and disclose
> The greatest genius of the world
> Enjoying still his calm repose.
>
> The air is full of woodland scents,
> Around are hedgerows trim and green,
> Close-growing intercrossed bamboos
> Replace the painted doorway screen.
> But look within and books you see
> By every couch, near every chair;
> And you may guess that common men
> Are very seldom welcomed there.
> The hut seems far from human ken,
> So far, one might expect to find
> Wild forest denizens there, trained
> To serve in place of human kind.
> Without a hoary crane might stand
> As warden of the outer gate;
> Within a long-armed gibbon come
> To offer fruit upon a plate.
> But enter; there refinement reigns;

Brocaded silk the lutes protect,
And burnished weapons on the walls
The green of pines outside reflect.
For he who dwells within that hut
Is talented beyond compare,
Although he lives the simple life
And harvest seems his only care.
He waits until the thund'rous call
Shall bid him wake, nor sleep again;
Then will he forth and at his word
Peace over all the land shall reign.

Yuan-te soon arrived at the door of the retreat, dismounted and knocked at the rough door of the cottage. A youth appeared and asked what he wanted.

Yuan-te replied, "I am Liu Pei, General of the Han Dynasty, Marquis of Ichengt'ing, Magistrate of Yuchou and Uncle of the Emperor. I am come to salute the Master."

"I cannot remember so many titles," said the lad.

"Then simply say that Liu Pei has come to enquire after him."

"The master left this morning early."

"Whither has he gone?"

"His movements are very uncertain. I do not know whither he has gone."

"When will he return?"

"That also is uncertain. Perhaps in three days, perhaps in ten."

The disappointment was keen.

"Let us go back since we cannot see him," said Chang Fei.

"Wait a little time," said Yuan-te.

"It would be better to return," said Kuan Yu, "then we might send to find out when this man had come back."

So Yuan-te agreed, first saying to the boy, "When the master returns, tell him that Liu Pei has been."

They rode away. Presently Liu Pei stopped and looked back at the surroundings of the little cottage in the wood. The mountains were picturesque rather than grand, the water clear rather than profound, the plain was level rather than extensive, the woods luxuriant rather than extensive. Gibbons ranged through the trees and cranes waded in the shallow water. The pines and the bamboos vied with each other in verdure. It was a scene to linger upon.

While Liu Pei stood regarding it, he saw a figure coming down a mountain path. The man's bearing was lofty; he was handsome and dignified. He wore a comfortable-looking bonnet on his head and a black robe hung about his figure in easy folds. He used a staff to help him down the steep path.

"Surely that is he!" said Yuan-te.

He dismounted and walked over to greet the stranger, whom he saluted deferentially, saying, "Are you not Master Sleeping Dragon, Sir?"

"Who are you, General?" said the stranger.

"I am Liu Pei."

"I am not K'ung-ming, but I am a friend of his. My name is Ts'ui Chou-p'ing."

"Long have I known of you! I am very glad to see you, replied Yuan-te. "And now I pray you to be seated just where we are and let me receive your instruction."

The two men sat down in the wood on a stone and the two brothers ranged themselves by Liu Pei's side.

Chou-p'ing began, saying, "General, for what reason do you wish to see K'ung-ming?"

Liu Pei replied, "The Empire is in confusion and troubles gather everywhere. I want your friend to tell me how to restore order."

"You, Sir, wish to arrest the present disorder although you are a kindly man and, from the oldest antiquity, the correction of disorder has demanded stern measures. On the day that the founder of the Han dynasty first put his hand to the work and slew the wicked ruler of Ts'in, order began to replace disorder. Good government began with The Founder, (206 B.C.), and endured two hundred years; two centuries of tranquillity. Then came Wang Mang's rebellion and disorder took the place of order. Anon, arose Kuang-Wu, who restored the Dynasty, and order once more prevailed. We have had two centuries of order and tranquillity, and the time of trouble and battles is due. The restoration of peace will take time; it cannot be quickly accomplished. You, Sir, wish to get K'ung-ming to regulate times and seasons, to repair the cosmos; but I fear the task is indeed difficult and to attempt it would be a vain expenditure of mental energy. You know well that he who goes with the favour of Heaven travels an easy road, he who goes contrary meets difficulties. One cannot escape one's lot; one cannot evade fate."

"Master," replied Pei, "your insight is indeed deep and your words of wide meaning, but I am a scion of the House of Han and must help it. Dare I talk of the inevitable and trust to fate?"

Chou-p'ing replied, "A simple denizen of the mountain wilds is unfitted to discuss the affairs of Empire. But you bade me speak and I have spoken; perhaps somewhat madly."

"Master, I am grateful for your instruction. But know you whither K'ung-ming has gone?"

"I also came to see him and I know not where he is," said Chou-p'ing.

"If I asked you, Master, to accompany me to my poor bit of territory, would you come?"

"I am too dilatory, too fond of leisure and ease, and no longer have any ambitions. But I will see you another time."

And with these words he saluted and left.

The three brothers also mounted and started homeward. Presently Chang Fei said, "We have not found K'ung-ming and we have had to listen to the wild ravings of this so-called scholar. There is the whole result of this journey."

"His words were those of a deep thinker," replied Yuan-te.

Some days after the return to Hsinyeh, Yuan-te sent to find out whither K'ung-ming had returned and the messenger came back saying that he had. Wherefore Liu Pei prepared for another visit. Again Chang Fei showed his irritation by remarking, "Why must you go hunting after this villager? Send and tell him to come."

"Silence!" said Yuan-te, "The Teacher Meng, (Mencius) said, 'To try to see the sage without going his way is like barring a door you wish to enter.' K'ung-ming is the greatest sage of the day; how can I summon him?"

So Yuan-te rode away to make his visit, his two brothers with him as before. It was winter and exceedingly cold; angry clouds covered the whole sky. Before they had gone far a bitter wind began to blow in their faces and the snow began to fall. Soon the mountains were of jade and the trees of silver.

"It is very cold and the earth is frozen hard, no fighting is possible now." Said Chang Fei. "Yet we are going all this way to get advice which will be useless to us. Where is the sense of it? Let us rather get back to Hsinyeh out of the cold."

Yuan-te replied, "I am set upon proving my zeal to K'ung-ming, but if you, my brother, do not like the cold, you can return."

"I do not fear death; do you think I care for the cold? But I do care about wasting my brother's energies," said Chang Fei.

"Say no more," said Yuan-te, and they travelled on.

When they drew near the little wood they heard singing in a roadside inn and stopped to listen. This was the song:—

Although possessed of talent rare,
 This man has made no name;
Alas! the day is breaking late
 That is to show his fame.
 O friends you know the tale:
Th' aged man constrained to leave
 His cottage by the sea,
To follow in a prince's train
 His counsellor to be.
Eight hundred feudal chieftains met
 Who came with one accord;
The happy omen, that white fish,
 That leapt the boat aboard;
The gory field in distant wilds,
 Whence flowed a crimson tide,
And him acknowledged chief in war
 Whose virtues none denied;
That Kaoyang rustic, fond of wine,
 Who left his native place
And went to serve so faithfully
 The man of handsome face;
And one who spoke of ruling chiefs
 In tones so bold and free,
But sitting at the festive board
 Was full of courtesy;
And one, 'twas he who laid in dust
 Walled cities near four score—
But men of doughty deeds like these
 On earth are seen no more.
Now had these men not found their lord
 Would they be known to fame?
Yet having found, they served him well
 And so achieved a name.

The song ended, the singer's companion tapping the table sang:—

We had a famous emperor,
 Who drew his shining sword,
Cleansed all the land within the seas
 And made himself its lord.
In time his son succeeded him,
 And so from son to son
The lordship passed, held firm until

Four hundred years had run.
Then dawned a day of weaklier sons,
    The fiery virtue failed,
Then ministers betrayed their trust,
    Court intrigues vile prevailed.
The omens came; a serpent black
    Coiled on the dragon throne,
While in the hall of audience
    Unholy haloes shone.
Now bandits swarm in all the land
    And noble strives with chief,
The common people, sore perplexed,
    Can nowhere find relief.
Let's drown our sorrows in the cup,
    Be happy while we may,
Let those who wish run after fame
    That is to last for aye.

The two men laughed loud and clapped their hands as the second singer ceased. Yuan-te thought full surely the longed for sage was there, so he dismounted and entered the inn. He saw the two merry-makers sitting opposite each other at a table. One was pale with a long beard; the other had a strikingly refined face. Yuan-te saluted them and said, "Which of you is Master Sleeping Dragon?"

"Who are you, Sir?" asked the long-bearded one. "What business have you with Sleeping Dragon?"

"I am Liu Pei. I want to enquire of him how to restore tranquillity to the world."

"Well, neither of us is your man, but we are friends of his. My name is Shih Kuang-yuan and my friend here is Meng Kung-wei."

"I know you both by reputation," said Yuan-te smiling. "I am indeed fortunate to meet you in this haphazard way. Will you not come to the Sleeping Dragon's retreat and talk for a time? I have horses here for you."

"We idle folk of the wilds know nothing of tranquillising States. Do not trouble to ask, please. Pray mount again and go your way in search of Sleeping Dragon."

So he remounted and went his way. He reached the little cottage, dismounted and tapped at the door. The same lad answered his knock and he asked whether the Master had returned.

"He is in his room reading," said the boy.

Joyful indeed was Liu Pei as he followed the lad in. In front of the middle door he saw written this pair of scrolls:—

> By purity manifest the inclination:
> By repose affect the distant.

As he was looking at this couplet he heard some one singing in a subdued voice and stopped by the door to peep in. He saw a young man close to a charcoal brazier, hugging his knees while he sang:—

> The phoenix flies high, ah me!
> And only will perch on a *wutung* tree.
> The scholar is hid, ah me!
> Till his lord appear he can patient be.
> He tills his fields, ah me!
> He is well-content and I love my home,
> He awaits his day, ah me!
> His books and his lute to leave and roam.

As the song ended Yuan-te advanced and saluted saying, "Master, long have I yearned for you, but have found it impossible to salute you. Lately one Hsu spoke of you and I hastened to your dwelling, only to come away disappointed. This time I have braved the elements and come again and my reward is here; I see your face, and I am indeed fortunate."

"The young man hastily returned the salute and said, "General, you must be that Liu Pei of Yuchou who wishes to see my brother."

"Then, Master, you are not the Sleeping Dragon!" said Yuan-te, starting back.

"I am his younger brother, Chun. He has an elder brother, Chin, now with Sun in Chiangtung as a secretary. K'ung-ming is the second of our family."

"Is your brother at home?"

"Only yesterday he arranged to go a jaunt with Ts'ui Chou-p'ing."

"Whither have they gone?"

"Who can say? They may take a boat and sail away among the lakes, or go to gossip with the priests in some remote mountain temple, or wander off to visit a friend in some far away village, or be sitting in some cave with a lute or a chessboard. Their goings and comings are uncertain and nobody can guess at them."

"What very poor luck have I! Twice have I failed to meet the great sage."

"Pray sit a few moments and let me offer you some tea."

"Brother, since the master is not here I pray you remount and go," said Chang Fei.

"Since I am here, why not a little talk before we go home again?" said Yuan-te.

Then turning to his host he continued, "Can you tell me if your worthy brother is skilled in strategy and studies works on war?"

"I do not know."

"This is worse than the other," grumbled Chang Fei. "And the wind and snow are getting worse; we ought to go back."

Yuan-te turned on him angrily and told him to stop.

Chun said, "Since my brother is absent I will not presume to detain you longer. I will return your call soon."

"Please do not take that trouble. In a few days I will come again. But if I could borrow paper and pencil I would leave a note to show your worthy brother that I am zealous and earnest."

Chun produced the "four treasures" of the scholar and Yuan-te, thawing out the frozen brush between his lips, spread the sheet of delicate note-paper and wrote:—

"Pei has long admired your fame. He has visited your dwelling twice, but to his great disappointment he has gone empty away. He humbly remembers that he is a distant relative of the Emperor, that he has undeservedly enjoyed fame and rank. When he sees the proper government wrested aside and replaced by pretence, the foundation of the State crumbling away, hordes of bravos creating confusion in the country and an evil cabal behaving unseemly toward the rightful Prince, then his heart and gall are torn to shreds. Though he has a real desire to assist, yet is he deficient in the needful skill. Wherefore he turns to the Master, trusting in his kindness, graciousness, loyalty and righteousness. Would the Master but use his talent, equal to that of Lu Wang, and perform great deeds like Chang Tzu-fang, then would the Empire be happy and the throne would be secure."

"This is written to tell you that, after purification of mind with fasting and of body with fragrant baths, Pei will come again to prostrate himself in your honoured presence and receive enlightenment."

The letter written and given to Chun, Yuan-te took his leave, exceedingly disappointed at this second failure. As he was mounting he saw the serving lad waving his hand outside the hedge and heard him call out, "The old Master is coming".

Yuan-te looked and then saw a figure seated on a donkey leisurely jogging along over a bridge.

The rider of the donkey wore a cap with long flaps down to his shoulders and his body was wrapped in a fox fur robe. A youth followed him bearing a jar of wine. As he came through the snow he hummed a song:—

> 'Tis eve, the sky is overcast,
> The north wind comes with icy blast,
> Light snowflakes whirl adown until
> A white pall covers dale and hill.
> Perhaps above the topmost sky
> White dragons strive for mastery,
> The armour scales from their forms riven
> Are scattered o'er the world wind-driven.
> Amid the storm there jogs along
> A simple wight who croons a song.
> "O poor plum trees, the gale doth tear
> Your blossoms off and leave you bare."

"Here at last is the Sleeping Dragon," thought Yuan-te, hastily slipping out of the saddle. He saluted the donkey rider as he neared and said, "Master, it is hard to make way against this cold wind. I and my companions have been waiting long."

The rider got off his donkey and returned the bow, while Chuko Chun from behind said, "This is not my brother; it is his father-in-law, Huang Ch'eng-yen."

Yuan-te said, "I chanced to hear the song you were singing; it is very beautiful."

Ch'eng-yen replied, "It is a little poem I read in my son-in-law's house and I recalled it as I crossed the bridge and saw the plum trees in the hedge. And so it happened to catch your ear, noble Sir."

"Have you seen your son-in-law lately?" asked Yuan-te.

"That is just what I have come to do now."

At this Yuan-te bade him farewell and went on his way. The storm was very grievous to bear, but worse than the storm was the grief in his heart as he looked back at Sleeping Dragon Ridge.

> One winter's day through snow and wind
> A prince rode forth the sage to find;
> Alas! his journey was in vain,
> And sadly turned he home again.
>
> The stream stood still beneath the bridge
> A sheet of ice draped rock and ridge,
> His steed benumbed with biting cold
> But crawled as he were stiff and old.

The snow-flakes on the rider's head
Were like pear-blossoms newly shed,
Or like the willow-catkins light
They brushed his cheek in headlong flight.

He stayed his steed, he looked around,
The snow lay thick on tree and mound,
The Sleeping Dragon Ridge lay white
A hill of silver, glistening bright.

After the return to Hsinyeh the time slipped away till spring was near. Then Yuan-te east lots to find the propitious day for another journey in search of the sage. The day being selected he fasted for three days and then changed his dress ready for the visit. His two brothers viewed the preparations with disapproval and presently made up their minds to remonstrate.

The sage and the fighting man never agree,
A warrior despises humility.

The next chapter will tell what they said.

CHAPTER XXXVIII

PLAN FOR THREE KINGDOMS: THE SUNS AVENGE THEMSELVES

Nothing discouraged by two unsuccessful visits to the retreat of the sage whose advice he sought to secure, Liu Pei made preparations for a third visit. His brothers disapproved, and Kuan Yu said, "Brother, you have sought him twice, surely this is showing even too much deference. I do not believe in this fame of his for learning; he is avoiding you and dare not submit to the test. Why so obstinately hold this idea?"

"You are wrong, my brother. Duke Huan of Ch'i paid five visits to the 'Hermit of the Eastern Suburb' before he got to see his face. And my desire to see the sage is even greater than his."

"I think you are mistaken," said Chang Fei. "How can this villager be such a marvel of wisdom? You should not go again and, if he will not come, I will bring him with a hempen rope."

"Have you forgotten the great Prince Wen's visit to Chiang Tzu-ya, the old man of the Eastern Sea? If he could show such deference to a wise man, where am I too deferential? If you will not go, your brother and I will go without you," said Yuan-te.

If you two go, how can I hang back?" said Chang Fei.

"If you go, then you must be polite."

Fei said he would not forget himself, and the three set out. When they were half a *li* from the little cottage, Yuan-te dismounted, deciding to show his respect by approaching the house on foot. Very soon he met Chuko Chun, whom he saluted with great deference, enquiring whether his brother was at home.

"He returned last evening; you can see him today, General."

As he said this he went off with some swagger.

"Fortune favours me this time," said Yuan-te, "I am going to see the master."

"That was a rude fellow", said Fei, "it would not have hurt him to have conducted us to the house. Why did he go off like that?"

"Each one has his own affairs," said his brother. "What power have we over him?"

Soon the three stood at the door and they knocked. The serving lad came out and asked their business and Yuan-te said very deferentially, "I would trouble the servant of the genius, gentle page, to inform the Master that Liu Pei wishes to pay his respects to him."

"My Master is at home, but he is asleep."

"In that case do not announce me."

He bade his two brothers wait at the door quietly and he himself entered with careful steps. There was the man he sought, lying asleep on the couch, stretched on a simple mat. Yuan-te saluted him with joined hands at a respectful distance.

The time passed and still the sleeper did not wake. The two brothers left without, beginning to feel impatient, also came in and Chang Fei was annoyed at seeing his revered elder brother respectfully standing by while another slept.

"What an arrogant fellow is this Master?" said he. "There is our brother waiting, while he sleeps on perfectly carelessly. I will go to the back of the place and let off a bomb and see if that will rouse him."

"No, no; you must do nothing of the kind," whispered Kuan Yu, and then Yuan-te told them to go out again.

Just then he noticed that the Master moved. He turned over as though about to rise, but, instead, he faced the wall and again fell asleep. The serving lad made as if he would rouse his master, but Yuan-te forbade him to be disturbed and he waited yet another weary hour. Then K'ung-ming woke up repeating to himself the lines:—

> "Can any know what fate is his?
> Yet have I felt throughout my life,
> The day would come at last to quit
> The calm retreat for toil and strife."

As he finished he turned to the lad saying, "Have any of the usual people come?"

"Liu, the Uncle of the Emperor is here," said the boy. "He has been waiting some time."

"Why did you not tell me?" said he, rising from the couch. "I must dress."

He rose and turned into a room behind to dress. In a short time he re-appeared, his clothing properly arranged, to receive his visitor.

Then Yuan-te saw coming toward him a man rather below medium height with a refined face. He wore a head-wrap and a long crane-white gown. He moved with much dignity as though he was rather more than mortal.

Yuan-te bowed saying, "I am one of the offshoots of the Han family, a simple person from Cho. I have long known the Master's fame, which has indeed thundered in my ear. Twice I have come to visit you, without success. Once I left my name on your writing table; you may have my note."

K'ung-ming replied, "This hermit is but a dilatory person by temperament. I know I have to thank you for more than one vain visit and I am ashamed to think of them."

These courteous remarks and the proper bows exchanged, the two men sat in their relative positions as host and guest and the serving lad brought tea. Then K'ung-ming said, "From your letter I know that you grieve for both people and government. If I were not so young and if I possessed any talent, I would venture to question you."

Yuan-te replied, "Ssuma Hui and Hsu Shu have both spoken of you; can it be that their words were vain? I trust, O Master, that you will not despise my worthlessness but will condescend to instruct me."

"The two men you speak of are very profound scholars. I am but a peasant, a mere farmer, and who am I that I should talk of Empire politics? Those two misled you when they spoke of me. Why do you reject the beautiful jewel for a worthless pebble?"

"But your abilities are world embracing and marvellous. How can you be content to allow time to pass while you idle away life in these secluded haunts? I conjure you, O Master, to remember the inhabitants of the world and remove my crass ignorance by bestowing instruction upon me."

"But what is your ambition, General?"

Yuan-te moved his seat nearer to his host and said, "The Hans are sinking; designing ministers steal away their authority. I am weak, yet I desire to restore the State to its right mind. But my ignorance is too vast, my means are too slender and I know not where to turn. Only you, Master, can lighten my darkness and preserve me from falling. How happy should I be if you would do so!"

K'ung-ming replied, "One bold man after another has arisen in various parts of the Empire ever since the days of the great rebel Tung Cho. Ts'ao Ts'ao was not so powerful as Yuan Shao, but he overcame him by seizing the favourable moment and using his men properly. Now he is all-powerful; he rules an immense army and, through his control of the Court, the various feudal lords as well. You cannot think of opposing him. Then the Suns have held their territory in Chiangtung for three generations. Their position may not appear too secure, but they have popularity to appeal to. You can gain support but win no success there. Chingchou on the north rests on the two rivers Han and Mien; their interests lie in all to the south of them; on the east they touch Wu and on the west they extend to the ancient states Pa and Shu. This is the area in which decisive battles have to be won and one must hold it in order to be secure and Heaven has virtually made it yours. Yichou is an important place, fertile and extensive, a country favoured of Heaven and that through which the Founder of Han obtained the Empire. Its ruler Liu Chang is ignorant and weak. The people are noble and the country prosperous, but he does not know how to hold it all, and all the able men of the district are yearning for an enlightened prince. As you are a scion of the Family, well known throughout the land as trusty and righteous, a whole-hearted hero, who greatly desires to win the support of the wise, if you get possession of Yi and Ching, if on the west you are in harmony with the Jung tribes, on the south win over I and Yueh, make an alliance with Sun Ch'uan, and maintain good government, you can await confidently the day when heaven shall offer you the desired opportunity. Then you may depute a worthy leader to go to the north-east while you take command of an expedition to the north-west, and will you not find the warmest welcome prepared for you by the people? This done the completion of the task will be easy. The Hans will be restored. And I will be your adviser in all these operations if you will only undertake them."

He paused while he bade the lad bring out a map. As this was unrolled K'ung-ming went on, "There you see the fifty four divisions of Ssuch'uan. Should you wish to take the overlordship you will yield to Ts'ao Ts'ao in the north till the time of Heaven become, to Sun Ch'uan in the south till the position may become favourable. You, General, will be the Man and complete the trinity. Chingchou is to be taken first as a home, the west next for the foundation of domination. When you are firmly established you can lay your plans for the attainment of the whole Empire."

As K'ung-ming ceased his harangue, Yuan-te left his place and saluted him, saying, "Your words, O Master, render everything so clear that meseems the clouds are swept aside and I see the clear sky. But Chingchou belongs to Liu Piao, my kinsman, and Yichou to another kinsman; I could hardly take the land from them."

"I have studied the stars and I know Liu Piao is not long for this world; the other is not the sort of man to endure. Both places will certainly fall to you."

Yuan-te bowed his acknowledgments. And so, in one conversation, K'ung-ming proved that he, who had lived in complete retirement all his life, knew and foresaw the three fragments into which the Empire was to break. True, indeed, is it that throughout all the ages no one has ever equalled his intelligence and mastery of the situation.

> Behold, when Liu Pei frets that he is weak,
> Then "Sleeping Dragon" is not far to seek;
> When he desires to know how things will hap,
> The Master, smiling, shows him on the map.

"Though I be of small repute and scanty virtue," said Yuan-te, "I hope, O Master, you will not despise me for my worthlessness, but will leave this retreat to help me. I will assuredly listen most reverently to your words."

K'ung-ming replied, "I have long been happy on my farm and am fond of my leisure. I fear I cannot obey your command."

Yuan-te wept. "If you will not, O Master, what will become of the people?"

The tears rolled down unchecked upon the lapel and sleeves of his robe. This proved to K'ung-ming the sincerity of his desire and he said, "General, if you will accept me, I will render what trifling service I can."

Then Yuan-te was delighted. He called in Kuan and Chang to make their bow and brought out the gifts he had prepared. K'ung-ming refused them all.

"These are not gifts to engage your services, but mere proof of my regard," said Yuan-te.

Then the presents were accepted. They all remained that night at the farm. Next day Chuko Chun returned and his brother said to him, "Uncle Liu has come thrice to see me and now I must go with him. Keep up the farm in my absence and do not let the place go to ruin for, as soon as my work is accomplished, I will certainly return."

Then, turning from his humble home,
He thought of peaceful days to come,
When he should take the homeward way
And ne'er beyond the valley stray.
But duty kept him in the west,
And there he found his place of rest.

An old poem may be quoted here:—

The Founder of Han seized his gleaming blade
And at Mangtang the blood of the white snake flowed.
He conquered Ts'in, destroyed Ch'u and entered Hsienyang.
After two centuries of rule the line was near broken,
But Kuang-Wu, the great, restored the glory at Loyang.
And his children occupied the throne
Till decay began in the days of Huan and Ling.
The Emperor Ling removed the capital to Hsuch'ang,
And, within the four seas, all was confusion.
Bold spirits started up in fierce contention.
Ts'ao Ts'ao, seized the favourable moment
And the Imperial authority passed into his hands,
While the Suns made to themselves
A glorious heritage east of the river,
Solitary and poor, Liu Pei wandered from place to place,
Till he found a haven in Hsinyeh.
Sorely distressed he was at the sorrows of the people,
But the Sleeping Dragon conceived a noble ambition,
Within his breast were thoughts
Of great things to be accomplished by force of arms.
Then, because of the parting words of Hsu Shu,
And by the thrice repeated visits to his retreat,
The great hero found and knew his mentor.
When the age of K'ung-ming was but thrice nine years,
He turned from his books, put aside his lute
And left the peaceful fields he had loved,
Under his guidance Chingchou was taken
And the Land of the Four Streams conquered.
He unrolled great schemes, as one all knowing,
In speech, he went to and fro in the world,
The sound of war drums rolled from his tongue,
The words from his heart stirred one to the utmost depths,
The dragon pranced, the tiger glared,
And peace was brought to the world.
Through all the ages his fame shall never decay.

After taking leave of the younger brother, Yuan-te and his followers left for Hsinyeh, with K'ung-ming as companion. When they took up their abode there, K'ung-ming was treated as a master, eating at the same table, sleeping on the same couch as Liu Pei. They spent whole days conversing over the affairs of the Empire.

K'ung-ming said, "Ts'ao Ts'ao is training his men for naval service and hence certainly intends to invade the country south of the river. We ought to send our spies to ascertain what he is really doing."

So spies were despatched.

Now after Sun Ch'uan had succeeded to the heritage of his father and brother he sent far and wide to invite men of ability to aid him. He established lodging places for them in Wu, and directed Ku Yung and Chang Hung to welcome and entertain all those who came. And year by year they flocked in, one recommending another. Among them were K'an Tse, of Kueichi; Yen Chun, of P'engch'eng; Hsueh Tsung, of P'eihsien; Ch'eng Ping, of Junan; Chu Huan, of Wuchun; Lu Chi of the same place; Chang Wen, of Wu; Ling T'ung, of Kueichi and Wu Ts'an of Wuch'eng; and all these scholars were treated with great deference.

Some able leaders came also, Lu Meng, of Junan; Lu Hsun, of Wuchun; Hsu Sheng, of Langya; P'an Chang, of Tungchun and Ting Feng of Luchiang. Thus Sun Ch'uan obtained the assistance of many men of ability both in peace and war and all well with him.

In the seventh year of "Established Tranquillity" Ts'ao Ts'ao had broken the power of Yuan Shao. Then he sent a messenger to Chiangtung ordering Sun Ch'uan to send his son to court to serve in the retinue of the Emperor. Sun, however, hesitated to comply with this request and the matter was the subject of much discussion. His mother, the lady Wu, sent for Chou Yu and Chang Chao and asked their advice.

The latter said, "He wishes a son to be present at court as a hostage whereby he has a hold upon us, as formerly was the case with all the feudal chiefs. If we do not comply with this request he will doubtless attack the territory. There is some peril."

Chou Yu said, "Our lord has succeeded to the heritage and has a large army of veterans and ample supplies. He has able men ready to do his bidding, and why should he be compelled to send a hostage to any man? To send a hostage is to be forced into joining Ts'ao, and to carry out his behests, whatever they be. Then we shall be in his power. It would be better not to send, but rather to wait patiently the course of events and prepare plans to attack."

"That is also my opinion," said the Dowager.

So Sun Ch'uan dismissed the messenger but did not send his son. Ts'ao Ts'ao resented this and had since nourished schemes for the destruction of the Suns. But their realisation had been delayed by the dangers on the north and, so far, no attack had been made.

Late in the eighth year, Sun Ch'uan led his armies against Huang Tsu and fought on the Great River, where he was successful in several battles. One of Sun's leaders, Ling Ts'ao, led a fleet of light vessels up the river and broke into Hsiak'ou but was killed by an arrow. He left a son, Liug T'ung, fifteen years of age, who led another expedition to recover his father's corpse and was so far successful. After that, as the war was inclined to go against him, Sun Ch'uan turned again to his own country.

Now Sun Ch'uan's brother, Sun I, was Prefect of Tanyang. He was a hard man and given to drink and, in his cups, very harsh to his men, ordering the infliction of severe floggings. Two of his officers, Kuei Lan and Tai Yuan, bore their chief a grudge and sought to assassinate him. They took into their confidence one Pien Hung, of the escort, and the three plotted to kill their master at a great assembly of officials at Tanyang amid the banquets and junketings.

Sun's wife was skilled in divination and on the day of the great banquet she cast a most inauspicious lot. Wherefore she besought her husband to stay away from the assembly. But he was obstinate and went. The faithless guardsman followed his master in the dusk when the gathering dispersed, and stabbed him with a dagger. The two prime movers at once seized their accomplice and beheaded him in the market place. Then they went to Sun's residence, which they plundered. Kuei Lan was taken with the beauty of the dead Prefect's wife and told her that as he had avenged the death of her husband she must go with him, or he would slay her. The wife pleaded that it was too soon after her husband's death to think of re-marriage but promised to be his after the mourning sacrifices.

She thus obtained a respite, which she utilised to send for two old Generals of her husband's, Sun Kao and Fu Ying. They came and she tearfully told her tale.

"My husband had great faith in you. Now Kuei and Tai have compassed his death and have laid the crime on Pien Hung. They have plundered my house and carried off my servants and slaves. Worse than this Kuei Lan insists that I shall be his wife. To gain time I have pretended to favour this proposal and I pray you now to send the news to my husband's brother and beg him to slay these two miscreants and avenge this wrong. I will never forget your kindness in this life or the next."

And she bowed before them. They wept also and said, "We were much attached to our master and now that he has come to an untimely end we must avenge him. Dare we not carry out your behests?"

So they sent a trusty messenger. On the day of the sacrifices the lady called in her two friends and hid them in a secret chamber. Then the ceremonies were performed in the great hall. These over, she put off her mourning garb, bathed and perfumed herself, and assumed an expression of joy. She laughed and talked as usual, so that Kuei Lan rejoiced in his heart, thinking of the pleasure that was to be his.

When night came she sent a slave girl to call her suitor to the Palace, where she entertained him at supper. When he had well drunk she suggested that they should retire and led him to the chamber where her friends were waiting. He followed without the least hesitation. As soon as she entered the room she called out, "Where are you, Generals?" Out rushed the two men, and the drunken man, incapable of any resistance, was despatched with daggers.

Next she invited Tai Yuan to a supper and he was slain in similar fashion. After that, she sent to the houses of her enemies and slew all therein. This done, she resumed her mourning garb and the heads of the two men were hung as a sacrifice before the coffin of her husband.

Very soon her brother-in-law came with an army, and hearing the story of the deeds of the two generals from the widow, gave them office and put them over Tanyang. When he left he took the widow to his own home to pass the remainder of her days. All those who heard of her brave conduct were loud in praise of her virtue:—

> Full of resource and virtuous, few in the world are like her,
> Guilefully wrought she and compassed the death of the lusty
>   assassins,
> Faithful servants are always ready to deal with rebellion,
> None can ever excel that heroine famous in East Wu.

The brigandage that had troubled Wu had all been suppressed and a large fleet (of seven thousand) keels were in the Yangtse River ready for service. Sun Ch'uan appointed Chou Yu to be the Admiral-in-Chief.

In the twelfth year (207 A.D.) the Dowager Lady Wu, feeling her end approaching, called to her the two advisers Chou Yu and Chang Chao and spoke thus:—"I came of a family of Wu, but losing my parents in early life, my brother and I went into Yueh, and then I married into this family. I bore my husband four sons, not without premonitions of the greatness to be theirs. With my first, I dreamed of the moon and with my second, Ch'uan, of the sun, which omens were interpreted by the soothsayer as signs of their great honour. Unhappy Ts'e died young, but Ch'uan inherited and it is he whom I pray you both to assist with one accord. Then may I die in peace."

And to her son she said, "These two you are to serve as they were your masters and treat them with all respect. My sister and I both were wives to your father, and so she is also a mother to you and you are to serve her after I am gone as you now serve me. And you must treat your sister with affection and find a handsome husband for her."

Then she died and her son mourned for her, but of that and her burial nothing will be said.

The following year they began to discuss an attack upon Huang Tsu. Chang Chao said the armies should not move during the period of mourning; however, Chou Yu, more to the point, said that vengeance should not be postponed on that account; it could not wait upon times and seasons. Still Sun Ch'uan halted between two opinions and would not decide.

Then came Lu Meng, the Commander of the North, who said to his master, "While I was at Lungchiushuiki'ou one of Huang Tsu's captains, Kan Ning by name, offered to surrender. I found out all about him. He is something of a scholar, is forceful, fond of wandering about as a knight-errant. He assembled a band of outlaws with whom he roamed over the rivers and lakes where he would terrorise everybody. He wore a bell at his waist and at the sound of this bell every one fled and hid. He fitted his boats with sails of Ssuch'uan brocade and people called him the 'Pirate with Sails of Silk.'

"Then he reformed. He and his band went to Liu Piao, but they left him when they saw he would never accomplish anything and now they would serve under your banner, only that Huang Tsu detains them at Hsiak'ou. Formerly when you were attacking Huang Tsu, he owed the recovery of Hsiak'ou to this same Kan Ning, whom he treated with liberality, but when Su Fei, the Commander-in-Chief, recommended him for promotion, Huang Tsu said he was unsuited for any high position as, after all, he was no more than a pirate.

"So Kan Ning became a disappointed and resentful man. Su Fei tried to win him over to good humour and invited him to wine parties and said, 'I have put your name forward many times but our chief says he has no place suitable for you. However, time slips away and man's life is not very long. One must make the most of it. I will put you forward for the magistracy of Ohsien, whence you may be able to advance.' So Kan Ning got away from Hsiak'ou and would have come to you then, but he feared that he would not be welcomed, since he had assisted Huang Tsu and killed Ling Ts'ao. I told him you were always ready to welcome able men and would nourish no resentment for former deeds. After all, every man was bound to do his best for his master. He would come with alacrity if he only felt sure of a welcome. I pray you to express your pleasure."

This was good news for Sun Ch'uan and he said, "With his help I could destroy Huang Tsu." Then he bade Lu Meng bring Kan to see him.

When the salutations were over, the chief said, "My heart is entirely captivated by your coming; I feel no resentment against you. I hope you will have no doubts on that score and I may as well tell you that I desire some plan for the destruction of Huang Tsu."

He replied, "The dynasty is decadent and without influence. Ts'ao Ts'ao will finally absorb the country down to the river unless he is opposed. Liu Piao provides nothing against the future and his sons are quite unfitted to succeed him. You should lay your plans to oust him at once before Ts'ao Ts'ao anticipates you. The first attack should be made on Huang Tsu, who is getting old and avaricious, so that every one hates him. He is totally unprepared for a fight and his army is undisciplined. He would fall at the first blow. If he were gone, you would control the western passes and could conquer Pa and Shu (Szech'uan). And you would be securely established."

"The advice is most valuable," said Sun Ch'uan, and he made his preparations. Chou Yu was appointed Commander-in-Chief; Lu Meng was van-leader; Tung Hsi and Kan Ning were sub-leaders. Sun Ch'uan himself would command the main army of ten legions.

The spies reported that Huang Tsu, at the news of an expedition against him, called his officers together to consult. He placed Su Fei in chief command. He also appointed van-leaders, and other officers, and prepared for defence. He had two squadrons of ships under the command of Ch'en Chiu and Teng Lung. On these he placed strong bows and stiff crossbows to the number of more than a thousand and secured the boats to heavy hawsers so that they formed a barrier in the river.

At the approach of the men of Wu the drums beat for the ships to attack. Soon arrows and bolts flew thick, forcing back the invaders, who withdrew till several *li* of water lay between them and the defenders.

"We must go forward," said Kan Ning to his colleague.

So they chose a hundred light craft and put picked men on them, fifty to a boat. Twenty were to row the boats and thirty to fight. These latter were armoured swordsmen. Careless of the enemy's missiles these boats advanced, got to the defenders' fleet and cut the hawsers of their ships so that they drifted hither and thither in confusion. Kan Ning leaped upon one boat and killed Teng Lung. Ch'en Chiu left the fleet and set out for the shore. Lu Meng dropped into a small boat and went among the larger ships setting them on fire. When Ch'en Chiu had nearly reached the bank, Lu reckless of death went after him, got ahead and struck him full in the breast so that he fell.

Before long Su Fei came along the bank with reinforcements, but it was too late; the armies of Wu had already landed and there was no hope of repelling them. Su Fei fled into the open country, but he was made prisoner. He was taken to Sun Ch'uan who ordered that he be put into a cage-cart and kept till Huang Tsu should be captured. Then he would execute the pair. And the attack was pressed; day and night they wrought to capture Hsiak'ou.

> He sees his ships cut loose and burned,
> By the "Silk-sailed Pirate" he once spurned.

For Huang Tsu's fate, see next chapter.

Now Sun Ch'uan fought against Hsiak'ou. When Huang Tsu recognised that he was beaten and could not maintain his position, he abandoned Chianghsia and took the road to Chingchou. Kan Ning, foreseeing this, had laid an ambush outside the east gate. Soon after the fugitive, with a small following, had burst out of the gate he found his road blocked.

From horseback, Huang Tsu said, "I treated you well in the past, why do you now press me so hard?"

Kan Ning angrily shouted, "I did good service for you and yet you treated me as a pirate. Now what have you to say?"

There was nothing to be said, and Huang turned his horse to escape. But Kan Ning thrust aside his men and himself rode in pursuit. Then he heard a shouting in his rear and saw Ch'eng P'u coming up. Fearing lest this other pursuer should overpass him and score the success he desired for himself, Kan fitted an arrow to his bow and shot at the fugitive. Huang was hit and fell from his steed. Then Kan Ning cut off his head. After this, joining himself to Ch'eng P'u, the two returned bearing the ghastly trophy to their lord. Sun Ch'uan ordered them to place it in a box to be taken back home and offered as a sacrifice to the manes of his father.

Having rewarded the soldiers for the victory and promoted Kan Ning, Sun Ch'uan next discussed the advisability of sending a force to hold Chianghsia. But his adviser, Chang Chao, said it was useless to try to hold one city alone. It would be better to return home and prepare for the expedition that Liu Piao would send in revenge. They would defeat him, push home the attack and capture his district.

Sun Ch'uan saw the advice was wise so he left Chianghsia and led his army home to the east.

Now Su Fei was still confined, but he got some one to go to Kan Ning to beg him to plead for mercy. Kan Ning had expected this although the prisoner had said no word and he was averse from leaving his friend and one-time protector to perish. "I should not have forgotten him even if he had said nothing," said Kan.

When the army had reached Wuhui the victor gave orders for Su Fei's execution that his head might be offered with that of Huang Tsu. Then Kan Ning went in to his lord and said, weeping, "Long ago, if it had not been for Su Fei, my bones would have been rotting in some ditch and how then could I have rendered service under your banner? Now he deserves death, but I cannot forget his kindness to me and I pray you take away the honours you have bestowed on me as a set-off to his crime."

Sun Ch'uan replied, "Since he once showed kindness to you, I will pardon him for your sake. But what can be done if he runs away?"

"If he be pardoned and escape death he will be immeasureably grateful and will not go away. If he should, then will I offer my life in exchange."

So the condemned man escaped death and only one head was offered in sacrifice. After the sacrificial ceremonies a great banquet was spread in honour of the victories. As it was proceeding suddenly one of the guests burst into loud lamentations, drew his sword and rushed upon Kan Ning. Kan hastily rose and defended himself with the chair on which he had been sitting. The host looked at the assailant and saw it was Ts'ao T'ung, whose father had fallen under an arrow shot by Kan Ning. The son was now burning to avenge his father's death.

Hastily leaving his place, Sun Ch'uan checked the angry officer, saying, "If he slew your noble father, then remember each was fighting for his lord for whom he was bound to exert himself to the utmost. But now that you are under one flag and are of one house you may not recall an ancient injury. You must regard my interests continually."

Ts'ao Ling beat his head upon the floor and cried, saying, "But how can I not avenge this? It is a blood feud and we may not both live under the same sky."

The guests interfered, beseeching the man to forgo his revenge, and at last he ceased from his murderous intention. But he sat glaring wrathfully at his enemy.

So soon after Kan Ning was despatched with half a legion and a squadron of ships to guard Hsiak'ou, where he was beyond the reach of his enemy's wrath. Then Sun Ch'uan promoted Ts'ao Ling and so he was somewhat appeased.

From about this time Wu enlarged her fleets, and men were sent to various points to guard the river banks. The brother of the chieftain was placed in command at Wuhui and Sun Ch'uan himself, with a large army, camped at Ch'aisang. Chou Yu, the Commander-in-Chief of the forces, was on the P'oyang Lake training the naval forces, and general preparations were made for defence and attack.

Here our story digresses to follow the adventures of Liu Pei. By his spies he had tidings of the doings in the lower portion of the great river, and knew of the death of Huang Tsu. So he consulted K'ung-ming as to his action. While they were discussing matters, there arrived a messenger from Liu Piao, begging Liu Pei to go to see him. K'ung-ming advised him to go and said, "This call is to consult you about avenging Huang Tsu. You must take me with you and let me act as the circumstances direct. There are advantages to be got."

Leaving his second brother in command at Hsinyeh, Liu Pei set forth, taking Chang Fei with half a company as his escort. On the way he discussed the course of action with his adviser, who said, "First you must thank him for having saved you from the evil that was planned against you at Hsiang-yang. But you must not undertake any expedition against Wu; say you must return to Hsinyeh to put your army in good order."

With this admonition Liu Pei came to Chingchou and was lodged in the guest-house. Chang Fei and the escort camped without the walls. In due course Liu Pei and K'ung-ming were received, and after the customary salutations, the guest apologised for his conduct.

The host said, "Worthy brother, I know you were the victim of a vile plot and I should have put the prime mover to death for it had there not been so universal a prayer for mercy. However, I remitted that penalty. I hope you do not consider that I was wrong."

"Mao had little to do with it; I think it was due to his subordinates," replied Pei.

Piao said, "Chianghsia is lost, as you know; Huang is dead. So I have asked you to come that we might take measures of vengeance."

"Huang was harsh and cruel and never used his men in the proper way; that was the real cause of his fall. But have you reflected what Ts'ao Ts'ao may do on the north if we attack the south?"

"I am getting old and weak and I am unable to manage affairs properly; will you aid me, brother? After I am gone you will have this district.

"Why do you say this, my brother? Think you that I am equal to such a task?"

Here K'ung-ming glanced at Liu Pei who continued, "But give me a little time to think it over."

And at this point he took his leave. When they had reached their lodging, K'ung-ming said, "Why did you decline his offer of the district."

"He has always been most kind and courteous. I could not take advantage of his weakness."

"A perfectly kindly and gracious lord," sighed K'ung-ming.

Soon after the son of Liu Piao was announced and Liu Pei received him and led him in. The young man began to weep saying, "My mother cannot bear the sight of me. My very life is in danger. Can you not save me, Uncle?"

"My worthy nephew, this is a family affair. You should not come to me."

K'ung-ming, who was present, smiled. Liu Pei turned to him to know what he should do.

"This is a family affair; I cannot touch it!" replied K'ung-ming.

The young man soon left and when Yuan-te was saying good-bye he whispered, "I will get K'ung-ming to return your call and you can talk with him. He will advise you."

Liu Chi thanked him and left. Next day when the call was to be returned Yuan-te pretended to be suffering from colic and made that an excuse to send K'ung-ming to return the call. The adviser went, and when he had reached the Palace, dismounted and was led in, Liu Chi conducted him into one of the inner rooms and when the tea had been brought, said, "I am an object of my stepmother's dislike; can you advise me what to do?"

"As a mere stranger guest I can hardly have anything to do with your own 'bone and flesh' matters. If I did, and the story got abroad, much harm might ensue."

With this he rose to take leave. But Chi was unwilling to say farewell. He said, "Your glory has turned in my direction, you cannot mean to go away so pointlessly."

He led his visitor into a private chamber and had refreshments brought. While they ate and drank Chi repeated his first request: what was he to do since his stepmother disliked him?

"It is not the sort of thing I can advise in," replied K'ung-ming, as he rose for the second time to take leave.

"Master, if you will not reply, that is well. But why incontinently leave me?"

So the adviser once more seated himself and Liu Chi said, "There is an ancient writing I should like to show you." And he led his visitor to a small upper room.

"Where is the writing?" said K'ung-ming.

Instead of answering Liu Chi wept, saying, "My stepmother cannot bear me; my life is in danger. O Master, will you not say a word to save me?"

K'ung-ming flushed and rose to go away. But he found the ladder by which they had mounted had been removed. Again Chi besought some advice, "Master, you fear lest it may get abroad! Is that why you are silent? Here we are between earth and sky and what you say will come out of your mouth directly into my ear. No other soul can hear. Now can you tell me what to do?"

"Sow not dissension among relatives," said K'ung-ming. "Is it possible for me to make any plan for you?"

"Then is my life indeed in danger," said the young man. "I will die at your feet."

So saying, he pulled out a dagger and threatened to make an end of himself.

K'ung-ming checked him. "There is a way," said he.

"I pray you tell me."

"You have heard of Shen Sheng and Ch'ung Erh, have you not? Shen Sheng stayed at home and died; his brother went away and lived in peace. Now that Huang Tsu is gone and Chianghsia is weakly defended, why do you not ask to be sent there to guard it? Then you would be out of the way of harm."

Chi thanked him. Then he called to his people to restore the ladder and he escorted K'ung-ming down to the level ground.

K'ung-ming returned to Yuan-te and related the whole interview. The young man soon acted on the advice given him, but his father would not at first consent to let him go. To settle his doubts he sent for Yuan-te, who said, "Chianghsia is important and your son is the most suitable man to defend it. You must let him go. The south-east will be defended by your son; the north-west I will look after."

"I hear that Ts'ao Ts'ao has been training a naval force and I am afraid he has intentions against us. We must be on our guard."

"I know all about it; you need feel no anxiety," said Yuan-te.

He took leave of his relative and went home while Liu Chi received command of three companies and went to guard Chianghsia.

At this time Ts'ao Ts'ao suppressed the three high officers of State and exercised their functions himself. He appointed as his general secretaries or *Ts'ao-Ch'uan*, Mao Chieh and Ts'ui Yen, and as literary secretary, Ssuma I, grandson of Ssuma Sui and son of Ssuma Fang. Thus he was strong in literary talent.

He then called his military officers to a council to discuss an expedition against the south. Hsiahou Tun opened the debate saying, "Liu Fei is drilling his army at Hsinyeh, and is a source of danger. He should be destroyed."

Accordingly he was appointed Commander-in-Chief and four assistants were given him. With these he led ten legions to Powangch'eng, whence he could observe Hsinyeh.

"Hsun Yu was opposed to this and said, "Liu Pei is a famous warrior and he has lately taken to himself as his director of training Chuko Liang. Caution is needed."

Tun replied, "Liu Pei is a mean rat. I will certainly take him prisoner."

"Do not despise him," said Hsu Shu. "Remember he has Chuko Liang to help him and so he is like a tiger who has grown wings."

Ts'ao Ts'ao said, "Who is this Chuko Liang?"

"He is also called K'ung-ming, and has taken a Taoist cognomen of 'Sleeping Dragon.' He is a perfect genius, god and devil combined, the greatest marvel of the age. Do not despise him."

"How does he stand as compared with you?" asked Ts'ao.

"There is no comparison. I am a mere glow-worm spark; he is the glory of the full moon," replied Hsu Shu.

"You are mistaken," replied Tun. "This Chuko Liang of yours is of no account. Who would fear him? If I do not take him and his master prisoners in the first battle, then here is my head, a free gift to our lord, the minister."

"Hasten to comfort me with news of victory," said Ts'ao Ts'ao.

Hsiahou Tun hastened to depart.

The advent of K'ung-ming and the extravagant deference shown him did not please Liu Pei's sworn brothers who grumbled, saying, "He is very young although he is clever and learned. Our brother really treats him too well. We have not seen any evidence of his wonderful skill."

Liu Pei replied, "You do not know his worth. To me it seems as if the fish had got into the water again. Pray do not discuss this matter further, my brothers."

They withdrew, silent but dissatisfied. One day a man presented Liu Pei with a yak's tail and he at once put it in his cap as an ornament. K'ung-ming came in and noticed it at once. "Then you have renounced all ambition, my lord; you are just going to attend to this sort of thing," he quietly remarked.

Yuan-te snatched off his cap and flung it away. "I was only amusing myself with the thing," replied he.

"How do you think you stand compared with Ts'ao Ts'ao?" asked K'ung-ming.

"Inferior."

"Yes; your army is less than one legion and the chances are ten thousand to one that he will attack. How can we meet him?"

"I am greatly distressed about it; but I see no way."

"You might recruit and I will train them. Then we might be able to oppose him."

So recruiting began and three companies were enlisted. K'ung-ming set about drilling them diligently.

Soon they heard that Hsiahou Tun was leading an army of ten legions against them. When he heard it Chang Fei said to his brother, Kuan Yu, "We will get this K'ung-ming to go and fight them."

Just at that moment they were summoned to their brother, who asked their advice.

"Why not send the 'Water' brother?" said Chang Fei.

"For method I rely on K'ung-ming; but for action I put my faith in you, my brothers. Are you going to fail me?"

They went out and K'ung-ming was called. "I fear your brothers will not obey me," said K'ung-ming. "Wherefore, if I am to direct the campaign, you must give me a seal of office and a sword of authority."

So Yuan-te gave him both. Armed with these ensigns of power he assembled the officers to receive their orders.

"We will go just to see what he will do," said one brother to the other.

In the assembly K'ung-ming spoke saying, "On the left of Powang are hills called Yushan. On the right is a forest, Anlin. There we will prepare an ambush. Kuan Yu will go to the former place with one company. He will remain there quiescent till the enemy has passed, but when he sees a flame in the south, that will be the signal to attack. He will first burn their baggage train. Chang Fei will go to a valley behind the forest. When he sees the signal he is to go to the old stores depot at Powang and burn that. Kuan P'ing and Liu Feng will take half a company each, prepare combustibles and be ready with them beyond Powang Slope. The enemy will arrive about dusk and then they can start the blaze."

"Chao Yun, now recalled from Fanch'eng, is to lead the attack, but he is to lose and not win. And Liu Pei is to command the reserve. See that each one obeys these orders and let there be no mistakes."

Then said Kuan Yu, "All of us are to go out to meet the enemy, but I have not yet heard what you are going to do."

"I am going to guard the city."

Chang Fei burst into a laugh, "We are to go out to bloody battle and you are to stay quietly at home quite comfortable."

"Here is the sword and here the seal," replied the strategist, displaying the emblems of authority. "Disobedience of orders will be death."

Liu Pei said, "Do you not understand that the plans elaborated in a little chamber decide success over thousands of *li*? Do not disobey the command, my brothers."

Chang Fei went out smiling cynically.

Kuan Yu remarked, "Let us await the result. If he fail then we can look to it."

The brothers left None of the officers understood anything of the general line of strategy and, though they obeyed orders, they were not without doubts and misgivings.

K'ung-ming said to Liu Pei, "You may now lead your men to the hills and camp till the enemy shall arrive tomorrow evening. Then you are to abandon the camp and move away retreating till the signal is seen. Then you will advance and attack with all force. The two Mi and I will guard the city."

In the city he prepared banquets to celebrate the victory and also prepared the books to record exceptional services. Liu Pei noted all these things with not a little trouble in his heart.

Ts'ao Ts'ao's army in due course reached Powang. Then half of them, the veterans, were told off for the first attack and the remainder were to guard the baggage train and supplies. Thus they marched in two divisions. The season was autumn and a chilly wind began to blow.

They pressed forward. Presently they saw a cloud of dust ahead of them and the general ordered the ranks to be reformed. He questioned the guides as to the name of the place. They told him the place in front was Powang Slope and behind them was the Lok'ou Stream. Then Hsiahou Tun rode to the front to reconnoitre, leaving Yu Chin and Li Tien to finish setting out the battle array.

Presently he began to laugh and, when they asked the cause of this merriment, he replied, Hsu Shu praised Chuko Liang to the very skies as something more than human. But now that I see how he has placed his men and the stuff he has put into his vanguard, it seems to me that he is sending dogs or sheep against tigers and leopards. I bragged a little when I said I would take him prisoner, but I am going to make good my boast."

Then he rode forward at full speed. Chao Yun rode to meet him and Tun opened a volley of abuse. "You lot, followers of Liu Pei, are only like wraiths following devils."

This angered Chao Yun and a combat began. In a little time Chao Yun turned and retreated as if he was worsted. Tun pressed after him and kept up the chase for some ten *li*. Then Chao suddenly turned again and offered fight, but only to retreat after a few passes.

Seeing these tactics Han Hao, one of Tun's captains, rode up to his chief and urged him to use caution saying he feared he was being inveigled into an ambush.

"With such antagonists as these I should not fear a score of ambushes," replied Tun, pressing forward eagerly.

Just as he reached the slope he heard the roar of a bomb and out came Liu Pei to attack. "Here is your ambush," said Hsiahou Tun, laughing. "I will get to Hsinyeh this evening before I have done."

He urged his men forward and his opponents retired in measure as he advanced.

As evening came on, thick clouds overcast the whole sky. The wind increased but the leader still urged his men after the retreating foe. The two captains came to a narrow part of the road with reeds and rushes thick all round them.

"Those who despise the enemy are beaten," said Li Tien to Yu Chin. "Away south there the roads are narrow, and streams and mountains make the country difficult. The forests are dense and if the enemy used fire we should be lost."

"You are right," replied Chin. "I will get on and warn the Commander. Perhaps he will stop. You can halt those who come up."

Yu Chin rode forward shouting at the top of his voice. Hsiahou Tun saw him coming up and asked what was the matter. Chin told him of the state of the country and reminded him of the danger of fire. His ferocity had then somewhat abated and he turned his steed toward his main body.

Then there arose a shout behind him. A rushing noise came from in the reeds and great tongues of flame shot up here and there. These spread and soon the fire was in "the four quarters and the eight sides," and fanned by a strong wind.

The Ts'ao troops were thrown into confusion and trampled each other down. Many perished. Chao Yun turned on them again. The Commander-in-Chief dashed through the fire and smoke to escape.

Now Li Tien saw that things were going very badly so he turned to get back to Powangch'eng but fell upon a body of men in the way, led by Kuan Yu. He dashed into their midst and managed to get clear. Yu Chin saw the supplies were being destroyed and there was nothing left to guard, so he escaped along a bye-path. Two other captains, who came to try to save the baggage train, met Chang Fei and one of them was slain forthwith, but the other escaped. Next morning the countryside was strewn with corpses and drenched with blood.

> The armies met on Powang Slope
>> And K'ung-ming fought with fire;
> A perfect strategist, he bent
>> All men to his desire.
> But poor Ts'ao Ts'ao, his enemy,
>> He trembled in his shoes
> Before the man, who'd never fought
>> But yet could armies use.

Hsiahou Tung drew up the battered remains of his army and led them back to the capital.

K'ung-ming ordered his armies to collect, and as Kuan and Chang rode homeward they confessed to each other that the new strategist was a fine fellow. Before long they met him seated in a light carriage and they dismounted and bowed before him. The remaining bodies came in. The spoil was distributed among the soldiers and all returned to Hsinyeh, where the populace lined the roads to bid them welcome.

"We owe our lives to the Prince," they cried to Liu Pei.

Said K'ung-ming, "Hsiahou Tun has been driven off, but Ts'ao Ts'ao will come with a stronger force."

"And what shall we do?" replied Liu Pei.

"My plan is quite ready," said K'ung-ming.

> Always battles, nowhere rest for horse or man;
> Must rely on ruses, dodging where one can.

The plan prepared against Ts'ao Ts'ao will be unfolded in the next chapter.

CHAPTER XL

When Yuan-te asked how his adviser hoped to repel Ts'ao Ts'ao, K'ung-ming replied, "This is a small city and unfitted for our lengthy occupation. Liu Piao is ill and failing fast, so this is the time to take his district as a base where we may be safe against Ts'ao Ts'ao."

"You speak well, Master, but Liu Piao has shown me great kindness and I could not hear to serve him an ill turn."

"If you do not take this opportunity you will regret it ever after," said K'ung-ming.

"I would rather perish than do what is wrong."

"We will discuss it again," replied K'ung-ming.

When Hsiahou Tun reached the capital he presented himself to his master in bonds and craved death. But his master loosed him and let him tell his tale. And he said, "I was the victim of Chuko Liang's evil machinations; he attacked with fire."

"As a soldier from your youth you should have remembered that fire was a likely weapon in narrow roads."

"Li Tien and Yu Chin reminded me; I am sorry enough now."

Ts'ao Ts'ao rewarded his two captains who had warned their leader.

"Liu Pei as strong as he is now certainly is a menace to our existence and he must be quickly destroyed," said Hsiahou Tun.

"He is one of my anxieties," replied Ts'ao. "Sun Ch'uan is the other. The rest do not count. We must take this chance to sweep the south clean."

Then orders were issued to prepare an army of fifty legions, in five divisions of ten legions each. Each had two leaders, except the fifth, which Ts'ao Ts'ao himself led. The van was commanded by

Hsu Ch'u. The seventh moon of the thirteenth year was fixed for the march.

The high officer, K'ung Jung, offered a remonstrance. He said, "Liu Pei and Liu Piao are both of the Imperial House and should not be attacked without grave reasons. Sun Ch'uan in the six districts is terrible as a crouching tiger and, with the Great River as his defence, he is very secure. If, Sir Minister, you undertake this unjustifiable expedition, you will forfeit the respect of the world, I fear."

"All three of them are disobedient ministers and rebels and how can I fail to punish them?" replied Ts'ao.

He was angry, and bade the adviser go from his presence. Presently he gave formal orders that he would put to death any one who remonstrated on the subject of his expedition.

K'ung Jung went forth from the palace sadly. Casting his eyes up to heaven, he cried, "Where is the chance of success when the perfectly inhumane attacks the perfectly humane? He must be defeated."

One of the clients of the historian Ch'i Lu, whom K'ung Jung had always treated contemptuously and disdainfully, happened to hear this apostrophe and told his patron who carried the tale to Ts'ao Ts'ao. He also added to it that K'ung habitually spoke disrespectfully of the Chief Minister and had been very friendly with Mi Heng. In fact the insults that Mi Heng had hurled at Ts'ao Ts'ao had been deliberately arranged and intrigued by K'ung. K'ung Jung and Mi Heng seemed to admire each other hugely and Mi used to say, "Confucius is not dead" and the other used to reply "Yen Hui has risen again."

Ch'i Lu's tale angered Ts'ao, who ordered the arrest of the historian and sent T'ing Wei to carry it out.

Now K'ung Jung had two sons, both young, who were sitting at home playing *wei-ch'i*, when one of their servants ran in and said, "Your father has just been carried off for execution; why do you not run away?"

The youths replied, "When the nest is pulled down are the eggs left unbroken?"

Even at that moment the same officer came and carried off the whole household. The two youths were beheaded. The father's corpse was exposed in the streets.

The Prefect of the Metropolis, Chih Hsi, wept over the corpse. This public exhibition of sympathy re-kindled Ts'ao's anger and he was going to punish it with death. However, this additional cruelty was prevented by the adviser Hsun Yu, who said, "You should not slay a righteous man who came to mourn over his friend's corpse. He had often warned his friend, K'ung Jung, against the danger his severe rectitude might lead him into."

Chih Hsi took up the remains of father and sons and buried them.

> K'ung Jung, who dwelt on the north sea shore,
> A noble reputation bore;
> With him all guests warm welcome found,
> And ceaselessly the wine went round.
> For skill in letters he was famed,
> In speech, he dukes and princes shamed,
> Historians his merits tell,
> Recorders say that he did well.

After wreaking his wrath on K'ung Jung, Ts'ao issued the order to march. Hsun Yu was left in command of the capital.

About this time the Prefect of Chingchou became seriously ill and he summoned Liu Pei to his chamber. He went accompanied by his two brothers and the adviser. Liu Piao said, "The disease has attacked my very vitals and my time is short. I confide my orphans to your guardianship. My son is unfit to succeed to my place, and I pray you, my brother, to administer the district after my death."

Liu Pei wept, saying, "I will do my utmost to help my nephew; what else could I do, indeed?"

Even at this moment came the news of the march of Ts'ao Ts'ao's armies and Liu Pei, taking hasty leave of his kinsman, was forced to hurry to his station. The evil tidings aggravated the sick man's condition and he began to make his last arrangements. In his testament he appointed Yuan-te the guardian of his son Liu Chi, who was to succeed in the lordship.

This arrangement greatly angered his wife the Lady Ts'ai. She closed the inner doors against all and confided to her own partizans, of whom her brother and Chang Yun were her confidants, the keeping of the outer gates.

The heir was at Chianghsia and he came to make filial enquiries as soon as his father's condition became serious. But Ts'ai Mao refused him admittance and said, "Your father sent you to guard Chianghsia. Such a very responsible post should by no means have been quitted without orders. Suppose it was attacked, what might not happen? If your father sees you he will be very angry and it will make him worse. That would be most undutiful and you should return to your command at once."

Liu Chi stood out for some time, but admittance was denied him in spite of his tears. So he returned to his post. Meanwhile his father rapidly grew worse. He anxiously looked for his son, but he came not. Suddenly he uttered piercing shrieks and then passed away.

> When the Yuans were lords of the north,
> And Piao held the bank of the river,
> It seemed, so strong were they both,
> That they would endure for ever.
> But the women folk troubled their states,
> And, meddling, confusion made;
> It was mournful indeed to see
> How quickly the house decayed.

So the Prefect died. Then the widow and her partizans took counsel together and forged a testament conferring the lordship of Chingchou on the second son Liu Ts'ung before they published the news of the death.

The wrongful heir was then fourteen years of age. He was no fool, so he assembled the officials and said, "My father has passed away and my elder brother is at Chianghsia. More than that, our uncle is at Hsinyeh. You have made me lord, but if my brother and uncle come here with an army to punish me for usurping the lordship, what explanation can I offer?"

At first no one replied. Then a secretary Li Kuei, rose and said, "You speak well. Now hasten to send letters of mouring to your brother and ask him to come and take his inheritance. Also call upon Yuan-te to come and assist in the administration. Then shall we be safe against our enemies on both north and south. I consider this the most excellent plan."

But Ts'ai Mao replied harshly, "Who are you to speak thus wildly and oppose the testament of our late lord?"

Li began to abuse him, "You and your party have fabricated this testament, setting aside the rightful heir. Now the whole district is in the hands of the Ts'ao family and if our dead lord knew your doings he would slay you."

Ts'ai Mao ordered the lictors to take him away to execution. He was hurried out, but his tongue ceased not.

So the younger son was placed in his father's seat and the Ts'ai clan shared among them the whole military authority of the district. The defence of Chingchou was confided to Teng I and Liu Hsien, while Lady Ts'ai and her son took up their residence in Hsiangyang so as to be out of the reach of the rightful heir and his uncle. They interred the remains of the late Prefect on the east of Hsiangyang. No notice of the death was sent to Liu Chi, the son, or to his uncle.

Liu Ts'ung arrived at Hsiangyang, but, before he had had time to recover from the fatigue of the journey, the startling news of the approach of a great army came in. He summoned K'uai Yueh and Ts'ai Mao and others to ask counsel. One of the secretaries, Fu Sun, offered his advice, saying, "Not only are we threatened by a great army, but the elder son, who is the real heir, at Chianghsia, and his uncle at Hsinyeh, are to be reckoned with. These two have not been notified of the death, and they will resent that. We shall be in sad case if they also march against us. But if you will adopt my suggestion then our people will be as steady as Mount T'ai and our young lord's position and rank will be assured."

"What is your plan?" asked the young lord.

"To offer the whole district to Ts'ao Ts'ao, who will treat our young master most liberally."

"What advice!" said Liu Ts'ung angrily. "Am I to yield my heritage to another before I have even fairly succeeded to it?"

"The advice is good," said K'uai Yueh. "Opportunism is a policy and possibilities need consideration. In the name of government, Ts'ao is fighting against his neighbours. If our lord oppose him he will be termed contumacious. Beside, any misfortune on our borders before our young lord is well established will react upon the internal administration and our people will be panic-stricken at the mere news of the approach of a hostile army. How could we then offer any resistance?"

Liu Ts'ung replied, "It is not that I disagree with you, but I should be a laughing-stock to the whole world were I to abandon my heritage without an effort."

He was interrupted by a speaker who said, "If their advice is good, why not follow it?"

They turned toward the speaker who was a certain Wang Ts'an of Shangyang, a lean, cadaverous individual much below the middle height of a man.

However, his talents did not conform to his physical appearance. When he was yet a youth he went to visit Ts'ai Yung, then a vice-president, and although many guests of exalted rank were present, the host hastened to welcome the newcomer with the greatest deference. The others were astonished and asked why he was so respectful to a mere youth.

"He is a young man with the highest gifts; were I only like him—," said Ts'ai.

Wang was widely read and had a most retentive memory, better than any of his contemporaries. If he glanced at a roadside monument as he passed, he remembered every word of the inscription. If he saw people playing *wei-ch'i* and the board was suddenly overthrown, he could replace every pip in its proper place. He was a good mathematician and his poems were exquisite. At seventeen he was appointed a court official but did not take up the appointment. When the disturbance in the empire grew serious he sought refuge in Chingchou, where he was received with great honour as guest of the Prefect.

What he said was this, General, how do you compare with Ts'ao Ts'ao?"

"Inferior," replied Liu Ts'ung.

Wang continued, "Ts'ao has many soldiers and bold leaders; he is able and resourceful. He took Lu Pu and broke the power of Yuan Shao. He pursued Liu Pei into Lung and destroyed Wu Huan. The destruction of such firmly established men shows his invincible character. Now he is on the way here and it will be very difficult to withstand him. The plan proposed is the best you can expect and you should not delay and hesitate till it is too late for aught but regret."

"Worthy Sir, you indeed speak to the point; I must inform my mother," said the young ruler.

But just then they saw his mother appear from behind a screen; she had been listening to all that was said.

"Why refer to me when three such gentlemen coincide in their opinions?" said she.

So he decided, and the letter of surrender was composed and entrusted to one Sung Chung to convey secretly to Ts'ao Ts'ao. Sung went straight to Wanch'eng and presented the letter. It was received with joy and the bearer well rewarded. The submission was accepted and Sung was told to tell his master to go out to Ts'ao Ts'ao in the open country and he was to be confirmed in perpetual tenure of his land.

Sung Chung left the city and took the homeward way. He had nearly reached the ferry when he fell in with a party of horse. On a closer look he saw the leader was Kuan Yu. The messenger tried to escape observation, but was presently captured and taken to the leader to be questioned. At first he prevaricated but on being closely questioned told the whole story. Then he was carried off to Hsinyeh and made to retell his story to Liu Pei who heard it with lamentations.

Chang Fei said. "This being so, I propose that we put this fellow to death, then cross the river, attack Hsiangyang and make an end of the Ts'ai tribe and Liu Ts'ung as well. Then we can attack Ts'ao Ts'ao."

But Yuan-te replied, "Just shut your mouth. I have something more to say." Then turning to the prisoner he shouted, "When they did all this why did you not come to tell me? As things are now there is nothing to be gained by killing you. You may go."

Sung Chung stammered his thanks, threw his arms over his head and ran away. Yuan-te was very sad.

Presently a certain I Chi, a messenger from his nephew, was announced. Yuan-te was very fond of this man and went down the steps to welcome him.

Then said I Chi, "The heir has heard that his father is dead, but his stepmother and her family are keeping back the news so that they may set up Liu Ts'ung. He knows the news is true, as he sent a special messenger to find out. He thinks you, O Prince, may not know and has sent me to inform you and his letter begs you to lead all the men you can to Hsiangyang to help him assert his claims."

Yuan-te opened and read the letter. Then he said, "Yes, you know that the younger son has usurped the lordship, but you have not heard that he has already sent to offer the district to Ts'ao Ts'ao."

This news shocked I Chi. "How know you this?" he asked.

Liu Pei told of the capture of Sung Chung. Chi said, "You can go to Hsiangyang as if to attend the mourning ceremonies and so draw Liu Ts'ung into coming out of the city to welcome you. Then you can seize him, slay his party and take the district."

"Your advice is good," said K'ung-ming, "and my lord ought to take it."

Liu Pei wept, saying, "In his last interview my brother confided his son and heir to my care. If I lay hands upon another son and seize upon the inheritance, how shall I be able to look my brother in the face when I meet him by and bye beyond the grave?"

"If you do not act in this way now how will you repel Ts'ao Ts'ao who has already reached Wanch'eng? said K'ung-ming.

"Our best plan is to take refuge in Fanch'eng," replied Yuan-te.

Just about this time the spies came to say that Ts'ao's army had reached Powang. So I Chi was sent off with instructions to take measures for the defence of Chianghsia, while Liu Pei and K'ung-ming discussed plans for meeting the enemy.

K'ung-ming bade his master take heart. As he had seen the last army destroyed by fire, so would he see this one also the victim of a ruse. He said, "This is no place to live in; we will move over to Fanch'eng."

Then notices were posted at all the gates that all the people, without any exception, were to follow their rulers at once to the new city to escape danger. Boats were prepared and the people sent away under the direction of Sun Ch'ien. Mi Chu saw to the safe conveyance of the families of the officials.

Then the officers assembled for orders. Kuan Yu was to go to the White River. His men were to carry bags to fill with sand and earth to dam the river till the enemy should be heard, about the third watch next day. Then the waters were to be freed to drown one of the armies. He was then to march down river. Chang Fei was to go to Poling Ferry, where the current was slow. After the waters of the White River had been let loose on Ts'ao's men they would try to get over the river at the ferry. They were to be attacked. Chao Yun was to divide three companies into four parties and take one to the east gate. The other three were for the other gates. The roofs of the houses within the city walls were piled with sulphur nitre and other combustibles.

The intention was to set fire to the city when the army of the enemy had entered it for shelter. There would be a strong breeze next day in the evening which would fan the flames When this wind began to blow, fire arrows were to be shot into the city from all sides. When the flames were high there was to be a great shouting outside to add to the general terror. The east gate was to be left free for escape, but the flying men were to be smitten after passing the gate. Fanch'eng was the rallying centre after the battle.

Other orders were given to Mi Fang and Liu Feng to take command of two companies, one half with red flags and the other half with black. They were to go to Magpie Tail Slope (Hsiwei P'o), about thirty *li* from the city and camp. When they saw the Ts'ao army coming along they were to move right and left to confuse them so that they should be afraid to advance further.

All the orders given, the various leaders went their way to take up their positions and await the burning of the city. K'ung-ming and Liu Pei went away to an eminence whence they could watch what happened and where they would await the reports of victory.

Ts'ao Hung and Ts'ao Jen, with their ten legions, preceded by Hsu Ch'u leading three companies of mailed men, marched toward Hsinyeh. They formed a mighty host. They reached Magpie Tail Slope about noon. Looking ahead, they saw what seemed a goodly army with many black and red flags. Hsu Ch'u pressed forward. As he neared the flags moved from side to side and he hesitated. He began to think it unwise to advance and called a halt. Finally it was decided to go no farther then, and the leader rode back to the main body to see Ts'ao Jen.

"Those men are only make-believe," said Ts'ao Jen. "Advance, there is no ambush. I will hasten up the supports."

So Hsu Chiu rode to his own command again and advanced. When he reached the wood where he had seen the flags he saw no one at all. It was then late in the afternoon but he decided to move on. Then he heard from the hills the sound of musical instruments and, looking up, saw on the hill top two umbrellas surrounded by many banners. There sat Liu Pei and K'ung-ming quietly drinking.

Angry at their coolness, he sought for a way up, but logs of wood and great stones were thrown down and he was driven back. Further, from the rear of the hills came a confused roar. He could find no way to attack and it was getting late.

Then Ts'ao Jen arrived and ordered an attack on Hsinyeh that he might have a place to rest in. They marched to the walls and found the gates wide open. They entered and found a deserted city. No one was visible.

"This shows they are done," said Ts'ao Hung, "They have all run away, people and all. We may as well occupy the city and rest our men ready for the morrow."

The soldiers were fatigued with marching and hungry as well, so they lost no time in scattering among the houses and setting about preparing food in the deserted kitchens. The leaders took up their quarters in the *yamen*.

After the first watch the wind began to blow. Soon after the gate guards reported that a fire had started.

"The careless men have let sparks fly about," said the General.

He thought no more about it just then, but along came other reports of like nature and soon he realised that fires breaking out in all quarters were not due to accident. So he gave orders to evacuate the city. Soon the whole city seemed on fire and a red glow hung in the sky. The army was beset with fire fiercer than it had been at Powang.

> Thrice wicked was Ts'ao, but he was bold;
> Though all in the capital he controlled,
> Yet with this he was not content,
> So southward his ravaging army went.
> But, the autumn wind aiding, the Spirit of Fire
> Wrought to his army destruction dire.

Officers and men dashing through the smoke and fire in utter confusion sought some way of escape, and hearing that the east gate was free they made for that quarter. Out they rushed pell-mell, many being trodden down and trampled to death. Those who got through took the road to the east.

But presently there was a shouting behind them and Chao Yun's company came up and attacked. Then Ts'ao's men scattered, each fleeing for his life. No stand was made. A little later Mi Chu came. The fleeing general then had very few followers and those left him were scorched and burned and very wearied.

They directed their way to the Paiho, joyfully remembering that the river was shallow and fordable. And they went down into the stream and drank their fill, men shouting and horses neighing.

Meantime Kuan Yu, higher its course, had dammed the river with sandbags so that its waters were collected in a lake. Toward evening he had seen the red glow of the burning city and began to look out for his signal. About the fourth watch he heard down stream the sounds of men and horse and at once ordered the breaking of the dam. The water rushed down in a torrent and overwhelmed the men just then in the bed of the river. Many were swept away and drowned. Those who escaped made their way to where the stream ran gently and got away.

Presently they reached the ferry at Powang. Here, where they thought there would be safety, they found the road barred.

"You Ts'ao brigands!" shouted Chang Fei. "Come and receive your fate!"

> Within the city the red flame leaps out:
> On the river bank black anger is met.

What happened will appear in later chapters.

The last chapter closed with the attack made by Chang Fei as soon as his brother had let loose the waters on the doomed army. He met with Hsu Ch'u and a combat began, but a fight with such a warrior was not to Hsu's taste and he ran away. Chang Fei followed till he came upon Liu Pei and K'ung-ming and the three went up stream till they came to the boats that had been prepared, when they all crossed over and marched toward Fanch'eng. As soon as they disembarked K'ung-ming ordered the boats and rafts to be burned.

Ts'ao Jen gathered in the remnants of his army and camped at Hsinyeh, while his colleague went to tell their lord the evil tidings of defeat.

"How dare he, this rustic fool!" exclaimed Ts'ao Ts'ao angrily.

He then hastily sent an overwhelming army to camp near the place and gave orders for enormous works against the city, levelling hills and turning rivers to launch a violent assault on Fanch'eng from every side at once.

Then Liu Yeh came in to see his lord and said, "Sir, you are new to this district and you should win over the people's hearts. Liu Pei has moved all the people from Hsinyeh to Fanch'eng. If we march through the country, the people will be ground to powder. It would be well to call upon Liu Pei first to surrender, which will prove to the people that you have a care for them. If he yield then we get Chingchou without fighting.

Ts'ao agreed and asked who would be a suitable messenger. The reply was Hsu Shu.

"He is a close friend and he is here with the army," said Liu Yeh.

"But he will not come back," objected Ts'ao.

"If he does not return he will be a laughing stock to the whole world; he will come back."

Hsu Shu was sent for, and Ts'ao said, "My first intention was to level Fanch'eng with the ground, but out of pity for its people you may carry an offer to Liu Pei, that if he will surrender he will not only not be punished but he shall be given rank. But if he hold on his present misguided course the whole of his followers shall be destroyed. Now you are an honest man and so I confide this mission to you, and I trust you will not disappoint me."

Hsu Shu said nothing but accepted his orders and went to the city, where he was received by both Liu Pei and K'ung-ming. They enjoyed a talk over old times before Shu mentioned the object of his mission. Then he said, "Ts'ao has sent me to invite you to surrender, thereby making a bid for popularity. But you ought also to know that he intends to attack the city from every point, that he is damming up the Paiho waters to be sent against you, and I fear you will not be able to hold the city. You ought to prepare."

Liu Pei asked Shu to remain with them, but he said that that was impossible, for all the world would ridicule him if he stayed.

"My old mother is dead and I never forget my resentment. My body may be over there, but I swear never to form a plan for him. You have the 'Sleeping Dragon' to help you and need have no anxiety about the ultimate achievement of your undertaking. But I must go."

And he took his leave. Liu Pei felt he could not press his friend to stay. He returned to Ts'ao Ts'ao's camp and reported that Liu Pei had no intention of surrender. This angered Ts'ao who gave orders to begin the siege. When Liu Pei asked what K'ung-ming meant to do he replied that they would abandon. Fanch'eng and take Hsiangyang.

"But what of the people who have followed us? They cannot be abandoned."

"You can tell them to do as they wish. They may come if they like, or remain here."

They sent Kuan Yu to prepare boats and told Sun Ch'ien to proclaim to the people that Ts'ao was coming, that the city could not be defended, and those who wished to do so might cross the river with the army. All the people cried, "We will follow the prince even if it be to death."

They started at once, some lamenting, some weeping, the young helping the aged and parents leading their children, the strong soldiers carrying the women. As the crowds crossed the river from both banks arose the sound of lamentation.

Yuan-te was much affected as he saw all this from the boat. "Why was I ever born," said he, "to be the cause of all this misery to the people?"

He made to leap overboard, but they held him back. All were deeply sympathetic. When the boat reached the southern shore he looked back at the weeping crowds waiting still on the other bank and was again moved to tears. He bade Kuan Yu hasten the boats before he mounted and rode on.

When Hsiangyang came in sight they saw many flags flying on the walls and that the moat was protected by *chevaux de frise*. Yuan-te checked his horse and called out, "Liu Ts'ung, good nephew, I only wish to save the people and nothing more. I pray you quickly to open the gates."

But Liu Ts'ung was too frightened to appear. Ts'ai Mao and Chang Yun went up to one of the fighting towers and ordered the soldiers to shoot arrows down on those without the walls. The people gazed up at the towers and wept aloud.

Suddenly there appeared a captain, with a small following, who cried out, "You are two traitors. The princely Liu is a most upright man and has come here to preserve his people. Why do you repulse him?"

All looked at this man. He was of middle height, with a face dark brown as a ripe date. He was from Iyang and named Wei Yen. At that moment he looked very terrible, whirling his sword as if about to slice up the gate guards. They lost no time in throwing open the gate and dropping the bridge. "Come in, Uncle Liu," cried Yen," and bring your men to slay these traitors!"

Chang Fei plunged forward to take him at his word, but was checked by his brother, who said, "Do not frighten the people!"

Thus Wei Yen let in Liu Pei. As soon as he entered he saw a captain galloping up with a few men. The newcomer yelled, "Wei Yen, you nobody! how dare you create trouble? Do you not know me, the Generalissimo Wen P'ing?"

Wei Yen turned angrily, set his spear and galloped forward to attack the generalissimo. The soldiers joined in the fray and the noise of battle rose to the skies.

"I wanted to preserve the people and I am only causing them injury," cried Yuan-te distressed. "I do not wish to enter the city."

"Chiangling is an important point; we will first take that as a place to dwell in," said K'ung-ming.

"That pleases me greatly," said Yuan-te.

So they led the people thither and away from Hsiangyang. Many of the inhabitants of that city took advantage of the confusion to escape and they also joined themselves to Yuan-te.

Meanwhile, within the inhospitable city, Wei Yen and Wen P'ing fought. The battle continued for four or five hours, all through the middle of the day, and nearly all the combatants fell. Then Wei Yen got away. As he could not find Yuan-te he rode off to Ch'angsha and sought an asylum with the Prefect, Han Yuan.

Yuan-te wandered away from the city that had refused shelter. Soldiers and people, his following numbered more than a hundred thousand. The carts numbered scores of thousands and the burden bearers were innumerable. Their road led them past the tomb of Liu Piao and Yuan-te turned aside to bow at the grave. He lamented, saying, "Shameful is thy brother, lacking both in virtue and in talents. I refused to bear the burden you wished to lay upon me, wherein I was wrong. But the people committed no sin. I pray your glorious spirit to descend and rescue these people."

His prayer was fraught with sorrow and all those about him wept.

Just then a scout rode up with the news that Fanch'eng was already occupied and that men were preparing boats and rafts to cross the river. The captains knew that Chiangling was a defensible place, but they said, "With this crowd we can only advance very slowly and when can we reach the city? If Ts'ao Ts'ao pursue, we shall be in a parlous state. Our counsel is to leave the people to their fate for a time and press on to the city."

But Yuan-te wept, saying, "The success of every great enterprise depends upon humanity; how can I abandon these people who have joined me?"

Those who heard him repeat this noble sentiment were greatly affected.

> In time of stress his heart was tender toward the people,
> And he wept as he went down into the ship,
> Moving the hearts of soldiers to sympathy.
> Even today, in the countryside,
> Fathers and elders recall the Princely One's kindness.

The progress of Yuan-te , with the crowd of people in his train, was very slow.

"The pursuers will be upon us quickly," said K'ung-ming. "Let us send Kuan Yu to Chiangk'ou for succour. Liu Chi should be told to bring soldiers and prepare boats for us at Chiangling."

Yuan-te agreed to this and wrote a letter which he sent by the hands of Kuan Yu and Sun Ch'ien. Chang Fei was put in command of the rear guard. Chao Yun was told to guard the aged and the children, while the others ordered the march of the people. They only travelled a short distance daily and the halts were frequent.

Meanwhile Ts'ao Ts'ao was at Fanch'eng, whence he sent soldiers over the river toward Hsiangyang. He summoned Liu Ts'ung, but he was too afraid to answer the call. No persuasion could get him to go. One, Wang Wei, said to him privately, "Now you can overcome Ts'ao Ts'ao if you are wise. Since you have announced surrender and Liu Pei has gone away, he will relax his precautions and you can catch him unawares. Send a well-prepared but unexpected force to waylay him in some commanding position and the thing is done. If you were to take Ts'ao prisoner your fame would run throughout the empire and the land would be yours for the taking. This is a sort of opportunity that does not recur and you should not miss it."

The young man consulted Ts'ai Mao, who called Wang an evil counsellor and spoke to him harshly. "You are mad; you know nothing and understand nothing of destiny," said Mao.

Wang Wei angrily retorted, calling his critic the betrayer of his country, and saying he wished he could eat him alive. The quarrel waxed deadly but eventually peace was restored.

Then Ts'ao Mao and Chang Yun went to Fanch'eng to see Ts'ao Ts'ao. Mao was by instinct specious and flattering, and when his host asked concerning the resources of the district, he replied, "There are five legions of horse, fifteen of foot and eight of marines. Most of the money and grain are at Chiangling; the rest is stored at various places. There are ample supplies for a year."

"How many war vessels are there? Who is in command?" said Ts'ao.

"The ships, of all sizes, number seven thousand and we two are the commanders."

Upon this Ts'ao conferred upon Ts'ao Mao the title of Marquis, Guardian of the South and Admiral-in-Chief of the Naval Force and Chang Yun was his Vice-Admiral with the title of Marquis *Tsu-shun*.

When they went to thank Ts'ao for these honours he told them he was about to propose to the throne that Liu Piao's son should be perpetual prefect of Chingchou in succession to his late father. With this promise for their young master and the honours for themselves they retired.

Then Hsun Yu asked Ts'ao why these two evident self-seekers

and flatterers had been treated so generously. Ts'ao replied, "Do I not know all about them? Only in the north country, where I have been, they know nothing of war by water and these two men do. I want their help for the present. When my end is achieved I can do as I like with them."

Liu Ts'ung was highly delighted when his two chief supporters returned with the promise Ts'ao had given them. Soon after he gave up his seal and military commission and proceeded to welcome Ts'ao Ts'ao, who received him very graciously.

Ts'ao next proceeded to camp near Hsiangyang. The populace, led by Ts'ao Mao, welcomed him with burning incense, and he on his part put forth proclamations couched in comforting terms.

Ts'ao Ts'ao presently entered the city and took his seat in the residence in state. Then he summoned K'uai Yueh and said to him graciously, "I do not rejoice so much at gaining Chingchou as at meeting you, I-tu."

He made K'uai Prefect of Chiangling and Marquis of Fanch'eng; his other adherents were all ennobled. Liu Ts'ung became Governor of Ch'ingchou in the north and was ordered to proceed to his district forthwith. He was greatly frightened and said he had no wish to become an actual official; he wished to remain in the place where his father and mother lived.

Said Ts'ao, "Your governorship is quite near the capital and I have sent you there as a full official to remove you from the intrigues of this place."

In vain Liu Ts'ung declined the honours thus thrust upon him; he was compelled to go and he departed, taking his mother with him. Of his friends, only Wang Wei accompanied him. Some of his late officers escorted him as far as the river and then took their leave. Then Ts'ao called his trusty officer Yu Chin and bade him follow up Liu Ts'ung and put him and his mother to death.

Yu Chin followed the small party. When he drew near he shouted, "I have an order from the great Minister to put you both to death, mother and son; you may as well submit quietly."

The Lady Ts'ai threw her arms about her son, lifted up her voice and wept. Yu Chin bade the soldiers get on with their bloody work. Only Wang Wei made any attempt to save his mistress and he was soon killed. The two, mother and son, were soon finished and the murderer returned to report his success. He was richly rewarded.

Next Ts'ao Ts'ao sent to discover and seize the family of K'ungming, but they had already disappeared. It was much to Ts'ao's disgust that the search was fruitless.

So Hsiangyang was settled. Then Hsun Yu proposed a further

advance. He said, "Chiangling is an important place, and very rich; if Liu Pei gets it, it will be difficult to dislodge him."

"How could I have overlooked that?" said Ts'ao.

Then he called upon the officers of Hsiangyang for one who could lead the way. They all came except Wen P'ing.

Ts'ao sent for him and soon he came also. "Why are you late?" asked Ts'ao.

"To be a minister and see one's master lose his own boundaries is most shameful. Such an one has no face to show to any man and I was too ashamed to come."

His tears fell fast as he finished this speech. Ts'ao admired his loyal conduct and rewarded him with office and a title, and also bade him open the way.

The spies returned and told how Liu Pei was hampered by the crowds of people who had followed him. And he was then only three hundred *li* away. Ts'ao decided to take advantage of his plight so chose out five companies of tried horsemen and sent them after the cavalcade, giving them a limit of a day and a night to come up therewith. The main army would follow.

As has been said Liu Pei was travelling with a huge multitude of followers, to guard whom he had taken what precautions were possible. Kuan Yu had been sent to Chianghsia. One day K'ung-ming came in and said, "There is as yet no news from Chianghsia; what are we to do?"

"I wish that you yourself would go there," said Liu Pei. "Liu Chi would remember your former kindness to him and consent to anything you proposed."

K'ung-ming said he would go and set out with Liu Feng, the adopted son of Liu Pei, taking an escort of half a company.

A few days after, while on the march in company with three of his intimate captains, a sudden whirlwind rose just in front of Yuan-te, and a huge column of dust shot up into the air hiding the face of the sun. Yuan-te was frightened and asked what that might portend. Chien Yung, who knew something of the mysteries of nature, took the auspices by counting secretly on his fingers. Pale and trembling he announced that a calamity was threatening that very night. He advised his lord to lead the people to their fate and flee quickly. But he refused to think of it.

"If you allow your pity to overcome your judgment, then misfortune is very near," said Chien.

Thus spake Chien Yung to his lord, who then asked what place was near. His people replied that Tangyang was quite close and there was a very famous hill near it called Chingshan or Prospect Hill. Then Yuan-te bade them lead the way thither.

The season was late autumn, just changing to winter, and the icy wind penetrated to the very bones. As evening fell, long-drawn howls of misery were heard on every side. At the middle of the fourth watch, two hours after midnight, they heard a rumbling sound in the north-west. Yuan-te halted and placed himself at the head of his own guard of two companies to meet whatever might come. Presently Ts'ao's men appeared and made a fierce onslaught. Defence was impossible, though Yuan-te fought desperately. By good fortune just at the crisis Chang Fei came up, cut his way through, rescued his brother and got him away to the east. Presently they were stopped by Wen P'ing.

"Turncoat! Can you still look men in the face?" cried Yuan-te.

Wen P'ing was overwhelmed with shame and led his men away. Chang Fei, now fighting, now flying, protected his brother till dawn.

By that time Liu Pei had got beyond the sound of battle and there was time to rest. Only a few of his men had been able to keep near him. He knew nothing of the fate of his captains or the people. He lifted up his voice in lamentation saying, "Myriads of living souls are suffering from love of me, and my captains and my loved ones are lost. One would be a graven image not to weep at such loss."

Still plunged in sadness presently he saw hurrying toward him Mi Fang, with an enemy's arrow still sticking in his face. He exclaimed, "Chao Yun has gone over Ts'ao Ts'ao!"

Yuan-te angrily bade him be silent. "Do you think I can believe that of my old friend?" cried he.

"Perhaps he has gone over," said Chang Fei. "He must see that we are nearly lost and there are riches and honours on the other side."

"He has followed me faithfully through all my misfortunes. His heart is firm as a rock. No riches or honours would move him."

"I saw him go away north-west," said Mi Fang.

"Wait till I meet him," said Chang Fei. "If I run against him I will kill him."

"Beware how you doubt him," said Yuan-te. "Have you forgotten the circumstances under which your brother had to slay two men to ease your doubts of him? Chao Yun's absence is due to good reason wherever he has gone, and he would never abandon me."

But do you think Chang Fei was convinced? Then Chang Fei

with a score of his men, rode to Ch'angpan Bridge. Seeing a wood near the bridge, an idea suddenly struck him. He bade his followers cut branches from the trees, tie them to the tails of the horses and ride to and fro so as to raise a great dust as though an army were concealed in the wood. He himself took up his station on the bridge facing the west with spear set ready for action. So he kept watch.

Now Chao Yun, after fighting with the enemy from the fourth watch till daylight, could see no sign of his lord and, moreover had lost his lord's family. He thought bitterly within himself, "My master confided to me his family and the young lord; and I have lost them. How can I look him in the face? I can only go now and fight to the death. Whatever happen I must go to seek the women and my lord's son."

Turning about he found he had but two score followers left. He rode quickly to and fro among the scattered soldiers seeking the lost women. The lamentations of the people about him were enough to make heaven and earth weep. Some had been wounded by arrows, others by spears; they had thrown away their children, abandoned their wives, and were flying they knew not whither in crowds.

Presently he saw a man lying in the grass and recognised him as Chien Yung.

"Have you seen the two mothers?" cried he.

Chien replied, "They left their carriage and ran away taking O-tou in their arms. I followed but on the slope of the hill I was wounded and fell from my horse. The horse was stolen. I could fight no longer and I lay down here."

Chao Yun put his colleague on the horse of one of his followers, told off two soldiers to support him and bade him ride to their lord and tell him of the loss. "Say," said he, "that I will seek the lost ones in heaven or hell, through good or evil, and if I find them not I will die in the desert."

Then he rode off toward Ch'angpan Slope. As he went a voice called out, "General Chao, where are you going?"

"Who are you?" said Chao Yun, pulling up.

"One of the Princely One's carriage guards. I am wounded."

"Do you know anything of the two ladies?"

"Not very long ago I saw the Lady Kan go south with a party of other women. Her hair was down and she was barefooted."

Hearing this, without even another glance at the speaker, Chao Yun put his horse at full gallop toward the south. Soon he saw a small crowd of persons, male and female, walking hand in hand.

"Is the Lady Kan among you?" he called out.

A woman in the rear of the party looked up at him and uttered a loud cry. He slipped off his steed, stuck his spear in the sand and wept, "It was my fault that you were lost. But where are the Lady Mi and our young lord?"

She replied, "I and she were forced to abandon our carriage and mingle with the crowd on foot. Then a band of soldiers came up and we were separated. I do not know where they are. I ran for my life."

As she spoke a howl of distress rose from the crowd of fugitives, for a company of soldiers appeared. Chao Yun recovered his spear and mounted ready for action. Presently he saw among the soldiers a prisoner bound upon a horse; and the prisoner was Mi Chu. Behind him followed a captain ripping a huge sword. The men belonged to the army of Ts'ao Jen and the Captain was Shunyu Tao. Having captured Mi Chu he was just taking him to his chief as a proof of his prowess.

Chao Yun shouted and rode at the captor who was speedily unhorsed and his captive was set free. Then taking two of the horses Chao Yun set the lady on one and Mi Chu took the other. They rode away toward Ch'angpan Slope.

But there, standing grim on the bridge, was Chang Fei. As soon as he saw Chao Yun he called out, "Tzu-lung, why have you betrayed my brother?"

"I fell behind because I was seeking the ladies and our young lord," said Chao Yun. "What do you mean by talking of betrayal?"

"If it had not been that Chien Yung arrived before you I should hardly have spared you."

"Where is the master?" said Chao Yun.

"Not far away, in front there."

"Conduct the Lady Kan to him; I am going to look for the Lady Mi," said Chao Yun to his companion, and he turned back along the road by which he had come.

Before long he met a captain armed with an iron spear and carrying a sword slung across his back, riding a curvetting steed and leading a half score of other horsemen. Without uttering a word Chao Yun rode straight toward him and engaged. At the first pass he disarmed his opponent and brought him to earth. His followers galloped away.

This fallen officer was no other that Hsiahou En. Ts'ao Ts'ao's sword-bearer, and the sword on his back was his master's. Ts'ao Ts'ao had two swords, one called *I-t'ien* (Trust in God) and the other *Ch'ing-kung*. *I-t'ien* was the weapon he usually wore at his side, the other being carried by his sword-bearer. *Ch'ing-kung* would cut clean through iron as though it were mud and no sword had so keen an edge.

When Chao Yun thus fell in with Ts'ao's sword-bearer the later was simply plundering, depending upon the authority implied by his office. Least of all thought he of such sudden death as met him at Chao Yun's hands.

So Chao Yun got possession of a famous sword. The name *Ch'ing-kung* was chased in gold characters so that he recognised its value at once. He stuck it in his belt and again plunged into the press. Just as he did so he turned his head and saw he had not a single follower left; he was quite alone.

Nevertheless not for a single instant thought he of turning back, he was too intent upon his quest. To and fro, back and forth, he rode questioning this person and that. At length a man said, "A woman with a child in her arms, and wounded in the thigh so that she cannot walk, is lying over there through that hole in the wall."

Chao Yun rode to look and there, beside an old well behind the broken wall of a burned house, sat the mother clasping the child to her breast and weeping.

Chao was on his knees before her in a moment.

"My child will live then since you are here," cried the Lady Mi. "Pity him, O General; protect him, for he is the only son of his father's flesh and blood. Take him to his father and I can die content."

"It is my fault that you have suffered," replied Chao Yun. "But it is useless to say more. I pray you take my horse while I will walk beside and protect you till we get clear."

She replied, "I may not do that. What would you do without a steed? But the boy here I confide to your care. I am badly wounded and cannot hope to live. Pray take him and go your way. Do not trouble more about me."

"I hear shouting," said Chao. "The soldiers will be upon us again in a moment. Pray mount quickly."

"But really I cannot move," she said. "Do not let there be a double loss!" And she held out the child toward him as she spoke.

"Take the child," cried she. "His life and safety are in your hands."

Again and again Chao Yun besought her to get on his horse, but she would not. The shouting drew nearer and nearer, Chao Yun spoke harshly saying. "If you will not do what I say, what will happen when the soldiers come up?"

She said no more. Throwing the child on the ground she turned over and threw herself into the old well. And there she perished.

> The warrior relies upon the strength of his charger,
> Afoot, how could he bear to safety his young prince?
> Brave mother! who died to preserve the son of her husband's line;
> Heroine was she, bold and decisive!

Seeing that the lady had resolved the question by dying there was nothing more to be done. Chao Yun filled in the well with the rubbish that lay about lest the dead body should suffer shame. Then he loosened his armour, let down the heart-protecting mirror and placed the child in his breast. This done he slung his spear and re-mounted.

He had gone but a short distance when he saw Yen Ming, one of Ts'ao Ts'ao's minor captains. This warrior used a double edged, three pointed weapon and he offered battle. However, Chao Yun disposed of him after a very few bouts and dispersed his men.

As the road cleared before him he saw another detachment barring his way. At the head of this was a captain of rank exalted enough to display a banner with his name Chang Ho. Chao Yun never waited to parley but attacked. However, this was a more formidable antagonist and half a score bouts found neither any nearer defeat. But Chao, with the child in his bosom, could only fight with the greatest caution and so he decided to flee. Chang Ho pursued and as Chao thought only of thrashing his steed to get away, and little of the road, suddenly he went crashing into a pit. On came his pursuer, spear at poise. Suddenly a brilliant flash of light seemed to shoot out of the pit and the fallen horse leapt with it into the air and was again on firm earth.

> A bright glory surrounds the child of the imperial line,
>   now in danger,
> The powerful charger forces his way through the press
>   of battle,
> Bearing to safety him who was destined to sit on the
>   throne two score years and two;
> And the general thus manifested his godlike courage.

This apparition frightened Chang Ho, who abandoned the pursuit forthwith and Chao Yun rode off. Presently he heard shouts behind, "Chao Yun, Chao Yun, stop!" and at the same time he saw ahead of him two captains who seemed disposed to dispute his way. Two in front and two following, his state seemed desperate, but he quailed not.

As the men of Ts'ao came pressing on he drew Ts'ao Ts'ao's own sword to beat them off. Nothing could resist it. Armour, clothing, it went through without effort and blood gushed forth in fountains wherever it struck. So the four captains were soon beaten off and Chao Yun was once again free.

Now Ts'ao Ts'ao from a hill top saw these deeds of derring-do and a captain showing such valour that none could withstand him, so he asked of his followers whether any knew the man. No one recognised him, so Ts'ao Hung galloped down into the plain and shouted to the hero asking him his name.

"I am Chao Tzu-lung of Ch'angshan, replied Chao Yun.

Ts'ao Hung returned and told his lord, who said, A very tiger of a leader! I must get him alive." Whereupon he sent gallopers to all detachments with orders that no arrows were to be fired from an ambush at any point Chao Yun should pass; he was to be taken alive.

And so Chao Yun escaped most imminent danger, and O-tou's safety, bound up with his saviour's, was also secured. On this career of slaughter which ended in safety, Chao Yun, bearing in his bosom him who was to be known as The Later Lord, cut down two banners, took three spears and slew of Ts'ao's captains half a hundred, all men of renown.

> Blood dyed the fighting robe and crimsoned his buff coat;
> None dared engage the terrible warrior at Tangyang;
> In the days of old lived the brave Chao Yun,
> Who fought in the battlefield for his lord in danger.

Having thus fought his way out of the press Chao Yun lost no time in getting away from the battle field. His battle robe was soaked in blood.

On his way, near the rise of the hills, he met with two other bodies of men under two brothers, Chung Chin and Chung Shen. One of these was armed with a massive axe, the other a halberd. As soon as they saw Chao Yun they knew him and shouted, "Quickly dismount and be bound!"

> He has only escaped from the tiger's cave,
> To risk the deep pool's sounding wave.

How Chao Yun escaped will be next related.

CHAPTER XLII

CHANG FEI'S GREAT FIGHT AT CH'ANGPAN
SLOPE: LIU PEI, DEFEATED, GOES TO
HANCHINGK'OU

As related in the last chapter two brothers appeared in front of our warrior, who rode at them with his spear ready for a thrust. Chung Chin was leading, flourishing his battle-axe. Chao Yun engaged and very soon unhorsed him. Then he galloped away. Chung Shen rode up behind ready with his halberd and his horse's nose got so close to the other's tail that in Chao Yun's back heart-protecting mirror he could see the play of the reflection of his weapon. Then suddenly, and without warning, Chao Yun wheeled round his horse so that he faced his pursuer and their two steeds struck breast to breast. With his spear in his left hand he warded off the halberd strokes and in his right he swung the sword *Ch'ing-kung*. One slash and he had cut through both helmet and head; Chung Shen fell to the ground, a corpse with only half a head on his body. His followers fled and Chao Yun retook the road toward Long Slope Bridge.

But in his rear arose another tumultuous shouting, seeming to rend the very sky, and Wen P'ing came up behind. However, although the man was weary and his steed highspent, Chao Yun got close to the bridge where he saw standing, all ready for any fray, his brother in arms.

"Help me, I-te!" he cried and crossed the bridge.

"Hasten!" cried Chang Fei, "I will keep back the pursuers."

About twenty *li* from the bridge he saw Yuan-te with his followers reposing in the shade of some trees. He dismounted and drew near, weeping. The tears also started to Yuan-te's eyes when he saw his faithful follower.

Still panting from his exertions, Chao Yun gasped out, "My fault—death is too light a punishment. The Lady Mi was severely wounded; she refused my horse and threw herself into a well. She is dead and all I could do was to fill in the well with the rubbish that lay around. But I placed the babe in the breast of my fighting robe and have won my way out of the press of battle. Thanks to the little lord's grand luck I have escaped. At first he cried a good deal, but for some time now he has not stirred or made a sound. I fear I may not have saved his life after all."

Then he opened his robe and looked; the child was fast asleep.

"Happily, Sir, your son is unhurt," said Chao as he drew him forth and presented him in both hands. Yuan-te took the child but threw it aside angrily, saying, "To preserve that suckling I very nearly lost a great captain."

Chao Yun picked up the child again and, weeping, said, "Were I ground to powder I could not prove my gratitude."

> From out Ts'ao's host a tiger rushed,
>   His wish but to destroy;
> Though Liu Pei's consort lost her life,
>   Chao Yun preserved her boy.
> "Too great the risk you ran to save
>   This child," the father cried.
> To show he rated Chao Yun high,
>   He threw his son aside.

Wen P'ing and his company pursued Chao Yun till they saw Chang Fei's bristling moustache and fiercely glaring eyes before them. There he was seated on his battle steed, his hand grasping his terrible serpent-like spear, guarding the bridge. They also saw great clouds of dust rising above the trees and concluded they would fall into an ambush if they ventured across the bridge. So they stopped the pursuit, not daring to advance further.

In a little time several other captains came up, but none dared advance, frightened not only by Chang Fei's fierce look, but lest they should become victims of a ruse of the terrible Chuko Liang. As they came up they formed a line on the west side, halting till they could inform their lord of the position.

As soon as the messengers arrived and Ts'ao Ts'ao heard about it he mounted and rode to the bridge to see for himself. Chang Fei's fierce eye scanning the hinder position of the army opposite him saw the silken umbrella, the axes and banners coming along and concluded that Ts'ao Ts'ao came to see for himself how matters stood. So in a mighty voice he shouted, "I am Chang I-te of Yen; who dares fight with me?"

At the sound of this thundrous voice a terrible quaking fear seized upon Ts'ao and he bade them take the umbrella away.

Turning to his followers he said, "Kuan Yu said that his brother Chang Fei was the sort of man to go through an army of a hundred legions and take the head of its commander-in-chief; and do it easily. Now here is this terror in front of us and we must be careful."

As he finished speaking again that terrible voice was heard, "I am Chang I-te of Yen; who dares fight with me?"

Ts'ao, seeing his enemy so fierce and resolute, was too frightened to think of anything but retreat and Chang Fei, seeing a movement going on in the rear, once again shook his spear and roared, "What mean you, cowards? You will not fight nor do you run away."

This roar had scarcely begun when one of Ts'ao's staff reeled and fell from his horse terror-stricken, paralysed with fear. The panic touched Ts'ao Ts'ao, and spread to his whole surroundings and he and his staff galloped for their lives. They were as frightened as a suckling babe at a clap of thunder or a weak woodcutter at the roar of a tiger. Many threw away their spears, dropped their casques and fled, a wave of panic-stricken humanity, a tumbling mass of terrified horses. None thought of aught but flight, and those who ran trampled the bodies of fallen comrades under foot.

> Chang Fei was wrathful; and who dared
> To accept his challenge? Fierce he glared;
> His thundrous voice rolled out, and then
> In terror fled Ts'ao's armed men.

Panic stricken Ts'ao Ts'ao galloped westward with the rest, thinking of nothing but getting away. He lost his headdress and his loosened hair streamed behind him. Presently Chang Liao and Hsu Ch'u came up with him and seized his bridle; fear had deprived him of all self-control.

"Do not be frightened," said Chang Liao. "After all Chang Fei is but one man and not worthy of extravagant fear. If you will only return and attack you will capture your enemy."

By that time Ts'ao had somewhat overcome his panic and become reasonable. Two captains were ordered back to the bridge to reconnoitre.

Chang Fei saw the disorderly rout of the enemy but he dared not pursue. However, he bade his score or so of dustraising followers to cut loose the branches from their horses' tails and come to help destroy the bridge. This done he went to report to his brother and told him of the destruction of the bridge.

"Brave as you are, brother, and no one is braver, you are no strategist," said Liu Pei.

"What mean you, brother?"

"Ts'ao Ts'ao is very deep. You are no match for him. The destruction of the bridge will bring him in pursuit."

"If he ran away at a yell of mine, think you he will dare return?"

"If you had left the bridge he would have thought there was an ambush and would not have dared to pass it. Now the destruction of the bridge tells him we are weak and fearful, and he will pursue. He does not mind a broken bridge. His legions could fill up the biggest rivers that we could get across."

So orders were given to march and they went by a bye-road which led diagonally to Hanching and then took the road to Minyang.

The two captains sent by Ts'ao to reconnoitre near Ch'angpan Bridge returned, saying, "The bridge has been destroyed, Chang Fei has left."

"Then he is afraid," said Ts'ao.

He at once gave orders to set a legion at work on three floating bridges to be finished that night.

Li Tien said, "I fear this is one of the wiles of Chuko Liang; so be careful."

"Chang Fei is just a bold warrior, but there is no guile about him," said Ts'ao Ts'ao.

He gave orders for immediate advance.

Liu Pei was making all speed to Hanching. Suddenly there appeared in his track a great cloud of dust whence came loud rolls of drums and shoutings. Yuan-te was dismayed and said, "Before us rolls the great river; behind is the pursuer. What hope is there for us?"

But he bade Chao Yun organise a defence.

Now Ts'ao Ts'ao in an order to his army had said, "Liu Pei is a fish in the fish kettle; a tiger in the pit. Catch him this time, or the fish will get back to the sea and the tiger escape to the hills. Therefore every captain must use his best efforts to press on."

In consequence every leader bade those under him hasten forward. And they were pressing on at great speed when suddenly soldiers appeared from the hills and a voice cried, "I have waited here a long time."

The leader who had shouted this bore in his hand the Black Dragon sword and rode "Red Hare," for indeed it was no other than Kuan Yu. He had gone to Chianghsia for help and had returned with a whole legion. Having heard of the battle he had taken this very road to intercept pursuit.

As soon as Kuan Yu appeared Ts'ao stopped and said to his officers, "Here we are, tricked again by that Chuko Liang."

Without more ado he ordered a retreat. Kuan Yu followed him some ten *li* and then drew off to act as guard to his elder brother on his way to the river. There boats were ready and Yuan-te and family went on board. When all were settled comfortably in the boat Kuan Yu asked where was his sister, the second wife of his brother. Then Yuan-te told him the story of Tangyang.

"Alas!" said Kuan Yu. "Had you taken my advice that day of the hunting in Hsut'ien we should have escaped the misery of this day."

"But," said Yuan-te, "on that day it was 'Ware damage when pelting rats.' "

Just as he spoke he heard war-drums on the south bank. A fleet of boats, thick as a flight of ants, came running up with swelling sails before the fair wind. He was alarmed.

The boats came nearer. There he saw the white clad figure of a man wearing a silver helmet who stood in the prow of the foremost ship. He cried, "Are you all right, my uncle? I am very guilty."

It was Liu Chi. He bowed low as the ship passed, saying, "I heard you were in danger from Ts'ao Ts'ao and I have come to aid you."

Yuan-te welcomed him with joy and his soldiers joined in with the main body and the whole fleet sailed on, while they told each other their adventures.

Unexpectedly in the south-west there appeared a line of fighting ships swishing up before a fair wind. Liu Chi said, "All my men are here and now there is an enemy barring the way. If they are not Ts'ao Ts'ao's ships they must be from Chiangtung. We have a poor chance. What now?"

Yuan-te went to the prow and gazed at them. Presently he made out a figure in a turban and Taoist robe sitting in the bows of one of the boats and knew it to be K'ung-ming. Behind him stood Sun Ch'ien.

When they were quite near Yuan-te asked K'ung-ming how he came to be there. And he reported what he had done, saying, "When I reached Chianghsia I sent Kuan Yu to land at Hanching with reinforcements, for I feared pursuit from Ts'ao Ts'ao and knew the road you would take. So I prayed your nephew to go to meet you while I went to Hsiak'ou to muster as many men as possible."

The new-comers added to their strength and they began once more to consider how their powerful enemy might be overcome.

Said K'ung-ming, "Hsiak'ou is strong and a good strategical

point; it is also rich and suited for a lengthy stay. I would ask you, my lord, to make it a permanent camp. Your nephew can go to Chianghsia to get the fleet in order and prepare weapons. Thus there will be two threatening angles to our position. If we all return to Chianghsia the position will be weakened."

Liu Chi replied, "The Adviser-General's words are excellent, but I would rather my uncle stayed awhile in Chianghsia till the army was in thorough order. Then he could go to Hsiak'ou."

"You speak to the point, nephew," replied Yuan-te. Then leaving Kuan Yu with half a legion at Hsiak'ou he, with K'ung-ming and his nephew, went to Chianghsia.

When Ts'ao Ts'ao saw Kuan Yu with a force ready to attack he feared lest a greater number were hidden away behind, so he stopped the pursuit. He also feared lest Yuan-te should take Chiangling, so he marched thither with all haste.

The two officers in command at Chingchou had heard of what happened at Hsiangyang and, knowing that there was no chance of successful defence against Ts'ao Ts'ao's armies, they led out the people of Chingchou to the outskirts and offered submission. Ts'ao entered the city and, after restoring order and confidence, he released Han Sung and gave him the dignified office of Director of Ambassadorial Receptions. He rewarded the others.

Then said Ts'ao Ts'ao, "Liu Pei has gone to Chianghsia and may ally himself with Wu and the opposition to me will be greater. Can he be destroyed?

Hsun Yu said, "The splendour of your achievements has spread wide. Therefore you might send a messenger to invite Sun Ch'uan to a grand hunting party at Chianghsia and you two could seize Liu Pei, share Chingchou with Sun and make a solemn treaty. Sun will be too frightened not to come over to you and your end will be gained."

Ts'ao agreed. He sent the letters by a messenger and he prepared his men, horse and foot and marines. He had in all eighty-three legions, but he called them a hundred. The attack was to be by land and water at the same time.

The fleet advanced up the river in two lines. On the west it extended to Chinghsia, on the east to Ch'ihuang in Hupeh. The stockades stretched three hundred *li*.

At this point the narrative must digress. The story of Ts'ao Ts'ao's movements and successes reached Sun Ch'uan, then in camp at Ch'aisang. He assembled his strategists to decide on a scheme of defence.

Lu Su said, "Chingchou is contiguous to our borders. It is strong and defensive, its people are rich. It is the sort of country that an emperor or a king should have. Liu Piao's recent death gives an excuse for me to be sent to convey condolence and, once there, I shall be able to talk over Liu Pei and the officers of the late prefect to combine with you against Ts'ao. If Liu Pei does as I wish, then success is yours."

Sun Ch'uan thought this a good plan, so he had the necessary letters prepared, and the gifts, and sent Lu Su with them.

All this time Liu Pei was at Chianghsia where, with K'ung-ming and Liu Ch'i, he was endeavouring to evolve a good plan of campaign.

K'ung-ming said, "Ts'ao Ts'ao's power is too great for us to cope with. Let us go over to Wu and ask help from Sun Ch'uan. If we can set north and south at grips we ought to be able to get some advantage from our mediary position between them."

"But will they be willing to have anything to do with us?" said Yuan-te. "It is a large and populous country and Sun Ch'uan has ambitions of his own."

K'ung-ming replied, "Ts'ao with his army of a hundred legions holds the Han and the Yangtse. Chiangtung will certainly send to find out all possible about the position. Should any messenger come I shall borrow a little boat and make a little trip over the river and trust to my little lithe tongue to set north and south at each other's throats. If the southern men win, we will assist in destroying Ts'ao in order to get Chingchou; if the north win, we shall profit by the victory to get Chiangnan. So we shall get some advantage either way."

"That is a very fine view to take," said Yuan-te. "But how are you going to get hold of any one from the south to talk to?"

Liu Pei's question was answered by the arrival of Lu Su, and as the ship touched the bank and the envoy came ashore, K'ung-ming laughed, saying, "It is done!"

Turning to Liu Ch'i he asked, "When Sun Ts'e died did your country send any condolences?"

"Is it likely there would be any mourning courtesies between them and us while there was the death of a father to avenge?"

"Then it is certain that this envoy does not come to present condolences but to spy out the land."

So he said to Yuan-te, "When Lu Su asks about the movements of Ts'ao Ts'ao, you will know nothing. If he press the matter, say he can ask me."

Having thus prepared their scheme they sent to welcome the envoy, who entered the city in mourning garb. The gifts having been accepted, Liu Ch'i asked Lu Su to meet Yuan-te. When the introductory ceremonies were over the three men went to one of the inner chambers to drink a cup of wine. Presently Lu Su said to Yuan-te, "By reputation I have known you a long time, Uncle Liu, but till today I have not met you. I am very gratified at seeing you. You have been fighting Ts'ao Ts'ao, though, lately, so I suppose you know all about him. Has he really so great an army? How many, do you think, he has?"

"My army was so small that we fled whenever we heard of his approach; so I do not know how many he had."

"You had the advice of Chuko K'ung-ming and you used fire on Ts'ao Ts'ao twice. You burned him almost to death so that you can hardly say you know nothing about his men," said Lu.

"Without asking my adviser I really do not know the details."

"Where is K'ung-ming? I should like to see him," said Lu.

So they sent for him and he was introduced. When the ceremonies were over Lu Su said, "I have long admired your genius but have never been fortunate enough to meet you. Now that I have met you I hope I may speak of present politics."

Replied K'ung-ming, "We know all Ts'ao Ts'ao's infamies and wickednesses, but to our regret we were not strong enough to withstand him. That is why we avoided him."

"Is the Imperial Uncle going to stay here?"

"The Princely One is an old friend of Wu Ch'en, Prefect of Ts'angwu and intends to go to him."

"He has few men and insufficient supplies, he cannot ensure safety. How can he receive the Uncle?" said Lu.

"His place is not one to remain in long, but it is good enough for the present. We can make other plans for the future."

Lu said, "Sun Ch'uan is strongly posted and is exceedingly well supplied. He treats able men and scholars with the greatest courtesy and so they gather round him. Now if you are seeking a plan for your Prince you cannot do better than send some friend to confer with him."

"There have never been any relations between my master and yours," said K'ung-ming. "I fear there would be nothing but a waste of words. Besides, we have no one to send."

"Your elder brother is there as adviser and is longing to see you. I am but a simple wight but I should be pleased to discuss affairs with my master and you."

"But he is my Director-in-Chief," said Yuan-te, "and I cannot do without him. He cannot go."

Lu Su pressed him. Yuan-te pretended to refuse permission.

"It is important; I pray you give me leave to go," said K'ung-ming.

Then Yuan-te consented. And they soon took leave and the two set out by boat for Sun Ch'uan's headquarters.

> A little boat sailed down the stream
> With Chuko well content;
> For he could see his enemies
> To black perdition sent.

The result of this journey will appear in the following chapter.

CHAPTER XLIII

CHUKO LIANG DISPUTES WITH THE SCHOLARS: LU SU DENOUNCES THE MAJORITY OPINION

In the boat on the way to Ch'aisang the two travellers beguiled the time by discussing affairs. Lu Su impressed upon his companion the necessity of concealing from Sun Ch'uan the truth about the magnitude of Ts'ao Ts'ao's army.

"I do not promise to do what you ask," replied Chuko Liang, "but I shall know how to reply."

When the boat arrived K'ung-ming was lodged in the guests' quarters and Lu Su went alone to see his master. He found him actually at a council, assembled to consider the situation. Lu Su was summoned thereto and questioned at once upon what he had discovered.

"I know the general outline, but I want a little time to prepare my report," replied he.

Then Sun Ch'uan produced Ts'ao Ts'ao's letter and gave it to Su. "That came yesterday. I have sent the bearer of it back and this gathering is to consider the reply," said he.

Lu Su read the letter, which said, "When I, the solitary one, received the imperial command to punish a fault my banners went south and Liu Ts'ung became my prisoner, while his people flocked to my side at the first rumour of my coming . Under my hand are a hundred legions and I have many able captains. My desire is, General, that we go on a great hunting expedition into Chianghsia and together attack Liu Pei. We will share his land between us and we will swear perpetual amity. If happily you would not be a mere looker-on I pray you reply quickly."

"What have you decided upon, my lord?" asked Lu as he finished the letter.

"I have not yet decided."

Then Chang Chao said, "It would be imprudent to withstand Ts'ao's many legions backed by the imperial authority. Moreover your most important defence against him is the Long River (Yangtse) and since Ts'ao has gained possession of Chingchou the river is his ally against us. We cannot withstand him, and the only way to tranquillity, in my opinion, is submission."

"The words of the speaker accord with the manifest decree of providence," echoed all the assembly.

Sun Ch'uan remaining silent and thoughtful, Chang Chao again took up the argument. "Do not hesitate, my lord. Submission to Ts'ao means tranquillity for the people of Wu and safety for the inhabitants of Chiangnan."

Sun Ch'uan still remained silent, his head bent in deep thought. Presently he arose and paced slowly out at the door and Lu Su followed him. Outside he took Lu by the hand, saying, "What do you desire?"

"What they have all been saying is very derogatory to you. A common man might submit; you cannot."

"Why? How do you explain that?"

"If people like us submitted we could just return to our village, and everything would go on as before. If you submit, whither will you go? You will be created a Marquis, perhaps. You will have one carriage, no more, one saddle horse, that is all. Your retinue will be half a score. Will you be able to sit facing the south and call yourself by the kingly title of 'the solitary'? Each one in your crowd of hangers-on is thinking for himself, is purely selfish, and you should not listen to them, but take a line of your own and that quickly. Determine to play a bold game."

Sun Ch'uan sighed, "They all talk and talk, they miss my point of view. Now you have just spoken of a bold game and your view is the same as mine. Surely God has expressly sent you to me. Still Ts'ao is now the stronger by all Yuan Shao's army and he has possession of Chingchou. I fear he is almost too powerful to contend with."

"I have brought back with me Chuko Liang, the brother of our Chuko Chin. If you questioned him he would explain clearly."

"Is 'Master Sleeping Dragon' really here?"

"Really here; in the guest-house."

"It is too late to see him today. But tomorrow I will assemble my officials and you will introduce him to all my best. After that we will debate the matter."

With these instructions Lu Su retired. Next day he went to the guest-house and conveyed Sun's commands to the guest, particularly saying, "When you see my master tomorrow, say nothing of the magnitude of Ts'ao's army."

K'ung-ming smiled, saying, "I shall act as circumstances dictate, you may be sure I shall make no mistakes."

K'ung-ming was then conducted to where the high officers, civil and military to the number of two score and more, were assembled. They formed a dignified conclave as they sat in stately ranks with their tall headdresses and broad girdles.

Chang Chao sat at the head and K'ung-ming first saluted him. Then, one by one, he exchanged the formal courtesies with them all. This done he took his seat in the guest's chair. They, on their part, noted with interest his refined and elegant manner and his commanding figure, thinking within themselves, "Here is a man fitted for discourse."

Chang Chao led the way in trying to bait the visitor. He said, "You will pardon the most insignificant of our official circle, myself, if I mention that people say you compare yourself with those two famous men of talent, Kuan Chung and Yo I. Is there any truth in this?"

"To a trifling extent I have compared myself with them," replied K'ung-ming.

"I have heard that Liu Pei made three journeys to visit you when you lived in retirement in your simple dwelling, and that when you consented to serve him he said he was as lucky as a fish in getting home to the ocean. Then he desired to possess the district about Chingchou and Hsiangyang. Yet today all that country belongs to Ts'ao Ts'ao. I should like to hear your account of all that."

K'ung-ming thought, "This Chang is Sun Ch'uan's first adviser and unless I can nonplus him I shall never have a chance with his master." So he replied, "In my opinion the taking of the district around the Han River was as simple as turning over one's hand. But my master Liu is both righteous and humane and would not stoop to filching the possession of a member of his own house. So he refused the offer of succession. But Liu Ts'ung, a stupid lad, misled by specious words, submitted to Ts'ao and fell victim to his ferocity. My master is in camp at Chianghsia, but what his future plans may be cannot be divulged at present."

Be it so; but your words and your deeds are something discordant. You say you are the equal of the two famous ones. Well, Kuan Chung as Minister of Duke Kuan, put his master at the very head of the feudal nobles, making his master's will supreme in all the land. Under the able statesmanship of Yo I the feeble country of Yen conquered Ch'i reducing nearly four score of its cities. These two were men of most commanding and conspicuous talent. When you lived in retirement you smiled scornfully at ordinary people, passed your days in idleness, nursing your knees and posing in a superior manner, implying that if you had control of affairs Liu Pei would be more than human; he should bring good to everybody and remove all evil; rebellion and robbery would be no more. Poor Liu, before he obtained your help, was an outcast and a vagabond, stealing a city here and there where he could. With you to help him he was to become the cynosure of every eye and every lisping school boy was to say that he was a tiger who had grown wings. The Hans were to be restored and Ts'ao and his faction exterminated. The good old days would be restored and all the men who bad been driven into retirement by the corruption of political life would wake up, rub the sleep out of their eyes and be in readiness to lift the cloud of darkness that covered the sky and gaze up at the glorious brilliancy of the sun and moon, to pull the people out of fire and water and put all the world to rest on a couch of comfort. That was all to happen forthwith. Why then, when you went to Yuchou, did not Ts'ao's army throw aside their arms and armour and flee like rats? Why could you not have told Liu Piao how to give tranquillity to his people? Why could you not aid his orphan son to protect his frontiers? Instead you abandoned Hsinyeh and fled to Fanch'eng; you were defeated at Tangyang; you fled to Hsiak'ou with no place to rest in. Thus, after you had joined Liu Pei, he was worse off than before. Was it thus with Kuan Chung and Yo I? I trust you do not mind my blunt speech."

K'ung-ming waited till he had closed his oration, then laughed and said, "How can the common birds understand the long flight of the roc? Let me use an illustration. A man has fallen into a terrible malady. First the physician must administer hashish, then soothing drugs until his viscera shall be calmed into harmonious action. When the sick man's body shall have been reduced to quietude, then may he be given strong meats to strengthen him and powerful drugs to correct the disorder. Thus the disease will be quite expelled and the man restored to health. If the physician does not wait till the humours and pulse are in harmony, but throws in his strong drugs too early, it will be difficult to restore the patient. My master suffered defeat at Junan and went to Liu Piao. He had then less than one company of soldiers and only three captains. That was indeed a time of extreme weakness. Hsinyeh was a secluded, rustic town with few inhabitants and scanty supplies, and my master only retired there as a temporary refuge. How could he even think of occupying and holding it? Yet, with insufficient force, in a weak city, with untrained men and inadequate supplies, a camp was burned, two leaders and their army were nearly drowned and were frightened into running away. I doubt whether your two ancient heroes would have done any better. As to the surrender of Liu Ts'ung, Liu Pei knew nothing of it. And he was too noble and to righteous to take advantage of a kinsman's straits to seize his inheritance. As for the defeat at Tangyang it must be remembered that Liu Pei was hampered with a huge voluntary following of common people, with their aged relatives and their children, whom he was too humane to abandon. He never thought of taking Chiangling, but willingly suffered with his people. This is a striking instance of his magnanimity. Small forces are no match for large armies. Victory and defeat are common episodes in every campaign. The great Founder of the Hans suffered many defeats at the hands of Hsiang Yu, but he finally conquered at Haihsia and that battle was decisive. Was not this due to the strategy of Han Hsin who, though he had long served his master, had never won a victory. Indeed real statesmanship, the restoration of stable government is a master plan far removed from the vapid discourses and debates of a lot of bragging babblers and specious and deceitful talkers, who, as they themselves say, are immeasureably superior to the rest of mankind but who, when it comes to deeds and decisions to meet the infinite and constant vicissitudes of affairs, fail to throw up a single capable man. Truly such people are the laughing stock of all the world."

Chang Chao found no reply to this diatribe but another in the assembly lifted up his voice, saying, "But what of Ts'ao Ts'ao's present position? There he is, encamped with many legions and numberless leaders. Whither he goes he is invincible and whither he looks he is fearsome. He has taken Chianghsia already, as we see."

The speaker was Yu Fan and K'ung-ming replied, "Ts'ao has acquired the swarms of Yuan Shao and stolen the crowds of Liu Piao. Yet I care not for all his legions."

Yu Fan smiled icily, "When you got thrashed at Tangyang and in desperation sent this way and that to ask help, even then did you not care? But do you think big talk really takes people in?"

"Liu had a few companies of scrupulous soldiers to oppose to a hundred legions of fierce brutes. He retired to Hsiak'ou for breathing space. The soldiers of Chiangtung are good and there are ample supplies and the Long River is a defence. Is now a time for him to bend the knee before a renegade, to be careless of his honour and reputation? As a fact Liu is not the sort of man to fear such a rebel as Ts'ao."

Yu Fan had nothing to reply. Next, one Pu Chih, who was among those seated, said, "Will you talk of our land of Wu with a tongue like the tongues of Chang I and Su Ch'in of old?"

K'ung-ming replied, "You regard those two as mere speculative talkers: you do not recognise them also as heroes. Su Ch'in bore the prime minister's seals of six federated states; Chang I was twice prime Minister of Ch'in. Both were men of conspicuous ability who brought about the reformation of their governments. They are not to be compared with those who quail before the strong and overbear the weak, who fear the dagger and run away from the sword. You, Sir, have listened to Ts'ao Ts'ao's crafty and empty rhodomontade and it has frightened you into advising surrender. Dare you ridicule Su Ch'in and Chang I?"

Pu Chih was silenced. Then suddenly another interjected the question, "What do you think of Ts'ao Ts'ao?"

It was Hsueh Tsung who had spoken and K'ung-ming replied, "Ts'ao is one of the rebels against the dynasty; why ask about him?"

"You are mistaken," said Hsueh Tsung. "The Hans have outlasted their allotted time and the end is near. Ts'ao already has two-thirds of the empire and people are turning to him. Your master has not recognised the fateful moment and to contend with a man so strong is to try to smash stones with eggs. Failure is certain."

K'ung-ming angrily replied, "Why do you speak so undutifully, as if you knew neither father nor prince? Loyalty and filial duty are the essentials of a man's being. For a minister of Han correct conduct demands that one is pledged to the destruction of any one who does not follow the canon of a minister's duty. Ts'ao's forbears enjoyed the bounty of Han, but instead of showing gratitude, he nourishes in his bosom thoughts of rebellion. The whole world is incensed against him and yet you would claim for him the indication of destiny. Truly you are a man who knows neither father nor prince, a man unworthy of any words, and I decline to argue with you farther."

The blush of shame overspread Hsueh's face and he said no more. But another, one Lu Chi, took up the dispute and said, "Although Ts'ao Ts'ao overawes the Emperor and in his name coerces the nobles, yet he is the descendant of a minister, while your master, though he says he is descended from a prince, has no proof thereof. In the eyes of the world he is just a weaver of mats, a seller of straw shoes. Who is he to strive with Ts'ao?"

K'ung-ming laughed and replied, "Are you not that Lu who

pocketed the orange when you were sitting among Yuan Shao's guests? Listen to me; I have a word to say to you. Inasmuch as Ts'ao Ts'ao is a descendant of a minister of state he is by heredity a servant of the Hans. But now he has monopolised all state authority and knows only his own arbitrary will, heaping every indignity upon his lord. Not only does he forget his prince, but he ignores his ancestors; not only is he a rebellious servant of Han, but the renegade of his family. Liu Pei of Yuchou is a noble scion of the imperial family upon whom the Emperor has conferred rank, as is recorded in the annals. How then can you say there is no evidence of his imperial origin? Beside, the very founder of the dynasty was himself of lowly origin, and yet he became emperor. Where is the shame in weaving mats and selling shoes? Your mean, immature views are unfit to be mentioned in the presence of scholars of standing."

This put a stop to Lu Chi's flow of eloquence, but another of those present said, "K'ung-ming's words are overbearing and he distorts reason. It is not proper argument and he had better say no more. But I would ask him what classical canon he studied."

K'ung-ming looked at his interlocutor, who was named Yen Chun, and said, "The dryasdusts of every age select passages and choose phrases; what else are they good for? Do they ever initiate a policy or manage an affair? I Yin, who was a farmer in Hsin and Tzu-ya, the fisherman of the Wei River, Chang Liang and Ch'en P'ing, Teng Yu and Keng Yen all were men of transcendent ability, but I have never enquired what classical canon they followed or on whose essays they formed their style. Would you liken them to your rusty students of books, whose journeyings are comprised between their brush and their inkstone, who spend their days in literary futilities, wasting both time and ink?"

No reply was forthcoming ; the speaker hung his head with shame. But another disputant, Ch'eng Te-shu by name, suddenly shouted, "You are mightily fond of big words, Sir, but they do not give any proof of your scholarship after all. I am inclined to think that a real scholar would just laugh at you."

K'ung-ming replied, "There are scholars and scholars. There is the noble scholar, loyal and patriotic, of perfect rectitude and a hater of any crookedness. The concern of such a scholar is to act in full sympathy with his day and leave to future ages a fine reputation. There is the scholar of the mean type, a pedant and nothing more. He labours constantly with his pen, in his callow youth composing odes and in hoary age still striving to understand the classical books completely. Thousands of words flow from his pen but there is not a solid idea in his breast. He may, as did Yang Hsiung, glorify the age with his writings and yet stoop to serve a tyrant such as Mang. No wonder Yang threw himself out of a window; he had to. That is the way of the scholar of mean type. Though he composes odes by the hundred, what is the use of him?"

Ch'eng could make no reply. The other officers now began to hold this man of torrential speech in wholesome fear. Only two of them had failed to challenge him, but when they would have tried to pose K'ung-ming, suddenly some one appeared from without and angrily shouted, "This is not paying fit respect to a guest. You have among you the most wonderful man of the day and you all sit there trying to entangle him in speech while our arch enemy Ts'ao Ts'ao is nearing our borders. Instead of discussing how to oppose him you are all wrangling and disputing."

All eyes turned toward him; it was Huang Kai, of Lingling, who was master of the commissariat of Wu. He turned to address K'ung-ming, saying, "There is a saying that though something may be gained by talk there is more to be got by silence. Why not give my lord the advantage of your valuable advice instead of wasting time in discussion with this crowd?

"They did not understand," replied K'ung-ming, "and it was necessary to enlighten them, I had to speak."

As Huang Kai and Lu Su led the guest toward their master's apartments, they met his brother Chuko Chin. K'ung-ming saluted him with the deference due to an elder brother and Chin said, "Why have you not been to see me, brother?"

"I am now in the service of Liu of Yu chou and it is right that public affairs precede private obligations. I cannot attend to any private matters till my work is done. You must pardon me brother."

"After you have seen the Marquis you will come and tell me your news," said he as he left.

As they went along to the audience chamber Lu Su again cautioned K'ung-ming against any rash speech. The latter nodded but made no other reply. When they reached the hall Sun Ch'uan came down the steps to welcome his guests and was extraordinarily gracious. After the mutual salutations the guest was given a chair while the Marquis's officials were drawn up in two lines, on one side the civil, on the other the military. Lu Su stood beside K'ung-ming and listened to his introductory speech.

As K'ung-ming spoke of Yuan-te's intentions, he glanced up at his host. He noted the grey eyes and brown beard and the dignified commanding air of the man and thought within himself, "Certainly in appearance this is no common man. He is one to be incited perhaps, but not to be persuaded. It will be better to see what he has to say first, then I will try to stir him to action."

The serving of tea being now finished, Sun Ch'uan began with the usual gracious ceremonial expressions.

"Lu Su has often spoken of your genius" said the host; "it is a great pleasure to meet you. I trust you will confer upon me the advantage of your instruction."

"I am neither clever nor learned" was the reply, it humiliates me to hear such words."

"You have been at Hsinyeh lately and you helped your master to fight that decisive battle with Ts'ao Ts'ao, so you must know exactly the measure of his military strength."

"My master's army was small and his generals were few; the city was paltry and lacked supplies. Hence no stand could be made against such a force as Ts'ao Ts'ao had."

"How many men has he in all?"

"Horse and foot, land and marine, he has a hundred legions."

"Is there not some doubt about that?" said Sun Ch'uan.

"None whatever; when Ts'ao Ts'ao went to Yenchou he had the twenty legions of Chingchou. He gained fifty or sixty legions when Yuan Shao fell. He has thirty or forty legions newly recruited in the capital. Lately he has acquired twenty or thirty legions in Chingchou. And if these be reckoned up the total is not less than a hundred and fifty. Hence I said a hundred for I was afraid of frightening your officers."

Lu Su was much disturbed and turned pale. He looked meaningly at the bold speaker, but K'ung-ming would not see. Sun Ch'uan went on to ask if his arch enemy had a corresponding number of leaders.

"He has enough administrators and strategists to control such a host and his capable and veteran leaders are more than a thousand; perhaps more than two thousand."

"What will be Ts'ao Ts'ao's next move now that he has overcome Chingchou and Ch'u?"

"He is camped along the river and he has collected a fleet. If he does not intend to invade your territory, what can be his intentions?"

"Since that is his intention, it is a case of fight or not fight. I wish you would decide that for me."

"I have something I could say, but I fear, Sir, you would not care to hear it."

"I am desirous of hearing your most valuable opinion."

"Strife has prevailed for a long time and so you should raise your army and Liu Pei should collect his forces south of the Han River, to act with you in contest for the empire against Ts'ao Ts'ao. Now Ts'ao has overcome most of his difficulties and his recent conquest of Chingchou has won him great and wide renown. Though there might be one bold enough to tackle him, yet there is no foothold for such. That is how Liu Pei has been forced to come here. But, General, I wish you to measure your forces and decide whether you can venture to meet him and that without loss of time. If you cannot, then follow the advice of your councillors; cease your military preparations and yield; turn your face to the north and serve."

Sun Ch'uan did not reply. But his guest went on, "You have the reputation of being reasonable but I know also you are inclined to hesitate. Still this matter is most important and evil will be quickly upon you if you do not decide."

Then replied Sun, "If what you say represents the actual conditions, why does not Liu Pei yield?"

"Well, you know Ts'ien Heng, that hero of the state of Ch'i; his character was too noble for him to submit to any shame. It is necessary to remember that Liu Pei also is an off-shoot from the dynastic family, beside being a man of great renown. Every one looks up to him. His lack of success is simply the will of Heaven but manifestly he could not bow the knee to any one."

These last words touched Sun Ch'uan to the quick and he could not control his anger. He shook out his sleeves, rose and left the audience chamber. Those present smiled at each other as they dispersed.

But Lu Su was annoyed and reproached K'ung-ming for his maladroit way of talking to Sun. "Luckily for you my lord is too large-minded to rebuke you to your face for you spoke to him most contemptuously."

K'ung-ming threw back his head and laughed. "What a sensitive fellow it is!" cried he. "I know how Ts'ao Ts'ao could be destroyed, but he never asked me; so I said nothing.

"If you really do know how that could be done I will certainly beg my lord to ask you."

"Ts'ao Ts'ao's hosts in my eyes are but as swarms of ants. I have but to lift my hand and they will be crushed."

Lu Su at once went into his master's private room, where he found him still very irritable and angry. "Kung-ming insulted me too deeply," said Sun.

"I have already reproached him," said Lu Su, "and he laughed and said you were too sensitive. He would not give you any advice without being asked for it. Why did you not seek advice from him, my lord?"

At once Sun's anger changed to joy. He said, "So he had a plan ready and his words were meant to provoke me. I did despise him for a moment and it has very nearly lost me."

So he returned to the audience chamber where the guest was still seated and begged K'ung-ming to continue his speech. He spoke courteously saying, "I offended you just now, I hope you are not implacable."

"And I also was rude," replied K'ung-ming. "I entreat pardon."

Host and guest retired to the inner room where wine was served. After it had gone round several times, Sun Ch'uan said, "The enemies of Ts'ao Ts'ao were Lu Pu, Liu Piao, Yuan Shao, Yuan Shu, his brother, Liu Pei and my poor self. Now most of these are gone and only Liu Pei and I remain. I will never allow the land of Wu to be dictated to by another. The only one who could have withstood Ts'ao Ts'ao was Liu Pei, but he has been defeated lately and what can he do now against such force?"

K'ung-ming replied, "Although defeated, Liu Pei still has Kuan Yu with a legion of veterans. And Liu Ch'i still leads the men of Chianghsia, another legion. Ts'ao Ts'ao's army is far from home and the men are worn out. They made a frantic effort to come up with my master, and the light horse marched three hundred *li* in a day and a night. This was the final kick of the crossbow spring and the bolt was not swift enough to penetrate even the thin silken vesture of Lu. The army can do no more. They are northern men, unskilled in water warfare, and the men of Chingchou are unwilling supporters. They have no desire to help Ts'ao. Now if you, General, will assist Liu Pei, Ts'ao will certainly be broken and he must retire northwards. Then your country and Chingchou will be strong and firmly established. But the scheme must be carried out without delay and only you can decide."

Sun Ch'uan joyfully replied, "Your words, master, open up the road clearly. I have decided and shall have no further doubts."

So the orders were issued forthwith to prepare for a joint attack on Ts'ao Ts'ao. And he bade Lu Su bear the news of his decision to all his officers. He himself escorted K'ung-ming to the guest quarters and saw to his comfort.

When Chang Chao heard of the decision he met his colleagues and said to them, "He has fallen into the trap set by this K'ung-ming."

They went in a body to their lord and said, "We hear you are going to Ts'ao Ts'ao; but how do you stand when compared with

Yuan Shao ? In those days Ts'ao was comparatively weak and yet he overcame. What is he like today with his countless legions? He is not to be lightly attacked and to listen to Chuko Liang's advice to engage in a conflict is like carrying fuel to a fire."

Sun Ch'uan made no reply and Ku Yung took up the argument. "Liu Pei has been defeated and he wants to borrow our help to beat his enemy. Why must our lord lend himself to his schemes? Pray listen to our leader's words."

Doubts again surged up in the mind of Sun Ch'uan. When the troop of advisers had retired, Lu Su came in saying, "They came to exhort you not to fight, but to compel you to surrender simply because they wish to secure the safety of their families. They distort their sense of duty to serve their own ends and I hope you will not take their advice."

Sun Ch'uan being sunk in thought and saying nothing, Lu Su went on, "if you hesitate you will certainly be led astray by the majority and—"

"Retire for a time," said his master. "I must think it over carefully."

So Lu Su left the chamber. Among the soldiers some wished for war, but of the civil officers, all were in favour of surrender and so there were many discussions and much conflict of opinion. Sun Ch'uan went to his private apartments greatly perplexed. There his worry was easily discernible and he neither ate nor slept. He was quite unable to decide finally upon a course of action.

Then the Lady Wu asked him what so troubled him, and he told her of the threatened danger and the different opinions his advisers held one and another and all his doubts and fears. If he fought, he might fail; and if he offered to surrender, perhaps Ts'ao Ts'ao would reject his proposal.

Then she replied, "Have you forgotten the last words of my sister?"

As to one recovering from a fit of drunkenness, or waking out of a dream, so came to him the dying words of the mother who bore him.

His mother's advice he called to mind,
"In Chou Yu's counsels you safety find."

What happened will be told in the next chapter.

CHAPTER XLIV

K'UNG-MING STIRS CHOU YU TO ACTION: SUN CH'UAN DECIDES TO ATTACK TS'AO TS'AO

The dying message which the Lady Wu recalled to Sun Ch'uan's memory was, "For internal matters consult Chang Chao; for external policy Chou Yu."

Wherefore Chou Yu was summoned.

But he was already on the way. He had been training his naval forces on Lake P'oyang when he heard of the approach of Ts'ao Ts'ao's hosts and had started for Ch'aisengchun without loss of time. So, before the messenger ordered to call him could start, he had already arrived. As he and Lu Su were close friends the latter went to welcome him and told him of all that had happened.

"Have no anxiety," said Chou Yu, "I shall be able to decide this. But go quickly and beg K'ung-ming to come to see me."

So Lu Su went to seek out K'ung-ming. Chou Yu had many other visitors. First came Chang Chao and his faction to find out what might be afoot. They were received , and after the exchange of the usual commonplaces, Chang Chao said, "Have you heard of our terrible danger?"

"I have heard nothing," said Chou Yu.

"Ts'ao Ts'ao and his hordes are encamped up the river. He has just sent letters asking our lord to hunt with him in Chianghsia. He may have a desire to absorb this country but, if so, the details of his designs are still secret. We prayed our master to give in his submission and so avoid the horrors of war, but now Lu Su has returned bringing with him the Commander-in-Chief of Liu Pei's army, Chuko Liang. He, desiring to avenge himself for the recent defeat, has talked our lord into a mind for war and Lu Su persists in supporting him. They only await your final decision."

"Are you and yours unanimous in your opinions?"

"We are perfectly unanimous," said Chang.

Chou said, "The fact is I have also desired to submit for a long time. I beg you to leave me now and tomorrow we will see our master and I shall make up his mind for him."

So they took their leave. Very soon came the military party led by Ch'eng P'u. They were admitted and duly enquired after their host's health. Then the leader said, "Have you heard that our country is about to pass under another's government?"

"No; I have heard nothing," replied the host.

"We helped General Sun to establish his authority here and carve out this kingdom, and to gain that end we fought many a battle before we conquered the country. Now our lord lends his ear to his civil officers and desires to submit himself to Ts'ao Ts'ao. This is a most shameful and pitiful course and we would rather die. than follow it, so we hope you will decide to fight and you may depend upon our struggling to the last man."

"And are you unanimous, Generals?" asked Chou Yu.

Huang Kai suddenly started up and smote his forehead saying, "They may take my head but I swear never to surrender."

"Not one of us is willing to surrender," cried all the others.

"My desire also is to decide matters with Ts'ao Ts'ao on the battlefield. How could we think of submission? Now I pray you retire, Generals, and when I see our lord I will settle his doubts."

So the war party left. They were quickly succeeded by Chuko Ching and his faction. They were brought in and, after the usual courtesies, Ching said, "My brother has come down the river saying that Liu Pei desires to ally himself with our lord against Ts'ao Ts'ao. The civil and military hold different opinions as to the course to be pursued, but as my brother is so deeply concerned I am unwilling to say much on either side. We are awaiting your decision."

"And what do you think about it?" asked Chou Yu.

"Submission is an easy road to tranquillity, while the result of war is hard to foretell."

Chou Yu smiled, "I shall have my mind made up. Come tomorrow to the palace and the decision shall be announced."

The trimmers took their leave. But soon after came Lu Meng with his supporters, also desirous of discussing the same thing, and they told him that opinions differed greatly, some being for peace and others for war. One party constantly disputed with the other.

"I must not say much now, replied Chou Yu, "but you will see tomorrow in the palace, when the matter will be fully debated."

They went away leaving Chou Yu smiling cynically.

About eventide Lu Su and K'ung-ming came and Chou Yu went out to the main gate to receive them. When they had taken their proper seats, Lu Su spoke first, saying, "Ts'ao Ts'ao has come against the south with a huge army. Our master cannot decide whether to submit or give battle and waits for your decision. What is your opinion?"

Chou Yu replied, "We may not oppose Ts'ao Ts'ao when he acts at the command of the Emperor. Moreover, he is very strong and to attack him is to take serious risks. In my opinion, opposition would mean defeat and, since submission means peace, I have decided to advise our lord to write and offer surrender."

"But you are wrong," stammered Lu Su. "This country has been under the same rule for three generations and cannot be suddenly abandoned to some other. San Ts'e said that you were to be consulted on matters beyond the border and we depended upon you to keep the country as secure and solid as Mount T'ai. Now you adopt the view of the weaklings and propose to yield! I cannot believe you mean it."

Replied Chou Yu, "The six districts contain countless people. If I am the means of bringing upon them the misery of war they will hate me. So I have decided to advise submission."

"But do you not realise our lord's might and the strength of our country? If Ts'ao does attack it is very uncertain that he will realise his desire."

The two wrangled for a long time, while K'ung-ming sat smiling with folded arms. Presently Chou Yu asked why he smiled thus and he replied, "I am smiling at no other than your opponent Lu Su, who knows nothing of the affairs of the day."

"Master," said Lu Su, "What do you mean?"

"Why, this intention to submit is perfectly reasonable; it is the one proper thing."

"There!" exclaimed Chou Yu, "K'ung-ming knows the times perfectly well and he agrees with me."

"But, both of you, why do you say this?" said Lu.

Said K'ung-ming, "Ts'ao is an excellent commander, so good that no one dares oppose him. Only very few have ever attempted it and they have been exterminated; the world knows them no more. The only exception is Liu Pei, who did not understand the conditions and vigorously contended against him, with the result that he is now at Chianghsia in a very parlous state. To submit is to secure the safety of wives and children, to be rich and honoured. But the dignity of the country would be left to chance and fate— However, that is not worth consideration."

Lu Su interrupted angrily, "Would you make our lord crook the knee to such a rebel as he?"

"Well," replied K'ung-ming, "there is another way, and a cheaper; there would be no need to 'lead the sheep and shoulder wine pots' for presents, nor any need to yield territory and surrender seals of office. It would not even be necessary to cross the river yourselves. All you would require is a simple messenger and a little boat to ferry a couple of people across the river. If Ts'ao only got these two persons under his hand, his hordes and legions would just drop their weapons, furl their banners and silently vanish away."

"What two persons could cause Ts'ao Ts'ao to go away as you say?" asked Chou Yu.

"Two persons who could be easily spared from this populous country. They would not be missed any more than a leaf from a tree or a grain of millet from a granary. But if Ts'ao could only get them, would he not go away rejoicing!"

"But who are the two?" asked Chou Yu again.

"When I was living in the country they told me that Ts'ao was building a pavilion on the Chang River; it was to be named the Bronze Bird Pavilion. It is an exceedingly handsome building and he has sought throughout all the world for the most beautiful women to live in it. For Ts'ao really is a sensualist."

"Now there are two very famous beauties in Chiantung, born of the Ch'iao family. So beautiful are they that birds alight and fishes drown, the moon hides her face and the flowers blush for shame at sight of them. Ts'ao has declared with an oath that he only wants two things in this world, the imperial throne in peace and the sight of those two women on the Bronze Bird Terraces. Given these two he would go down to his grave without regret. This expedition of his, his huge army that threatens this country, has for its real aim these two women. Why do you not buy these two from their father for any sum however large and send them over the river? The object of the army being attained, it will simply be marched away. This is the use that Fan Li made of the famous beauty Hsi Shih."

"How do you know he so greatly desires these two?" said Chou Yu.

"Because his son, who is an able writer, at the command of his father wrote a poem 'An Ode to the Bronze Bird Terrace,' the theme only allowing allusions to the family fitness for the throne. He has sworn to possess these two women. I think I can remember the poem, if you wish to hear it. I admire it greatly."

"Try," said Chou Yu.

So he recited the poem:—

Let me follow in the footsteps of the enlightened ruler that I may
 rejoice,
And ascend the storied terrace that I may gladden my heart,
That I may see the wide extent of the palace,
That I may gaze upon the plans of the virtuous one.
He has established the exalted gates high as the hills,
He has builded the lofty towers piercing the blue vault,
He has set up the beautiful building in the midst of the heavens,
Whence the eye can range over the cities of the west.
On the banks of the rolling River Chang he planned it,
Whence abundance of fruits could be looked for in his gardens.
The two towers rise, one on either flank,
This named Golden Phoenix, that Jade Dragon.
He would seize the two Ch'iao; these beautiful ladies of the south-
 east,
That he might rejoice with them morning and evening.
Look down; there is the grand beauty of an imperial city,
And the rolling vapours lie floating beneath.
He will rejoice in the multitude of scholars that assemble,
Answering to the felicitous dream of King Wen.
Look up; and there is the gorgeous harmony of spring-time,
And the singing of many birds delighting the ear;
The lofty sky stands over all.
The house desires success in its double undertaking,
That the humane influence may be poured out over all the world,
That the perfection of reverence may be offered to the Ruler.
Only the richly prosperous rule of Huan and Wen
Could compare with that of the sacred understanding
What fortune! what beauty!
The gracious kindness spreads afar,
The imperial family is supported,
Peace reigns over all the world,
Bounded only by the universe.
Bright as the glory of the sun and moon,
Ever honourable and ever enduring,
The Ruler shall live to the age of the eastern emperor,
The dragon banner shall wave to the farthest limit.
His glorious chariot shall be guided with perfect wisdom,
His thoughts shall reform all the world,
Felicitous produce shall be abundant,
And the people shall rest firm.
My desire is that these towers shall endure for ever,
And that joy shall never cease through all the ages.

Chou Yu listened to the end but then suddenly jumped up in a tremendous rage. Turning to the north and pointing with his finger he cried, "You old rebel; this insult is too deep!"

K'ung-ming hastily rose too and, as if to soothe him, said, "But remember Shan Yu. The emperor gave him a princess of the family to wife although he had made many incursions into our territory. That was the price of peace. You surely would not grudge two more women from among the people."

"You do not know, Sir," replied Chou Yu. "Of those two women you mentioned, the elder is the widow of Sun Ts'e, our late ruler, and the younger is my wife."

K'ung-ming feigned the greatest astonishment and said, "No indeed; I did not know. I blundered; a deadly fault; a deadly fault!"

"One of us two has to go, either the old rebel or I; we shall not both live. I swear that," cried Chou Yu.

"However, such a matter needs a good deal of thought," replied K'ung-ming. "We must not make any mistake."

Chou Yu replied, "I hold a sacred trust from my late lord, Sun Ts'e; I would not bow the knee to any such as Ts'ao. What I said just now was to see how you stood. I left the lake with the intention of attacking the north, and nothing can change that intention, not even the sword at my breast or the axe on my neck. But I trust you will lend an arm and we will smite Ts'ao Ts'ao together."

"Should I be happy enough not to be rejected I would render such humble service as I could. Perhaps presently I might be able to offer a plan to oppose him."

"I am going to see my lord tomorrow to discuss this matter," said Chou Yu.

K'ung-ming and Lu Su then left. Next day at dawn Sun Ch'uan went to the council chamber, where his officials, civil and military, were already assembled. They numbered about three score in all. The civil, with Chang Chao at their head, were on the right; the military, with Ch'eng P'u as their leader, were ranged on the left. All were in full ceremonial dress and the swords of the soldiers clanked on the pavement. Soon Chou Yu entered and, when Sun Ch'uan had finished the usual gracious remarks, he said, "I hear that Ts'ao Ts'ao is encamped on the river and has sent a despatch to you, my lord, I would ask what your opinion is."

Thereupon the despatch was produced and handed to Chou Yu. After reading it through he said, smiling, "The old thief thinks there are no men in this land that he writes in this contemptuous strain."

"What do you think, Sir?" asked Sun Ch'uan.

"Have you discussed this with the officials?" asked Chou Yu.

"We have been discussing this for days. Some counsel surrender and some advise fight. I am undecided and therefore I have asked you to come and decide the point."

"Who advise surrender?" asked Chou Yu.

"Chang Chao and his party are firmly set in this opinion."

Chou Yu then turned to Chang Chao and said, "I should be pleased to hear why you are for surrender, Master."

Then Chang Chao replied, "Ts'ao Ts'ao has been attacking all opponents in the name of the Emperor, who is entirely in his hands. He does everything in the name of the government. Lately he has taken Chingchou and thereby increased his prestige. Our defence against him was the river, but now he also has a large fleet and can attack by water. How can we withstand him? Wherefore I counsel submission till some chance shall offer."

"This is but the opinion of an ill-advised student," said Chou Yu. "How can you think of abandoning this country that we have held for three generations?"

"That being so," said Sun Ch'uan, "where is a plan to come from?"

"Though Ts'ao Ts'ao assumes the name of a Minister of the empire, he is at heart a rebel. You, O General, are able in war and brave. You are the heir to your father and brother You command brave and tried soldiers, and you have plentiful supplies. You are able to overrun the whole country and rid it of every evil There is no reason why you should surrender to a rebel. Moreover, Ts'ao has undertaken this expedition in defiance of all the rules of war. The north is unsubdued and Ma T'eng and Han Sui threaten his rear and yet he persists in his southern march. This is the first point against Ts'ao. The northern men are unused to fighting on the water; Ts'ao is relinquishing his well-tried cavalry and trusting to ships. That is the second point against him. Again, we are now in full winter and the weather is at its coldest so there is no food for the horses. That is the third point against. Soldiers from the central state marching in a wet country among lakes and rivers will find themselves in an unaccustomed climate and suffer from malaria. That is the fourth point against. Now when Ts'ao's armies have all these points against them, defeat is certain, however numerous they may be, and you can take Ts'ao captive just as soon as you wish. Give me a few companies of veterans and I will go and destroy him."

Sun Ch'uan started up from his place saying, "The rebellious old rascal has been wanting to overthrow the Hans and set up himself for years. He has rid himself of all those he feared, save only myself, and I swear that one of us two shall go now. Both of us cannot live.

What you say, noble friend, is just what I think, and Heaven has certainly sent you to my assistance."

"Thy servant will fight a decisive battle," said Chou Yu, "and shrink not from any sacrifice. Only, General, do not hesitate."

Sun Ch'uan drew the sword that hung at his side and slashed the table in front of him, exclaiming, "Let any other man mention surrender and he shall be served as I have served this table."

Then he handed the sword to Chou Yu, at the same time giving him a commission as Commander-in-Chief, Ch'eng P'u being second in command. Lu Su was also nominated as assistant.

In conclusion Sun said, "With this sword you will slay any officer who may disobey your commands."

Chou Yu took the sword and turning to the assembly said, "You have heard our lord's charge to me, to lead you to destroy Ts'ao; you will all assemble tomorrow at the river-side camp to receive my orders. Should any be late or fail, then the full rigour of military law, the seven prohibitions and the fifty-four penalties there provided, will be enforced."

He took leave of Sun Ch'uan and left the chamber; the various officers also went their several ways. When Chou Yu reached his own place he sent for K'ung-ming to consult over the business in hand. He told him of the decision that had been taken and asked for a plan of campaign.

"But your master has not yet made up his mind, said K'ung-ming. "Till he has, no plan can be decided upon."

"What do you mean?"

"In his heart he is still fearful of Ts'ao's numbers and frets over the inequality of the two armies. You will have to explain away those numbers and bring him to a final decision before anything can be effected."

"What you say is excellent," said Chou Yu and he went to the palace that night to see his master. Sun Ch'uan said, "You must have something of real importance to say if you come like this at night."

Chou Yu said, "I am making my dispositions tomorrow; you have quite made up your mind?"

"The fact is," said Sun Ch'uan, "I still feel nervous about the disparity of numbers. Surely we are too few. That is really all I feel doubtful about."

"It is precisely because you have this one remaining doubt that I am come. And I will explain. Ts'ao's letter speaks of a hundred legions of marines, and so you feel doubts and fears and do not wait to consider the real truth. Let us examine the case thoroughly. We find that he has of Central State soldiers, say, fifteen or sixteen legions, and many of them are sick. He only got seven or eight legions from the Yuans and many of those are of doubtful loyalty. Now these sick men and these men of doubtful loyalty seem a great many but they are not at all fearsome. I could smash them with five legions. So, my lord, have no further anxiety."

Sun Ch'uan patted his general on the back saying, "You have explained my difficulty and relieved my doubts. Chang Chao is an old fool who constantly baulks my expeditions. Only you and Lu Su have any real understanding of my heart. Tomorrow you and he and Ch'eng P'u will start and I shall have a strong reserve ready with plentiful supplies to support you. If anything goes agley you can at once send for me and I will engage with my own men."

Chou Yu left; but in his innermost heart he said to himself, "If that K'ung-ming can gauge my master's thoughts so very accurately he is too clever for me and will be a danger. He will have to be put out of the way."

He sent a messenger over to Lu Su to talk over this last scheme. When he had laid it bare, Lu Su did not favour it. "No, no," said he, "it is self-destruction to make away with your ablest officer before Ts'ao shall have been destroyed."

"But K'ung-ming will certainly help Liu Pei to our disadvantage."

"Try what his brother Chuko Chin can do to persuade him; It would be an excellent thing to have these two in our service."

"Yes, indeed," replied Chou Yu.

Next morning at dawn Chou Yu went to his camp and took his seat in the council tent. The lictors took up their stations right and left and the officers ranged themselves in lines to listen to the orders.

Now Ch'eng P'u, who was older than Chou Yu, was very angry at being passed over, so he made a pretence of indisposition and stayed away from this assembly. But he sent his son to represent him. Chou Yu addressed the gathering, saying, "The law knows no partiality and you will all have to attend to your several duties. Ts'ao is now more absolute than ever was Tung Cho, and the Emperor is really a prisoner in Hsuch'ang, guarded by the most cruel soldiers. We have a command to destroy Ts'ao and with your willing help we shall advance. The army must cause no hardship to the people anywhere. Rewards for good service and punishments for faults shall be given impartially."

Having delivered this charge he told off Han Tang and Huang Kai as leaders of the van, and ordered the ships under his own command to get under way and go to Sanchiangk'ou. They would get orders by and bye. Then he appointed five armies with two officers over each while Lu Fan and Chu Chih were appointed inspectors, to move from place to place and keep the various units up to their work and acting with due regard to the general plan. Land and marine forces were to move simultaneously. The expedition would soon start.

Having received their orders each returned to his command and busied himself in preparation. Ch'eng P'u's son returned and told his father what arrangements had been made and Ch'eng P'u was amazed at their skill. Said he, "I have always despised Chou Yu as a mere student who would never be a general, but this shows that he has a leader's talent. I must support him." So he went over to the quarters of the Commander-in-Chief and confessed his fault. He was received kindly and all was over.

Next Chou Yu sent for Chuko Chin and said to him, "Evidently your brother is a genius, a man born to be a king's counsellor. Why then does he serve Liu Pei? Now that he is here I wish you to use every effort to persuade him to stay with us. Thus our lord would gain able support and you two brothers would be together, which would be pleasant for you both. I wish you success."

Chin replied, "I am ashamed of the little service I have rendered since I came here and I can do no other than obey your command to the best of my ability."

Thereupon he went away to his brother, whom he found in the guest-house. The younger brother received him and when he had reached the inner rooms K'ung-ming bowed respectfully and, weeping, told his experiences since they parted and his sorrow at their separation. Then Chin, weeping also, said, "Brother, do you remember the story of Po I and Shu Ch'i, the brothers who would not be separated?"

"Ah, Chou Yu has sent him to talk me over," thought K'ung-ming. So he replied, "They were two of the noble people of old days; yes, I know."

"Those two, although they perished of hunger near the Shouyang Hills, yet never separated. You and I, born of the same mother and suckled at the same breast, yet serve different masters and never meet. Are you not ashamed when you think of such examples as Po I and Shu Ch'i?"

K'ung-ming replied, "You are talking now of love, but what I stand for is duty. We are both men of Han and Liu Pei is of the family. If you, brother, could leave Wu and Join me in serving the rightful branch, then on the one side we should be honoured as Ministers of Han and on the other we should be together as people of the same flesh and blood should be. Thus love and duty would both receive their proper meed. What do you think of it, my brother."

"I came to persuade him and lo! it is I who am being talked over," thought Chuko Chin. He had no fitting reply to make so he rose and took his leave. Returning to Chou Yu he related the story of the interview.

"What do you think?" asked Chou Yu.

"General Sun has treated me with great kindness and I could not turn my back on him," replied Chin.

"Since you decide to remain loyal, there is no need to say much; I think I have a plan to win over your brother."

> The wisest men see eye to eye,
> For each but sees the right;
> But should their several interests clash,
> They all the fiercer fight.

The means by which Chou Yu tried to get the support of K'ung-ming will be described in the next chapter.

CHAPTER XLV

TS'AO TS'AO LOSES SOLDIERS:
CHIANG KAN VICTIM OF A RUSE

Chou Yu was very annoyed by the words of Chuko Chin and a fierce hatred for K'ung-ming took root in his heart. He nourished a secret resolve to make away with him. He continued his preparations for war and when the men were all mustered and ready he went in for a farewell interview with his lord.

"You go on first, noble Sir," said Sun Ch'uan. "I will then march to support you."

Chou Yu took his leave and then, with Ch'eng P'u and Lu Su, marched out with the army. He invited K'ung-ming to accompany the expedition, and when he cheerfully accepted, the four embarked in the same ship. They set sail and the flotilla made for Hsiak'ou.

About sixty *li* from "Three River Mouths" the fleet anchored near the shore and Chou Yu built a stockade on the bank near the middle of their line with the West Hills as a support. Other camps were made near his. K'ung-ming, however, took up his quarters in a small ship.

When the camp dispositions were complete Chou Yu sent to request K'ung-ming to come and give him advice. He came, and after the salutations were ended Chou Yu said, "Ts'ao Ts'ao thought he had fewer troops than Yuan Shao, nevertheless overcame him because he followed the advice given by Hsu Yu to destroy his supplies. Now Ts'ao Ts'ao has over eighty legions while I have but five or six. In order to defeat him his supplies must be destroyed first. I have found out that the main depot is at Chut'ieh Hill. As you have lived hereabout you know the topography quite well and I wish to entrust the task of cutting off supplies to you and your colleagues Kuan Yu, Chang Fei and Chao Yun. I will assist you with a company. I wish you to start without delay. In this way we can best serve our masters."

K'ung-ming saw through this at once. He thought to himself, "This is a ruse in revenge for my not having been persuaded to enter the service of Wu. If I refuse I shall be laughed at. So I will do as he asks and trust to find some means of deliverance from the evil he intends."

Therefore he accepted the task with alacrity, much to the joy of Chou Yu. After the leader of the expedition had taken his leave, Lu Su went to Chou Yu secretly and said, "Why have you set him this task?"

"Because I wish to compass his death without appearing ridiculous. I hope to get him killed by the hand of Ts'ao Ts'ao and prevent his doing further mischief."

Lu Su left and went to see K'ung-ming to find out if he suspected anything. He found him looking quite unconcerned and getting the soldiers ready to march. Unable to hold his tongue, however, he put a tentative question, "Do you think this expedition will succeed?"

K'ung-ming laughingly replied, "I am an adept at all sorts of fighting, with foot, horse and chariots on land and on the water. There is no doubt of my success. I am not like you and your friend, only capable in one direction."

"What do you mean by our being capable only in one direction?" said Lu Su.

"I have heard the street boys in your country singing:—

> To lay au ambush, hold a pass,
>   Lu Su is the man to choose;
> But when you on the water fight,
>   Chou Yu is the man to use.

You are only fit for ambushes and guarding passes on land, just as he only understands fighting on the water."

Lu Su carried this story to Chou Yu, which only incensed him the more against K'ung-ming.

"How dare he flout me, saying I cannot fight a land battle? I will not let him go. I will go myself with a legion and cut off Ts'ao Ts'ao's supplies."

Lu Su went back and told this to K'ung-ming, who smiled and said, "He only wanted me to go on this expedition because he wanted Ts'ao Ts'ao to kill me. And so I teased him a little. But he cannot bear that. Now is the critical moment and the Marquis Wu and my master must act in harmony if we are to succeed. If each one tries to harm the other the whole scheme will fail. Ts'ao Ts'ao is no fool and it is a usual thing with him to attack an enemy through his supplies. Do you not think he has already taken double precautions against any surprise of his own depot? If Chou Yu tries he will be taken prisoner. What he ought to do is to bring about a decisive naval battle, whereby to dishearten the northern men, and then find some other means to defeat them utterly. If you could persuade him what was his best course it would be well."

Without loss of time, Lu Su went to Chou Yu to relate what K'ung-ming had told him. Chou shook his head when he heard it and beat the ground with his foot, saying, "This man is far too clever; he beats me fifty to one. He will have to be done away with or my country will suffer."

Said Lu Su, "This is the moment to use men; you must think of the country's good first of all. When once Ts'ao Ts'ao is defeated you may do as you please."

Chou had to confess the reasonableness of this.

It is now time to speak of Liu Pei. He had ordered his nephew Liu Ch'i to hold Chianghsia while he and the bulk of the army returned to Hsiak'ou. Thence he saw the opposite bank thick with banners and flags and glittering with every kind of arms and armour. He knew then that the expedition from Wu had started. So he moved all his force from Chianghsia to Fank'ou.

Then he assembled his officers and said to them, "K'ung-ming went to Wu some time ago and no word has come from him, so I know not how the business stands. Will any one volunteer to go to find out?"

"I will go," said Mi Chu.

So presents were prepared and gifts of flesh and wine, and Mi Chu prepared to journey to Wu on the pretext of offering a congratulatory feast to the army. Mi Chu set out in a small ship and went down river. He stopped opposite the camp and the soldiers reported his arrival to Chou Yu, who ordered him to be brought in. Mi Chu bowed low and expressed the respect which Liu Pei had for Chou Yu and offered the various gifts. The ceremony of reception was followed by a banquet in honour of Mi Chu. Mi said, "K'ung-ming has been here a long time and I desire that he may return with me."

"K'ung-ming is making plans with me and I could not let him return," said Chou Yu. "I also wish to see Liu Pei that we may make joint plans, but when one is at the head of a great army one cannot get away even for a moment. If your master would only come here it would be very gracious on his part."

Mi Chu agreed that Liu Pei might come and presently took his leave. Then Lu Su asked Chou Yu the reason for his desiring Liu Pei to come.

"Liu Yuan-te is the one bold and dangerous man and must be removed. I am taking this opportunity to persuade him to come, and when he shall be slain a great danger will cease to threaten our country."

Lu Su tried to dissuade him from this scheme but Chou Yu was deaf to all he said. He even issued orders for half a hundred executioners to be ready to hide within the lining of his tent if Liu Pei decided to come and arranged to drop a cup as a signal for them to fall on and slay him.

Mi Chu returned and told Liu Pei that his presence was desired by Chou Yu. Suspecting nothing Liu Pei at once ordered them to prepare a fast vessel to take him without loss of time. Kuan Yu was opposed to his going saying that Chou Yu was artful and treacherous and there was no news from K'ung-ming.

Yuan-te replied, "I have joined my forces to theirs in this attack on our common enemy. If Chou Yu wishes to see me and I refuse to go, it is a betrayal. Nothing will succeed if both sides nourish suspicions."

"If you have finally decided to go, then will I go with you," said Kuan Yu.

"And I also," cried Chang Fei.

But Yuan-te said, "Let Kuan Yu come with me while you and Chao Yun keep guard. Chien Yung will hold Ohsien. I shall not be away long."

So leaving these orders, Liu Pei embarked with his brother on a small boat. The escort did not exceed a score. The light craft travelled very quickly down the river. Liu Pei rejoiced greatly at the sight of the war vessels in tiers by the bank, the soldiers in their breastplates and all the pomp and panoply of war. All was in excellent order.

As soon as he arrived the guards ran to tell Chou Yu.

"How many ships has he?" asked Chou.

They replied, "Only one; and the escort is only about a score."

"His fate is sealed," said Chou Yu.

He sent for the executioners and placed them in hiding between the outer and inner tents, and when all was arranged for the assassination he contemplated, he went out to receive his visitor.

Liu Pei came with his brother and escort into the midst of the army to the Commander's tent. After the salutations Chou Yu wished Liu Pei to take the upper seat, but he declined saying, "General, you are famous through all the country, while I am a nobody. Do not overwhelm me with too great deference."

So they took the positions of simple friends and refreshments were brought in.

Now by chance K'ung-ming came on shore and heard that his master had arrived and was with the Commander-in-Chief. The news gave him a great shock and he said to himself, "What is to be done now?" He made his way to the reception tent and stole a look therein. He saw murder written on Chou Yu's countenance and noted the assassins hidden within the walls of the tent. Then he got a look at Liu Pei, who was laughing and talking quite unconcernedly. But when he noticed the redoubtable figure of Kuan Yu near his master's side he became quite calm and contented.

"No danger," said he, and he went away to the river bank to await the end of the interview.

Meanwhile the banquet of welcome proceeded. After the wine had gone around several times Chou Yu picked up a cup to give the signal agreed upon. But at that moment he saw so fierce a look upon the face of the trusty henchman who stood, sword in hand, behind his guest, that he hesitated and hastily asked who he was.

"That is my brother, Kuan Yun-ch'ang," replied Yuan-te.

Chou Yu, quite startled, said, "Is he the slayer of Yen Liang and Wen Ch'ou?"

"Exactly; he it is," replied Liu Pei.

The sweat of fear broke out all over Chou Yu's body and trickled down his back. Then he poured out a cup of wine and presented it to Kuan Yu. Just then Lu Su came in and Yuan-te said to him, "Where is K'ung-ming? I would trouble you to ask him to come."

"Wait till we have defeated Ts'ao Ts'ao," said Chou Yu, "then you shall see him."

Yuan-te dared not repeat his request, but Kuan Yu gave him a meaning look which Yuan-te understood and rose, saying, "I would take leave now; I will come again to congratulate you when the enemy has been defeated and your success shall be complete."

Chou Yu did not press him to remain, but escorted him to the great gates of the camp, and Yuan-te left. When he reached the river bank they found K'ung-ming awaiting them in their boat.

Yuan-te was exceedingly pleased but K'ung-ming said, "Sir, do you know in how great danger you were today?"

Suddenly sobered, Yuan-te said, "No; I did not think of danger."

"If Yun-ch'ang had not been there you would have been killed," said K'ung-ming.

Yuan-te, after a moment's reflection, saw that it was true. He begged K'ung-ming to return with him to Fanch'eng, but he refused. "I am quite safe," said he. "Although I am living in the tiger's mouth, I am as steady as Mount T'ai. Now, my lord, return and prepare your ships and men. On the twentieth day of the eleventh month send Chao Yun with a small ship to the south bank to wait for me. Be sure there is no miscarriage."

"What are your intentions?" said Yuan-te.

"When the south-east wind begins I shall have to return."

Yuan-te would have questioned him further, but K'ung-ming pressed him to go. So the boat started up river again while K'ung-ming returned to his temporary lodging.

The boat had not proceeded far when appeared a small fleet sweeping down with the current, and in the prow of the leading vessel stood a tall figure armed with a spear. It was Chang Fei, who had come down fearing lest his brother might be in some difficulty from which the strong arm of Kuan Yu might even be insufficient to rescue him.

Of the return of the three brothers nothing will be said. After Chou Yu, having escorted Yuan-te to the gate of his camp, had returned to his quarters Lu Su soon came to see him.

"When you had cajoled Yuan-te into coming, why did you not carry out your plan?" asked Lu.

"Because of that Kuan Yu; he is a very tiger and he never left his brother for a moment. If anything had been attempted he would certainly have had my life."

Lu Su knew that he spoke the truth. Then suddenly they announced a messenger with a letter from Ts'ao Ts'ao. Chou Yu ordered them to bring him in and took the letter. But when he saw the superscription "The First Minister of Han to Commander-in-Chief Chou," he fell into a frenzy of rage, tore the letter to fragments and threw them on the ground.

"To death with this fellow!" cried he.

"When two countries are at war their emissaries are not slain," said Lu.

"Messengers are slain to show one's dignity and independence," replied Chou.

The unhappy bearer of the letter was decapitated and his head sent back to Ts'ao Ts'ao by the hands of his escort.

Chou Yu then decided to move. The van under Kan Ning was

to advance, supported by two wings. Chou Yu would lead the remainder in support. The next morning the early meal was eaten in the fourth watch and the ships got under weigh in the fifth with a great beating of drums.

Ts'ao Ts'ao was greatly angered when he heard that his letter had been torn to fragments and he resolved to attack forthwith. His advance was led by Ts'ao Mao and others of the Chingchou officers who had joined his side. He went as hastily as possible to the meeting of the three rivers and saw the ships of Wu sailing up. In the bow of the foremost ship stood a fine figure of a warrior who cried, "I am Kan Ning; I challenge any one to combat."

Ts'ai Mao sent his young brother to accept the challenge, but as his ship approached Nan King shot an arrow and Ts'ai Hsun fell. Kan Ning pressed forward, his crossbowmen keeping up a heavy discharge which Ts'ao's men could not stand. The wings also joined in.

Ts'ao's men, being mostly from the dry plains of the north, did not know how to fight effectually on water and the southern ships had the battle all their own way. The slaughter was very great. However, after a contest lasting till afternoon Chou Yu thought it more prudent, in view of the superior numbers of his enemy, not to risk further the advantage he had gained. So he beat the gongs as the signal to cease battle and recall the ships.

Ts'ao was worsted, but his ships returned to the bank, where a camp was made and order was restored. Ts'ao sent for his defeated leaders and reproached them saying, "You did not do your best. You let an inferior force overcome you."

Ts'ai Mao defended himself saying, "The Chingchou marines have not been exercised for a long time and the others have never been trained for naval warfare at all. A naval camp must be instituted, the northern men trained and the Chingchou men drilled. When they have been made efficient they will win victories."

"If you know what should be done, why have you not done it?" said Ts'ao Ts'ao. "What is the use of telling me this? Get to work."

So Ts'ao Mao and Chang Yun organised a naval camp on the river bank. They established twenty-four "Water Gates," with the large ships outside as a sort of rampart, and under their protection the smaller ships went to and fro freely. At night when the lanterns and torches were lit the very sky was illuminated and the water shone red with the glare. On land the smoke of the camp fires could be traced for three hundred *li* without a break.

Chou Yu returned to camp and feasted his victorious fighting men. A messenger bore the joyful tidings of victory to his master in Wu. When night fell Chou Yu went up to the summit of one of the hills and looked out over the long line of bright lights stretching toward the west, showing the extent of the enemy's camp. He said nothing, but a great fear came in upon him.

Next day Chou Yu decided that he would go in person to find out the strength of the enemy. So he bade them prepare a small squadron which he manned with strong, hardy men armed with powerful bows and stiff crossbows. He also placed musicians on each ship. They set sail and started up the stream. When they got opposite Ts'ao Ts'ao's camp the heavy stones that served as anchors were dropped and the drums and trumpets began while Chou Yu scanned the enemy's naval camp. What he saw gave him no satisfaction for everything was most admirable. He enquired whether any one knew the names of the admirals and they told him Ts'ai Mao and Chang Yun.

"They have lived in our country a long time," said he, "and are thoroughly experienced in naval warfare. I must find some means of removing them before I can effect anything."

Meanwhile on shore the sentinels had told Ts'ao that the enemy craft were spying upon them and he ordered out some ships to capture the spies. Chou Yu saw the commotion on shore and hastily gave the order to unmoor and sail down stream. The squadron at once got under way and scattered; to and fro went the oars and each ship seemed to fly. Before Ts'ao's ships could get out after them they were all far away. Ts'ao's ships took up the chase but soon saw pursuit was useless. They returned and reported their failure.

Again Ts'ao found fault with his officers and said, "The other day you lost a battle and the soldiers were greatly dispirited. Now the enemy have spied out our camp. What can be done?"

In eager response to his question one stepped out, saying, "When I was a youth Chou Yu and I were fellow students and pledged friends. My three-inch tongue is still good and I will go over and persuade him to surrender."

Ts'ao, rejoiced to find so speedy a solution, looked at the speaker. It was Chiang Kan of Kiukiang, one of the secretary staff in the camp.

"Are you a good friend of Chou Yu's?" said Ts'ao.

"Rest contented, O Minister," replied Kan. "If I only get on the other side of the river I shall succeed."

"What preparations are necessary?" asked Ts'ao.

"Just a youth as my servant and a couple of rowers; nothing else."

Ts'ao offered him wine, wished him success and sent him on his way.

Clad in a simple white robe and seated in his little craft, the messenger reached Chou Yu's camp and bade the men say that an old friend Chiang Kan wished to see him. The commander was in his tent at a council when the message came, and he laughed as he said to those about him, "A guest is coming." Then he whispered certain instructions in the ear of each one of them and they went out to await his arrival.

Chou Yu received his friend in full ceremonial garb. A crowd of officers in rich silken robes were about him. The guest appeared, his sole attendant a lad dressed in a simple blue gown. He bore himself proudly as he advanced and Chou Yu made a low obeisance.

"You have been well I hope since last we met," said Chiang Kan.

"You have wandered far and suffered much in this task of emissary in the Ts'ao cause," said Chou.

"I have not seen you for a very long time," said the envoy much taken aback, "and I came to visit you for the sake of old times. Why do you call me an emissary for the Ts'ao cause?"

"Though I am not so clever a musician as Shih Kuang, yet I can comprehend the thought behind the music," replied Chou.

"As you choose to treat your old friend like this I think I will take my leave," said Chiang.

Chou Yu laughed again and taking Kan by the arm, said, "Well, I feared you might be coming on his behalf to try to persuade me. But if this is not your intention, you need not go away so hastily."

So they two entered the tent; and when they had exchanged salutes and were seated as friends, Chou Yu bade them call his officers that he might introduce them. They soon appeared civil and military officials, all dressed in their best. The military officers were clad in glittering silver armour and the staff looked very imposing as they stood ranged in two lines.

The visitor was introduced to them all. Presently a banquet was spread, and while they feasted the musicians played songs of victory and the wine circulated merrily. Under its mellowing influence Chou Yu's reserve seemed to thaw and he said, "He is an old fellow student of mine and we are pledged friends. Though he has arrived here from the north he is no artful pleader so you need not be afraid of him."

Then he took off the sword which he wore as Commander-in-Chief and handed it to T'aishih Tzu, saying, "You take this and wear it for the day as master of the feast. This day we meet only as friends and if any one shall begin a discussion of the questions at issue between Ts'ao Ts'ao and our country just slay him."

T'aishih Tzu took the sword and seated himself in his place. The guest was not a little overcome, but he said no word.

Chou Yu said, "Since I assumed command I have tasted no drop of wine, but today as an old friend is present and there is no reason to fear him, I am going to drink freely."

So saying he quaffed a huge goblet and laughed loudly.

The rhinoceros cups went swiftly round from guest to guest till all were half drunk. Then Chou Yu, laying hold of the guest's hand, led him outside the tent. The guards who stood around all braced themselves up and seized their weapons.

"Do you not think my soldiers a fine lot of fellows?" said Chou.

"Strong as bears and bold as tigers," replied Chiang Kan.

Then Chou Yu led him to the rear of the tent whence he saw the grain and forage piled up in mountainous heaps.

"Do you not think I have a fairly good store of grain and forage?"

"It is quite true as I have heard that your men are brave and your supplies ample."

Chou Yu pretended to be quite intoxicated and went on, "When you and I were students together, we never looked forward to a day like this did we?"

"For a genius like you it is nothing extraordinary," said the guest.

Chou Yu again seized his hand and they sat down. "When a really great man has found his proper lord then, in his service, he relies upon the right feeling between prince and minister outside, and at home he is firm in the kindly feeling of relatives. His words must be obeyed, his plans must be followed out. He is independent of good or evil fortune. He takes as his models such men as Su Ch'in, Chang I, Lu Chia and Li Sheng so that they seem to live again. His words pour forth like a rushing river, his tongue is as a sharp sword. Is it possible to move such as I am?"

He burst into a loud laugh as he finished and Chiang Kan's face had become clay-coloured. Chou Yu then led his guest back into the tent and again they fell to drinking. Presently he pointed to the others at table and said, "These are all the best and bravest of the land of Wu; one might call this 'The Meeting of Heroes'."

They drank on till daylight failed and continued after lamps had been lit. Chou Yu even gave an exhibition of sword play and sang this song:—

> When a man is in the world, O,
>   He ought to do his best.
> And when he's done his best, O,
>   He ought to have his rest.
> And when I have my rest, O,
>   I'll quaff my wine with zest.
> And when I'm drunk as drunk can be,
>   I'll sing the madman's litany.

A burst of applause greeted the song. By this time it was getting late and the guest begged to be excused. "The wine is too much for me," said he. His host bade them clear the table and as all the others left Chou Yu said, "It is many a day since I shared a couch with my friend, but we will do so tonight."

Putting on the appearance of irresponsible intoxication he led Chiang Kan into the tent and they went to bed. Chou Yu simply fell, all dressed as he was, and lay there emitting uncouth grunts and groans, so that to the guest sleep was impossible. He lay and listened to the various camp noises without and his host's thund'rous snores within. About the second watch he rose and looked at his friend by the dim light of the small lamp. He also saw on the table a heap of papers and looking at them furtively, saw they were letters. Among them he saw one marked as coming from Chang Yun and Ts'ai Mao. He read it and this is what it said:—"We surrendered to Ts'ao Ts'ao, not for the sake of pay but under stress of circumstances. Now we have fooled these northern soldiers into admitting us to their camp but, as soon as occasion offers, we mean to have the rebel's head to offer as a sacrifice to your banner. From time to time there will be reports as occasions serve but you may trust us. This is our humble reply to your letter."

"Those two were connected with Wu in the beginning," thought Chiang Kan, so he secreted the letter in his dress and began to examine the others. But at that moment Chou Yu turned over and so Kan hastily blew out the light and went to his couch.

Chou Yu was muttering as he lay there and his guest, carefully listening, made out, "Friend, I am going to let you see Ts'ao's head in a day or two."

Chiang Kan hastily made some reply to lead on his host to say more. Then came, "Wait a few days; you will see Ts'ao's head. The old wretch!"

Chiang tried to question him as to what he meant, but Chou Yu was fast asleep and seemed to hear nothing. Chiang lay there on his couch wide awake till the fourth watch was beating. Then some one came in, saying, "General, are you awake?" At that moment as if suddenly awakened from the deepest slumber, Chou Yu started up and said, "Who is this on the couch?"

The voice replied, "Do you not remember, General? You asked your old friend to stay the night with you; it is he, of course."

"I drank too much last night," said Chou Yu in a regretful tone, "and I forgot. I seldom indulge to excess and am not used to it. Perhaps I said many things I ought not."

The voice went on, "A man has arrived from the north."

"Speak lower," said Chou Yu, and turning toward the sleeper he called him by name. But Chiang Kan affected to be sound asleep and made no sign.

Chou Yu crept out of the tent, while Kan listened with all his ears. He heard the man say, "Chang and Ts'ai, the two commanders, have come."

But listening as he did with straining ears he could not make out what followed. Soon after Chou Yu re-entered and again called out his companion's name. But no reply came, for Chiang Kan was pretending to be in the deepest slumber and to hear nothing. Then Chou Yu undressed and went to bed.

As Chiang Kan lay awake he remembered that Chou Yu was known to be meticulously careful in affairs and if in the morning he found that a letter had disappeared he would certainly slay the offender. So he lay there till near daylight and then called out to his host. Getting no reply he rose, dressed and stole out of the tent. Then he called his servant and made for the camp gate.

"Whither are you going, Sir?" said the watchmen at the gate.

"I fear I am in the way here," replied Kan, "and so I have taken leave of the General for a time. So do not stop me."

He found his way to the river bank and re-embarked. Then, with flying oars, he hastened back to Ts'ao's camp. When he arrived Ts'ao asked at once how he had sped and he had to acknowledge failure.

"Chou Yu is very clever and perfectly high-minded," said he, "nothing that I could say moved him in the least."

"Your failure makes me look ridiculous," said Ts'ao.

"Well, if I did not win over Chou Yu, I found out something for you. Send away these people and I will tell you," said Chiang.

The servants were dismissed and then Chiang Kan produced the letter he had stolen from Chou Yu's tent. He gave it to Ts'ao. Ts'ao was very angry and sent for the two at once. As soon as they appeared he said, "I want you two to attack."

Ts'ai Mao replied, "But the men are not yet sufficiently trained."

"The men will be well enough trained when you have sent my head to Chou Yu, eh?"

Both officers were dumb-founded, having not the least idea what this meant. They remained silent for they had nothing to say. Ts'ao bade the executioners lead them away to instant death. In a short time their heads were produced.

By this time Ts'ao had thought over the matter and it dawned upon him that he had been tricked. A poem says:—

> No one could stand against Ts'ao Ts'ao,
>   Of sin he had full share,
> But Chou Yu was more treacherous,
>   And caught him in a snare.
> Two officers to save their lives,
>   Betrayed a former lord,
> Soon after, as was very meet.
>   Both fell beneath the sword.

The death of these two naval commanders caused much consternation in the camp and all their colleagues asked the reason for their sudden execution. Though Ts'ao knew he had been victimised he would not acknowledge it. So he said the two men had been remiss and so had been put to death. The others were aghast, but nothing could be done. Two other officers, Mao and Yu by name, were put in command of the naval camp .

Spies took the news to Chou Yu, who was delighted at the success of his ruse.

"Those two were my only source of anxiety," said he. "Now they are gone, I am quite happy."

Lu Su said, "General, if you can continue like this you need not fear Ts'ao."

"I do not think any of them saw my game," said Chou Yu, except Chuko Liang. He beats me, and I do not think this ruse was hidden from him. You go and sound him. See if he knew."

> Chou's treacherous plot succeeded well,
> Dissension sown, his rivals fell.
> Drunk with success was he, but sought
> To know what cynic K'ung-ming thought.

What passed between Lu Su and K'ung-ming will next be related.

CHAPTER XLVI

K'UNG-MING "BORROWS" SOME ARROWS: HUANG KAI ACCEPTS A PUNISHMENT

The gossip Lu Su departed on his mission and found K'ung-ming seated in his little craft.

"There has been so much to do that I have not been able to come to listen to your instruction," said Lu Su.

"That is truly so," said K'ung-ming, "and I have not yet congratulated the Commander-in-Chief."

"What have you wished to congratulate him upon?"

"Why Sir, the matter upon which he sent you to find out whether I knew about it or not. Indeed I can congratulate him on that."

Lu Su turned pale and gasped. "But how did you know, Master?"

"The ruse succeeded well thus played off on Chiang Kan. Ts'ao has been taken in this once, but he will soon rise to it. Only he will not confess his mistake. However, the two men are gone and your country is freed from a grave anxiety. Do you not think that a matter for congratulation? I hear Mao Chieh and Yu Chin are the new admirals, and in their hands lie both good and evil for the fate of the fleet."

Lu Su was quite dumbfounded; he stayed a little time longer passing the time in making empty remarks, and then took his leave. As he was going away K'ung-ming cautioned him against letting Chou Yu know that his new rival had guessed his ruse. "I know he is jealous and he only seeks some chance to do me harm."

Lu Su promised; nevertheless he went straight to his chief and related the whole thing just as it happened.

"Really he must be got rid of," said Chou Yu, "I have quite decided to put the man out of the way."

"If you slay him, will not Ts'ao Ts'ao laugh at you?"

"Oh, no; I will find a legitimate way of getting rid of him so that he shall go to his death without resentment."

"But how can you find a legitimate way of assassinating him?"

"Do not ask too much; you will see presently."

Soon after all the officers were summoned to the main tent and K'ung-ming's presence was desired. He went contentedly enough. When all were seated Chou Yu suddenly addressed K'ung-ming, saying, "I am going to fight a battle with the enemy soon on the water: what weapons are the best?"

"On the great river arrows are the best," said K'ung-ming.

"Your opinion and mine agree. But at the moment we are short of them. I wish you would undertake to supply about a hundred thousand for the naval fight. As it is for the public service you will not decline, I hope!"

"Whatever task the Commander-in-Chief lays upon me I must certainly try to perform," replied K'ung-ming. "May I enquire by what date you require the hundred thousand arrows?"

"Could you have them ready in ten days?"

"The enemy will be here very soon; ten days will be too late," said K'ung-ming.

"In how many days do you estimate the arrows can be ready?"

"Let me have three days; then you may send for your hundred thousand."

"No joking, remember," said the General. "There is no joking in war time."

"Dare I joke with the Commander-in-Chief? Give me a formal military order and if I have not completed the task in three days I will take my punishment."

Chou Yu, secretly delighted, sent for the secretaries and prepared the commission then and there. Then he drank to the success of the undertaking and said, "I shall have to congratulate you most heartily when this is accomplished."

"This day is not to count," said K'ung-ming. "On the third from tomorrow morning send five hundred small boats to the river side to convey the arrows."

They drank a few more cups together and then K'ung-ming took his leave. After he had gone, Lu Su said, "Do you not think there is some deceit about this?"

"I think he has signed his own death warrant," said Chou. "Without being pressed in the least he asked for a formal order in the face of the whole assembly. If he grew a pair of wings he could not escape. Only I will just order the workmen to delay him as much as they can, and not supply him with materials, so that he is sure to fail. And then, when the certain penalty is incurred, who can criticise? You can go and enquire about it all and keep me informed."

So off went Lu Su to seek K'ung-ming, who at once reproached him with having blabbed about the former business, "He wants to hurt me, as you know, and I did not think you could not keep my secret. And now there is what you saw today and how do you think I can get a hundred thousand arrows made in three days? You will simply have to rescue me."

"You brought the misfortune on yourself and how can I rescue you?" said Lu.

"I look to you for the loan of a score of vessels, manned each by thirty men. I want blue cotton screens and bundles of straw lashed to the sides of the boats. I have good use for them. On the third day I have undertaken to deliver the fixed number of arrows. But on no account must you let Chou Yu know, or my scheme will be wrecked."

Lu Su consented and this time he kept his word. He went to report to his chief as usual, but he said nothing about the boats. He only said K'ung-ming was not using bamboo or feathers or glue or varnish, but had some other way of getting arrows.

"Let us await the three days' limit," said Chou Yu, puzzled though confident.

On his side Lu Su quietly prepared a score of light swift boats, each with its crew and the blue screens and bundles of grass complete and, when these were ready, he placed them at K'ung-ming's disposal. His friend did nothing on the first day, nor on the second. On the third day at the middle of the fourth watch, K'ung-ming sent a private message asking Lu Su to come to his boat.

"Why have you sent for me, Sir?" asked Lu Su.

"I want you to go with me to get those arrows."

"Whither are you going?"

"Do not ask: you will see."

Then the twenty boats were fastened together by long ropes and moved over to the north bank. The night proved very foggy and the mist was very dense along the river, so that one man could scarcely see another. In spite of the fog K'ung-ming urged the boats forward.

There is a poem on these river fogs:—

Mighty indeed is the Yangtse River!
Rising far in the west, in the mountains of Omei and Min,
Ploughing its way through Wu, east flowing, resistless,
Swelled by its nine tributary streams, rolling down from the far
    north,
Aided and helped by a hundred rivulets swirling and foaming,
Ocean receives it at last welcoming, joyful, its waters.
Therein abide sea-nymphs and water gods,
Enormous whales a thousand fathoms long,
Nine-headed monstrous beasts yclept *t'ien-wu*,
Demons and uncouth creatures wondrous strange.
In faith it is the home and safe retreat
Of devils black, and sprites, and wondrous growths,
And eke the battle ground of valiant men.
At times occur strange strife of elements,
When darkness strives on light's domain t'encroach,
Whereat arises in the vaulted dome of blue
White wreaths of fog that toward the centre roll.
Then darkness falls, too dense for any torch
T'illumine; only clanging sounds can pass.
The fog at first appears, a vaprous wreath
Scarce visible. But thickening fast, it veils
The southern hills, the Painted leopard's home.
And spreads afar, until the northern sea
Leviathans are mazed and lose their course.
And denser yet it touches on the sky,
And spreads a heavy mantle o'er the earth.
Then, wide as is the high pitched arch of heaven,
Therein appears no single rift of blue.
Now mighty whales lead up their wives to sport
Upon the waves, the sinuous dragons dive
Deep down and, breathing, swell the heaving sea,
The earth is moist as with the early rains,
And spring's creative energy is chilled.
Both far and wide and high the damp fog spreads,
Great cities on the eastern bank are hid,
Wide ports and mountains in the south are lost,
Whole fleets of battle ships, a thousand keels,
Hide in the misty depths; frail fishing boats
High riding on a wave are seen—and lost.
The gloom increases and the domed sky
Grows dark and darker as the sun's light fails.

The daylight dies, dim twilight's reign begins,
The ruddy bills dissolve and lose their hue.
The skill of matchless Yu would fail to sound
The depth and height; and Li Lou's eye, though keen,
Could never pierce this gloom. Now is the time,
O sea and river gods, to use your powers.
The gliding fish and creeping water folk
Are lost; there is no track for bird or beast.
Fair P'englai Isles are hidden from our sight,
The lofty gates of heaven have disappeared.
Nature is blurred and indistinct, as when
A driving rain storm hurries o'er the earth.
And then, perhaps, within the heavy haze
A noisome serpent vents his venom foul
And plagues descend, or impish demons work
Their wicked wills.
Ills fall on men but do not stay,
Heaven's cleansing breath sweeps them away,
But while they last the mean ones cry,
The nobler suffer silently.
The greatest turmoil is a sign
Of quick return to state benign.

The little fleet reached Ts'ao Ts'ao's naval camp about the fifth watch and orders were given to form line lying prows west, and then to beat the drums and shout.

"But what shall we do if they attack us?" exclaimed Lu Su.

K'ung-ming replied with a smile, "I think the fleet will not venture out in this fog; go on with your wine and let us be happy. We will go back when the fog lifts."

As soon as the shouting from the river was heard by those in the camp the two commanders ran off to report to their chief, who said, "Coming up in a fog like this means that they have prepared an ambush for us. Do not go out, but get all the force together and shoot at them."

He also sent orders to the soldier camps to despatch six companies of archers and crossbowmen to aid the marines.

The naval forces were then lined up on the bank to prevent a landing. Presently the soldiers arrived and a legion and more men were shooting down into the river, where the arrows fell like rain. By and bye K'ung-ming ordered the boats to turn round so that their prows pointed east and to go closer in so that many arrows might hit them.

The drums were kept beating till the sun was high and the fog began to disperse, when the boats got under way and sailed down stream. The whole twenty boats were bristling with arrows on both sides. As they left, all the crews derisively shouted, "We thank you, Sir Minister, for the arrows."

They told Ts'ao Ts'ao, but by the time he came the light boats helped by the swift current were a long way down river and pursuit was impossible. Ts'ao Ts'ao saw that he had been duped and was very sorry, but there was no help for it.

On the way down K'ung-ming said to his companion, "Every boat must have five or six thousand arrows and so, without the expenditure of an ounce of energy, we must have more than ten myriad arrows, which tomorrow can be shot back again at Ts'ao Ts'ao's army to his great inconvenience."

"You are really superhuman," said Lu Su. "But how did you know there would be a thick fog today?"

"One cannot be a leader without knowing the workings of heaven and the ways of earth. One must understand the secret gates and the inter-dependence of the elements, the mysteries of tactics and the value of forces. It is but an ordinary talent. I calculated three days ago that there would be a fog today and so I set the limit at three days. Chou Yu would give me ten days, but neither artificers nor material, so that he might find occasion to put me to death as I knew, but my fate lies with the Supreme and how could Chou Yu harm me?"

Lu Su could not but agree. When the boats arrived half a company were in readiness on the bank to carry away the arrows. K'ung-ming bade them go on board the boats, collect them and bear them to the tent of the Commander-in-Chief. Lu Su went to report that the arrows had been obtained and told Chou Yu by what means.

Chou Yu was amazed and sighed sadly, saying, "He is better than I; his methods are more than human."

> Thick lies the fog on the river,
> 　　Nature is shrouded in white,
> Distant and near are confounded,
> 　　Banks are no longer in sight.
> Fast fly the pattering arrows,
> 　　Stick in the boats of the fleet.
> Now can full tale be delivered,
> 　　K'ung-ming is victor complete.

When, shortly after his return, K'ung-ming went to the tent of the Commander-in-Chief he was welcomed by Chou Yu, who came forward to greet him, saying, "Your superhuman predictions compel one's esteem."

"There is nothing remarkable in that trifling trick," replied he.

Chou Yu led him within and wine was brought.

Chou Yu said, "My lord sent yesterday to urge me to advance, but I have no master plan ready; I wish you would assist me, Master."

"But where should I, a man of poor, everyday ability, find such a plan as you desire?"

"I saw the enemy's naval camp just lately and it looked very complete and well organised. It is not an ordinary place to attack. I have thought of a plan, but I am not sure it will answer. I should be happy if you would decide for me."

"General," replied K'ung-ming, "do not say what your plan is but each of us will write in the palm of his hand and see whether our opinions agree."

So pen and ink were sent for and Chou Yu first wrote on his own palm, and then passed the pen to K'ung-ming who also wrote. Then getting close together on the same bench each showed his hand to the other, and both burst out laughing, for both had written the same word, "Fire."

"Since we are of the same opinion," said Chou Yu, "there is no longer any doubt. But our intentions must be kept secret."

"Both of us are public servants and what would be the sense of telling our plans? I do not think Ts'ao Ts'ao will be on his guard against this although he has had two experiences. You may put your scheme into force."

They finished their wine and separated. Not an officer knew a word of the general's plans.

Now Ts'ao Ts'ao had expended a myriad arrows in vain and was much irritated in consequence. He deeply desired revenge. Then Hsun Yu proposed a ruse, saying, "The two strategists on the side of the enemy are Chou Yu and Chuko Liang, two men most difficult to get the better of. Let us send some one who shall pretend to surrender to them but really be a spy on our behalf and a helper in our schemes. When we know what is doing we can plan to meet it."

"I had thought of that myself," replied Ts'ao. "Whom do you think the best man to send?"

"Ts'ai Mao has been put to death, but all the clan and family are in the army and the two younger brothers are junior generals. You have them most securely in your power and may send them to surrender. The ruler of Wu will never suspect deceit there."

Ts'ao Ts'ao decided to act on this plan and in the evening summoned the two men to his tent, where he told them what he wished them to do. And he promised them rich rewards if they succeeded. "But do not betray me," added he.

"Our families are in Chingchou and that place is yours," replied they. "Should we dare betray? You need have no doubts, Sir. You will soon see the heads of both Chou Yu and Chuko Liang at your feet."

Ts'ao Ts'ao gave them generous gifts and soon after the two men, each with his half company, set sail with a fair wind for the opposite bank.

Now as Chou Yu was preparing for the attack the arrival of some ships was announced. They bore the two younger brothers of Ts'ai Mao, who had come as deserters. They were led in and, bowing before the general, said, weeping, "Our innocent brother has been put to death and we desire vengeance. So we have come to offer allegiance to you. We pray you to appoint us to the vanguard."

Chou Yu appeared very pleased and made them presents. Then he ordered them to join Kan Ning in leading the van. They thanked him and regarded their scheme as already a success.

But he gave Kan Ning secret orders, saying, "They have come without their families and so I know their desertion is only pretence. They have been sent as spies and I am going to meet their ruse with one of my own. They shall have some information to send. You will treat them well, but keep a careful guard over them. On the day our soldiers start they shall be sacrificed to the flag. But be very careful that nothing goes wrong."

Kan Ning went away, and Lu Su came in to tell Chou Yu that every one agreed in thinking the surrender of the two feigned and said they should be rejected.

"But they wish to revenge the death of their brother," said the General. "Where is the pretence? If you are so suspicious you will receive nobody at all."

Lu Su left much piqued and went to see K'ung-ming to whom he told the story. K'ung-ming only smiled.

"Why do you smile?" said Lu Su.

"I smile at your simplicity. The General is playing a game. Spies cannot easily come and go so these two have been sent to feign desertion that they may act as spies. The General is meeting one ruse with another. He wants them to give information. Deceit is not to be despised in war and his scheme is the correct one to employ."

Then Lu Su understood. That night as Chou Yu was sitting in his tent, Huang Kai came to see him privately. "You have surely some wise plan to propose that you come at night like this."

Huang Kai replied, "The enemy are more numerous than we and it is wrong to delay. Why not burn them out?"

"Who suggested that to you?"

"I thought of it myself, nobody suggested it," replied Huang.

"I just wanted something like this and that is why I kept those two pretended deserters. I want them to give some news. The pity is that I have no one to feign desertion to the other side and work my plan."

"But I will carry out your plan," said Huang Kai.

"But if you cannot show some injury you will not be believed," said Chou.

"The Sun family have been very generous to me and I would not resent being crushed to death to repay them," said Huang.

The General thanked him saying, "If you would not object to some bodily suffering then our country would indeed be happy."

"Kill me; I do not mind," repeated Huang Kai as he took his leave.

Next day the drums called all the officers together to the General's tent and K'ung-ming came with the others. Chou Yu said, "The enemy's camps extend about three hundred *li* so that the campaign will be a long one. Each leader is to prepare supplies for three months."

Scarcely had he spoken when Huang Kai started up, crying, "Say not three months; be ready for thirty months, and even then it will not be ended. If you can destroy them this month then all is well. If you cannot, then it were better to take Chang Chao's advice, throw down your weapons, turn to the north and surrender."

Chou Yu's anger flared up and he flushed, crying, "Our lord's orders were to destroy Ts'ao Ts'ao and whoever mentioned the word surrender should be put to death. Now, the very moment when the two armies are to engage, you dare talk of surrender and damp the ardour of my men! If I do not slay you, how can I support the others?"

He ordered the lictors to remove Huang Kai and execute him without delay.

Kai then flamed up in turn, saying, "This is the third generation since I went with General P'o-lo (Sun Chien) and we overran the south-east; whence have you sprung up?"

This made Chou Yu perfectly furious and Huang Kai was ordered to intant death. But Kan Ning interfered. Said he, "He is a veteran officer of Wu; pray pardon him."

"What are you prating about?" cried Chou Yu. "Dare you come between me and my duty?" Turning to the lictors he ordered them to drive him forth with blows.

The other officials fell on their knees entreating pity for Huang Kai. "He is indeed most worthy of death, but it would be a loss to the army; we pray you forgive him. Record his fault for the moment and after the enemy shall have been defeated then put him to death."

But Chou Yu was implacable. The officers pleaded with tears. At length he seemed moved, saying, "Had you not interceded he should certainly have suffered death. But now I will mitigate the punishment to a beating. He shall not die."

He turned to the lictors and bade them deal the culprit one hundred blows. Again his colleagues prayed for remission but Chou Yu angrily pushed over the table in front of him and roared to the officers to get out of the way and let the sentence be executed.

So Huang Kai was stripped, thrown to the ground and fifty blows were given. At this point the officers again prayed that he be let off. Chou Yu sprang from his chair and pointing his finger at Huang Kai said, "If you dare flout me again you shall have the other fifty. If you are guilty of any disrespect, you shall be punished for both faults!"

With this he turned into the inner part of the tent, growling as he went, while the officers helped their beaten colleague to his feet. He was in a pitiable state. His back was cut in many places and the blood was flowing in streams. They led him to his own quarters and on the way he swooned several times. His case seemed most pitiable.

Lu Su went to see the suffering officer and then called on K'ung-ming in his boat. He related the story of the beating and said that though the other officers had been cowed into silence he thought K'ung-ming might have interceded. "You are a guest and not under his orders. Why did you stand by with your hands up your sleeves and say never a word?"

"You insult me," said K'ung-ming smiling.

"Why do you say that? I have never insulted you, never since the day we came here together."

"Do you not know that that terrible beating was but a ruse? How could I try to dissuade him?"

Then Lu Su began to perceive and K'ung-ming continued, "Ts'ao

Ts'ao would not be taken in unless there was some real bodily suffering. Now he is going to send Huang Kai over as a deserter and he will see to it that the two Ts'ao spies duly tell the tale. But when you see the General you must not tell him that I saw through the ruse. You say that I am very angry like the others."

Lu Su went to see Chou Yu and asked him why he had so cruelly beaten a proved and trusty officer.

"Do the officers resent it?" asked Chou.

"They are all upset about it."

"And what does your friend think?"

"He also resents it in his heart, and thinks you have made a mistake."

"Then I have deceived him for once," said Chou gleefully.

"What mean you?" cried Lu.

"That beating that Huang Kai got is part of my ruse. I am sending him to Ts'ao Ts'ao as a deserter and so I have supplied a reason for desertion. Then I am going to use fire against the enemy."

Lu Su kept silence but he recognised that K'ung-ming was again right.

Meanwhile Huang Kai lay in his tent, whither all his brother officers went to condole with him and enquire after his health. But Kai would say never a word; he only lay sighing deeply from time to time.

But when the strategist K'an Tse came, Kai told them to bring him to the room where he lay. Then he bade the servants go away and Tse said, "Surely you must have some serious quarrel with the General."

"I have none," said Kai.

"Then this beating is just part of a ruse?"

"How did you guess?" said Kai.

"Because I watched the General and I guessed about nine tenths of the truth."

Huang said, "You see I have been very generously treated by the Sun family, all three of them, and have no means of showing my gratitude except by offering to help in this ruse. True I suffer, but I do not regret that. Among all those I know in the army there is not one I am intimate with except yourself. You are true and I can talk with you as a friend."

"I suppose you wish me to present your letter proposing to come over; is that it?"

"Just that; will you do it?" said Huang.

K'an Tse consented joyfully.

> Even the warrior's body is but a stake in the game,
> The friend so ready to help him proves that their hearts are the
>   same.

K'an's reply will be read in the next chapter.

CHAPTER XLVII

K'AN TSE PRESENTS THE TREACHEROUS
LETTER: P'AN T'UNG SUGGESTS CHAINING
THE SHIPS TOGETHER

This K'an Tse was from Shanyin, a son of a humble family. He loved books, but as he was too poor to buy he used to borrow. He had a wonderfully tenacious memory, was very eloquent and no coward. Sun Ch'uan had employed him among his advisers and he and Huang Kai were excellent friends. The latter had thought of him to present the treacherous letter as his gifts made him most suitable. K'an Tse accepted with enthusiasm, saying, "When you, my friend, have suffered so much for our lord, could I spare myself? No; while a man lives he must go on fulfilling his mission or he is no better than the herbs that rot in the field."

Huang Kai slipped off the couch and came over to salute him.

"However, this matter must speed," continued K'an Tse; there is no time to lose."

"The letter is already written," said Huang Kai.

K'an Tse received it and left. That night he disguised himself as an old fisherman and started in a small punt for the north shore, under the cold, glittering light of the stars.

Soon he drew near the enemy's camp and was captured by the patrol. Without waiting for day they informed their General, who said at once, "Is he not just a spy?"

"No," said they, "he is alone, just an old fisherman; and he says he is an adviser in the service of Wu named K'an Tse, and he has come on secret business."

"Bring him," said Ts'ao Ts'ao and he was led in. Ts'ao was seated in a brilliantly lighted tent. He was leaning on a small table and as soon as he saw the prisoner, he said, "You are an adviser of Wu; what then are you doing here?"

People say that you greedily welcome men of ability; I do not think your question a very proper one. Friend Huang, you made a mistake," said K'an.

"You know I am fighting against Wu and you come here privately. Why should I not question you?"

"Huang Kai is an old servant of Wu, one who has served three successive rulers. Now he has been cruelly beaten, for no fault, before the face of all the officers in Chou Yu's camp. He is grievously angry about this and wishes to desert to your side that he may be revenged. He discussed it with me, and as we are inseparable, I have come to give you his letter asking whether you would receive him."

"Where is the letter?" said Ts'ao.

The missive was produced and presented. Ts'ao Ts'ao opened it and read:—"I, Huang Kai, have been generously treated by the Sun family and have served them single-heartedly. Lately they have been discussing an attack with our forces on the enormous army of the central government. As every one knows our few are no match for such a multitude and every officer of Wu, wise or foolish, recognises that quite well. However, Chou Yu who, after all, is but a youth and a shallow minded simpleton, maintains that success is possible and rashly desires to smash stones with an egg. Beside this he is arbitrary and tyrannical, punishing for no crime, and leaving meritorious service unrewarded. I am an old servant and for no reason have been shamed in the sight of men Wherefore I hate him in my heart.

"You, O Minister, treat men with sincerity and are ready to welcome ability and so I, and those under my leadership, desire to enter your service whereby to acquire reputation and remove the shameful stigma. The commissariat, weapons and the supply ships will also come over to you. In perfect sincerity I state these matters; I pray you not to doubt me."

Leaning there on the low table by his side, Ts'ao turned this letter over and over and read it again and again. Then he smacked the table, opened his eyes wide with anger saying, "Huang Kai is trying to play the personal injury trick on me, is he? And you are in it as the intermediary to present the letter. How dare you come to sport with me?"

He ordered the lictors to thrust forth the messenger and take off his head. K'an Tse was hustled out, his face untroubled. On the contrary, he laughed aloud. At this Ts'ao told them to bring him back and harshly said to him, "What do you find to laugh at now that I have foiled you and your ruse has failed?"

"I was not laughing at you; I was laughing at my friend's simplicity."

"What do you mean by his simplicity?"

"If you want to slay, slay; do not trouble me with a multitude of questions."

"I have read all the books on the art of war and I am well versed in all ways of misleading the enemy. This ruse of yours might have succeeded with many, but it will not do for me."

"And so you say that the letter is a vicious trick?" said K'an.

"What I say is that your little slip has sent you to the death your risked. If the thing was real and you were sincere, why does not the letter name a time? What have you to say to that?"

K'an Tse waited to the end and then laughed louder than ever, saying, "I am so glad you are not frightened, but can still boast of your knowledge of the books of war. Now you will not lead away your soldiers. If you fight, Chou Yu will certainly capture you. But how sad to think I die at the hand of such an ignorant fellow!"

"What mean you? I, ignorant?"

"You are ignorant of any strategy and a victim of unreason; is not that sufficient?"

"Well then, tell me where is any fault in my navy."

"You treat wise men too badly for me to talk to you. You can finish me and let there be an end of it."

"If you can speak with any show of reason, I will treat you differently."

"Do you not know that when one is going to desert one's master and become a renegade one cannot say exactly when the chance will occur? If one binds one's self to a fixed moment and the thing cannot be done just then, the secret will be discovered. One must watch for an opportunity and take it when it comes. Think; is it possible to know exactly when? But you know nothing of common sense; all you know is how to put good men to death. So you really are an ignorant fellow."

At this Ts'ao changed his manner, got up and came over to the prisoner bowing, "I did not see clearly; that is quite true. I offended you and I hope you will forget it."

"The fact is that Huang Kai and I are both inclined to desert to you; we even yearn for it as a child desires its parents. Is it possible that we should play you false?"

"If you two could render me so great a service, you shall certainly be richly rewarded."

"We do not desire rank or riches; we come because it is the will of heaven and the plain way of duty."

Then wine was set out and K'an Tse was treated as an honoured guest. While they were drinking some one came in and whispered in Ts'ao's ear. He replied, "Let me see the letter." Whereupon the man pulled out and gave him a letter, which evidently pleased him.

"That is from the two Ts'ais," thought K'an Tse. "They are reporting the punishment of my friend and that will be a proof of the sincerity of his letter."

Turning toward K'an Tse, Ts'ao said, "I must ask you to return to settle the date with your friend: as soon as I know I will have a force waiting."

"I cannot return; pray, Sir, send some other man you can trust."

"If some one else should go the secret would out."

K'an Tse refused again and again but at last gave way, saying, "If I am to go I must not wait here; I must be off at once."

Ts'ao offered him gold and silks, which were refused. Tse started left the camp and re-embarked for the south bank, where he related all that had happened to Huang Kai.

"If it had not been for your persuasive tongue then I had undergone this suffering in vain," said Huang.

"I will now go to get news of the two Ts'ais," said K'an Tse.

"Excellent," said Huang.

He went to the camp commanded by Kan Ning and when they were seated he said to his host, "I was much distressed when I saw how disgracefully you were treated for your intercession on behalf of Huang Kai."

Kan Ning smiled. Just then the two Ts'ais came, and host and guest exchanged glances. The former said, "The truth is the General is over confident and he reckons us as nobody. We count for nothing. Every one is talking of the way I was insulted. Aiya!" and he shouted and gritted his teeth and smacked the table in his wrath.

K'an Tse leaned over toward his host and said something in a very low voice, at which Kan Ning bent his head and sighed.

The two visitors and spies gathered from this that both Kan and K'an were ripe for desertion and determined to probe them.

"Why, Sir, do you anger him? Why not be silent about his injuries?" said they.

"What know you of our bitterness?" said K'an Tse.

"We think you seem much inclined to go over to Ts'ao Ts'ao," said they.

K'an Tse at this lost colour: Kan Ning started up and drew his sword, crying, "They have found out; they must die to keep their mouths shut."

"No, no," cried the two in a flurry. "Let us tell you something quite secret."

"Quick, then," cried Kan Ning.

So Ts'ao Ho said, "The truth is that we are only pretended deserters, and if you two gentlemen are of our way of thinking we can manage things for you."

"But are you speaking the truth?" said Kan.

"Is it likely we should say such a thing if it were untrue?" cried both at the same moment.

Kan Ning put on a pleased look and said. "Then this is the very heaven-given chance."

"You know we have already told Ts'ao of the Huang Kai affair and how you were insulted."

"The fact is I have given the Minister a letter on behalf of Huang Kai and he sent me back again to settle the date of his desertion," said K'an.

"When an honest man happens upon an enlightened master his heart will always be drawn toward him," said Kan Ning.

The four then drank together and opened their hearts to each other. The two brothers Ts'ai wrote a private letter to their master saying that Kan Ning had agreed to join in their plot and play the traitor, and K'an Tse also wrote and they sent the letters secretly to Ts'ao Ts'ao. Kan's letter said that Huang had found no opportunity so far. However, when he came his boat could be recognised by a black, indented flag. That would mean he was on board.

However, when Ts'ao Ts'ao got these two letters he was still doubtful and called together his advisers to talk over the matter. Said he, "On the other side Kan Ning has been put to shame by the Commander-in-Chief whom he is prepared to betray for the sake of revenge. Huang Kai has been punished and sent K'an Tse to propose that he should come over to our side. Only I still distrust the whole thing. Who will go over to the camp to find out the real truth?"

Then Chiang Kan spoke up, saying, "I failed in my mission the other day and am greatly mortified. I will risk my life again and, this time, I shall surely bring good news."

Ts'ao Ts'ao approved of him as messenger and bade him start. He set out in a small craft and speedily arrived in Chiangnan landing near the naval camp. Then he sent to inform Chou Yu, who hearing who it was chuckled, saying, "Success depends upon this man."

Then he called Lu Su and told him to call P'ang T'ung to come and do certain things for him.

This P'ang T'ung was from Hsiangyang. His other name was Shih-yuan and he had gone to the east of the river to get away from the strife. Lu Su had recommended him to Chou Yu, but he had not yet presented himself. When Chou Yu sent to ask what scheme of attack he would recommend against Ts'ao Ts'ao, P'ang T'ung had said to the messenger, "You must use fire against him. But the river is wide and if one ship is set on fire the others will scatter unless they are fastened together so that they must remain in one place. That is the one road to success."

Lu Su took this message to the General, who pondered over it and then said, "The only person who can manage this is P'ang T'ung himself."

"Ts'ao Ts'ao is very wily," said Lu Su, "how can P'ang T'ung go?"

So Chou Yu was sad and undecided. He could think of no method till suddenly the means presented itself in the arrival of Chiang Kan. He at once sent instructions to P'ang T'ung how to act and then sat himself in his tent to await his visitor Chiang Kan.

But the visitor became ill at ease and suspicious when he saw that his old student friend did not come to welcome him and he took the precaution of sending his boat into a retired spot to be made fast before he went to the General's tent.

When Chou Yu saw him he put on an angry face and said, "My friend, why did you treat me so badly."

Chiang Kan laughed and said, "I remembered the old days when we were as brothers and I came expressly to pour out my heart to you. Why do you say I treated you badly?"

"You came to persuade me to betray my master, which I would never do unless the sea dried up and the rocks perished. Remembering the old times I filled you with wine and kept you to sleep with me. And you, you plundered my private letters and stole away with never a word of farewell. You betrayed me to Ts'ao Ts'ao and caused the death of my two friends on the other side and so caused all my plans to miscarry. Now what have you come for? Certainly it is not out of kindness to me and I care no more for our old friendship; it is cut in two, destroyed. I would send you back again, but within a day or two I shall attack that rebel and, if I let you stay in my camp, my plans will leak out. So I am going to tell my attendants to conduct you to a certain retired hut in the western hills and keep you there till I shall have won the victory. Then I will send you back again."

Chiang Kan tried to say something but Chou Yu would not listen. He turned his back and went into the recesses of his tent. The attendants led the visitor off, set him on a horse and took him away over the hills to the small hut, leaving two soldiers to look after him.

When Chiang Kan found himself in the lonely hut he was very depressed and had no desire to eat or sleep. But one night, when the stars were very brilliant, he strolled out to enjoy them. Presently he came to the rear of his lonely habitation and heard, near by, some one crooning over a book. Approaching with stealthy steps he saw a tiny cabin half hidden in a cliff whence a slender beam or two of light stole out between the rafters. He went nearer and peeping in, saw a man reading by the light of a lamp near which hung a sword. And the book was Sun Wu's "Art of War."

"This is no common person," thought he and so he knocked at the door. The door was opened by the reader, who bade him welcome with cultivated and refined ceremony. Chiang Kan enquired his name and the host replied that he was P'ang T'ung, sometimes known as Shih-yuan.

"Then you are surely The Master known as 'Phoenix Fledgeling,' are you not?"

"Yes; I am he."

"How often have I heard you talked about! You are famous. But why are you hidden away in this spot?"

"That fellow Chou Yu is too conceited to allow that any one else has any talent and so I live here quietly. But who are you, Sir?"

"I am Chiang Kan."

Then P'ang T'ung made him very welcome and led him in and the two sat down to talk.

"With your gifts you would succeed anywhere," said Chiang Kan. "If you would enter Ts'ao Ts'ao's service I would recommend you to him."

"I have long desired to get away from here and if you, Sir, will present me there is no time like the present. If Chou Yu heard of my wish he would kill me, I am sure."

So without more ado they made their way down the hill to the water's edge to seek the boat in which Chiang had come. They embarked and, rowing swiftly, they soon reached the northern shore. At the central camp Chiang landed and went to seek Ts'ao Ts'ao to whom he related the story of the discovery of his new acquaintance.

When Ts'ao Ts'ao heard that the newcomer was Feng-ch'u, or the "Phoenix Chick" Master, he went to meet him, made him very welcome and soon they sat down to talk on friendly terms.

Ts'ao Ts'ao said questioningly, "And so Chou Yu in his youth is conceited and annoys his officers and rejects all their advice; I know that. But your fame has been long known to me and now that you have been gracious enough to turn my way I pray you not to be niggardly of your advice."

"I, too, know well that you are a model of military strategy," said P'ang T'ung, "but I should like to have one look at your disposition."

So horses were brought and the two rode out to the lines, host and visitor on equal terms, side by side. They ascended a hill whence they had a wide view. After looking all round P'ang T'ung remarked, "Sun Wu, come to life again, could not do better, nor Jang Chu if he reappeared. All accords with the precepts. The camp is beside the hill and is flanked by a forest. The front and rear are within sight of each other. Gates of egress and ingress are provided and the roads of advance and retirement are bent and broken."

"Master, I entreat you not to overpraise me, but to advise me where I can make further improvements," said Ts'ao.

Then the two men rode down to the naval camp, where twenty four openings were arranged facing the south. The cruisers and the battleships were all lined up so as to protect the lighter craft which lay inside. There were channels to pass to and fro and fixed anchorages and stations.

P'ang T'ung surveying all this smiled, saying, "Sir Minister, if this is your method of warfare, you enjoy no empty reputation." Then pointing to Chiangnan he went on, "Chou, my friend, Master Chou, you are finished; you will have to die."

They rode back to the chief tent and wine was brought. They discussed military mattes and P'ang T'ung held forth at length. Remarks and comments flowed freely between the two, and Ts'ao formed an exalted opinion of his new adherent's abilities and treated him with the greatest honour.

By and bye the guest seemed to have succumbed to the influence of many cups and said, "Have you any capable medical men in your army?"

"What for?" said Ts'ao.

"There is a lot of illness among the marines and you ought to find some remedy."

The fact was that at this time Ts'ao's men were suffering from the climate; many were vomiting and not a few had died. It was a source of great anxiety to him and when the newcomer suddenly mentioned it, of course he had to ask advice.

P'ang T'ung said, "Your marine force is excellent, but there is just one defect; it is not quite perfect."

Ts'ao pressed him to say where the imperfection lay.

"I have a plan to overcome the ailment of the men so that no one shall be sick and all fit for service."

"What is this excellent scheme?" said Ts'ao.

"The river is wide and the tides ebb and flow. The winds and waves are never at rest. Your men from the north are unused to ships and the motion makes them ill. If your ships, large and small, were classed and divided into thirties, or fifties, and joined up stem to stem by iron chains and boards spread across them, to say nothing of men being able to pass from one to the next, even horses could move about on them. If this were done, then there would be no fear of the wind and the waves and the rising and falling tides."

Coming down from his seat Ts'ao Ts'ao thanked his guest saying, "I could never defeat the land of Wu without this scheme of yours."

"That is my idea," said P'ang T'ung, "it is for you to decide about it."

Orders were then issued to call up all the blacksmiths and set them to work, night and day, forging iron chains and great bolts to lock together the ships. And the men rejoiced when they heard of the plan.

> In Red Wall's fight they used the flame,
> The weapon here will be the same.
> By P'ang's advice the ships were chained,
> Else Chou had not that battle gained.

P'ang T'ung further told Ts'ao Ts'ao saying, "I know many bold men on the other side who hate Chou Yu. If I may use my little tongue in your service I can induce them to come over to you and if Chou Yu be left alone you can certainly take him captive. And Liu Pei is of no account."

"Certainly if you could render me so great a service I would memorialise the throne and obtain for you one of the highest offices," said Ts'ao.

"I am not doing this for the sake of wealth or honours, but from a desire to succour mankind. If you cross the river I pray you be merciful."

"I am Heaven's means of doing right and could not bear to slay the people."

P'ang T'ung thanked him and begged for a document that would protect his own family. Ts'ao Ts'ao asked where they lived. He replied that they lived by the river bank and Ts'ao Ts'ao ordered a protection to be prepared. Having sealed it he gave it to P'ang T'ung who said, "You should attack as soon as I have gone but do not let Chou Yu know anything."

Ts'ao Ts'ao promised secrecy and the wily traitor took his leave. Just as he was about to embark he met a man in a Taoist robe, with a bamboo comb in his hair, who stopped him saying, "You are very bold. Huang Kai is planning to use the 'personal injury ruse' and K'an Tse has presented the letter of pretended desertion. You have proffered the fatal scheme of chaining the ships together lest the flames may not completely destroy them. This sort of mischievous work may have been enough to blind Ts'ao Ts'ao but I saw it all."

P'ang T'ung become helpless with fear, his three *hun* flown away, his seven *po* scattered.

> By guileful means one may succeed,
> The victims too find friends in need.

The next chapter will tell who the stranger was.

CHAPTER XLVIII

BANQUET ON THE YANGTSE; TS'AO TS'AO'S SONG: THE NORTHERN MEN FIGHT ON THE CHAINED SHIPS

In the last chapter P'ang T'ung was brought up with a sudden shock when some one seized him and said he understood. Upon turning to look at the man he saw it was Hsu Shu, an old friend, and his heart revived. Looking around and seeing no one near he said, "It would be a pity if you upset my plan; the fate of the people of all the eighty-one districts is in your hands."

Hsu Shu smiled. "And what of the fate of these eighty-three legions of men and horse?" said he.

"Do you intend to wreck my scheme?"

"I have never forgotten the kindness of Uncle Liu, nor my oath to avenge the death of my mother at Ts'ao Ts'ao's hands. I have said I would never think out a plan for him. So am I likely to wreck yours now, brother? But I have followed the army thus far and after they shall have been defeated, good and bad will suffer alike and how can I escape? Tell me how I can secure safety and I sew up my lips and go away."

P'ang T'ung smiled, "If you are as high-minded as that there is no great difficulty."

"Still I wish you would instruct me."

So P'ang T'ung whispered something in his ear, which seemed to please Hsu Shu greatly, for he thanked him most cordially and took his leave. Then P'ang T'ung betook himself to his boat and left for the southern shore.

His friend gone, Hsu Shu mischievously spread certain rumours in the camp, and next day were to be seen everywhere men in small groups, some talking, others listening, heads together and ears stretched out, till the camps seemed to buzz. Some of the men went to Ts'ao Ts'ao and told him that a rumour was running around that Han Sui and Ma T'eng had attacked the capital. This troubled Ts'ao

Ts'ao, who called together his advisers to council. Said he, "The only anxiety I have felt in this expedition was about the possible doings of Han Sui and Ma T'eng. Now there is a rumour running among the men, and though I know not whether it be true or false, it is necessary to be on one's guard."

At this point Hsu Shu said, "You have been kind enough to give me an office, Sir, and I have really done nothing in return. If I may have three companies I will march at once to San Pass and guard it. If there be any pressing matter I will report at once."

"If you would do this I should be quite at my ease. There are already men beyond the Pass, who will be under your command, and now I will give you three companies of horse and foot and Tsang Pa shall lead the van and march quickly."

Hsu Shu took leave of the Minister and left in company with Tsang Pa. This was P'ang's scheme to secure the safety of Hsu Shu.

A poem says:—

> Ts'ao Ts'ao marched south, but at his back
> There rode the fear of rear attack.
> P'ang T'ung's good counsel Hsu Shu took,
> And thus the fish escaped the hook.

Ts'ao Ts'ao's anxiety diminished after he had thus sent away Hsu Shu. Then he rode round all the camps, first the land forces and then the naval. He boarded one of the large ships and thereon set up his standard. The naval camps were arranged along two lines and every ship carried a thousand bows and crossbows.

While he remained with the fleet occurred the full moon of the eleventh month of the twelfth year of "Established Tranquillity." The sky was clear; there was no wind and the river lay unruffled. He prepared a great banquet, with music, and thereto invited all his captains. As evening drew on the moon rose over the eastern hills in its immaculate beauty and beneath it lay the broad belt of the river like a band of pure white silk. It was a great assembly and all the guests were clad in gorgeous silks and embroidered robes and the arms of the fighting men glittered in the moonlight. The officers, civil and military, were seated in their proper order of precedence.

The setting, too, was exquisite. The Nanping hills were outlined as in a picture; the boundaries of Ch'aisang lay in the east; the river showed west as far as Hsiak'ou; on the south lay the Hills of Fan, on the north was the "Black" Forest. The view stretched wide on every side.

Ts'ao's heart was jubilant and he harangued the assembly, "My one aim since I enlisted my first small band of volunteers has been the removal of evil from the State and I have sworn to cleanse the country and restore tranquillity. Now there is only left this land of Chiangnan to withstand me. I am at the head of a hundred legions. I depend upon you, gentlemen, and have no doubt of my final success. After I have subdued Chiangnan there will be no trouble in all the country. Then we shall enjoy wealth and honour and revel in peace."

They rose in a body and expressed their appreciation saying, "We trust that you may soon report complete victory and we shall all repose in the shade of your good fortune."

In his elation Ts'ao Ts'ao bade the servants bring more wine and they drank till late at night. Warmed and mellowed, the host pointed to the south bank saying, "Chou Yu and Lu Su know not the appointed time. Heaven is aiding me bringing upon them the misfortune of the desertion of their most trusted friends."

"O Minister, say nothing of these things lest they become known to the enemy," said Hsun Yu.

But the Minister only laughed. "You are all my trusty friends," said he, "both officers and humble attendants. Why should I refrain?"

Pointing to Hsiak'ou he continued, "You do not reckon for much with your puny force, Liu Pei and Chuko Liang. How foolish of you to attempt to shake T'aishan! I am now fifty-four and if I get Chiangnan I shall have the wherewithal to rejoice. In the days of long ago the late noble Ch'iao and I were great friends and we came to an agreement on certain matters, for I knew his two daughters were lovely beyond words. Then by some means they became wives to Sun Ts'e and Chou Yu. But now my palace of rest is built on the Chang River and victory over the south will mean that I marry these two fair women. I will put them in my palace and they shall rejoice my declining years. My desires will then be completely attained."

He smiled at the anticipation.

Tu Mu, a poet of the T'ang Dynasty, in one poem says:—

> A broken halberd buried in the sand,
>   With deep rust eaten,
> Loud tells of ancient battles on the strand,
>   When Ts'ao was beaten.
> Had eastern winds Chou's plan refused to aid
>   And fan the flame,
> Two captives fair, locked in the Bronze Bird's shade,
>   Had gone to shame.

But suddenly amid the merriment was heard the hoarse cry of a raven flying toward the south.

"Why does the raven thus cry in the night?" said Ts'ao to those about him.

"The moon is so bright that he thinks it is day," said they, "and so he leaves his tree."

Ts'ao laughed; by this time he was quite intoxicated. He set up his spear in the prow of the ship and poured a libation into the river and then drank three brimming goblets. As he lowered the spear he said, "This is the spear that broke up the Yellow Turbans, captured Lu Pu, destroyed Yuan Shao and subdued his brother, whose armies are now mine. In the north it reached to Liaotung and it stretched out over the whole south. It has never failed in its task. The present scene moves me to the depths and I will sing a song in which you shall accompany me.

And so he sang:—

> When goblets are brimming then song is near birth,
> But life is full short and has few days of mirth,
> Life goes as the dew drops fly swiftly away,
> 'Neath the glance of the glowing hot ruler of day.
> Man's life may be spent in the noblest emprise,
> But sorrowful thoughts in his heart oft arise.
> Let us wash clean away the sad thoughts that intrude,
> With bumpers of wine such as Tu K'ang once brewed.
> Gone is my day of youthful fire
> And still ungained is my desire.
> The deer feed on the level plain
> And joyful call, then feed again.
> My noble guests are gathered round,
> The air is trilled with joyful sound.
> Bright my future lies before me,
> As the moonlight on this plain;
> But I strive in vain to reach it.
> When shall I my wish attain?
> None can answer; and so sadness
> Grips my inmost heart again.
> Far north and south,
> Wide east and west,
> We safety seek;
> Vain is the quest.
> Man's heart oft yearns
> For converse sweet,

And my heart burns
When old friends greet.
The stars are paled by the full moon's light,
The raven wings his southward flight,
And thrice he circles round a tree,
No place thereon to rest finds he.
They weary not the mountains of great height,
The waters deep of depth do not complain,
Duke Chou no leisure found by day or night
Stern toil is his who would the Empire gain.

The song made they sang it with him and were all exceedingly merry; save one guest who suddenly said, "When the great army is on the point of battle and lives are about to be risked, why do you, O Minister, speak such ill words?"

Ts'ao turned quickly toward the speaker, who was Liu Fu, the Governor of Yangchou. This Liu sprang from Hofei. When first appointed to his post he had gathered in the terrified and frightened people and restored order. He had founded schools and encouraged the people to till the land. He had long served under Ts'ao Ts'ao and rendered valuable service.

When he spoke Ts'ao dropped his spear to the level and said, "What ill-omened words did I use?"

"You spoke of the moon paling the stars and the raven flying southward without finding a resting place. These are ill-omened words."

"How dare you try to belittle my endeavour?" cried Ts'ao, very wrathful; and with that he smote Liu Fu with his spear and slew him.

The assembly broke up and the guests dispersed in fear and confusion. Next day, when he had recovered from his drunken bout, Ts'ao Ts'ao was very grieved at what he had done and when the murdered man's son came to crave the body of his father for burial, Ts'ao wept and expressed his sorrow.

"I am guilty of your father's death; I was drunk yesterday. I regret the deed exceedingly. Your father shall be interred with the honours of a minister of the highest rank."

He sent an escort of soldiers to take the body home for burial.

A few days after this the two leaders of the naval force came to say the ships were all connected together by chains as had been ordered, and all was now ready. They asked for the command to start.

Thereupon the leaders of both land and naval forces were

assembled on board a large ship in the centre of the squadron to receive orders. The various armies and squadrons were distinguished by different flags, the central naval squadron, yellow; the leading squadron, red; the rear squadron, black; the left, blue, and the right, white. On shore the horsemen had a red flag; for the vanguard, black; blue and white for the rearguard and the wings respectively. Hsiahou Tun and Ts'ao Hung were in reserve and the general staff was under the leadership of Hsu Ch'u and Chang Liao. The other leaders were ordered to remain in camp, but ready for action.

All being ready, the squadron drums beat the roll thrice and the ships sailed out under a strong north-west wind on a trial cruise and when they got among the waves they were found to be as steady and immoveable as the dry land itself. The northern men showed their delight at the absence of motion by capering and flourishing their weapons. The ships moved on, the squadrons keeping quite distinct. Fifty light cruisers sailed to and fro keeping order and urging progress.

Ts'ao Ts'ao watched his navy from the General's terrace and was delighted with their evolutions and manœuvres. Surely this meant complete victory. He ordered the recall and the squadrons returned in perfect order to their base.

Then Ts'ao Ts'ao went to his tent and summoned his advisers. He said, "If Heaven had not been on my side, should I have got this excellent plan from the Phoenix Chick? Now that the ships are attached firmly to each other, one may traverse the river as easily as walking on firm earth."

"The ships are firmly attached to each other," said Ch'eng Yu, "but you should be prepared for an attack by fire so that they can scatter to avoid it."

The General laughed. "You look a long way ahead," said he, "but you see what cannot happen."

"He speaks much to the point" said Hsun Yu, "why do you laugh at him?"

"Any one using fire depends upon the wind. This is now winter and only west winds blow. You will get neither east nor south winds. I am on the north-west and the enemy is on the south bank. If they use fire they will destroy themselves. I have nothing to fear. If it was the tenth moon, or early spring, I would provide against fire."

"The Minister is indeed wise," said the others in chorus. "None can equal him."

"With northern men unused to shipboard I could never have crossed the river but for this plan," said Ts'ao.

Then he saw two of the secondary leaders stand up and they said, "We are from the north, but we are also sailors. Pray give us a small squadron and we will seize some of the enemy's flags and drums for you that we may prove ourselves adepts on the water."

The speakers were two men who had served under Yuan Shao, named Chiao Ch'u and Chang Nan.

"I do not think naval work would suit you two, born and brought up in the north," said Ts'ao. "The Chiangnan men are thoroughly accustomed to ships. You should not regard your lives as a child's plaything."

They cried, "If we fail, treat us according to army laws."

"The fighting ships are all chained together, there are only small, twenty-men boats free. They are unsuitable for fighting."

"If we took large ships where would be the wonderful in what we will do? No; give us a score of the small ships and we will take half each and go straight to the enemy's naval port. We will just seize a flag, slay a leader and come home."

"I will let you have the twenty ships and half a company of good, vigorous men with long spears and stiff crossbows. Early tomorrow the main fleet shall make a demonstration on the river and I will also tell Wen P'ing to support you with thirty ships."

The two men retired greatly elated. Next morning, very early, food was prepared and at the fifth watch all was ready for a start. Then from the naval camp rolled out the drums and the gongs clanged, as the ships moved out and took up their positions, the various flags fluttering in the morning breeze. And the two intrepid leaders with their squadron of small scouting boats went down the lines and out into the stream.

Now a few days before the sound of Ts'ao Ts'ao's drums had been heard on the southern bank and the watchers had seen their enemy's fleet manoeuvring in the open river. Chou Yu had watched the manoeuvres from the top of a hill till the fleet had gone in again. So when the sound of drums was again heard all the army went up the hills to watch the fleet. All they saw was a squadron of small ships bounding over the waves. But as they came nearer the news was taken to the leader who called for volunteers to go out against them. Han Tang and Chou T'ai offered themselves. They were accepted and orders were issued to the camps to remain ready for action but not to move till told.

Han and Chou sailed out each with a small squadron of five ships in line.

The two braggarts from the north really only trusted to their boldness and luck. Their ships came down under the powerful strokes of the oars and as they neared the two leaders put on their heart-protectors, gripped their spears and each took his station in the prow of the leading ship of his division. Chino's ship led and as soon as he came near enough his men began to shoot at Han Tang, who fended off the arrows with his buckler. Chiao twirled his long spear as he engaged his opponent. But, at the first thrust, he was killed.

His comrade with the other ships was coming up with great shouts when Chou T'ai sailed up at an angle and these two squadrons began shooting arrows at each other in clouds. Chou T'ai fended off the arrows with his shield and stood gripping his sword firmly till his ships came within a few feet of the enemy's ships when he leaped across and cut down Chang Nan. Chang's dead body fell into the water. Then the battle became confused and the attacking ships rowed hard to get away. The southerners pursued but soon came in sight of Wen P'ing's supporting fleet. Once more the ships engaged and the men fought with each other.

Chou Yu with his officers stood on the summit of a mountain and watched his own and the enemy ships out on the river. The flags and the ensigns were all in perfect order. Then he saw Wen P'ing and his own fleets engaged in battle and soon it was evident that the former was not a match for his own sailors. Wen P'ing turned about to retire, Chou and Han pursued. Chou Yu fearing lest his sailors should go too far, then hoisted the white flag of recall.

To his officers Chou Yu said, "The masts of their ships stand thick as reeds; Ts'ao himself is full of wiles; how can we destroy him?"

No one replied, for just then the great yellow flag that flapped in the breeze in the middle of Ts'ao's fleet suddenly fell over into the river.

Chou Yu laughed. "That is a bad omen," said he.

Then an extra violent blast of wind came by and the waves rose high and beat upon the bank. A corner of his own flag flicked Chou Yu on the cheek and suddenly a thought flashed through his mind. He uttered a loud cry, staggered and fell backward. They picked him up; there was blood upon his lips and he was unconscious. Presently, however, he revived.

> And once he laughed, then gave a cry,
> T'is hard to ensure a victory.

Chou Yu's fate will appear as the story unfolds.

CHAPTER XLIX

ON THE SEVEN STARS ALTAR CHUKO SACRIFICES TO THE WINDS: AT THE THREE RIVERS CHOU YU LIBERATES FIRE

In the last chapter Chou Yu was seized with sudden illness as he watched the fleets of his enemy. He was borne to his tent and his officers came in multitudes to enquire after him. They looked at each other saying, "What a pity our general should be taken ill when Ts'ao's legions threaten so terribly! What would happen if he attacked?"

Messengers with the evil tidings were sent to Wu while the physicians did their best for the invalid. Lu Su was particularly sad at the illness of his patron and went to see K'ung-ming to talk it over.

"What do you make of it?" said K'ung-ming.

"Good luck for Ts'ao Ts'ao; bad for us," said Lu.

"I could cure him," said K'ung-ming laughing.

"If you could the State would be very fortunate," said Lu.

He prayed K'ung-ming to go to see the sick man. They went, and Lu Su entered first. Chou Yu lay in bed, his head covered by a quilt.

"How are you, General?" said Lu.

"My heart pains me; every now and again I feel faint and dizzy."

"Have you taken any remedies?"

"My gorge rises at the thought; I could not."

"I saw K'ung-ming just now and he says he could heal you. He is just outside and I will call him if you like."

"Ask him to come in."

Chou bade his servants help him to a sitting position and K'ung-ming entered.

"I have not seen you for days," said he. "How could I guess that you were unwell?"

"How can any one feel secure? We are constantly the playthings of luck, good or bad."

"Yes; Heaven's winds and clouds are not to be measured. No one can reckon their comings and goings, can they?"

Chou Yu turned pale and a low groan escaped him, while his visitor went on, "You feel depressed, do you not? As though troubles were piling up in your heart?"

"That is exactly how I feel."

"You need cooling medicine to dissipate this sense of oppression."

"I have taken a cooling draught, but it has done no good."

"You must get the humours into good order before the drugs will have any effect."

Chou Yu began to think K'ung-ming knew what was really the matter and resolved to test him. "What should be taken to produce a favourable temper?"

"I know one means of producing a favourable temper," replied K'ung-ming.

"I wish you would tell me."

K'ung-ming got out writing materials, sent away the servants and then wrote a few words:—"One should burn out Ts'ao; all is ready, but there is no east wind," this he gave to the sick general, saying "That is the origin of your illness."

Chou Yu read the words with great surprise and it confirmed his secret opinion that K'ung-ming really was rather more than human. He decided that the only course was to be open and tell him all. So he said, "Since you know the cause of the disease, what do you recommend as treatment? The need of a remedy is very urgent."

"I have no great talent," said K'ung-ming, "but I have had to do with men of no ordinary gifts from whom I have received certain magical books. I can call the winds and summon the rains. Since you need a south-east breeze, General, you must build an altar on the Nanping Mountains, the Altar of the Seven Stars. It must be nine feet high, with three steps, surrounded by a guard of one hundred and twenty men bearing flags. On this altar I will work a spell to procure a strong south-east gale for three days and three nights. Do you approve?"

"Never mind three whole days;" said Chou Yu, "one day of strong wind will serve my purpose. But it must be done at once and without delay."

"I will sacrifice for a wind for three days from the twentieth day of the moon; will that suit you?"

Chou Yu was delighted and hastily rose from his couch to give the necessary orders. He commanded that five hundred men should be sent to the mountains to build the altar and he told off the guard of one hundred and twenty to bear the flags and be at the orders of K'ung-ming.

K'ung-ming took his leave, went forth and rode off with Lu Su to the mountains where they measured out the ground. He bade the soldiers build the altar of red earth from the south-east quarter. It was two hundred and forty feet in circuit, square in shape, and of three tiers, each of three feet, in all nine feet high. On the lowest tier he placed the flags of the twenty-eight "houses" of the heavens; on the east seven, with blue flags, on the north seven, with black flags, on the west seven, with white flags, and on the south seven, with red flags. Around the second tier he placed sixty-four yellow flags, corresponding to the number of the diagrams of the Book of Divination, in eight groups of eight. Four men were stationed on the highest platform, each wearing a Taoist headdress and a black silk robe embroidered with the phoenix and confined with wide sashes. They wore scarlet boots and square-cut skirts. On the left front stood a man supporting a tall pole bearing at its top a plume of light feathers to show by their least movement the wind's first breathing. On the right front was a man holding a tall pole whereon was a flag with the symbol of the seven stars to show the direction and force of the wind. On the left rear stood a man with a sword, and on the right rear a man with a censer. Below the altar were two score and four men holding flags, umbrellas, spears, lances, yellow banners, white axes, red bannerols and black ensigns. And these were spaced about the altar.

On the appointed day K'ung-ming, having chosen a propitious moment, bathed his body and purified himself. Then he robed himself as a Taoist, loosened his locks and approached the alter.

He bade Lu Su retire saying, "Return to the camp and assist the General in setting out his forces. Should my prayers avail not, do not wonder."

So Lu Su left him. Then he commanded the guards on no account to absent themselves, to maintain strict silence and to be reverent; death would be the penalty of disobedience.

Next with solemn steps he ascended the altar, faced the proper quarter, lighted the incense and sprinkled the water in the basins. This done he gazed into the heavens and prayed silently. The prayer ended he descended and returned to his tent. After a brief rest he allowed the soldiers by turns to go away to eat.

Thrice that day he ascended the altar and thrice descended; but there was no sign of the wind.

Here it may be related that Chou Yu with Ch'eng P'u and Lu Su and a certain number of military officials on duty, sat waiting in the tent till the wished-for wind should blow and the attack could be launched. Messengers were also sent to Sun Ch'uan to prepare to support the forward movement.

Huang Kai had his fire ships ready, a score of them. The fore parts of the ships were thickly studded with large nails, and they were loaded with dry reeds, wood soaked in fish oil and covered with sulphur, saltpetre and other inflammables. The ships were covered in with black oiled cloth. In the prow of each was a black dragon flag with indentations. A fighting ship was attached to the stern of each to propel it forward. All were ready and awaited orders to move.

Meanwhile Ts'ao Ts'ao's two spies, the brothers Ts'ai, were being guarded carefully in an outer camp far from the river bank and daily entertained with feasting. They were not allowed to know of the preparations. The watch was so close that not a trickle of information reached the prisoners.

Presently, while Chou Yu was anxiously awaiting in his tent for the desired wind, a messenger came to say that Sun Ch'uan had anchored at a place eighty-five *li* from the camp, where he awaited news. Lu Su was sent to warn all the various commanders to be ready, the ships and their weapons, sails and oars, all for instant use, and to impress upon them the penalties of being caught unprepared. The soldiers were indeed ready for the fight and yearning for the fray.

But the sky remained obstinately clear and as night drew nigh no breath of air stirred.

"We have been cajoled," said Chou Yu. "Indeed what possibility is there of a south-east wind in mid-winter?"

"K'ung-ming would not use vain and deceitful words," replied Lu Su.

Towards the third watch the sound of a movement arose in the air. Soon the flags fluttered out. And when the general went out to make sure he saw they were flowing toward the north-west. In a very short time the south-east wind was in full force.

Chou Yu was, however, frightened at the power of the man whose help he had invoked. "Really the man has power over the heavens and authority over the earth; his methods are incalculable, beyond the ken of god or devil. He cannot be allowed to live to be a danger to our land of Wu. We must slay him soon to fend off later evils."

So he resolved to commit a crime to remove his dangerous rival. He called two of the captains of his guard, Ting Feng and Hsu Sheng, and bade each take a party, one along the river, the other along the road, to the altar on the mountains. As soon as they got there, without asking questions or giving reasons, they were to seize and behead K'ung-ming. They might expect a solid reward if they brought his head.

The two went off on their nefarious errand, one leading dagger-and axe-men going as fast as oars could propel them along the river, the other at the head of archers and bowmen on horseback. The south-east wind buffeted them as they went on their way.

> High was raised the Seven Stars' Altar,
> On it prayed the Sleeping Dragon
> For an eastern wind, and straightway
> Blew the wind. Had not the wizard
> Exercised his mighty magic
> Nought had Chou Yu's skill availed.

Ting Feng first arrived. He saw the guards with their flags, dropped off his steed and marched to the altar, sword in hand. But he found no K'ung-ming. He asked the guards; they told him he had just gone down. Ting Feng ran down the hill to search. There he met his fellow and they joined forces. Presently a simple soldier told them that the evening before a small, fast boat had anchored there near a sand spit and K'ung-ming had been seen to go on board. Then the boat had gone up river. So they divided their party into two, one to go by water, the other by land.

Hsu Sheng bade his boatmen put on all sail and take every advantage of the wind. Before very long he saw the fugitive's boat ahead and when near enough, stood in the prow of his own and shouted, "Do not flee, O Instructor of the Army! The General requests your presence."

K'ung-ming, who was seated in the stern of his boat, just laughed aloud, "Return and tell the General to make good use of his men. Tell him I am going up river for a spell and will see him again another day."

"Pray wait a little while," cried Hsu. "I have something most important to tell you."

"I knew all about it, that he would not let me go and that he wanted to kill me. That is why Chao Yun was waiting for me. You had better not approach nearer."

Seeing the other ship had no sail, Hsu Sheng thought he would assuredly come up with it and so maintained the pursuit. Then when he got too close Chao Yun fitted an arrow to the bowstring and, standing up in the stern of his boat, cried, "You know who I am and I came expressly to escort the Instructor. Why are you pursuing him? One arrow would kill you, only that would cause a breach of the peace between two houses. I will shoot and just give you a specimen of my skill."

With that he shot, and the arrow whizzed overhead cutting the rope that held up the sail. Down came the sail trailing in the water and the boat swung round. Then Chao Yun's boat hoisted its sail and the fair wind speedily carried it out of sight.

On the bank stood Ting Feng. He bade his comrade come to the shore and said, "He is too clever for any man; and Chao Yun is bravest of the brave. You remember what he did at Tangyang Slope. All we can do is to return and report."

So they returned to camp and told their master about the preparations that K'ung-ming had made to ensure safety. Chou Yu was indeed puzzled at the depth of his rival's insight. "I shall have no peace day or night while he lives," said he.

"At least wait till Ts'ao is done with," said Lu Su.

And Chou Yu knew he spake wisely. Having summoned the leaders to receive orders, first he bade Kan Ning take with him the false deserter Ts'ai Chung and his soldiers and go along the south bank, showing the flags of Ts'ao Ts'ao, till they reached the "Black" Forest (Wu Lin) just opposite the enemy's main store of grain and forage. Then they were to penetrate as deeply as possible into the enemy's lines and light a torch as a signal. Ts'ai Chung's brother was to be kept in camp for another purpose.

The next order was for T'aishih Tzu; he was to lead two companies as quickly as possible to Huangchou and cut the enemy's communications with Hofei. When near the enemy he was to give a signal and if he saw a red flag he would know that Sun Ch'uan was at hand with reinforcements.

These two had the farthest to go and started first. Then Lu Meng was sent into Wu Lin (the "Black" Forest) with three companies as a support. Kan Ning was ordered to set fire to the camp. A fourth party was to go to the borders of Iling and attack as soon as the signal from the forest was seen. A fifth party of three companies went to Hanyang to fall upon the enemy along the river. Their signal was a white flag and a sixth division supported them.

When these six parties had gone off, Huang Kai got ready his fire ships and sent a soldier with a note to tell Ts'ao Ts'ao that he was coming over that evening. Four fighting ships were told off to support Huang Kai.

The four squadrons, each of three hundred ships, were placed under four commanders, Han Tang, Chou T'ai, Chiang Ch'in and Ch'en Wu. The score of fire ships preceded them. Chou Yu and Ch'eng P'u went on board one of the large ships to direct the battle. Their guards were Ting Feng and Hsu Sheng. Lu Su, K'an Tse and the advisers were left to guard the camp. Ch'eng P'u was greatly impressed with Chou Yu's ordering of the attack.

Then came a messenger bearing a mandate from Sun Ch'uan making Lu Hsun leader of the van. He was ordered to go to Ch'ihuang. The Marquis himself would support him. Chou Yu also sent a man to the western hills to make signals and to hoist flags on the Nanping Mountains.

So all being prepared they waited for dusk.

Here it is necessary to diverge from the direct narrative to say that Yuan-te was at Hsiak'ou anxiously awaiting the return of his adviser. Then appeared a fleet, led by Liu Ch'i, who had come to find out how matters were progressing. Yuan-te sent to call him to the battle tower and told him of the south-east wind that had begun to blow and that Chao Yun had gone to meet K'ung-ming. Not long after a single sail was seen coming up before the wind and he knew it was K'ung-ming, the Instructor of the Army. So he and Liu Ch'i went down to meet the boat. Soon the vessel reached the shore and K'ung-ming and Chao Yun disembarked.

Yuan-te was very glad and after they had enquired after each other's well-being K'ung-ming said, "There is no time to tell of any other things now. Are the soldiers and ships ready?"

"They have long been ready," replied Yuan-te. "They only await you to direct how they are to be used."

The three then went to the tent and took their seats. K'ung-ming at once began to issue orders. "Chao Yun, with three companies is to cross the river and go to the Wu Lin by the minor road. He will choose a dense jungle and prepare an ambush. Tonight, after the fourth watch, Ts'ao Ts'ao will hurry along that way. When half his men have passed, the jungle is to be fired. Ts'ao Ts'ao will not be wholly destroyed but many will perish."

"There are two roads," said Chao Yun. "One leads to the southern districts and the other to Chingchou. I do not know by which he will come."

"The south road is too dangerous; Ts'ao Ts'ao will certainly pass along the Chingchou road, so that he may get away to Hsuch'ang."

Then Chao Yun went away. Next K'ung-ming said to Chang

Fei, "You will take three companies over the river to cut the road to Iling. You will ambush in the Hulu Valley. Ts'ao Ts'ao, not daring to go to South Iling, will go to North Iling. Tomorrow, after the rain, he will halt to refresh his men. As soon as the smoke is seen to rise from their cooking fires you will fire the hill side. You will not capture Ts'ao Ts'ao but you will render excellent service."

So Chang Fei left. Next was called Mi Chu, Mi Fang and Liu Feng. They were to take command of three squadrons and go along the river to collect the weapons that the beaten soldiers would throw away.

The three left. Then K'ung-ming said to Liu Ch'i, "The country around Wuch'ang is very important and I wish you to take command of your own troops and station them at strategic points. Ts'ao Ts'ao, being defeated, will flee thither, and you will capture him. But you are not to leave the city without the best of reasons."

And Liu Ch'i took leave.

Then K'ung-ming said to Yuan-te, "I wish you to remain quietly and calmly in Fank'ou while Chou Yu works out his great scheme this night."

All this time Kuan Yu has been silently waiting his turn but K'ung-ming said no word to him. When he could bear this no longer he cried, "Since I first followed my brother to battle many years ago I have never been left behind. Now that great things are afoot is there no work for me? What is meant by it?"

"You should not be surprised. I wanted you for service at a most important point only that there was a something standing in the way that prevented me from sending you," said K'ung-ming.

"What could stand in the way? I wish you would tell me."

"You see Ts'ao Ts'ao was once very kind to you and you cannot help feeling grateful. Now when his soldiers have been beaten he will have to flee along the Huayung road and if I sent you to guard it you would have to let him pass. So I will not send you."

"You are most considerate, Instructor. But though it is true that he treated me well, yet I slew two of his most redoubtable opponents by way of repayment, beside raising a siege. If I happened upon him on this occasion I should hardly let him go."

"But what if you did?"

"You could deal with me by military rules."

"Then put that in writing."

So Kuan Yu wrote a formal undertaking and gave the document to K'ung-ming.

"What happens if Ts'ao Ts'ao does not pass that way?" said Kuan Yu.

"I will give you a written engagement that he will pass." Then he continued, "On the hills by the Huayung Valley you are to raise a heap of wood and grass to make a great column of smoke and mislead Ts'ao Ts'ao into coming."

"If Ts'ao Ts'ao sees a smoke he will suspect an ambush and will not come." said Kuan Yu.

"You are very simple," said K'ung-ming. "Do you not know more of war's ruses than that? Ts'ao Ts'ao is an able leader but you can deceive him this time. When he sees the smoke he will take it as a subterfuge and risk going that way. But do not let your kindness of heart rule your conduct."

Thus was his duty assigned Kuan Yu and he left, taking his adopted son, P'ing, Chou Ts'ang and a half company of swordsmen.

Said Liu Pei, "His sense of rectitude is very profound; I fear if Ts'ao Ts'ao should come that way that my brother will let him pass."

"I have consulted the stars and Ts'ao the rebel is not fated to come to his end yet. I have purposely designed this manifestation of kindly feeling for Kuan Yu to accomplish and so act handsomely."

"Indeed there are few such far-seeing men as you are," said Yuan-te.

The two then went to Fank'ou whence they might watch Chou Yu's evolutions. Sun Chuan and Chien Yung were left on guard.

Ts'ao Ts'ao was in his great camp in conference with his advisers and awaiting the arrival of Huang Kai. The southeast wind was very strong that day and Ch'eng Yu was insisting on the necessity for precaution, But Ts'ao laughed saying, "The Winter Solstice depends upon the sun and nothing else; there is sure to be a south wind at some one or other of its recurrences. I see nothing to wonder at."

Just then they announced the arrival of a small boat from the other shore with a letter from Huang Kai. The bearer of the letter was brought in and presented it. It stated that Chou Yu had kept such strict watch that there had been no chance of escape. But now some grain was coming down river and Huang Kai had been named as escort commander, which would give him the opportunity he desired. He would slay one of the known captains and bring his head as an offering when he came. That evening at the third watch, if boats were seen with dragon toothed flags, they would be the grain boats.

This letter delighted Ts'ao Ts'ao who, with his officers, went to the naval camp and boarded a great ship to watch for the arrival of Huang Kai.

In Chiangtung, when evening fell, Chou Yu sent for Ts'ao Ho

and bade the soldiers bind him. The unhappy man protested that he had committed no crime but Chou Yu said, "What sort of a fellow are you, think you, to come and pretend to desert to my side? I need a small sacrifice for my flag and your head will serve my purpose. So I am going to use it."

Ts'ai Ho being at the end of his tether unable to deny the charge suddenly cried, "Two of your own side, K'an Tse and Kan Ning, are also in the plot!"

"Under my directions," said Chou Yu.

Ts'ai Ho was exceedingly repentant and sad, but Chou Yu bade them take him to the river bank where the black standard had been set up and there, after the pouring of a libation and the burning of paper, he was beheaded, his blood being a sacrifice to the flag.

This ceremony over the ships started and Huang Kai took his place on the third ship. He merely wore breast armour and carried a keen blade. On his flag were written four large characters "Van Leader Huang Kai". With a fair wind his fleet sailed toward Ch'ihp'i, or Red Wall.

The wind was strong and the waves ran high. Ts'ao Ts'ao in the midst of the central squadron eagerly scanned the river which rolled down under the bright moon like a silver serpent writhing in innumerable folds. Letting the wind blow full in his face Ts'ao Ts'ao laughed aloud for was he not now to obtain his desire?

Then a soldier pointing to the river said, "The whole south is one mass of sails and they are coming up on the wind."

Ts'ao Ts'ao went to a higher point and gazed at the sails intently and his men told him that the flags were black and dragon shaped, and indented, and among them there flew one very large banner on which was a name Huang Kai.

"That is my friend the deserter," said he joyfully. "Heaven is on my side today."

As the ships drew closer Ch'eng Yu said, "Those ships are treacherous. Do not let them approach the camp."

"How know you that?" asked Ts'ao Ts'ao.

And Ch'eng Yu replied, "If they were laden with grain they would lie deep in the water. But these are light and float easily. The south-east wind is very strong and if they intend treachery, how can we defend ourselves?"

Ts'ao Ts'ao began to understand. Then he asked who would go out to stop them, and Wen P'ing volunteered. "I am well used to the waters," said he.

Thereupon he sprang into a small light craft and sailed out, followed by a half score cruisers which came at his signal. Standing in the prow of his ship he called out to those advancing toward them, "You southern ships are not to approach; such are the orders of the Minister. Stop there in mid stream."

The soldiers all yelled to them to lower their sails. The shout had not died away when a bowstring twanged and Wen P'ing rolled down into the ship with an arrow in the left arm. Confusion reigned on his ship and all the others hurried back to their camp.

When the ships were about a couple of *li* distant, Huang Kai waved his sword and the leading ships broke forth into fire, which, under the force of the strong wind, soon gained strength and the ships became as fiery arrows. Soon the whole twenty dashed into the naval camp.

All Ts'ao Ts'ao's ships were gathered there and as they were firmly chained together not one could escape from the others and flee. There was a roar of bombs and fireships came on from all sides at once. The face of the three rivers was speedily covered with fire which flew before the wind from one ship to another. It seemed as if the universe was filled with flame.

Ts'ao Ts'ao hastened toward the shore. Huang Kai, with a few men at his back, leaped into a small boat, dashed through the fire and sought Ts'ao Ts'ao. He, seeing the imminence of the danger, was making for the land, Chang Liao got hold of a small boat into which he helped his master; none too soon, for the ship was burning. They got Ts'ao Ts'ao out of the thick of the fire and dashed for the bank.

Huang Kai seeing a handsomely robed person get into a small boat guessed it must be Ts'ao Ts'ao and pursued. He drew very near and he held his keen blade ready to strike, crying out, "You rebel! do not flee. I am Huang Kai."

Ts'ao Ts'ao howled in the bitterness of his distress. Chang Liao fitted an arrow to his bow and aimed at the pursuer, shooting at short range. The roaring of the gale and the flames kept Huang Kai from hearing the twang of the string and he was wounded in the shoulder. He fell and rolled over into the water.

> He fell in peril of water
> When flames were high;
> Ere cudgel bruises had faded,
> An arrow struck.

Huang Kai's fate will be told in the next chapter.

CHAPTER L

CHUKO LIANG FORESEES THE HUAYUNG EPISODE: KUAN YUN-CH'ANG RELEASES TS'AO TS'AO

The last chapter closed with Huang Kai in the water wounded, Ts'ao Ts'ao rescued from immediate danger and confusion rampant among the soldiers. Pressing forward to attack the naval camp Han Tang was told by his soldiers that some one was clinging to the rudder of his boat and shouting to him by his familiar name. Han Tang listened carefully and in the voice at once he recognised that Huang Kai was calling to him for help.

"That is my friend Huang Kai," cried he and they quickly pulled the wounded leader out of the water. Then they saw Huang Kai was wounded for the arrow still stuck. Han bit out the shaft of the arrow but the point was deeply buried in the flesh. They hastily pulled off his wet garments and cut out the metal arrowhead with a dagger, tore up one of the flags and bound up the wound. Then Han Tang gave his friend his own fighting robe to put on and sent him off in a small boat back to camp.

Huang Kai's escape from drowning must be taken as proof of his natural affinity for, or sympathy with, water. Although it was the period of great cold and he was heavy with armour when he fell into the river yet he escaped with life.

In this great battle at the junction of the rivers, when fire seemed to spread wide over all the wide surface of the water, when the earth quaked with the roar of battle, when land forces closed in on both wings and four battle squadrons advanced on the front, when the ferocity of fire answered the clash of weapons and weapons were aided by fire, under the thrusts of spears and the flights of arrows, burnt by fire and drowned by water, Ts'ao Ts'ao lost an incalculable number of men. And a poet wrote:—

When Wei and Wu together strove

> For the mastery,
> In Red Cliff fight the towering ships
> Vanished from the sea,
> For there the fierce flames, leaping high,
> Burned them utterly.
> So Chou Yu for his liege lord
> Got the victory.

And another poem runs:—

> The hills are high, the moon shines faint,
> The waters stretch afar;
> I sigh to think how oft this land
> Has suffered stress of war;
> And I recall how southerners
> Shrank from the northmen's might,
> And how a favouring eastern gale
> Helped them to win the fight.

Leaving for a while the story of the slaughter on the river it is time to follow Kan Ning. He made Ts'ao Chung guide him into the innermost recesses of Ts'ao Ts'ao's camp. Then he slew him with one slash of his sword. After this he set fire to the jungle, and at this signal Lu Meng put fire to the grass in half a score places near to each other. Then other fires were started, and the noise of battle was on all sides.

Ts'ao Ts'ao and the faithful Chang Liao, with a small party of horsemen, fled through the burning forest. They could see no road in front; all seemed on fire. Presently Mao Chieh and Wen P'ing, with a few more horsemen, joined them. Ts'ao Ts'ao bade the soldiers seek a way through. Chang Liao pointed out that the only suitable road was through the "Black" Forest and they took it.

They had gone but a short distance when they were overtaken by a small party of the enemy and a voice cried, "Ts'ao Ts'ao, stop!" It was Lu Meng, whose ensign soon appeared against the fiery background. Ts'ao Ts'ao urged his small party of fugitives forward bidding Chang Liao defend him from Lu Meng. Soon after he saw the light of torches in front and from a gorge there rushed out another force. And the leader cried "Ling T'ung is here!"

Ts'ao Ts'ao was scared; his liver and gall both seemed torn from within. But just then on his half right he saw another company approach and heard a friendly cry "Fear not, O Minister, I am here to rescue you."

The speaker was Hsu Huang and he attacked the pursuers.

A move to the north seemed to promise escape, but soon they saw a camp on a hill top. Hsu Huang went ahead to reconnoitre and found the officers in command were Ma Yen and Chang I, who had once been in the service of Yuan Shao. They had three companies of northern men in camp. They had seen the sky redden with the flames, but knew not what was afoot so dared make no move.

This turned out lucky for Ts'ao Ts'ao who now found himself with a fresh force. He sent these two, with a company, to clear the road ahead while the others remained as guard. And he felt much more secure.

The two went forward, but before they had gone very far they heard a shouting and a party of soldiers came out, the leader of them shouting, "I am Kan Hsing-pa of the land of Wu." Nothing daunted the two leaders would engage, but the redoubtable Kan Ning cut down Ma Yen, and when his brother warrior Chang I set his spear and dashed forward, he too fell beneath a stroke from the fearsome sword. Both leaders dead, the soldiers fled to give Ts'ao Ts'ao the bad news.

At this time Ts'ao Ts'ao expected aid from Hofei for he knew not that Sun Ch'uan was barring the road. But when Sun saw the fires and so knew that his men had won the day he ordered Lu Hsun to give the answering signal. T'aishih Tzu seeing this came down and his force joined up with that of Lu Hsun and they went against Ts'ao.

As for Ts'ao Ts'ao he could only get away toward Iling. On the road he fell in with Chang Ho and ordered him to protect the retreat. He pressed on as quickly as possible. At the fifth watch he was a long way from the glare and he felt safer. He asked the name of the place where they were. They told him it was west of the "Black" Forest and north of Itu. Seeing the thickly crowded trees all about him, and the steep hills and narrow passes, he threw up his head and laughed. Those about him asked why he was merry and he said he was only laughing at the stupidity of Chou Yu and the ignorance of Chuko Liang. If they had only set an ambush there, as he would have done, why, there was no escape.

He had scarcely finished his explanation when from both sides came a deafening roll of drums and flames sprang up to heaven. Ts'ao Ts'ao nearly fell off his horse, he was so startled. And from the side dashed in a troop, with Chao Yun leading, who cried, "I am Chao Tzu-lung and long have I been waiting here."

Ts'ao Ts'ao ordered Hsu Huang and Chang Ho to engage this new opponent and he himself rode off into the smoke and fire. Chao Yun did not pursue; he only captured his banners and Ts'ao Ts'ao escaped.

The faint light of dawn showed a great black cloud all around, for the south-east wind had not ceased. Suddenly began a heavy down-pour of rain, wetting every one to the skin, but still Ts'ao Ts'ao maintained his headlong flight till the starved faces of the men made a halt imperative. He told the men to forage in the villages about for grain and the means of making a fire. But when these had been found and they began to cook a meal another pursuing party came along and Ts'ao Ts'ao again was terrified. However, these proved to be friends escorting some of his advisers whom he saw with joy.

When giving the order to advance again he asked what places lay ahead, and they told him there were two roads; one was the highway to South Iling and the other a mountain road to the north of Iling.

"Which is the shorter way to Chiangling?" asked Ts'ao Ts'ao.

"The best way is to take the south road through Huluk'ou," was the reply.

So he gave orders to march that way. By the time Huluk'ou was reached the men were almost starving and could march no more; horses too were worn out. Many had fallen by the roadside. A halt was then made, food was taken by force from the villagers, and as there were still some boilers left they found a dry spot beside the hills where they could rest and cook. And there they began to prepare a meal, boiling grain and roasting strips of horse-flesh. Then they took off their wet clothes and spread them to dry. The beasts, too, were unsaddled and turned out to graze.

Seated comfortably in a somewhat open spot Ts'ao Ts'ao suddenly looked up and began to laugh loud and long. His companions, remembering the sequel of his last laugh, said, "Not long since, Sir, you laughed at Chou Yu and Chuko Liang; that resulted in the arrival of Chao Yun and great loss of men to us. Why do you now laugh?"

"I am laughing again at the ignorance of the same two men. If I was in their place, and conducting their campaign, I should have had an ambush here, just to meet us when we were tired out. Then, even if we escaped with our lives, we should suffer very severely. They did not see this and therefore I am laughing at them."

Even at that moment behind them rose a great yell. Thoroughly startled, Ts'ao Ts'ao threw aside his breastplate and leaped upon his horse. Most of the soldiers failed to catch theirs and then fires sprang up on every side and filled the mouth of the valley. A force was arrayed before them and at the head was the man of Yen, Chang Fei, seated on his steed with his great spear levelled.

"Whither wouldst thou flee, O rebel?" shouted he.

The soldiers grew cold within at the sight of the terrible warrior. Hsu Ch'u, mounted on a barebacked horse, rode up to engage him and two comrades galloped up to his aid. The three gathered about Chang Fei and a melee began, while Ts'ao Ts'ao made off at top speed. The other leaders set off after him and Chang Fei pursued. However, Ts'ao Ts'ao by dint of hard riding got away and gradually the pursuers were out-distanced.

But many had received wounds. As they were going the soldiers said, "There are two roads before us; which shall we take?"

"Which is the shorter?" asked Ts'ao Ts'ao.

"The high road is the more level, but it is fifty *li* longer than the bye road which goes to Huayungtao. Only the latter road is narrow and dangerous, full of pits and difficult."

Ts'ao Ts'ao sent men up to the hill tops to look around. They returned saying there were several columns of smoke rising from the hills along the road. The high road seemed quiet.

Then Ts'ao Ts'ao bade them lead the way along the bye-road.

"Where smoke arises there are surely soldiers," remarked the officers. "Why go this way?"

"Because the Book of War says that the hollow is to be regarded as solid and the solid as hollow. That fellow Chuko Liang is very subtle and has sent men to make those fires so that we should not go that way. He has laid an ambush on the high road. I have made up my mind and I will not fall a victim to his wiles."

"O Minister, your conclusions are most admirable. None other can equal you," said the officers.

And the soldiers were sent along the highway. They were very hungry and many almost too weak to travel. The horses too were spent. Some had been scorched by the flames and they rode forward resting their heads on their whips; the wounded struggled on to the last of their strength. All were soaking wet and all were feeble. Their arms and accoutrements were in a deplorable state, and more than half had been left upon the road they had traversed. Few of the horses had saddles or bridles, for in the confusion of pursuit they had been left behind. It was the time of greatest winter cold and the suffering was indescribable.

Noticing that the leading party had stopped Ts'ao Ts'ao sent to ask the reason. The messenger returned to report that by reason of the rain water collected in the pits and the mire the horses could not move. Ts'ao Ts'ao raged.

He said, "When soldiers come to hills they cut a road, when they happen upon streams they bridge them; such a thing as mud cannot stay an army."

So he ordered the weak and wounded to go to the rear and come on as they could, while the robust and able were to cut down trees, and gather herbage and reeds to fill up the holes. And it was to be done without delay, or death would be the punishment of the disobedient or remiss.

So the men dismounted and felled trees and cut bamboos, and they levelled the road. And because of the imminence and fear of pursuit a party was told off to hasten the workers and slay any that idled.

The soldiers made their way along the shallower parts, but many fell, and cries of misery were heard the whole length of the way.

"What are you howling for?" cried Ts'ao Ts'ao. "The number of your days is fixed. Any one who howls shall be put to death."

The remnant of the army, now divided into three, one to march slowly, a second to fill up the waterways and hollows and a third to escort Ts'ao Ts'ao, gradually made its way over the precipitous road. When the going improved a little and the path was moderately level, Ts'ao Ts'ao turned to look at his following and saw he had barely three hundred men. And these lacked clothing and armour and were tattered and disordered.

But he pressed on, and when the officers told him the horses were quite spent and must rest, he replied, "Press on to Chingchou and there we shall find repose."

So they pressed on. But they had gone only a few *li* when Ts'ao Ts'ao flourished his whip and broke once again into loud laughter.

"What is there to laugh at?" asked the officers.

"People say those two are able and crafty; I do not see it. They are a couple of incapables. If an ambush had been placed here we should all be prisoners."

He had not finished this speech when the explosion of a bomb broke the silence and a half company of men with swords in their hands appeared and barred the way. The leader was Kuan Yu holding the famous Black Dragon sword, bestriding the "Red Hare" steed. At this sight the spirits of the soldiers left them and they gazed into each others' faces in panic.

"Now we have but one course;" said Ts'ao Ts'ao, "we must fight to the death."

"How can we?" said the officers. "The men are scared, the horses are spent."

Ch'eng Yu said, "I have always heard that Kuan Yu is haughty to the proud but kindly to the humble; he despises the strong, but is gentle with the weak. He discriminates between love and hate and is always righteous and true. You, O Minister, have shown him kindness, and if you will remind him of that we shall escape this evil."

Ts'ao Ts'ao agreed to try. He rode out to the front, bowed low and said, "General, I trust you have enjoyed good health."

"I had orders to await you, O Minister," replied he, bowing in return, "and I have been expecting you these many days."

"You see before you Ts'ao Ts'ao, defeated and weak. I have reached a sad pass and I trust you, O General, will not forget the kindness of former days."

"Though indeed you were kind to me in those days, yet I slew your enemies for you and relieved the siege of Paima. As to the business of today, I cannot allow private feelings to outweigh public duty."

"Do you remember my generals, slain at the five passes? The noble man values righteousness. You are well versed in the histories and must recall the action of Yu-kung, the archer, when he found his master Tzu-cho in his power."

Kuan Yu was indeed a very mountain of goodness and could not forget the great kindness he had received at Ts'ao Ts'ao's hands, and the magnanimity he had shown over the deeds at the five passes. He saw the desperate straits to which his benefactor was reduced and tears were very near to the eyes of both. He could not press him hard. He pulled at the bridle of his steed and turned away saying to his followers, "Break up the formation."

From this it was evident that his design was to release Ts'ao Ts'ao, who then went on with his officers, and when Kuan Yu turned to look back they had all passed. He uttered a great shout and the soldiers jumped off their horses and knelt on the ground crying for mercy. But he also had pity for them. Then Chang Liao, whom he knew well, came along and was allowed to go free also.

> Ts'ao Ts'ao, his army lost, fled to the Huayung Valley;
> There in the throat of the gorge met he Kuan Yu.
> Grateful was Kuan, and mindful of former kindness,
> Wherefore slipped he the bolt and freed the imprisoned dragon.

Having escaped this danger Ts'ao Ts'ao hastened to get out of the valley. As the throat opened out he glanced behind him and saw only two score and seven horsemen. As evening fell they reached Nanchun and they came upon what they took to be more enemies. Ts'ao Ts'ao thought the end had surely come, but to his delight they were his own men and he regained all his confidence. Ts'ao Jen, who was the leader, said that he had heard of the misfortunes of his master, but he was afraid to venture far from his charge else he would have met him before.

"I nearly missed you as it was," said Ts'ao Ts'ao.

The fugitives found repose in the city, where Chang Liao soon joined them. He also praised the magnanimity of Kuan Yu.

When Ts'ao Ts'ao mustered the miserable remnant of his host he found nearly all were wounded and he bade them rest. Ts'ao Jen poured the wine of consolation whereby his master might forget his sorrows. And as Ts'ao drank among his familiars he became exceedingly sad.

Wherefore they said, "O Minister, when you were in the cave of the tiger and trying to escape you showed no sign of sorrow; now that you are safe in a city, where you have food and the horses have forage, where all you have to do is to prepare for revenge, suddenly you lose heart and grieve; why thus?"

Replied Ts'ao Ts'ao, "I am thinking of my friend Kuo Chia; had he been alive he would not have let me suffer this loss."

He beat his breast and wept, saying "Alas for Feng-hsiao! I grieve for Feng-hsiao! I sorrow for Feng-hsiao!"

The reproach shamed the advisers. Next day Ts'ao Ts'ao called Ts'ao Jen and said, "I am going to the capital to prepare another army for revenge. You are to guard this district and, in case of necessity, I leave with you a sealed plan. You are only to open the cover when hard-pressed, and then you are to act as directed. Wu will not dare to look this way."

"Who is to guard Hofei and Hsiangyang?"

"Chingchou is particularly your care and Hsiahou Tun is to hold Hsiangyang. As Hofei is most important I am sending Chang Liao thither with good aids. If you get into difficulties send at once to tell me."

Having made these dispositions Ts'ao Ts'ao set off at once with a few followers. He took with him the officers who had come over to his side when Chingchou fell into his hands.

Ts'ao Jen placed Ts'ao Hung in charge of the south of Iling.

After having allowed the escape of Ts'ao Ts'ao, Kuan Yu found his way back to headquarters. By this time the other detachments had returned bringing spoil of horses and weapons and supplies of all kinds. Only Kuan Yu came back empty-handed. When he arrived Chuko Liang was with his brother congratulating him on his success. When Kuan Yu was announced K'ung-ming got up and went to welcome him, bearing a cup of wine.

"Joy! O General," said he. "You have done a deed that overtops the world. You have removed the country's worst foe and ought to have been met at a distance and felicitated.

Kuan Yu muttered inaudibly and K'ung-ming continued, "I hope it is not because we have omitted to welcome you on the road that you seem sad."

Turning to those about him he said, "Why did you not tell us he was coming?"

"I am here to ask for death," said Kuan Yu.

"Surely Ts'ao Ts'ao came through the valley?"

"Yes; he came that way, and I could not help it; I let him go."

"Then whom have you captured?"

"No one."

"Then you remembered the old kindness of Ts'ao Ts'ao and so allowed him to escape. But your acceptance of the task with its conditions is here. You will have to suffer the penalty."

He called in the lictors and told them to take away Kuan Yu and put him to death.

> Kuan Yu risked life when he spared Ts'ao
>> In direst need,
> And age-long admiration gained
>> For kindly deed.

What actually befell will be seen in the next chapter.

CHAPTER LI

K uan Yu had died there but for his elder brother, who said to
the great strategist, "We three pledged ourselves to live and
die together. Although my brother Yun-ch'ang has offended
I cannot bear to break our oath. I hope you will only record this
against him and let him atone later for the fault by some specially
meritorious service."

So the sentence was remitted. In the meantime Chou Yu
mustered his officers and called over his men, noted the special
services of each and sent full reports to his master. The soldiers who
had surrendered were all transported across the river. All this done
they spread the feast of victory.

The next step was to attack and capture Nanchun. The van of
the army camped on the river bank. There were five camps and the
general's tent was in the centre. He summoned his officers to a
council. At this moment Sun Ch'ien arrived with congratulations
from Liu Pei. Chou Yu received him and, having saluted in
proper form, Ch'ien said, "My lord sent me on this special mission
to felicitate the General on his great virtue and offer some
unworthy gifts."

"Where is Yuan-te?" asked Chou Yu.

"He is now encamped at Yuchiangk'ou."

"Is K'ung-ming there?" asked Chou Yu, taken aback.

"Both are there," said Ch'ien.

"Then return quickly, and I will come in person to thank
them."

The presents handed over, Sun Ch'ien was sent back forthwith
to his own camp. Then Lu Su asked Chou Yu why he had started
when he heard where Liu Pei was camped.

"Because," replied Chou Yu, "camping there means that he has
the intention of taking Nanchun. Having spent much military

energy and spared no expenditure, we thought the district should fall to us easily. Those others are opposed to us and they wish to get the advantage of what we have already accomplished. However, they must remember that I am not dead yet."

"How can you prevent them?" asked Lu Su.

"I will go myself and speak with them. If all goes well, then, let it be so; in case it does not, then I shall immediately settle up Liu Pei without waiting for Nanchun to be taken."

"I should like to accompany you," said Lu Su.

The General and his friend started, taking with them a guard of one squadron of light horse. Having arrived at Yuchiangk'ou they sought out Sun Ch'ien, who, in turn, went in to see Yuan-te and told him Chou Yu had come to render thanks.

"Why has he come?" asked Yuan-te of his all-wise adviser.

"Is it likely he would come out of simple politeness? Of course he has come in connection with Nanchun."

"But if he brings an army, can we stand against it?" asked Yuan-te.

"When he comes you may reply thus and thus."

Then they drew up the warships in the river and ranged the soldiers upon the bank and when the arrival of Chou Yu was formally announced, Chao Yun, with some horsemen, went to welcome him. When Chou Yu saw what bold men they looked he began to feel uncomfortable, but he went on his way. Being met at the camp gates by Liu Pei and K'ung-ming, he was taken in to the chief tent, where the ceremonies were performed and preparations for a banquet had been made.

Presently Liu Pei raised his cup in felicitation on the recent victory gained by his guest. The banquet proceeded and after a few more courses Chou Yu said, "Of course you are camped here with no other idea than to take Nanchun?"

"We heard you were going to take the place and came to assist. Should you not take it then we will occupy it."

Chou Yu laughed. "We of the east have long wished for this district. Now that it is within our grasp we naturally shall take it."

Liu Pei said, "There is always some uncertainty. Ts'ao Ts'ao left Ts'ao Jen to guard the district and you may be certain that there is good strategy behind him to say nothing of his boldness as a warrior. I fear you may not get it."

"Well, if we do not take it then, Sir, you may have it, said Chou Yu.

"Here are witnesses to your words," said Liu Pei, naming those at table. "I hope you will never repent what you have just said."

Lu Su stammered and seemed unwilling to be cited as one of the witnesses but Chou Yu said, "When the word of a noble man has gone forth it is ended; he never regrets."

"This speech of yours, Sir, is very generous," interjected K'ung-ming. "Wu shall try first, but if the place does not fall there is no reason why my lord should not capture it."

The two visitors then took their leave and rode away. As soon as they had left Liu Pei turned to K'ung-ming and said, "O Master, you bade me thus reply to Chou Yu, but though I did so I have turned it over and over in my mind without finding any reason in what I said. I am alone and weak, without a single foot of land to call my own. I desired to get possession of Nanchun that I might have, at least, a temporary shelter, yet I have said that Chou Yu may attack it first and if it fall to Wu, how can I get possession?"

K'ung-ming laughed and replied, "First I advised you to attack Chingchou, but you would not listen; do you remember?"

"But it belonged to Liu Piao and I could not bear to attack it then. Now it belongs to Ts'ao Ts'ao I might do so."

"Do not be anxious," replied the adviser. "Let Chou Yu go and attack it; some day, my lord, I shall make you sit in the high places thereof."

"But what design have you?"

"So and so," replied K'ung-ming.

Yuan-te was satisfied with the reply, and only strengthened his position at Chiangk'ou. In the meantime Chou Yu and Lu Su returned to their own camp and the latter said, "Why did you tell Liu Pei that he might attack Nanchun?"

"I can take it with a flick of my finger," replied Chou Yu, "but I just manifested a little pretended kindliness."

Then he enquired among his officers for a volunteer to attack the city. One Chiang Ch'in offered himself, and was put in command of the vanguard, with Hsu Sheng and Ting Feng as helpers. He was given five companies of veterans and they moved across the river. Chou Yu promised to follow with supports.

On the other side Ts'ao Jen ordered Ts'ao Hung to guard Iling and so hold one corner of a triangular defence. When the news came that Wu had crossed the river Han, Ts'ao said, "We will defend and not offer battle."

But Niu Chin said impetuously, "To let the enemy approach the walls and not offer battle is timidity. Our men, lately worsted, need heartening and must show their mettle. Let me have half a company of veterans and I will fight to a finish."

Ts'ao Jen could not withstand this offer and so the half company went out of the city. At once Ting Feng came to challenge the leader and they fought a few bouts. Then Ting Feng pretended to be defeated, gave up the fight and retreated into his own lines. Niu Chin followed him hard. When he had got within the Wu formation, at a signal from Ting Feng, the army closed round and Niu Chin was surrounded. He pushed right and left, but could find no way out. Seeing him in the toils, Ts'ao Jen, who had watched the fight from the wall, donned his armour and came out of the city at the head of his own bold company of horsemen and burst in among the men of Wu to try to rescue his colleague. Beating back Hsu Sheng he fought his way in and presently rescued Niu Chin.

However, having got out he saw several score of horsemen still in the middle unable to make their way out, whereupon he turned again to the battle and dashed in to their rescue. This time he met Chiang Ch'in on whom he and Niu Chin made a violent onslaught. Then the brother Ts'ao Shun came up with supports and the great battle ended in a defeat for the men of Wu.

So Ts'ao Jen went back victor, while the unhappy Chiang Ch'in returned to report his failure. Chou Yu was very angry and would have put to death his hapless subordinate but for the intervention of the other officers.

Then he prepared for another attack where he himself would lead. But Kan Ning said, "General, do not be in too great hurry; let me go first and attack Iling, the supporting angle of the triangle. After that the conquest of Nanchun will be easy."

Chou Yu accepted the plan and Kan, with three companies, went to attack Iling.

When news of the approaching army reached him Ts'ao Jen called to his side Ch'en Chiao, who said, "If Iling be lost then Nanchun is lost too. So help must be sent quickly."

Thereupon Ts'ao Shun and Niu Chin were sent by secret ways to the aid of Ts'ao Hung. Ts'ao Shun sent a messenger to the city to ask that they should cause a diversion by a sortie at the time the reinforcements should arrive.

So when Kan Ning drew near, Ts'ao Hung went out to meet and engage him. They fought a score of rounds, but Ts'ao Hung was overcome at last and Kan Ning took the city. However, as evening fell the reinforcements came up and the captor was surrounded in the city he had taken. The scouts went off immediately to tell Chou Yu of this sudden change of affairs which greatly alarmed him.

"Let us hasten to his rescue," said Ch'eng P'u.

"This place is of the greatest importance," said Chou Yu, "and I am afraid to leave it undefended lest Ts'ao Jen should attack."

"But he is one of our first leaders and must be rescued," said Lu Meng.

"I should like to go myself to his aid, but whom can I leave here in my place?" said Chou Yu.

"Leave Lin T'ung here," said Lu Meng; "I will push on ahead and you can protect my advance. In less than ten days we shall be singing the pæan of victory."

"Are you willing?" said Chou Yu to the man who was to act for him.

"If the ten day period is not exceeded I may be able to carry on for that time; I am unequal to more than that."

"Ling's T'ung consent pleased Chou Yu who started at once, leaving a legion for the defence of the camp. Lu Meng said to his chief, "South of Iling is a little-used road that may prove very useful in an attack on Nanchun. Let us send a party to fell trees and barricade this road so that horses cannot pass. In case of defeat the defeated will take this road and will be compelled to abandon their horses, which we shall capture."

Chou Yu approved and the men set out. When the main army drew near Iling, Chou Yu asked who would try to break through the besiegers and Chou T'ai offered himself. He girded on his sword, mounted his steed and burst straight into the Ts'ao army. He got through to the city wall.

From the city wall Kan Ning saw the approach of his friend Chou T'ai and went out to welcome him. Chou T'ai told him that the Commander-in-Chief was on the way to his relief and Kan Ning at once bade the defenders prepare from within to support the attack of the rescuers.

When the news of the approach of Chou Yu had reached Iling the defenders had sent to tell Ts'ao Jen, who was at Nanchun and they prepared to repel the assailants. So when the army of Wu came near they were at once attacked. Simultaneously Kan Ning and Chou T'ai attacked on two sides and the men of Ts'ao were thrown into confusion. The men of Wu fell on lustily and the three leaders all fled by a bye-road, but, finding the way barred with felled trees and other obstacles, they had to abandon their horses and go afoot. In this way the men of Wu gained some five hundred steeds.

Chou Yu, pressing on as quickly as possible toward Nanchun, came upon Ts'ao Jen and his army marching to save Iling. The two armies engaged and fought a battle which lasted till late in the evening. Then both drew off and Ts'ao Jen withdrew into the city.

During the night he called his officers to a council. Then said

Ts'ao Hung, "The loss of Iling has brought us to a dangerous pass; now it seems the time to open the letter of the Minister our Chief and see what plans he arranged for our salvation in this peril."

"You but say what I think," replied Ts'ao Jen. Whereupon he tore open the letter and read it. His face lighted up with joy and he at once issued orders to have the morning meal prepared at the fifth watch. At daylight the whole army moved out of the city but they left a semblance of occupation in the shape of banners on the walls.

Chou Yu went up to the tower of observation and looked over the city. He saw that the flags along the battlements had no men behind them and he noticed that every man carried a bundle at his waist behind so that he was prepared for a long march. Thought Chou Yu to himself, "Ts'ao Jen must be prepared for a long march."

So he went down from the tower of observation and sent out an order for two wings of the army to be ready. One of these was to attack and, in case of its success, the other was to pursue at full speed till the clanging of the gongs should call them to return. He took command of the leading force in person and Ch'eng P'u commanded the other. Thus they advanced to attack the city.

The armies being arrayed facing each other, the drums rolled out across the plain. Ts'ao Hung rode forth and challenged, and Chou Yu, from his place by the standard, bade Han Tang respond. The two champions fought near two score bouts and then Ts'ao Hung fled. Thereupon Ts'ao Jen came out to help him and Chou T'ai rode out at full speed to meet him. These two exchanged a half score passes and then Ts'ao Jen fled.

His army fell into confusion. Thereupon Chou Yu gave the signal for the advance of both his wings and the men of Ts'ao were sore smitten and defeated. Chou Yu pursued to the city wall, but Ts'ao's men did not enter the city. Instead, they went away northwest. Han Tang and Chou T'ai pressed them hard.

Chou Yu, seeing the city gates standing wide open and no guards upon the walls, ordered the raiding of the city. A few score horsemen rode in first, Chou Yu followed and whipping his steed. As he galloped into the enclosure around the gate, Ch'en Chiao stood on the defence tower. When he saw Chou Yu enter, in his heart he applauded the god-like perspicacity of the Minister Ts'ao Ts'ao.

Then was heard the clap-clap of a watchman's rattle. At this signal the archers and crossbowmen let fly and the arrows and bolts flew forth in a sudden fierce shower, while those who had won their way to the van of the inrush went headlong into a deep trench. Chou Yu managed to pull up in time, but turning to escape, he was wounded in the left side and fell to the ground. Niu Chin rushed out from the city to capture the chief, but Hsu Sheng and Ting Feng at the risk of their lives got him away safe. Then the men of Ts'ao dashed out of the city and wrought confusion among the men of Wu, who trampled each other down and many more fell into the trenches. Ch'eng P'u tried to draw off, but Ts'ao Je and Ts'ao Hung came toward him from different directions and the battle went hardly against the men from the east, till help came from Ling T'ung, who bore back their assailants. Satisfied with their success Ts'ao led his men into the city, while the losers marched back to their own camp.

Chou Yu, sorely wounded, was taken to his own tent and the army physician called in. With iron forceps he extracted the sharp bolt and dressed the wound with a lotion designed to counteract the poison of the metal. But the pain was intense and the patient rejected all nourishment. The physician said the missile had been poisoned and the wound would require a long time to heal. The patient must be kept quiet and especially free from any irritation, which would cause the wound to re-open.

Thereupon Ch'eng P'u gave orders that each division was to remain in camp. Three days later Niu Chin came within sight and challenged the men of Wu to battle, but they did not stir. The enemy hurled at them taunts and insults till the sun had fallen low in the sky, but it was of no avail and Niu withdrew.

Next day Niu Chin returned and repeated his insulting abuse. Ch'eng P'u dared not tell the wounded general. The third day, waxing bolder, the enemy came to the very gates of the stockade, the leader shouting that he had come for the purpose of capturing Chou Yu.

Then Ch'eng P'u called together his officers and they discussed the feasibility of retirement into Wu that he might seek the opinion of the Marquis.

Ill as he was Chou Yu still retained control of the expedition. He knew that the enemy came daily to the gates of his camp and reviled him although none of his officers told him. One day Ts'ao Jen came in person and there was much rolling of drums and shouting. Ch'eng P'u, however, steadily refused to accept the challenge and would not let any one go out. Then Chou Yu summoned the officers to his bedside and said, "What mean the drums and the shouting?"

"The men are drilling," was the reply.

"Why do you deceive me?" said Chou Yu angrily. "Do I not know that our enemies come day by day to our gates and insult us?

Yet Ch'eng P'u suffers this in silence and makes no use of his powers and authority."

He sent for Ch'eng P'u and, when he arrived, asked him why he acted thus.

"Because you are ill and the physician said you were on no account to be provoked to anger. Wherefore, although the enemy challenged us to battle, I kept it from you."

"And if you do not fight what think you should be done?" said Chou Yu.

And they all said they desired to return to the east till he had recovered from his wound, when they would make another expedition.

Chou Yu lay and listened. Suddenly he sprang up, crying, "The noble man who has eaten of his lord's bounty should die in his lord's battles; to return to one's home wrapped in a horse's hide is a happy fate. Am I the sort of man to bring to nought the grand designs of my country?"

So speaking he proceeded to gird on his armour and he mounted his horse. The wonder of the officers only redoubled when their General placed himself at the head of some hundreds of horsemen and went out of the camp gates toward the enemy, then fully arrayed. Ts'ao Jen, their general, stood beneath the great standard.

At sight of the opponents Ts'ao Jen flourished his whip and began to hurl abuse at them, "Chou Yu, you babe! I think your fate has met you. You dare not face my men."

The stream of insult never ceased. Presently Chou Yu could stand it no longer. Riding out to the front he cried, "Here I am, base churl; look at me!"

The whole Ts'ao army were taken aback. But Ts'ao Jen turned to those about him and said, "Let us all revile him!" And the whole army yelled insults.

Chou Yu grew angry and sent P'an Chang out to fight. But before he had delivered his first blow Chou Yu suddenly uttered a loud cry, and he fell to the ground with blood gushing from his mouth.

At this the Ts'ao army rushed to the battle and the men of Wu pressed forward to meet them. A fierce struggle waged around the General's body, but he was borne off safely and taken to his tent.

"Do you feel better?" asked Ch'eng P'u anxiously.

"It was a ruse of mine," whispered Chou Yu in reply.

"But what avails it?"

"I am not suffering, but I did that to make our enemies think I was very ill and so oppose them by deceit. I will send a few trusty men to pretend desertion and tell them I am dead. That will cause them to try a night raid on the camp and we shall have an ambush ready for them. We shall get Ts'ao Jen easily."

"The plan seems excellent," said Ch'eng P'u.

Soon from the tent there arose the sound of wailing as for the dead. The soldiers around took up the cry and said one to another, "The General is dead of his wound," and they all put on the symbols of mourning.

Meanwhile Ts'ao Jen was consulting with his officers. Said he, "Chou Yu lost his temper and that has caused his wound to re-open and brought on that flow of blood. You saw him fall to the ground and he will assuredly die soon."

Just then there came in one who said that a few men had come over from the enemy asking to be allowed to join the army of Ts'ao; among them were two of Ts'ao's men who had been made prisoners.

Ts'ao Jen sent for the deserters and questioned them. They told him a story of Chou Yu's wound and death that day. The leaders were all in mourning. They had deserted because they had been put to shame by the second in command.

Pleased at this news Ts'ao Jen at once began to arrange to make a night attack on the camp and, if possible, get the head of the dead general to send to the capital.

"Success depends upon promptitude, so act without delay," said Ch'en Chiao.

Niu Chin was told off as van leader, Ts'ao Jen himself led the centre, while the rear was commanded by Ts'ao Hung and Ts'ao Shun. Ch'en Chiao, and a few men, were left to guard the city.

At the first watch they left the city and took the way toward Chou Yu's camp. When they drew near not a man was visible, but flags and banners and spears were all there, evidently to keep up an appearance of preparation. Feeling at once that they had been tricked they turned to retreat. But a bomb exploded and this was the signal for an attack on all four sides. The result was a severe defeat for the raiders and the army of Ts'ao Jen was entirely broken and scattered abroad so that no one part of the beaten army could aid the other.

Ts'ao Jen, with a few horsemen got out of the press and presently met Ts'ao Hung. The two leaders ran away together and by the fifth watch they had got near Nanchun. Then they heard a beating of drums and Lin T'ung appeared barring the way. There was a small skirmish and Ts'ao Jen went off at an angle. But he fell in with Kan Ning, who attacked him vigorously. Ts'ao Jen dared not go back to Nanchun, but he made for Hsiangyang along the main road. The men of Wu pursued him for a time and then desisted.

Chou Yu and Ch'eng P'u then made their way to Nanchun where they were startled to see flags on the walls and every sign of occupation. Before they had recovered from their surprise there appeared one who cried, "Pardon, General; I had orders from my chief to take this city. I am Chao Tzu-lung of Ch'angshan."

Chou Yu was fiercely angry and gave orders to assault the city, but the defenders sent down flights and flights of arrows and his men could not stay near the rampart. So he withdrew and took counsel. In the meantime he decided to send a force to capture Chingchou and another to take Hsiangyang. Nanchun could be taken later.

But even as these orders were being given the scouts came in hurriedly to report that Chuko Liang, suddenly producing a military commission, had induced the guards of Chingchou to leave it and go to the rescue of Chou Yu. Whereupon Chang Fei had occupied the town. Soon after another messenger came to say that Hsiahou Tun, at Hsiangyang, had received from Chuko Liang despatches, supported by a commission in due form, saying that Ts'ao Jen was in danger and needed help, whereupon Hsiahou Tun had marched off and Kuan Yu had seized that town.

Thus the two towns that Chou Yu wanted had fallen, without the least effort, into the hands of his rival Liu Pei.

"How did Chuko Liang get this military commission with which he has imposed on the captains?" asked Chou Yu.

Ch'eng P'u replied, "He seized that of Ch'en Chiao; and so has got all this district into his power."

Chou Yu uttered a great cry for at that moment his wound had suddenly burst open.

> A city falls, but not to us the gain;
> The guerdon is another's; ours the pain.

The next chapter will say what befell Chou Yu.

CHAPTER LII

CHUKO LIANG TALKS CUNNINGLY
TO LU SU: CHAO YUN, BY A RUSE,
CAPTURES KUEIYANG

Chou Yu's anger at seeing that his rival, K'ung-ming, had surprised Nanchun, and at hearing the same news of Chingchou and Hsiangyang, was but natural. And this sudden fit of rage caused his wound to re-open. However, he soon recovered. All his officers besought him to accept the situation, but he said, "What but the death of that bumpkin, Chuko, will assuage my anger? If Ch'eng P'u can but aid me in an attack on Nanchun I can certainly restore it to my country."

Soon Lu Su came in, to whom Chou Yu said, "I simply must fight Liu Pei and Chuko Liang till it is decided which shall have the upper hand. I must also recapture the city. Perhaps you can assist me."

"It cannot be done," replied Lu Su. "We are now at grips with Ts'ao Ts'ao and victory or defeat is undecided. Our lord has not been successful in overcoming Hopei. Do not fight near home, or it will be like people of the same household destroying each other and should Ts'ao Ts'ao take advantage of this position to make a sudden descent we should be in a parlous condition. Further, you must remember that Liu Pei Ts'ao Ts'ao are united by the bonds of old friendship and, if the pressure becomes too great, Liu Pei may relinquish these cities, offer them to Ts'ao Ts'ao and join forces with him to-attack our country. That would be a real misfortune."

"I cannot help being angry" said Chou Yu, "to think that we should have used our resources for their benefit. They get all the advantage."

"Well, let me go and see Yuan-te and talk reason to him. If I can arrive at no understanding then attack at once."

"Excellent proposal!" cried all present.

So Lu Su, with his escort, went away to Nanchun to carry out his proposal and try to arrange matters. He reached the city wall and summoned the gate, whereat Chao Yun came out to speak with him.

"I have something to say to Liu Yuan-te," said he; "I wish to see him."

"My lord and Chuko Liang are in Chingchou," was the reply.

Lu Su turned away and hasted to Chingchou. He found the walls bedecked with flags and everything in excellent order. In his heart he admired the sight, and thought what an able man was the commander of that army.

The guards reported his arrival and K'ung-ming ordered them to throw wide the gate. He was led to the government house and, after the usual exchange of salutes, K'ung-ming and his visitor took their respective seats. Having finished the tea, Lu Su said, "My master, the Marquis Wu, and the Commander of his army, Chou Yu, have sent me to lay before the Imperial Uncle their views. When Ts'ao Ts'ao led his huge host south-ward he gave out that it was for the conquest of Chiangnan; really his intention was to destroy Liu Pei. Happily our army was able to repulse that mighty host and so saved him. Wherefore Chingchou with its nine districts ought to belong to us. But by a treacherous move your master has occupied Chingchou and Hsiangyang, so that we have spent our treasure in vain and our armies have fought to no purpose. The Imperial Uncle has reaped the benefits to the full. This is not as it should be."

K'ung-ming replied, "Tzu-ching, you are a man of high intelligence; why do you hold such language? You know the saying, that all things turn to their owner. These places have never belonged to Wu, but were of the patrimony of Liu Piao, and though he is dead, his son remains. Should not the uncle assist the nephew to recover his own? Could my master have refrained?"

"If the nephew Liu Ch'i, the rightful heir, had occupied these cities there would have been something to say. But he is at Chianghsia and not here."

"Would you like to see him?" said K'ung-ming.

At the same time he ordered the servants to request Liu Ch'i to come. Thereupon he at once appeared, supported by two attendants. Addressing Lu Su he said, "I am too weak to perform the correct ceremonies; I pray you pardon me, Tzu-ching."

Lu Su said not a word; he was too much taken aback. However, he recovered himself presently and said, "But if the heir had not been here, what then?"

"The heir is living but from day to day; should he go, then—there will be something to talk about."

"Should he die, then you ought to return these cities to us."

"You state the exact facts," said K'ung-ming.

Then a banquet was prepared and, that over, Lu Su took his leave. He hastened back to his own camp and gave Chou Yu an account of his mission.

"But what is there for us in the chance of Liu Ch'i's death?" said Chou Yu. "He is in his very first youth. When will these places fall to us?"

"Rest content, General; let me guarantee the return of these places."

"But how can you?" asked Chou Yu.

"Liu Ch'i has indulged too freely in wine and women; he is a wreck and rotten to the core, miserably emaciated and panting for breath. I will not give him half a year's life. Then I will go to Liu Pei and he will be unable to deny the request."

But Chou Yu was still unmollified. Suddenly came a messenger from Sun Ch'uan, who said, "Our lord is laying siege to Hofei but in several battles has had no victory. He now orders you to withdraw from here and go to Hofei to help him."

Thereupon Chou Yu marched back to Ch'aisang. Having reached home he began to give attention to the recovery of his health. He sent Ch'eng P'u with the marine and land forces to Hofei ready for Sun Ch'uan's call.

Liu Pei was exceedingly well satisfied with the possession of his new territory and his thoughts turned to more ambitious schemes. Then a certain man came to him to suggest a plan. This man was I Chi and, remembering the kindly feeling of other days, Yuan-te received him most graciously. When he was seated, and his host had asked what he proposed, he said, "You wish for a plan to accomplish yet greater deeds; why not seek wise men and ask them?"

"Where are these wise men to be found?" asked Yuan-te.

I Chi replied, "In this district there is a certain family named Ma, five brothers, all of whom are known as men of ability. The youngest is called Ma Su, or Ma Yu-ch'ang. The ablest is Ma Liang, or Chi-ch'ang, who has white hairs in his eyebrows, and the villagers have a little rhyming couplet that means there are five sons in the family Ma but white eyebrows is the best of them. You should get this man to draw up a plan for you."

So Yuan-te told them to request his presence. Ma Liang came and was received with great respect. He was asked to suggest a plan for the security of the newly acquired district and he said, "Attacked as it is on all sides this district is not one in which one is permanently secure. You should let Liu Ch'i remain here till he is recovered from his present illness, the actual protection of the place being left in the hands of trusty friends. Obtain an Edict appointing him Governor and the people will be content. Then conquer Wuling, Changsha, Kueiyang and Linling and with the resources you will thus acquire you will have the means for further plans. That should be your policy."

"Which of the four districts should be first taken?" asked Liu Pei.

"The nearest, Linling, which lies in the west of Hsiang (Hunan). The next is Wuling and after these the other two."

Ma Liang was given an appointment as secretary, with I Chi as his second. Then Yuan-te consulted K'ung-ming about sending Liu Ch'i to Hsiangyang, so that Yun-ch'ang could be free to return. Next they made preparations to attack Linling, and Chang Fei was to lead the van. Chao Yun was to guard the rear while Yuan-te and K'ung-ming were to command the main body. A legion and a half were left to hold Chingchou. Mi Chu and Liu Feng were left to guard Chiangling.

The Prefect of Linling was Liu Tu. When danger thus threatened he called in his son Liu Hsien and they discussed the case. The son was very self-confident and said to his father, "Have no anxiety. They may have the known and famous warriors, Chang Fei and Chao Yun, but we have our leader, Hsing Tao-yung, who is match for any number of men. He can withstand them."

So Liu Hsien, with the famous leader, was entrusted with the defence. At the head of a full legion they made a camp about thirty *li* from the city, with the shelter of hills and a river. Their scouts brought news that K'ung-ming was close at hand with one army. Hsing Tao-jung decided to check his advance and went forth to oppose him. When both sides were arrayed, Hsing rode to the front. In his hand he held a battle-axe called Cleaver of Mountains. In a mighty voice he cried, "Rebels, how comes it that you have dared to enter our territory?"

From the centre of the opposing army, where appeared a cluster of yellow flags, there came out a small four-wheeled carriage in which sat, very erect, a certain man dressed in white, with a turban on his head. In one hand he held a feather fan, with which he signed to the warrior to approach. At the same time he said, "I am Chuko K'ung-ming, of Nanyang, whose plans broke up the countless legions of Ts'ao Ts'ao so that nothing of them returned whence they started, How then can you hope to oppose me? I now offer you peace and it will be well for you to surrender."

Hsing laughed derisively. "Their defeat was owing to the plan of Chou Yu; you had nothing to do with it. How dare you try to deceive me?"

So saying he swung up his battle-axe and came running toward K'ung-ming. But he turned his carriage and retired within the lines which closed up behind him. Hsing still came rushing on. As he reached the array the men fell away on both sides and let him enter. Well within he looked round for his chief opponent. Seeing a yellow flag moving along quietly he concluded that K'ung-ming was with it and so followed it. When the flag had gone over the shoulder of a hill it stopped. Then suddenly as if the earth had opened and swallowed it up, the four-wheeled carriage disappeared, while in its place came a ferocious warrior, with a long spear in his hand and mounted on a curvetting steed. It was Chang Fei, who dashed at Hsing with a tremendous roar.

Nothing daunted Hsing Tao-jung whirled up his battle-axe and went to meet Chang Fei. After four or five bouts he saw that there was no chance of victory for him, so he turned his horse and ran. Chang Fei pursued, the air shaking with the thunder of his voice.

Then the ambushed men appeared. Tao-jung, nothing daunted, rushed into their midst. But in front appeared another warrior barring the way, who called out, "Do you know me? I am Chao Tzu-lung of Ch'angshan."

Hsing Tao-jung knew that all was over; he could neither fight nor fly. So he dismounted and gave in. He was fettered and taken to camp, where were Yuan-te and K'ung-ming. The former ordered him out to execution, but K'ung-ming hastily checked him.

"We will accept your submission if you capture Liu Hsien for us," said he.

The captive accepted the offer without the least hesitation, and when K'ung-ming asked how he intended to do it, he replied, "If you will set me free, I shall be cunning of speech. If you raid the camp this evening you will find me your helper on the inside. I will make Liu Hsien a prisoner and will hand him over to you. He being captured, his father will surrender at once."

Yuan-te doubted the good faith of the man, but K'ung-ming said he knew he could answer for him. Wherefore he was set free and went back to camp, where he related all that had occurred.

"What can we do?" asked Liu Hsien.

"We can meet trick with trick. Put soldiers in ambush tonight outside our camp while within everything will appear as usual. When K'ung-ming comes we shall capture him."

The ambush was prepared. At the second watch a troop came out of the darkness and appeared in the gate. Each man carried a torch and they began to set fire to all about them. Out dashed Liu Hsien and Hsing Tao-jung and the incendiaries forthwith fled. The two warriors pursued them, but the fugitives ran and then suddenly disappeared at about ten *li* from the camp. Much surprised the two turned to wend their way back to their own camp.

It was still burning for no one had extinguished the flames. Soon from behind them came out Chang Fei. Liu Hsien called out to his companion not to enter the burning camp, but to go with him to attack K'ung-ming's stockade.

Thereupon they turned again, but at a distance of ten *li* Chao Yun and a troop suddenly debouched upon their road. Chao Yun attacked and Hsing Tao-jung fell. Liu Hsien turned to flee, but Chang Fei was close upon him and made him prisoner. He was thrown across a horse, bound and taken to camp. When he saw K'ung-ming he laid blame on his fallen comrade saying he had listened to his evil counsel and this deed was not his own wish. K'ung-ming ordered them to loose his bonds, had him properly dressed and gave him wine to cheer him and help him forget his troubles. When he was recovered he was told to go to his father and persuade him to yield.

"And if he does not, the city shall be destroyed and every one put to death," said K'ung-ming as he left.

The son returned to the city and told his father these things. Liu Tu at once decided to yield and forthwith hoisted the flag of surrender, opened the gates, and went out taking his seal of office with him. He was re-appointed to his prefectship, but his son was sent to Chingchou for service with the army.

The people of Linling all rejoiced greatly at the change of rulers. Yuan-te entered the city, calmed and re-assured the people and rewarded his army.

But he at once began to think of the next move and asked for an officer to volunteer to take Kueiyang, Chao Yun offered, but Chang Fei vehemently proposed himself for the command of the expedition. So they wrangled and contended.

Then said K'ung-ming, "Undoubtedly Chao Yun was first to volunteer, wherefore he is to go."

Still Chang Fei opposed and insisted on going. They were told to decide the dispute by drawing lots and Chao Yun drew the winning lot. Chang Fei was still very angry and grumbled, "I would not have wanted any helpers: just three companies and I would have done it."

"I also only want three companies," said Chao Yun. "And if I fail I am willing to suffer the penalties."

K'ung-ming was pleased that he recognised his responsibility so fully, and with the commission gave him three companies of veterans.

Though the matter was thus settled Chang Fei was discontented and pressed his claim till Yuan-te bade him desist and retire.

With his three companies Chao Yun took the road to Kueiyang. The Prefect Chao Fan soon heard of his approach and hastily called his officers to take counsel. Two of them, Ch'en Ying and Pao Lung, offered to meet the invaders and turn them back.

These two warriors belonged to Kueiyang and had made themselves famous as hunters. Ch'en used a "Flying Fork" and Pao could draw a bow with such force that he had been known to send an arrow through two tigers. So strong were they, as well as bold.

They stood before Chao Fan and said, "We will lead the way against Liu Pei."

The Prefect replied, "I know that Liu Pei is of the Imperial family: K'ung-ming is exceedingly resourceful: Kuan Yu and Chang Fei are very bold. But the commander of this force is Chao Tzu-lung who, on one occasion, faced a hundred legions and never blenched. Our small force here cannot stand against such people. We shall have to yield."

"Let me go out to fight," said Ch'en Ying. "If I cannot capture Chao Yun then you can yield."

The Prefect could not resist him and gave his consent. Then Ch'en Ying, with three companies, went forth and soon the two armies came within sight of each other. When Ch'en Ying's army was drawn up he girded on his "Flying Fork" and rode to the front. Chao Yun gripped his spear and rode to meet him. Chao Yun began to rail at Ch'en Ying, saying, "My master is the brother of Liu Piao to whom belonged this land. Now he is supporting his nephew the heir and son of Liu Piao. Having taken Chingchou I am come to soothe and comfort the people here. Why then do you oppose me?"

"We are supporters of the Minister Ts'ao and are no followers of your master," was the reply.

Chao Yun, waxing angry, firmly grasped his spear and rode forward. His opponent twirled "Flying Fork" and advanced. The horses met, but after four or five encounters Ch'en Ying, realising that there was no hope of victory, turned and fled. Chao Yun followed. Suddenly turning, Ch'en Ying got close to Chao Yun and flung the fork. Chao Yun deftly caught it and threw it back. Ch'en Ying dodged away, but Chao Yun soon caught him up, seized Ch'en Ying, dragged him out of the saddle and threw him to the ground. Then he called up his soldiers and they bound the prisoner. He was taken to the camp, while his men scattered and fled.

"I thought you would not dare a combat with me," said Chao Yun to the prisoner when they had returned to camp. "However, I am not going to put you to death. You are free. But persuade your master to yield."

Ch'en Ying asked pardon, put his hands over his head and fled like a frightened rat. When he reached his city he told the Prefect all these things.

"My original desire was to yield, but you insisted on fighting and this is what it has brought you to."

So spoke the Prefect. He bade Ch'en begone and then prepared his letter of submission and put up his seal. With a small party he went out of the city and wended his way to Chao Yun's camp. Chao received him graciously, offered him wine and then accepted the seal of office. After the wine had gone round several times Chao Fan became talkative, General, your surname is the same as mine, and five centuries ago we were one family. You are from Chenting and so am I. Moreover we are from the same village. If you do not mind we might swear brotherhood. I should be very happy."

Chao Yun was pleased and they compared ages. They were of the same year. However, Chao Yun was the elder by four months and so Chao Fan made his bow as younger brother. The two men, having so many things in common, were very pleased with each other and seemed fitted to be close friends.

At eventide the feast broke up and the late Prefect returned to his dwelling. Next day he requested Chao Yun to enter the city, where, after he had assured the people of their safety, Chao Yun went to a banquet at the *ya-men*. When they had become mellow with wine the Prefect invited Chao Yun into the inner quarters, where wine was again served. When Chao Yun was a little intoxicated, his host bade a woman come forth and offer a cup of wine to the guest.

The woman was dressed entirely in white silk and her beauty was such as to overthrow cities and ruin states.

"Who is she?" asked Chao Yun.

"My sister-in-law; her maiden name was Fan."

Chao Yun at once changed his look and treated her with deference. When she had offered the cup the host told her to be seated and join the party but Chao Yun declined this addition to the evening and the lady withdrew.

"Why did you trouble your sister-in-law to present wine to me, brother?" asked Chao Yun.

"There is a reason," said the host smiling. "I pray you let me tell you. My brother died three years ago and left her a widow. But this cannot be regarded as the end of the story. I have often advised her to marry again, but she said she would only do so if three conditions were satisfied in one man's person. The suitor must be famous for literary grace and warlike exploits, secondly, handsome and highly esteemed and, thirdly, of the same name as our own. Now where in all the world was such a combination likely to be found? Yet here are you, brother, dignified, handsome and prepossessing, a man whose name is known all over the wide world and of the desired name. You exactly fulfil my sister's ambitions. If you do not find her too ugly, I should like her to marry you and I will provide a dowry. What think you of such an alliance, such a bond of relationship?"

But Chao Yun rose in anger, shouting, "As I have just sworn brotherhood with you, is not your sister-in-law my sister-in-law? How could you think of bringing such confusion into the relationship."

Shame suffused Chao Fan's face and he said, "I only thought of being kind to you; why are you so very rude to me?"

He looked right and left to his attendants with murder in his eye. Chao Yun raised his fist and knocked him down. Then he strode out of the place, mounted and rode out of the city.

Chao Fan at once called in his two fighting men. Ch'en Ying said, "He has gone away in a rage, which means that we shall have to fight him."

"I greatly fear you will lose," said Chao Fan.

"We will pretend to be deserters," said Pao Lung, "and so get among his men. When you challenge him we will suddenly catch him."

"We shall have to take some others with us," said Ch'en.

"Half a company will be ample," said Pao.

So in the night the two men and their followers ran over to Chao Yun's camp to desert.

Chao Yun understood the trick they would play, but he called them in and they said, "When Chao Fan tempted you with that fair lady he wanted to make you drunk and get you into the private apartments so that he might murder you and send your head to Ts'ao Ts'ao. Yes; he was as wicked as that even. We saw you go away in anger and we thought that would mean grave trouble for us and so we have deserted."

Chao Yun listened with simulated joy, and he had wine served to the two men, and pressed them to drink so that they were quite overcome. When this was done he had both bound with cords, called up their followers and asked them whether this was real or pretended desertion and they told him the truth. Then he gave the soldiers wine and said, "Those who wanted to harm me are your leaders and not you. If you do as I tell you shall be well rewarded."

The soldiers threw themselves to the ground and promised obedience. Thereupon the two leaders were beheaded. The half company were made to lead the way and act as screen for a whole company of horsemen and the party set out at full speed for Kueiyang. When they got there they summoned the gate and said that they had slain Chao Yun and had got back. And they wished to speak with the Prefect.

Those on the wall lighted flares and inspected those at the gate. Surely enough they wore the uniforms of their own people and Chao Fan went out to them. He was immediately seized and made prisoner. Then Chao Yun entered the city, restored order and sent off swift messengers to Yuan-te who at once, with his adviser, came to Kueiyang.

When they had taken their seats the late Prefect was brought in and placed at the foot of the steps. In response to K'ung-ming's questions he related the history of the proposed marriage.

Said K'ung-ming to Chao Yun, "But this seems a fine project; why did you receive the proposal so roughly?"

"Chao Fan and I had just sworn brotherhood and so marriage with his sister-in-law would have called down on my head universal blame. That is one reason. Another is that I should have made his sister fail to keep her dutiful chastity. And thirdly I did not know whether I might trust such a proposal from one who had just yielded to force. My lord, your position as a recent victor was one of danger and could I risk the failure of your plans for the sake of a woman?"

"But now that the plan has been carried out and we are victors would you care to marry her?"

"There are plenty of women in the world. All my fear is for my reputation. What is a family to me?"

"You are indeed right honourable," said Yuan-te.

Chao Fan was released and restored to the prefectorate. Chao Yun was conspicuously rewarded.

But Chang Fei was angry and disappointed. "So Tzu-lung gets all the praise and I am worth nothing," cried he. "Just give me three companies and I will take Wuling and bring you the Prefect."

This pleased K'ung-ming, who said, "There is no reason why you should not go, but I will only require one condition of you."

Wondrous, the plans of the general, so doth he conquer in battle;
Soldiers keenly competing gain renown in the fighting.

The condition that K'ung-ming made will appear in the next chapter.

CHAPTER LIII

KUAN YU, FROM A SENSE OF RIGHTEOUSNESS, RELEASES HUANG CHUNG: SUN CH'UAN FIGHTS A GREAT BATTLE WITH CHANG LIAO

What K'ung-ming required from Chang Fei was a formal recognition of responsibility for success. Said he, "When Chao Yun went on his expedition he gave written guarantee of being responsible for success and you ought to do the same now that you are starting for Wuling. In that case you may have men and start."

So Chang Fei gave the required document and received joyfully the three companies of soldiers he had demanded. He set out at once and travelled without rest till he reached Wuling.

When the Prefect of Wuling, Chin Hsuan by name, heard that an expedition against him was afoot he mustered his officers and recruited brave soldiers and put his weapons in order ready for the struggle. And his army moved out of the city.

A certain secretary, Kung Chih, remonstrated with his chief for opposing a scion of the imperial house, saying, "Liu Yuan-te is of the Hans, and recognised as an uncle of the Emperor. All the world knows he is kindly and righteous. Added to that his brother Chang Fei is extraordinarily bold. We cannot face them in battle with hope of success. Our best course is to give in."

But his master angrily replied, "Do you want to play the traitor and take the side of the rebels and help them?"

He called in the lictors and told them to put Kung to death. The other officers interceded for him, saying, "It augers ill to start an expedition by slaying your own men."

So the Prefect merely sent Kung Chih away. He himself led the army out of the city. After marching twenty *li* he met with Chang Fei's army.

Chang Fei at once rode to the front, spear ready to thrust, and opened with a shout. Chin Hsuan turned to his officers and asked who would go out to fight him, but no one replied; they were too afraid.

So the Prefect himself galloped out, flourishing his sword. Seeing him advance Chang Fei shouted in a voice of thunder. Poor Chin was seized with panic, turned pale and could not go on. He turned his steed and fled. Then Chang Fei and his army went in pursuit and smote the fugitives, chasing them to the city wall.

Here the fugitives were greeted by a flight of arrows from their own wall. Greatly frightened, Chin Hsuan looked up to see what this meant and there was Kung Chih, who had opposed him, standing on the wall.

"You brought defeat upon yourself because you opposed the will of God," cried the traitor. "I and the people with me are determined to yield to Liu Pei."

Just as he finished speaking an arrow wounded Chin Hsuan in the face and he fell to the ground. Thereupon his own men cut off his head, which they forthwith presented to Chang Fei. Kung Chih then went out and made formal submission and Chang Fei bade him take his letter and the seal to Kueiyang to Liu Pei, who was pleased to hear of Chang Fei's success and gave the prefectship to Kung Chih. Soon after Yuan-te came in person and soothed the people.

This done he wrote to his other brother telling him I-te and Tzu-lung had gained a district each. Kuan at once wrote back and said that Changsha was yet to be taken and if he was not thought too feeble he would like to be sent to attack it. Yuan-te agreed and sent Chang Fei to relieve his brother, whom he ordered to return and prepare for an expedition to Changsha. Kuan Yu came and went in to see his elder brother and K'ung-ming.

At this interview K'ung-ming said that the other two successful warriors had done their work with three companies. The Prefect of Changsha, Han Yuan, was not worth mentioning, but there was a certain general with him, named Huang Chung, who had to he reckoned with.

"Huang Chung," said K'ung-ming, "is a native of Nanyang. He used to be in the service of Liu Piao and was a colleague of Liu P'an, when he was in command of Changsha. After Liu Piao's death he joined Han Yuan when he took command of the district. Now, although he is nearly sixty he is a man to be feared and a warrior of a thousand. You ought to take a larger number of men."

Kuan Yu replied, "General, what makes you damp another man's ardour to fight and do away with your own dignity? I do not think the old leader need be discussed and I do not think I require three companies of men. Give me my own half company of swordsmen and I will have the heads of both our enemies to sacrifice to our standard."

Yuan-te resisted this decision of Kuan Yu, but Kuan would not give way. He just took his half company and set out.

"If he is not careful how he attacks Huang Chung there will be a mishap," said K'ung-ming. "You must go to support him."

Yuan-te accordingly, at the head of another and larger party, set out toward Changsha.

The Prefect of Changsha was of hasty temperament with small compunction in matters of life and death and was universally hated. When he heard of the army coming against him he called his veteran leader, Huang, to ask advice. The latter said, "Do not be distressed; this sword of mine and my bow are equal to the slaughter of all who may come."

Huang Chung had been very strong and could bend the two hundred catty bow and was a most perfect archer. When he referred to his one-time prowess a certain man spoke up and said, "Let not the old General go out to battle. Trust to my right arm and you shall have this Kuan a prisoner in your hands."

The speaker was named Yang Ling. The Prefect accepted his offer and told off a company to go with him and they quickly rode out of the city. About fifty *li* from the city they observed a great cloud of dust approaching and soon distinguished the invaders. Yang Ling set his spear and rode to the front to abuse and fight. Kuan Yu made no reply to the abuse, but rode forward flourishing his sword. The warriors soon met and in the third encounter Yang Ling was cut down. Kuan Yu's company dashed forward and pursued the defeated force to the city wall.

When the Prefect heard of this reverse he ordered the veteran Huang Chung to go out while he went up on the city wall to watch the fight.

Huang Chung took his sword and crossed the drawbridge at the head of his men. Kuan Yu, seeing an old leader riding out, knew it must be Huang Chung. He halted his men and placed them in line with their swords at the point. Then sitting there on horseback he said, "He who comes is surely Huang Chung, eh?"

"Since you know me, how dare you come within my boundaries?" replied the veteran.

"I have come expressly to get your head."

Then the combat began. They fought a hundred and more bouts and neither seemed nearer victory. At this point the Prefect, fearing some mishap to his veteran general, beat the gong to retreat and the battle ceased, one side going into the city and the other camping ten *li* away to the rear.

Kuan Yu thought in his heart that the fame of the veteran opposed to him was well merited. He had fought a hundred bouts and discovered never a weak spot. He determined that in the next encounter he would use a feint (or "Parthian" stab) and so overcome him.

Next day, the early meal eaten, Kuan Yu came to the city wall and offered his challenge. The Prefect seated himself on the city wall and bade his veteran warrior go out to accept it and, at the head of a few horsemen, he dashed across the drawbridge. The two champions engaged and at the end of half a hundred bouts neither had the advantage. On both sides the soldiers cheered lustily.

When the drums were beating most furiously, suddenly Kuan Yu wheeled round his horse and fled. Of course Huang Chung followed. Just as the moment for the feint arrived Kuan Yu heard behind him a tremendous crash and turned to see his pursuer lying prone upon the ground. His steed had stumbled and thrown him. Kuan Yu turned, raised his sword in both hands, and cried in a fierce tone, "I spare your life, but quick! get another horse and come again to battle."

Huang Chung pulled his horse to its feet hastily, leapt upon its back and went into the city at full speed. The prefect was astonished and asked for an account of the accident. "The horse is too old," replied Huang.

"Why did you not shoot since your arm is so perfect?" asked the Prefect.

"I will try again tomorrow," said Huang. "Then I will run away as if overcome and so tempt him to the drawbridge and then shoot him."

The Prefect gave the veteran a grey horse that he usually rode himself; Huang thanked him and retired.

But he could not forget Kuan Yu's generous conduct, nor could he understand it. He could not make up his mind to shoot the man who had spared his life. Yet if he did not shoot he betrayed his duty as a soldier. It was very perplexing and the whole night spent in thinking it over found him still undecided.

At daybreak a man came in saying that Kuan Yu was near the wall and challenging them again. So Huang Chung gave orders to go out.

Now Kuan Yu, having fought for two days and not having overcome Huang Chung, was very ill at ease. So he called up all his dignity when he went forth to fight that day. When they had got to the thirtieth bout Huang Chung fled as if he was overcome. Kuan Yu pursued.

As he rode away Huang Chung thought in his heart, "He spared me only yesterday and I cannot bear to shoot him today. Putting up his sword he took his bow and twanged the string only; no arrow flew. Kuan Yu dodged, but seeing no arrow in the air, he re-took the pursuit. Again Huang twanged an arrowless bowstring and again Kuan dodged, but no arrow came. Then he said to himself, "He cannot shoot," and pressed on in pursuit.

As they neared the city wall, the veteran stopped on the drawbridge, fitted an arrow, pulled the bow and sent an arrow flying that just hit the base of the plume on Kuan's helmet. The soldiers shouted at the display of marksmanship. Kuan Yu was taken aback and set off for camp with the arrow still sticking. Then he heard that Huang Chung's skill was said to be equal to piercing a willow leaf at a hundred paces and he understood that he owed this warning in the shape of an arrow in his plume to gratitude, for sparing the veteran the preceding day.

Both withdrew. But when the veteran leader went up on the wall to see the Prefect, he was at once seized. "What have I done?" cried Huang Chung.

"I have seen these last three days that you were fooling me; you were slack the day before yesterday, which proved you had some sinister intention. Yesterday, when your horse stumbled and he spared you, it showed that you were in league with him. And today you twice twanged a vain bowstring, while at the third shot you only hit your opponent's helmet. Dare you say there is no secret understanding in all this? If I do not put you to death it will assuredly redound to my own hurt."

The Prefect ordered him to be executed outside the city gate. The intercession of the officers he met by saying that any one who pleaded for the condemned would be regarded as in the plot.

The executioners had hustled the old man out of the city and the sword was in the air and on the point of descending, when a man suddenly dashed in, cut down the lictor and rescued Huang Chung.

"Huang Chung is our bulwark," shouted he, "to destroy him is to destroy the Changsha people. This Han is too fierce and cruel, too lightly values good men and is too arrogant toward his officers. We ought rather to kill him, and those who will, let them follow me."

All eyes turned toward this bold speaker, who was bronzed and had eyes like the Cowherd's star. Some of them knew him as Wei Yen, a native of Iyang. He had followed Liu Pei from Hsiangyang but, unable to come up with him, had gone into the service of Han Yuan. Han Yuan took exception to his arrogant carriage and lack of polish and neglected him. And so he had come to this place.

After the rescue of Huang Chung he called upon the people to make an end of the Prefect. He waved his arm and shouted to the people. Soon he had a following of several hundreds. Huang Chung could not stop them. In a very short time Wei had dashed up on the wall and the Prefect lay dead. Taking his head, Wei Yen rode off out of the city to lay the bloodstained trophy at the feet of Kuan Yu, who forthwith went into the city to restore confidence.

When the people were all quiet, Kuan sent to request Huang Chung to come to see him, but the old general pleaded illness. Next he sent the good news to his brother and to K'ung-ming and asked them to come.

Soon after Kuan Yu had left to capture Changsha, Liu Pei and K'ung-ming had followed him up with supports in case of need. While on the march a black flag was furled backwards and a crow flew over from north to south croaking thrice as it passed.

"What good or evil things do these omens presage?" asked Yuan-te.

With hands hidden within his long sleeves, K'ung-ming performed a rapid calculation on his fingers of the auspices and replied, "Changsha is taken and a great leader mastered. We shall know soon after noon."

Sure enough a simple soldier presently came galloping along with the welcome tidings of the capture of the city and saying that the two city warriors who had aided them were near waiting the arrival of Liu Pei. Soon after they arrived Liu Pei entered the city, where he was escorted to the magistracy and heard the recital of Huang Chung's deeds.

Yuan-te went in person to Huang's house and enquired for him, whereupon he came forth and yielded formally. He requested to be permitted to bury the remains of the late Prefect on the east of the city.

> Lofty as is heaven above earth was the spirit of the captain,
> Who, even in his old age, suffered sorrows in the south;
> Cheerfully had he approached death, with no thought of
>   resentment,
> But, bowing before the conquerer, he hung his head and was
>   ashamed.
> Praise the sword, gleaming snow-white, and the glory of super-
>   human bravery,

Consider the mail-clad steed snuffing the wind and rejoicing in the
    battle,
That warrior's name shall stand high and its brightness be
    undiminished,
While the cold moon sheds her light on the waters of Hsiang and
    T'an.

Yuan-te was generous toward the veteran leader who had come
under his banner. But when Wei Yen was introduced, K'ung-ming
suddenly ordered him to be thrust forth and put to death.

"He has merit; he has committed no fault," exclaimed Yuan-te.
"Why slay him?"

But K'ung-ming replied, "Ingratitude; to eat a man's bread and
slay him is most disloyal; to live on his land and offer his territory
to another is most wrong. I see the bone of treachery at the hack of
his head and he will certainly turn against his master. Wherefore it
is well to put him to death and prevent him from doing harm."

"If we slay this man others who may wish to surrender will be
deterred by the danger. I pray you forgive him."

K'ung-ming pointed his finger at Wei Yen and said, "You are
pardoned. You would do well to be perfectly faithful to your lord as
well as grateful. Do not let a single thought stray elsewhere or I will
have your head by fair means or foul."

Wei Yen went away muttering to himself.

Having given in with good grace, Huang Chung introduced a
nephew of Liu Piao, named P'an, then living in Yuhsien near by.
Yuan-te employed him in the administration of Changsha.

All being tranquil at Changsha, Yuan-te and his army returned
to Chingchou. The name Yuchiangk'ou was changed to Kungan
and soon all was prosperous. Taxes were freely paid and able men
from all sides came to assist in the administration. Guards were
placed at strategic points.

It is time to return to Chou Yu. When he went to Ch'aisang to
recover from his wound he left Kan Ning in command at Lingchun
and Ling T'ung at Hanyang. The fleet was shared between these
two places to be ready to move when required. The remainder of
the force was under Ch'eng P'u and he went to Hofei, where Sun
Ch'uan had been since the fight at Red Wall. He was still fighting
the northern army and in half a score encounters, small and great,
neither had gained a decided advantage. He could not approach
the city but entrenched himself about fifty *li* away.

When he heard of the coming of reinforcements he was very
pleased and went in person to meet and welcome the leaders. Lu Su

was in advance of the main body and Sun Ch'uan dismounted and stood by the roadside to greet him. As soon as he saw this, Lu Su slid out of the saddle and made his obeisance.

But the officers were amazed at the attitude of Sun Ch'uan, and still more so when Sun Ch'uan asked Lu Su to remount and ride by his side. Presently he said secretly to Lu Su, "I, the Lone One, dismounted to greet you as you saw; was that manifestation enough for you?"

"No," replied Lu Su.

"Then what further can I do?"

"I want to see your authority and virtue spread over the four seas and enfold the nine provinces and you yourself playing your part as Emperor. Then will my name be inscribed in the annals and I shall indeed be known."

Sun Ch'uan clapped his hands and laughed gleefully.

When they reached the camp a banquet was prepared and the services of the new arrivals were praised and glorified.

The destruction of Hofei was one day under discussion when one came in to say that Chang Liao had sent a written challenge to battle. Sun Ch'uan tore open the cover and what he read therein made him very wrath. "This Chang has insulted me grossly," said he, "he hears that Ch'eng P'u has arrived and sends a challenge. Tomorrow, O newly-come warriors, you shall see me fight with him. You shall have no share in the battle."

Orders were given that next morning the army would move out of camp and advance on Hofei. Early in the morning, when they had advanced about halfway, they met the army of Ts'ao and prepared for battle. Sun Ch'uan, with helmet and breastplate of silver, rode to the front with Sung Ch'ien and Chia Hua, each armed with a *ch'i* halberd to support him and guard him one on each side.

When the third roll of the drum ceased, the centre of the Ts'ao array opened to allow the exit of three warriors, all fully armed. They were Chang Liao, supported by Li Tien and Yo Chin. Chang Liao, the central figure, especially designated Sun Ch'uan as the object of his challenge. Sun Ch'uan took his spear and was about to accept the challenge, when the ranks behind him were broken by T'aishih Tzu, who galloped forth with his spear ready to thrust. Chang Liao whirled up his sword to strike the newcomer and the two fought near a hundred bouts without a decisive blow.

Then said Li Tien to Yo Chin, "He there opposite us with the silver helm is Sun Ch'uan; could I but capture him the loss of our four score legions would be amply avenged."

So speaking he rode out, alone, just one man and one sword, and went sidelong toward the two combatants. Then suddenly, swift as a flash of lightning, he ran forward and slashed at Sun. But Sun Ch'uan's two guards were too quick for him. Up went the two *ch'i* guarding their lord's head. The blow fell, but on the crossed *ch'i* which were shorn through near the head, and in another moment they were hammering away on the head of Yo Chin's steed with the shafts of their broken weapons and forcing him back.

Sung Ch'ien snatched a spear from a soldier near and went in pursuit of Yo Chin, but Li Tien, on the other side, fitted an arrow to his bow and aimed at Sung's heart from behind. And he fell as the bowstring twanged.

Then T'aishih Tzu, seeing a squadron of horse in motion toward him, left off the fight with Chang Liao and returned to his own line. At this Chang Liao fell on in a swift attack and the army of Wu, thrown into confusion, scattered and fled.

Chang Liao, having distinguished Sun Ch'uan in the distance, galloped in pursuit and had nearly come up with him, when Ch'eng P'u happily rushed in from one side of the line of fight, stayed the pursuit and saved his master, Chang Liao withdrew to Hofei. Sun Ch'uan was escorted back to his main camp, where his beaten soldiers gradually rejoined him and their ranks were reformed.

When Sun knew of the death of Sung Ch'ien he was greatly pained and wept aloud.

But Chang Hung, the recorder, reproached him saying, "My lord, you relied too much upon your martial prowess and lightly engaged in battle with a formidable enemy. Every man in the army was chilled with fear and you lost a general and some of your banners. It is not for you to exhibit prowess on the actual battlefield and encroach upon the duties of a captain. Rather curb and repress such physical feats as those of Meng Pen and Hsia Yu and contemplate schemes of exercising princely virtues with the hegemony of all the feudal states. It is because of your ill-regulated action in engaging in battle that Sung Ch'ien perished at the hands of your enemies. Hereafter you should regard as most important your personal safety."

"Yes; it is indeed a fault," said Sun Ch'uan. "I will reform."

Soon after T'aishih Tzu entered the tent and said, "In my command there is a certain Ko Ting, brother of a groom named Hou Ts'ao in the army of Chang Liao. This Hou Ts'ao is deeply resentful on account of a punishment inflicted upon him and is anxious to be revenged. He has sent over to say that he will show a signal tonight when he has assassinated Chang Liao in revenge for the death of your late leader Sung Ch'ien. I wish to take some men over to await this signal to attack."

"Where is this Ko Ting?" asked Sun Ch'uan.

"He has mingled with the enemy and gone into the city. Let me have five companies."

Chuko Ching said, "Chang Liao is full of guile, I think you will find him prepared for your coming. Be careful."

As T'aishih Tzu urged his chief to let him go, and Sun Ch'uan was deeply hurt by the death of his captain, the permission was given and the force started.

Now here it must be said that T'aishih Tzu and this Ko Ting were natives of the same place. Ko had made his way into the city without detection, found his brother and the two had arranged their plot. Ko also told him that T'aishih Tzu would come over that night to help them and asked what they should do.

His brother, the groom, said, "As the men of Wu are far away I fear they cannot be here tonight, so we will make a huge bonfire of straw and then you can rush out and cry treachery. That will throw all into confusion and will give a chance to kill Chang Liao."

"This is an excellent plan," said Ko Ting.

Now after the victory Chang Liao returned to the city and rewarded his men but he issued orders that no one was to doff his armour or sleep. His attendants said, "You have gained a great victory today and the enemy are far away. You might doff your armour and get some repose."

But Chang Liao replied, "That is not the way of a leader. A victory is no reason for rejoicing, nor should a defeat cause sadness. If the men of Wu suspect that I am unprepared, they will attack and we must be ready to repel them. Be ready tonight and be doubly careful."

Scarcely had he said this than a fire started and cries of "Treachery!" arose. Many rushed to tell the leader, who went out and called together his guard of about half a score. They took up a commanding position in the way.

Those about him said, "The shouts are insistent; you ought to go and see what it means."

"A whole city cannot be traitors," said he. "Some discontented person has frightened the soldiers. If I see any one doing so I will slay him."

Soon after this Li Tien dragged up Ko Ting and his fellow-traitor. After a few brief questions they were beheaded. Then arose a great noise, shouting and the rolling of drums was heard outside the gate.

"That means the men of Wu are there to help," said Chang Liao. "But we will destroy them by a simple ruse."

He bade them light torches and yell "Treachery! Rebellion!" and throw open the city gates and let down the drawbridge.

When T'aishih Tzu saw the gates swing open he thought his scheme was going well and in full confidence rode in at the gate But just at the entrance a signal bomb suddenly exploded and the enemy arrows came down on him like pelting rain. Then he knew he had fallen into a snare and turned to ride out. But he was wounded in many places. And in the pursuit that followed more than half the men of Wu were cut off. As he drew near his own lines a rescue force came to his aid and the Ts'ao soldiers ceased from pursuit.

Sun Ch'uan was exceedingly sad when he learned that his faithful captain had been grievously wounded and when Chang Chao prayed him to cease from war he was content. They gathered in their men to their ships and sailed to Nanhsu and Junchou where they camped.

Meanwhile T'aishih Tzu was dying. When his lord sent to ask how he fared, he cried, "When a worthy man is born into a turbulent world, he has to be a soldier and gird on a three feet sword. I have not rendered great service. Why must I die before I have attained my desire?"

These were his last words; he was forty-one years of age.

> Single minded and perfectly loyal,
> Such was T'aishih, in Tunglai born,
> Far distant frontiers rang with his exploits,
> Riding or archery, all men he excelled,
> One in Pohai who admired his valour
> Cared for his mother while he was fighting,
> How he joyed in the battle at Shent'ing!
> Dying, he spake as a hero;
> All through the ages men sigh for his fate.

Sun Ch'uan was exceedingly grieved when this second of his leaders died. He gave orders to bury his remains most honourably outside the north wall on Ku Hill and took his son, T'aishih Hsiang, into his own palace to be brought up.

When Yuan-te heard of the series of misfortunes that had befallen Wu and of their retirement to Nanhsu, he and K'ung-ming discussed their plans. Said K'ung-ming, "I was studying the sky and saw a falling star in the north-west. The Imperial family is to suffer a loss."

He had scarcely said this when they brought news of the death of Liu Ch'i, son of Liu Piao.

Yuan-te at once began to wail bitterly. But his adviser said to him, "Life and death are beyond our control, wherefore weep not, my lord, for grief harms the body. Rather consider what is necessary to be done. Send some one to assume control and make arrangements for the interment."

"Who can go?" asked Yuan-te.

"No other than Kuan Yu."

So they sent him to guard the city of Hsiangyang.

Liu Pei at once began to feel troubled about his promise to surrender Chingchou on the death of Liu Ch'i, but K'ung-ming did not consider this a matter of moment. He said he would have somewhat to say to any one who came to ask fulfilment of the promise. In half a month it was announced that Lu Su would come to mourn at the funeral.

> To claim the promise one will come,
> But they will send him empty home.

What reply K'ung-ming made may be read in the next chapter.

CHAPTER LIV

THE DOWAGER MARCHIONESS SEES HER
SON-IN-LAW AT A TEMPLE: LIU, THE
IMPERIAL UNCLE, TAKES A WORTHY CONSORT

Yuan-te and K'ung-ming went out of the city to welcome the envoy of Wu and led him to the guest-house. After the usual greetings, Lu Su said, "Hearing of the death of your nephew, my lord has prepared some gifts and sent me to take his place at the funeral sacrifices. General Chou Yu also sends greetings to the Imperial Uncle and to you, Master Chuko."

Both rose at once and thanked him for the courtesy. Then the gifts were handed over and a banquet prepared, and while it was in progress, the guest brought up the real object of his visit.

"You said, Sir, that Chingchou should be returned to us after the death of Liu Ch'i. Now that that event has happened rendition becomes due and I should be glad to know when the transfer can take place."

"We will discuss that later; in the meantime let us go on with our wine," said Yuan-te.

So the feasting continued. Some time later Lu Su returned to the subject, but this time his host remained silent. However, K'ung-ming, changing colour, said, "Tzu-ching, you are unreasonable. You should have waited till some other spoke of this matter. From the very foundation of the empire by our illustrious ancestor the great heritage has descended in due course till today when, unhappily, evil doers have risen among the powerful and they have seized upon such portions as they could. But with God's favour and help unity is nearly restored. My lord is a scion of the Imperial house, a great great grandson of the Emperor Hsiao-Ching. Now, as the Emperor's Uncle, should he not have a share of the Empire? Moreover, Liu Ching-hsing (Liu Piao) was my lord's elder brother and there is certainly nothing extraordinary in one brother's succession to another's estate. What is your master? The son of a petty official on the banks of the Ch'ient'ang River, absolutely without merit so far as the State is concerned. Just because he is powerful he holds actual possession of a certain amount of territory, which has whetted his insatiable appetite till he now desires to swallow the whole country. The land is the estate of the Liu family and my lord, who is of that name, has no share thereof, while your master, whose name is Sun, would dispute with, and even fight him. Beside, at the battle at Ch'ihpi (Red Wall) my lord did good service and acquired great merit while his captains risked their lives. Was it solely the strength of your men of Wu that won that fight? Had I not brought that south-east wind that meant so much for Chou Yu, could he have done anything? Had Chiangnan been conquered, it is needless to say that two beauties you wot of would now be gracing the Bronze Bird Palace, and as for yourself, insignificant though your family be, could you have been sure to survive? Just now my lord did not reply because he was willing to believe rather that a scholar of your abilities would understand without a detailed explanation, and I trust now that you will."

This speech absolutely shut the guest's mouth for a time and he said no word in reply. But after an interval he said, "What you say, K'ung-ming, I think is devoid of reason, and means much unpleasantness for me."

"What unpleasantness?" asked K'ung-ming.

The guest replied, "When Liu Pei was in serious straits at Tangyang I conducted you across the river and introduced you to my lord. I opposed Chou Yu when he was going to capture Chingchou, and then it came about that the place was to be ours when the young man died. And I pledged myself to that. Now how can I go back and say you break your promise? Both my lord and Chou Yu will hold me guilty. I would not mind death so much, but I fear that my master will be very wrathful and make war on the Imperial Uncle, who will have no place of refuge and he will look ridiculous in the eyes of the world for no reason."

Replied K'ung-ming, "I care not for Ts'ao Ts'ao with his hundred legions and the Emperor in name at his back, and do you think I fear such a youngster as your Chou Yu? However, as it may cause you some loss of consideration I will try to persuade my master to put the matter in writing and give you a paper to the effect that he is temporarily occupying Chingchou as a base and when he can obtain possession of some other city this shall be returned to you. What think you Wu would say to this?"

"Wait till what other place was obtained?" said Lu Su.

"My master can scarcely think of attacking the capital yet, but

Liu Chang in Ssuch'uan is ignorant and weak and my master will attack him. If he get the western province then this place will be given up to you."

Lu Su had no alternative and accepted the offer. Yuan-te with his own hand wrote the pledge and sealed it. Chuko K'ung-ming being named as guarantor also signed the document.

"Since I belong to this side of the compact and one can hardly have a guarantor of the same party I would trouble you, Tzuching, also to sign. It will look better when you reach Wu again," said K'ung-ming.

Lu Su said, "I know that your master is perfectly honourable and will adhere to the bargain."

And so he signed. Then he received the document in formal style and took his departure. He was sent off with every mark of great respect, both Yuan-te and K'ung-ming attending him to his boat. There the adviser delivered him a last exhortation, "When you see your master, speak discreetly and explain fully so as not to create a bad impression. If he reject our document we may get angry and we will take his whole country. The one thing now is for our two houses to live in harmony and not give our common enemy an opportunity against us."

Lu Su went down into his ship. He reached Ch'aisang and there saw Chou Yu, who said, "Well, how did you speed with your demand for Chingchou?"

"Here is the document," said Lu Su, giving it to Chou Yu to read.

"You have been victimised by Chuko," said Chou, stamping his foot with irritation. "In name it may be temporary occupation but in fact it is humbug. They say the place is to be returned when they get the west. Who knows when that will be? Suppose ten years; then it will be ten years before they give us Chingchou. What is the use of such a document as this? And you are a guarantor of its due performance! If they do not give us the city, you get into trouble. Suppose our lord finds you in the wrong, what then?"

Lu Su was dumbfounded. When he had somewhat recovered his self-possession, he said, "I think Yuan-te will be true to me."

"You, my friend, are simple and sincere; Liu Pei is a scoundrelly adventurer; and Chuko Liang is a slippery customer. They and you are utterly different."

"What then is to be done?" cried Lu Su distressfully.

"You are my dear friend and your kindness in freely offering your store of grain to relieve my necessity is still fresh in my memory. Of course I will save you. Do not be anxious, but wait a few days till we get news of what is doing on the north of the river and then we can decide upon a plan."

Lu Su passed some very uneasy days. Then the scouts came back saying that in Chingchou everything seemed in excellent order and the flags were flying everywhere, while outside the city they were building a magnificent mausoleum for the Lady Kan, wife of Liu Pei. All the soldiers were in mourning.

When Chou Yu knew who was dead, he said to his friend, "My scheme is made. You will see Liu Pei just stand still to be bound and we shall get Chingchou like turning a hand."

"What is the main-spring of your plan?" said Lu Su.

"Liu Pei will want to re-marry and our lord has a sister. She is a veritable amazon, whose women guards number many hundreds, all armed with weapons of war. Her apartments also are full of such things. I will write to our lord to send an intermediary to arrange that the lady shall wed Liu Pei at her family home and thus we shall entice him to Nanhsu. But instead of marrying a wife, he will find himself a prisoner, and then we will demand Chingchou as ransom. When they have handed over the city I shall find something else to say and nothing will fall on your head."

Lu Su was very grateful. Then Chou Yu wrote letters to his master and a swift boat was chosen to take Lu Su to see the Marquis of Wu.

After the lending of Chingchou had been discussed, Lu Su presented the document given him by Liu Pei. "What is the use of such nonsense as this?" said Sun Ch'uan, when he had read it.

"There is another letter from General Chou and he says that if you will employ his scheme you can recover Chingchou," replied Lu.

Having read that letter the Marquis was more pleased and began to consider who was the best man to send. Suddenly he cried, "I have it; Lu Fan is the man to send."

He called Lu Fan and said to him, "I have just heard that Liu Yuan-te has lost his wife. I have a sister whom I should like to marry to him and so make a bond of union between our two houses. Thus we should be united against Ts'ao and in support of the House of Han. You are the one man to be intermediary and I hope you will go to Chingchou and see to this."

Under these orders Lu Fan at once began to prepare his ships for the voyage and soon started.

Yuan-te was greatly distressed at the death of the Lady Kan, fretting for her day and night. One day when he was talking with his adviser they announced the arrival of Lu Fan. He had come on a mission from Wu.

"One of Chou Yu's devices," said the adviser smiling, "and it is all on account of this city. I will just retire behind the screen and listen. But you, my lord, agree to whatever the messenger proposes. Then let the messenger be taken to the guest-house while we arrange what is to be done."

So the envoy was introduced. Bows having been exchanged, host and guest being seated in due order and the tea drunk, Yuan-te opened the interview.

"You must have some commands for me, Sir, since you come thus."

"News has just been received that you, O Imperial Uncle, have just been bereaved of your consort. I venture to hope you would not object to an advantageous match and I have come to propose one. Are you disposed to listen?"

"To lose one's wife in middle age is truly a great misfortune," said Liu Pei. "While her body is still warm I cannot listen to proposals for another marriage."

Lu Fan said, "A man without a wife is like a house without a ridge pole. At your age one should not live an incomplete life. I am come on the part of the Marquis of Wu, who has a sister, beautiful as she is accomplished and well fitted to be a mate for you. Should the two families become allied as formerly were Ts'in and Chin, then that ruffian Ts'ao would never dare so much as look this way. Such an alliance would be to the benefit of both our houses and of the State. I hope, O Imperial Uncle, that you will fairly consider the proposal. However, since the young girl's mother is dotingly fond of her she does not wish her to go far away, and so I must ask you to come into our country for the wedding."

"Does the Marquis know of your coming?"

"How dare I come without his knowledge?"

"I am no longer young," said Liu Pei. "I am fifty and grizzled. This fair damsel, the sister of the Marquis, is now in the flower of her youth and no mate for me."

"Although the damsel is a woman yet in mind she surpasses many a man, and she has said she will never wed any one who is unknown to fame. Now, Sir, you are renowned throughout the four seas. Marriage with you would be the chaste maiden mating with the born gentleman. Of what consequence is the difference in age?"

"Sir, stay here awhile and I will give you a reply tomorrow," said Liu Pei.

So that day the envoy was entertained at a banquet and then conducted to the guest house to repose, while, late as it was, Yuan-te and K'ung-ming discussed their plans.

"I knew what he had come about," said the adviser. "While he was talking I consulted the oracle and obtained an excellent sortilege. Wherefore you may accept the proposal and send Sun Ch'ien back with this envoy to arrange the details. When the promise has been ratified we will choose a day and you shall go to complete the ceremony."

"How can I thus go into enemy territory? Chou Yu has wanted to slay me for a long time."

"Let Chou Yu employ all his ruses; think you he can get beyond me? Let me act for you and his calculations will always fail halfway. Once Sun Ch'uan's sister is in your power there will be no fear for Chingchou."

Still Yuan-te doubted in his mind. However, the messenger was sent to Wu, with definite instructions, and travelled thither with Lu Fan. At the interview Sun Ch'uan said, "I wish my sister could induce Yuan-te to live here with us. He would come to no harm."

Sun Ch'ien took his leave, and returning to Chingchou he told the bridegroom elect that Sun Ch'uan's sole desire was for him to go over and complete the marriage.

However, Yuan-te feared and would not go. K'ung-ming said he had prepared three plans but they needed Chao Tzu-lung to carry them out. Wherefore he must go as guard. So he called in Chao Yun, gave him three silken bags and whispered in his ear saying, "Here are three schemes enclosed in three bags. When you escort our lord to Wu you will take these with you and act as they direct."

Chao Yun hid the three silken bags in his breast so that they should be at hand when required.

K'ung-ming next sent the wedding gifts, and when these had been received the preliminaries were settled.

It was then the early winter of the fourteenth year of "Established Tranquillity" (209 A.D.) and the bridegroom elect, his escort and the intermediary, left Chingchou with a fleet of ten fast ships to sail down the river to Nanhsu. K'ung-ming remained to guard and rule the City.

But Liu Pei was far from feeling comfortable. They arrived and the ships were made fast. This done the time had come for the first of the silken bags to be opened. And so it was; and thereupon Chao Yun gave each of the soldiers of his half company his instructions and they went their several ways. Next he told Liu Pei what he was to do; that he was to pay his visit first to Ch'iao "*Kuo-lao*," who was the father-in-law of Sun Ts'e and of Chou Yu. He resided in Nanhsu and to his house, "leading sheep and bearing wine jars," went the bridegroom elect. Having made his obeisance he explained that as Lu Fan had arranged he had come to marry a wife.

In the meantime the half company of the escort, all in gala dress, had scattered over the town buying all sorts of things, as they said, for the wedding of Liu Pei with the daughter of the House of Wu. They spread the news far and wide and the whole town talked about it.

When Sun Ch'uan heard of Yuan-te's arrival he bade Lu Fan wait upon him and take him to the guest-house. Meanwhile Ch'iao *Kuo-lao* went to the Dowager of Wu, mother of Sun Ch'uan, to congratulate her on the happy event.

"What happy event?" ejaculated the old lady.

"The betrothal of your beloved daughter to Yuan-te. And he has arrived too, as surely you know."

"My poor old self does not know," said the Dowager, "I have heard nothing of all this."

She at once summoned her son and also sent her servants out into the town to see what was going about. They quickly returned to say that the whole town knew of the coming wedding, and the bridegroom was then at the guest-house. Moreover, he had come with a large escort and the men were spending freely, buying pork and mutton and fruits, all in readiness for the wedding feasting. They also told her the names of the intermediaries on each side, and said they were in the guest-house too.

The Dowager was terribly taken aback and upset so that, when Sun Ch'uan arrived, he found his mother beating her breast and weeping bitterly.

"What has disturbed you, mother?" asked he.

"What you have just done," said she. "You have treated me as a nonentity. When my elder sister lay dying, what did she tell you?"

Sun Ch'uan began to be frightened, but he said boldly, "Please speak out plainly, mother; what is this great sorrow?"

"When a son is grown he takes a wife, and when a girl is old enough she goes to her husband. And that is right and proper. But I am the mother and you ought to have told me that your sister was to become the wife of Liu Pei. Why did you keep me in the dark? It was my place to promise her in marriage."

"Whence comes this story?" said the Marquis, really much frightened.

"Do you pretend ignorance? There is not a soul in the city who does not know! But you have succeeded in keeping me in the dark."

"I heard it several days ago," said Ch'iao. "And I came just now, to offer my felicitations."

"There is no such thing," said Sun. "It is just one of the ruses of Chou Yu to get hold of Chingchou. He has used this means to inveigle Liu Pei here and hold him captive till Chingchou is restored to us. And if they will not give it back, then Liu Pei will be put to death. That is the plot. There is no real marriage."

But the Dowager was in a rage and vented her wrath in abusing Chou Yu. "He is a pretty sort of a governor over the eighty-one districts if he cannot find any means of recovering one city except making use of my child as a decoy. Truly this is a fine deed, to spoil the whole of my child's life and condemn her to perpetual widowhood because he wants to use the fair damsel ruse to slay a man! Who will ever come to talk of marriage with her after this?"

Said Ch'iao *Kuo-lao*, "By this means you may indeed recover Chingchou but you will be a shameful laughing stock to all the world. What can be done?"

Sun Ch'uan had nothing to say; he could only hang his head, while the Dowager abused his general.

Ch'iao tried to soothe her. "After all Liu, the Imperial Uncle, is a scion of the reigning family. You can do nothing better now than to welcome him as a son-in-law and not let this ugly story get abroad."

"I am afraid their ages do not match," interposed Sun Ch'uan.

"Liu is a very famous man," said Ch'iao. "There can be no shame in having such a son-in-law."

"I have never seen him," said the Dowager. "Arrange that I may get a look at him tomorrow at the Gentle Dew Temple. If he displeases me, you may work your will on him. But if I am satisfied with him then I shall simply let the girl marry him."

Now Sun Ch'uan was above all things filial and at once agreed to what his mother said. He went out, called in Lu Fan and told him to arrange a banquet for the morrow at the temple so that the Dowager might see the bridegroom.

"Why not order Chia Hua to station some men in the wings of the temple? Then if the Dowager be not pleased we can call them out and fall upon him," said Lu Fan.

Accordingly the ambush was prepared and ruffians posted to act as the Dowager's attitude might determine.

When Ch'iao took his leave and had reached his house, he sent to tell Yuan-te that on the morrow the Dowager wished to see him and she was well disposed.

Yuan-te and his faithful henchman discussed their plans. Chao
Yun said, "The morrow bodes rather ill than well. However, the
escort shall be there."

Next day the Dowager and Ch'iao went to the Temple of Gentle
Dew as had been arranged. Sun Ch'uan came with a number of his
strategists, and when all were assembled Lu Fan was sent to the
guest house to request Yuan-te to come. He obeyed the summons,
but as a precaution he put on a light coat of mail under his brocaded
robe. His followers too took their swords upon their backs and
followed close. He mounted his steed and the cavalcade set out for
the temple. At the door of the temple he met Sun Ch'uan on whom
the visitor's brave demeanour was not lost. After they had
exchanged salutations, Sun led Liu Pei into the presence of his
mother.

"Just the son-in-law for me!" said the Dowager delighted with
the appearance of Liu Pei.

"He has the air of an emperor and a look like the sun," remarked
Ch'iao. "When one remembers also that his fair fame has spread
over the whole earth, you may well be congratulated on getting
such a noble son-in-law."

Liu Pei bowed, in acknowledgment of his reception. Soon after
they were all seated at the banquet in the temple, Chao Yun entered
and took his place beside Yuan-te.

"Who is this?" asked the Dowager.

This is Chao Yun of Ch'angshan."

"Then he must be the hero of Tangyang Slope, who saved the
little O-tou."

"Yes; this is he," replied Yuan-te.

"A fine captain!" said the Dowager, and she gave him wine.

Presently Chao Yun said to his master, "I have seen a lot of
armed ruffians hidden away in the purlieus of the temple. They can
be there for no good and you should ask the Dowager to get them
sent away."

Thereupon Liu Pei knelt at the feet of the Dowager and,
weeping, said, "If you would slay me, let it be here."

"Why do you say this?" asked she.

"Because there are assassins in hiding in the wings of the temple;
what are they there for if not to kill me?"

The Dowager wrathfully turned on Sun Ch'uan. "What are
armed men doing there today when Yuan-te is to become my son-
in-law and the pair are my son and daughter?"

Sun Ch'uan said he did not know and sent Lu Fan to enquire. Lu
Fan put the blame on Chia Hua. The Dowager summoned him and

upbraided him severely. He had nothing to say and she told them to put him to death. But Yuan-te interceded saying that it would do him harm and make it hard for him to stay at her side.

Ch'iao *Kuo-lao* also interceded and she only ordered the captain out of her presence. His men also scattered and ran like frightened rats.

By and bye, strolling out of the banquet room into the temple grounds, Yuan-te came to a boulder. Drawing his sword he looked up to heaven and prayed saying, "If I am to return to Chingchou and achieve my intent to become a chief ruler, then may I cleave this boulder asunder with my sword, but if I am to meet my doom in this place then may the sword fail to cut this stone."

Raising his sword he smote the boulder. Sparks flew in all directions; and the boulder lay creft in twain.

It happened that Sun Ch'uan had seen the blow and he said, "Why do you thus hate that stone?"

Yuan-te replied, "I am near my fifth decade and have so far failed to rid the State of evil; I greatly regret my failure. Now I have been accepted by the Dowager as her son-in-law, and this is a critical moment in my life. So I implored of Heaven a portent that I might destroy Ts'ao as I would that boulder and restore the dynasty. You saw what happened."

"That is only to blind me," thought Sun. Drawing his own sword he said, "And I also ask of Heaven an omen, that if I am to destroy Ts'ao I may also cut this rock."

So he spoke. But in his secret heart he prayed "If I am to recover Chingchou and extend my borders, may the stone be cut in twain."

He smote the stone and it split in twain. And to this day there are cross cuts in the stone, which is still preserved.

One who saw this relic wrote a poem:—

> The shining blades fell and the rock was shorn through,
> The metal rang clear and the sparks widely flew.
> Thus fate then declared for the dynasties two
> And the tripartite rule there began.

Both put up their swords and returned hand in hand to the banquet hall. After some more courses Sun Ch'uan gave his master a warning look and Liu Pei said, "I pray you to excuse me as my drinking powers are very small." Wherefore Sun Ch'uan escorted him to the gate. As they walked down looking at high land and rolling river spreading in glorious panorama before their eyes, Yuan-te exclaimed, "Really this is the finest scene in the whole world!"

These words are recorded on a tablet in the Temple of the Gentle Dew and one who read them wrote a poem:—

> From the river-side hills the rain clears off,
>> And the black clouds roll away,
> And this is the place of joy and mirth
>> And never can sorrow stay.
> And here two heroes of ages past
>> Decided their parts to play,
> And the lofty heights flung back wind and wave
>> Then, as they do today.

Yes, they stood both entranced by the beautiful scene. And gradually along the vast river the wind whipped the waves into snowy foam and raised them high toward heaven. And in the midst of the waves appeared a tiny leaf of a boat riding over the waves as if all was perfect calm.

"The southern people are sailors and the northern men riders; it is quite true," sighed Liu Pei.

Sun Ch'uan hearing this remark took it as a reproach to his horsemanship. Bidding his servants lead up his steed he leaped into the saddle and set off, full gallop, down the hill. Then wheeling he came up again at the same speed.

"So the southerners cannot ride, eh?" said he laughing.

Not to be outdone Liu Pei lifted the skirts of his robe, jumped upon his horse and repeated the feat.

The two steeds stood side by side on the declivity, the riders flourishing their whips and laughing.

Thence forward that hillside was known as the "Slope where the Horses Stood" and a poem was written about it.

> Their galloping steeds were of noble breed,
>> And both of spirit high,
> And the riders twain from the hill-crest gazed
>> At the river rolling by.
> One of them mastered the far off west,
>> One ruled by the eastern sea;
> And the name of the hill to this very day
>> Brings back their memory.

When they rode side by side into Nanhsu the people met them with acclamations. Yuan-te made his way to the guest-house and there sought advice from Sun Ch'ien as to the date of the wedding. Sun Ch'ien advised that it be fixed as early as possible so that no further complications could arise. So next day Yuan-te went to

Ch'iao "*Kuo-lao*" and told him in plain words that it was clear the people of the place meant harm to him and he could not stay there long. He must return soon.

"Do not be anxious," said Ch'iao. "I will tell the Dowager and she will protect you."

He saw the Dowager and she was very angry when she heard the reason for Liu Pei's desire to leave.

"Who would dare harm my son-in-law?" cried she.

But she made him move into the library of the Palace as a precaution and she chose a day for the celebration of the wedding. But his soldiers could not keep guard at the library. Yuan-te explained to his hostess and when she understood this she gave her son-in-law rooms in her own Palace so that he might be quite safe.

Yuan-te was very happy and there were fine banquets and the bride and bridegroom duly plighted their troth. And when it grew late and the guests had gone the newly wedded pair walked through the two lines of red torches to the nuptial apartment.

To his extreme surprise Yuan-te found the chambers furnished with spears and swords and banners and flags, while every waiting-maid had girded on a sword.

> Walls hung with spears the bridegroom saw,
> And armed waiting-maids;
> His heart fell back on all its fears
> Of well-laid ambuscades.

What happened will be related in the next chapter.

CHAPTER LV

YUAN-TE ROUSES THE SPIRIT OF HIS BRIDE:
K'UNG-MING A SECOND TIME ANGERS
HIS RIVAL

The bridegroom turned pale; bridal apartments lined with weapons of war and waiting maids armed! But the housekeeper said, "Do not be frightened, O honourable one. My lady has always had a taste for warlike things and her maids have all been taught fencing as a pastime. That is all it is."

"Not the sort of thing a wife should ever look at," said Liu Pei. "It makes me feel cold and you may have them removed for a time."

The housekeeper went to her mistress and said, "The weapons in your chamber displease the handsome one; may we remove them?"

The Lady Sun laughed, saying, "Afraid of a few weapons after half a life time spent in slaughter!"

But she ordered their removal and bade the maids take off their swords while they were at work. And the night passed happily enough.

Next day Yuan-te distributed gifts among the maids to secure their good will. He also sent Sun Ch'ien to Chingchou with news of the wedding, while he gave himself up to feasting and enjoyment. The Dowager loved him more every day.

The results of the plot to destroy Liu Pei were thus very different from the originators' intention. Sun Ch'uan sent to his general to say that his mother had insisted upon marrying her daughter to their proposed victim and so by juggling with the fictitious they had made it real. What was to be done?

The news troubled Chou Yu, but eventually he thought out another scheme which he embodied in a letter sent to his master. Here is the outline of the missive:—"Contrary to expectation the plot that I, Chou Yu, contrived has turned the wrong way.

However, since by juggling with deceit we have ended in a solid truth our future plans must start from the actual present facts. To the boldness of the adventurer is added the aid of such great captains as Kuan, Chang and Chao Yun, not to mention that Liu Pei has a strategist like Chuko. He is not the man to remain long in a lowly position. Wherefore I can think of no better plan than to enervate him by surrounding him with softness and keeping him in Wu, a prisoner of luxury. Therefore build for him a fine Palace to blunt the edge of his determination and surround him with sensuous luxury. In this way the affection of his brothers will be alienated and Chuko will be driven away. When this result has been attained we can smite him and so end a great matter. If we be at all careless I fear the recumbent dragon may fly to the skies; it is no beast to be kept in a pond.

"My lord, I pray you to consider this thoroughly."

The letter was shown to Chang Chao who said, "My idea is identical with his. Liu Pei began life in a humble position and for years has been a wanderer. He has never tasted the delights of wealth. Give him the means of luxury, a beautiful dwelling, fair women, gold and silken attire, and as he enjoys them the thoughts of K'ung-ming and his brothers will fade away and they, on their side, will be filled with rancour. Thus can we lay our plans for recovering Chingchou. I recommend action as Chou Yu says and quickly."

Sun Ch'uan then set about re-decorating the eastern Palace and laying out the grounds. He filled the rooms with beautiful furniture for his sister and her husband. He also sent fair damsels and musicians by the score, and many and beautiful vessels in gold and silver, and silken stuffs. And his mother was delighted at his kindness to her son-in-law.

Indeed Liu Pei was soon so immersed in sensuous pleasure that he gave no thought to return. Chao Yun and the company under him led an idle life in the front portion of the eastern Palace, save that at times they went outside the city for archery and horse-racing. And thus passed the year.

Suddenly Chao Yun remembered the orders he had received and the three bags with the plans in them. It was time to open the second one for the end of the year was nigh. His orders were only to open the third when danger was very near and there appeared no way out.

As already remarked, the year was drawing to a close and Chao Yun saw his lord daily becoming more and more the slave of pleasure. Liu Pei never appeared among his guards now. So the bag was opened and in pursuance of the wonderful scheme thereby discovered, Chao Yun went to the hall of the Palace and asked to see his master. The maid in attendance went within and said, "Chao Yun has some important matter on which to see the master."

Yuan-te called him in and asked what the business was. Chao Yun assumed an attitude of great concern and said, "My lord, you are living happily secluded in these beautiful apartments; do you never think of Chingchou?"

"But what is the matter that you seem so disturbed?" asked Liu.

"Today early K'ung-ming sent a messenger to say that Ts'ao Ts'ao was trying to avenge his last defeat and was leading fifty legions to attack Chingchou, which was in great danger. And he wished you to return."

"I must speak to my wife," said Yuan-te.

"If you consult her she will be unwilling for you to return. It would be better to say nothing but to start this evening. Delay may do great damage."

"Retire for a time; I must act discreetly," said Liu Pei.

Chao Yun urged the need to return several times more, but finally went away.

Yuan-te went into his wife's rooms and began to weep silently. Seeing his tears the Lady Sun said, "Why are you so sad, my husband?"

Yuan-te replied, "I have been driven hither and thither all my life. I was never able to do my duty to my parents nor have I been able to sacrifice to my ancestors. I have been very unfilial. The new year is at hand and its approach disquiets me greatly."

"Do not try to deceive me," said the Lady Sun. "I heard and I know all. Just now Chao Yun came to tell you Chingchou was threatened and you wish to return home. That is why you put forward this excuse."

Then Yuan-te fell on his knees and said, "Why should I dissemble, O wife, since you know? I do not wish to go, but if Chingchou be lost I shall be an object of ridicule to every one. I do desire to go, but I cannot leave you. Now you know why I am grieved."

She replied, "I am your handmaid and whithersoever you go it is my duty to follow."

"Yes; your heart is right, but the difficulty is your mother and the Marquis; they will be unwilling. If you would have pity on me and let me go for a time—."

And again the tears gushed forth.

"Do not be so sad, my husband," said the Lady Sun. "I will

implore my mother to let us go and she will surely allow it."

"Even supposing the Dowager permits I am sure the Marquis will hinder."

The Lady Sun said nothing for a long time while she weighed the matter thoroughly. Presently she spoke, "On New Year's Day you and I will go to court and present our congratulations. Then we will give the excuse of a sacrifice on the river bank and go away without formal leave. Will that suit you?"

Yuan-te knelt at her feet and expressed his gratitude. "I should be never so grateful," said he. "Dead or alive I would remember your love. But this must be a perfect secret."

This having been decided and the arrangements made, Chao Yun received secret orders to lead out his company and be on the road on New Year's morn. He was told they were going away.

Sun Ch'uan held a grand court on the New Year's Day of the fifteenth year of "Established Tranquillity." Liu Pei and his bride went into the Dowager's presence and the Lady Sun said, "My husband has been thinking of his ancestors, who lie in Cho, and grieves that he cannot do his duty by them. Today we wish to go to the river side and offer sacrifices towards the North. It is our duty to inform you."

"A very filial proceeding," said the Dowager. I should not think of stopping you. Although you have never known your husband's parents yet you may go with him to sacrifice as it is proper for a wife to do."

Both thanked the Dowager and went out, rejoicing at having so far hoodwinked Sun Ch'uan. The Lady Sun got into her carriage taking only a little clothing with her, while Yuan-te followed with a small escort. They went out of the city and met Chao Yun at the place arranged. Then with a guard in front and rear they left the precincts of the city, travelling as quickly as they could.

That day, at the new year banquet, Sun Ch'uan drank freely so that he had to be helped to his chamber, and the guests left. Before very long the escape of the fugitives became known, but it was then dark and when they tried to tell Sun Ch'uan they could not rouse him. He slept heavily until the fifth watch.

The next morning, when Sun Ch'uan heard the story he asked advice of his counsellors. Chang Shao said, "They have got away today but trouble will surely come of it; therefore pursue after them without loss of time."

So Ch'en Wu and P'an Chang, with a half-company of veterans, were sent out with orders to use all speed both by day and by night and bring back the fugitives.

They left. Sun Ch'uan's anger burned hot against Yuan-te. In his wrath he seized his jade inkstone and dashed it to the ground where it shivered to pieces.

Said Ch'eng P'u, "My lord, your wrath is in vain, for I do not think your men will catch the runaways."

"Will they dare to disobey my order?" said Sun Ch'uan.

"Our young lady had always delighted to look upon war and is very fierce and determined. All the officers fear her. Now she has gone with her husband of her own free will and those sent in pursuit, if once they look upon her countenance, will not dare to lay hands on her."

Sun Ch'uan's wrath burned the more fiercely at these words. He drew the sword girded at his side and called up Chiang Ch'in and Chou T'ai saying, "You two take this sword and bring back the heads of my sister and Liu Pei. And if you do not I will put you to death."

With this order they set out in pursuit, leading a whole company. Meanwhile Yuan-te and his wife were pressing forward with all speed. When night fell they rested for a time by the roadside, but not for long. Just as they reached the confines of Ch'aisang they turned and saw a great cloud of dust and the soldiers said that a force was coming in pursuit.

"What shall we do if they come up with us?" said Yuan-te excitedly to Chao Yun.

"My lord, you go on in front and I will prevent pursuit."

As they turned the foot of a hill they saw a troop of soldiers blocking their road in front. Two captains were there and they bellowed, "Liu Pei, dismount and yield yourself captive. We are here by order of General Chou and you have kept us waiting long."

Now the thought had come to Chou Yu that Yuan-te would try to flee, and so he had sent Hsu Sheng and Ting Feng, with three companies, to intercept him at this critical spot. They had made a camp there and kept a lookout from the hill-tops, for Chou had calculated that he would certainly pass that way. So when Liu Pei and his cavalcade appeared they all buckled on their arms and barred the way.

Greatly fearing, Yuan-te rode back to consult Chao Yun, to whom he said, "In front a force barring the road; in rear pursuers. There is no escape. What can we do?"

"Do not be alarmed, my lord. The great strategist gave me three plans enclosed in three silken bags. Two have been used and have answered admirably. There is yet the third and my orders were to open the bag in such a strait as this. This is a day of great danger such as calls me to open the bag."

Thereupon he opened the bag and handed it to Yuan-te. As soon as Yuan-te had seen the contents he hastened to the Lady Sun's carriage and began to weep, saying, "I have something private to say, and I must tell you."

"What have you to tell me, my husband? Tell me the whole truth," replied she.

"Your brother and Chou Yu formerly made a plot for you to marry me, not for your sake, but to get me into their power and hold me so that they might recover Chingchou. They were set on my murder, and you were the bait with which to hook me. Careless of consequences I came, for I knew that the spirit of a man dwelt in your bosom and you would pity me. Lately I heard that harm was intended me and so I made danger to Chingchou the excuse to escape. Happily for me you have remained true and come with me. But now the Marquis is pursuing us and Chou Yu's men are in front. Only you, my wife, can extricate us from this danger and if you refuse, then slay me where I stand that I may thus show my gratitude for your kindness."

The Lady Sung grew angry and said, "Then does my brother forget that I am his sister? How will he ever look me in the face? I can extricate us from this danger."

Thereupon she bade her people push the carriage to the front. She rolled up the blind and herself called out, "Hsu Sheng, Ting Feng, are you turned traitors then?"

The two captains slid out of their saddles, dropped their arms and stood meekly in front of the carriage.

"We are no traitors," said they. "We have the General's orders to camp here and await Liu Pei."

"Chou Yu is an interfering scoundrel," cried she. "We of the land of Wu have never harmed you, and Yuan-te, the Uncle of the Great Family, is my husband. I have already told my mother and my brother of our journey and now I find you with an army at the foot of these hills preventing our passage. Is it that you would plunder us of our valuables?"

The two captains mumbled dissent; they would not dare such a thing. "We pray you, O Lady, to stay your anger. This is no plan of ours; we do but obey our General's orders."

"So you fear Chou Yu and not me!" cried she scornfully. "Think you that if he slay you I will not slay him?"

She broke into a torrent of abuse of Chou Yu. Then she bade them push her carriage forward.

The two leaders thought within themselves, "We are but men of lowly rank, we dare not dispute with the Lady Sun." Beside they saw Chao Yun was bursting with wrath. So they ordered their men to stand aside and leave the road clear.

The cavalcade had only gone a little distance when up came the pursuers. The two captains told the new-comers what had happened. "You were wrong to let them pass," said Ch'en and P'an. "We have orders from the Marquis himself to arrest them."

Thereupon all four went in pursuit. When the noise of the approaching force reached the ears of Yuan-te he said to his wife, "They are again pursuing us; what now?"

"Husband, go on in front. I and Chao Yun will keep them off."

So Yuan-te and a small company went on toward the river bank, while Chao Yun reined up beside the lady's carriage and set out his men ready for battle. And when the four men came up they dismounted and stood with folded arms.

"What are you doing here, Captains?" asked the Lady Sun.

"We have orders from our lord to request you and Yuan-te to return."

Calmly but bitterly she said, "So this is the sort of fools you are! You would make dissension between brother and sister. But I am a wife on my way to my husband's home. Nor am I leaving clandestinely, for I had my mother's gracious permission. Now we, husband and wife, are going to Chingchou and if even my brother were here himself he would let us pass in all politeness. But you, because you have weapons in your hands, would slay us!"

She abused the four men to their faces so that they looked from one to another in shame. And each in his heart thought, "Say what one will, after all they two are brother and sister and the Dowager is the controlling power. Sun Ch'uan is most obedient and would never dare oppose his mother's decision. When the reaction comes, then indeed we shall certainly be found in the wrong. We had better be kind." Another thing was that one of the two they sought, Yuan-te, was not there and Chao Yun looked angry and dangerous. Finally, muttering to themselves, they gave way and with one accord retired and left the road open. The Lady Sun passed through.

"We four will go to see the General and report," said Hsu Sheng.

But that did not please them all and they stood irresolute. Presently they saw a column of men sweeping down on them like a hurricane. These were Chiang and Chou with their company.

"Have you fellows seen Liu Pei?" they cried as they rushed up.

"He has just passed along."

"Why did you not arrest him?"

"Because of what the Lady Sun said."

"That is just as the Marquis feared and so he gave us this sword and told us first to slay his sister and then Liu Pei. And if we disobey he will put us to death."

"What can be done? They are far away by now."

Chiang Ch'in said, "After all they are but a few and on foot; they cannot travel very fast. Let Hsu and Ting go to Chou Yu to tell him, and he can send fast boats to pursue them on the river while we follow up on the bank. We must get them either on water or land and we must not listen to what they say."

Whereupon two went back to report and two to the river bank. Meanwhile Liu Pei had got a long way from Ch'aisang and reached Liulangpu. He now felt calmer. He went along the bank of the river seeking a boat, but there was no craft on the broad bosom of the stream. He bowed his head in deep sorrow. Chao Yun bade him be of good courage seeing that he had just escaped from the tiger's jaws and had not far to go.

"I suspect K'ung-ming has something prepared for us," said he.

But his master was despondent. His thoughts were back to the pleasures he had enjoyed but a few hours since in the house of his wife, and the tears rolled down his cheeks. A poem has been written on this episode.

> By the bank of the deep flowing Yangtse
> Once was a wedding,
> And the ruling houses of two states yet to be
> Were allied by marriage.
> See the beautiful maiden stepping slowly
> To the golden bridal chamber!
> Yet was the marriage but a ruse.
> Its author vainly imagined that a hero,
> Sinking in amorous toils,
> Would forget his high intent and great resolve.

Yuan-te bade the captain of his guard go along the bank to seek some boats. Then the soldiers told him there was a huge cloud of dust on the road. Ascending one of the hills he looked back whence they had come and saw the whole earth as it were covered with an advancing host. He sighed and said, "We have fled before them now for days, worn out our men and jaded our horses, and all to die in a strange place."

He watched them coming nearer and nearer. Then as things began to look most desperate he saw a line of some twenty boats all in the act of setting their sails.

"By good luck here are some ships," said Chao Yun. "Let us get on board, row to the further bank and see what can be done."

Yuan-te and his bride hastened down the bank and went into a ship. The soldiers were embarked. Then they saw in the hold of the ship some one in Taoist dress, who came up with a smile, saying, "My lord, again you see Chuko Liang. He has waited a long time."

"All the men on board were from Chingchou, and Yuan-te rejoiced at the sudden happy turn of affairs.

Before long the pursuers reached the bank. K'ung-ming pointed to them and laughed, saying, "I foresaw this a long time ago. You may return and tell your General not to use the fair damsel trick again."

Those on the bank sent a flight of arrows at the ships but they were already too far away. The four officers on the bank looked very foolish.

As the boats were sailing along a great noise was heard on the river behind them and there appeared a huge fleet of war ships, sailing under the flag of Chou Yu. He also was there in command of the fleet and he was supported by Huang Kai and Han Tang. They seemed like a drove of horses and came along swift as a falling star. They gained on the fugitives rapidly.

K'ung-ming ordered the boats to row over to the north bank, and the party landed. They had started off away from the shore before Chou Yu could land. Chou Yu's men, naturally, were all afoot but they kept up the pursuit, following as quickly as they could. When they reached the borders of Huangchou, Liu Pei and his party were not far away, and so they pressed the pursuit. But there were only horses for a few in front and suddenly the rolling of drums struck Chou Yu's ears and from out a gully dashed a troop of swordsmen led by Kuan Yu. Chou Yu was too surprised and unprepared to do anything but flee.

Chou Yu fled for his life and Kuan Yu pursued. At different points other captains came out and attacked, so that the men of Wu suffered a great defeat and Chou Yu barely escaped. As he came to the river and was going down into his ship the soldiers on the bank jeered at him on account of the miscarriage of his scheme for the restoration of tranquillity. All he had done was to give his enemy a wife and lose his soldiers. He was so annoyed that he would have gone up the bank to fight again, but his captains restrained him. He was very despondent and felt ashamed to face his master and confess utter defeat and failure.

All at once he cried aloud and fell back in a swoon. His wound had re-opened. The captains came to his help but it was long before he recovered consciousness.

> Twice had he played his trick
> And twice had he lost the game;
> His heart was full of resentment,
> He was overwhelmed with shame.

The fate of Chou Yu will appear in the next chapter.

CHAPTER LVI

A BANQUET IN THE BRONZE BIRD PAVILION:
K'UNG-MING PROVOKES CHOU YU
A THIRD TIME

The ambuscade into which Chou Yu had fallen had been prepared by the orders of K'ung-ming and was triple. However, Huang Kai and Han Tang contrived to get clear and found refuge in the ships, though with the loss of many men. When Chou Yu was in safety and looked about him he saw Yuan-te and the Lady Sun quietly resting on a hill top. How could such a sight fail to put him in a rage? And with the access of rage his wound, not yet healed, burst open once again. He swooned and fell. They raised him and his ship set sail. He was allowed to depart undisturbed, while Yuan-te proceeded to Chingchou, where were great rejoicings in honour of his recent marriage.

Meanwhile Chou Yu had gone to Ch'aisang while Chiang Ch'in and those with him bore the sad tidings to Sun Ch'uan. He was angry beyond words and his first thought was to send an army under Ch'eng P'u to take Chingchou. Chou Yu also wrote from his sick bed urging his lord to take vengeance. But Chang Chao knew better and said it could not be done.

Said he, "Ts'ao Ts'ao has never forgotten his defeat, but he dares not attempt to avenge himself while the Sun family are friendly with Liu Pei. If in any moment of anger you two fall upon each other, Ts'ao will certainly seize the opportunity and your position will be dangerous."

Ku Yung supported him, saying, "Beyond all doubt Ts'ao Ts'ao has his spies here. As soon as he hears of any rift in the friendship between Sun and Liu he will desire to come to an understanding with the latter and Liu Pei, who fears your power, will accept his offer and take his side. Such an alliance will be a continual menace to the land south of the river. No; the plan for the occasion is to

secure the friendship of Liu Pei by memorialising that he be made
Governor of Chingchou. This will make Ts'ao Ts'ao afraid to send
any army against the south-east. At the same time it will raise
kindly feelings in the heart of Liu Pei and win his support. You will
be able to find some one who will provoke a quarrel between Ts'ao
and Liu and set them at each other and that will be your
opportunity. In this way you will succeed."

"These are good words," said Sun Ch'uan, "but have I a
messenger who can accomplish such a mission?"

"There is such a man, one whom Ts'ao respects and loves."

"Who is he?"

"What prevents you from employing Hua Hsin? He is ready
to hand."

Wherefore Hua Hsin was given letters and bidden go to the
capital, whither he proceeded at once and sought to see Ts'ao Ts'ao.
They told him that Ts'ao and all his friends were at Yehchun,
celebrating the completion of the Bronze Bird Pavilion. So thither
he went.

Ts'ao had indeed never forgotten his great defeat and nourished
schemes to avenge it, but he feared the combination of his two
chief enemies and that fear restrained him.

In the spring of the fifteenth year the great Pavilion was
completed and Ts'ao invited a vast assembly to celebrate its
inauguration with banquets and rejoicings. The pleasaunce was on
the bank of the Chang River. The Bronze Bird Terrace stood in the
centre, flanked by two others named the Terrace of the Jade
Dragon and the Terrace of the Golden Phoenix. Each tower was a
hundred feet high and a bridge connected them. Gold and jade
vied with each other in the many apartments.

At the opening ceremony Ts'ao Ts'ao wore a golden headdress
inlaid with jewels and a robe of green brocaded silk, girded with a
belt of jade. On his feet were pearl-encrusted shoes. So clad he
took his seat as host, while his officers, civil and military, were
drawn up below the terrace.

For the military officers was arranged an archery competition
and one of his attendants brought forth a robe of red crimson
Ssuch'uan silk as a prize. This was suspended from one of the
drooping branches of a willow tree, beneath which was the target.
The distance was a hundred paces. The competitors were divided
into two bands, those of his own family being dressed in red and
the others in green. They all had carved bows and long arrows and
were mounted. They stood holding in their steeds till the signal
should be given for the games to begin. Each was to shoot one

arrow and the robe was the guerdon for hitting the target in the red; misses were to pay a forfeit of drinking a cup of cold water.

As soon as the signal was given a red-robed youth rode quickly forth. He was Ts'ao Hsiu. Swiftly he galloped to and fro thrice. Then he adjusted the notch of his arrow to the string, pulled the bow to its full and the arrow flew straight to the bullseye.

The clang of the gongs and the roll of the drums announced the feat, which astonished them all. And Ts'ao, as he sat on the terrace, was delighted. "A very promising colt of my own," said he to those about him, and he sent a messenger for the red robe that the winner might receive it from his own hands.

But suddenly from the green side rode out one who cried, "It were more fitting to let outsiders compete for the Minister's silken robe; it is not right that members of the family monopolise the contest."

Ts'ao Ts'ao looked at the speaker, who was one Wen P'ing. And some of the officers cried, "Let us see what his shooting is like!"

So Wen P'ing fitted an arrow to the string and fired also from horseback while galloping. To the surprise of the onlookers he also made a bullseye, which was honoured by another salute from gongs and drums.

"Quickly bring me the robe," cried Wen P'ing.

But at once from the ranks of the red-robed another competitor dashed forward, shouting fiercely, "How can you win what has been already won? But let me show you how I can shoot an arrow that shall overcome both your shots."

He drew his bow to the full and the arrow flew straight to the heart of the red. The surprised onlookers saw that this new competitor was Ts'ao Hung, who now became also a claimant for the robe.

However, yet another archer came forth from the green robed ranks, playing with his bow and crying, "What is there amazing in your shooting, you three? See how I can shoot."

This man was Chang Ho. He put his horse to the gallop, then turned his back and, shooting backwards, also hit the centre of the red.

Thus four arrows were now sticking in the bullseye and all agreed that it was marvellous archery.

"I think the robe should be mine," said Chang Ho.

Before he could finish speaking a fifth competitor came out from the red robes and shouted, "You shot backwards; but that is commonplace enough. Look while I shoot better than you all."

The speaker was Hsiahou Yuan. He galloped off to the very

limit of the butts and then bending his body over backwards he sent his arrow right in among the other four.

As the gongs and drums broke out Yuan put aside his bow and rode up saying, "Is not that a better shot than any of its predecessors?"

Then came out another from the greens who cried, "Leave the robe there for me, Hsu Huang, to win."

"What can you do that is better than my shot?" said Yuan.

"That you hit the bullseye is no great feat. You will see me win the silken robe after all."

So speaking, Hsu Huang fitted an arrow to his bow. Then looking around he aimed at the willow twig from which the robe hung down and shot thereat so true that his arrow cut it through and the robe fluttered to the ground. At once Hsu Huang dashed along, picked up the robe and slipped it on. Then riding swiftly to the terrace he thanked the Minister. No one present could withhold unstinted praise and Hsu was turning to ride away when another green clad captain leaped out saying, "Where would you go with that robe? Quickly leave it for me!"

All eyes turned to this man who was Hsu Ch'u. Hsu Huang cried, "The robe has already been adjudged to me; would you dare take it by force?"

Hsu Chiu made no reply but galloped up to snatch the robe. As his horse drew near Huang struck at his rival a blow with his bow. But Hsu Ch'u seized the bow with one hand while with the other he simply lifted his opponent out of his seat. Wherefore Hsu Huang let go the bow and the next moment lay sprawling on the ground. Hsu Ch'u slipped out of the saddle too and they began to pommel each other with their fists. Ts'ao Ts'ao sent one to separate them, but in the struggle the robe had been torn and soiled. He called the angry rivals before him and they came, one darting fierce looks of hate, the other grinding his teeth with rage.

"Never mind the robe; I see only your magnificent courage, said Ts'ao smiling. "What does a robe more or less matter?"

Whereupon he called the captains to him one by one and to each he presented a robe of Ssuch'uan silk. They thanked him for the generous gifts and he then commanded them to take their seats in due order. Then to the strains of a band of music, wherein each performer vied with all the others, the naval and military officers took their places. Civil officers of repute and captains of renown drank one to another, and hearty felicitations were exchanged.

Ts'ao looked around to those about him saying, "Since the military officers have competed in mounted archery for our enjoyment and displayed their boldness and their skill, you, gentlemen scholars, stuffed full of learning as you are, can surely mount the terrace and present some complimentary odes to make the occasion a perfect success."

"We are most willing to obey your commands," they replied, all bowing low.

At that time there was a band of four scholars named, Wang Lang, Chung Yao, Wang Ts'an and Ch'en Lin, and each of them presented a poem. Every poem sang the praises of Ts'ao Ts'ao's valuable services and great merits and said he was worthy to receive the highest trust of all.

When Ts'ao Ts'ao had read them he laughed saying, "You gentlemen are really too flattering. As a fact I am but an ignoramus who began life with a simple bachelor's degree. And when the troubles began I built me a little cottage in the country near Ch'iaotung, where I could study in spring and summer and spend the rest of the year in hunting till the empire was once more tranquil and I could emerge and take office. To my surprise I was chosen for a small military office which changed my intentions and I determined to repress the rebellion and so make a name for myself. I thought that I might win an inscription on my tomb to the effect that it covered the remains of the Marquis Ts'ao, who had restored order in the west. That would have been ample for a life's work. I recall now how I destroyed Tung Cho and smote the Yellow Turbans; then I made away with Yuan Shu and broke the power of Lu Pu; next I exterminated Yuan Shao and at the death of Liu Piao I had subdued the whole empire. As a Minister of State I have attained the topmost pinnacle of honour and I have no more to hope for. Were it not for poor me, I know not how many there would be styling themselves Emperor and dubbing themselves princes. Certain there be who, seeing my great authority, think I have some ulterior aim. But they are quite wrong. I ever bear in mind what Confucius said of Chou Kung, that he was perfectly virtuous, and this saying is ever engraven on my mind. An I could I would do away with my armies and retire to my fief with my simple title of Marquis Wuping. Alas! I cannot. I am afraid to lay down my military powers lest I should come to harm. Should I be defeated, the State would totter and so I may not risk real misfortune for the sake of an empty reputation for kindness. There be some of you who do not know my heart."

As he closed they all rose and bowed their heads saying, "None are your equals, O Minister, not even Duke Chou or the great Minister I Yin."

A poem has been written referring to this:—

Had Duke Chou, the virtuous, died, while foul-mouthed slander
    was spreading her vile rumours;
Or Wang Mang, the treacherous, while he was noted for the
    deference paid to learned men;
None would have known their real characters.

After this oration Ts'ao Ts'ao drank many cups of wine in quick succession till he became very intoxicated. He bade his servants bring him pencil and inkstone that he might compose a poem. But as he was beginning to write they told him that the Marquis of Wu had sent Hua Hsin as an envoy and presented a memorial to appoint Liu Pei governor of Ching-chou and that Sun Ch'uan's sister was now Liu Pei's wife, while on the river Han the greater part of the nine districts was under Liu Pei's rule.

Ts'ao Ts'ao was seized with quaking fear at the news and threw the pen on the floor. Ch'eng Yu said to him, "O Minister, you have been among fighting men by myriads and in danger from stones and arrows many a time and never quailed. Now the news that Liu Pei has got possession of a small tract of country throws you into a panic. Why is it thus?"

Ts'ao Ts'ao replied, "Liu Pei is a dragon among men. All his life hitherto he has never found his element, but now that he has obtained Chingchou it is as if the dragon, once captive, had escaped to the mighty deep. There is good reason for me to quake with fear."

"Do you know the reason of the coming of Hua Hsin?" said Ch'eng.

"No; I know not," said the Minister.

"Liu Pei is Sun Ch'uan's one terror and he would attack him were it not for you, O Minister. He feels you would fall upon him while he was smiting his enemy. Wherefore he has taken this means of calming Liu Pei's suspicions and fears and at the same time directing your enmity toward him and from himself."

Ts'ao Ts'ao nodded; "Yes," he said.

Ch'eng Yu continued, "Now this is my plan to set Sun and Liu at one another and give you the opportunity to destroy both; it can be done easily."

"What is your plan?" asked Ts'ao.

"The one prop of Wu is Chou Yu; remove it by memorialising that Chou be appointed Prefect of Nanchun. Then get Ch'eng P'u made Prefect of Chianghsia and cause the Emperor to retain this Hua Hsin in the capital to await some important post. Chou Yu will assuredly attack Liu Pei and that will be our chance. Is not the scheme good?"

"Friend Ch'eng, you are a man after my own heart."

Wherefore he summoned the emissary from Wu and overwhelmed him with gifts. That day was the last of the feastings and merry-makings and Ts'ao, with all the company, returned to the capital where he forthwith presented a memorial assigning Chou Yu and Ch'eng P'u to the posts he wished, and Hua Hsin was retained at the capital with a post of dignity.

The messenger bearing the commissions for their new offices went down to Wu and both Chou Yu and Ch'eng P'u accepted the appointments. Having taken over his command the former thought all the more of the revenge he contemplated and, to bring matters to a head, he wrote to Sun Ch'uan asking him to send Lu Su and renew the demand for the rendition of Chingchou.

Wherefore Lu Su was summoned and his master said to him, "You are the guarantor in the loan of Chingchou to Liu Pei. He still delays to return it and how long am I to wait?"

"The writing said plainly that the rendition would follow the occupation of Ssuch'uan."

Sun Ch'uan shouted back, "Yes it said so. But so far they have not moved a soldier to the attack. I will not wait till old age has come to us all."

"I will go and enquire?" said Lu Su.

So he went down into a ship and sailed to Chingchou.

Meanwhile Liu Pei and K'ung-ming were at Chingchou gathering in supplies from all sides, drilling their men and training their armies. From all quarters men of learning flocked to their side. In the midst of this they heard of Lu Su's coming and Liu Pei asked K'ung-ming what he thought of it.

K'ung-ming replied, "Just lately Sun Ch'uan concerned himself with getting you appointed Governor of Chingchou; that was calculated to inspire Ts'ao Ts'ao with fear. Ts'ao Ts'ao obtained for Chou Yu the Prefectship of Nanchun; that was designed to stir up strife between our two houses and set us fighting so that he might accomplish his own ends. This visit of Lu Su means that Chou Yu, having taken over his new governorship, wishes to force us out of this place."

"Then how shall we reply?"

"If he introduce the subject you will at once set up loud lamentations. When the sound of lamentation is at its height I will appear and talk over your visitor."

Thus they planned and Lu Su was duly received with all honour.

When the salutations were over and host and guest were about to be seated, Lu Su said, "Sir, now that you are the husband of a daughter of Wu you have become my lord, and I dare not sit in your presence."

Liu Pei laughed. "You are an old friend," said he. "Why this excessive humility?"

So Lu Su took his seat. And when tea had been served the guest said, "I have come at the order of my master to discuss the subject of Chingchou. You, O Imperial Uncle, have had the use of the place for a long time. Now that your two houses are allied by marriage, there should be the most friendly relations between you and you should hand it back to my master."

At this Yuan-te covered his face and began to cry.

"What is the matter?" asked the guest.

Yuan-te only wept the more bitterly.

Then K'ung-ming came in from behind a screen saying, "I have been listening. Do you know why my lord weeps so bitterly."

"Really I know not."

"But it is easy to see. When my lord got the temporary occupation of Chingchou he gave the promise to return it when he had got the west country. But reflect. Liu Chang of Ichou is my lord's younger brother and both of them are blood relations of the ruling family. If my lord were to move an army to capture another city he fears the blame of the ignorant. And if he yield this place before he has another, where could he rest? Yet, while he retains this place it seems to shame you. The thing is hard on both sides and that is why he weeps so bitterly.

The close of K'ung-ming's speech seemed to move Yuan-te to greater grief for he beat his breast and stamped his feet and wept yet more bitterly."

Lu Su attempted to console him saying, "Be not so distressed, O Uncle; let us hear what K'ung-ming can propose."

"I would beg you to return to your master and tell him all. Tell him of this great trouble and entreat him to let us stay here a little longer."

"But suppose he refuse; what then?" said Lu Su.

"How can he refuse since he is related by marriage to my master?" said K'ung-ming. "I shall expect to hear glad tidings through you."

Lu Su was really the first of generous men and seeing Yuan-te in such distress he could do no other than consent and say he would do so. Yuan-te and K'ung-ming both thanked him most cordially and after a banquet the emissary went down into his ship to return. On the way he called in to see Chou Yu and told him. But Chou stamped his foot with rage and said, "My friend, you have been fooled again. Long ago when Liu Pei was dependent on Liu Piao he always cherished the intention to supplant him; think you that he really pities Liu Chang of Shu? This sort of evasive policy will certainly cause you much trouble. However, I have a scheme which I think K'ung-ming will not be able to get the better of. Only you will have to make another journey."

"I should be pleased to hear your fine scheme," said Lu Su.

"Do not go to see our master. Return to Chingchou and say to Liu Pei that since his family and the Suns are related by marriage they really form but one house, and since he has qualms about attacking the west we will do it for him. We will march an army under this pretext, but really go to Ching-chou, and we shall take him unprepared. The road to the west runs through his city and we will call upon him for supplies. He will come out to thank the army and we will assassinate him whereby we shall revenge ourselves and at the same time remove a source of future evil."

This seemed an excellent plan to Lu Su and he returned at once to Chingchou. Before receiving him Yuan-te talked over the matter with his adviser.

Said K'ung-ming, "He has not seen the Marquis, he has called in at Ch'aisang and he and Chou Yu have decided upon some scheme, which he is to talk you into accepting. However, let him talk; only watch me and when I nod my head then agree to whatever he may propose."

Lu Su was then admitted and said, "The Marquis of Wu praises the noble virtue of the Imperial Uncle and after consultation with his officers he has determined to take the western kingdom on his behalf and, that done, Chingchou can be exchanged for it without further delay. However, when the army marches through it will be expected of you to contribute some necessary supplies."

K'ung-ming here nodded his head rapidly, at the same time saying, "We could hardly have hoped for such kindness," while Yuan-te saluted with joined hands and said, "This is due to your friendly efforts on our behalf."

"When the brave army arrives we shall certainly come out to meet it and entertain the soldiers," said K'ung-ming.

Lu Su felt great satisfaction and was quite happy at his success; he took his leave and went homeward. But Yuan-te as yet did not understand.

"What is their intention?" said he.

His adviser smiled. "Chou Yu's end is very near. The ruse he is now trying would not take in a boy."

"Why?"

"This is the ruse known as 'borrow a road to exterminate Kuo.' Under the pretence of taking the west they intend to capture this place, and when you go out to compliment the army you will be seized and they will dash into the city which they hope to find unprepared."

"And what are we to do?"

"Have no anxiety; all we have to do is to prepare a hidden bow to get the fierce tiger; to spread the enticing bait to hook the great leviathan. Wait till Chou Yu comes; if he is not killed he will be nine-tenths a corpse. We will call in Chao Yun for orders and give him secret instructions and I will dispose the others."

And Yuan-te was glad.

> Let Chou Yu lay what plans he will,
> K'ung-ming anticipates his skill;
> That river land fair bait did look,
> But he forgot the hidden hook.

Lu Su hastened back to Chou Yu to tell him that all was going as he desired and Yuan-te would come out to welcome the army. And Chou Yu laughed with glee, saying, "At last! Now they will fall into my trap."

He bade Lu Su prepare a petition for the information of the Marquis and he ordered Ch'eng P'u to bring up reinforcements. He himself had nearly recovered from the arrow wound and felt well. He made his dispositions for the advance, telling off the leaders of the van and wings. The army numbered five legions and Chou Yu marched with the second division. While voyaging in his ship he was always smiling to think how he was to have K'ung-ming at last.

At Hsiak'ou he enquired if there was any one to welcome him. They told him the Imperial Uncle had sent Mi Chu to greet him and he was called.

"What of the preparations for the army?" asked Chou Yu as soon as Mi Chu came.

"My master has seen to that; all is prepared," said Mi.

"Where is the Imperial Uncle?" asked Chou.

"He is at Chingchou, waiting outside the walls to offer you the cup of greeting."

"This expedition is on your account," said Chou Yu. "When one undertakes so long a march and such a task the rewards for the army must be very substantial."

Having got this idea of what Chou Yu expected, Mi Chu returned to his own city, while the battle ships in close order sailed up the river and took their places along the bank. As they went on the most perfect tranquillity seemed to reign on all sides. Not a ship was visible anywhere, and no one hindered. Chou Yu pressed forward till he came quite near Chingchou and still the wide river lay calm. But the spies who came back reported two white flags flying on the city walls.

Still not a man was seen and Chou Yu began to feel suspicious. He had his ship navigated in shore and he himself landed on the bank, where he mounted a horse and, with a small army of veterans under three captains, travelled along the land road.

By and bye he came to the city wall. There was no sign of life. Reining in his steed he bade them challenge the gate. Then some one from the wall asked who was there. The men of Wu replied that it was their General in person. Immediately was heard the thud of a club and the wall became alive with men all armed. And from the tower came out Chao Yun who said, "Why are you here, General?"

"I am going to take the west for you," replied Chou Yu, "do you not know?"

"K'ung-ming knows that you want to try the ruse of 'borrowing a road to destroy Kuo.' And so he stationed me here. And my master bade me say that he and the ruler of the west country are both members of the reigning family so that he could not think of such baseness as attacking Shu. If you people of Wu do so, he will be forced to go away into the mountains and become a recluse. He could not bear to lose the confidence of mankind."

At this Chou Yu turned his horse as if to return. Just then his scouts came up to say that armed bands were moving toward him from all sides, and Kuan Yu and Chang Fei led two of them. Their number was unknown but the sound of their tramping shook the heavens. They said they wanted to capture Chou Yu.

At these tidings Chou Yu's excitement became so intense that he fell to the ground with a great cry, and the old wound re-opened.

> The game was now too deep; in vain he sought
> A countermove; his efforts came to nought.

Later chapters will show what was Chou Yu's fate.

In the last chapter it was said that a sudden rage filled the bosom of Chou Yu and he fell to the ground. Then he was carried to his boat. It only added to his rage and mortification to be told that his enemies and rivals could be seen on the top of one of the hills apparently feasting and enjoying some music. He lay grinding his teeth with vexation. "They say I shall never be able to get Ssuch'uan! But I will; I swear I will."

Soon after Sun Ch'uan's brother Yu arrived and Chou Yu told him his vexations. "My brother sent me to assist you," said Sun Yu.

Sun Yu ordered the army to press forward and they got to Pach'iu. There they stopped, for the scouts reported large forces under Liu Feng and Kuan P'ing barring the river route. This failure did not make the General any calmer.

About this time a letter from K'ung-ming arrived, which ran like this:— "Since our parting at Ch'aisang I have thought of you often. Now comes to me a report that you desire to take The Western Land of Streams, which I regret to say I consider impossible. The people are strong and the country is precipitous and defensible. The governor may be weak within, but he is strong enough to defend himself. Now indeed, General, you would go far and you would render great services, yet can any one foretell the final result? No; not even Wu Ch'i the great General could say for certain, nor could Sun Wu be sure of a successful issue. Ts'ao Ts'ao suffered severe defeat at Ch'ihpi; think you he will ever cease to hope for revenge? Now if you undertake a long expedition, will he not seize the occasion to fall upon Chiangnan and grind it to powder? Such a deed would be more than I could bear and I venture to warn you of the possible danger if haply you may condescend to regard it."

The letter made Chou Yu feel very sorrowful and he sighed

deeply. He called for paper and a pen and wrote to the Marquis Wu and, having done this, he said to his assembled officers, "I have honestly tried to do my best for my country but my end is at hand. The number of my days is accomplished. You must continue to aid our master till his end shall be achieved—"

He stopped; for he had swooned. Slowly he regained consciousness and as he looked up to heaven he sighed heavily, "O God, since thou madest me; why didst thou also create Liang?"

Soon after he passed away; he was only thirty-six.

> The battle at Ch'ihpi made him famous;
> Though young in years he gained a veteran's reputation.
> Deep feeling, his music declared its intensity;
> Subtle, with excess hospitality he foiled a plot;
> Persuasive, he once obtained a large gift of grain;
> Capable he led an army of millions.
> Pach'iu was his deathbed, there his fate met him.
> Sadly indeed they mourned him.

After his death his captains sent his dying memorial to the Marquis of Wu, who was most deeply affected and wept aloud at the sad tidings of his death. When he opened the letters he saw that Lu Su was named as the dead general's successor. This is the letter:—

"Possessing but ordinary abilities, there was no reason why I should have been the recipient of your confidence and high office, but I have not spared myself in the leadership of the great army under my command that thereby I might prove my gratitude. Yet none can measure life and the number of our days is ordained by fate. Before I could achieve even my poor intentions my feeble body has failed me. I regret it without measure. I die with Ts'ao Ts'ao threatening and our northern borders disturbed and with Liu Pei in your family as though you were feeding a fierce tiger. None can foretell the fate of the empire in these weary days of stress and of peculiar anxiety for you.

"Lu Su is most loyal, careful in all matters and a fitting man to succeed to my office. When a man is near death his words are wise and if I may haply retain your regard I may die but I shall not decay."

"He should have been a king's counsellor, cried Sun Ch'uan, amid his tears. "He has left me, alas! too soon, and whom have I to lean upon? But he recommends his friend and I can do nothing better than take that advice."

Whereupon he appointed Lu Su to the vacant command.

He also saw that the coffin of his beloved general was sent to Ch'aisang ready for the funeral sacrifices.

The night of Chou Yu's death K'ung-ming was gazing up at the heavens when he saw a bright star fall to the earth. "Chou Yu is dead," said he with a smile. At dawn he sent to tell Yuan-te, who sent men to find out, and they came back to say it was true; he had died.

"Now that this has come to pass what should we do?" said Yuan-te.

"Lu Su will succeed," said K'ung-ming. "And I see in the heavens signs of an assembly of captains in the east so I shall go. The mourning for Chou Yu will serve as a pretext. I may find some able scholar there to be of help to you."

"I am afraid lest the captains of Wu harm you," said Liu Pei.

"While Chou Yu lived I did not fear; is there anything to dread now that he is gone?"

However, he took Chao Yun as commander of his escort when he embarked for Pach'iu, and on the road he heard of Lu Su's succession to the late general's post. As the coffin of Chou Yu had been sent to Ch'aisang, K'ung-ming continued his journey thither and, on landing, was kindly received by Lu Su. The officers of Wu did not conceal their enmity but the sight of the redoubtable Chao Yun, always close at hand, kept them from trying to hurt K'ung-ming.

The officers brought by K'ung-ming were arranged in order before the bier and he himself poured the libation. Then he knelt and read this threnody:—

"Alas, Kung-chin! Hapless are you in your early death. Length of days is in the hands of God, yet do men suffer and my heart is deeply grieved for you. I pour this libation that your spirit may enjoy its fragrance.

"I lament you. I lament your younger days passed in the companionship of Po-fu, when, preferring eternal principles to material wealth, you abode in a humble cottage.

"I lament your ripe strength when you guarded distant Pach'iu, putting fear into the heart of Liu Piao, destroying rebels and ensuring safety.

"I lament the grace of your manhood. Married to a fair maid of the Ch'iao family, son-in-law of a minister, you were such as would add lustre to the Han Court.

"I lament your resolute purpose when you opposed the pledge-giving. As in the beginning your wings drooped not, so in the end your pinions spread wide.

"I lament your abandon, when your false friend, Chiang, came to you at Poyang. There you manifested your lofty ideals.

"I lament your magnificent talents, proved in civil administration as in military science. With fire attacking the fierce enemy you brought his strength to weakness.

"I recall you as you were but yesterday, bold and successful, and I weep your untimely death. Prostrate I weep tears of sorrow. Loyal and upright in heart, noble and spiritual by nature, your life has been but three decades but your fame will endure for ages.

"I mourn for your affection. My bowels writhe with sorrow and my deep-seated sadness will never cease. The very heavens are darkened. The army is sad; your lord sheds tears; your friends weep floods.

"Scanty of ability am I, yet even of me you begged plans and sought schemes to aid Wu to repulse Ts'ao, to restore the Hans and comfort the Lius. But with you as the firm corner stone and your perfect dispositions, could the final result cause any anxiety?

"Alas, my friend! The quick and the dead are ever separate; they mingle never. If in the deep shades spirits have understanding you now read my inmost heart, yet hereafter there will be none on earth to comprehend.

"Alas, the pain!

"Deign to accept this my sacrifice."

The sacrifice finished, K'ung-ming bowed to the ground and keened while his tears gushed forth in floods. He was deeply moved.

Those who stood on guard by the bier said one to another, "People lied when they said these two were enemies; look at the sincerity shown in sacrifice." And Lu Su was particularly affected by the display of feeling and thought, "Plainly K'ung-ming loved him much, but Kung-chin was not broadminded enough and would have done him to death."

> Before the Sleeping Dragon emerged from his Nanyang retreat
> Many brilliant men had descended upon this earth;
> Since, O azure Heaven, ye made Kung-ching
> Why needed dusty earth produce a K'ung-ming?

Lu Su gave a banquet for K'ung-ming after which the guest left. Just as he was embarking his arm was clutched by a person in Taoist dress who said with a smile, "You exasperated literally to death the man whose body lies up there; to come here as a mourner is an open insult to Wu. It is as good as to say they have no other left."

At first K'ung-ming did not recognise the speaker but very soon he saw it was no other than P'an T'ung, or the "Phoenix Fledgeling." Then he laughed in his turn, and they two hand in hand went down into the ship, where they talked heart to heart for a long time. Before leaving, K'ung-ming gave his friend a letter and said, "I do not think that Sun will use you as you merit. If you find life here distasteful, then you may come to Chingchou and help to support my master. He is liberal and virtuous and will not disdain what you have spent your life in learning."

Then they parted and K'ung-ming went alone to Chingchou.

Lu Su had the coffin of Chou Yu taken to Wuhu, where Sun Ch'uan received it with sacrifices and lamentations. The dead leader was buried in his native place.

His family consisted of two sons and a daughter, the sons being named Hsun and Yin. Sun Ch'uan treated them with tenderness.

Lu Su was not satisfied that he was the fittest successor to his late chief and said, "Chou Kung-chin was not right in recommending me, for I have not the requisite ability and am unfitted for this post. But I can commend to you a certain able man, conversant with all knowledge, and a most capable strategist, not inferior to Kuan Chung or Yo I, one whose plans are as good as those of Sun Wu and Wu Ch'i, the most famous masters of the Art of War. Chou Yu often took his advice and K'ung-ming believes in him. And he is at hand."

This was good news for Sun, who asked the man's name, and when he heard it was P'ang T'ung, he replied, "Yes; I know him by reputation; let him come."

Whereupon P'ang T'ung was invited to the Palace and introduced. The formal salutations over, Sun Ch'uan was disappointed with the man's appearance, which was indeed extraordinary. He had bushy eyebrows, a turned-up nose, a dark skin and a stubby beard. So he was prejudiced against him.

"What have you studied," asked he, "and what are you master of?"

P'ang T'ung replied, "One must not be narrow and obstinate; one must change with circumstances."

"How does your learning compare with that of Chou Yu?" asked Sun.

"My learning is not to be compared with his in the least; mine is far greater."

Now Sun Ch'uan had always loved his late general and he could not bear to hear him disparaged. This speech of P'ang's only increased his dislike. So he said, "You may retire, Sir; I will send for you when I can employ you."

P'ang T'ung uttered one long sigh and went away. When he had gone Lu Su said, "My lord, why not employ him?"

"What good would result; he is just one of those mad fellows."

"He did good service at the Red Wall fight, however, for it was he who got Ts'ao Ts'ao to chain his ships together."

"It was simply that Ts'ao wished to chain his ships together. No credit was due to this fellow. In any case I give you my word that I will not employ him. That much is certain."

Lu Su went out and explained to P'ang T'ung that the failure was not due to lack of recommendation, but simply a whim of Sun Ch'uan's and he must put up with it. The disappointed suitor hung his head and sighed many times without speaking.

"I fear you are doomed to constant disappointment here," said Lu Su. "There is nothing you can hope for, eh?"

But still P'ang T'ung was silent.

"With your wonderful gifts of course you will be successful whithersoever you may go. You may take my word for that. But to whom will you go?"

"I think I will join Ts'ao Ts'ao," said P'ang T'ung suddenly.

"That would be flinging a gleaming pearl into darkness. Rather go to Liu Pei, who would appreciate you and employ you fittingly."

"The truth is that I have been thinking of this for a long time," said P'ang T'ung. "I was only joking just now."

"I will give you a letter to Liu Pei, and if you go to him you must try to maintain peace between him and my lord and get them to act together against Ts'ao Ts'ao."

"That has been the one desire of my life."

He took the letter offered by Lu Su and soon made his way to Chingchou. He arrived at a moment that K'ung-ming was absent on an inspection journey, but the doorkeeper announced him and said he had come to throw in his lot with Liu Pei. He was received, for he was no stranger in name.

When P'ang T'ung was admitted he made the ordinary salutation but did not make an obeisance and this, coupled with his ugly face, did not please his host.

"You have come a long and arduous journey," said Liu Pei.

At this point the suitor should have produced his letters from K'ung-ming and Lu Su, but did not. Instead he replied, "I hear, O Imperial Uncle, that you are welcoming the wise and receiving scholars, wherefore I have come to join your service."

"The country is decently peaceful now and unfortunately there is no office vacant. But away to the northeast there is a small magistracy, Leiyanghsien, which needs a chief. I can offer you that post until there should be something more fitting."

P'ang T'ung thought this rather poor welcome for a man of his talent. But his friend was absent, so he could do nothing but control his annoyance and accept. He took his leave and started.

But when he arrived at his post he paid no attention to business at all; he gave himself up entirely to dissipation. The taxes were not collected nor were lawsuits decided. News of this reaching Liu Pei, he was angry and said, "Here is this stiff-necked pedant throwing my administration into disorder."

So he sent Chang Fei to the district with orders to make a general inspection of the whole district and look into any irregularities and disorders. But as he thought there might be some tact needed Sun Ch'ien was also sent as coadjutor.

In due course the inquisitors arrived at Leiyanghsien, where they were received by the officials and welcomed by the people at the boundary. But the magistrate did not appear.

"Where is the magistrate?" asked Chang Fei.

"Ever since his arrival, a hundred days ago and more, he has attended to no business, but spends his days from morn to night in wine-bibbing and is always intoxicated. Just now he is sleeping off a debauch and is not yet risen."

This raised Chang Fei's choler and he would have dismissed the offender forthwith had not his colleague said, "P'ang T'ung is a man of great ability and it would be wrong to deal with him thus summarily. Let us enquire into it. If he is really so guilty we will punish his offence."

So they went to the magistracy, took their seats in the hall of justice and summoned the magistrate before them. He came with dress all disordered and still under the influence of wine.

"My brother took you for a decent man," said Chang Fei, angrily, "and sent you here as magistrate. How dare you throw the affairs of the district into disorder?"

"Do you think I have done as you say, General ?" said P'ang T'ung. "What affairs have I disordered?"

"You have been here over a hundred days and spent the whole time in dissipation. Is not that disorderly?"

"Where would be the difficulty in dealing with the business of a trifling district like this? I pray you, General, to sit down for a while till I have settled the cases."

Thereupon he bade the clerks bring in all the arrears and he would settle them at once. So they brought in the piles of papers and ordered the suitors to appear. They came and knelt in the hall while the magistrate, pencil in hand, noted this and minuted that, all the while listening to the pleadings. Soon all the difficulties and disputes were adjusted, and never a mistake was made, as the satisfied bows of the people proved. By midday the whole of the cases were disposed of and the arrears of the hundred days settled and decided. This done the magistrate threw aside his pencil and turned to the inquisitors saying, "Where is the disorder? When I can take on Ts'ao Ts'ao and Sun Ch'uan as easily as I can read this paper, what attention from me is needed for the business of this paltry place?"

Chang Fei was astonished at the man's ability, rose from his seat and crossed over saying, "You are indeed a marvel, Master. I have not treated you respectfully enough but now I shall commend you to my brother with all my might."

Then P'ang T'ung drew forth Lu Su's letter and showed it to Chang Fei.

"Why did you not show this to my brother when you first saw him?" asked Chang Fei.

"If I had had a chance I would have done so. But is it likely that one would just take advantage of a letter of commendation to make a visit?"

Chang Fei turned to his colleague and said, "You just saved a wise man for us."

They left the magistracy and returned to Liu Pei to whom they related what had happened. Liu Pei then seemed to be conscious of his error and said, "I have been wrong; I have behaved unjustly to a sage."

Chang Fei then gave his brother the letter in which Lu Su had recommended P'ang T'ung. Opening it he read:— "P'ang Shih-yuan is not the sort of man to be met with in any day's march. Employ him in some capacity where extraordinary talent is required and his powers will declare themselves. Beware of judging him by his looks or you may lose the advantage of his abilities and some other will gain him. This would be a misfortune."

While he was feeling cast down at the mistake he had made, as shown by the letter, they announced the return of K'ung-ming. Soon he entered the hall and the first question he put after the formal salutations was "Is Instructor-General P'ang quite well?"

"He is in charge of Leiyang," replied Yuan-te, "where he is given to wine and neglects his business."

K'ung-ming laughed. "My friend P'ang has extraordinary abilities and ten times my knowledge. I gave him a letter for you, my lord. Did he present it?"

"This very day I have received a letter, but from Lu Su. I have had no letter written by you."

"When a man of transcendant abilities is sent to a paltry post he always turns to wine out of simple ennui," said K'ung-ming.

"If it had not been for what my brother said, I should have lost a great man," said Yuan-te. Then he lost no time, but sent Chang Fei off to the north to request P'ang T'ung to come to Chingchou. When he arrived Liu Pei went out to meet him and at the foot of the steps asked pardon for his mistake. Then P'ang T'ung produced the letter that K'ung-ming had given him. What Yuan-te read therein was this:—"As soon as the "Phoenix Fledgeling" shall arrive he should be given an important post." Liu Pei rejoiced indeed as he read it, for had not Ssuma Hui said of the two men, Sleeping Dragon and Phoenix Fledgeling, that any man who obtained the help of either of them could restore the empire when he would? As he now had them both surely the Hans would rise again.

Then he appointed P'ang T'ung as Chuko Liang's assistant and gave him general's rank, and the two famous strategists began training the army for its work of subjugation.

News of these doings came to the capital and Ts'ao Ts'ao was told of Liu Pei's two strategists and of the army in training and the stores he was accumulating and the league between his two chief enemies. And he knew that he had to expect an attack sooner or later. So he summoned his strategists to a council.

Said Hsun Yu, "Sun Ch'uan should be first attacked, because of the recent death of their ablest general Chou Yu. Liu Pei will follow."

Ts'ao Ts'ao replied, "If I go on such a distant expedition, Ma T'eng will fall upon the capital. While I was at Ch'ihpi there were sinister rumours of this and I must guard against it."

Hsun Yu said, "The best thing that occurs to stupid me is to obtain for Ma the title of 'Subduer of the South' and send him against Wu. Thus he can be enticed to the capital and got rid of. Then you can have no fear of marching southward."

Ts'ao Ts'ao approved and soon Ma T'eng was summoned from Hsiliang, in the west.

Ma T'eng, called also Ma Shou-ch'eng, was a descendant of the famous leader Ma Yuan, styled General, "Queller of the Waves." His father's name was Ma Su. He had held a minor magistracy in the reign of Emperor Huan, but had lost it and drifted west into Shensi where he got amongst the *Ch'iang*, one of whose women he took to wife. She bore him a son, Ma T'eng. Ma T'eng was rather over the common height, and bold-looking. He was of a mild disposition and very popular. But in the reign of Emperor Ling these *Ch'iangs* made trouble and then Ma T'eng raised a force and put it down. For his services he received the tile of General, "Corrector of the West." He and Han Sui, who was known as "Guardian of the West," were pledged brothers.

On receipt of the summons to the capital he took his eldest son, Ma Ch'ao, into his confidence and told him some of his former life. "When Tung Ch'eng got the Girdle Edict" from the Emperor, we formed a society, of which Liu Pei was one, pledged to put down rebellion. However, we accomplished nothing, for Tung was put to death and Liu was unfortunate, while I escaped to the west. However, I hear that Liu Pei now holds Chingchou and I am inclined to carry out the plan we made so long ago. But here I am summoned by Ts'ao Ts'ao and what is to be done?"

Ma Ch'ao replied, "Ts'ao Ts'ao has the command of the Emperor to call you and if you do not go that will mean disobeying an imperial command and you will be punished. Obey the summons in so far as to go to the capital, where you may be able to arrange to carry out your original intention."

But his nephew, Ma Tai, held other opinions and opposed this. Said he, "Ts'ao's designs are unfathomable and if you go, Uncle, I fear you will suffer."

"Let me lead the army against the capital," said Ma Ch'ao. "Can we not purge the empire of evil?"

But his father said, "You must take command of the *Ch'iang* troops for the defence of our territory here. I will take with me your two brothers and your cousin. When Ts'ao knows that you have the *Ch'iang* at your call and that Han Sui is prepared to assist, he will hardly dare to work any harm to me."

"Father, if you must go be careful not to enter the city till you know exactly what plots and machinations are afoot."

"I will certainly take great care, so do not be too anxious," said the father.

The order of march was prepared. The governor took five companies, with his two sons as leaders of the van and his nephew bringing up the rear. These set out along the tortuous road to the capital. At twenty *li* distance they camped.

When Ts'ao heard of Ma T'eng's arrival he called to him Huang K'uei, one of his officers, and said to him, "Ma T'eng is to be sent against the south and I shall send you as adviser. You are first to go to his camp and express my congratulations on his arrival and say that as Hsiliang is so distant and transport very difficult, he is not to take too large an army of his own. I will send a large force. Also tell him to come in soon for audience of the Emperor. I will send him supplies."

With these instructions Huang K'uei went to Ma T'eng, who brought out wine and entertained him well. In his cups the messenger grew confidential and said, "My father perished at the hands of Li and Kuo and I have always nourished resentment. Now there is another rebel in power wronging our prince."

"Who is that?" asked Ma.

"The wrong doer is that rebel Ts'ao, of course. Do you mean to say you do not know?"

However, Ma was careful. He thought it very likely that these words were but a trap for him so he pretended to be greatly shocked and begged his guest to be careful lest he be overheard.

But he cared not. "Then you have quite forgotten, the 'Girdle Edict,' eh?" shouted he.

Ma T'eng began to see he was sincere and presently became confidential in turn and told his guest all his schemes.

"He wants you to go in to audience; there is no good intention there. Do not go." said Huang K'uei. "You lead your men up close to the city and get Ts'ao Ts'ao to come and review them and when he comes, assassinate him."

They two settled how this plan could be worked out and the messenger, still hot with anger and excitement, returned to his home.

Seeing him so disturbed in mind his wife asked him what was wrong. But he would tell her nothing. However, he had a concubine, born of the Li family, called "Fragrance of the Spring." And it happened that she had an intrigue with the wife's younger brother, Miao-tse, who much desired to marry her. The concubine who also saw her lord's displeasure, spoke of it to her paramour, and he told her she could probably draw from him what was wrong by a leading question. "Ask him what is the truth about two men, Liu Pei and Ts'ao Ts'ao? Who is the wicked one."

That evening Huang K'uei went to the apartments of his concubine and she presently put the question proposed by her lover. Her lord, still rather intoxicated, said, "You are only a woman; still you know right from wrong as well as I. My enemy and the man I would slay if I could, is Ts'ao Ts'ao."

"But why? And if you wish to slay him, why do you not do something?" said she.

"I have done something. I have settled with General Ma to assassinate Ts'ao at the review."

"Fragrance of the Spring" of course told her paramour, who told

Ts'ao Ts'ao, and he made his arrangements to defeat the scheme. He called up certain trusty captains and gave them orders for the morrow and, this done, he arrested Huang K'uei and all his household.

Next day, as arranged, Ma and his western men came close up to the wall and among the flags and banners he discerned that of the Minister himself, whereby he knew that he would hold the review in person.

So he rode forward. Suddenly a bomb exploded and at this signal there appeared bodies of armed men right and left and in front, so that the western men were quite hemmed in. Ma T'eng then saw the mistake he had made and he and his two sons fought valiantly to free themselves from the trap. The youngest son soon fell. Father and son rode this way and that, seeking a way out, but failed on every side. Both were sorely wounded and when their steeds fell from their many arrow wounds, both were captured.

Ma T'eng and his son, and the miserable wretch who could not keep his counsel, were brought before Ts'ao. Huang loudly protested his innocence. Ts'ao then called in the witness Miao-tse.

"That worthless scoundrel has spoiled all my plans!" cried Ma T'eng. "Now I cannot slay the rebel and purge my country. But it is the will of God."

Father and son were dragged forth, the father uttering volleys of abuse all the time. And so three men came to harm in this adventure.

> The son and father share one niche of fame,
> For purest loyalty their praise the same.
> To their own hurt the rebels they withstood,
> Content to die to make their pledges good.
> In blood the solemn oath they did indite
> To slay the wicked and preserve the right.
> A worthy father's worthy son by western bride,
> Old Fu-po's name his grandson glorified.

"I desire no other reward than the lady, 'Fragrance of the Spring' as wife," said the betrayer.

Ts'ao smiled and said, "For the sake of a woman then you have brought a whole household to death. What advantage would there be in preserving such a miscreant?"

So he bade the executioners put both the traitor and the woman to death, with the Huang household. Those who saw the fearful vengeance sighed at its cruelty.

> Through passion base a loyal man was slain,
> And she who shared his passion shared his fate;
> The man they served was pitiless in hate,
> And thus a mean man's treachery was vain.

Ts'ao Ts'ao did not desire to rouse the rancour of the men of Hsiliang, wherefore he proclaimed to them, "The intended treachery of your leaders was theirs alone." However, he sent to secure the passes so that Ma Tai should not escape.

As has been said, Ma Tai led the rearguard. Before long the fugitives from the main army came and told him what had occurred at the capital. This frightened him so much that he abandoned his army and escaped disguised as a trader.

Having slain Ma T'eng, Ts'ao Ts'ao decided to set out on his expedition to the south. But then came the disquieting news of the military preparations of Liu Pei, whose objective was said to be Ssuch'uan. This caused him alarm, for, as he said, the bird's wings would be fully grown if he obtained possession of the west. He recognised the difficulty, but from among his counsellors there arose one who said, "I know how to prevent Liu Pei and Sun Ch'uan from helping each other and both Chiangnan and Hsich'uan will be yours."

> Chill death struck down the heroes of the west,
> Calamity approached the bold men of the south.

The next chapter will unfold the scheme.

CHAPTER LVIII

AN EXPEDITION FOR REVENGE:
EXPEDIENTS TO CON-CEAL IDENTITY

"What is this good plan of yours, friend Ch'en?" asked Ts'ao of the speaker, who was a civilian in his service named Chi'en Ch'un.

Ch'en replied, "Your two principal enemies are now firm allies, close as lips and teeth. But Liu Pei wants Hsich'uan and if you, O Minister, send a mighty host against Sun Ch'uan, he must ask help from his friend Liu, who, having his heart set on the west, will refuse it. Sun without this aid cannot stand and will become so weak that Chiangtung will be yours for the taking and Chingchou will follow in a tap of the drum. The west will follow and the whole Empire is yours."

"Those are my thoughts put into words," replied Ts'ao Ts'ao.

The expeditionary force of thirty legions set out for the south. Chang Liao of Hofei was in command of the supply department.

Sun Ch'uan speedily heard of the move and called in his advisers. At the council Chang Chao said, "Let us send to Lu Su to tell him to write at once to Liu Pei that he may help us. They are good friends and Liu will certainly respond favourably. Beside, since Liu Pei and Sun Ch'uan are now connected by marriage, there is no risk of refusal. With the support of Liu Pei there is no danger to our country."

Sun Ch'uan listened to this advice and sent to Lu Su bidding him to ask help from Liu Pei. Accordingly, on receipt of this command, a letter was written to Liu Pei, who after reading it, retained the messenger at the guest-house till K'ung-ming could arrive from Nanchun. As soon as he arrived Liu Pei showed him the letter. The adviser said, "It is not necessary for Chiangnan troops to move, nor need we send ours. I can prevent Ts'ao Ts'ao from even daring to look in a south-easterly direction."

So he wrote a reply telling Lu Su he could lay aside all anxiety and rest content, for should the northern army approach, they would be forced backward at once.

The letter was given to the messenger and then Liu Pei asked his adviser how he could hope to roll back the huge army that Ts'ao had prepared to bring south.

He replied, "Ts'ao Ts'ao's chief fear is Hsiliang. Now just lately he has slain Ma T'eng and his son as well, and the men of Hsiliang are grinding their teeth with rage. Now you must write and ask Ma Ch'ao to march through the pass and Ts'ao will have no leisure to think of any expedition to the south."

The letter was written, sent by a trusty hand and duly delivered.

Now Ma Ch'ao was in Hsiliang. One night he had a vision. In his dream he saw himself lying out on a snowy plain and many tigers were coming up and biting him. He awoke in a fright and began to wonder what the dream portended. Failing to explain it, he told the dream to his officers. One of them ventured to say the portent was evil. This was one, P'ang Te, a junior officer.

"What is your interpretation?" asked Ma Ch'ao.

"Meeting with tigers on a snowy plain is a very inauspicious subject to dream about. Assuredly our old General is in trouble at the capital."

And at that moment one came in in hot haste and cast himself on the earth weeping and crying, "Both your uncle and your brother are dead."

It was Ma Tai and he told the story of the evil that had fallen through Huang K'uei and the plotted assassination that had miscarried and become known. They two had been put to death in the market place and he had escaped in disguise.

Ma Ch'ao fell to the ground and wept bitterly, grinding his teeth with rage at his enemy Ts'ao. They lifted him to his feet and led him away to repose.

Soon after arrived a messenger with a letter from Liu Pei, which read like this:—"In these latter days of the hapless Hans, when the rebellious and tyrannical Ts'ao monopolises all power, to the injury of the Emperor and the wretchedness of the people, I, Liu Pei, recall that I and your father were recipients of an edict and we swore to exterminate the recreant. Now your father has suffered death at the hands of the tyrant and you must avenge him. As the holy books say, you cannot let the same sky cover you nor the same sun shine upon you and your father's murderer. If you can lead your men to attack Ts'ao on one side I will march my armies to prevent his retreat and he will be taken and all his evil crew can be exterminated. Then and thus will your father be avenged and the Hans can be restored. I might add more but I will await your reply."

Wiping his tears, Ma Ch'ao wrote a reply which was returned by the bearer.

The Hsiliang army was then mustered; horse and foot were assembled. Just before the day that had been fixed for the start the Governor of the district, Han Sui, sent for Ma Ch'ao, to whom he showed a letter from Ts'ao Ts'ao promising the Marquisate of Hsiliang as a reward for sending Ma Ch'ao a prisoner to the capital.

"Bind us both, Uncle, and send us thither; you need not move a single spear," said the younger man prostrating himself.

But Han Sui raised him saying, "Your father and I were sworn brothers; think you I would harm you? Rather will I help if you are going to fight."

Ma Ch'ao expressed his gratitude. The unhappy bearer of Ts'ao Ts'ao's letter was dragged forth and beheaded. This done the two took count of their armies. Han Sui had eight divisions under as many commanders, all to be relied upon to follow Han Sui, while the younger man had twenty legions counting those under P'ang Te and Ma Tai. Such were the forces with which they could attack Ch'angan the capital.

The commander of that city was Chung Yu. As soon as he heard what was afoot he sent a fleet messenger to Ts'ao and prepared for defence. He led his force out into the open plain and arrayed it for battle.

Ma Tai, with a legion and half, came on first, pouring over the countryside like a flood. Chung Yu would parley with him, but he came forward, sword in hand, to attack. However, the defender did not take the challenge but turned and fled. Ma Tai followed in pursuit. Soon the main body of the invaders arrived and they surrounded the city, which Chung Yu set about defending.

Ch'angan had been the capital of the western Hans and so was well fortified with a solid wall and a deep moat, safe against the most terrific attacks. The new armies besieged the city for ten days without success. Then P'ang Te proposed a plan. Said he, "Since the land about the city is barren and the water bitter, the people must have communication with the country around in order to live. Further they have no fuel. Ten days of siege must have exhausted the supplies in the city, wherefore if we relax for a time—well, you will see. We shall capture the city without moving a finger."

"Your plan seems excellent," said Ma Ch'ao, when he heard what it was.

Thereupon they sent orders to each division to retire and Ma

Ch'ao covered the retreat. Next day Chung Yu went up on the walls to look around and saw that the besiegers had gone. However, suspecting a ruse, he sent out spies, who returned to say the soldiers had really moved away to a distance. Wherefore he felt much relieved and allowed both soldiers and people to go out into the country to cut the much-needed firewood and bring in water. The city gates, thrown wide open, were thronged with those passing in and out.

This continued for five days and then they heard that Ma Ch'ao's army was returning. A panic ensued. The people rushed into the city and the gates were once more barred.

The captain of the west gate was Chung Chin, brother of Chung Yu. About the third watch of the night a torch was seen moving just inside the gate and when the captain went to see what was wrong, and was passing the gateway, a man suddenly galloped up and slashed at him with a sword. At the same time he shouted "Here is P'ang Te!" The captain of the gate was taken aback, could not defend himself and was cut down. The gate guard was soon disposed of, the gates were shattered and the soldiers outside came pouring in. Chung Yu escaped by the opposite gate and left the City in the hands of his enemies. He reached Chang Pass, where he fortified himself and sent news of the misfortune to Ts'ao Ts'ao.

Ts'ao Ts'ao threw aside all plans for his expedition to the south when Ch'angan was lost. He at once ordered that the unfortunate Chung Yu at Chang Pass should be replaced by Ts'ao Hung and Hsu Huang, who had a legion under their command. They were told to hold the Pass at all costs for at least ten days, or they should pay for its loss with their heads. After ten days the Pass would be no concern of theirs, for Ts'ao Ts'ao would be there with the main army.

The two captains made all haste to the Pass and took over the command from Chung Yu. They confined themselves to defence and though Ma Ch'ao appeared every day and reviled and said shameful things of the three generations of Ts'ao Ts'ao's family, the guardians of the Pass remained quiet. But Ts'ao Hung fretted at the daily insults and would have led the defenders out to fight had not his colleague restrained him.

"Ma Ch'ao only wishes to provoke you to come out, but remember our orders and go not. The Minister has some master plan."

So spake Hsu Huang. But the advice was hard to follow for Ma Ch'ao's men took turns in reviling the defenders of the Pass, resting neither day nor night. And Hsu Huang found it hard to curb his colleague's impatience.

Thus it continued till the ninth day. Then the defenders saw that their enemies had turned all their horses loose and were lolling about on the grass and sleeping as if quite fatigued. Thereupon Ts'ao Hung bade them saddle his horse, told off three companies and soon this small force was dashing down to catch the besiegers unprepared. They at once fled leaving their steeds and throwing aside their weapons. Ts'ao Hung could not resist pursuit and chased them.

At this time Hsu Huang was higher up the road taking in cartloads of grain and forage; but when he heard what his impulsive colleague had done he hastily got some men together and went to his rescue. He shouted to Ts'ao Hung to return.

Suddenly a great shouting arose near him and out dashed Ma Tai to attack. Both Ts'ao and Hsu turned to flee, but the drums rolled and two bodies of men came out from behind the hills. Then a battle began which went against them from the first. The Ts'ao men fell fast, but some of them thrust through the press and made for the Pass. Their enemies came in close pursuit and they had to abandon their post and flee whither they could find a way.

Ts'ao Hung made all haste to his master to give him the evil tidings.

"When I gave you the limit of ten days, why did you leave the Pass on the ninth?"

"Those men from Hsiliang hurled every sort of insult at us," replied Ts'ao Hung, "And when I thought I had them unprepared I took the opportunity. But I fell victim to their cunning."

"You are young and impetuous. But, Hsu Huang, you ought to have known."

"He would not listen though I told him many times. And that day I was taking in stores in another part of the Pass. As soon as they told me I felt sure there would be some misfortune and so I hastened after him, but it was too late."

Ts'ao Ts'ao was annoyed and ordered Ts'ao Hung to be put to death. But his brother-officers begged that he might be pardoned, and as he had confessed his fault, he was allowed to go free and unpunished.

Ts'ao Ts'ao advanced to Chang Pass and Ts'ao Jen said it would be well to establish a strong stockade before attacking. So trees were felled and a strong stockade built. They made three camps and Ts'ao himself was in the centre one.

Soon after, Ts'ao and all his officers in a body rushed to attack the Pass. They ran against the Hsiliang men posted on two sides, halted and formed their array. This done, Ts'ao rode to the centre standard whence he looked at his opponents.

He saw before him a body of fine men, every one with the bearing of a hero. And the leader, Ma Ch'ao, was worthy of them, with his pale face and red lips, his supple hips and broad shoulders, his deep voice and fierce strength. He was wearing a silver helmet and gripped a long spear as he sat there on his charger. P'ang Te and Ma Tai supported him and Ts'ao Ts'ao admired him in his secret heart. However, Ts'ao urged forward his steed and shouted to Ma Ch'ao, "Why are you arrayed against the Hans, whom your father and grandfather served faithfully?"

Ma ground his teeth and cursed Ts'ao Ts'ao for a rebel, a betrayer of both prince and people, the murderer of his father and brother. "My hate for you is to the death; the same sky shall not continue to cover us for I will take you captive and satiate my appetite on your living flesh."

With this he set his spear and rode over toward Ts'ao Ts'ao as if to slay him. But Yu Chin came out from behind and engaged Ma Ch'ao in battle. These two fought some half score bouts and then Yu Chin had to flee. Chang Ho, however, took his place and the two heroes exchanged a score of passes. Then Chang Ho, too, ran away.

Next to come forth was Li T'ung. Ma Ch'ao's martial prowess was now at its height and he made short work of Li T'ung, who went out of the saddle at the first blow. Then Ma Ch'ao flourished his spear at the men behind him as a signal for them to come on, which they did like a flood. They overwhelmed Ts'ao's men and Ma Ch'ao and his colleague rode forward to try to capture Ts'ao Ts'ao.

They came close. Ts'ao heard one of his pursuers shout to another, "That is he in the red dress!" So he hastily tore off his red robe and threw it away. He also heard one say "That is Ts'ao Ts'ao with the long beard!" At once Ts'ao took the sword that he wore at his side and sawed off some of the beard. Yet again a soldier recognised him and told Ma Ch'ao that Ts'ao had now cut his beard, whereupon the order went forth to capture short beards. And then Ts'ao Ts'ao wrapped the corner of a flag about neck and jowl and fled.

> Panic seized upon the soldiers at T'ung Pass;
> Frightened, Meng-te flung off his brocade robe

And, terror-stricken, sawed his beard off with a sword.
The fame of Ma Ch'ao rose even to the sky.

Ts'ao had got clear of the battle and was getting calmer. Then again the sound of hoofs fell upon his ears and on looking round he perceived Ma Ch'ao quite close. He and those near were panic-stricken, and all scattered for their lives, careless of the fate of their captain.

"Ts'ao Ts'ao, do not flee!" cried Ma coming nearer.

The whip dropped from Ts'ao Ts'ao's nerveless hand as he saw his enemy coming closer and closer. But just as Ma had levelled his spear for a thrust Ts'ao slipped behind a tree, changed the direction of his flight and so escaped, while Ma struck the tree. He quickly pulled out his spear but the delay gave the fugitive an advantage although it did not quite free him from pursuit, for Ma Ch'ao was soon again galloping on his track. As they drew near the slope of some hills a bold captain suddenly appeared, who cried, "Do not hurt my lord!"

This was Ts'ao Hung and he went toward Ma Ch'ao, whirling his sword. Ma Ch'ao was stopped and this saved Ts'ao Ts'ao's life. Ts'ao Hung and Ma Ch'ao fought half a hundred bouts till both began to grow weary and become uncertain of their strokes. And when, shortly after, Hsiahou Yuan appeared with a half score of horse, Ma Ch'ao found it prudent to retire.

Then Ts'ao Ts'ao was escorted to his camp. Although he had lost Ts'ao Jen yet the camps were still unharmed and the losses had not been great.

As he sat in his tent Ts'ao said, "Had I not spared Ts'ao Hung I should have fallen at the hands of Ma Ch'ao today." So he called in his rescuer and rewarded him well. And they got together the scattered men and strengthened the camp, deepening the moat and raising the rampart. Ma Ch'ao came daily and challenged any one to combat and abused them all shamefully, but, by the order of the General these insults were treated with silent contempt.

"Our enemies use long spears," said the officers. "We will meet them with bows and crossbows."

"They may have long spears," replied Ts'ao Ts'ao, "but whether I give battle or not depends on my decision. How can they thrust at us if we do not go out? All you have to do is to take no notice of them and they will speedily retire."

The officers wondered. They said one to another, "The Minister came out on this expedition of his own will and was foremost in the fight; why does he accept defeat so easily?"

After some days the spies reported that Ma Ch'ao had been reinforced by the *Ch'iang*, the tribesmen beyond the frontier. Ts'ao Ts'ao took the news gleefully. His officers asked him why the news pleased him and Ts'ao Ts'ao replied, "Wait till I have defeated them and I will explain."

Three days later there was a report of further reinforcements and Ts'ao not only smiled but gave a banquet. His officers ridiculed him in secret.

Then said Ts'ao Ts'ao, "You gentlemen laugh because I cannot destroy Ma Ch'ao. Well then, can any one of you propose a plan?."

Then rose Hsu Huang and said, "O Minister, you have a large force here and the enemy are strongly posted beyond the Pass. This means that on the west side of the river they are unprepared. If you can get an army secretly across the river and block the ferry you will cut off their retreat, and if you can smite them on the north side of the river they can get no reinforcements and must fail."

"What you propose is just what I think," said, Ts'ao Ts'ao.

So Hsu Huang was placed over four companies and with Chu Ling marched to the west of the river and hid in the gullies. They were to wait till Ts'ao Ts'ao crossed the river to the north so that both could strike together.

Then Ts'ao Ts'ao ordered Ts'ao Hung to prepare boats and rafts at the ferry. Ts'ao Jen was left in command of the camps.

Ts'ao Ts'ao himself crossed the River Wei, and when Ma Ch'ao heard of the new military movements he said, "I understand. The Pass is left, rafts are being prepared; that means that he is going to cross to the north side and cut off my retreat. I must coast along the river and keep him off. If I can do that his food will run short within twenty days and that will cause a mutiny. I will travel along the south bank and attack."

Han Sui did not approve this plan. He quoted the military maxim to strike when troops were half over the river. "Attack from the south bank when his army is in the act of crossing and his men will be drowned in the river," said he.

"Uncle, your words are good," replied Ma Ch'ao. And the spies went forth to find out the time of crossing the river.

When Ts'ao Ts'ao's preparations were complete and all was ready he sent three parties of soldiers over the river first. They reached the ferry at the first sign of dawn and the veterans were sent over first and lay out a camp. Ts'ao and his guard took up station on the south bank to watch the crossing.

Very soon the sentinels reported the approach of a General dressed all in white, whom everyone knew must be Ma Ch'ao. This terrified them and they made a rush to get into the boats. The river bank became a scene of shouting men struggling who could first embark. Ts'ao Ts'ao sat watching and never stirred. He only issued orders to stop the confusion. Meanwhile the yelling of the men and the neighing of the horses of the approaching army came nearer and nearer. Suddenly a captain jumped out of one of the boats and shouted to Ts'ao. "The rebels are close! Get into a boat, O Minister."

"The rebels are near; why not?" replied Ts'ao simply to the speaker, who was Hsu Ch'u. And he turned round to look at them.

As a fact Ma Ch'ao was very close, not a hundred paces away, and Hsu Ch'u laid hold of Ts'ao and dragged him down the bank. The boat had already pushed off and was ten feet from the bank but Hsu Ch'u took Ts'ao Ts'ao on his back and leaped on board. The boat was small and in danger of being overturned, wherefore Hsu Ch'u drew his sword and chopped away at the hands clinging to the side so that the men fell back into the water.

The boat went down stream, Hsu Ch'u standing in the prow poling as hard as he could. His master crouched out of sight at his feet.

When Ma Ch'ao saw the boat in mid-stream drifting down with the current he took his bow and arrows and began to shoot. He also ordered his brave captains to go along the river and shoot so that a shower of arrows fell about the boat. Hsu Ch'u fearing Ts'ao Ts'ao would be wounded, protected him with a saddle which he held over him with his left hand, for Ma Ch'ao's shooting was not in vain. Many of the men working the boat were wounded. Some had fallen overboard, while more lay in the bottom of the boat. The boat itself got out of control and was whirled hither and thither by the current. Hsu Ch'u straddled over the tiller and tried thus to guide the boat while he poled with one hand and with the other held the protecting saddle over Ts'ao Ts'ao's head.

Then the Magistrate of Weinan, Ting P'ei, who from a hill top saw that Ts'ao Ts'ao was very closely pressed, nay, even in danger of his life, drove out from his camp all the cattle and horses there, so that they scattered over the hillside. This was too much for the born herdsmen of the plains. At sight of the beasts, they left the river and ran off to secure them. Nor had they any inclination to pursue their enemy.

And so Ts'ao Ts'ao escaped. As soon as they reached the northern shore the boat was scuttled. The rumour had spread that Ts'ao Ts'ao was on the river and in danger, so all his officers came to his aid. But he was now safe on shore. Hsu Ch'u's double armour was stuck full of arrows. His officers escorted Ts'ao Ts'ao to the

camp where they made their obeisance and expressed the hope that
he had not suffered seriously.

"The rebels very nearly caught me today," said he smiling.

"They would have got across the river had they not been
enticed away by the freeing of the cattle and horses. said Hsu Ch'u.

"Who was it that drew them off?" said Ts'ao Ts'ao.

Some one who knew told him. Before long the Magistrate Ting
came in to pay his respects and Ts'ao Ts'ao thanked him.

"I should have been a prisoner but for your happy thought," said
he. And the Magistrate received a rank in the army.

"Though they have gone, yet they will assuredly return
tomorrow," said Ting P'ei. "You must prepare to repel them."

"My preparations are all made," was the reply.

Ts'ao Ts'ao ordered his captains to spread themselves along the
river bank and throw up mounds as shelters for camps. If they saw
the enemy approaching the soldiers were to be withdrawn from
behind the mounds, leaving the ensigns all flying, so as to give the
impression that each camp contained a garrison. Along the river
they were to dig ditches and put up sheds, thus to entice the
enemy there and their men would stumble into the pits and fall
easy victims.

Ma Ch'ao returned to Han Sui and told him how he had nearly
captured Ts'ao Ts'ao, but a certain bold captain had taken Ts'ao on
his back and leaped with him into a boat.

Han Sui replied, "I have heard that Ts'ao Ts'ao had a body guard
of the bravest and strongest soldiers under the command of Tien
Wei and Hsu Ch'u. They are called the Tiger Guards. Now as Tien
Wei is dead, the man you saw must have been Hsu Ch'u. He is both
brave and powerful and goes by the name of Tiger-lust. You will do
well to avoid him."

"I know his name, too," said Ma.

"Ts'ao Ts'ao now means to attack our rear," continued Han Sui;
"let us attack first, before he can establish camps and stockades. If
once he can do that it will be difficult to dislodge him."

"My idea is that we should hold the north bank and prevent him
from crossing."

"Worthy nephew, keep guard here while I go along the bank of
the river and fight Ts'ao Ts'ao."

"If you will take P'ang Te as your van-leader, I am content," said
Ma Ch'ao.

So Han Sui and P'ang Te, with five legions, went away down to
the river, while Ts'ao again warned his captains to entice the enemy.

P'ang Te was in advance with a goodly squadron of iron-clad horsemen and they burst along at full speed. Then there arose a confused shouting as they all went plunging into the ditches prepared for them. P'ang Te soon leaped out, gained the level ground and laid about him with all his might. He slew many men and presently got out of the thick of the fight.

But Han Sui had also been involved and P'ang went afoot to try to aid him. On the way he met Ts'ao Jung, whom he cut down. Then mounting the dead man's steed he rode forward fiercely, slaying as he passed. He reached his leader whom he led away south-east. The men of Ts'ao Ts'ao pursued him, but Ma Ch'ao came with reinforcements and drove them off. He rescued a great number and they continued fighting till evening when they withdrew and mustered their men. Some officers were missing and a couple of hundred men had been killed when they fell into the pits.

Ma Ch'ao and Han Sui discussed what should next be done. "If we give the enemy time, he will make himself strong on the north bank. I think we can do no better than to raid his camp tonight."

"We must have a force and supports for it," said Han Sui.

So it was decided that Ma Ch'ao should lead the striking force with P'ang Te and Ma Tai as supports. They would start at nightfall.

Now Ts'ao's men were on the north bank of the Wei and he gave his captains orders, saying, "The rebels will try to surprise us as they are deceived by my not having set up stockades. You will place your men in ambush."

At nightfall Ma Ch'ao sent out a small scouting party, which seeing nothing, penetrated deep into the enemy's lines. Presently the signal was given. Out leapt the hidden men and in a few moments the whole scouting party were killed. And close at hand came the main army.

> Wait for the foe all undismayed,
> Place your men in ambuscade.
> Captains striving to outvie
> Are not beaten easily.

Who got the advantage will presently be told.

CHAPTER LIX

The fight narrated in the last chapter lasted till morn when each side drew off, Ma Ch'ao camping on the Wei River, whence he kept up harassing attacks both day and night. Ts'ao Ts'ao, also camped in the bed of the same river, began to construct three floating bridges out of his rafts and boats so as to facilitate communication with the south bank. Ts'ao Jen established a camp on the river, which he barricaded with his carts and waggons.

Ma Ch'ao determined to destroy this camp, so his men collected straw and each man marched with a bundle and took fire with him. Han Sui's men were to fight. While one party attacked, the other party piled up the straw, which they lit, and soon there was a fierce fire all around. The defenders could do nothing against it so they abandoned the camp and ran away. All the transport and bridges were destroyed. It was a great victory for the Hsiliang army and gave them the command of the River Wei.

Ts'ao Ts'ao was sad at the failure to make good his strong camp and fearful of his defencelessness. Then Hsun Yu proposed a mud wall. So three legions were set to build a mud rampart. The enemy seeing this harassed the workmen with perpetual attacks at different points so that the work went slowly. Beside the soil was very sandy and the wall would not stand but collapsed as fast as it was built. Ts'ao Ts'ao felt helpless.

It was the ninth month and the fierce cold of winter was just coming on. Ominous clouds covered the sky day after day with never a break. One day as Ts'ao Ts'ao sat in his tent, very disheartened, a stranger was announced and was led in. He was an old man who said he had a suggestion to offer. He was tall, sparely built and spiritual looking. He gave his name as Lou Tzu-po and said he came from Chingchao. He was a recluse and a Taoist, his religious name being Meng-mei or "Plum-blossom Dreamer." Ts'ao Ts'ao received him with great courtesy and presently the venerable one began, "O Minister, you have long been striving to make a camp on the river. Now is your opportunity; why not begin?"

"The soil is too sandy to stand," said Ts'ao. But If you have some other plan to propose, pray tell me what it is, O hermit."

"You are more than human, O Minister, in the art of war, and you surely know the times and seasons. It has been overcast for many days and these clouds foretell a north wind and intense cold. When the wind begins to blow you should hurry your men to carry up the earth and sprinkle it with water. By dawn your wall will be complete."

Ts'ao Ts'ao seized upon the suggestion. He offered his aged visitor a reward but he would receive nothing.

That night the wind came down in full force. Every man possible was set to earth-carrying and wetting. As they had no other means of carrying water they made stuff bags which they filled with water and let out the water over the earth. And so as they piled the earth they froze it solid with water, and by dawn the wall was finished and stood firm.

When his scouts told Ma Ch'ao that the enemy had built a wall, and he had ridden out and seen it, he was greatly perplexed and began to suspect help from the gods.

However, very soon after he got his whole army together and sounded an attack. Ts'ao Ts'ao himself rode out of the camp, with only the redoubtable Hsu Ch'u in attendance, and advanced toward the enemy. Flourishing his whip he called out, "I, Meng-te, am here alone and I beg Ma Ch'ao to come out to parley with me."

Thereupon Ma Ch'ao rode out, his spear set ready to thrust.

"You despised me because I had no wall to my camp but lo! in one single night, God has made me a wall. Do you not think it time to give in?"

Ma Ch'ao was so enraged that he almost rushed at Ts'ao Ts'ao, but he was not too angry to notice the henchman behind him, glaring in angry fashion, who held a gleaming sword in his grip. He thought this man could be no other than Hsu Ch'u, so he determined to find out. With a flourish of his whip he said, "Where is the noble 'Tiger Marquis' that I hear you have in your camp?"

At this Hsu lifted his sword and roared, "I am Hsu Ch'u of Ch'iaochun!" From his eyes shot gleams of supernatural light and his attitude was so terror-striking that Ma dared not move. He turned his steed and retired.

Ts'ao Ts'ao and his doughty follower returned to their camp and as they two passed between the armies not a man there but felt a quiver of fear.

"They know our friend Hsu Ch'u over there as Marquis Tiger," said Ts'ao Ts'ao when he returned.

And thereafter the soldiers all called him by that name.

"I will capture that fellow Ma tomorrow," said Hsu.

"Ma Ch'ao is very bold," said his master. "Be careful."

"I swear to fight him to the death," said Hsu.

Then he sent a written challenge to his enemy saying that the "Tiger Marquis" challenged Ma Ch'ao to a decisive duel on the morrow.

Ma Ch'ao was very angry when he received the letter. "Dare he insult me so?" cried he. Then he wrote his pledge to slay, Tiger-lust on the morrow.

Next day both armies moved out and arrayed in order of battle. Ma Ch'ao gave P'ang Te and Ma Tai command of the two wings, while Han Sui took the centre. Ma Ch'ao took up his station in front of the centre and called to Tiger-lust to come out. Ts'ao Ts'ao, who was on horseback by the standard, turned and said, "He is no less bold than Lu Pu."

As he spoke, Hsu Ch'u rode forth whirling his sword and the duel began. They fought over a hundred bouts and neither had the advantage. But then, their steeds being spent with galloping to and fro, each retired within his own lines and obtained a fresh mount. The contest was renewed and a hundred more encounters took place, still without victory to either.

Suddenly Hsu Ch'u galloped back to his own side, stripped off his armour, showing his magnificent muscles and, naked as he was, leaped again into the saddle and rode out to continue the battle.

Again the champions engaged, while both armies stood aghast. Thirty bouts more, and Hsu, summoning up all his force, plunged toward Ma with his sword held high to strike. But Ma avoided the stroke and rode in with his spear pointing directly at his opponent's heart. Throwing down his sword, Hsu dashed aside the spear, which passed underneath his arm.

Then ensued a struggle for the spear and Hsu by a mighty effort snapped the shaft so that each held one half. Then the duel was continued, each belabouring the other with the pieces of the broken spear.

At this point Ts'ao Ts'ao began to fear for his champion and so ordered two of his captains to go out and take a hand. At this P'ang Te and Ma Tai gave the signal to their armoured horsemen to attack. They rode in and a melee began in which Ts'ao's men were worsted and the great champion Hsu Ch'u received two arrow wounds in the shoulder. So the men of Ts'ao retreated to their stockade, Ma Ch'ao following them to the river. Ts'ao's men lost more than half their number.

Ts'ao barred his gates and allowed none to go out. Ma Ch'ao went down to the river. When he saw Han Sui he said, "I have seen some wicked fighters, but none to match that man. He is aptly nicknamed Tiger-lust."

Thinking that by strategy he might get the better of Ma Ch'ao, Ts'ao Ts'ao secretly sent two bodies of men across the river to take up position so that he might attack in front and rear.

One day from his ramparts, Ts'ao Ts'ao saw Ma Ch'ao and a few horsemen ride close up to the walls and then gallop to and fro like the wind. After gazing at them for a long time he tore off his helmet and dashed it on the ground saying, "If that Ma is not killed may I never be buried!"

Hsiahou Yuan heard him and his heart burned within him. He cried, "May I die here at once if I do not destroy that rebel!"

Without more ado he flung open the gates and rode out with his company. Ts'ao Ts'ao tried to stop this mad rush, but it was no good, so, fearing, he might come to grief, he rode out after him. At sight of the men of Ts'ao, Ma Ch'ao faced his men about extended them in line and, as the enemy approached, dashed forward to the attack. Then noticing Ts'ao himself among them he left Hsiahou and rode straight for Ts'ao. Panic seized Ts'ao and he rode for his life, while his men were thrown into confusion.

It was during the pursuit of this portion of the Ts'ao army that Ma Ch'ao was told of the force on the other bank of the river. Realising the danger he abandoned the pursuit, called in his men and went to his own camp, there to consult with Han Sui.

"What now? Ts'ao has crossed the river and we can be attacked in the rear," said Ma.

A certain Li K'an said, "Then you had better come to an agreement; sacrifice some territory and make peace. Then both can repose through the winter and await the changes and chances that may come with the spring warmth."

"He is wise," said Han Sui, "and I advise the same."

But Ma Ch'ao hesitated. Others exhorted him to make peace and at length he agreed. So Yang Ch'iu and Hou Hsuan were sent as messengers of peace to the camp of Ts'ao Ts'ao.

"You may return; I will send my reply," said Ts'ao when they had declared the purport of their mission. And they left.

Then Chia Yu said to Ts'ao Ts'ao, "What is your opinion, O Minister?"

"What is yours?" asked Ts'ao.

"War allows deceit, therefore pretend to agree. Then we can try some means of sowing suspicions between Han and Ma so that we may thereby destroy both."

Ts'ao clapped his hands for very joy. "That is the best idea of all! Most suitable! You and I agree in our ideas; I was just thinking of that."

So an answer was returned saying, "Let me gradually withdraw my soldiers and I will give back the land belonging to you on the west of the river." And at the same time Ts'ao ordered the construction of a floating bridge to help in the withdrawl.

When the reply arrived, Ma Ch'ao said to Han Sui, "Although he agrees to peace, yet he is evil and crafty. We must remain prepared against his machinations. Uncle, you and I will take turns in watching Ts'ao and Hsu Huang on alternate days. So shall we be safe against his treachery."

They agreed and began the regular alternate watch. Soon Ts'ao got to know what they were doing and he turned to Chia Hsu saying, "I am succeeding."

"Who keeps the look out on this side tomorrow?" asked Ts'ao. "Han Sui."

Next day Ts'ao at the head of a large party of his captains rode out of the camp and the officers presently spread out right and left, he himself remaining a solitary rider visible in the centre. Han Sui did not know that Ts'ao had come out. Presently Ts'ao called out, "Do any of you soldiers want to see Ts'ao Ts'ao? Here I am quite alone. I have not four eyes nor a couple of mouths, but I am very knowing."

The soldiers turned pale with fright. Then Ts'ao called up a man and told him to go and see Han Sui and say "Sir, the Minister humbly asks you to come and confer with him." Thereupon Han went out, and seeing Ts'ao wore no armour, Han also threw off his and rode out clad in a light robe. Each rode up to the other till their horse's heads nearly touched and there they stood talking.

Said Ts'ao, "Your father and I took our degrees at the same time and I used to treat him as an uncle. You and I set out on our careers at the same time, too, and yet we have not met for years. How old may you be now?"

"I am forty six," replied Han.

"In those old days in the capital we were both very young and never thought about middle age. If we could only restore tranquillity to the State, that would be a matter of rejoicing."

After that they chatted long about old times, but neither said a word on military matters. They gossiped for a couple of hours before they took leave of each other.

It was not long before some one told Ma Ch'ao of this meeting and he went over to his ally to ask about it.

"What was it Ts'ao Ts'ao came out to discuss today?" said he.

"He just recalled the old days when we were together in the capital."

"Did he say nothing about military matters?"

"Not a word; and I could not talk about them alone."

Ma Ch'ao went out without a word but he felt suspicious.

When Ts'ao returned to his camp he said to Chia Hsu, "Do you know why I talked with him thus publicly?"

"It may be an excellent idea," said Hsu, "but it is not sufficient simply to estrange two people. I can improve on it and we will make them quarrel and even kill each other."

"What is your scheme?"

"Ma Ch'ao is brave but not very astute. You write a letter with your own hand to Han himself and put in it some rambling statements about some harm that is going to happen. Then blot it out and write something else. Afterwards you will send it to Han, taking care that Ma shall know all about it. He will demand to read the letter, and when he sees that the important part of the letter has been changed, he will think that Han Sui has made the changes lest his secrets should leak out. This will fit into the private talk you had with Han the other day and the suspicion will grow until it has brought about trouble. I can also secretly corrupt some of his subordinates and get them to widen the breach and we can settle Ma Ch'ao."

"The scheme looks excellent," said Ts'ao, and he wrote the letter as suggested, and then erased and changed it, after which he sealed it securely and sent it across to Han Sui.

Surely enough some one told Ma Ch'ao about the letter, which increased his doubts, and he came to Han Sui's quarters to ask to see it. Han gave it to him and the erasures and alterations struck Ma at once.

"Why are all these alterations here?" asked he.

"It came like that; I do not know."

"Does any one send a rough draft like this? It seems to me, Uncle, that you are afraid I shall know something or other too well and so you have changed the wording."

"It must be that Ts'ao has sealed up the rough draft by mistake."

"I do not think so. He is a careful man and would not make such a mistake. You and I, Uncle, have been allies in trying to slay the rebel; why are you turning against me now?"

"If you doubt my word I will tell you what you can do. Tomorrow, in full view of the army, I will get Ts'ao Ts'ao to come out and talk. You can hide in behind the ranks ready to kill me if I am false."

"That being so I shall know that you are true, Uncle."

This arrangement made, next day Han Sui with five captains in his train, rode to the front while Ma Ch'ao concealed himself behind the great standard. Han Sui sent over to say that he wished to speak to the Minister.

Thereupon at his command, Ts'ao Hung, with a train of ten horsemen rode out, advanced straight to Han Sui, leaned over to him and said, loudly enough to be heard plainly, "Last night the Minister quite understood there is no mistake." Then without another word on either side he rode away.

Ma Ch'ao had heard. He gripped his spear and started galloping out to slay his companion in arms. But the five captains checked him and begged him to go back to camp. When Han Sui saw him, he said, "Nephew, trust me, really I have no evil intentions."

But think you that Ma Ch'ao did? Burning with rage he went away. While Han Sui talked over the matter with his five captains.

"How can this be cleared up?"

"Ma Ch'ao trusts too much to his strength," said Yang Ch'iu, one of them. "He is always inclined to despise you, Sir. If we overcome Ts'ao Ts'ao do you think he will give way to you? I think you should rather take care of your own interests, go over to the Minister's side and you will surely get rank one day."

"I was his father's pledged brother and could not bear to desert him," said Han Sui.

"It seems to me that as things have come to this pass you simply have to now."

"Who would act as go-between?" asked Han.

"I will," said Yang Ch'iu.

Then Han Sui wrote a private letter which he confided to Yang Ch'iu, who soon found his way over to other camp. Ts'ao Ts'ao was only too pleased, and he promised that Han Sui should be made Marquis of Hsiliang and Yang Ch'iu its Prefect. The other confederates should be rewarded in other ways. When the preparations for the act of treachery were complete a bonfire was to be lighted in Han's camp and all would try to do away with Ma Ch'ao.

Yang Ch'u went back and related all this to his chief and Han Sui felt elated at the success of his overtures. A lot of wood was collected in camp at the back of his tent ready for the signal blaze and the five captains got ready for the foul deed. It was decided that Ma Ch'ao should be persuaded into coming to a banquet and there they would slay him then.

All this was done, but not without some hesitation and delay, and some news of the plot reached Ma Ch'ao. He found out the careful preparations that had been made and resolved to act first. Leaving Ma Tai and P'ang Te in reserve, he chose a few trusted men and with stealthy steps made his way into Han Sui's tent. There he found Han Sui and his five confederates deep in conversation. He just caught a word or two that Yang Ch'iu said, "We must not delay, now is the time."

In burst Ma Ch'ao raging and yelling, "You herd of rebels! Would you dare to plot against me?"

They were taken aback. Ma Ch'ao sprang at Han Sui and slashed at his face. Sui put up his hand to ward off the blow and it was cut off. The five drew their swords and set on Ma Ch'ao and his men who rushed outside, followed by the five who slashed away, but were kept at bay by Ma Ch'ao's wonderful swordsmanship. And as the swords flashed, the red blood flowed. Soon one of the five was down and a second disabled; then the other three fled.

Ma Ch'ao ran back into the tent to finish Han Sui but the servants had removed him. Then a torch was lit, and soon there was commotion all through the camp. Ma Ch'ao mounted his horse, for P'ang Te and Ma Tai had now arrived, and the real fight began. Ts'ao's men poured in from all sides and the Hsiliang men fought with each other.

Losing sight of his companions, Ma Ch'ao and a few of his men got to the head of the floating bridge over the Wei just about dawn. There he fell across Li K'an coming over the bridge. Ma Ch'ao set his spear and rode at him full tilt. Li K'an let go his spear and fled. Lucky for him it seemed at first that Yu Chin came up in pursuit. But unable to get near enough to seize Ma Ch'ao, Yu Chin sent an arrow flying after him. Ma Ch'ao's ear caught the twang of the bowstring and he dodged the arrow, which flew on and killed Li K'an. Ma Ch'ao turned to attack his pursuer, who galloped away and then he returned and took possession of the bridge.

Quickly Ts'ao's men gathered about him and the fiercest among them, the Tiger Guards, shot arrows at Ma Ch'ao, which he warded off with his spear shaft so that they fell harmless to the earth. Ma Ch'ao and his men rode to and fro striking a blow wherever there was a chance, but the enemy were very thick about him and he could not force his way out. In desperation he made a dash northwards and got through, but quite alone. Of his followers every one fell.

Still he kept on dashing this way and that till he was brought down by a crossbow bolt. He lay upon the ground and his enemies were pressing in. But at the critical moment a troop came in from the north-west and rescued him. P'ang Te and Ma Tai had come up in the very nick of time.

Thus Ma Ch'ao was rescued and they set him on one of the soldiers' horses and he again took up the battle. Leaving a trail of blood in his rear he got away north-west.

Hearing that his enemy had got away, Ts'ao Ts'ao ordered his captains to pursue him day and night and offered rewards for him dead or alive. For his head the reward was a thousand taels and the marquisate of a fief of a myriad families. If any one captured Ma the reward was the rank of general. Consequently the pursuit was warm as every one was anxious to win renown and reward. Meanwhile careless of all but flight Ma galloped on and one by one his followers dropped by the way. The footmen who were unable to keep up were captured till very few remained and only some score of riders were left. They travelled toward Shensi.

Ts'ao Ts'ao in person joined the pursuit and got to Anting, but there Ma Ch'ao was still far in advance so he gave up and returned. Gradually the captains did the same, all coming back to Ch'angan. Poor Han Sui, with the loss of his left hand, was an invalid, but he was rewarded with the marquisate and his confederates, the five captains, were given rank and office.

Then orders were given to lead the whole army back to the capital. Yang Fou, a military officer of rank, came to Ch'angan to point out the danger of withdrawal. "Ma Ch'ao has the boldness of Lu Pu and the heart of a barbarian. Unless you destroy him this time he will come again and he will be both bolder and stronger, and the whole of this district will be lost to the Throne. Wherefore you should not withdraw your army."

Ts'ao said, "I would be quite willing to finish the subjugation but there is much to do in the capital and the south is still to conquer. So I cannot remain. But you, Sir, might secure this country for me. Do you consent?"

Yang Fou did consent. And he brought to Ts'ao Ts'ao's notice Wei K'ang, who was made Governor, with joint military powers. Just before Yang Fou left he said to Ts'ao Ts'ao, "A strong force ought to be left in Ch'angan, as a reserve in case they be required."

"That has been already dealt with," replied Ts'ao.

Contentedly enough Yang Fou took leave and went away.

His captains asked Ts'ao to explain his recent policy, since the first out-break at T'ung Pass and he replied, "The rebel first held the Pass. Had I forthwith taken the east the rebels would have defended the camps one by one and mustered at all the ferries, and I should never have got across the river. So I massed men against T'ung Pass and made the rebels guard the south so that the west was left open. Thus Hsu Huang and Chu Ling could cross over and I was able later to cross over to the north. Then I made the raised road and the mud rampart to deceive the enemy and cause them to think I was weak and thus embolden them up to the point of attacking without proper preparation. Then I used the clever device of causing dissension in their ranks and was able in one day to destroy the stored up energy of all their forces. It was a thunder clap before you could cover your ears. Yes indeed; the mutations of the art of war can be called infinite."

"But one thing more puzzled us," said the officers, "and we ask you to explain it. When you heard the enemy was reinforced you seemed to grow happier. Why was that?"

"Because the Pass was distant and if the rebels had taken advantage of all defensible points and held them, they could not have been quelled in less than a couple of years. When they came on altogether they made a multitude but they were not unanimous. They easily quarrelled and, disunited, were easily overcome. So I had reason to rejoice that they came on altogether."

"Indeed no one can equal you in strategy," said his officers, bowing low before him.

"Still, remember that I rely on you," said Ts'ao.

Then he issued substantial rewards to the army and appointed Hsiahou Yuan to the command at Ch'angan. The soldiers who had surrendered were distributed among the various troops. Hsiahou Yuan recommended Feng I, and one, Chang Chi, of Kaoling, as his aids.

So the army returned to the capital where it was welcomed by the Emperor in his State chariot. As a reward for his service Ts'ao Ts'ao was given the court privileges of omitting his distinctive name when he was received in audience and of proceeding toward the dais without assuming the appearance of frantic haste. Further he might go to court armed and booted, as did the Han Minister, Hsiao Ho, of old. Whence his prestige and importance waxed mightily.

The fame of these doings penetrated west into Hanchung, and

one of the first to be moved to indignation was Chang Lu, Prefect of Hanning. This Chang Lu was a grandson of Chang Ling who retired to Mount Humin, in Ssuch'uan, where he had composed a work on Taoism for the purpose of deluding the multitude.

Yet all the people respected him, and when he died his son, Chang Heng, carried on his work, and taught the same doctrines. Disciples had to pay a fee in rice, five measures. The people of his day called him the Rice Thief.

Chang Lu, his son, styled himself Master Superior and his disciples were called commonly devil soldiers. A headman was called Libationer and those who made many converts were called Chief Libationers. Perfect sincerity was the ruling tenet of the cult and no deceit was permitted. When any one fell ill an altar was set up and the invalid was taken into the Room of Silence where he could reflect upon his sins and confess openly. Then he was prayed for. The director of prayers was called Superintending Libationer.

When praying for a person they wrote his name on a slip and his confession and made three copies thereof, called "The writing of the Three Officers." One copy was burned on the mountain top as a means of informing Heaven; another was burned to inform Earth; and the third was sunk in water to tell the Controller of the Waters. If the sick person recovered he paid as fee five measures of rice.

They had Public Houses of Charity wherein the poor found rice and flesh and means of cooking. Any wayfarer was allowed to take of these according to the measure of his appetite. Those who took in excess would invite punishment from on high. Offences were pardoned thrice; afterwards offenders were punished. They had no officials but all were subject to the control of the Libationers.

This sort of cult had been spreading in Hanchung for some thirty years and had escaped repression so far because of the remoteness of the district. All the Government did was to give Chang a title and take means to secure from him a full quota of tribute.

When the reports of Ts'ao Ts'ao's success against the west, and his prestige and influence, reached the Hanchung people they met to consult, for they feared lest, T'eng and Ma being overcome, they would be next invaded. This Chang proposed to the assembly that he should assume the title of Prince of Hanning and superintend the defence.

In reply one Yen Pu said, "The families of this province are reckoned by myriads and there are ample supplies of everything.

This place is a natural stronghold. Now Ma Ch'ao's soldiers are newly defeated. The fugitives from the Tzuwu Valley are very numerous. My advice is that as Liu Chang of Ichou is weak we should take possession of Hsich'uan and then you may style yourself Prince as soon as you like."

This speech greatly pleased Chang Lu, who then began to concert measures with his brother to raise an army.

Stories of the movement reached Hsich'uan. It is necessary here to say a few words about the west. The governor was Liu Chang, a son of Liu Yen, a descendant from a Prince of the Imperial House. The Prince had been moved out to Ching-ling some generations ago and the family had settled there. Later, Liu Yen became an official and when he died in due course, his son was recommended for the vacant Prefectship of Ichou. There was enmity between the Perfect and the Changs because some of the latter's relatives had been put to death.

When he knew of the danger, Liu Chang despatched one P'ang Hsi as Prefect of Pahsi to ward off Chang Lu. But Liu Chang had always been feeble, and when he received news from his lieutenant of Chang Lu's movements his heart sank within him for fear and he hastily called in his advisers.

At the council one haughtily said, "My Master, be not alarmed, I am no genius but I have a bit of a healthy tongue and with that I will make Chang Lu afraid even to look this way."

> When plots did grow about the west,
> It suited Chingchou's plans best.

The speaker's name and lineage will be told in the next chapter.

CHAPTER LX

CHANG SUNG TURNS THE TABLES
ON YANG HSIU: OCCUPATION OF
SHU DISCUSSED

The man who proposed the plan spoken of in the last chapter was Chang Sung, who belonged to Ichou and held the small office of *pieh-chia*, or Supernumerary Charioteer. His appearance was grotesque. He had a broad forehead, protuberant at the temples like a countryman's hoe, and a pointed head. His nose was flat and his teeth protruded. He was a dwarf in stature but had a deep voice like a great bell.

"What proposal have you to offer that may avert this danger?"

"My proposal is that we gain the support of Ts'ao Ts'ao. As we know, he has made a clean sweep of the Empire. Lu Pu went first and both the Yuans followed, all exterminated. Lately he has destroyed Ma Ch'ao. In short he is the one man against whom no one can stand. Therefore, my lord, prepare me worthy gifts to take to the capital and I will get Ts'ao Ts'ao to march an army against Hanchung, which will keep this Chang Lu occupied so that we shall be left alone."

This met Liu Chang's views and so he prepared gold and pearls and rich stuffs, worthy presents for the man of power. And when these were ready he appointed Chang Sung his emissary. Chang Sung in the meantime occupied his leisure in secretly copying maps and plans of the west country. When all was ready he started with a small escort.

They heard this in Chingchou and K'ung-ming sent a trusty person to the capital to keep him informed as to all the doings.

Chang Sung arrived in Hsutu, and, after he had established himself in his lodging, he made daily visits to the Minister's Palace to try to obtain an interview. But his last success had filled Ts'ao Ts'ao with insufferable pride and he did nothing but give banquets.

He never appeared except for the most important affairs, and even carried on the business of the state in his own residence. So Chang Sung waited many days. But when he got to know the persons who were nearest the Minister, he bribed them and obtained an audience.

Ts'ao Ts'ao was seated in the high place, and after his visitor had finished his salutations, he said, "Your Master Liu Chang has sent no tribute for several years; why?"

"Because the roads are dangerous and thieves and robbers infest them. Intercourse is restricted."

Ts'ao interrupted in a loud harsh voice, "What thieves and robbers are there when I have cleansed the country?"

"How can you say the land is tranquil when one sees Sun Ch'uan in the south, Chang Lu in the north, Liu Pei in the west and every one of these with armies reckoned in legions? The weakest of them has half a score."

The mean appearance of the emissary had prejudiced Ts'ao Ts'ao from the outset, and when he heard these blunt words he suddenly shook out his sleeves, rose and left the hall. Those in attendance were annoyed with Chang Sung and said, "How can you behave so rudely when you come on a mission? Your whole attitude was blunt and discourteous. Happily for you our lord remembered you had come from afar and did not take open notice of your fault. The best thing for you is to go home again as quickly as you can."

But Chang Sung smiled. "We have no plausible flatterers and glib talkers in our western country," said he.

At this, one from below the steps called out, "So you call us plausible and glib then; and you have none such in your country, eh?"

Chang Sung looked around and saw the speaker was a man with thin delicate eyebrows crossing narrow eyes set in a pale spirituel face. He asked his name. It was Yang Hsiu, a son of Yang Piao. The young man was then employed in the commissariat of the Minister. He was deeply read and had the reputation of being a clever controversialist, as Chang Sung knew. So on one side was a desire to confound and on the other overweening pride in his own ability, with contempt for other scholars. Perceiving the ridicule in Chang Sung's speech Yang Hsiu invited him to go to the library where they could talk more freely. There, after they had got settled in their respective places, Yang Hsiu began to talk about the west country.

"Your roads are precipitous and wearisome," said Yang.

"But at our lord's command we travel, even through fire and water; we never decline," replied Chang.

"What sort of a country is this Shu?"

"Shu is a name for the group of districts known of old as Ichou. The roads are intersected by streams and the land bristles with steep mountains. The circuit is over two hundred marches and the area thirty thousand square *li*. The population is dense, villages being so close that the crowing of cocks in one waken the people in the next, and the dogs barking in this excite the curs in that. The soil is rich and well cultivated and droughts or famines are equally unknown. Prosperity is general and the music of pipes and strings can always be heard. The produce of the fields is piled mountain high. There is no place its equal."

"But what of the people?"

"Our administrators are talented as Hsiang-ju (Ssuma Hsiang-ju): our soldiers able as Fu-po (Ma Yuan): our physicians are expert as Chung-ching; our diviners are profound as Chun-p'ing (Yen Tsun). Our schools of philosophy and our culture stand forth as models and we have more remarkable men than I can enumerate. How should I ever finish the tale of them?"

"And how many such as you, Sir, do you think there are at the orders of your Governor?"

"Our officers are all geniuses; wise, bold, loyal, righteous and magnanimous. As for poor simpletons like me, they are counted by hundreds; there are cartloads of them; bushels of them. No one could count them."

"What office may you hold then?"

Chang Sung replied, "Mine can hardly be called an office. I am a Supernumerary Charioteer. But, Sir, what State affairs may you control?"

"I am an Accountant in the Palace of the Minister," replied Yang.

"They say that members of your family held office for many generations and I do not understand why you are not in court service actually assisting the Emperor, instead of filling the post of a mere clerk in a private Palace."

Yang Hsiu's face suffused with shame at this rebuke, but he mastered himself and replied, "Though I am among the minor officials, yet my duties are of great importance and I am gaining experience under the Prime Minister's guidance. I hold the office for the sake of the training."

Chang Sung smiled, "If what I have heard is true, Ts'ao Ts'ao's learning throws no gleaming light on the way of Confucius or

Mencius, nor does his military skill illumine the art of Sun or Wu. He seems to understand the doctrine of brute force and holding on to what advantages he can seize, but I see not how he can give you any valuable training or enlighten your understanding."

"Ah, Sir; that comes of dwelling in out-of-the-way parts. How could you know of the magnificent talents of the great Minister? But I will show you something."

He called up an attendant and bade him bring a book from a certain case. He showed this to his guest, who read the title "The New Book of Meng-te." Then he opened it and read it through from the beginning, the whole thirteen chapters. They all dealt with the art of war.

"What do you take this to be?" asked Chang Sung, when he had finished.

"This is the great Minister's discussion of the art of ancient and modern war composed on the model of Sun's treatise. You may be disdainful of the Minister's talents but will this not go down to posterity?"

"This book! Every child in Shu knows this by heart. What do you mean by calling it a new book? It was written by some obscure person of the time of the Warring States (Chou Dynasty, about 320 B.C.) and Ts'ao Ts'ao has plagiarised it. But he has deceived no one but you, Sir."

But what is the use of your sarcastic insult in saying that your school children know the book by rote? It has never been given to the world although copies have been made. It belongs to his private library."

"Do you disbelieve me? Why, I know it and could repeat it."

Then he repeated the whole book, word for word, from beginning to end.

"You remember it like this after only one reading! Really you are marvellous."

> He boasted not a handsome face,
> Nor was his body blessed with grace.
> His words streamed like a waterfall,
> He read a book and knew it all.
> Shu's glories could he well rehearse,
> His lore embraced the universe.
> Or text or note of scholiast
> Once read, his memory held fast.

At leave-taking Yang Hsiu said, "Remain a while in your

lodgings till I can petition our Minister to give you another interview."

Chang Sung thanked him and left. By and bye Yang Hsiu went to see Ts'ao Ts'ao on the matter of receiving the emissary from the west and said, "Sir, why did you formerly treat Chang Sung so off-hand."

"He spoke very rudely; that is why."

"But you bore with Mi Heng; why not with this man?"

"Mi Heng's reputation for scholarship stood highest of all and I could not bear to put him to death. But what ability has this Chang?"

"To say nothing about his speech being like the River of Heaven, nothing daunts his talent for dialectic. I happened to show him your new treatise; he read it over once and could repeat it. From this it is evident he is cultured and has a prodigious memory. There are few like him in the world. But he said the book was the work of an obscure person of a few hundred years back and every school boy in his country knew it."

"It only shows that the ancients and I are in secret sympathy," replied Ts'ao.

However, he ordered the book to be torn up and burned.

"Then may I bring him to see you, Sir, that he may see the glory of our court."

Ts'ao Ts'ao grudgingly consented, saying, "I am reviewing troops tomorrow on the western parade-ground. You may bring him there and let him see what my army looks like. He will be able to talk about it when he goes home. When I have dealt with the south I shall take the west in hand."

Hence the very next day Yang Hsiu took Chang Sung over to the west parade ground, where a review of the Tiger Guard was to be held. There were five legions of them, and when drawn up in order, they made a very brave show with their gleaming helmets and bright new uniforms. Their drums rolled to shake the heavens and their weapons glittered in the sun. Their discipline and order were perfect; their gay banners fluttered in the breeze. They looked ready to fly even, so alert and smart were they.

Chang Sung glanced at them contemptuously. After a long time Ts'ao Ts'ao called up Chang Sung and, pointing to his army, said, "Have you ever seen such fine bold fellows in your country?"

"We never see this military parade in Shu; we govern men by righteousness."

Ts'ao Ts'ao changed colour and looked hard at the bold speaker, who gazed back at him without the least sign of fear. Yang Hsiu shot a quick glance at him, but Ts'ao went on, "I regard the rat-class of the world [There is a pun here; the characters for "rat" and "Shu" are read the same] as of no more importance than so many weeds, and for my army to reach a place is to overcome it, to give battle is to conquer, to besiege is to take. Those who are with me, live; but those who oppose me, die. Do you understand?"

"O Minister, I know well that when you march out your army you always conquer. I knew it when you attacked Lu Pu at P'uyang; and when you fought Chang Hsiu at Wangch'eng; and when you met Chou Yu at the Red Wall; and when Hua Yung encountered Kuan Yu; and on that day when you cut off your beard and threw away your robe at the Pass; and when you hid in a boat to escape the arrows on the Wei River. On all these occasions no one could stand against you."

It made Ts'ao Ts'ao very angry to be thus twitted with his misfortunes and he said, "You stuck-up pedant! How dare you thus bring up all my failures?"

He called to his attendants to eject the bold disputant and put him to death.

Yang Hsiu ventured to argue with him saying, "You may behead him, but he came from Shu bearing tribute and his death would have a very evil effect on all distant peoples."

But Ts'ao Ts'ao was too angry to be reasonable and persisted. However, Hsun Yu also remonstrated and Chang Sung was not put to death. But he was beaten and ejected. He returned to his lodging and left the city that night, reflecting upon what he had intended and what he had accomplished.

Thought he, "I did not expect such arrogance when I came with the intention of giving him a province. When I get back Liu Chang will expect great things. Now I am returning empty handed and a failure to endure the laughter of my fellow countrymen. I will not go back. I have heard of the virtues of Liu Pei and I will go to him and see what manner of man he is. Then I can decide what to do."

So with his little escort and following he made for Chingchou. He had reached the boundaries of Yingchou (Wuch'ang) when he met a troop of horsemen, at the head of whom rode a captain in simple undress, who pulled up, saying, "Surely you are the Charioteer Chang."

"I am he," said Chang Sung.

The captain quickly dismounted and humbly said, "I have expected you these many days. I am Chao Yun."

Chang Sung dismounted and returned the salutation saying, "Then you are no other than Chao Tzu-lung, of Ch'angshan."

"No other," was the reply. "And my lord Liu Yuan-te bade me await you here and offer you refreshment after your long and toilsome journey."

At this some soldiers brought forward wine and food which they offered kneeling.

Chang Sung said, "I am come because the world says Liu Pei is liberal and kindly disposed."

After a few cups of wine the two retook the road toward Chingchou, which they neared next day at evening. They went to the guest-house. Here they found a large number of men who received the visitor with the beating of drums and every sign of respect. And the officer in command, bowing low, said, "My brother sent me to meet you after your long and dusty journey and prepare the guest house for your reception. My name is Kuan."

So Chang Sung and Chao Yun dismounted and entered the rest-house, where hosts and guest exchanged formal salutations and took their seats. In a short time refreshments were served and both men were most diligent in their attention to the traveller. This roadside banquet was prolonged to the time of setting the watch, when they prepared for rest.

Next morning, after the early meal, they mounted and continued their journey. Very soon they met Yuan-te himself, with an escort, and his two chief advisers, deferentially standing by the roadside.

As soon as he recognised them, Chang Sung dismounted and walked toward them. Yuan-te received him with extreme respect.

"Your exalted name has been long known to me," said Yuan-te, "it has reverberated through my ears. My one regret is that cloudy hills and long distances have hitherto prevented me from enjoying the advantage of your instruction. Hearing that you were passing through, I have come to meet you and if you would be willing to notice me and condescend to rest for a time in my desolate city, thus allowing me to satisfy my long disappointed desire to see you, I should indeed hold myself fortunate."

Naturally the traveller's vanity was tickled and he joyfully remounted. They rode bridle to bridle into the city. When they reached the residence again they exchanged profound salutations and compliments before they took their various places as host and guest. And then a banquet was served. But all throughout Yuan-te refrained from saying a word about Shu; he only chatted on general and common things.

The visitor noted this steady avoidance and resolved to probe his host's thoughts.

"How many districts are there in Chingchou, where you are now, O Imperial Uncle?"

K'ung-ming replied, "Chingchou is only ours temporarily; we have borrowed it from Wu. They are always sending messengers to demand its return. However, now that our lord has married the daughter his position is more secure. But it is still temporary."

"Wu is large," said Chang Sung, "yet their six districts and their eighty one departments do not satisfy them. The people are strong and the land is fruitful."

Said P'ang T'ung, "Our lord, being of the dynastic family, certainly cannot merely occupy two districts. Those others, thievish as they are, may indeed seize upon as much territory as they are strong enough to hold, but such deeds are not according to the wise man's heart."

"Noble Sirs, pray say no more: what virtue have I that I should expect anything from the future?" said Liu Pei.

"Not so, indeed," said Chang Sung. "Illustrious Sir, you are of the lineage of Han; your noble character is widely known. No one could say that your fate excludes all thought of occupying territory, where you might begin to set up authority and take an Emperor's position."

Yuan-te deprecated such a suggestion, "Sir, you go too far; this really is too much."

The next three days were spent in banquets and wine-parties but all the time no mention was made of the western province. And when, at the end of that time, Chang Sung took leave, his host was at the ten *li* rest-house to bid him farewell and offer refreshment. When the moment came for the parting Liu Pei raised his wine-cup and said, "I am sincerely grateful that you deigned to come here. You have prolonged your visit to three days, but now the moment of parting has come. Who knows when I may have the privilege of receiving your instructions again?"

As he said this the tears flowed, but he hid them while Chang Sung, willing to believe that this emotion was on his account, thought how wonderfully kind and noble his host must be to be thus affected. Quite overcome, he decided to speak about Hsich'uan. So he said, "I have thought that I, too, would come to you one day, but so far I have found no way. I see Sun Ch'uan on the east, always ready to pounce; I see Ts'ao Ts'ao on the north, greedy to swallow. So this is not a wholly desirable place for you to remain in."

"I know this but too well," said Liu Pei, "but I have no secure place to go to."

"Ichou is well protected, has much fertile soil, is populous and well governed. Its scholars are attracted by your virtue. If you marched your armies westward you could easily become a real power there and restore the glory of the Hans."

"But how dare I attempt this? The ruler is also of the Imperial House. The whole province is devoted to him for his good deeds, and no other man could attain such a hold."

"I am no traitor," said Chang Sung, "but in your presence I feel constrained to be perfectly open and plain. Liu, the prefect of Ichou, is naturally weak and can neither use the wise nor employ the capable. Then again Chang Lu threatens the north. People are distracted and would gladly welcome an appreciative ruler. The journey I have just made was to propose to support Ts'ao Ts'ao and place the province under him, but I found him rebellious and set on evil, proud and arrogant. So I have turned aside to you. If you will take Hsich'uan, you will have a base from which to deal with Hanchung when you will, and the whole country beside. You will continue the rightful line and your name will live in history. Would not that be real fame? If then you think of taking our country I am willing to do what little I can as an ally within. But do you contemplate such a step?"

"I am deeply grateful that you think so well of me. But the Prefect being a member of the family, I should lay myself open to general execration were I to attack him."

"When a hero finds himself in the world, his duty is to work out his destiny, to exert himself and perform his task as best as he can, to press forward among the foremost. At the moment the position is that, if you fail to seize this opportunity, some other will take possession and you will regret when too late."

"And I have heard much of the difficult nature of the country, its many high mountains and numerous streams, and its narrow roads. How could such a country be invaded?"

Then Chang Sung drew the map from his sleeve. "I am so deeply affected by your virtue that I offer you this map of the country, whereby its roads and rivers may be known."

Yuan-te unrolled the map; it was covered with notes, on the lie of the land, lengths and widths, and such matters. Strategical points on rivers and hills were shown, and store-houses and granaries and treasuries. Everything was plainly stated.

Chang Sung went on, "Sir, you can prepare your plans promptly.

I have two friends who will certainly help you. And when they come to see you, you may be perfectly frank with them. Their names are Fa Cheng and Meng Ta."

Yuan-te thanked him with joined hands. Said he, "As the blue mountains grow not old and the green waters always remain, so shall I never forget. And when I shall have accomplished my task you shall have no mean reward."

"I look for no reward. Having met with an enlightened lord I felt compelled to unbosom myself to him."

Chang Sung left soon after and Kuan Yu escorted him for a long distance.

After arrival in Ichou, Chang Sung lost no time in sending for his friends, Fa Cheng and Meng Ta. The former was the first to come and he was told of Ts'ao Ts'ao's arrogance and haughtiness toward men of parts. "As for the man himself," said he, "he is a man to grieve with but not a man to rejoice with. I have promised Ichou to Liu Pei, the Imperial Uncle, and I want your especial advice and assistance."

"I think Liu Chang incapable," said Fa Cheng, "and I have felt drawn to Liu Pei for some time past. So we are in sympathy here."

Shortly after Meng Ta arrived. Meng Ta and Fa Cheng were fellow townsmen. When Meng Ta entered the room and saw the other two in earnest and secret conversation, he said, "I know what you two are about; you are scheming to hand over Ichou to somebody."

"It is really so; you have guessed right," said Chang Sung. "But to whom ought it to go?"

"There is but one; Liu Pei, said Meng Ta.

All three clapped their hands and laughed.

Then said Fa Cheng to Chang Sung, "You will see our lord tomorrow; what about that?"

"I shall recommend that you two be sent to Chingchou on a mission."

They thought that a suitable scheme. And when the lately arrived messenger saw his master and was asked how he had fared, Chang Sung said, "Ts'ao Ts'ao is a rebel who desires to get the whole country into his hands. I need hardly tell you that. But he also hankers after this district."

"Then what will become of us?" said Liu Chang.

"I have a plan to check both our enemies. Liu, the Imperial Uncle, now in Chingchou, is a relative of yours and he is generous and well disposed. This is a matter of common knowledge. Ts'ao

Ts'ao was simply overwhelmed at the result of the battle at Red Wall and Chang Lu more so. Now my plan is that you ally yourself with your distinguished relative against Ts'ao Ts'ao and Chang Lu."

"I have been thinking thus for a long-time, can you recommend a suitable emissary?"

"The only ones are Fa Cheng and Meng Ta."

These two were summoned and, meanwhile, a letter was prepared. Fa Cheng was to proceed as emissary to open up friendly relations and Meng Ta would follow in due course with an army to welcome Liu Pei into the west country.

While still discussing the details of the policy, a person forced his way in, his face all running with sweat, and cried out, "My lord; your land will be lost to you and pass to another if you listen to Chang Sung."

Chang Sung turned a startled look on the intruder, who was a certain Huang Ch'uan of Hsiliang, an accountant in the Prefect's Palace.

The Prefect said, "Why do you use such language? Yuan-te is of my family and so I am seeking his support."

Said Huang Ch'uan, "I know all about him; he is liberal-minded to gain people to his side and his softness can overcome the hardest. He is bolder than any other. He gains men's hearts from afar off and those near him look up to him. He also has the wisest advisers and the boldest warriors. But if you call him here as a soldier, think you that he will be content to remain in a lowly condition? And if you treat him as an honoured guest, can a State stand two rulers? Hear me, my lord, and you stand secure as Mount T'ai; be deaf to my words and your position is as precarious as a pile of eggs. This Chang Sung has lately come home through Chingchou where he has certainly been plotting with Liu Pei. Slay this man; and make an end of Liu Pei. That will be for the happiness of this land."

"But how else am I to fend off my two enemies?"

"Fortify your country; dig out your moats and raise your ramparts. Then you can wait on events."

"If these rebels invade this land the position will be critical, as when fire singes one's eyebrows. It is idle talk to tell me to wait on events."

No notice was taken of Huang Ch'uan, and Fa Cheng was about to set out when another interfered, crying, "No, No." This was a secretary, Wang Lei.

With bowed head Wang Lei stood and said, "My lord will bring misfortune upon himself if he listens to this Chang Sung."

"Not so; I make an alliance with Liu Yuan-te in order to withstand Chang Lu."

"A Chang Lu invasion would be but a skin disease. Liu Pei's entry into this country would be a mortal malady. Liu Pei is an unscrupulous bravo; he was once in Ts'ao Ts'ao's service and plotted against him. Then he hung on to Sun Ch'uan and seized Chingchou. This shows his character and his designs. Think you that you two can dwell together? If you invite him, then Hsich'uan is lost."

"No more wild talk!" cried Liu Chang angrily. "Yuan-te is of my clan and family and will not ravish me of my possessions."

He bade the lictors escort both men outside and ordered Fa Cheng to set out. So he did; and before long came to Chingchou. When the salutations were over he presented his letter, which Yuan-te opened and read.

"I, Liu Chang, a younger brother of our family, now write to General Liu Yuan-te. From my humble place long have I gazed in your direction, but the roads of Shu are precipitous and I have failed to send my tribute. This is to my shame. The victims of misfortune aid each other and those in trouble support each other. If friends act thus, how much more should members of the same family? Now Chang Lu is mustering an army of invasion on my northern frontier, much to the injury of my tranquillity. Wherefore I send this letter that you may know of my distress and if you remember the kindly bonds of family and will play a brotherly part and lead your armies to destroy these ruffians, you will be my eternal protector and I shall be ever grateful. This letter leaves much unsaid, but I await your coming."

This letter greatly pleased Yuan-te. He made a banquet for the bearer thereof, and when they had mellowed themselves with wine, he dismissed the attendants and spoke to Fa Cheng in confidence.

"Friend, I have long admired you, and Chang Sung extolled your virtues. I shall always feel grateful for this opportunity of hearing you."

Fa Cheng bowed. "That is too great praise for a humble emissary from Shu. But they say that horses always neighed in recognition of Po Lo, the supreme judge of horses, and when a man has found his lord he dies for him. Have you thought further of Chang Sung's proposals, General?"

"I have always been a wanderer, often in suffering and sorrow. I have often thought of the wren for even that tiny bird has a twig to rest on; and of the cunning hare, that secures safety with three openings to its burrow. Does not a man need at least a shelter? Your land of Shu is fertile and a temptation, but its ruler is of my family and I cannot plot against him."

"Yes; Ichou is a very paradise. But without a ruler it cannot exist. Liu Chang knows not how to use the wise man and his heritage must speedily pass to another. Today it is offered to your hands and you must not miss the opportunity. You know the saying, that the leader in the hunt gets the quarry. If you will only consent, I will serve you to the death."

Yuan-te signified his gratitude. Said he, "Let me reflect for a time and take advice."

The banquet terminated and the guest left. K'ung-ming conducted Fa Cheng to his lodging while his master sat thinking. Then P'ang T'ung said, "You must decide; not to decide is foolish. You are of high intelligence, my lord, and why do you hesitate?"

"What should my reply be?" asked Yuan-te.

"You know these surroundings and with them you cannot attain your ends. Now before you lies a populous, fertile and rich land, a base with the greatest possibilities. You have the promise of assistance from two men within and it seems like a gift of providence. Why hesitate?"

"Now there are two men in the world as mutually antagonistic as fire and water. My opposite is Ts'ao Ts'ao. He is impetuous and I am long suffering; he is cruel and I am humane; he feigns, while I am true. In all particulars I act the direct contrary to him. I refuse to risk the loss of the confidence and trust of the world for a trifling advantage."

P'ang T'ung smiled at these sentiments. "My lord's words are quite in accord with abstract rectitude, but such ideas scarcely suit the days of rebellion. There are other ways of fighting than with warlike weapons, but to adhere too obstinately to the idea of abstract rectitude is to do nothing. One must be an opportunist, annex the weak and attack the wilfully deluded: seize the recalcitrant and protect the docile. These were the teachings of T'ang and Wu. If after the settlement you reward with righteousness and make of the land a great country, will you be guilty of a breach of trust? Remember if you do not take it now another will.

Yuan-te, a prey to confused emotions, replied, "These words are as jewels; they should be engraven on my very heart."

Thereupon he summoned K'ung-ming to settle the details of an army to march west.

K'ung-ming said, "This is an important place and must be well defended."

Liu Pei replied, "I, P'ang T'ung and my two captains Huang Chung and Wei Yen will go into Hsich'uan; you and our three best captains, my two brothers and Chao Tzu-lung, can defend Chingchou."

Kuan Yu was told off for Hsiangyang and the narrow pass of Ch'ingni, Chang Fei went along the river and Chao Yun camped at Chiangling. For the march westward, Huang Chung led the van, Wei Yen had the rearguard, while Yuan-te moved in the centre. P'ang T'ung was commander of the whole army.

Just as the five legions were starting there came Liao Hua to surrender; he and his men were attached to Kuan Yu.

It was in the winter that the expedition started. Soon they met the force under Meng Ta, five companies, to act as escort into Ichou. Liu Pei informed Liu Chang that he had started and the latter sent orders to the districts along the road to entertain them well on the march.

The Prefect proposed to go out in person to welcome Liu Pei and ordered carriages to be prepared and tents and banners. All the escort were dressed in glittering armour. At this the accountant, Huang Ch'un, the sturdy opponent of the invitation to Liu Pei, again remonstrated.

"My lord, if you go out you will be exposed to danger. I have been in your service for many years and I would prevent you from being the victim of another's wiles. I pray you reflect."

Chang Sung said, "His words are those of one who would sow discord in a family and encourage the power of the robbers who threaten you. Assuredly such action is to your detriment."

Liu Chang then spoke angrily to Huang Ch'uan saying, "I have decided, and why do you oppose me?"

The objector bowed his head and wept. Then approaching nearer he seized hold of the Prefect's robe with his teeth to hinder him. Liu Chang angrily shook his robe and rose from his seat, but Huang Ch'uan still held on till two of his teeth fell out. Then the lictors forced him away and he retired, still crying.

As Liu Chang was starting another man cried, "My lord, do you neglect the loyal words of your faithful Huang Ch'uan to go to your death?"

And he threw himself prostrate at the steps in remonstrance. He was one, Li K'uei, of Chienning.

"The prince may have Ministers who remonstrate with him and the father may have sons who oppose," said he. Huang Ch'uan has spoken faithfully and you ought to listen. To let Liu Pei into this land is to welcome the tiger into your gates."

"Yuan-te is my brother and will not harm me," said the Prefect. "And any other who shall oppose me shall suffer death."

So Li K'uei was thrust out.

"The officers of Shu regard the safety of their families and no longer render you service. The captains are arrogant and each has some scheme of his own to further. If you do not get Liu Pei to oppose the enemy without and your own people oppose you within, surely you are on the road to ruin."

So spoke Chang Sung and the Prefect replied that he knew the plan was for his advantage. Whereupon he mounted his horse to ride out to Elm Tree Bridge.

Then it was reported to him that Wang Lei had suspended himself, head downwards, at the city gate. In one hand he held a written remonstrance and in the other a knife. "And he says that if you heed him not he will cut the rope and die at your feet," concluded the messenger.

Liu Chang went to the gate, took the writing and read:— "Good medicine is bitter in the mouth but good for the disease; faithful words offend the ear but are good for the conduct. Of old the king of Ch'u listened not to Ch'u Yuan, but attended the meeting at Wukuan and was captured. Sir, you are thoughtlessly leaving your place to go to welcome Liu Pei, but I fear there is a way out and none in. Could you but behead Chang Sung in the market-place and have nothing to do with this league with Liu Pei, it would be for the happiness of old and young, and assure the safety of yourself."

Anger rose in his breast as he read.

"Why do you insult me when I go to meet a kindly man? I feel as if I were about to enjoy the delight of seeing a brother?"

At this Wang Lei gave a great cry, severed the rope and fell to the ground battered and dead.

> Head downwards at the city gate one hung,
> A last remonstrance in his outstretched hand,
> Resolved that, were his words rejected, he
> Would not survive defeat. Sincere was he
> Who, desperate, held to Liu Chang's silken robe
> Until his broken teeth released their grip.
> Sincere indeed, but how can he compare
> With stern Wang Lei, who went to awful death?

Liu Chang with a great company went out to welcome his clansman and there followed many waggons laden with supplies and rich stuffs.

Liu Pei's advanced guard had arrived at Shuchu. During the march the people had brought presents, and Liu Pei had given an order to pay for everything, under penalty of death for disobedience. Thus no one suffered and the people came out in trusting crowds to watch the soldiers marching by and welcome them in every way. Liu Pei soothed them with very gracious words.

Then Fa Cheng secretly showed P'ang T'ung a letter from Chang Sung advocating the assassination of Liu Chang near the place of welcome.

P'ang T'ung said, "Say nothing about this; after the two Lius have met there may be opportunities but this is too early to talk. Any plot would leak out."

So nothing was said. Fouch'eng, where the meeting was to take place, is three hundred and sixty *li* from Ch'engtu. Liu Chang arrived first and sent messengers to welcome Liu Pei. The two armies camped on the bank of the Fou River. Liu Pei went into the city to see the Prefect and they met cordially as brothers should. Both shed a few tears, and by and bye they began a heart-to-heart talk. Then followed a banquet and after this each returned to his own camp.

The Prefect said, "How ridiculous have been proved the fears of Huang Ch'uan and Wang Lei! They do not understand the force of family affection. I see he is really a kindly and noble man, and with him as a support I shall fear neither Ts'ao nor Chang. And I owe all this to Chang Sung."

To show his gratitude he took off the green silken robe he wore and sent it as a gift to Chang Sung, together with five hundred *liang* of gold.

However, some of his officers were not so content and a group of them bade him beware.

"Do not rejoice too soon, O Master," said they, "for Liu Pei is hard enough within in spite of his mild exterior. You have not sounded him yet and should be on your guard."

"You are all too anxious," said he, laughing, "my brother is no double-dealer, I am sure."

When Liu Pei had returned to his own tent, P'ang T'ung came in to ask what impression he had of his host of that day.

He seems a very honest man," said Liu Pei.

"He is good enough, but some of his servants are discontented at this turn of affairs and I would not guarantee there will be no murders. If you took my advice you would have Liu Chang assassinated at the return banquet. A hundred ruffians behind the arras, a signal from you, and the deed would be accomplished. All that would be needed then would be a rush on the capital. No sword need be drawn, no arrow fitted to the string."

"He is a brother of my house and has treated me with sincerity. I am a new-comer and so far unknown in this land. Such a deed would be abhorrent to all the world and these people would resent it. I will not establish myself by such means."

"The scheme is not mine; it originated in a private letter from Chang Sung, who says it will have to be done some time."

At this moment Fa Chung came in and said, "This is not for ourselves; it is the will of heaven."

"Liu Chang and I are of the same house and I would shudder at harming him."

"Sir, you are wrong. If you act not as we propose, then Chang Lu will take Shu in revenge for the death of his mother. What is there for you at the end of your long march? Advance, and success is yours; retreat and you have nothing. And delays are most dangerous. At any moment this scheme may leak out and another will reap the profit. This is the day when Heaven smiles on you. Act before Liu Chang suspects you; establish yourself."

So urged Fa Cheng and P'ang T'ung backed it.

> Their lord, by argument, they tried
> From rectitude to turn aside.

What Liu Pei hid in his heart will be explained in the next chapter.

END OF VOLUME I